SPARKTOPIA

NEW YORK TIMES BESTSELLING AUTHOR
JA HUSS

Copyright © 2024 by JA Huss
ISBN: 978-1-957277-35-6

No part of this book may be reproduced or resold in any form or by any electronic or mechanical means, including information storage and retrieval systems, without written permission from the author, except for the use of brief quotations in a book review.

This is a work of fiction. Names, characters, businesses, places, events and incidents are either the products of the author's imagination or used in a fictitious manner. Any resemblance to actual persons, living or dead, or actual events is purely coincidental.

Edited by RJ Locksley
Cover and Interior Design by JA Huss

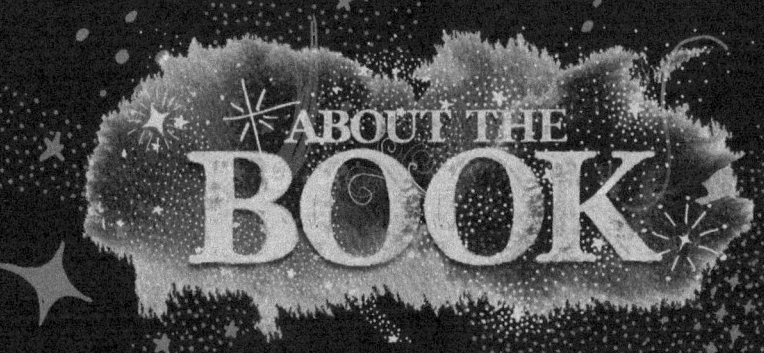

ABOUT THE BOOK

Spark is light, Spark is magic, Spark is power.

Spark is everything and it blooms inside the bodies of Tau City's young women. Once a decade, in exchange for enough power to keep the city modern and comfortable, a Spark Maiden must be sacrificed to their mysterious tower god in a ritual called The Extraction.

Ten Maidens are Chosen, but only one enters the tower as a sacrifice, never to be seen again. The nine leftovers are elevated to celebrity status and spend the next decade living in the luxurious Maiden Tower, wearing couture gala gowns, and partying with the city's most interesting and beautiful people. Every young woman in Tau City wants to be a Spark Maiden because the odds have always been in their favor.

Until now.

One by one, the greedy god has summoned the leftover Spark Maidens into sacrifice. When Clara Birch, Spark Maiden number nine, gets the call, she fully expects her fiancé, Finn Scott, the Extraction Master's son, to save her.

Spoiler alert: He's not going to.

At the same time, a rebellion is brewing. The forgotten underclass is plotting the end of the god and his tower with strategically-placed Rebel spies that will bring it all down. Jasina Bell is a young woman on a mission to make history and she will stop at nothing to get the fame she deserves.

When Clara is forced into the tower against her will, she makes an unexpected discovery. There is no god—just a man, one willing to do what Finn Scott wouldn't: save Clara Birch.

Even if it means destroying the entire world to do so.

PART 1

"We all know the victor takes the spoils. And in this case, it's the villain who writes the history books. Make no mistake, the Godslayer will continue to be humanity's biggest threat until he is stopped. In the meantime, we must purge these romantic ideas of his sinister quest while we still can. If truth matters at all, we cannot—*we must not*—let these animals have their way with it. Especially if it's a child's picture book. The fragile, malleable little minds of children everywhere are being warped by the images portrayed on the pages of this atrocity. Burn it. Burn every copy. Ban it. Never let it see the light of day again."

—Leena Peel, Editor-in-Chief, *Tau City Metro News*

CHAPTER ONE

Spark leaks out of my fingertips as cyan-blue light when I stroke the curve of Finn Scott's muscled shoulder. It leaves a trace of glow on his skin that takes many more seconds to disappear today than it did ten years ago. We're in his quarters—in his bed, specifically—hiding from the festival going on outside.

Not really hiding, I guess. What we just did wasn't wrong and if anyone saw us come in here—or sees us leave —they wouldn't even blink.

Clara Birch and Finn Scott have been a 'thing' for… well, our entire lives. Which totals up to nearly three decades.

But I'm a Spark Maiden and he's the Extraction Master's son and I technically still have three months left in service to the tower god before Finn and I can officially and publicly declare our love.

Right now, in bed next to me, he is absently tracing a fingertip up and down my outer thigh. And this simple touch of his is enough to send a chill up my whole body.

"Clara?"

"Hmm." I sigh the word out with eyes closed, picturing our future.

"You're the best thing that ever happened to me. I wish we could stay like this forever."

Now I smile and turn, pressing my face into his neck. "Pretty soon we're gonna be spending so much time together, you're gonna get sick of me."

He chuckles and I hear this happiness as a rumble coming from his chest.

In just three months we will be this close to each other every night. We will make love, and wake up together, and breakfast, and he will go to work as his father's new apprentice, and I will have babies and turn his quarters into our home.

This new life will be the complete opposite of how I have lived for the past ten years, up on the ninth floor of the Maiden Tower, surrounded by luxury. A celebrity, of sorts.

"We should get going." Finn's other hand, the one not caressing my thigh, is busy playing with my hair as he says this.

I moan and turn a little so we're facing each other. Our mutual smiles are genuine. "Not yet." This comes out a little bit whiny, but I feel I have earned this tiny objection.

"They're gonna start missing you." He's pulling strands of hair away from my face now. We kiss, letting it linger, well aware that we need to get back to the Choosing Festival outside, but unwilling to break apart.

I sigh, knowing he's right, but reluctant to give up this time with him. So I stall with more words. "Trust me. I'm not missed. They're busy with the Little Sisters today. I'm old news now."

Finn chuckles. "Not exactly. I mean, seven, Clara. It's… precariously close, don't you think?"

"Wow." I sit up a little, blinking at his audacity. Because that was not just impolite, but actually *rude*. "Well, that's certainly one way to pull me out of my postcoital bliss. Thanks for reminding me."

"Sorry." He offers me a weak smile, then pushes a few errant strands of long, blonde hair away from my face. "I just don't want you to get in trouble."

"That's not why you said that. And I'm mad that you're worrying about it. There are only three months left, I'm number nine, and the last call was over a year ago now. Whatever crisis the god was having that required so many Spark Maidens, I think it's been remedied."

Finn sighs, not quite agreeing, but not willing to say it out loud, either. He's worried and he wants me to allay his feelings, but he's looking for something more than what I just gave him. What I just said is the same thing everyone says.

But the truth is, no one knows what's going on with the god in the tower. What we do know is that seven Spark Maidens in ten years is too many.

The Extraction is a tradition here in Tau City. But it's more than that. Spark is what the god uses to power the city. Every ten years the Extraction Master ranks the most powerful Spark Maidens in order from one to ten. And on Extraction Day itself, the god calls number one into the tower to take as his own.

Being number nine in the Spark Maiden line-up comes with a whole lot of peace of mind because one is supposed to be the limit. The other nine are Maidens-in-Waiting. We get celebrity status. We live in the Maiden Tower surrounded by luxury. We wear the best dresses, attend the best parties, and have a whole staff of maids and helpers. It's a fantasy life that every little girl dreams about as she grows up.

If you're one of the nine Maidens-in-Waiting in normal years there is no need to worry about being called up for Extraction. There have only been a handful of times, in over a thousand years of history, where *two* Spark Maidens were Extracted in the same decade.

But this has not been a normal Extraction period. As Finn pointed out, we are on Maiden number seven now. Those bells have rung seven times in the last ten years. And each time one of my friends walked into the tower, never to be seen again.

They don't return, you see. They don't come back.

Still, there are only three months left. I'm safe. I *know* I'm safe.

And this feeling of safety is elevated because of what's been happening outside while Finn and I took this opportunity to reunite after months of not seeing each other. Because today marks the first official pre-Extraction Choosing.

This morning there were three hundred and twenty-seven young women between the ages of eighteen and twenty-four on the tower stage. All of whom were calmly, but anxiously, awaiting the calling of names. All of whom were desperate to be Chosen.

After the ceremony was over there were only seventy-five Chosen left.

But over the course of the next three months that number will dwindle to ten. Then, finally, on Extraction Day itself, number one will be sent into the tower and my duty to the god will end.

The remaining nine Spark Maidens, in a normal Extraction period, do not enter the tower. They move into the Maiden Tower, get all the celebrity perks, and are generally just emissaries for the Extraction process itself.

I have spent the last decade speaking to young girls who dream of being Chosen, occasionally presiding over their spark training, supporting various political agendas, going to elite parties, and accepting gifts, and coin, and the attention of up-and-coming young men.

When the decade is over and the Maidens-in-Waiting leave their service, they are rich. We pay no coin for anything while we live in the tower. In fact, all our appearances and services come with a price. The coin is collected by the Matrons in our name and held in accounts until our duty has ended.

My time as a Spark Maiden came with all those luxuries. My accounts are overflowing with coin. Even with all the extra-stressful bell ringing, it was mostly good. And if the bells weren't ringing, it was mostly fun.

But my heart belongs to Finn Scott. My heart has always belonged to Finn Scott. And our happy ending is so close, I can taste it. In three months, when the new Maidens are sworn in on Extraction Day, my status of Spark Maiden will finally be nullified, I will be free to take what the god has given me in exchange for being one of the Chosen, and I will start a brand-new life with the man I love.

I've been planning our wedding for over a year now. Nothing has been set up but as soon as I am free, those plans will be put into motion.

Finn leans in and kisses me again. "I'm sorry. I didn't mean to upset you. I know you're safe. I *know* you are." He touches my cheek as he says this, giving the words a little more weight.

He knows I'm safe.

Well, that must mean that Aldo—his father, who is the Extraction Master and in charge of this whole thing—must've said something to him.

I open my mouth to start asking questions about this, but Finn doesn't give me a chance. He gets out of bed and holds his hand out to me. "Come on. Let's get back. There is no way they're not missing you and I don't want to risk the wrath of the god, not to mention my father. This could be considered cheating, after all. I don't wanna tarnish your record."

I feel relieved that he gave me this assurance that I am safe. Normally, he does not talk about his father's work. It's forbidden. But his last point is a little ridiculous, so I scoff as well.

Spark Maidens are not permitted to have a committed relationship during our service time, but we are allowed to date. There is no rule about sex in the Extraction manual, but we are expected to represent the god, so all our actions are judged. If you're sleeping around and people start talking, demerits are added to your Maiden record and the day we are set free from our obligations, these demerits are read aloud in public for all to hear.

We are not formally judged for them, but opinions are formed on that day. If you have a tarnished record, then your prospects suffer. And what is the point of giving up ten years of your life if you're not going to collect the reward at the end?

I take Finn's hand and allow him to pull me out of his bed, sighing as I do this. The spark inside me flares up and I look him in the eyes as I touch the tip of my finger to his chest, dragging it down his pecs, then over his abs, leaving a trace of cyan-blue light behind. Then I coo, in my most sultry voice, "I have zero demerits, Finn Scott. Even if I did get marked, it would not affect my future."

He pulls me close until we are face to face and we kiss. It's a nice, kinda long kiss. And when we pull apart, I look him in the eyes as the words flow out of him like poetry. "You're my future. And the god can't take you away from me, Clara Birch. Not ever. Our love is destiny."

We stare into each other's eyes like the stupid teenagers we haven't been in years, and then giggle like those long-ago versions of us as well. He spins me around and slaps my butt. "Get dressed. Let's go join the party."

I scoot forward, squealing, and start picking up my clothes. His private quarters are bigger than most since his family has been running the Extraction for many generations now, but it's still in the Extraction District so it's got the same cozy feel I remember from his childhood apartments when we were kids. Smooth, slate floors, and river-stone half walls that turn into a warm gray plaster near the domed ceilings make up the most charming parts of it.

Just past the foot of the bed there is a half-circle fireplace made out of the same river-stone rock that lines the walls. And the wooden side tables are dotted with lit candelabras—powered by spark, not flames. All the fabric on the pillows, blankets, and rugs are neutral shades of cream, and tan, and blue. This soothing and cozy charm is multiplied when the round windows dotting both the ceiling and the walls allow rays of hazy sunshine to filter through from outside.

Everything about Finn's quarters says… comfort.

Simple comforts though. Nothing like the luxurious rooms we have over in the Maiden District. But it's nice and I can easily picture myself living here with him.

These quarters are new because his father has finally allowed him to start his apprenticeship as the next Extraction Master and this is my first visit, but now that I've seen it, I will be picturing myself sleeping in this bed next to him and living in this space with him every moment until I am free.

I know it's only three more months, but when my gown is back on, my hair back in place, and I'm sliding my feet into my hand-embroidered silk slippers, my heart begins to ache and a sadness floods through me.

I look over my shoulder at Finn, who has been put back together as well—looking so debonair in his gorgeous cream-colored linen tunic and slate-blue vest, I actually sigh. His family always did have the best tailors—the Extraction Master is pretty much the highest status one can have in Tau City. And one day, Finn will take his father's place and I will stand by his side. We will rule the highest levels of society—in a benevolent way, of course.

Finn comes towards me, hands automatically going to my waist and pulling me close. "What's got you sighing?"

I stare up at him, marveling at how handsome a man he's grown into over the last decade. Same shoulder-length, but messy blond hair. Same deep and penetrating blue eyes. But his shoulders are broad and muscular now. His jaw set with that hard, squared-off chin and covered in just the right amount of golden stubble.

He was still a boy of eighteen when I was Chosen and now he's a man. Did I miss something and not realize it? It didn't feel that way as time was passing. Finn and I were never really apart, we just led separate lives. But we're not kids anymore and it just right now occurs to me that we gave up something irreplaceable so I could be a Spark Maiden.

Our youth.

We're only twenty-eight, it's not like we're old. But still, it feels like a loss.

"I want this to be over now, Finn. I don't wanna go back to the Maiden Tower. I wanna stay here with you and never leave."

He smiles as he kisses me. "Three months. We're practically there, Clara. Nothing will get in the way."

"I know. But I want it now."

"We've waited ten years. We'll be together forever before we know it."

Then he pulls away, slips his hand around to the small of my back, and guides me over to the door.

Being with him feels like going home. And home is something that was always precarious with me as a child because my mother died when I was twelve and my father died just before I was Chosen. Finn Scott and his parents are all that's left of my humbler beginnings as a valet's daughter living in one of the serene and cozy, though not as glamorous, neighborhoods on a tertiary canal just past the Extraction Tower. My father was Aldo's personal assistant. As has been every male in my father's line.

Until now.

I don't even know who the present valet is because I am not male, so the position was given to another family and I didn't follow the news. I didn't want to know.

All those generations, all that inheritance—gone in a blink with the birth of a daughter.

It was part of the reason my father encouraged me to try for the Spark Maidens. I was not blessed with much natural spark and probably would not have bothered pledging if he hadn't urged me the way he did. He knew I would not inherit anything when he died and he couldn't stand the thought of me being left coinless.

Being Spark Maiden number nine wasn't *my* dream, but I did it anyway because my father worried about me so much and it was such a simple thing to be part of the Choosing process when you're young like that. You just show up and learn manners, and propagate your tiny bits of spark, and get educated in society things, and anyway, it's all free. So why not? What else was there to do? *All* the up-city girls were in these classes. If I didn't go, I'd have been labeled weird and made an outcast.

I don't remember having companions other than Finn before signing up as a Pledge. But after… even in the early, early days during my twelfth year, there were groups of girls around me who wanted to be friends. And, even after all the tower drama, two of them still are.

Never, did I ever expect to be part of 'the ten.' And getting drawn as number nine was an especially nice perk. A near promise that I had made it, that I would not walk into that tower for Extraction, and my reward, after another decade of service, was all but guaranteed.

All of that is still true. But only partially for the obvious reasons.

Finn is reaching for the door to his quarters, but then suddenly goes stiff and stops, bracing himself and looking at me with wide eyes. "What was that?"

I shrug, confused. "What was… what?"

"You didn't feel that?" He stands up straight again, looking around. Then lets go of my hand and walks across the room to the window.

"What are you doing?"

"You really didn't feel that?"

"No. I didn't feel anything." I join him at the window, peering out at the festival going on down below. He's got a nice view. His place is not inside the Extraction Tower, but it's practically next door. So I can see the canal, and the Maiden Tower across the way, and hundreds of people celebrating Choosing Day.

Nothing looks out of the ordinary to me, but Finn continues to look.

"What did you feel?" I ask him.

He lets out a long breath and drags his gaze from the window. "It was like a... crash. Or a... boom. Something... big."

"Hmmm. Well, I don't know, Finn. I didn't feel any of that." Then a terrible idea hits me. "You don't think it's a spark outage?"

He must see the panic in my eyes because his whole demeanor changes. He calms. His eyes droop a little, like nothing interesting at all is happening, and then he smiles. "No. Absolutely not. Look." He points out the window. "Don't you think if there was a spark outage people would be freaking out?"

I do think that, but he was the one who looked out the window in the first place. So he thought it might be a spark outage and he went to check.

"It was nothing." He shrugs at me. "I probably imagined it. Forget I ever said anything, OK?" Then he's kissing me again, murmuring words into my mouth. "I love you, Clara Birch. You're my future and our love is destiny."

I smile into the kiss, placated. "I love you too."

We press our foreheads together and sigh, lingering in this embrace for one more moment.

When we leave Finn's quarters and I go one way while he goes the other, I can't entirely suppress the feeling of being set loose. Of being untethered and adrift.

Like he's my everything. And he is. He's my anchor to

this world. His is the only family I have left. Yes, I have friends, but family is something different.

I take one more look over my shoulder and smile when I find Finn looking over his shoulder taking one more look at me. Then he winks, looks forward again, and walks up the stairs that lead to the heart of the Extraction District.

A moment later he has disappeared around a corner and another long sigh leaves me. But I gather up the skirts of my gown and head towards the bridge that will take me across the cyan-blue canal and deposit me into the Maiden District where my duties as Maiden-in-Waiting number nine await.

I resist the urge to stop in the middle of the bridge to enjoy the view. It's late afternoon now and I've always liked the way the light bounces off the tower and shimmers across the canal at this time of day. But the smooth, sandy beach awaiting me on the other side of the canal is a whole other temptation. One I don't have the strength to fight.

Once in the sand I kick off my slippers and carry them as I walk parallel to the flagstone pavers that lead into the Maiden District.

Even after ten years, sinking my toes into the sand on my way home every evening is a luxury I don't take for granted. There are other beaches in Tau City, of course, since there are miles of canals winding through the districts. But none of them are like the one reserved especially for the Maidens. It's groomed twice a day and the sand is so white it sparkles.

Another ache fills my heart when I have to step back on to the rocks and leave the water behind. Which is silly. I've lost nothing. There is no reason for the ache.

But logic doesn't seem to apply when it comes to matters of the heart. Finn and I are soulmates, but so far, we've been denied our full love. And even though we've managed to sustain our attraction and longing over the past ten years, I feel like there is always a limit. That even the love of soulmates can wobble when the star-crossing goes on for too long.

Three more months, Clara. That's it. Just three more months and the stars will align instead of cross.

Hopping on one foot, then the other, I put my slippers back on as I approach the Maiden gate. I am waved through with a nod by a guard and then hurriedly make my way through the entrance and towards the stairs that will take me up into our tower.

Haryet Chettle—Maiden number eight—and Gemna Hatley—Maiden number ten—also live in the upper levels with me. On floors eight and ten, respectively, because those are their numbers. Imogen Gibson was Spark Maiden number one in our group. She went into the tower on Extraction Day itself, of course. The leftover nine all came to live here and this is where we've been ever since.

Each Spark Maiden gets her own floor filled with rooms. All kinds of rooms. Dining rooms, and dressing rooms, and bathrooms, and bedrooms, and entertaining rooms. In the first year, every floor had a different party going on in the evenings, some loud and exciting with lots of drinking, others calm and meant for dining and stimulating conversation.

But the parties ended years ago now. After Lucy Fisher, Spark Maiden number four, was Extracted. That's when it kinda hit home that something was wrong in that god's tower.

Haryet, Gemna, and I still live up on our assigned floors at the top. It didn't even occur to us that we might move down. Or maybe it did and we just didn't want to tempt fate by lowering our numbers, even in this small, silly way.

We have been best friends for ten years now. Not a single night has gone by since we moved into the Maiden Tower that we didn't say goodnight to each other. It's crazy how much time I've spent with these two women and I'm not gonna lie, I think I will be a little lost without them once I move in with Finn.

Though it will be the good kind of lost. The kind that comes with brand-new beginnings.

The other Maidens who came before us are gone, of course. We are the last ones left after all that crazy bell-ringing in the middle of the night. This is how our god in the tower lets us know that for whatever reason, he needs another Maiden to keep the Spark flowing through Tau City.

So all the floors below us are empty now. And since the communal rooms are so massive, and the ceilings so high, even the soft steps of my slippers are enough to cause an echo all around me as I climb the stairs.

I hate the silence, but it's as if the god himself is listening to my thoughts, because suddenly there is a commotion of noise coming towards me from a hallway.

I pause, not understanding what this commotion might mean. But then feel foolish as a large group of Spark Maiden wannabes comes into the living space. At this stage of the Choosing we call them Little Sisters and they are bright, and young, and excited because regardless of what kind of luxury they grew up in, the Maiden Tower is a whole new definition of extravagance. They all want to be here to experience it.

Almost everything in the Maiden Tower is decorated in the same color palette—cream and other light-colored neutrals, with just a little touch of sun-faded blue sprinkled about. The dormitory, where these Little Sisters will spend the rest of the Choosing time, is the only exception to this scheme because the color palette is reversed. Everything is blue in their dorm with just little touches of the neutrals that dominate here. Blue is how they segregate 'them' from 'us.' Because blue is the color of spark and as Little Sisters, they have not yet perfected the spark inside them.

As a Maiden, however, I could light up the night if I want to.

Not as spectacularly as Spark Maidens with lower numbers, of course. Being number nine means that while my spark display was definitely better than most during our group's final Choosing, it was nowhere close to the fireworks Imogen Gibson could set off with her performance.

All these Little Sisters are wearing blue day dresses, mostly long ones woven out of linen, and each of them have a little accent scarf or a belt made of leather as an accessory. Dressmaking is considered a desirable skill for those wanting to be Spark Maidens. So all these girls made these dresses with their own hands. In fact, they are probably wearing their finest work since it's the very first Choosing, and therefore, the very first time they are on public display.

Tonight is their first gala and they are practically bursting with excitement. Some of them are even displaying tiny bits of spark, mostly as static in their hair or a miniscule glint of light in their eyes. But it really is just tiny bits because they are probably trying to hold it in. Tonight, at the gala, they will light themselves up for the very first time—at least in public. And no one wants to give away what they have planned to astonish Finn's father, Aldo, the Extraction Master.

Spark display is the number one criterion for being Chosen as a Maiden and my time at the first gala is probably my fondest memory of this whole journey.

Compared to most of my fellow Maidens, my spark is rather limited. And back then, as a Little Sister, it was only in my fingertips. But that night, during the first gala, I managed to make spark drawings in the air with my blue light. I drew stupid things—hearts, and simple flowers, and arrows. But no one had ever done that before. Yes, it was basic—especially compared to Imogen, who actually blew a bubble of blue light around her entire body and floated up in the air for six whole seconds—but it was also surprising, so it made people gasp with delight and clap their hands with laughter.

It made them happy. I was the girl who made them happy.

"Ladies, simmer down and please stay in a triple line!" The Matron in charge of the Little Sisters calls this out as she claps her hands. She's an older woman who isn't around much, so her name escapes me at the moment. Sometimes, when a Maiden's duty is over, she joins the Order and becomes a Matron. Their job is to train up the Pledges and keep the Little Sisters in line. This one's tone becomes sharper when a group in back takes too long to form up. "Do I need to remind you that you're being judged on this?" Though I can't see the Matron's face, I can almost hear the raised eyebrow.

Which makes me chuckle and scurry up the stairs that lead to my floor.

But I take a moment to look back at them when I get to the next landing. And when I do this, my gaze finds the girl in back who is responsible for all that Matronly attention. She's tall, with long, flowing auburn hair, and even from up here I get a little lost in those brilliant blue eyes when she directs her gaze right at me. She gives them a good roll. Like she's bored or something.

So brazen.

Or, maybe, just so arrogant.

I turn away without acknowledging her and hurry up the next flight of stairs, eager to get home. When I enter my quarters, I find Haryet and Gemna sitting on my reception room couch, giggling like schoolgirls.

"What's so funny?" I close the door behind me, kick my slippers off, and then skip across the bone-colored flagstone floor, bouncing onto the couch next to them. I sink back into the overstuffed cushions and lay my feet across Haryet's lap.

Gemna answers. "Oh, we were just talking about the

new Little Sisters and started remembering how silly we were back then."

Haryet sighs. "Goodness, that was so long ago. And I know people say that all the time, but it really was!" Her eyes go big when she says this, directing them right at me. "Ten years, Clara! Where did the time go?"

Both Gemna and Haryet are blonde and blue-eyed like me. We could be literal sisters. But Gemna is taller and her face is squarer, while Haryet is petite and her face is in the shape of a heart.

The fact that we're almost always dressed alike really contributes to the whole 'sisters' look. We don't choose our clothes for events. They are chosen for us. And every moment, from this day forward, all the way up to Extraction Day itself, is part of the process. Both for us, who are leaving the Maidens behind, and them, the Little Sisters who will advance up.

I blow out a breath and sink a little further into the cushions. "I don't know. It feels like forever, doesn't it? But at the same time, it went by so fast."

Both of my best friends hum out their agreement.

"It's just about over, girls," I tell them. "And we're not girls anymore. I saw them, by the way. The Little Sisters downstairs in their blue dresses. And it's really weird to think that this is all over and in just three months we will be free, and rich, and moving on."

My friends both laugh. Then Gemna gets up, offering one hand to me and the other to Haryet. "Come on, let's get ready for the gala. There aren't many left, ya know? We should make the most of these end times. Because who knows, we might spend the rest of our lives being ordinary people. Taking care of husbands, and raising children, and playing cards on Sunday nights like our mammas did."

Haryet squeals. "Never!" And we both let Gemna pull us to our feet.

But as they leave me and go to their own floors to get ready, I can't help but think that the boring life Gemna just described doesn't really sound boring to me.

I hope that's what my life is. That's the plan, anyway. I just want to marry Finn Scott and spend the rest of my days taking care of him and raising our family. My mother died when I was twelve, but even back when she was alive, she was sick. So sick, she never got a chance to play cards with the ladies on Sunday nights like the other wives. I wouldn't mind doing that every week. I wouldn't mind that at all.

After entering my bedroom, I stop in front of my full-length mirror and stare at the woman I've turned into over the past decade. My dress is high fashion traditional. Long, and layered, and made of copper-colored silk and cream-colored linen. I'm wearing a single-strand necklace made of gold that I was gifted on the last Maiden anniversary. My long hair is still a honey-colored blonde, not much different than it was when I first came here.

I touch my face. I don't have any wrinkles. I'm only twenty-eight, but some aging would be expected, and my face looks just as smooth and unblemished today as it was ten years ago as far as I can tell.

But those blue eyes of mine are different. They have seen things now. They understand this world a little better. They definitely know what's important and what's not.

This is when my gaze wanders over to the large adjoining room, which is my closet. That's where tonight's gown has been draped over my dressing stand. It's a beautiful dress made of glimmering champagne silk, with the highest-quality linen, and there are thousands of tiny hand-blown glass beads all across the bodice. And when the sun from my spectacular floor-to-ceiling windows finds the dress, they sparkle in a most magnificent way.

It's such a pretty scene, I wish that the official photographers were here to take a picture. Something I could keep and look back on. But photography uses a lot of spark, so photographs are only taken at galas and Extractions.

Next to the gown is another stand that holds all the accessories I will be wearing tonight. Every bit of this is donated by the best outfitters in the Tau City Canal District. Right down to the lingerie and the jewelry.

Do I love the fact that I've been wearing the best dresses and jewelry for the last ten years? Of course I do. But it's not important to me. I've had my share. It's time for the Little Sisters to enjoy this lifestyle now. Time for them to show off and for me to fade into the background a little.

I just want the family I've been dreaming of. That's all. I would give up every dress, every ring, and bracelet, and earring to get that.

But that's not to say that I can't enjoy the time I have left.

So I strip off my finery, wash up, and by the time I'm stepping out of the shower my lady's maid has arrived to sparkle me back up.

CHAPTER TWO

*M*atron Bell, my auntie, is angry with me. I know this because of the way she directs those dark, pitted eyes of hers in my direction every time I so much as make a whisper of noise during our tour of the Maiden Tower. She pulled me aside this morning and gave me a long, boring lecture on how I am not here to enjoy myself, I am here to do a job, and if I embarrass her, or any of the other Matrons, there will be severe consequences.

I controlled my urge to roll my eyes during that lecture —mostly because she was looming over me like a bitter matriarch—but here, in this great hall, and among the other Little Sisters, I do not have the fortitude.

The eye-roll wasn't meant for Clara Birch, but it's aimed in her direction on the stairwell above me when it comes out.

She flashes me a disapproving look and then turns and continues her way up into the tower. As she is number nine, she has a long climb.

As a newly minted Little Sister, I will be housed in the dorm with the other seventy-four girls who just made it past the First Choosing. And even though I understand that I am here to do a job, I can hardly contain my excitement.

Technically, this is the second Choosing, but the first one happens internally, done by the Matrons and not by the Extraction Master, so it's not officially a Choosing, merely a whittling down.

Every Extraction year comes with hundreds of Pledges, little girls who all made an initial vow to the god when they were twelve. This is the official beginning of service. Then, each year thereafter, the Pledges make that same vow again.

Lots of girls drop out before they ever reach the age of Extraction. But still, there were three hundred and twenty-seven of age Pledges during this initial whittling down.

One hundred of us got through to the next level. And even though we weren't yet in the dorms, all one hundred of us were presented to the Extraction Master—Aldo Scott—three days ago and this morning seventy-five names were called out on the Tower stage.

That's us. The official Little Sisters for the one-hundred-and-twenty-first Extraction.

Three weeks from now there will be another Choosing and twenty-five girls will move out of the dorm and then there will be fifty left.

These fifty will spend the next three weeks getting ready for the next Choosing that will leave a lean twenty-five.

The final Choosing is the one everyone shows up for. The whole city shuts down for three days and there is a carnival, and feasts, and galas, and finally, standing on the tower stage, the top ten are announced and number one is sent through the doors and the nine left over are awarded gigantic, luxurious Maiden Tower apartments, and a yearly stipend that no Maiden in the history of the Extraction has ever managed to spend. There is an endless supply of expertly crafted handmade gowns and dresses, the best perfumes and lingerie, and more eligible men to go out on the town with than anyone could ever hope to choose from.

Most Maidens find their future husbands during this time. Clara Birch was an exception, since she was already in love with Finn Scott. But even if she didn't officially date the men she spent her evenings with, she still went out with them. It's required.

But Clara never got close to the men. And everyone in the city talks about how Finn Scott is waiting for his one true love to be released from the god's service, oohing and ahing over them like their love is so special. As if they've been celibate. Come on. We all know Clara and Finn have the occasional tryst and from the mussed-up, just-fucked look of Clara Birch's hair it's pretty clear where she just came from.

"Jasina!"

My head snaps to attention. "Yes!"

Matron Bell, my auntie, claps her hands as she yells. "Keep up!"

The group started to move on while I was daydreaming, so they are all a couple dozen steps ahead of me now.

I nod, bowing my head a little—"Yes, Matron"—then scurry to catch up with the group.

The Little Sister dorm is a hotly-guarded secret. It's here on the ground level on the Maiden Tower, but it has its own four-story wing that is locked and empty at all times, except for the three months out of every decade when it is filled with Little Sisters for the Choosing. All growing up, us hopefuls have dreamed of the day when we move into the tower.

All Little Sisters and Maidens alike start their journey into the god's service in the same way, cloistered together with your competitors. No one, absolutely no one but Matrons and Little Sisters is allowed inside. And even though every decade there are sixty-five girls who leave the tower behind, Unchosen, none of them ever broke the vow of secrecy about what it all looks like or how it's laid out.

It feels unnecessarily... clandestine. I mean, who cares? It's a dorm. I don't get it. But rules are rules. My Little Sister class got the same sermon this morning as every other entering Little Sister class. "If you say anything about the dorm in public, you will immediately forfeit your right to be here and be escorted out."

We're only midway through the tour of the Maiden Tower at present, but from what I've seen so far, it's been *way* undersold. The common rooms are open and airy, the roof above us so far away details must be left to the imagination, but I hear there's a dining room up there at the very tippy top. Closed now, because with only three Maidens left, it was pointless to throw parties anymore.

But now that the Little Sisters are moving in, I bet they will open that dining room back up. We live in the dorm, but we can go into any of the common areas without invitation. Back when nine women used to call this tower home it might be seen as rude to venture upstairs where they live. But now? Who cares? I'm sure all of us have the same plans—stay away from Haryet's, Clara's, and Gemna's floors, but explore *every* other nook and cranny of the place.

After all, some of us will only be here a few short weeks. Everyone wants to make the most of it.

Just as these words are forming in my head, we come around a corner and the whole group—all seventy-five of us—gasp in unison. There is a silence immediately after this gasp, and then... excitement. Squealing, and chatter, and giggling, and dancing, and jumping, and wide eyes with open mouths.

Because we have finally gotten our first look at the Little Sister dorm and it is spectacular.

I pictured a large room with many beds. Perhaps a little nightstand to put things on and a dresser of drawers. All those things are here in this real-life version of the dorm, but to say my imagination came up lacking is an understatement.

I don't know what to look at first. The curved, rounded walls that make the entire massive room look like the inside of a sandstone cave? The mature trees growing out of cracks in the plaster? Or the thick, woody roots spanning the walls—which are four stories tall and dotted with more balconies than I can count?

All that is amazing, but my gaze floats down to the floor where a canal made out of polished blue stone cuts the long, colossal room in half. Just like the real one outside cuts the city down the middle like a bright, blue line.

I'm smiling, and stunned, and shivers erupt, causing my body to have a slight spark display that presents as a tingle across my face where my freckles are. I'm here. And it feels like a dream, something meant for princesses in storybooks from long ago, not a down-city girl who grew up with no spark at all in her humble childhood home.

But the canal is just the start of this most magnificent space. On either side of the teal-colored canal 'water' there is a plush, buff-colored carpet made to look like sand.

While I do not see bedrooms, per se, there are a hundred nooks with beds in them, each one with a special feature to make it unique. Like a terrace, for nooks on the upper floors, or a comfy and semi-private sitting area for those here on the ground. Some beds are on the 'beachy' carpet and others sit directly on the polished turquoise 'canal.' Looking past those first nooks, through round, cut-out windows in the plaster walls, I can see more spaces. More nooks. Like it goes on forever.

The walls are covered in artwork and shelves, which are lined with plants and small decorative items like stained-glass bowls, or books, or vases.

Staircases line the walls every twenty feet or so and dozens of girls are already climbing them, hoping to find their perfect spot to call home on a higher level. And the sewing rooms—my god. The sight of them actually causes me to sigh. They have machines here in up-city. Not foot-petal ones, like I've been using my whole life, but machines powered by the god with the magic of spark. Machines that can sew all kinds of different stitches and handle all kinds of delicate fabrics.

But I will think about that later because Ceela, Britley, Harlow, and Lucindy have all formed up around me. We do not rush the stairs, we remain calm because we were given instructions.

"I presume it's all down that way?" Britley is pointing to the far end of the dorm, which feels like a million miles away from where we're standing.

Ceela begins reciting our instructions from memory. "'Follow the canal all the way down to the end and you will find an area meant to house five. Claim this space and we will be in touch.'"

"All right then, girls." Harlow nods her head with firm resolve. "Let's go make ourselves at home."

Lucindy takes my hand, squeezes it and squeals. Just once. Just a small one. Then gives me a great big all-teeth smile that is part wince. I squeeze her hand back, smiling as well. Being a Little Sister is a job for us. A very important job. But that doesn't mean we can't enjoy all the luxury that comes with it.

Minutes later, having come to the end of the canal, we arrive at a large, open living space outfitted with five separate bedroom nooks, each with an attached private bathroom. All the nooks are different, nothing is the same, but they're all very similar with thick double-sized mattresses covered in linens so soft and fine, it takes my breath away when my fingertips dance over the surface. The pillows are stuffed with goose down, the blankets lined with fur, the towels in the bathroom are oversized and plush.

"Is this how they live?" Ceela asks, holding up a pillow from the bed she's chosen. "Like fuckin' royalty? While all the rest of us down-city shiver under scratchy, threadbare wool at night?"

Britley slaps her playfully. "Watch your mouth, Ceela. We're up-city girls now."

"*No.*" Harlow's interjection is severe and sharp. "We're not. We're always gonna be down-city girls. And we're here for a reason. Don't let the posh blankets fool ya, friends. This city is filled with evil and the god uses these fine things to capture souls. You're ready to sell out for a fuckin' pillow, are ya, Britley?"

Britley tsks her tongue. "You're such a downer, Harlow. Put your feet up and look around for once. This is life. Blink and you'll miss it. Enjoy it. Because your days are just as numbered as mine."

Harlow growls out her response. "There's plenty of time to sleep when you're dead, friend."

"OK," I say, inserting an arm between Britley and Harlow. "We're all on the same side, girls. Harlow, there's nothing wrong with enjoying what we have. Britley, it's fine to be excited, but don't let it go to your head."

They both nod, then sigh, murmuring apologies.

They don't have to listen to me. No one ever put me in charge. We're all equals. But they don't seem to mind taking orders from me when I give them. I think they might even… respect me. So I do my best to be impartial. I like them all equally, so it's not even hard.

And anyway, they all bring something unique to the team. Ceela is a trendsetter. She always has big, new ideas. Lucindy is thoughtful and pragmatic, preferring to work behind the scenes. Harlow always plays devil's advocate, refusing to say any idea is a good one, forcing us to consider every angle of a problem. And Britley is quick to stand next to me, no matter what. Because I am the niece of Matron Bell and I'm the only one who reports to her, so I get the final say in everything. Which really does make me a little bit special, I suppose.

Lucindy is the only one who's been quiet through all this and it takes me a moment to realize that it's because she's not even paying attention to us. She's looking at a bedroom nook all the way inside the interior rooms, not the one meant for her that is closest to the canal.

I make my way over to her, smiling as I round the corners of hallways and pass through other nooks. "Is this your pick?" I nod my head to the space she's in, which is just as gorgeously furnished as the others.

"I'm not sure. Look." Lucindy points up. And when I follow her pointing, I see there is a second level back here.

"Are those more bedrooms?"

Lucindy shrugs. "Not sure. Should we go look?"

I glance over my shoulder, but all the others have gone into their nooks to check them out thoroughly. So I turn back to Lucindy. "Sure. Do you see any stairs?"

There must be several dozen stairwells in this dorm, curving around walls or twisting around landings. But they are all along the canal. Surely there must be a stairwell back here to get us up to the second floor, but the only one we find actually leads down instead.

This is where we find even more rooms. So many more, I get the feeling that this dorm could hold several times the number of girls who just moved in. There are dining rooms, and seating rooms, and sewing rooms, and even a couple of kitchens.

Lucindy looks at me, bewildered. "What is all this?"

"I'm not sure," I tell her.

"It's like they had hundreds of us down here in the old days, not just seventy-five. Why would they need hundreds of Little Sisters?"

"Why, indeed." I say this, but it comes out barely above a whisper because I'm distracted by another stairwell. I point at it. "There. Let's go up now."

Upstairs we can hear the other girls on the second level. Quite clearly, actually, because all the upper-story nook balconies are open to the canal room. But there are no doorways or hallways that connect this hidden second floor with the rest of the second floor.

Nor are there any bedrooms up here.

In fact, it's just a small open area. Completely empty except for a single door built into the far wall.

Lucindy stops at the top of the stairs, frowning as she plants her hands on her hips. "Well, this was a letdown." Then she turns and walks back down, calling out over her shoulder, "Are you coming? I want to check the wardrobes. Do you think we have new clothes yet?"

"Be right there," I call after her. Because I'm curious about the door. Everything in this place is so pretty, but this door is kind of ugly. Gray, and metal, and... well, that's pretty much it.

Strange. But whatever. I pull on the handle, but the door is locked. Part of me is relieved because it's the first day and I don't want to think about this weird space or this weird door. I just want to relish the fact that I live in this spectacular dorm. I want to go to the gala tonight, and dance, and laugh, and eat sweet things, and pretend like the god isn't the devil I know him to be. I want to be like all the up-city people who think that all this luxury is free.

Just one night. That's all I want. A few hours to appreciate the fact that after six years of classes, and lectures, and spark practice—I've made it.

I made it past the first Choosing. And sure, there was special treatment involved. I mean, I am *destined* to be here. But still, I put in the work. I deserve one night to shine, and be special, and be celebrated for the fruits of my labor.

So I go back down and rejoin my friends, putting the weirdness of the space and the mysterious door out of my mind.

Instead, I start poking through drawers (which contain nightclothes, and other comfort garments) and opening armoires (empty, because all our gala dresses are made specially for each event) and peeking into cupboards—which, depending on the space they're in, contain snacks and other small kitchen items or personal hygiene things.

When all that is done, I walk over to the sitting area right along the edge of our portion of the stone canal and flop back into the overstuffed and extraordinarily soft cushions as my gaze wanders. I watch other girls chat excitedly as they make themselves at home in their new Little Sister nooks.

The dorm is even more spectacular than I could've ever imagined. Just the color scheme alone is something I could look at all day. Except for the five of us, all the other Little Sisters are from up-city, so they're used to the trademark sun-bleached blue and soothing neutral tones. And, of course, I've seen my share of this up-city décor as well. I have been coming up here for classes since I pledged myself to the god when I was twelve.

But I am, and forever will be, from down-city where homes don't really have a décor. Furnishings are handmade out of scraps, mostly. There are some heirlooms, of course. Nice things a family has cherished over the generations, like a dining table or a glass-shaded lamp. But matching pillows and rugs? Sheer, billowing curtains that could be made into dozens of dresses? Quaint, round-paned windows in the walls and ceilings meant to direct sunlight into very specific areas of grand rooms?

No. Down-city is downtrodden. But we make do and we are happy with what we have.

And I'm not saying that the up-city girls are selfish, or wasteful, or entitled. I think, after all the years of social classes, all the years of learning polite manners and how to properly thank the god for your place in his world, that we've all come together at a certain level. They, the up-city girls, humbled themselves along the way, while us down-city girls accept the idea that there's more to life than what we were born with.

But only me and my friends come from down-city. Only the five of us understand how special this really is. As well as well as how fleeting it will be.

It was planned this way because we are a team and we are not here to relish in luxury as we giggle our way to the God's Tower stage to be Chosen. We are here to work.

That's why Auntie Bell was so cross with me this morning during the tour. That's why she gave me that infamous stink-eye of hers. "You have a purpose, Jasina." She looked down her nose at me when these words came out earlier. "You all have a purpose. The entire Rebellion is counting on you and your team to do this right. We won't ever get a better opportunity. Not even in a hundred years. This is our only chance and you had better take it seriously." She was shaking her finger at me by the end.

Of course I nodded dutifully, assuring her that all was under control.

And it is. I'm very serious about my job here.

Buuuuuut... this is the biggest moment of my life. She's a crazy old bat if she thinks I'm not gonna enjoy it.

This is *it* for me. Full stop.

There is no chance of me being one of the Chosen at the end of the Choosing because there will be no more Chosen.

The Extraction will die with us.

As will this god.

Ceela, Britley, Harlow, Lucindy, and I are here to make damn sure of it.

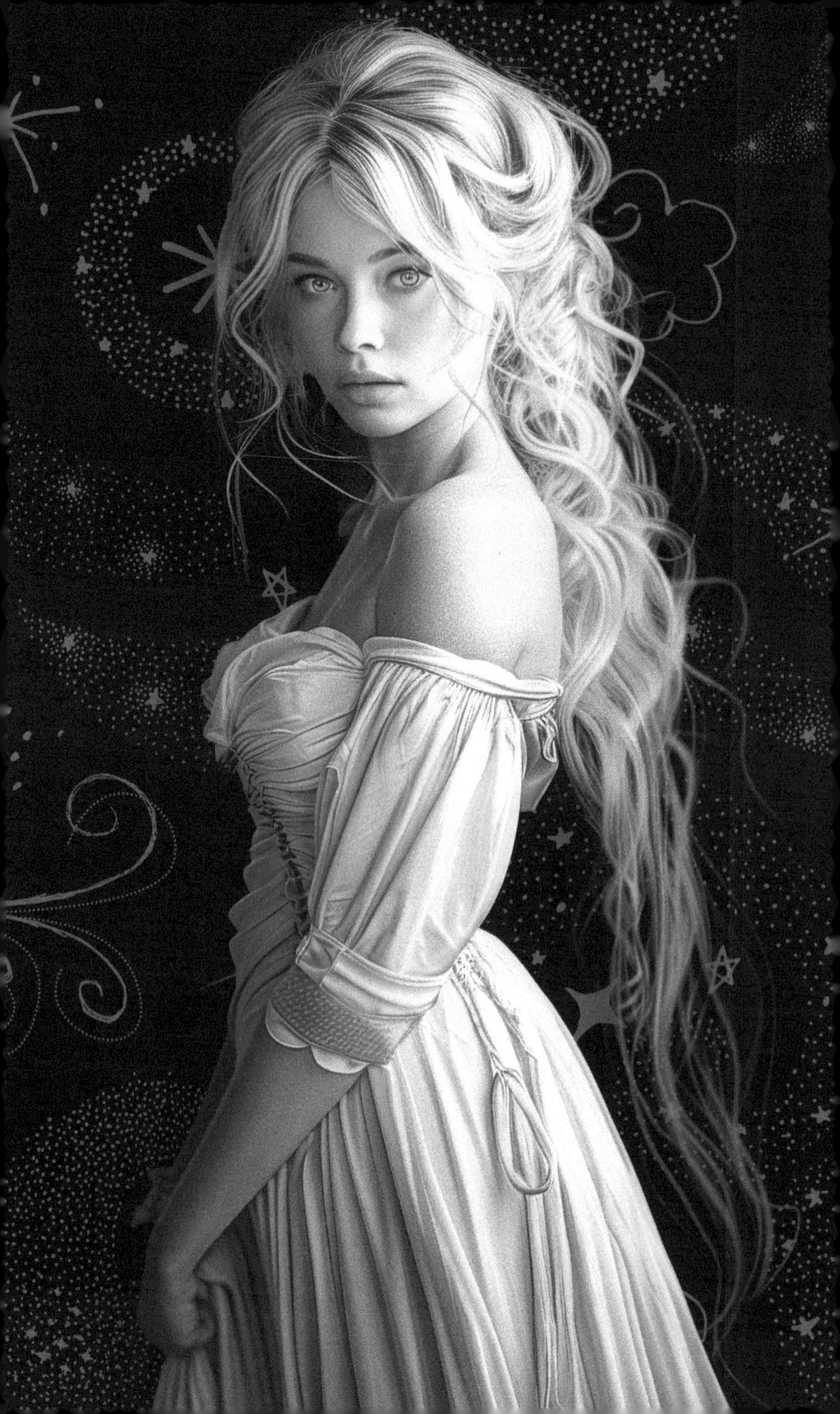

CLARA

CHAPTER THREE

An hour later I'm dressed and alone, standing in front of the floor-to-ceiling windows of my bedroom. If one were standing in the God's Tower looking down the central canal of Tau City, the Maiden Tower would be on the right bank and the Extraction Tower would be on the left.

So my view, looking out my windows, is of the canal and the Extraction District on the other side of it. Of course, the Extraction Tower dominates that view. But everything behind the tower is just as gorgeous because that's where you'll find all the many terraced neighborhoods built up along the sides of the rocky, desert cliffs.

Most of the buildings along the slope have square or rectangle-shaped main levels and a dome on top—which are decorative and a point of pride for everyone in the city. Especially when you're walking the wall and get a good look at them all. Tau City is exquisite from all angles, even down-city. But from the wall, from the air, from the bird's eye view—it's like looking down on perfection.

Some of the domes are deep and tall, while others are shallow or nearly flat, more like caps. Some of them are the color of the plaster—bone, or buff, or sand. But most are dull, sun-bleached shades of light blue. A few domes are trimmed in fancy hand-painted tiles, but most are ringed with thin, gold circles.

Not all the buildings are this shape though. Some are tall cones, almost obelisk-like, and mimic the shape of the sandstone formations that poke up from the desert landscape on the other side of the city walls, beyond our sheltered valley between the hills.

Even if I tried, I doubt I could dream up a more beautiful city. Of course, I have nothing to compare it to since the world beyond our walls ceased to exist more than a thousand years ago, after the wind took over the world and covered it in sand.

We call that event the Great Sweep, a time of extreme chaos that necessitated building protective walls around the city. First, to prevent the sands from covering us all up. But then, after the winds died down, it was to protect us from the predators that seemed to be everywhere, all at once. Very dangerous creatures that wanted to eat us.

That's why we needed the wall.

But no one thinks about that story very much anymore. It was so long ago. And not a single person, myself included, has ever seen anything on the other side of the wall but sand dunes and far-off mountains.

There are no monsters who want to eat us.

But no reason to go beyond the wall, either. Because we're all that's left. The last city standing after the Great Sweep covered the world in sand.

In school—before I pledged myself to the god in the

tower and my life turned into one long stream of lessons in etiquette, and culture, and tradition, and spark—I learned a little bit about why the Great Sweep happened. It had something to do with the speed of rotation of far-off planetary bodies and how they interacted with our planet and moons. I don't remember all the details, but I do know there were five moons before the Great Sweep and now there are only three.

A fascinating fact, in and of itself, but the historical bits that always piqued my interest the most were how my ancestors were able to harness the spark inside us and use it to make fantastic things. Like trains. There used to be train stations and trains where there is now desert. But all that old spark tech is in ruins and mostly covered by the dunes, which covers just about everything outside the walls of our little oasis.

There is nothing visible to the naked eye outside our little valley rimmed in towering red rock formations except sand dunes and a faint, rippling outline of mountains in the distance. I've never seen a stranger come to the wall asking to be let in.

And while there have not been any exploratory expeditions across the sand in my lifetime, there were hundreds in the early days, just after the Great Sweep.

No one ever came back. So… maybe they found a better place out there? Or, more likely, they just died.

It's just us. We're the last.

Our spark, the power that runs our city, comes from the god in the tower now.

He keeps us safe.

He keeps us fed and watered.

He keeps us happy and healthy.

And that's why, when the god in the tower demands Maidens come to him every ten years to keep us all alive, we send those Maidens right on in.

It's just one girl. And she's a volunteer, isn't she?

One girl in exchange for safety and spark to power the greenhouses and field irrigation so we can all eat? One girl in exchange for hot water and forced-air heating during the frigid nights? One girl in exchange for peace of mind so that we, the people of Tau City, might live long lives enriched in comforts and culture?

Yes. We all agree it's worth it. That's why there are seventy-five Little Sisters living in the Maiden Tower dorm at this very moment.

Of course, all of us enter this little arrangement thinking we'll be number two, don't we? Or ten, as it stands right now. None of us ever come in thinking we'll be number one.

Still, I have to take my hat off to Imogen Gibson. She didn't even squeal. Didn't even break her smile when her name was called as our number one. And that same night, as the bells were ringing, she stood in front of that massive black door that leads into the God's Tower with her back straight and her chin up and her spark on full display. It was so bright, it could light up the world.

And while the ritual is terrifying in the moments leading up to midnight on Extraction Day, after Imogen walked through, and the bells stopped ringing, and all the power shortages in up-city ceased to exist, and all the coffee machines worked perfectly once more, and the lights stopped flickering, and the elevators stopped skipping, and the faucets had hot water once again—we, the good people of Tau City, forgot our fear and started, once again, to count our blessings.

Because the spark from just one girl was enough to set things right.

Or so we thought.

Then the bells rang again, two years later, eight years early, and it was a shock. But we did have warnings. Nothing massive, but there were small signs. Machines struggled to work, lights crackled and dimmed, and a few heaters in the orchard gave out, causing an apple shortage that fall.

Well, we all thought. *Maybe the city has grown too much and we've been demanding more spark from the god than we thought?*

Yes, surely that was the problem.

So in went Spark Maiden number two—Marlowe Hughes—and all spark to up-city was strictly metered so we could keep track of what we used.

Three (mostly uneventful) years later, when the bells rang again, people were thoroughly confused. The metering worked. People conserved spark. We were using less than ever. And there were no signs of shortages. Everything was working just fine as far as anyone could tell.

So why was the god in the tower demanding yet another Spark Maiden?

Of course, Maiden number three—Mabel Paice, not to be confused with Maiden number five, Mabel Shaw—went in. This time things got worse. And the bells rang again just two weeks later. So in went Lucy Fisher.

Lucy Fisher was the breaking point for the people of Tau City. Two Spark Maidens in one decade? Weird, but OK. It had happened before.

Four, though?

No. No, no, no. This was abnormal. Something was very wrong. People panicked.

But, as one does when over time strange things return to normal, they forgot about it. When there were no more requests from the tower, we moved on with our lives, content that whatever the problem was, it had been fixed. This is what people do when times are good. No one wants to think about the bad times when nothing is wrong. What is the point of that?

There was no rhyme or reason for the next three called in—Mabel Shaw, Piper Adley, and Brooke Bayford. It was two years, then seven months, then eight months.

Brooke was the last and it's been over a year now. With just three months left of our service, Haryet, Gemna, and I can't help but hold our breath. It's been tense. But today feels… different. Like we've turned a corner.

To us, these Little Sisters are like a salvation.

We're going to make it.

And when I look at myself in the mirror, wearing this spectacular, handmade gala gown, it's enough to convince myself it's true.

"Are you ready?"

I turn and find tiny Haryet standing in my bedroom doorway all dressed up in her equally spectacular gown. It's also made of glimmering champagne silk, the highest-quality linen, and hand-blown glass beads. But it's shaped a little different, has a light blue sash that crosses her breasts, and more skirt layers than mine.

"You look stunning, Haryet."

She smiles and curtsies to me, lifting her skirts up as she bows her head. "So do you!"

"So do we all." I look past Haryet and find Gemna wearing her own version of our gowns.

She models for us, lifting up a hand to showcase her hair as she turns her head and cocks a hip. "Fab, right?"

We agree, laughing and smiling. But when that's done, there's a moment when we all go a little somber.

This is not the end. We're close, but not there yet. There are dozens of galas just like this one in our near future.

It just feels a little bit… *final*, for some reason.

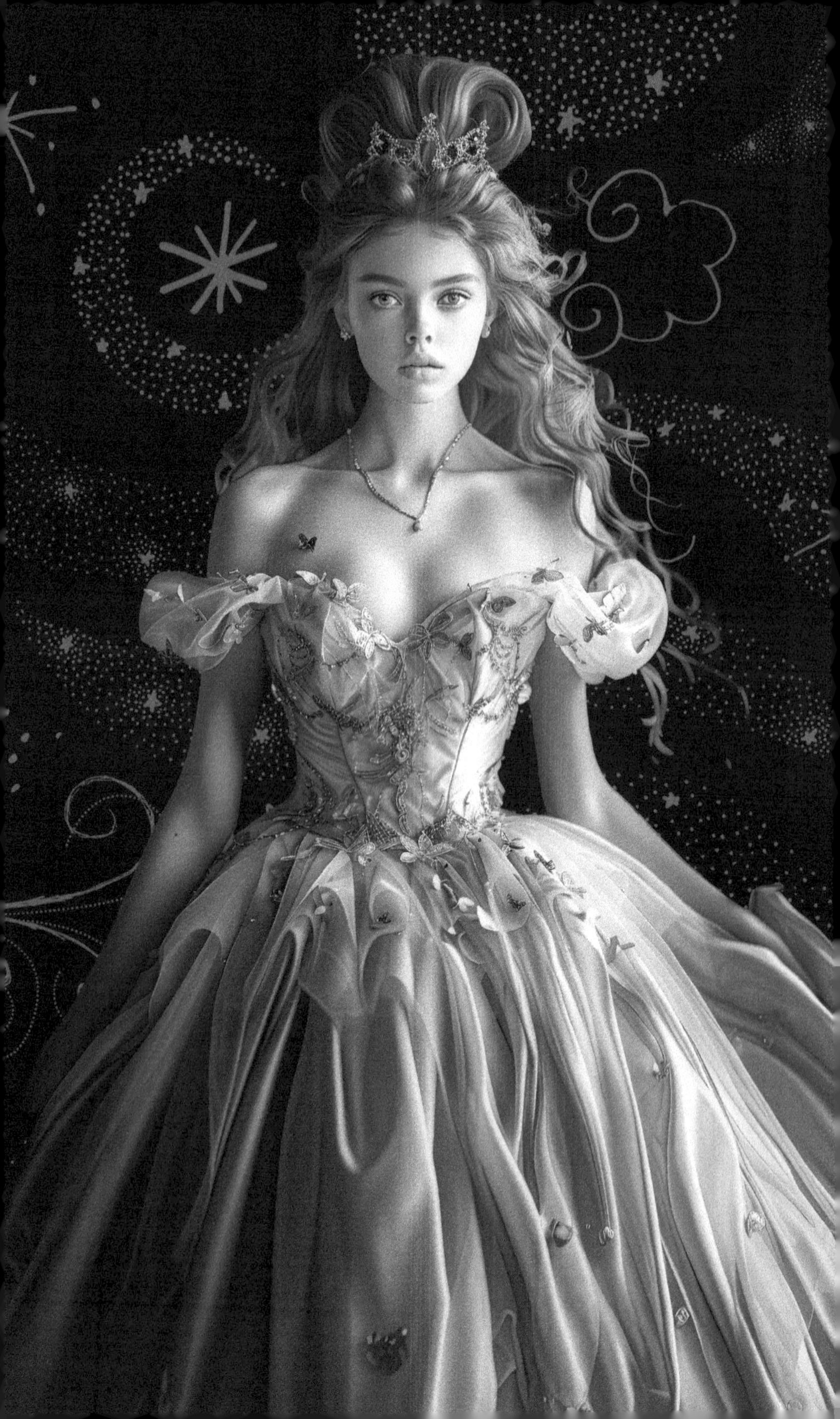

JASINA

CHAPTER FOUR

*A*s soon as the awe wears off, the five of us snap into action. Our first gala is in just two hours. We're not meant to have much time to pull ourselves together for the first Choosing ball, we're meant to have thought everything out ahead of time and the blue dresses we are all currently wearing are meant to be our gowns for the evening.

But every girl in Pledge, from the time they sign up at age twelve, secretly starts planning how she will amaze the Extraction Master on the first night because this is our first public display of spark.

There are about half a dozen girls who have a slight advantage in this area because they have exceptional spark displays. Spark display is genetic. You get what you get. But it's what you *do* with it that really matters.

And this is where my friends and I will shine.

We don't have the best breeding, we weren't blessed with up-city levels of genetic spark, but we are smart and we came prepared to stun. Because the five of us will be displaying our spark using our dresses. Embellishments, to be exact. Aside from the actual dresses we're currently wearing, the Little Sisters are only allowed to bring a modest-sized makeup case into the dorm. From now on everything else will be provided—including all the basics such as food, and clothes, and personal health items.

It doesn't even cross the minds of most Little Sisters to concentrate on making their dresses the one thing that sets them apart on the stage, because we have to wear the one we put on this morning to the gala tonight and the Choosing dress must always be made by our own hands.

And while every one of us looked very pretty in our handmade dresses, most of them were basic and simple. Because that's the tradition. This city does love its traditions, this whole Extraction thing being a prime example of that.

Also, these up-city girls are mostly unconcerned about their seamstress skills because... well, why should they be? All their lives they've had the coin to buy the clothes they wear. And anyway, dressmaking is only a modest percentage of the total score during the Choosings. Spark will be weighed the highest overall, of course. But even dancing is ranked higher than dressmaking.

Why worry about this dress when, in the past, it hasn't counted much?

So it hasn't even occurred to the up-city girls that they might make an impression by turning a simple dress into a beautiful gown with the addition of trimmings.

And no, I might not have the most powerful display of spark, but I *do* have spark. As do we all, or we wouldn't be here. And I know how to use it to my full advantage. All five of us do. That is how we, the down-city girls, will make ourselves stand out tonight.

Immediately after we all choose our spaces in the dorm the Matrons appear, clapping their hands and barking orders at us. Telling us to be ready in an hour because we have one final dress rehearsal in the ballroom.

My crew and I make the most of this hour. We find our modest-sized makeup cases on the carts lining the fake canal down the center of the room and rush right back to the sewing area in our space.

Inside my case I have yards, and yards, and yards of blue tulle. You can't stuff much fabric into a makeup case, not without ruining it, and there's very little time for sewing. But tulle is special in this regard. It's slightly wrinkled once I pull it out, but so is my day dress. It's linen and we all know what linen does in this heat. So when I wrap the secret skirts around my waist and fluff them up a little, I am transformed into something sexy and wild. A feminine creature men might dream of taming.

Which was my plan. The Extraction Master, Aldo Scott, is kind of old, but he's still a man. Men respond to beauty and when I pull out all the stops, I am more than beautiful. I am... tantalizing and sultry. Not exquisite in a Clara Birch way. But I see how the men look at me. Even the old ones.

And anyway, Aldo's retiring this year so his son, Finn Scott, will be right beside him tonight. He is *not* an old man and I don't care how attached he is to stupid Clara Birch, *all* men look.

He will definitely be looking at me tonight.

I labored over my skirts for more than a year, hand-stitching hundreds of handmade fabric butterflies into the tulle. Then I accented it with strings of shimmery, silver thread and tiny golden roses made of silk. Cheap silk, but who cares. The final result is something right out of a fairy tale.

And I didn't tell a soul about it. Which is why all four of my best friends are gaping at me in shock.

"Holy wow, Jasina!" Ceela's hand is over her mouth as she takes in my new look.

Britley comes over and bends down to get a better look at the details. "My goodness. Now we know why you turned down all those dates over the past year! How long did you work on this?"

"*So* long." I chuckle.

Harlow circles me with a critical eye, tapping her chin with her forefinger. "It's over-the-top, excessive, and pretentious." She stops in front of me, frowning. But then she bursts out laughing. "But that"—she points at the dress—"is a fabulous dress!"

Lucindy squeals, clapping her hands.

And then I compliment their dress embellishments too. We all brought extra tulle skirts. It's the only thing that could make this kind of impact and fit into a makeup case the size of a toaster. But each of our dresses are vastly different.

Harlow's skirt is gold and embellished with tiny brass fairy bells so every time she moves, she makes music.

Lucindy's skirt is blue, like mine, but it's not just tulle. She's ripped up tiny strips of dyed cotton and sewed them along the back to make a train that fluffs up in the wind she creates with her feet as she walks.

Ceela made her tulle into a huge bow that attaches at the small of her back and falls all the way down to the floor.

And Britley has not only made a skirt, but a capelet too. Her day dress was tailored, unlike all the other Little Sisters, who opted for full and fluffy. So this capelet makes her look mature and sophisticated instead of princess-y.

We stand in front of the massive, floor-to-ceiling mirrors in the sewing room and sigh.

But then the Matrons start calling us to line up, and while all my friends seem to have found time to pull their hair into something cultured and sophisticated, mine is still an untamed mess of auburn waves.

It's long and wild—like me. And I decide that it will just have to do.

When we get in the line of Little Sisters down the center canal of the dorm, every head turns to look at us. All eyes widen. Most with appreciation, but some with jealousy.

They all look gorgeous as well. Most of them have much nicer hair than me, though mine is pretty spectacular, wild and untamed as it is. And all of them have better makeup, since I didn't have time for that, either. But still, even though they look stunning, they are… the same. They are what the people of Tau City have come to expect from the first Choosing.

And the five of us are different.

This is when they all realize that we're down-city girls and not only that, we're sticking together. A team. Always a team.

And that's when they remember that this is a competition and turn back around to stare straight ahead.

I catch the eye of Auntie Bell after we start filing though the hallway to make our way over to the God's Tower event center, and she winks at me.

A knowing wink.

Not just because I look amazing and my seamstress talents are on full display, but because this is the beginning of the end for these galas.

It all starts here.

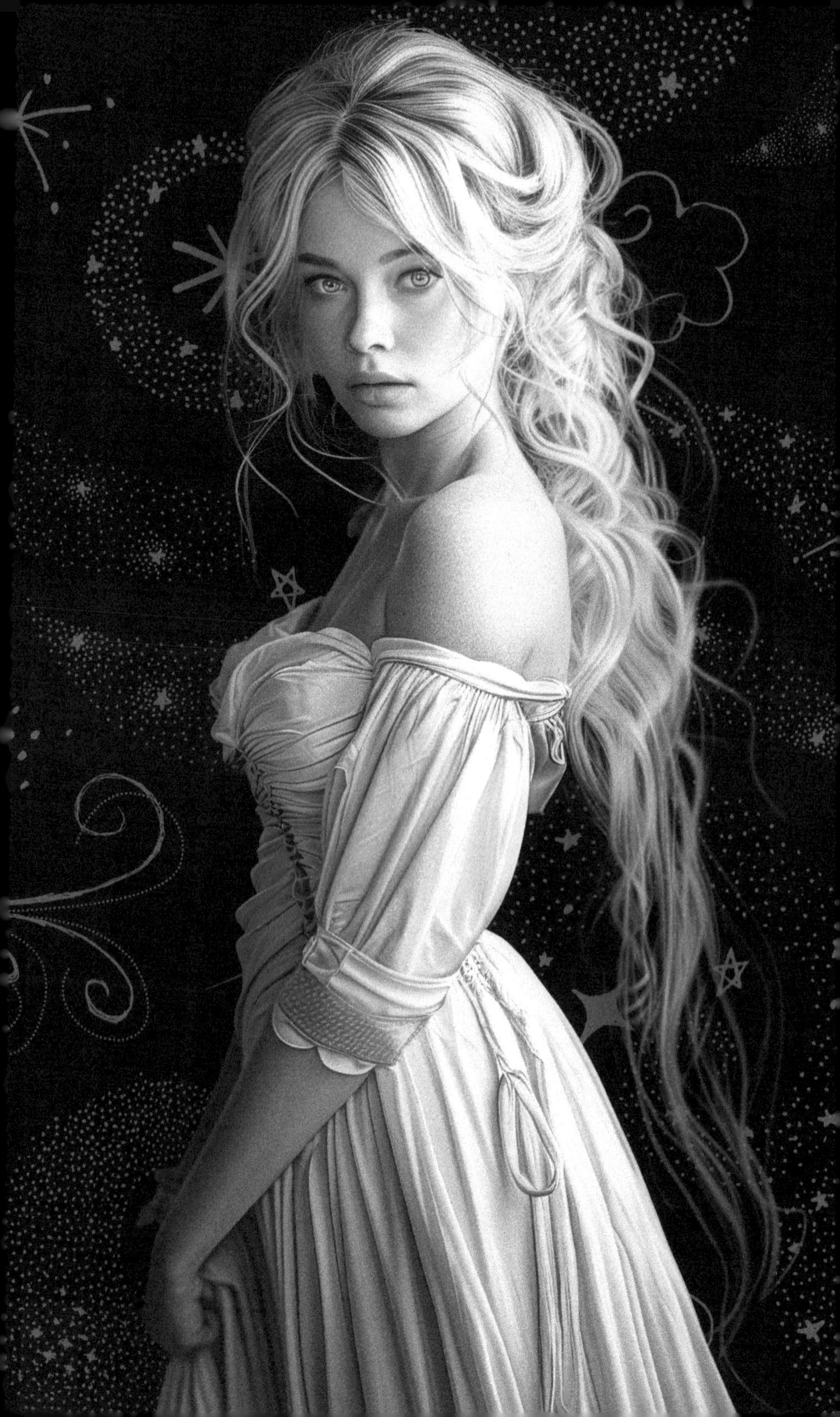

CLARA

CHAPTER FIVE

The God's Tower event center is unquestionably the most elaborate, over-the-top community building in Tau City. It is a giant four-story dome set in the middle of God's Lake with bridges leading back to both the Maiden and Extraction Districts like spokes on a wheel.

It's massive, but when compared to the God's Tower directly behind it, the event center comes off as miniature.

The ballroom inside is equally impressive—glossy, ice-blue floors lead up to a set of grand shallow steps at the top of the room, where balcony staircases feed into it. These balconies are supported by thick columns, meant to draw your eye up to the ceiling, which is a series of glass-paned windows surrounded by an intricate framework of silver-gray trusses.

You could get lost in that ceiling if you look too long. It's mesmerizingly beautiful.

At the top of the shallow stairs, right in the center of the stage, is a colossal, twenty-foot-wide glass globe with a hollow center and this is where Gemna, Haryet, and I presently stand, hidden by the dazzling gold light that shines outward, blinding the people in the ballroom.

Attendants are bustling all around us as we stand still and allow them do their jobs. Everything about the Maiden ceremonies is scripted, right down to the last detail. And we're used to this by now. So I am barely noticing the lighting people, and the makeup people, and the directors because I've been looking for Finn—dying to see him in whatever fancy suit the coordinators have planned—because the end of my Extraction Maiden tenure is the beginning of his.

In a way.

Because Finn's apprenticeship as Extraction Master begins tonight, he will be at his father's side through the whole thing, learning all the little details that make these galas so exciting and fun.

But I haven't seen him yet. And that's strange, isn't it? Come to think of it, I haven't seen Aldo, either. I lean in to Haryet's shoulder. "Have you seen Finn?"

"No. But I haven't been looking."

"I haven't seen him either. Have you, Gemna?"

"Nope. But I have seen both Mitchell and Jeyk, so he's gotta be around here somewhere."

Mitchell and Jeyk are Finn's best friends, so this assumption of Gemna's makes sense.

I look again. Granted, I don't have a great view of the main stage—it's much wider than the twenty-foot hole I can presently see through. Plus there are balconies and staircases on either side of the main stage and Finn could be in any of these out-of-sight locations. But I'm anxious to see him so I stare out of the hole, wishing for him to appear. It's only been a few hours since I left his quarters, but all the moments we spend apart feel like an eternity now that the end is so near.

I'm so ready to be done with the Maidens. So ready to just fall into a new life with him.

"Hey."

I jump in surprise, my hand over my heart, when Finn's voice is suddenly in my ear.

"Sorry. Didn't mean to scare you."

He's come up behind me, but I don't turn to look at him because attendants are already barking at me to keep still, and not to ruin my hair, and all kinds of other things. "Where have you been? I was looking for you."

He lets out a long breath, but no explanation is forthcoming. So despite the instructions of the attendants, I turn to look at Finn anyway. He's pale. And when I place my hand on his cheek, he's cold, too. "Are you sick?"

"No. But…" He hesitates. "But there was… an accident. I'll be presiding tonight."

"What kind of accident? Your father? Is he OK?"

"He's in the health center right now. They're calling the god—"

"*What?*" My mouth drops open in shock. Healing costs Tau City a lot of spark. It's used very sparingly these days. Of course, Tau City—for the most part—is filled to the brim with super-fit citizens, so health services have never been much of a drain on our spark rations. But still, even for the Extraction Master, they don't call the god for help with healing unless it's something *really* serious.

Finn exhales, interrupting the sense of hopelessness that begins creeping up my spine. "He's fine, Clara. He's…

gonna be fine. I just need to take over tonight and... it's... fine."

When things are fine, people don't feel the need to *insist* that things are fine.

I open my mouth, ready to pepper him with a barrage of questions, but then people are yelling at us both. At me to turn around, and at Finn to take his place. Music starts and it's not like we have a choice. I can just barely make out the Little Sisters entering the ballroom outside the globe. And then Finn is gone and I can't do anything but stare ahead and watch the show like everyone else.

I want to think about what Finn just said—especially the part about calling the god in the tower for help—but there's no time because suddenly, the whole place comes alive.

While I can't see the balconies or much of the stairwells, the scripted nature of the Extraction ceremonies means they are mostly predictable. Plus, it's the job of a Little Sister to memorize every movement. And even though it's been a long time since I was a Little Sister, I can see the patterns in my mind's eye.

With seventy-five girls in this first lineup of Chosen Little Sisters, the entrance is a very complicated affair and the choreography uses all eight of the balcony staircases to get everyone in quickly. Movement is coordinated like a dance, but no one is dancing. Just calmly trying to make sure they keep count of where they are and where they're supposed to be after the weaving serpentine entrance pattern is complete.

When the music stops there is a sea of girls in pretty blue dresses filling the entire circular area at the top of the ballroom, the space directly at the foot of the stage where our glass globe is.

Then the spotlights, which have been blocking us from view inside the globe, go out. This is the cue for Gemna, Haryet, and myself to walk forward and stand in front of the Little Sisters.

I'm in the center, because we always stand in numerical order on stage and I'm number nine, so I have the only spoken lines of the night. "Welcome, everyone," I say, projecting my voice to the very ends of the massive ballroom. "Welcome to the very first Choosing celebration of the one-hundred-and-twenty-first Tower God Extraction! Please give all seventy-five of our new Little Sisters the warmest of welcomes!"

Aside from the Extraction number, these lines never change. And although I have never said them myself, since this is my first time being center Maiden at the first Choosing celebration, I have known this day was coming for ten years now, so it all comes out in perfect order, just like it's supposed to.

Then Finn's voice is bounding through the ballroom. "Yes, welcome, everyone!"

He's stage left on a special landing halfway between the second level and the upper balconies, and the thing I immediately pick up about him is that he's calm. Like his father is not in the health center and the god has not been called upon to help him heal.

"You're probably wondering what I'm doing up here. Well, my father decided to throw me in the deep water and see if I could swim, so I'm taking over for him tonight—and I promise, Extraction Master, I will not disappoint!"

There's some chuckling here from the crowd as Finn pauses to look stage right and salute. We all look stage right, expecting Aldo to be there, smiling down at his son from the upper balcony or something.

But of course he's not there. Because he is in the health center.

Finn doesn't give the crowd time to wonder about this, or question where Aldo might be. He gives them just enough time to *think* they saw him, and then he's talking again.

I stop listening though. Because I'm suddenly caught up in this lie.

Because that's what he's doing. Finn is lying to the people. Trying to preserve the good mood of the night, I suppose.

But it kinda rubs me the wrong way. Aldo is injured and the god has been called in for special rations of spark. The proper thing to do here is to chuck these Little Sisters aside and have everybody bow their heads and pray for him. Begging the god to spare his life. Giving up every little bit of city spark we have available to heal him.

And that's not what happens. What happens is that things go on like Aldo is not injured and possibly dying.

I let out a breath, trying to control my... well, I'm not sure what I'm feeling, so I don't have a word for it. It's not anger, that's too strong. But it's much more than dissatisfaction.

But the ceremony goes on around me and then it's time

for Haryet, Gemna, and I to leave the stage and make our way up the stairs to a mezzanine platform on the same level where Finn is standing, only on the opposite side of the ballroom. He's already introducing Little Sister number ten by the time we take our seats.

I'm barely paying attention at this point. Much too worried about Aldo to care about these girls in blue as they muster up pathetic displays of spark power—case in point, this girl, number ten, is showing her spark through her eyes. Which are already blue so, yeah. Not only is this trick way overdone, but it has almost no effect.

Still, Finn smiles at her, clapping politely as she exits and he calls the next girl in line.

I want to get up and march right over to the health center to hold Aldo's hand and beg the god to make him well. But of course, there is no chance of that. I won't be getting out of here for hours, at least. Not until every last girl has been introduced and all the dancing is over.

I huff, making Haryet turn her head in my direction and whisper, "What's wrong?"

"Nothing. I'm... my feet hurt." It's the best I can come up with on the spot. I'm not much of a liar. Can't even remember the last time I told a lie, even one as small as this. But I suppose I *must* lie. Otherwise I'll just upset everyone.

I guess Finn came to the same conclusion, so maybe I'm overreacting.

Haryet lets out a breath, then reaches for my hand and gives it a squeeze. "Mine too, sister. But I'm busy picturing life after all this is over. And we're so close now, it doesn't even feel like a dream anymore." She gives my hand another squeeze, then lets go and straightens her back, pretending to pay attention.

I do the same. There isn't any point in getting worked up because there is nothing I can do. The only one with the power to change the situation would be Finn himself, and he just keeps going with the introductions, like he's not at all concerned about Aldo.

So I think maybe... maybe someone came and passed on a message right before the ceremony started letting him know that Aldo is fine. That the god listened and healed him up.

That's the only logical explanation for Finn's jovial mood, and as a little more time passes, I decide that's what happened. Aldo is fine and I can relax.

So that's what I do. I calm down, loosen up my tight shoulders, and listen attentively like I'm supposed to as each Little Sister walks across the stage in her simple, handmade blue dress while Finn calls out her name.

The spark displays are almost never dazzling the way Imogen's was when she was on this stage. She was a very special case. We all knew she was going to be number one.

But this next Little Sister is wearing something unexpected and different.

Haryet coos in my ear as I recognize the brazen, auburn-haired girl from earlier in the day as she takes her walk. "Ooo! That's Jasina Bell."

Gemna pipes in now. "That dress is gorgeous, isn't it, girls? Do you think she made it herself?"

"Not likely." Haryet laughs. "She comes from a long line of Maidens. I'm sure she had help."

I pay attention here, my curiosity getting the better of me. The dress she's wearing really is spectacular. It's blue, like all the others, but it's nothing like all the others. Typically, the first gala dresses are plain and simple, because they are the same dresses they've been wearing all day.

But Jasina Bell's dress doesn't look anything like the one I saw her in earlier. So many layers of flowing and fluttering skirts over a simple linen... this is when I realize she *is* wearing the one from earlier, except she's embellished it with the tulle, and the tulle has been decorated with... I squint and lean in. "What's that on her dress? Are those... butterflies?"

"Embroidered," Gemna says. "And look, it's sparkling."

"Woven silver?" Haryet postulates.

"And something gold too," I add.

And the moment I say this, it comes to life. The crowd gasps as all the tiny butterflies on her dress take flight and flutter around her. This is when we realize they are made of spark!

Not the actual embellishments on her dress, but electric blue light copies of them lift up off the tulle and float in the air around her. They don't do anything else, just float there. But this is such a different way to display spark that the entire ballroom erupts in cheers and clapping. And it goes on for so long, Finn has to stop them in order to make the girl leave the stage because she is soaking this moment up with every fiber of her being.

The whole thing is way over the top, but at the same time, it's... gorgeous. And even though projecting light into the air is a simple trick—hell, even I managed to do it during my first Choosing gala—it's not simple at all when combined with the butterflies on the dress.

It actually might be the most spectacular display of average spark I've ever seen. And by the sound of the reaction in the ballroom, everyone is agreeing with me.

"How many Maidens?" I ask Haryet and Gemna. "In her family, I mean."

"Four," Gemna replies. "But most were Chosen generations ago."

"One of them is a Matron now," Haryet adds.

Well. Now I remember the name of the Matron I saw leading that group of Little Sisters this afternoon. Matron Bell. Aunt, or great-aunt, or great-great-aunt of one Jasina Bell. Who will forever be known, from this day forward, as the Little Sister who wore the prettiest gown to the First Choosing in the whole entire history of the Choosings and stunned people with her spark butterflies.

Haryet interrupts my thoughts with a new statement. "I heard she got special treatment. You know, to get this far, since she's from down-city."

Gemna counters this with a huff. "Don't be jealous now, Haryet. This girl is as gorgeous as that dress. And her display of spark was creative and original. She doesn't need special treatment."

Gemna's right. Jasina is probably *the* most beautiful girl I've ever seen. And that's saying a lot, because every girl in the Extraction is beautiful and I've seen a lot of them.

I take Jasina's side for another reason as well, though. Because I maybe got special treatment myself. I'm not saying I didn't earn my place, but Aldo is like a father to me.

After my own father died, Aldo took me under his wing. I was already a part of the Extraction—girls sign up for that when they are twelve. But he helped me so much along the way after my parents died.

And number *nine*? It's practically a guarantee that I wouldn't go into that tower. So who's to say that he didn't give me this position simply because he loved me? And because his son loved me? And because he knew that one day, I really would be family?

I never asked, and I never would, but it's a logical conclusion even if it's not true.

Finally, all the introductions are over and Finn officially starts the ball by announcing the very first Dance of Sisters. Then the entire stage is filled with dancing girls in blue. At first, they do all the moves alone in their respective lines, but then young men enter, all wearing linen suits the color of sand. They weave their way through all the Little Sisters, and since I'm sitting in a balcony, I can see the patterns they are making as each one finds their partner and drifts off to the outer edge. When all the partners have been matched up, the dance truly begins with a waltz.

Haryet sighs, putting a hand to her heart. "My goodness, do you girls remember this night ten years ago the way I do?"

Gemna laughs. "I will never forget that night. Jeyk was my partner and he flirted with me non-stop. It was…" She sighs as well now. "It was the best night of my life, I think. And even though we've been to so many galas since then, this very first one was the absolute tippy-top!"

I smile as well, thinking back on this night again, this

time allowing myself to remember the details. Finn was my partner. We were dating for real at the time, but we knew that the moment I got in to the top ten it would be over. Not for real—well, yes for real, but it was just temporary and we both knew that. We were gonna wait for each other.

If I were making that promise to him today, I would understand that it was just a way to make ourselves feel better and the chances were very slim that we would still be in love ten years later. I was naïve back then. We both were. So we didn't understand that the odds were against us. We just carried on like it was already true.

Of course, we've seen each other nearly every day for the last decade of my service to the god in the tower. And we've had lots of meals together. Both private, at Finn's family home, as well as in public for gatherings and galas and such.

We even got together for a few trysts, like the one we had this afternoon. But all in all, he did his thing and I did mine. He didn't date anyone else, even though I never made a rule that he couldn't. And I didn't date anyone else, either. We didn't need the rule. We are in love. We only want each other.

He was my partner through all of it so my very first Dance of Sisters was with the man I loved. All the dances in my Choosing stage were with the man I loved. It was a good time. A fun time. A much more innocent time too.

I have been paired up with many a man for the galas that came after, of course, but none of them got anything out of me other than some light conversation. My heart belongs to Finn Scott. I haven't even imagined another. If something were to happen to him and we didn't get married, I would die a spinster.

"Will you miss it?"

I turn and look at Haryet, shaking my head. "I like the memories. It's been a great adventure and I have nothing but good things to say about my time in the Extraction. But I won't miss it."

She smiles and nods. "Me either."

Gemna dissents to my right. "I'll miss the maids." We all chuckle. "I mean, people have been picking up after me for ten years now, girls. That's a luxury you get used to quickly." Then she sighs and her real answer comes out. "But… it will be a relief, ya know?"

Both Haryet and I turn our heads to look at her, nodding.

"I'm number ten, girls. I'm not going into that tower. There was never any chance of it. But still, especially in these times, it's a weight on me and I want it to be over."

Haryet lets out a small laugh. "Oh, tell me about it. I'm number eight, Gemna. Remember when the bell rang for number seven?"

Gemna and I both huff. We remember. Haryet screamed like she woke up from a nightmare. But of course, it was worse than that because it wasn't a nightmare, it was reality.

After Brooke Bayford went in, Haryet was a mess. Jittery, and sensitive, and emotional. She had long bouts of insomnia, endless weeks of bloodshot eyes, and lost twelve pounds—which is way too much weight for someone so tiny. It made her look malnourished.

She got through it, of course. It's been over a year since

Brooke's bell rang. But it's horrifying to realize that your life could be over at any time and you have no control at all.

I can't even imagine what it's been like to be Haryet this past year. I want this to be over. For all of us. It's been a good decade, but it's also been a stressful decade. Probably the most stressful Extraction ever. Never, in the entire history of this contest, has a Spark Maiden with a number higher than two been called into the tower.

Three months.

It feels very far away when the bell could toll at any time.

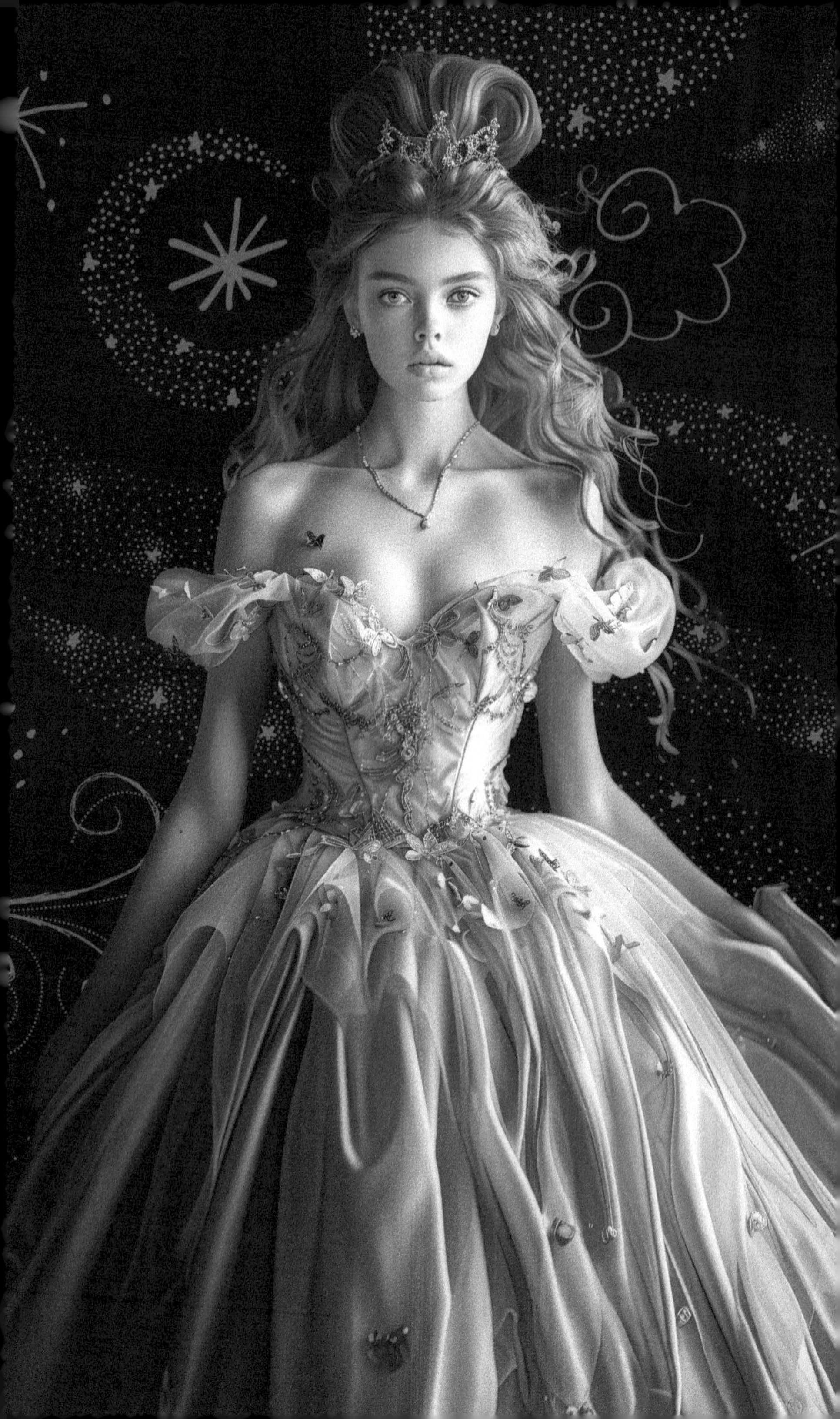

JASINA

CHAPTER SIX

The Dance of Sisters is the most stressful part about the Choosings because there are seventy-five girls, plus the boys we've been partnered up with. I guess we could just enter in two single-file lines and meet somewhere in the middle—it would get the job of getting us in here and with the right partner done in a much more efficient manner, but this is up-city and what is the point of a gala if you're not gonna put on a spectacle?

And so the Matron choreographers came up with the Dance of Sisters... oh, hundreds of years ago, probably. Maybe every Little Sister in the history of Tau City kicked off the first Choosing in this manner, I'm not sure. And it doesn't matter. For this is the way we begin tonight. Eight stairwells deliver lines of exquisitely dressed young men. But the boys closest to us are not the boys we have been partnered with. That's much too simple for a gala this important.

No, there are many steps to take and turns to make before we will end up with the boys chosen to be escorts for the Extraction. We are stuck with them for the duration.

So I count my steps and focus my attention on the other

hundred and forty-nine people dancing, and twirling, and walking across the glossy stone floor with me until finally, a good seven minutes after the young men have joined us, I am staring up at Donal Oslin.

Every boy here tonight is handsome. Just as every girl is pretty. That's a given. I mean, why spoil the night with ugly people when you have specimens such as us?

But Donal Oslin is a whole other kind of handsome. He's got dark hair that's always been a little bit too messy for his status in life. But no one seems to care because this tousled look only accentuates his perfect dimples flanking his charming smile.

And that's just where the handsome starts with Donal, because even covered by the flawless, sand-colored suit his body is on full display. His shoulders are broad and his chest wide, tapering down into a v-shape at his narrow waist. The shirt he's wearing under his jacket is so tight the ripped muscles of his stomach make a pattern of hills and valleys under the fabric.

I've seen him shirtless. We didn't practice this dance in suits and dresses. So it doesn't take much imagination on my part to conjure up a reliable image of what those muscles look like without clothes.

But Donal and I? Not a thing. He comes from an entirely different kind of family than I do.

Well, kind of.

The Oslins run the entire Tower District. Which doesn't sound particularly advantageous at first glance, since the Tower District is so small and consists only of the God's Tower, the bell tower, and the God's Tower event center.

But being the Tower District governor, which is Donal's father's title, is somewhat akin to being a king. He has final say over everything that happens here. It's a small kingdom, to be sure, as the only people who live in Tower District are the Oslins, the bellmakers, and the five families who take care of the event center and the grounds. But it's special and Prince Donal here understands, and uses, this unique station in life to his full advantage.

My family was special like that too, once upon a time. As bellmakers we were part of this small kingdom until the demotion that that got us sent down-city several generations back.

I can't tell if Donal finds the fact that my family used to live in the Tower District to be a threat or just an unfortunate reminder that nothing lasts forever, but regardless, he hates me.

And he's not shy about showing it.

At least to me. Donal here is much, much, *much* too cultured to ever make a scene in public. But he's got ways of jabbing me with insults so no one ever hears.

His right hand slips town to my waist and his left hand is waiting for me when I press my palm into it. Then we are dancing. He takes ceremony and circumstance all very seriously, so he waits until we've found our rhythm, making sure that all the other couples around us are on track as well, before he starts in on me.

"You look like a whore, Jasina. Why are your clothes always so… *slutty?*"

I don't even break my smile. Or eye contact. This is my moment, not his. He is nothing but a partner. Completely replaceable. I am *Chosen*. And I think this is part of the reason he's so mean to me when we dance. No one is looking at him tonight. His suit is very nice, but every partner in this ballroom is wearing that very same suit. It's nothing but a uniform.

My dress, on the other hand, is spectacular. My light display, while simple, was original and people loved it.

And he knows this. Everyone is looking at me and this dress and they are thinking about my spark. All the most spectacular photographs of this year's First Choosing will be of me.

Donal will probably be there for some of them—the society page writers can't *not* mention him—but he will be nothing but a small side note and I will be the main event.

When he doesn't get a rise out of me, he takes it a step further, squeezing my hand until the little bones of my fingers are being painfully pressed into each other. "It's always so over the top with you, Jasina. I get it, you've got no proper role models down-city—just the tavern sluts and the tattooed strippers—but come on." He pauses here to chuckle. "You've been coming up-city for etiquette classes for six years now, surely you've window-shopped the latest fashions. There's no excuse for all that… *fluff*."

He looks down at my tulle skirts for a moment, then back up at me, meeting my gaze. He smiles, his green eyes bright with wicked malice. And his next few words come out low, barely a whisper. "It's like you want everyone to see you as something for sale. Are you for sale, Jasina? How many coins will it cost me if I take you into a tunnel, push your face into a wall, lift up all that fluff, and fuck you in the ass?"

It's... gross. And it used to make me mad when he said things like this to me when we danced, but I forced myself to ignore him. He typically gives up if I don't give him a reaction. But I'm just tired of it now and I can't bite my tongue this time. "Donal," I say, my voice a low whisper, just as his was. "Your father doesn't even have enough coin to buy me, sweetie. Though he did try, much to your mother's dismay. So don't worry your pretty little head about how much I cost, dear boy, I'm *way* out of your league."

His mouth forms a chuckle, but I can see the anger dancing in his narrowed eyes.

He's about to retort with something equally hateful, but the music changes and this is our cue. A moment later I'm spinning away, right into the hands of my next partner.

Reid Bladen is the complete opposite of Donal Oslin, though they do run in the same crowd. Reid is Lucindy's partner, and this makes me very happy because he's everything Donal is not and Lucindy is the sweetest little rebel this war will ever see.

Also, Reid is a nice buffer as far as the opening dance goes. I get four minutes with him, then I move on to another of the boys in the same clique, Murray Gray, who is partnered with Ceela. But the time spent with each partner gets shorter and shorter after Reid, so I don't worry too much about who is guiding me across the glossy stone floors. And instead I concentrate on all the details around me.

Who is standing front-row of the crowded dancefloor

beyond the bright lights where the Little Sisters dance? Who is up in the balconies? Is anyone unhappy? Anyone have a frown? Who is laughing loudly? Who is already drunk?

I'm good with details and my memory has been trained to retain things since I was a small child, so this is what I do for the remainder of the dance—I soak it all up so I can report back later.

And then it's over. We stop and I clap. My ending partner is Bruce Cadwell, Harlow's date for the night, and he claps too. Sometimes he's mean to me, but he didn't say anything at all to me tonight and when I look up at him, I find his eyes searching the room until finally, they land on Harlow. Probably preoccupied with the idea he might get his face under that dress of hers.

I turn away from that, absolutely not looking around for Donal, and instead lift my gaze up to the balconies where the Maidens are.

Just the three of them now. Usually, there would be nine and the entire balcony would be overflowing with the big skirts of gorgeous silk dresses. But tonight, the balcony looks empty and they look lonely.

I follow Clara's gaze and find that she is staring at the balcony across the way.

Which is empty.

That's where Finn should be. Well, that's where Aldo should be if things were going to plan around here.

But things are not going to plan.

At least not for the Scott family.

And they might never go to plan again if the Rebellion has anything to say about it.

As soon as the clapping stops, the music starts again, signaling the second dance. This time, no partners. It's just us. And now that I can put Donal fully out of my mind and concentrate on my moment, and my friends, and my good fortune—that's what I do.

I dance, and I smile, and I laugh.

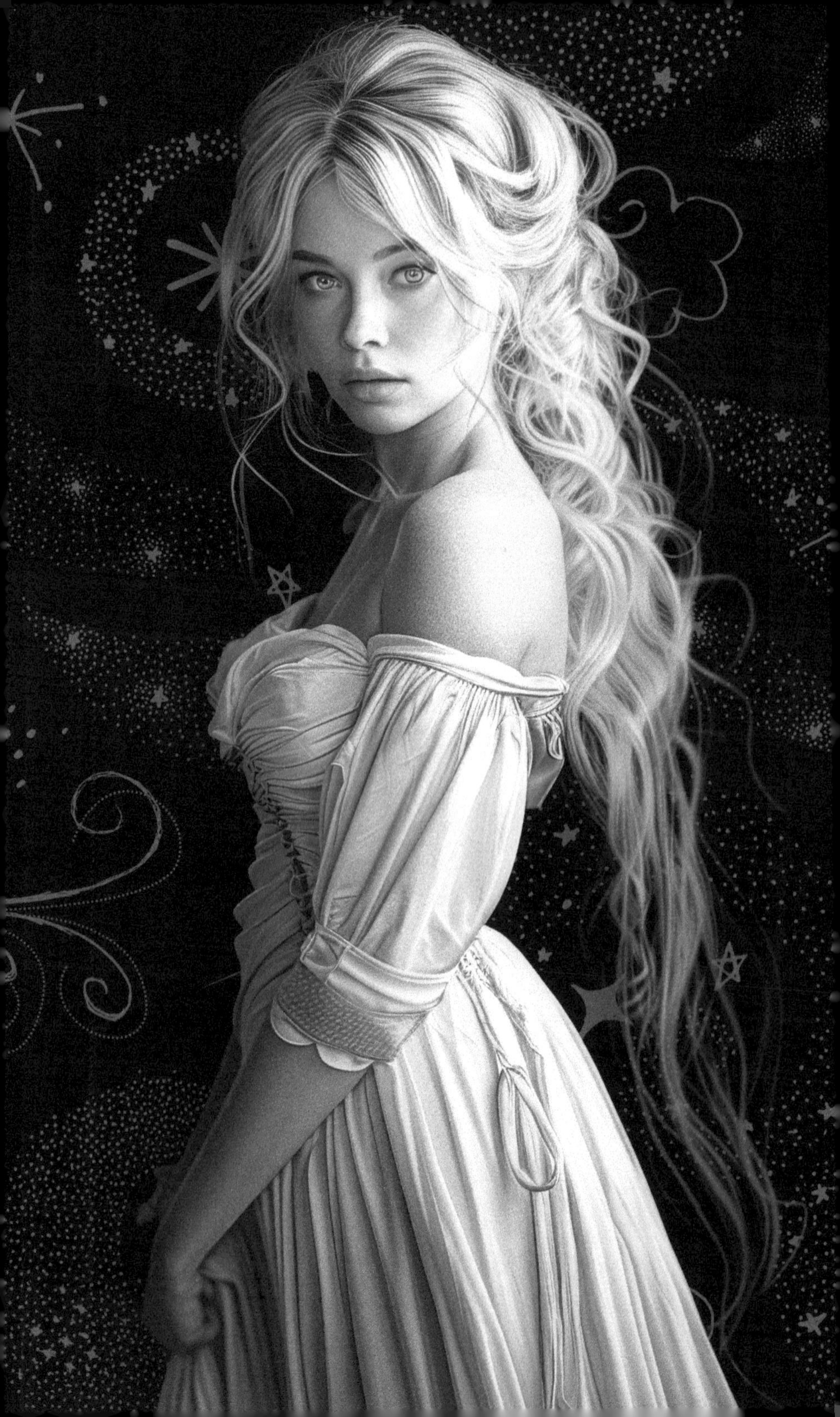

CLARA

CHAPTER SEVEN

The Little Sister solo dance goes on for another five minutes, but finally Finn appears on his balcony and announces the true start of the gala and everyone down on the floor, even the spectators in back, starts dancing.

This is our cue to descend the staircase like the proper Maidens we are and mingle, so that's what we do. I spend the whole time looking for Finn. I need an update on Aldo.

But he's missing again and without him, I'm adrift. I have no interest in this ball. I only had a vague interest in it before I learned about Aldo. More of a curiosity, really—wanting to get a glimpse of the next generation, I guess. But now, I just want to get the hell out of here.

I look around, trying to gauge how much negative attention it would draw if I slipped out and didn't tell anyone.

I don't know. If all nine of us Maidens were here, like it usually happens during these Choosing celebrations, no one would notice. But there are only three of us left and every time my gaze wanders around the crowd I find several sets of eyeballs trained right on me. People who raise their glasses of bubbly drink and give me a toast and a smile—for moral support, I suppose.

Still, I am determined to try. Because there is something really gross about being at this party while Aldo is in the health center, hurt. Possibly dying.

I walk quickly towards the nearest exit and slip outside before I can change my mind. When I come out into the cold night air, I pause to take a breath and get my bearings. I'm on the north side of the God's Tower event center, so I go right, heading for the bridge that leads over to the Extraction District. That's the health center Aldo would be at because that's his district.

I'm just about to step onto the bridge when I see two men coming towards me. I don't immediately recognize them because it's dark and there are shadows dancing on their faces from the spark lampposts that line the bridge on either side, so I just watch for a few seconds until I realize it's Jeyk and Mitchell, Finn's best friends.

A sigh of relief rushes out of my mouth with my words. "Where's Finn? I've been looking for him. Is he over there?" I nod my head in the direction of the Extraction District.

They don't say anything. Just pause in the middle of the bridge and stare at me.

"No." I start shaking my head. Because this silence is a sign of something bad coming. "*No.*" I say it again.

My eyes dart to their faces and I suddenly feel weak as a sick, sinking feeling builds in my gut. They start running towards me and both sets of hands catch me when I crumple to the ground. I don't faint. I wish I did, because then I'd be unconscious and time would stop, and I would not have to face the truth. At least not yet.

But my weakness was not a precursor to some fade-to-black moment and the only way forward is with the truth. "What happened? Tell me." I plead with my hands as both Jeyk and Mitchell continue to hold me up. "Tell me. Right now."

They look at each other. Then down at me. Mitchell is the one who answers. "He's... gone, Clara. And Finn—"

"No!" I yell this. "*No!* That's not what's happening. I just saw Aldo yesterday."

Jeyk takes a step forward, putting his hand on my bare shoulder. "Finn wants you to go home. He sent us to escort you home."

Time begins to slow and then, somehow, it just stops and the world around me suddenly ceases to exist. A sort of black tunnel forms in my field of vision as my mind spins with the truth. But I am unable to process it. Everything was fine this afternoon. Finn and I were trysting in his quarters. Aldo was fine. The world was fine. And now... it's not.

And I don't know what to do with this information.

I don't know how to process the death of Aldo. It's even worse than when I found out my own father died because I didn't understand death back then. I didn't understand fear, either.

But these days, after all the bell ringing from that fucking tower, and all those Maidens in the line-up before me, *missing*—I know what loss is. I know what fear is.

And I know, in my heart, that the death of Aldo is the

end of something. The end of... a reprieve, maybe. Because my life was so busy, and so full, and so cluttered with growing up and the Extraction that I didn't have time to think about the loss. I didn't have time to be afraid. There was a buffer around me and that buffer was Aldo.

Now he's gone and the harsh reality that was put on hold back when my mother died suddenly restarts and it's time now to face the truth. Everything that's happened to me in the past fifteen years suddenly catches up in a single moment. The death of my mother, the death of my father, my Choosing, my friends, the bells, the tower, the god.

And now this. Another loss.

The black tunnel vision fades and I begin to scream. Incoherent sentences start flowing out of my mouth, punctuated with swear words. Jeyk and Mitchell are holding me now, trying to calm me down, and then, out of nowhere, it seems, Matrons appear. A whole group of them yelling at me to be quiet as people come out of the event center, trying to figure out what is happening.

One of the Matrons leans into my ear and growls her words out. "Shut up, you stupid girl. Shut your mouth before you disrupt the entire city!"

And this is when I realize that the woman telling me this is Matron Bell. The pretty girl's aunt, or whatever. And I realize... she *did* pull strings for Jasina Bell. She did do this. The next thing I know, I slap her across the face.

Time slows down for me again and out of my fingers slides the cyan-blue light of spark. It makes a perfect handprint on her thick, wrinkled cheek and Matron Bell's facial expression changes as the realization sinks in that I just struck her.

Not only that, I assaulted her with spark.

Time suddenly speeds up again and she's about to slap me back, her hand in mid-air, when I'm saved by the ringing of the tower bells.

I blink. Then my mouth drops open.

Then someone else is yelling.

I whirl around and find Haryet, eyes cast up—looking at those fucking tower bells—*screaming*.

Because the god has just summoned her into his tower.

And this means I am next.

I am next.

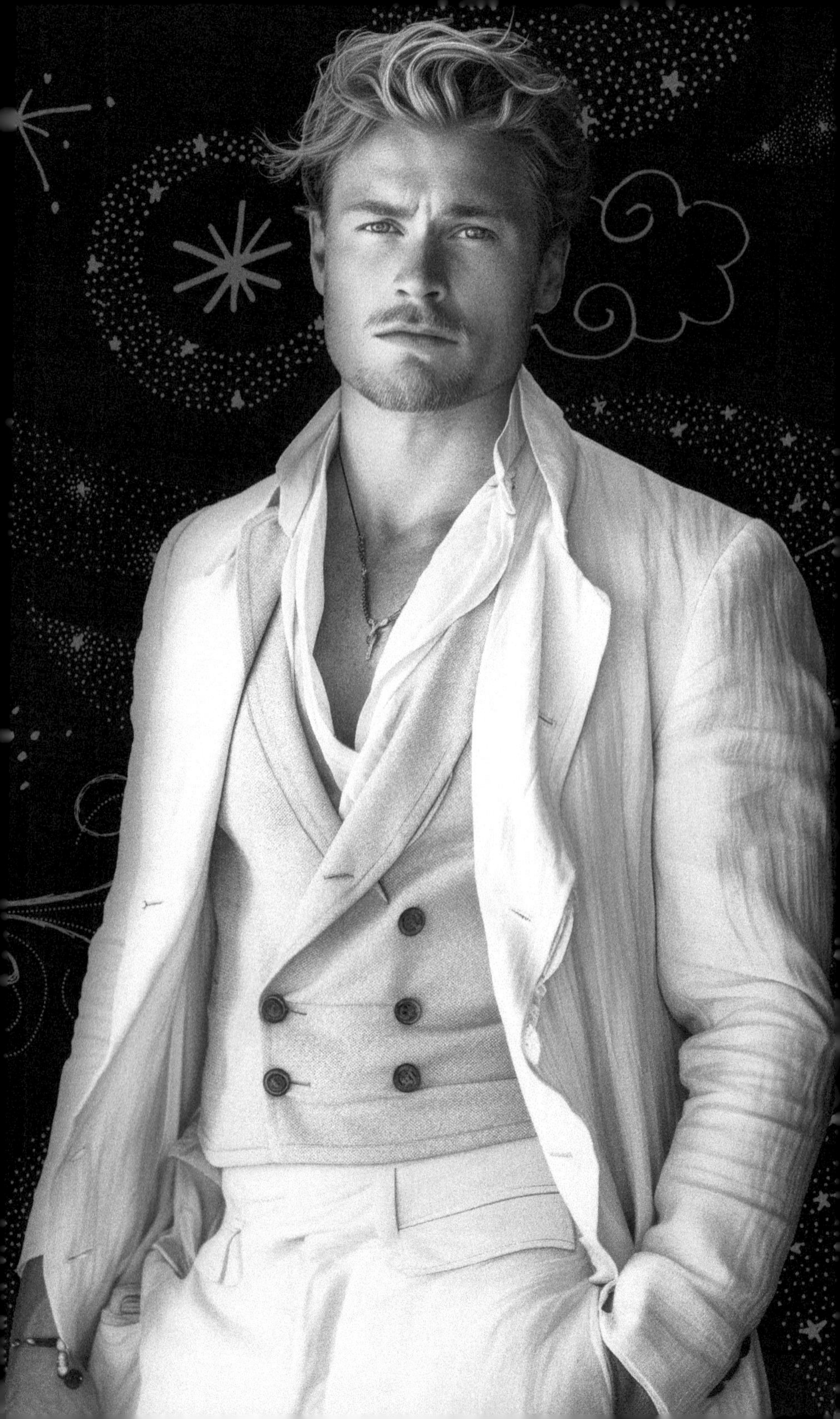

FINN

CHAPTER EIGHT

When the god in the tower rings the bells, the bells ring until that massive black door opens and the Maiden walks through. Then, and only then, will the people be free from the constant stress of being reminded that there is a god living inside the monstrous building at the top of our city who controls our fortunes and future through the power of spark.

The Maidens are a sacrifice. We train them up to display the spark inside them to their highest possible level. Then we choose the strongest one and give her to the god in the tower so he can... use her? Eat her? Kill her? No one knows what happens to the Spark Maidens in the tower, but we do know that it's a tradeoff.

In exchange for a woman, the god provides spark, and spark is what powers our city.

We all know this on some level. Even if the truth is buried deep down in the darkest corners of our minds.

But, then again, maybe not.

The people in Tau City are good. They are honest, and hardworking, and trustworthy. So if the Extraction Committee tells them that the sacrifice is really just a

Maiden called in for duty, the way a clerk or a maid might be called in to file records or clean bathrooms—neither of which are particularly desirable jobs, but it's just a job, after all—well, the good, honest, hardworking, trustworthy people of Tau City believe them.

But it's a lie and they are nothing but naïve.

And now look, those fucking bells are ringing—*again*. For the eighth time in a single decade. Like that fucking god, who has an insatiable appetite for beautiful, young, spark-filled women, realizes he's getting old, his power is waning, his youth is behind him, and he wants to use up as many girls as he can on his way out.

Which is what this means, this ringing of these fucking bells.

It means that this arrangement is over.

The god is dying.

Oh, it will take some time, so I am told. It will be another decade of sacrifices. That's why my father bothered with the next generation of Little Sisters.

He will want more, Finn. More, and more, and more. And you must feed him.

These were his last words to me in a letter.

What a fucking shit show.

I mean—I scoff—is this going to be recorded in our history? Finn Scott, age twenty-eight, received a written record of Aldo's Scott's final words and they were, *You must feed him.*

Feed him... *women.*

The god—our god—eats them? Rapes them? I don't know. No one bothered to tell me that. Probably because nobody else knows either. Not a single person who was not a sacrificial Spark Maiden has ever been inside that fucking tower.

I press my fingertips to my temples and rub little circles because I have a pounding headache that comes with a sinking feeling that this headache will follow me, will be here, haunting me, until the day I die.

The day someone kills me, more likely.

Because that's how my father died. He was killed.

Murdered.

No one on the Council even bothered to come up with an alternative story. Not even one for the masses, though that will happen. Murder is not a thing here. People do die by the hands of others, but it's a misunderstanding or an accident.

At least, that's how we record them—this is what I was told today while sitting next to my father's body in the morgue.

At no point in this day was my father in the health center.

He was dead when I arrived. And whoever the murderer was, they did more than just kill him. They slashed his face. They cut off his hands. There was a white sheet covering him so I didn't have to see the details, but there was so much blood, I didn't *need* to see the details.

That moment is burned into my mind. I will never stop imagining his desecrated body under that bloody sheet.

It was me and the members of the Council in that morgue. And that's where they handed me the letter he left and proceeded to slowly, and patiently, explain what was happening, what would happen next, and what part I would play in it. Not to mention the consequences if I didn't fall in line.

The god is dying.

The spark is dying.

We cannot let this happen because if the god dies, we go with him, and if we go, the human race is lost forever. Therefore, we must do everything we can to prolong the god's life by feeding him more Spark Maidens. Even if that means we feed him every Little Sister in this year's Extraction.

Which was a very convenient way to leave out the fact that Clara—the love of my life and future wife—would enter that tower long before any of those Little Sisters do.

This conversation with the Council took place less than thirty minutes after I last saw Clara when we left my quarters. Less than thirty minutes earlier I was in bed with Clara, filled with a sense of satisfaction. Dreaming about our very-near future where we would be married. There would be children. We would have a home together, and raise this family, and live out calm, easy, respectable lives.

And then I learned the truth.

That none of that will ever happen.

There was never even a remote chance that it would ever happen because our god's death has been a long time coming.

Everyone on the Council knew that the god was dying. And if we don't prolong his death by propping him up with more, and more, and *more* Spark Maidens, the entire city— the last city on the planet after the Great Sweep took everything out more than a thousand years ago—will disappear and all of humanity will go with it.

My entire life is a lie, not because everyone on the Council knew about the dying god, including my father, but because my family was given the position of Extraction Master for one reason and one reason only—because my great-great-great-great-grandfather was willing to lie to the people of Tau City and assure them that everything is going to plan.

Lie to them. Tell them it's fine.

And every Extraction Master who came after also agreed.

Including my father.

And now... *me*.

I AM LOOKING *out the window* of my new office watching as Clara loses her grip on reality and slaps one of the Matrons across the face. Even from fifteen floors up and across the canal, I can see the spark come out of her.

There is a struggle. It lasts longer than it probably should seeing that it's six Matrons, Jeyk, and Mitchell against one lone Spark Maiden, but Clara puts up a good fight.

Eventually, though, someone jabs her with a drug—

which is a pretty dear thing and I can count on one hand the number of times I've seen people given drugs in Tau City. It wouldn't be my first assumption if I wasn't able to see the cyan-blue liquid inside the syringe, but I can. It's not just glowing blue, it's pulsing. Like all the tumultuous emotions in the vicinity are giving it life.

A few moments later, Clara goes limp. Jeyk and Mitch are holding her up, but the Matrons push them aside, taking their places, then practically drag Clara back towards the Maiden Tower.

I didn't want the night to end this way. I don't want her to be alone, dealing with all that has happened. All that *is still* happening, the tolling bells remind me. But I am at a loss here. I don't know how to process the events of the day. And this muddled confusion goes beyond the death of my father and the ringing of the bells.

I step away from the window and turn my back to it, looking out at the office. My office, but up until a few hours ago, my father's office.

An office I didn't even know existed.

Mitch is the one who brought me up here. His father became my father's valet after Clara's father died and there wasn't a male child in her family to take his place. So Mitch knew about it because his father told him this afternoon. In fact, Mitch was probably getting his talk right about the same time I was getting mine from the Council. At any rate, his father thought it best that Mitch be the one to show it to me and help me deal with it.

So here I am. Dealing with it.

The problem is… I still don't understand what I'm looking at.

This is what I do know: The office is four stories tall and is located at the very top of the Extraction Tower. Which, from the outside, looks like a blue dome.

But from the inside—I turn back to the windows—it doesn't appear to be a dome at all. Because it's all made of glass. This makes me curious about all the other domes on the major towers. Are they all made of glass too? Do they contain an office inside?

I don't know. I don't really care.

It's very clear that my father didn't use most of the space in here. All the furnishings on the three floors below me are covered in blue sheets coated in dust.

But this floor—I turn back to look at the space around me—was used. Nothing is covered in sheets. There's a lot of dust, but Mitch said that's because my father didn't allow maids in here. Didn't allow anyone in here, not even cooks. Which makes sense from my point of view because he always came home for meals, even lunch.

The room is circular, of course, since it's part of the dome. And there's a giant stairwell that spirals up from down below and winds around a central core about twenty feet in diameter. There is a door along the wall, so obviously this central core is a room of some kind. But I don't even bother thinking about that right now. I just turn back to the window and stare down at the city. People are leaving the God's Tower event center. Almost all the spoke-y bridges that cross the canal are filled. But I'm not interested in them.

My eyes find the God's Tower. I'm interested in *that*. I am not quite eye-to-eye with it—the God's Tower is the tallest thing in Tau City, hands down. But from here, it's very close.

I feel a sense of... equality. Like the god in that tower and the Extraction Master in this one have some sort of understanding.

They look nothing alike.

In fact, the God's Tower doesn't look anything like the rest of the city. It is not built into the surrounding rocky hillside, for starters. There are no gentle corners and domed roofs. There are no neutral colors with blue accents. There are no golden lights shining from within.

If everything about Tau City is warm, and cozy, and inviting, then everything about the God's Tower is cold, and sharp, and repulsive.

It's black, for one. Not all of it. Some of it is a dark gray. And while there are lights coming from within, they are not a hazy gold mimicking sunshine. It's a very harsh white kind of light.

No one has ever been inside, so I can't say if it's cozy in there. But given what I can see from the dome of the Extraction Tower, I'm gonna have to say there is a one-hundred-percent chance that it's just as severe and hard on the inside as it is on the out.

It's a contradiction. It's always been in conflict with the city around it, and if I had to place a bet on that god being evil or good, just one look at the place he calls home is enough tip the scales in a certain direction.

How did I not see it?

How does everyone not see it?

Are they blind?

Are they stupid?

Willfully ignorant?

No. They are just naïve. And trusting. And good.

And it has just never occurred to them that the people they put all their faith in are nothing but liars.

I turn again, so my body is facing the Maiden Tower, and I realize that if I knew which of the windows in that tower across the canal belonged to Clara, I could wave to her from here. Though she wouldn't be able to see me. All she would see was a blue dome. But maybe I could see her.

The Maiden Tower is an enormous building for having never housed more than ten people at a time, except during the three months of Choosing when the Little Sisters live in ground-floor dorms. But most of the auxiliary buildings are classrooms and communal centers where thousands of teenage girls learn how to be good little ladies for the monster in the tower because god forbid they enter said tower not knowing which fucking fork to use while eating their salad.

It's so ridiculous. Actually, no that's the wrong word. It's gross. The way we send those teenage girls to those classes and how we have set up Extraction Day as some kind of contest to win.

And how, if you're Chosen, but not *actually* Chosen—i.e. you are numbers two through ten—then we will give you celebrity status. We, the good, honest, trustworthy people of Tau City, will give you coin, and pretty dresses, and gorgeous bedrooms, and a lady's maid to make you feel beautiful every single morning. So that you get through your day without having to think too hard about how your participation in this whole Extraction event is really just your tacit consent to sacrifice one of your friends to a god who lives in the tower that runs our city through the power of spark—which might as well be magic, that's how much we understand it.

Even after a thousand years, we know so little about how the world works. It's pathetic.

But that's not the point.

The point is that we pay them off with promises so that they never have to think about how close to death they actually are. Because while they are living in a very nice tower, and while they are wearing the very finest silk dresses, and while they are both entertaining the city and being entertained—what they're really doing is waiting to be a meal for that god in the tower, should his appetite for Spark Maidens ever increase.

Of course, none of them want to be number one, but they all know *someone* will.

And still, nearly every twelve-year-old girl in Tau City signs up to be a Pledge to the god. And their parents allow this. They allow their little girls to volunteer to be offerings. Thousands of them, every decade. And then they spend their entire teenage life learning how to be good little sacrifices so if they actually are Chosen, they don't scream in public when they end up standing in front of that black door, watching their friend disappear. Or, heavens forbid, they themselves have to walk through and vanish, never to be seen again.

Then these Chosen few—these sacrificial Spark Maidens—they spend the next decade getting paid to shut up about the fear they swallow every night with those fancy dinners. Bribes to make sure that the Little Sisters coming up after them don't think about how they will be killed, or raped, or *whatever*, should that god inside that tower ring a bell and make them walk through those doors.

I was there. I was there with Clara through this whole godforsaken ritual. I went with her to sign up when she turned twelve. I walked her to the classes every weekend. I was her partner for all the Choosings, I clapped when she was Chosen, I let out a breath when I learned she was number nine, and then I comforted her that night when Imogen Gibson walked through the tower doors lit up in bright blue spark.

But it was still just a *tradition*.

Then I watched the creeping fear build inside her as, time after time, the insatiable god called for more, more, more. I watched the relief on her face each night after one of her friends disappeared into the tower. Because it was over now and the fear could be forgotten. It was something to be tucked away. Put into a little compartment in her head where she didn't have to think too hard about what just actually happened.

And still, it was just our *custom*.

How did I not see it for what it was?

How did I fail Clara Birch so spectacularly?

I DON'T SLEEP.

I don't think anyone in the whole city sleeps because those fucking bells are ringing nonstop and they will continue to ring nonstop until the eighth Maiden—*say her name, at least, Finn. Say her fucking name. Give her that much respect*—they will ring until Haryet Chettle walks through those massive, black doors at midnight tonight, never to be seen again.

Only then will peace return to Tau City.

It's a form of torture, I now realize, the ringing of these bells.

But it's fine that I don't sleep because the people have now been told that Aldo Scott is dead and there needs to be a funeral *this morning* because there is no time for one tonight.

Aside from the mysterious office in the center of the dome, the dome contains a long tufted velvet couch, a desk, and two bookshelves filled with books. Last night the couch was facing the desk, like my father used to sit behind that desk and give speeches to tiny groups of sitting people.

But I swung the couch around and pushed it closer to the window. If I wasn't gonna sleep, I might as well stare at that clanging bell tower as I think up ways to ruin this god and bring his tower down.

I hate him. I have never met him, but I hate him. And I don't care if he's the one who keeps us warm at night and cool during the day. I don't care that he's the one who runs the irrigation to the fields and the heaters in the orchards. I don't care that he takes care of us. I want nothing more than to find a way into that tower and take him out.

Which is… concerning, to say the least. I've never been a violent guy. Sure, I'll play rough in sports. And if people fuck with me, I'll fight. But I've never had the urge to kill before and now I do.

Something has changed and for some reason I associate this change inside me with the rumbling I felt yesterday afternoon just before Clara and I left my quarters. She didn't feel it, but to me, it felt like the world shifted.

Maybe it was the death of my father? Maybe I felt it?

At any rate, I feel like a different person. Like the Finn who had a nice, sweet tryst with his soulmate yesterday afternoon is gone.

I get up off the couch and walk over to the window. It's a nice sunny day, as are almost all days in Tau City. It rains every once in a while, but for the most part, it's hot. The sweltering days are as predictable as the freezing nights.

So it's fuckin' sunny and it's the morning of my father's funeral.

Hundreds of small boats are lining up in the canals to take everyone from up-city to down-city, where my father's body will be laid to rest on a small boat, set aflame, and pushed out onto the canal. And we will all watch until the little inferno that makes the air smell like death floats its way into the lake on the edge of nothing.

Typically, this happens at night and the flaming boat is all very dramatic, but again, there is no room on the city schedule tonight because we're already booked for a fucking Extraction.

So this morning we'll boat down, watch as the body is set aflame, then we'll all go home and put it behind us. Because that's what the good citizens of Tau City do. They endure.

People are already queueing up to get into the boats along the canal down below. Many of them have probably already left. Others gather in small groups. It's a holiday. All city offices are closed because of the Extraction that will happen tonight and everyone in this part of town works in a city office of some kind, but they are still standing in line at the Magic Teacup for their morning dose of comfort. They are still grabbing a pastry from the Laughing Loaf. Still carrying on like this is all normal.

How did I not see it?

How could I have been so blind?

"Hello!" Mitch's voice drifts in from downstairs.

Then Jeyk is calling. "You up there, Finn?"

I don't answer them, but I hear footsteps, so they're coming up no matter what.

I've got my back to Jeyk and Mitch when they get to the top and step away from the stairs. A few seconds later they flank me. And we stand there like that for a few moments, just looking down at the people and the boats.

When they don't say anything, I snap. *"What?"*

Mitchell shrugs, his shoulder bumping mine. "We're just here for support, Finn."

"Yeah. We figured we'd keep you company on the Master boat." Jeyk nudges me with his elbow.

I sigh, then drop the tension in my shoulders as I try my best to be polite and thankful. "How did you guys even get up here? How did you get past security?"

Mitchell huffs. "We have our ways."

Jeyk scoffs. "Zander's in charge today. We slipped him a few coins."

Mitch side-eyes me. "What we did was promise that you'd keep him around as a regular. Give him a little promotion." He turns back to the view, leaving Jeyk and me at the windows. "Hope that's not a problem, because I don't like to be a liar."

Part of me is kinda pissed that Mitchell and Jeyk took it upon themselves to make a promise like that, but another part—a bigger part—is grateful that they're just acting like they normally would around me. Like I'm not the new Extraction Master. Like I don't now live in a secret… *palace*. Because that's what this place is. It's not an office. It's a fucking palace. And when I take all those sheets off the furniture on the lower levels, it's probably gonna be something spectacular.

"Thanks," I say, after a few moments of silence. "For… showing up."

They both just shrug.

I've been friends with these men since we were boys. As the Tau City Extraction Master my father was what amounts to a king in this town, but both Mitchell and Jeyk come from good, rich families too and they grew up in the Extraction District as well. The three of us have been nearly inseparable since we were six years old.

We all started out as engineers. That's what most young,

respectable men from up-city become because engineers work with the spark in all kinds of different ways. These days Jeyk is working in the Canal District, I've been working here in the Extraction District, and Mitch was offered a stipend to study bio-spark. So he stayed in school and has been… well, I don't actually know what he's been doing. He tells us things, I just usually stop listening one or two sentences in because it makes no sense.

I turn my head to look at them. "Did you guys see Clara?"

Jeyk sighs. "Not since last night. She was a mess. Tried to cross the bridge and get over here. She even slapped a Matron."

I nod. "I saw it. Even from all the way up here, I could see the cyan-blue light."

"Yeah. She left a perfect imprint of her hand in blue spark on Matron Bell's cheek." Mitch chuckles.

"It's not funny, Mitch. That's a major demerit."

Jeyk steps in front of me, focusing my attention on him. We stand mostly eye to eye, and that's what I'm looking at when he speaks—his crazy amber eyes. "No one cared, Finn. Nothing's gonna happen about it because a few seconds later the bells rang."

"Yep. They sedated her, the bells rang, and they carried her away." Mitchell is still looking out the windows.

Jeyk turns back to the view, joining Mitch. And then it just feels inevitable that I do the same.

My father loved Clara. He never said he played favorites for her when it came to the Maidens, but he did. I know he did. He chose her as a Maiden so she could pull herself up without my help through marriage. He made her number nine so she would never have to worry about being called into that tower.

And isn't it a little bit ironic that the night he dies is the night those bells ring? Which makes it the very same night that Clara Birch becomes the next Maiden up?

Is that why they killed him? Because he refused to do something he was told to do in regards to Clara?

I'll probably never know that. Unless we find the murderer and get a confession. Which seems very unlikely after the talk the Extraction Council gave me yesterday afternoon.

Mitchell sighs loudly, then turns away from the window and starts walking back to the stairs. "Let's go, Finn."

He's gonna be my number one, I realize. Because he's not afraid of me. Not afraid of telling me no or of ordering me around when it's in my best interest. Mitch is gonna stand at this door every day, guarding me from anyone and everything, until I die.

I don't think he knows this yet, but I do.

Jeyk will be who I will turn to when I have questions. He's smart. Way smarter than me and smarter than Mitch too, even though he wasn't offered a stipend to study biospark. He's more than a good spark engineer, he's a great spark engineer. Jeyk knows everything about Tau City. He understands the inner workings. His mind is filled with schematics. Courses of action and predictive analyses. He is strategic, almost to a fault, and will always look me in the eyes when he gives his opinion, even when I haven't asked for it.

I'm not alone. I have friends. Good friends.

Loyal friends who will stand by me, no matter what.

It is their duty now.

But I owe them something in return. Not just loyalty, but leadership.

Leaders don't hide from their duties. They steer the ship. They guide it through rocky waters. They deliver it to safe harbors. They don't lock themselves in their office so they can be sullen and petulant.

So I go downstairs and get into the boat that will deliver us to my father's funeral pyre.

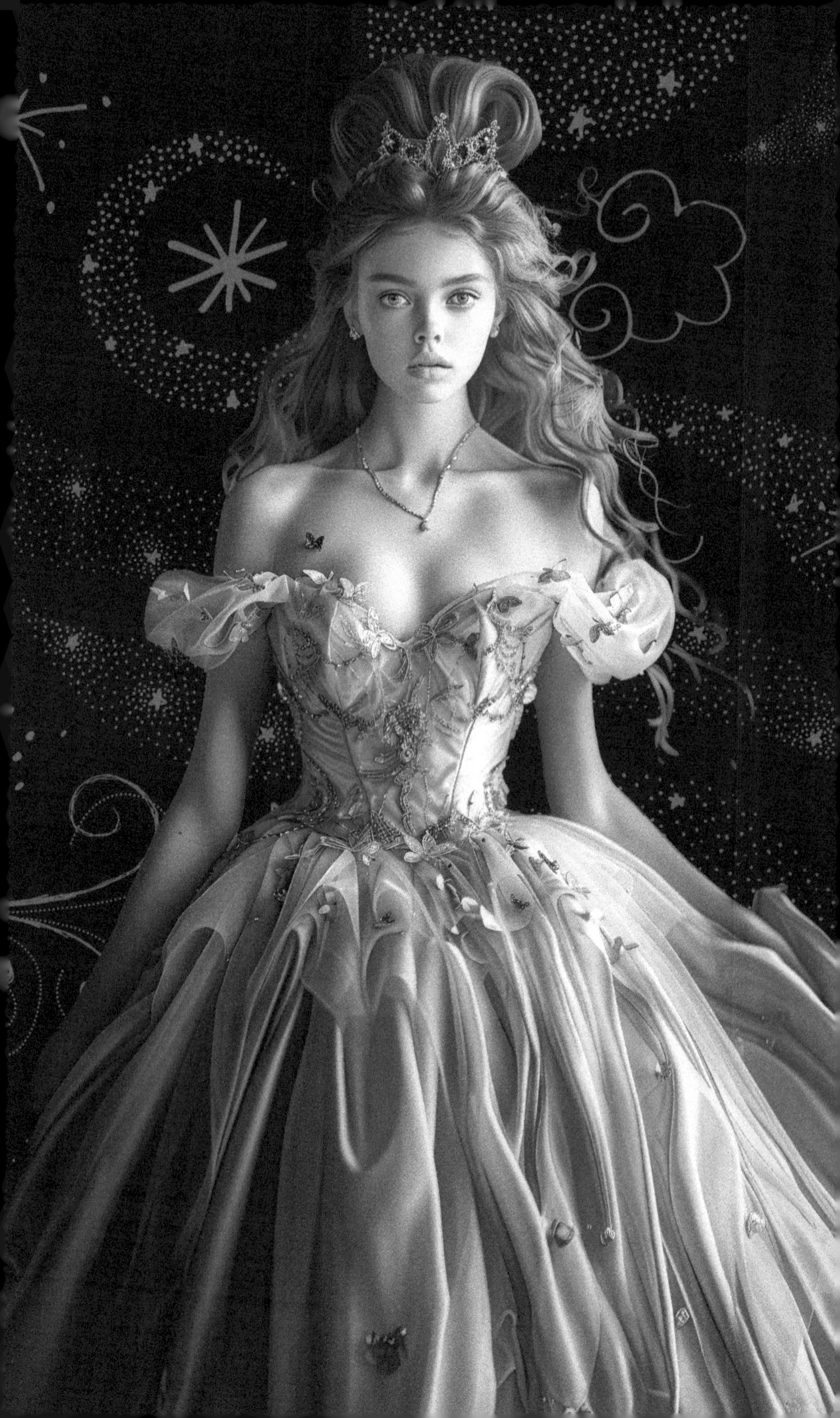

JASINA

CHAPTER NINE

Oh, how they howled. All night long. Just three women. But three is more than enough to make those anguished screams that echoed through the dorms last night.

Eight floors up—at least. They could've been in Gemna's quarters, and then it would've been ten. Or Clara's, and it would've been nine. But still, we could hear them. The entire dorm heard them.

Even we, the down-city rebels sent here to disrupt and tear things apart, felt their suffering.

Haryet Chettle's hours are now numbered.

Tonight, she dies.

Or maybe not. No one knows what happens to the Maidens. My best guess is that the god eats them. He devours them, and at the same time, he steals their spark. And this spark comes back to us as lights in lamps, or hot water from pipes, or heat in the orchards and greenhouses.

But I guess it's just as likely that he rapes them? Tortures them? Tears them to shreds?

He's an angry god, after all.

Because he's a dying god.
And we are part of the reason he's dying.

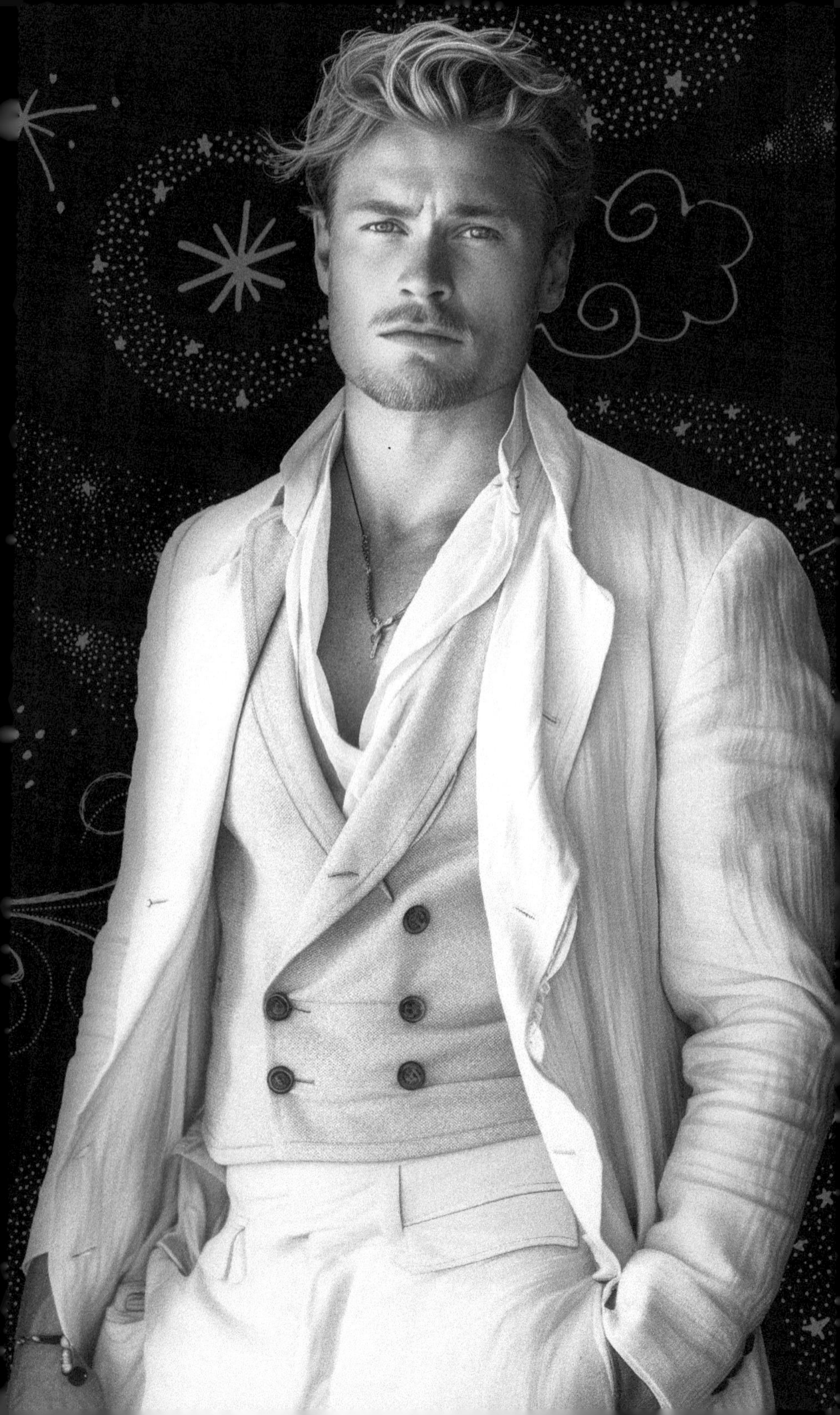

FINN

CHAPTER TEN

I can't seem to focus after I get in the boat with Jeyk and Mitchell and we start the long float down-city where the canal empties into the lake on the edge of nothing and where a pyre has been built.

It's weird and everything goes a little bit blurry. And I'm a little bit shocked—though I probably shouldn't be—that the entire city has turned up to pray for my father's soul as we burn his body until it is nothing but ash in the wind.

The bells ring the entire time.

Like it was planned this way.

Like the god himself is mourning the death of my father.

I am sitting as the ceremony happens. Elevated now, and alone on the dais meant only for the Extraction Master.

It takes six hours for the body to turn to dust and make all of down-city smell like death. How do they put up with it, that smell? People die every day. Bodies are burned every day and they don't get a private service. They pile all the previous day's bodies up into one boat and every night they all go up in flames together.

Every night there is an orange glow coming from down-city that makes all of us upwind thankful that we are not down here to smell it. How do these down-city people spend their whole lives in the vortex of that stench?

Mitchell comes down this way sometimes to drink and buy whores. But I haven't been down here for a funeral since Clara's father died years back. He got a private service. Not a grand one, like this, but it was nice.

Still, as nice as it can be, no one who lives up-city wants to be down here any longer than they have to.

There is a horn that blows when the Pyre Master decides that the body has been turned to ash and the funeral is over. And then... it's truly over. My father is gone and the grief flooding through my soul feels like the heaviest burden I have ever carried.

But there's something else inside me now too. I felt it the moment the Pyre Master declared my father to be dust.

It's a heat. It's an anger. It's the weight of my duty, but it's more than that. It's more the death, and the sadness, and the tolling bells that refuse to shut up.

I feel evil. Truly evil.

Because only an evil man would take part in these traditions we have.

Jeyk and Mitchell come up beside me as we leave, flanking me as the people part, giving us a path back to my boat. The good thing about being the last to arrive is that we are the first to go.

But it's Clara, waiting for me in her black dress and veil on the deck of the boat, who puts my upside-down world back into some kind of order.

"How did she get here?"

I'm mostly talking to myself when I say this, but Mitchell

answers. "I threatened those fucking Matrons. Told them they'd all be kicked out on their asses, freeloading days over for good, if they didn't have her waiting on this boat when you got here."

And despite everything that has happened in the last twenty-four hours, I smile.

Because Clara Birch is truly the only way I will get through the rest of this day.

I climb up onto the boat and Clara falls into my arms sobbing and apologizing at the same time. "Oh, Finn. I'm so sorry. I'm so, *so* sorry."

I hold on to her. Tight. Closing my eyes and letting out a sigh as we stand there, in front of the whole fucking city—letting them get a good long look at our grief—and forget about everything but her.

I just want to stay here like this. Capture this moment and hold it prisoner.

It's my father's funeral, which should be one of the very worst days of my life, but this moment right after is gonna stick with me. Because I know in my heart this is as good as it gets. My happiness peaked yesterday afternoon when I was dragging my fingertips up and down Clara's naked thigh after our tryst and the slipping started the moment she and I parted. We didn't know that the best moments were now behind us. That we had just lived through the good ol' days.

But I understand this now. It's never going to be this easy again. It's never going to be this good again. It's just going to get worse from here and if I don't appreciate every second of every day as the fall from grace happens, then I won't have anything left in the end. Not even the memories.

So I hold on to her. Tight. Keeping my eyes closed as the whole city watches our descent into despair.

She pulls back first, not saying anything. Just takes my hand and pulls me into the shade of the canopy positioned over the couches.

We sit while Mitchell and Jeyk busy themselves with the captain to give us some privacy and then start the journey back up the canal to the Extraction District.

"Thanks for coming."

Clara lays a hand on my face, staring straight into my eyes. "Of course I came."

This is when I notice that she's... *displaying*. "Clara! Your hands!"

She pulls her hand back from my face and looks at both of them the way one might look at something curious. Her spark was never magnificent. Only her fingertips displayed on her first Choosing night. But over the course of the rest of the Choosings the spark inside her grew and matured. It often happens this way for Little Sisters. And by the time the top ten are Chosen, most, if not all of them, display spark in a new way on Extraction Night itself.

It happened this way for Clara too. Little markings—symbols, kind of—started to appear on her hands. First, her palms. Then the backs of her hands. Then her wrists, and finally, on Imogen's Extraction night, when all nine Spark Maidens were still here with us, the spark inside Clara Birch leaked out as light all the way up to her elbows.

Since then, she's lost most of it. Which is also common,

since Maidens-in-Waiting don't have to practice their spark, as they are not meant to go into the tower.

She makes little spark drawings in the air sometimes. Or traces a finger across my skin, leaving a trail of spark behind. But the symbols... it's been years since I've seen the symbols.

Clara snaps out of the trance the spark cast over her and huffs. "Well. Look at that." And then, just as quick as it appeared, the spark fades until it goes out completely.

I suddenly have a keen interest in her spark and I want to ask her about it. About those symbols, specifically. But the timing is so wrong. So instead I say, "How is Haryet—"

But Clara pulls me into a hug before I can finish, whispering into my ear. "Don't think about tonight. Not yet. We only have room for this right now, so don't think about tonight."

Tonight. It's so close.

And we just did this last year and it hasn't even had a chance to feel like a long time ago yet. Not when there's supposed to be an entire decade of time between the tolling bells.

But I take her advice and I don't think about anything. I just sit and hold Clara in my arms as she holds me back, and I push the sight of her spark symbols, as well as the new anger and evil inside me, away as we float back up the canal.

When we arrive at the Extraction Tower, the four of us disembark, but then I turn to Mitchell and Jeyk. I'm gonna put them off and they are going to object because that's their job now—to keep me focused and on task as I fully integrate into my new role as Extraction Master. So I put up a hand to stop their objections before I speak. "I know we have a lot to do, but… give me one hour, OK?"

They both nod with somber faces, but don't try and talk me out of it.

Then I take Clara's hand and lead her to the elevator that will take us up to my new palace.

She leans in to me, once the elevator doors have closed, and discreetly whispers, so the liftman can't hear, "Where are we going?"

I let out a huff of air. Because she doesn't even know yet. She has no idea who I turned into since the last time we saw each other. So I just whisper back, "You'll see."

When we get to the top the liftman opens the doors for us and Clara and I exit. I put my hand in the small of her back, allowing myself to feel just the slightest bit of happiness as I watch her fascinated, wandering gaze as she takes in the luxurious hallway leading to the Extraction Master's office.

We stop in front of the massive, fifteen-foot double doors and finally that astonished gaze of hers finds mine. "What is this?"

I sigh. "My new home." Then I open the doors and she steps in, once again looking around, trying to see everything at once.

She's breathing heavy when she finds my eyes this time. "I don't understand…"

"This"—I pan my arms wide to indicate the whole of the palace—"was my father's office. Apparently. I never knew about it, but nonetheless, it's here. But it's much more than just an office. It's… well, a regular palace, as you can see."

"Oh." Her face crumples into a frown. Then, suddenly, she's crying, covering that beautiful face with her hands.

And I am so stupid. Why would she care about this place? Aldo's body was just burned in a pyre. The bells are still ringing for Haryet. This is the absolute worst day of Clara's life and I'm bragging about my new palace?

What the hell is wrong with me?

I put my arms around her. "Shhhh. It's OK." I want to explain that this is a good moment, she just doesn't realize it yet. But it's not the right time for that conversation. It's not even the right time for that thought.

So instead, I just hold her. Caressing her back with my fingertips. Because this is a terrible, awful day and she won't understand until it's too late that we are at the end of the best of times, so we need to enjoy it. And I don't want to tell her that—not yet. I don't want to kill all her hopes and dreams until I have no choice.

It takes a few minutes, but when she finally calms down, I lead her over to the nearest couch—sans blue sheet, courtesy of Mitch or Jeyk, I presume—and after we sit, I pull her into my arms and we let out that breath. A collective one. The one we've been holding, in our minds, at least, since the bells started ringing last night.

It's not over yet, of course, but we've come to terms with it. And in my experience, that's always half the battle.

We don't talk. We just sit. Not because there's nothing to say—there are millions of things to say—but because we don't know how to say them. The world doesn't make sense yet.

Instead, we kiss. And I am a little taken aback—not to mention slightly ashamed—to find that I am hungry for her.

There is no time for a tryst, there is so much to do before the ceremony tonight, but after, when the bells finally stop, I will bring her here and she will spend the night with me. Fuck that god. Fuck him and his tower too. Fuck the bells, fuck the Extraction, fuck the Matrons, and fuck the consequences.

She's mine and I might just take her prisoner. Keep her forever. Lock her up in some… upper palace room that I don't even know about yet, and never let her leave.

"What are you thinking about?" Clara's low whisper pulls me out of my anger, and shame, and lust and forces me to take a breath.

"You."

She snuggles into my neck, her mouth pressed against my skin just below my ear. I hold her as we lean into each other, trying to get through the moments.

"Where's your mother? I didn't see her at the funeral."

I blink. Squint. Then… I dunno. Get lost for a moment. Because Clara's right. I didn't see her either. And I didn't even notice that she wasn't there.

Clara pulls back a little, trying to see my face. "Finn?"

"Uh…" I have to lie. That's the only way out of this. "She was… sick. She couldn't come." I don't want to look Clara in the eyes as I say this lie, but I force myself to.

She's squinting her eyes in a severe look of confusion. "She didn't…" She can't even finish the sentence. Because it makes no sense.

My mother did not attend my father's *funeral?*

And I didn't even notice?

"I'll... check in on her. Don't worry." I drag my fingertips gently across Clara's cheek, forcing a smile. "She needs time."

Clara looks me in the eyes, the same way that Jeyk looks me in the eyes, and takes a moment to make herself believe the lie. Because why would she not believe me? She offers a small smile and then places her hand flat against my cheek. "Are you OK, Finn? I know that's a very stupid question, considering the circumstances, but you don't look OK."

I am not OK. There's something evil growing inside me, I can feel it. "I'm fine." This lie is too much. Even I know it. "I mean, I *will be* fine. Once this day is over."

She wants to question me. She wants to know more about my mother's absence, and this office that looks like a palace, and the bells—which are still ringing—and she probably wants to talk about how she's next.

But in the very next moment, there is a knock at the door, and I am saved from telling all the lies that would be necessary to explain away her unease because Mitch appears, telling us that there are things to do and places to be.

I rise up, standing in front of Clara, then offer her my hand. She hesitates, staring up into my eyes for a moment. Like she might ask all those questions in her head regardless of Mitchell's presence.

Her gaze is steady, her resolve firm. But then she sighs, looks away, and takes my hand. Allowing me to end the conversation and pull her to her feet.

But then I also pull her close and place my hands on her

cheeks, forcing her to focus on me. It takes a moment for her eyes to meet mine again. But she does. They are blue. Almost the same blue of the canals, and I've been comparing those eyes of hers to the canals down below for so many years now, it's almost impossible to think about water without picturing Clara's face.

"I'll see you tonight, OK?"

She nods her head, but she looks like she wants to cry. About Haryet, obviously. But for herself, too. And even Gemna. They thought they'd be safe. But when the Extraction climbs its way all the way up to Maiden number nine, it becomes pretty clear, pretty quick, that the god has every intention of taking each and every one of them.

Clara opens her mouth to say something and I know—I feel it in my gut—that it's going to be a question she won't like the answer to. So I place a fingertip on her lips and shake my head. "Tonight, Clara. We'll talk tonight."

Then Mitch is there, offering Clara his arm. She looks at him, then me, and gives in, taking his arm and letting him lead her out of my palace.

I wait until Mitchell comes back, then I ask, "Was my mother at the funeral?"

Mitch shakes his head, but doesn't say anything.

"I need to see her." I expect an objection, but he doesn't say anything to this, either. So I just walk past him, get in the elevator, take it down to the ground level, then travel the walkway that leads around and behind the Extraction Tower.

Behind every tower in Tau City there is a neighborhood that houses all the families who live in the districts. The homes are all attached, and built into the rocky hillside, with a canal view. There are dozens of canals in Tau City. Some are very small—just tiny streams with foot bridges that span only a few feet. But our family home is on a secondary canal that is big enough to have a bit of beach and I have many fond memories of swimming in that bright blue water as a kid. The sun tanning my skin brown as I spent hours and hours jumping off the boulders that line the banks and splashing around on hot days.

There are many levels to each neighborhood as well, since all the homes are built into the side of a cliff. It's beautiful, and serene, and when it's lit up with lampposts at night, it's even a little bit magical.

Our family quarters are located just a few minutes' walk from the tower for convenience and when I arrive, I find a guard standing on the porch outside our front door. He salutes me when I approach.

"What's going on here?" I ask.

"Sir... I... I was posted here."

"I can see that. *Why* are you posted here?" Of course, I can guess. My father was murdered. It's a logical thing to conclude that my mother might require protection. But that doesn't explain why she wasn't at the funeral.

"I don't know, sir." The guard shrugs. "I was told to report and someone will replace me in two hours."

I don't bother asking any more questions. He's telling the truth. So I wave him aside, open the door, step in, and close it behind me.

I immediately find myself looking straight into the eyes

of four Matrons. They are blocking the stairs that lead up to my parents' bedroom.

"What is going on? Why are you here? Where is my mother?"

The oldest Matron in the group, the one in the middle, takes a single step forward. Her face is nothing but a topography of wrinkles. She's not wearing the customary garb of blue tunic and cream scapular apron like the two Matrons on either side of her, but a long cape the color of the night sky. It's open in the front, trimmed in shimmering gold, and held together with a large gold brooch. Underneath the cape she's wearing a long dress the color of sand and embroidered with gold stars.

On her head is a crown of sorts. A tiara, but not a dainty one like the Little Sisters occasionally wear to balls during the Choosing. It's thick, and dull—made of iron, perhaps. It doesn't look precious, it looks… old. Ancient, like the woman wearing it. And out of place when contrasted with the dazzling gold brooch at her throat.

The outfit is over the top and far outside the parameters of tradition. Hell, just the fact that they are here, in my family home, implies a level of audacity I've never witnessed before from a Matron and the fact that they are blocking my way upstairs to check on my mother is a whole next level of insubordination.

"Answer me," I demand, looking the old one directly in the eyes.

She offers me a small smile, then folds her hands at her waist and bows her head as she speaks. "Your mother belongs to us now."

"What?" I blink at her, confused. "What are you talking about?"

The ancient Matron looks up at me once again, her eyes patient and soft. Like she is about to explain something very complicated to a small child. "It has never happened in your lifetime, so of course you are confused."

"What has never happened? What the hell is going on?"

"The death of the Extraction Master, of course. Your mother was the Extraction Mistress. So naturally—"

"Wait." I put up a hand to make her stop talking. "What do you mean Extraction *Mistress*? There's no such title."

"Oh, but there is, boy. Every Master has a Mistress, doesn't he?"

"Well…" I stop there. Because no. We don't. Obviously. Since I am not married. And my mother is not a Mistress. *She's* married, which means she's a… I can't even think the word that comes to mind. Because it suddenly makes perfect sense, but at the same time, it *can't* be.

"Of course you don't have a Mistress, Finn Scott. Yet, that is. You've only had the position for a single day. But you will. All Extraction Masters must have a Mistress. How do you think we get the next generation?"

"Well…" I say again. Then stop. Again.

"Never mind all that. We can discuss your options at a later date. Once you've had time to mourn and settle in."

"What does any of this have to do with my mother?"

"Finn."

I look up, startled at my mother's voice. She's on the landing between the first and second floors, her eyes bloodshot and tired-looking. Her smile, meant only for me and only as a pacifying gesture, is small. Barely enough to lift up the corners of her mouth.

But the thing that really disturbs me about her right now is what she's wearing. Because it's the exact same outfit as the ancient Matron standing in front of me. "Mother. What is going on? Why are you dressed like that?"

My mother's gaze finds the old one's. "Can you wait outside for a moment? I'll just need a minute."

The old Matron doesn't answer, just nods her head and motions for the rest of her group to leave.

When they're gone, I walk up to the stairs and offer my hand to my mother. She takes it and allows me to help her down. Then we turn and face each other. She has aged since I last saw her, which was only a couple weeks ago when I came for dinner.

I don't know what to say, and she knows this, so she starts first. "I'm sorry we didn't have a chance to talk before the funeral. It all happened..." She sighs. "It all happened so fast. And then the bells started ringing and there was just... no more time." She gives me a little shrug.

"But what does all this mean, Mother? Why are you dressed like that ancient Matron?" Of course I know the answer. I just can't seem to accept it.

"Because I am one of them, son. I was a Little Sister when your father became Extraction Master. He was about your age, in fact. That year the Choosing had a dual role. A courting for him so he could choose a suitable wife, and the Choosing, of course. And that is how you will experience it as well." Her smile is bigger this time, showing me a little bit of her teeth even. Then her hands come up to the collar of my shirt and she straightens it, like I am a small boy once again.

"You're leaving, aren't you."

She nods. "I did my job. My husband is gone and my son is grown. Now it's your turn to start a new legacy." Her smile grows even wider now. "With Clara."

I let out a breath, and with this breath goes a lot of tension. "She's not a Little Sister. She's a Maiden."

"It's not how it's normally done. But it's not forbidden. The important thing is that your future wife will be one of the Chosen. And Clara is. Quite a fantastic one, actually."

Now it's my turn to smile. And in this moment, I think... maybe it's all going to be OK? Maybe there's a reason for all this pain and uncertainty? Maybe we really will get married, and have our own son, and I will turn into my father, and Clara will turn into my mother, and everything about this life will be just fine?

If I can stomach the lies.

"I have to go, Finn. But I'll see you tonight at the Extraction for Haryet. I'll be with the Matrons, of course, not by your side." Then my mother places a hand on my cheek as she gives the other a small kiss.

Her robes swish as she turns towards the door.

"Wait. Will I see you again after that, Mother?"

Her head turns, just a little so she can look across her left shoulder, but she doesn't meet my gaze. "No, Finn. Our time together is over now and my place is in the Matron Tower."

A moment later she steps through the door.

And then she's gone.

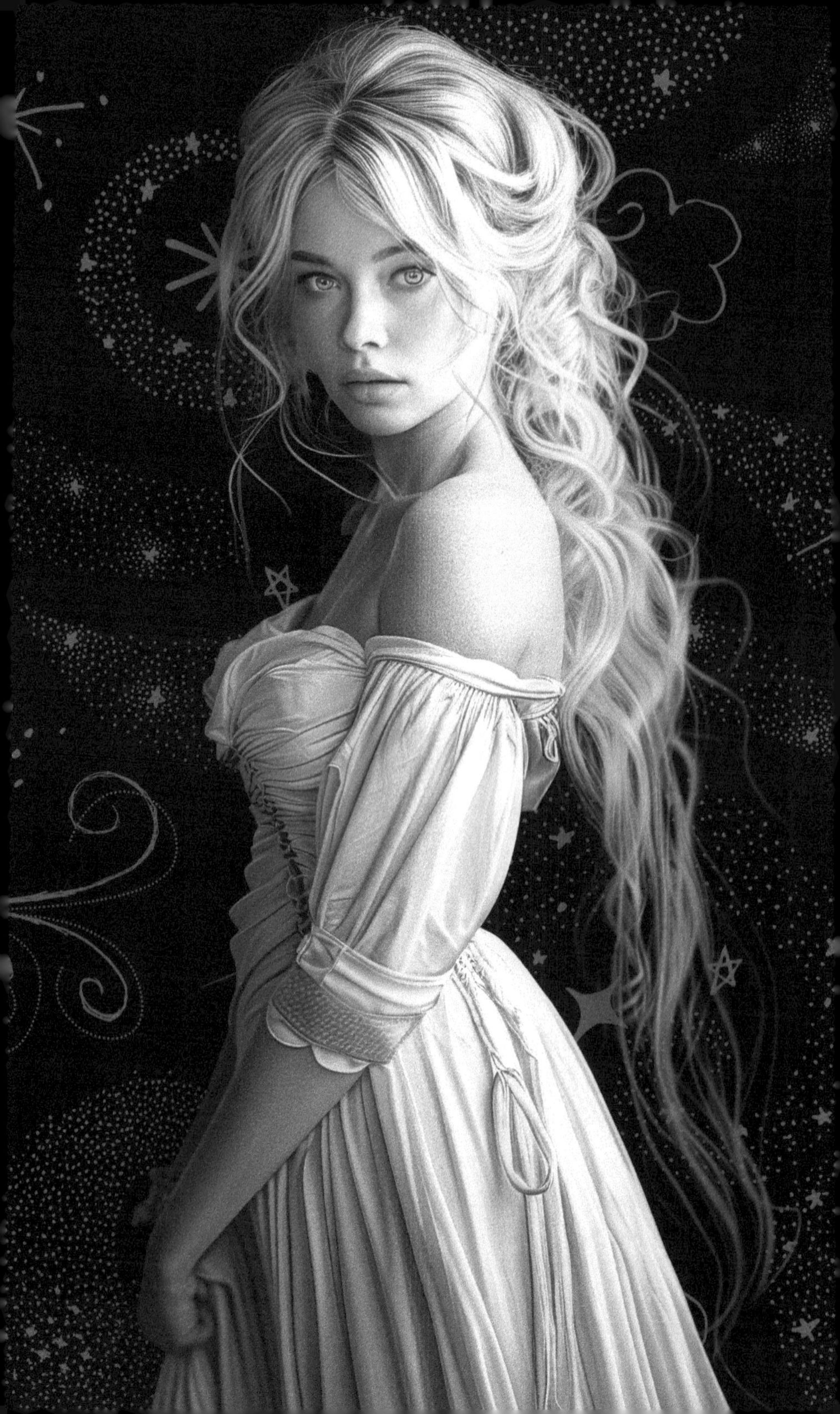

CLARA

CHAPTER ELEVEN

My head is swimming with emotions. Confusion, and sadness, and fear, and anxiety, and frustration. All of them, all at once. And those fucking bells will not stop tolling. Which only adds to my distress.

It's a form of torture, these bells. For all of us, but especially poor Haryet. She's crying, and even though our rooms are massive, and the walls substantial, and she is a whole floor below me—there is no way not to hear her wailing.

It's so heartbreaking.

But the worst thing is my reaction to it all because there's a part of me—a pretty substantial part at the moment—that just wants Haryet to walk through those doors, right now, in this very minute. Hell, there's a part of me that wants to push her through myself, just to make the wailing and tolling *stop*.

Which adds shame to the list of swirling emotions inside my head.

Stop it, Clara, I chastise myself. *You are not that selfish.*

Normally, anyway. But today is far, far, *far* from a

normal day and all I want to do is go back to Finn's quarters —not that palace of a place he took me to earlier, but his real quarters—and lie in bed with him, and let him put his arms around me, and believe his whispers when he tells me it's all going to be OK.

But that's not going to happen. I'm at home, he's at work, and this is the very last day I will ever spend with one of the dearest people to ever grace my life with her presence.

I get up, leave my room, and take the stairs down to Haryet's floor. When I peek into her doorway, I find a whole slew of Matrons surrounding her as the maids fuss over her dress for the Extraction.

My gaze darts over to the right where Gemna is standing off to the side, a scowl on her face as she watches Haryet be criticized and hushed for displaying her anguish.

I actually catch the words "poised, proper, polite," in the cacophony of scolding.

"OK," I say loudly. "That's enough. Every one of you needs to get the fuck out."

The whole group of them—Matrons and maids alike— turn to look at me in open-mouthed surprise.

"Don't look at me that way. Because I'm not about to apologize. This is Haryet's last day and it will not be ruined by the lot of you making her miserable with tongue-lashings and dress-fittings. Who gives a fuck what her dress looks like! The god? Who cares what that asshole thinks! He's stealing my friends! One by one, he's stealing *my friends*. And I"—I'm practically screaming now—"have had *enough!*" I point a shaking finger at the door. "Get out!"

There are a few seconds of absolute shocked silence. But

then they are all in motion at the same time and just a few moments later they are out in the hallway and I'm closing the doors in their faces.

My outburst has silenced Haryet as well, so even though the bells are still ringing, the clamor has been toned down several degrees. I go over to the windows—which are open because it's midday and hot as hell outside—and close them. And once they are all shut, the tolling fades and the feeling of discord begins to fade with it.

To a tolerable level, at least.

Then I turn back to a still-crying Haryet—though it is the silent kind now—and let out a long breath. "Sorry. But I couldn't take it anymore."

She sniffles, staring at me with wide eyes. Then walks over to her bed, sighs, and, even though there are still pins in the hem of her dress, she flops down onto it. "Thank you."

"Yeah." Gemna walks over and flops down next to Haryet. "That was amazing, Clara."

I huff, then smile. It kinda was. Though I'm sure, once all the drama is over, I will pay dearly for my outburst. I mean, last night I slapped a Matron with spark and today I was the picture of insubordination in front of a whole group of them. Not to mention the maids.

Oh, the gossip happening right now down in the servants' quarters must be epic.

One slip-up in a moment of high stress might be overlooked. But two in as many days?

Never.

But I don't care. I'm so relieved that they're gone, and so

thankful that Haryet has stopped crying and the bell-tolling has been toned down to a tolerable level, that I push it far, far away into the recesses of my mind to dwell and fret about on another day.

I walk over to the bed and lie down on the other side of Haryet, then put my arms around her and snuggle up to her neck like she's Finn. She doesn't have a steady man the way I do. Not that Finn and I have been very steady over the past decade, but it's more than all the others had. Much more. We're in love. Haryet has suitors, and gentlemen friends she's been ordered to entertain at parties and such, but no one to cling to the way I'm clinging to her now.

So she clings back.

And then Gemna has her arms around the both of us and this is how we stay. Silent, and all curled up together, and sleepy. Like it's just another hot afternoon and nothing special at all is happening tonight.

Haryet sighs again, and this time it's a heavy one. I can tell she wants to say something, but can't find the words. So I prod her on. I might never get another chance to have a private conversation with this woman, and this hurts me. I want all the words from Haryet right now. "What, Haryet? What are you not saying?"

"Oh... never mind."

Gemna rolls over onto her side. "No. Tell us." Gemna must feel the same way as I do because she adds, "Please," to the end of that sentence.

"It's just... unfair. And I know that's a stupid thing to say because I'm number eight. And it was always unfair, right? But... I don't understand this, girls. I don't get it. Why? Why does the god in the tower need so many of us? What has changed? Why now? Why not last time? I mean, it's just…"

"Unfair," I add. Because it is.

"It's more than unfair," Haryet continues. "It's pointless. Why do we need that god anyway? What does he do for us?"

Gemna kinda snickers. "Well, come on, Haryet. He gives us power. The spark is how everything runs around here."

"Not everything," Haryet counters. "Down-city doesn't have spark power."

"The farms do," I add. "The greenhouses do. That's how we get food. I mean, the climate here is pretty messed up. Without power how would we irrigate the fields? How would we keep the orchards warm at night?"

"Fire?" Haryet says. "And… well, I don't know about irrigation. But if the people in down-city can manage to live their whole lives without elevators, and electric lights, and hot water from the faucets, couldn't we *all* manage that?"

I shrug. "Sounds pretty depressing though, doesn't it?"

"You say that because you were born up-city. You don't know any different. But are these small luxuries worth the price of a woman?"

"Of course not," I say, slightly miffed at the turn in conversation. "I would trade all of it to save you."

Haryet turns her head towards me, her eyes less sad now, more resigned to her fate. "And I you, Clara."

"But that's all just a fantasy," Gemna adds. "Woulda, coulda, shoulda. We can't change it, girls. All we can do is meet our fate with grace."

I know what Haryet's thinking. Because I'm thinking the same thing. It's easy for Gemna to say that because she's number ten. She's not going into the tower tonight, nor is she next in line. There's still a possibility that I don't go in. I mean, there are only three months left. It's a pretty good possibility, actually.

But the chance of Gemna going in feels far away. A lot farther than three months.

If I don't go in, then she's definitely not going in. There is room to spare in her mind. And this extra space between fates is enough to give her hope.

I don't think I possess that same hope. I feel like it's all about to be ripped away.

Haryet smiles at me. "I wish I had someone like you, Clara."

"What do you mean?"

"Finn. He's the Master now. If those bells ring for you, he would save you. You're so lucky."

I don't say anything to that. It hadn't even occurred to me. Probably because his position is so new and came with such emotional trauma, I haven't had time to properly think about it. Would Finn intervene? If the bells rang for me?

It's a nice dream and we all lie on Haryet's bed, picturing this fantastical turn of events, for about an hour. But the maids return, sneaking in through some back door, bustling through the room and getting things ready. There's no way to put off what's coming. No one is coming to save her.

Haryet must be dressed. Gemna and I must be dressed. There is a dinner, and a gala, and then, of course, the Extraction itself.

This is reality and we live in it.

So I end up back in my own rooms, with my own maids, standing in front of my own mirror.

But that little bit of calm we conjured up while lying in Haryet's bed stays with me.

And I spend the rest of the afternoon daydreaming about how, if I am called for duty, Finn Scott would step in and save me.

It's a comfort. So much so, I let myself believe it.

And this is how I will manage to get through tonight.

With borrowed hope.

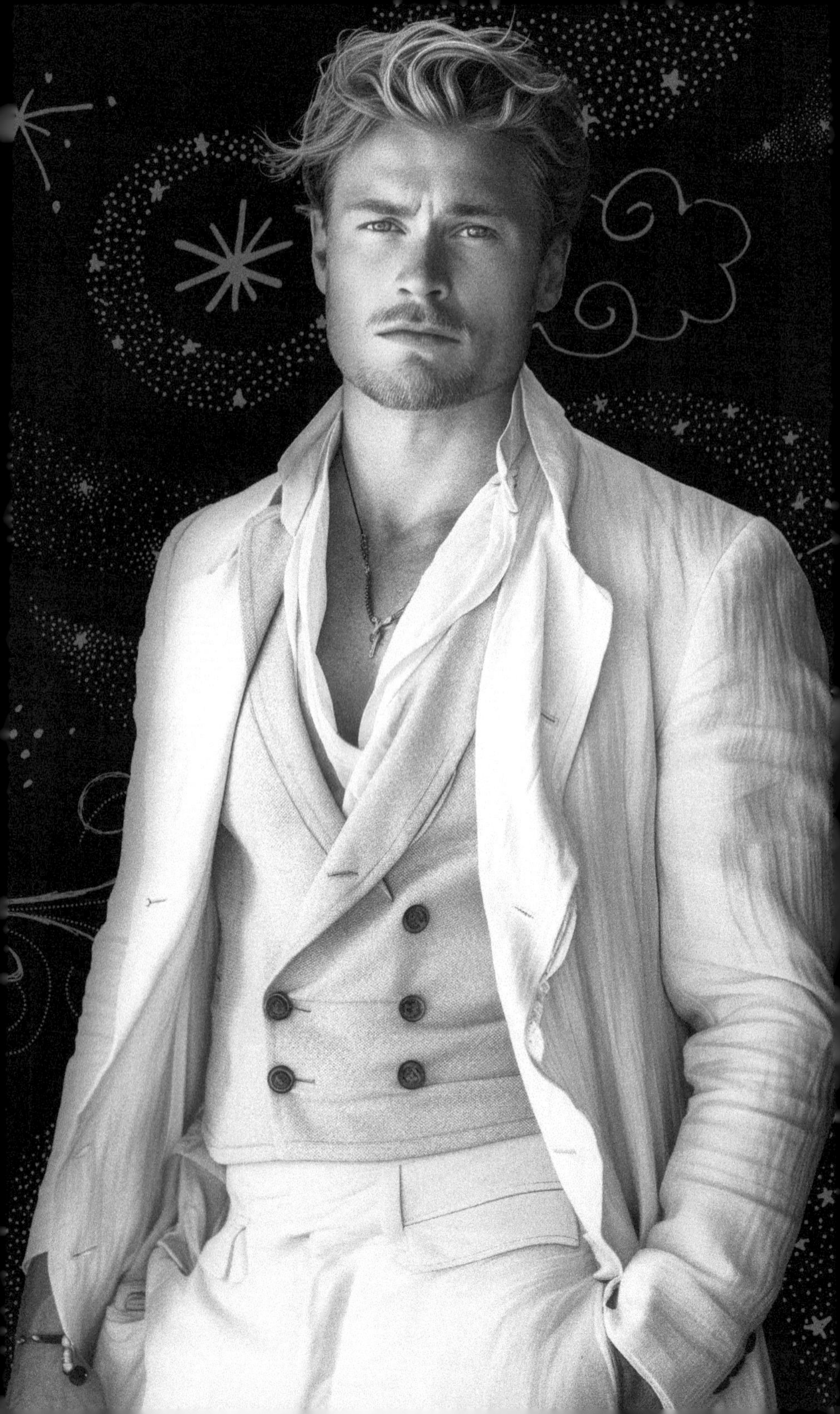

FINN

CHAPTER TWELVE

*A*fter I leave my childhood home and return to the palace, the rest of the afternoon goes by in a blur. Like time is nothing. Flowing quickly, the way the wind carried the dust during the Great Sweep.

Jeyk and Mitchell are here, and we don't go upstairs, just stay on the first floor, but there are dozens of others. Sorting out who was going to do what was a whole task in and of itself, since no one has been allowed up here since my father became Extraction Master decades ago.

Finally, Mitch starts barking orders like a general, scaring the servants, and cooks, and my father's panel of advisors—which is another thing to deal with, since I will need my own panel. Everyone gets busy with their assigned roles while Mitch and I go over an Extraction Master manual penned in my own father's handwriting, which details the entire night down to the last minute, starting with the feast at seven, followed by a gala at nine, the god's tribute ceremony in front of the tower at eleven-thirty, and then, at exactly midnight, Haryet Chettle will walk up to the massive black doors and they will open.

The moment she steps across the threshold, she will

disappear. And in that same moment, the bells will stop ringing and the entire city will let out a breath, relieved that it is now over.

And after the doors of the tower close, so is my job.

Ninety-nine percent of Tau City will probably never think of Haryet again.

Only Clara and Gemna will spend the rest of the night thinking about their friend.

Well, not Clara. Not if I can help it.

She's going to spend the night with me.

Fuck that god.

Those are the words running through my head all afternoon as Jeyk acts as emissary between the advisors and myself and Mitchell guides me through the ceremonial preparations, drilling me on the manual. We go through it page by page several times until a tailor appears stating that it is time for me to be dressed.

I have more Extraction ceremonies under my belt than any other Extraction Master in the history of Tau City. I've lived through eight of them. Eight in twenty-eight years. The first, of course, was when I was only eight years old myself. I don't remember much about that one, just that I was standing on the God's Tower stage with my father and mother. I didn't really pay attention to what was happening, just… kinda looked around and marveled at all the pomp and ceremony. I might even have enjoyed it.

The second was Imogen Gibson, Maiden number one in Clara's group. But aside from her spectacular display of spark as she entered the tower, it wasn't anything unusual. Of course it was sad. For some, I guess. Not for me personally. I didn't know Imogen. I danced with her a few times for the Little Sister dances, of course, but we never had a conversation. And anyway, she was meant to go in. She was number one. It was just... the way of things.

My third Extraction ceremony was Marlowe Hughes. And while two in one decade was rare, it was not unheard of. I maybe paid a little more attention to what was happening than I did the other two times. But it wasn't until we got to Maiden Number four, Lucy Fisher, that I really understood just how unusual this all was.

That was several years ago now. And three more ceremonies have happened since then, I barely need to study for tonight. I know all the words to say, I know what I'm supposed to do at each phase of the evening, I know where I'm supposed to stand and I've got it all timed down to the second.

But this is the first time I'll be the one in charge and I'll have to do it alone.

This is the first time I'll have to have that dance with Haryet and look her in the eyes. This is the first time I'll have to come to terms with the fact that I will be the one sending her through those doors. And she will disappear and never come back.

I will be the one to kill Haryet Chettle tonight at midnight, not my father. And I'm having a hard time coming to terms with it.

Who will I be tomorrow?

I'm not sure. All I really know is that I won't be Finn Scott. Not the way I am right now. The moment those tower doors close and Haryet is gone, I will be someone else.

"I don't wanna do this, Mitch."

He's in the middle of a sentence when I say this, but he stops mid-word and kinda stares at me for a moment. Then he straightens his back and lets out a breath. "I don't think your father did either. But… what choice do you have, ya know?"

"Isn't there always a choice? Even if they're all bad choices?"

Mitch actually scoffs. "Spoken like a true moralist. Don't you wonder why they do it?"

"Who?"

"The Spark Maidens. Don't you wonder why they actually go through with it? I mean, why don't they just refuse? What would people do? Throw them in?" He laughs. "That would really wake some people up, don't you think? So why do they do it?"

"Because they're… trained."

"Brainwashed, you mean?"

"That wasn't what I meant, no. It's just… they go to all those classes. Poised, polite, pretty or whatever."

"Poised, proper, and polite, you mean."

"Right. That. I know they don't *want* to go in, but it's tradition."

Mitch shakes his head at me, throwing an incredulous look in for good measure. "You really think that those girls walk into that tower with no idea whatsoever of what will happen to them on the other side because it's *tradition*?"

"Why else would they?"

"They're compelled, of course. It's the only logical answer."

"What? How?"

"How? Well, I'm not sure of the actual mechanism, but don't you think it's strange that they just… walk in without running? Because, if it were me, I'd run. No way in hell I'd give up my life for the greater good."

"Fucking hell, Mitch. That's selfish."

"Whatever. That's not the point. The point is, they're compelled. They don't have a choice."

I think about this for a moment, wondering if he's right. "My father never mentioned this."

"I have a suspicion that your father didn't tell you much of anything, Finn."

Well, I can't really say anything back to this because he's not wrong.

Mitch stares at me for a moment. And then, slowly, like he's making some kind of decision in the same moment, he raises one eyebrow at me. "Did he ever tell you about the Looking Glass?"

"What's a Looking Glass?"

His scoff is immediate and hearty. "See? You have no idea."

"And you do?"

"I don't know what it looks like, but I know he's got one in here."

"In where?"

Mitch ignores my question and looks over at the stairs that wind up to the fourth floor in a massive, graceful spiral. His eyes glide over to me. "What's up there?"

"A desk. A couch. Windows with a nice view. My father's personal collection of books."

"But there's a door too, right?" Mitch is practically smirking now. "One, perhaps, you've never seen the other side of?"

"Well… yeah. It leads to the… core, or whatever. That's what I've been calling the massive space in the middle of the upper dome."

"Let's go, then. That's where it is."

"That's where what is?"

But he's already walking towards the stairs and going up them by the time I shake myself out of my stupor and follow.

Mitchell stops at the top and I finish climbing the remaining steps and stand next to him. Then we both turn to the right and focus on the door. I walk over to it and try the handle. But it's locked.

"Where do you think we'd find the key?"

I look at Mitch and shrug. "Who needs a key? Just break the door."

He laughs. It's actually more of a scoff.

"What?" I ask. "It's my palace now. Who's gonna care? And anyway, it's literally Extraction Day. If there's information in there that I need, then get me in."

Mitch huffs out a breath, then snaps me a mock salute. "Yes, sir, Extraction Master."

It takes four good kicks to break the frame and pop the door open, but all in all, it was a pretty easy thing to do.

He waves a hand, inviting me to go first. "After you, Master."

"Shut up." But I do go first.

It's a dark room, so I stop once inside and feel along the walls for a switch. But the walls have a dramatic curve to them and they are exceptionally smooth, like glass. "I don't know—"

But then Mitch barks out, "Lights!" And the lights come on.

I look over my shoulder at him. "What the hell was that?"

"Voice commands. Rumor is—in school, at least—that there were rooms in the Extraction District with voice-activated spark power." Then he shrugs. "It felt appropriate."

When I look up, then around, I understand. This is not a room, it's a... sphere. It's like being inside a ball.

"Get out of the way." Mitch pushes me aside and closes the door. Then he takes a step back so we're standing shoulder to shoulder. "Ho-lee shit. What the fuck is this room, Finn?"

I'm as astonished and perplexed as he is. "I have no idea." We turn and walk over to a kind of desk in the center of the room. It's round with a cut-out in the middle. The actual desk part is flat with a slight curve upward on the outer edge. It's made of glass and clearly it is some kind of control panel. "Do you stand in the center?" I ask Mitch. "How do you get in? There isn't an opening."

Mitch runs a finger along the smooth glass top and then pauses. He looks up to smile at me as he lifts a portion of the desk up, creating an opening. "Your throne, my king." He waves a hand at me, inviting me inside the circle.

"You're stupid." But I do accept the invitation to walk in.

Mitch joins me, crowding me, because clearly this space was made for one person, not two. "What are you doing?"

"I wanna see." And then his fingers are sliding along the glass. Like he's looking for something. But after we've turned in a complete circle, tapping every part of the surface he possibly can, nothing happens.

A pounding on the door makes us both jump, then laugh. Mitch lifts the glass up, goes to the door, and opens just a crack so he can speak, but not enough that anyone can see inside.

I make out Jeyk's voice telling us time is short. So I look around the room, step out, and decide whatever this is—Looking Glass or not—the mystery will have to wait.

Because I've got a woman to Extract.

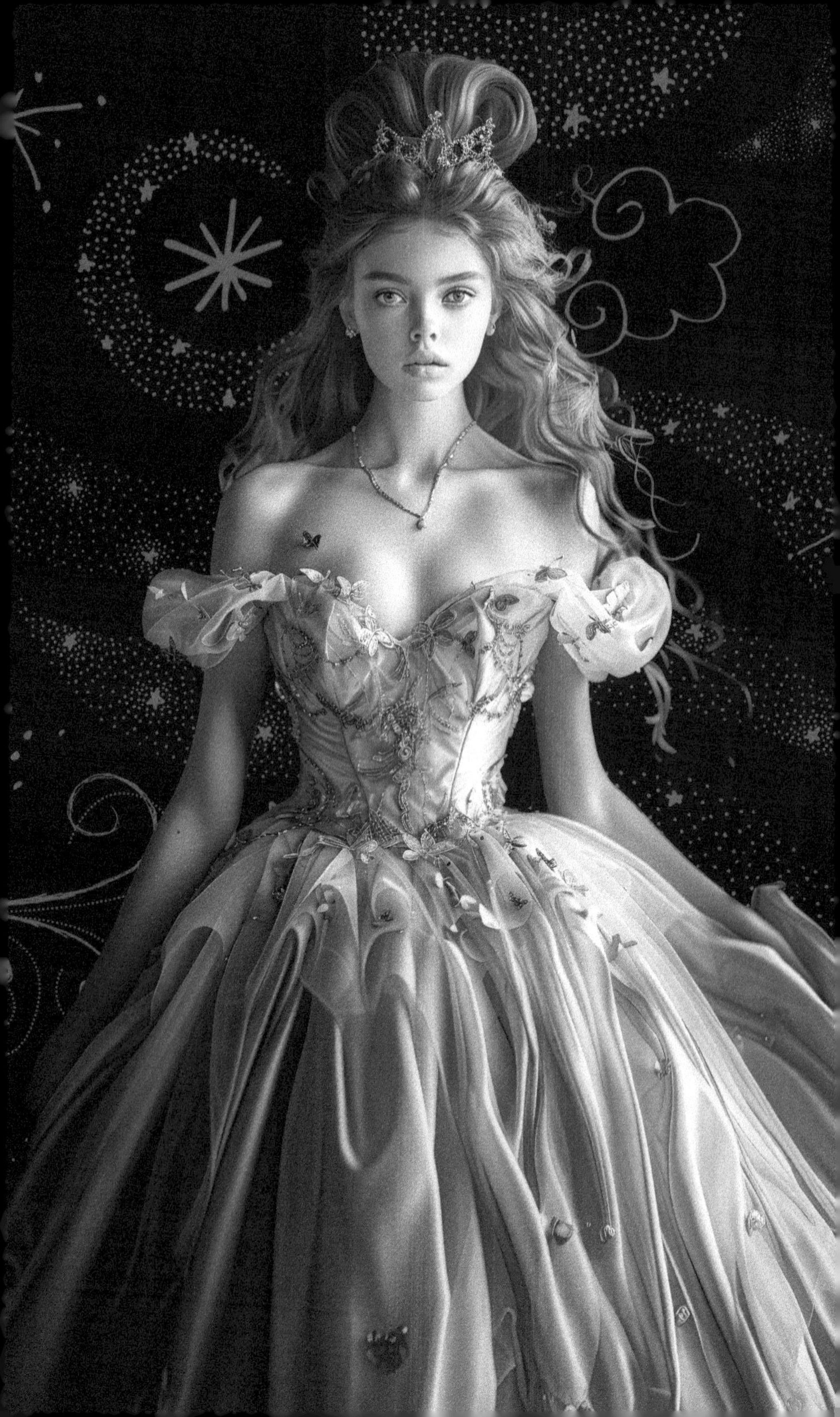

JASINA

CHAPTER THIRTEEN

*A**ttending the funeral is a drag.* It takes up so much of the day. We had to board the large boat before dawn so that everyone would be in place by the time Finn Scott, the new Extraction Master, arrived, so we had to wait around for hours, then again after the ceremony was over. Which took *sooooo* long.

Everyone was complaining about the smell. Which, of course, turned into a whole tirade about how gross down-city people are because they breathe the air of dead bodies every night.

The five of us got a lot of side-eye attention after that little comment.

It wouldn't have been such a bad experience if the boat was something nice. But there are seventy-five of us. The only boat big enough to transport all the Little Sisters at once was a mid-sized barge and we were packed in the cabin like canned fish for the ride down and back, so squished together I thought I was gonna suffocate.

Back in our little section of the dorm, everyone is feeling tired, and frustrated, and not the least bit beautiful because we've been wearing these dresses for two entire days now.

Not to mention feeling dirty. Though, as down-city girls, we would not admit the last part. We grew up in the ash. It's a part of us now. But being up-city full-time for couple of days is enough to make us question the practice of burning bodies like that so close to people.

"Look at me!" Britley is pointing to her sweat-stained dress. "My dress is a mess!"

"Look at mine!" Ceela points down to her feet. "Rosalit Bayner stepped on my hem getting out of the boat."

All four of us look down at Ceela's torn hem and gasp.

I walk over and put an arm around her shoulder. "Oh, Ceela. I'm so sorry. But it can be fixed."

"Fixed?" She scoffs. "We've got forty-five minutes to be lined up and ready. There's no time."

"There is," I insist. "Take it off and I'll take it to the sewing room and fix it."

Ceela pouts her lips. "But what about *your* dress?"

"Mine's fine. It's wrinkled and seen way too much action." The bad mood breaks and we laugh. "But it'll do."

Harlow huffs. "I'm gonna burn mine when I take it off tonight."

But Lucindy, ever the optimist, has a different idea. "We'll just tear the seams, wash the fabrics as best we can, and turn them all into something brand new." She beams a smile at us. Everyone but me groans.

"Come on, girls. She's right. Think positive. Everyone take your dresses off. We'll steam them and freshen ourselves up at the same time. It's an Extraction. It's... exciting, right?" I feel a little bad for calling it exciting for obvious reasons, but it is. I mean, I highly doubt a single Little Sister, in the whole history of Tau City, ever got to attend an Extraction. "It's special, girls. And while I do understand that we're here for a reason"—I shoot them each a knowing look—"we agreed to make the most of this experience, did we not?"

They perk up, just a little. Then mumble out agreements and start unzipping their dresses.

I take mine off as well, then hand it over to Ceela as I take hers. "Steam it. That's how you can repay me. I'll be back in twenty minutes and we'll still have plenty of time to steam yours too."

She leans in and kisses me on the cheek. "You're the best, Jasina. The absolute best."

I smile and then turn, not bothering to put something on over my corset and drawers. It's just us Little Sisters in the dorm and anyway, we're tucked so far in back there's no chance anyone will see me.

I make my way to the nearest sewing room, then rush over to a machine. I haven't had a chance to work the electric machines yet, but once I figure out how to turn the power on, it's pretty much the same as the foot-pedal model I grew up with. There are a lot of settings for fancy stitches that I have no clue how to use, but I don't need a fancy stitch to make a hem repair.

The mending goes quickly and soon, it's done. I stand up, gather up the dress, and I'm just about to head back in the direction of our space when I spy the spine of a book sticking out from a bookshelf just a few feet from me.

It's... enticing. Almost deliberately so. Because who in

their right mind can walk past this half-shelved book without pushing it back in?

Not me. I walk over, place my fingertip on the spine, and push it in. But as I'm doing this, I read the title. *"The Godslayer and His Courtesan."* I smile and pull it back out so I can study the cover.

I know the stories. The kid's versions, not this one—which is something much more than a child's tale because this is a thick tome and not a picture book. It actually has a subtitle that reads: *The Untold History.*

Interesting. Because this implies that it's not a myth, the way it was portrayed in the children's book I had as a child, but something more.

I like the story because it's a happy one. Kind of. I guess it depends on how you look at it. It starts out as a classic star-crossed lovers story, but there are adventures. Many adventures and many versions too.

I read them all as a child. The main characters never had names. Maybe in this serious version they do, but in the book I had as a child they were only known as the Godslayer and his Courtesan.

I've never thought about that title before. Courtesan makes sense for the girl, I guess. It's a little derogatory, if you ask me, but OK. Godslayer though? I don't remember ever knowing why they called him the Godslayer.

Weird.

"Jasina?"

I turn, startled, and find Ceela standing at the entrance that leads to this space. "You scared me."

She lifts up one shoulder in a half apology. "Sorry. I just

got worried when you didn't come back." She eyes the book I'm clutching to my chest. "What's that?"

"A book I found sticking out of the shelf. Do you remember the story of—"

"Jasina! We don't have time for this! Did you fix my dress?"

"Oh. Right. Yes." I thrust it at her. "All done. Let's go."

I put the back on the shelf and we both scurry back to our spaces to finish getting ready.

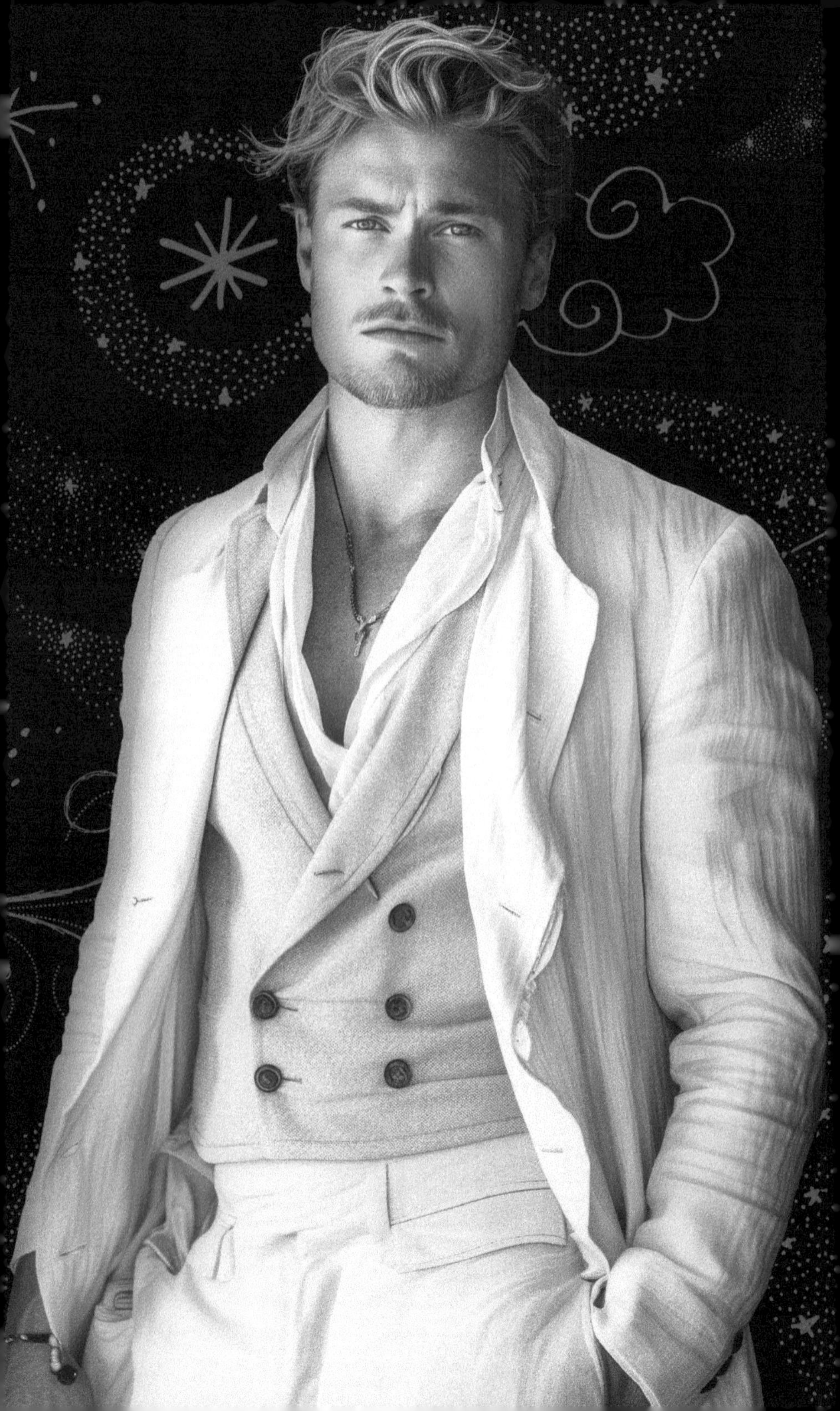

FINN

CHAPTER FOURTEEN

The rest of the evening passes just as quickly as the afternoon did. After Mitch and I left the viewing room we went back downstairs to deal with last-minute preparations for the dinner, gala, and ceremony.

I wanted to see Clara. So badly. I wanted to skip out on this entire night and take her in my arms, and make love to her, and kiss her all night long and live this day like it's a dream.

And then, maybe, when we woke up, we could've run away. Just walked out into the desert, leaving this whole city behind. We could've started over in a place with no tower and no god. Or hell, just dug a hole in the sand until we found an ancient train tunnel and spent the rest of our lives underground like the scholars who study that stuff do.

It wouldn't matter to me. I wouldn't care where we lived just as long as we got away from here before anything else had a chance to happen.

But it's a pointless fantasy because it's five minutes to seven and Mitchell, Jeyk, and I are already on our way to dinner. In five hours, the incessant bells will stop ringing and Haryet will be gone.

But how much time will that buy us? A year, like the last time?

Or will it be a week?

Will it be a day?

Maybe those bells never stop ringing?

Maybe Haryet walks through the door and they just keep going?

Maybe Clara will be gone tonight too?

It should be an absurd fear, but it's not. Because it could actually happen.

And the worst thing is, I couldn't do a thing about it.

Or… could I?

I stop walking halfway across the canal bridge and look at Mitch. "What happens if I refuse to let Haryet walk through the doors?"

He and Jeyk both stop abruptly and turn back to me. Mitch squints his eyes. "What?"

"What happens if I don't send her through? Has anyone ever done it?"

Surprisingly, it's Jeyk who answers me, not Mitch. "I asked that question once."

"To who?" I ask him.

"My father. And he said that his grandfather told him that your grandfather once refused."

"Really? My father never mentioned it. And I never knew my grandfather. He died long before—" I pause for a moment, trying on the idea that I should stop here. That I should forget I ever asked this question. Just wallow in my own ignorance for a while.

But I can't. I've already heard too much. "The god killed him?"

Jeyk's expression turns uncomfortable and he shrugs. "He wasn't the only one. The entire Council dropped dead. That was the night that Aldo became the Extraction Master and he was the one who sent the Maiden in. But Father said the worst part was that all the Maidens-in-Waiting, and even the Little Sisters who didn't get Chosen had to go in too."

"What?" This comes from Mitch. "That's bullshit."

Jeyk just shrugs. "Whatever. That's what he said."

"How would that even happen?" I ask. "I mean, did the god appear, or something, and then demand all this extra spark?"

"No." Jeyk shakes his head. "He said they just did it. The door didn't close after the first Maiden walked through. And then, all of a sudden, the other Maidens started walking towards the door too. People tried to stop them and they couldn't. It was like they were in a trance. Like they were compelled. Then all of that year's Unchosen did the same thing. They lost a hundred girls that night, not just one."

I let out a long breath and look at Mitch. He wants to object. He wants to say it's bullshit. But it was him, just a few hours ago, telling me that the only way these Maidens walk through is by compulsion. So he can't. Even if what Jeyk just told us is completely false, Mitch can't say shit.

But Jeyk isn't done. He keeps talking. "A lot of things like that have happened over the years, Finn. My father told me a lot of things about Tau City. He's worked in every single district. He has friends in all of them because he's the guy they turned to when they needed help with mechanicals. And sometimes, they couldn't pay. So he'd ask them questions about the past. What they saw, what they heard. This place doesn't run as smoothly as they tell us. Things—like *big* things—go wrong all the time. It's just, they don't put that in the history books, ya know? They just… don't tell anyone."

I don't respond. I just turn back to the bridge and continue walking.

Jeyk and Mitch follow behind me.

WHEN WE ARRIVE at the dining hall it's already packed with people. I can't sit with Clara—traditions—but she's sitting in a private elevated balcony, just like I am, and we are directly across from each other. Just like we were last night in the ballroom.

She seems to know I'm here, but I only get one small wave. Both Clara and Gemna are too busy consoling poor Haryet to pay attention to anything else.

Dinner is a long, boring affair and no one seems to be in the mood to party like they were last night. Of course, last night their Extraction Master wasn't dead—at least in their minds—and the eighth girl had not been called into the tower yet.

At nine o'clock, once the feast is over, the people sitting at the tables on the floor of the dining room begin migrating out and over to the God's Tower event center where the gala will be held.

The Maidens and myself will enter the gala last. I will dance with Haryet for at least thirty minutes while Tau City's elite class watch us, whispering and murmuring. Then I will hand her off to Mitchell and everyone will dance. Including me, including Clara. All the Maidens will dance with every man in the room and I will dance with every woman. Clara and I might get three minutes with each other.

But it's OK.

I keep telling myself that. Over and over again. It's OK. Because she's mine and I'm bringing her home with me tonight. She is spending the night with me tonight. I don't care what the Matrons say or how much they threaten her, or me, for that matter. I will have my night with Clara.

You never know, it could be my last. Who could predict the whims of a god we've never even seen, let alone understand?

Once it's my turn to leave the dining hall and make my way over to the gala, I go through the motions. I say all the right words to all the important people as I walk, and then, once I enter, wait for the applause to end while acting humble and unassuming. Then I meet up with Haryet on the dance floor so the gala can officially begin.

When I take her hand in mine, I realize it's shaking. But

then, when I place my other hand on her hip, I realize her whole body is shaking.

I've watched my father console all the others who came before Haryet, so I know he talked to them. Probably in that deep, soothing voice of his. Something I didn't inherit. And even though the Maiden always looked on the verge of a panic while he danced with them, they held it together. I don't recall a single one of them crying.

What was that Maiden motto again? Poised, polite, pretty? Something like that. At any rate, that's what the Spark Maidens going into the tower always looked like to me. Textbook examples of... well... Spark Maidens. All brainwashed up, as Mitch might say.

Haryet is not holding it together. I am not my father and I have no words—none at all—that could possibly console her.

I am sending this woman to her death tonight. In less than three hours, she will be gone.

Forgotten, except as a name in a list in a history book. If any more of those are written, that is. Which seems precarious at the moment. Because the god is dying.

I haven't told Mitch what the Council said yet. They told me not to tell anyone, ever, but there's no chance of that—I tell Mitch everything. But so much has happened in the last few days that the dying god isn't even at the top of my list.

"Finn?"

I look down at Haryet. Despite her red and swollen eyes, she still looks beautiful. She's so petite that she tips her chin all the way up to meet my gaze. This changes the shape of her face as I look down and makes her softer. Younger.

More vulnerable. Which is not the look I need right now. "Hmm?" I ask.

"If I live—"

"Haryet—"

"No, just listen. If I live—I mean, if I'm alive on the other side—I've decided to send a signal back. I don't know how, but I will. I made a promise to myself when Lucy Fisher went in that, if this ever happened to me, I would figure out what is going on. I hadn't thought about that in a while, but… it's all I have left, ya know? And so now I'm going in and that's my goal. Live, number one, but also find answers. So that neither Clara nor any Maiden ever again will have to feel the way I feel right now. I *will* find a way to tell Clara."

It's a dumb thing, I think. But I don't say that, of course. I just nod. "If anyone can do it, Haryet, it will be you."

And maybe I do have a little bit of my father inside me after all. Because this seems to finally set her at ease. Her shoulders drop, she lets out a long breath, and she presses her lips together as she forces herself to be stoic despite the large tears still rolling down her sweet cheeks.

She steps in closer to me and my arms automatically tighten around her. Then her cheek is on my chest and my chin is resting on her head.

I don't know if she closes her eyes, but I do. Because I can feel it. I can feel something bad coming.

Things are not going to go smoothly during my tenure as Extraction Master.

My three minutes with Clara begin at precisely eleven twenty-seven.

She falls into me. Head on my shoulder, arms wrapped around my back, gripping me tight. While I cross my hands at the small of her back in a possessive way.

I didn't want to watch her dance with all those men, but how could I not?

I didn't want to be jealous of them, but how could I not?

And I'm in a bad mood now. Which sucks. Because these three minutes are supposed to be my reprieve for the night. This tiny window of time where I could just be with the woman I love before I have to send her best friend into the God's Tower as a sacrifice.

Instead, I feel hot with anger and filled with resentment. Over everything. All of it. And my place in it. The death of my father, my missing mother—who isn't here. And now that I think about it, that whole situation is so fucked up, I can't even process it yet. In the span of two days I've lost both my parents and all my hope. Because this whole place is hopeless. I will never marry Clara. We will never have our own home together, or any children.

After an entire decade of patiently waiting, we will never get the reward we earned.

And I'm mad about it.

But by the time all these thoughts have run through my head, my three minutes with Clara are long gone, I've already missed my scheduled one minute dancing with Gemna, the gala is over, the clocktower has already chimed the half-past mark, and it's time to head outside to the God's Tower stage.

Clara pulls back, tipping her chin up in a small act of bravery, and meets my gaze. "Are you OK?"

"Am *I* OK?" I point to myself. "Are *you* OK?" I realize I should've asked this the moment she came to me for my dance, and I didn't. I was lost in my own pathetic self-pity.

Clara wants to say she is OK, but she's not. And so all that comes out of her mouth is a sigh.

I offer her my hand. "Walk with me?"

She pouts, but agrees.

Everyone is leaving the ballroom now, so it takes a good several minutes before we are outside again, breathing in the frigid night air.

Usually I like the chill of night. It's a dependable comfort that comes every twelve hours or so after a long, hot, stifling day.

But tonight, it's too much and Clara is shaking badly, her teeth chattering as we make our way over to the stage we will share as we send her best friend off to the god of Tau City.

A stranger god.

An unknown god.

Something foreign and irrelevant.

I hate him, I realize. I hate this god, and this job, and this city.

And I hate these feelings too. Because just a few days ago I was in love with all of it.

As we take our places, I notice that Mitch is taking care of Haryet. She, like Clara, is shaking uncontrollably, her teeth chattering so loud, I'm pretty sure even the people gathered at the far reaches of the tower stage can hear them.

I watch as Mitch holds her. Comforts her. Whispering things in her ear.

Clara snuggles up to me, unashamed at the public display of affection even though it's kind of forbidden for Spark Maidens.

Fuck it, though, right?

This whole thing is a charade, anyway.

We're sacrificing a woman to a god tonight and not a single person in this whole city will stand up and object.

Not even me.

There will be no discussion of Haryet tomorrow morning when people are lining up at the Magic Teacup or grabbing that morning pastry at the Laughing Loaf. They will forget about her immediately. For a year or two, at least. And then, when they are good and sure that the guilt of their silence that night has worn off, they will start praising her. They did that with Brooke Bayford, otherwise known as Maiden number seven. Just a few weeks ago I was walking across the canal bridge that leads to the Tower District and overheard a group of women discussing how beautiful Brooke looked on the night of her Extraction.

"Her hair was styled to look like a crown," a woman sighed as I walked past.

It irritated me at the time for reasons unknown. Reasons

I didn't have time to think about. But I understand it now. It's guilt. For the silence that is happening right in this very moment.

What is that old saying? All it takes for evil to prevail is for good men to remain silent.

But here's the thing: if the good men are silent, were they ever good in the first place?

I used to think I was, but I've been forced to reevaluate my high opinion of myself over the course of the day.

Mitchell steps away from Haryet and then Clara is giving my hand a squeeze and letting it go so she can join Gemna and the both of them can stand next to Haryet. Clara starts playing her part without being told. I mean, technically, I'm the one in charge here, so I should be the one leading the ceremony. But she's done this little ritual of standing on the tower stage next to one of her friends so many times now, she doesn't even need direction.

Which is good, I guess, for the sake of a seamless performance. Because I'm not capable of giving it.

I glance up at the clock tower and am a little shocked to see that it is eleven forty-seven.

Thirteen minutes. That's all the life that poor Haryet has left. Just thirteen minutes.

Mitch has reached me now. He leans in a little. "You're up. If we're gonna do this, let's do it."

I turn my head to look at him. "*If?*" Then I scoff. Because there is no question of 'if.' Not after what we learned on the bridge. Just the possibility that what Jeyk said is true is enough.

One girl or a hundred?

That's our choice.

Mitch just shrugs up one shoulder. "It's just a fuckin' expression, Finn." He doesn't look at me and these words come out tense.

Which makes me frustrated. So I take a moment to stew and stare out at the crowd of not-good men who will stay silent.

When I don't start the ceremony, Mitch growls at me. "Do your part, Finn. Don't leave Haryet up there like that. She's fuckin' terrified."

I look over at Haryet and while she's not sobbing or making a scene, she is still very much a mess. Gemna and Clara are standing on either side of her, holding her hands, looking straight ahead across the stage—at me, but not at me—with practiced, stoic looks on their faces. Behind them is a group of Matrons and once I notice them, I also notice that they are really shooting me some dirty looks.

Even my *mother*.

Which stuns me for a moment.

And then I just feel… ashamed. Because everyone here is doing their part with as much grace as they can muster and I'm the one who isn't living up to the standards.

This realization is enough to jolt me out of the state of shock I've been in all day and I step forward, taking my place in the center of the stage.

I turn and face the people, sucking in a breath and letting it out as I look down the central canal of Tau City. It's lit up cyan-blue, like it's made of spark itself. It gives off a glow that leaks across the shores, lighting up the city, just a little bit on either side of the water.

A line so bright.

These words hit my head and immediately come out of my mouth. "A line so bright." I don't say it loud enough, and the bells are still ringing, of course, but the people of Tau City know the speech by heart by now. Just as I do. So I clear my throat and continue, making my voice big. "That is what we are. A line so bright in the dead sandy world that resides outside the safety of these walls. We are what's left of the human race after the Great Sweep and every day that we exist is a blessing bestowed upon us by the god who resides inside the tower behind me."

All eyes of the city look at the monstrous, black tower where our god supposedly resides.

Everyone but me, because I am talking to them and must face forward.

I glance up at the clock tower and realize it's now eleven-fifty-four.

Six minutes.

And I still have more to say. So I put aside all the misgivings I have about being the person in charge of this woman's death and proceed. Because what choice do I have?

"Once a decade we Choose ten of Tau City's brightest Spark Maidens to represent us in the tower. While only one goes in, all the others stand in waiting. Ready to do their duty when the god calls." I look at Haryet when I say this. Look her straight in the eyes. She sucks in a breath so big, there's no way to miss it. But if there was any doubt, she adds to her resolve by lifting up her chin.

She's not crying now. She is doing her duty.

"With the ringing of the bells, the god has called and

Haryet Chettle, Maiden number eight, will answer his call tonight." I extend my hand in the direction of Haryet, Clara, and Gemna, then take a deep breath. "Join me now, Haryet. And I will walk you to the door."

Clara and Gemna give Haryet final bits of encouragement, and then drop their hands and take a step back. This step back—this separation of Haryet from the other Maidens—is what always jolts the Chosen one out of her stupor of shock and makes the moment real.

It separates Haryet from everyone else in Tau City now. Leaving her no choice but to see this stupid ritual through to the end.

Haryet joins me and I speak low now, my words only for the Maiden next to me. "Haryet, I'm so sorry. I'm just… so… sorry."

I don't know what my father told the Maidens as they stood up here next to him. That wasn't in the manual. It just said 'words of encouragement.' An apology isn't encouragement, but it's all I've got. So that's all I say.

"It's OK, Finn." Haryet pauses to breathe and lift her chin up a little. "I told you. I'm going in, I'm gonna find out what's happening, and I'm going to send back a signal." She looks up at me now, meeting my gaze. "I will do everything right inside there. I will do everything he tells me. Clara will not be called. I promise. She won't."

A short burst of air comes out of my mouth and I nod. "I know. Because… if anyone can do it, Haryet, it will be you."

And I find that I mean this. Really, really mean this. Also, I realize that her words have comforted *me*. I believe her. "I believe you."

This is the right thing to say because Haryet actually smiles. All the way up to her eyes.

Suddenly the bell tower bells are tolling, because they are ringing up midnight. A short song of only four notes. They sound completely different than God's Tower bells. Softer tones. More harmonious.

Haryet lets go of my hand and I have an almost uncontrollable urge to grab it back. To take her, and turn, and run down the line so bright. Which doesn't even make sense because it's water and I do not walk on water.

And anyway, she's already stepping forward towards the big black doors. So it's over. It's just over and I stay right where I am, eyes fixed as the doors begin to open. Leaning forward, like everyone else in this city, desperate to see past the darkness.

But it's no use. Even from here—mere steps away—there is nothing to see but black.

Sometimes the Maidens will look over their shoulder one final time before they step through, but not Haryet Chettle. She is afraid, but not scared. And I find, though it is the worst time to realize this, that I respect Haryet's resolve and I wish I'd taken the time to know her better. Because she is someone worth knowing.

It is in this same moment of realization that the clocktower bell reaches twelve gongs and Haryet Chettle steps across the threshold of the God's Tower.

All Spark Maidens display when they walk through the doors and Haryet is no different.

She glows bright blue like she's made of spark itself.

I stand there, unable to process it. What happens here on

this stage isn't natural. It's not right. But I've seen it so many times and it's such a part of my life that I can't imagine a world where a god in a tower at the top of your city doesn't steal women.

Then she's gone.

And the moment she disappears, the bells stop ringing.

If we, the people of Tau City, are a line so bright, then what comes after the bells stop ringing is a silence so loud.

***

*"FINN?" **Clara has been saying my name*** since we left, but I have not answered her. "Finn, talk to me. Please."

She's gripping my hand so tight I want to shake it off, but I find that I cannot let go. So instead, I just say nothing as the elevator doors open. We step in. Turn. Face the doors. And without comment, the liftman takes us up to the dome.

When the doors open we exit into the hallway, walk the short distance to the doors of the actual palace, and then I open them and wave her in.

This is the first time I've looked her in the eyes. I expect her to start back in, asking questions and trying to get answers out of me. But she must see something unfamiliar in my eyes when she looks back, because she doesn't even try. Just walks forward with a swish of her elaborate silk and linen gown.

And it's funny, I think. Well, not funny, actually. But... weird. Because I predicted this. The change in me. I knew I would be someone else after Haryet.

How could I not?

I step in after Clara, close the doors, and as she turns to look at me, I have an almost uncontrollable urge to be inside her.

She doesn't say anything. Just stares at me with bloodshot eyes, and downturned mouth, and... disappointment, I think.

I don't like to see her sad, of course. But the part about this look that stings is the disappointment. It feels like an accusation of failure.

I have so many things to say about this look she's giving me. I want to explain that it's out of my control, that I have no real power here, and anyway, isn't this what Haryet signed up for? Isn't this what they *all* signed up for? In exchange for pretty dresses, and luxurious quarters, and being invited to the best parties to rub shoulders with Tau City's most influential people, they promised to walk through those tower doors if the god called them in.

Not only that, they promised to do it as poised, proper, polite ladies.

I have to hand it to Haryet. In the end, she did her part. She tipped her chin up, squared her shoulders, and marched through those doors determined to... to save people. To save *Clara*.

And I know that Clara isn't privy to Haryet's last words —we haven't had a chance to discuss it yet—but that's what we would be discussing if she wasn't looking me in the eyes accusing me of failure.

I'm angry about this look she's giving me. It's not fair, I understand this, but I'm pissed. I don't want to be here. Unlike her, and all the other Spark Maidens, I didn't *choose* this path. I was born into it.

The sudden urge to yell at her—this woman that I love so dearly, and want so completely, and will never have a future with—the sudden urge to *blame her* for all of it is almost overwhelming. This impulse is so strong, I actually open my mouth to start the fight.

But in that same moment, Clara sighs. Tears spill out of her eyes and roll down her cheeks. She bows her head, breaking eye contact, to hide these tears, but then they just slide off her face and fall to the floor.

Get a hold of yourself, Finn. She's sad, and scared, and lost. She doesn't need a lecture right now, even if she does blame you.

Which is exactly what Mitchell would say to me, if he were here. And it's truly the best advice, even if it is only coming from my own inner voice.

So instead of starting a fight, I walk over to Clara—this woman that I love so much—place my hands on her cheeks, tilt her head up, and kiss her.

I'm still angry, but not at her. I'm angry at the world, and myself, and all the stupid traditions I am now obligated to continue. And the only way I know how to let go of it is to take control wherever I can.

And the only thing I have control over right now is how we put this night to bed. And I want to do that with sex.

So this is a passionate kiss. A greedy, hungry, insatiable

kiss. And while I'm kissing her, I'm pushing her backwards. She kisses me back with just as much longing, yearning to forget. Because that's all we're doing. That's all anyone's ever doing in this city. We're filling our lives with coffees, and pastries, and clothes, and galas, and the dreams of dreamers who think we're all free.

But, of course, we're not. We're living under the thumb of an insatiable god hungry for pretty women.

Stop thinking, that voice inside my head chastises. *Purge your feelings of guilt, and shame, and apathy with sex, Finn. It's what Clara wants too.*

And that voice in my head is right, I think. Because I can't recall a single conversation with Clara Birch about Imogen Gibson, or Marlowe Hughes, or Mabel P., or Lucy Fisher, or Mabel S., or Piper Adley, or Brooke Bayford.

So why would Haryet Chettle be any different?

Clara doesn't want to talk about Haryet, she wants to *forget* about Haryet.

Which just so happens to be a wish I am able to grant.

I'm still walking Clara backwards as I kiss her, but then the back of the couch is right there, pressing against her ass. I pull away, spin her around, place my hand right between her shoulder blades, and push her down, holding her in place for several seconds so she understands what I want her to do.

Which is stay still and follow my lead.

There is no way to get this gown off her in any kind of timely manner, and even if there was, the number of undergarments she's wearing pretty much make the attempt at getting her naked pointless. So I don't even bother trying.

Instead, I place my foot between her legs and kick one foot to the left, spreading that leg open a little wider. Clara gasps in surprise, but I don't stop, just do that same move again, spreading open her other leg until, as a pair, they are wider than her shoulders.

My hand is still firmly pressing down between her shoulder blades, so she is now breathing heavy and with effort. Her head has turned to the left, her eyes trying to see me over her shoulder, looking for guidance, but she's not able to fully meet my gaze.

I wait. There is silence in these waiting moments. Which is her way of giving me permission to continue.

So I lift my hand from her back, then lean down into her neck, biting her earlobe and making her squirm. My hand is lifting up the many layers of elaborate skirts, pushing them all up over her hips and exposing the gorgeous silk-lace lingerie covering her hips, and ass, and upper thighs. At the same time I whisper, "I love you," right into her ear.

She wants to say it back, almost gets part of a word out, but I shock her back into silence by grabbing the edge of that fine silk-lace underwear and ripping it open, giving me the access I need.

There's not going to be any talking. If she starts talking, I'll start talking, and I don't want to talk about anything right now. I just want sex.

A moment later I'm pushing a finger up inside her as I release my belt, open my pants, and pull out my cock, fisting it in my hand. Clara Birch is moaning loudly as this happens, arching her back and sending all the right signals, and I slide my finger along the streak of wetness between her legs.

I bend down a little, positioning myself at her entrance with one hand while I continue to stimulate her with the other, and then my finger slides out just as my cock slides in.

Clara's gasp of surprise, and possibly pain, is immediate. But I don't stop, or even consider going slower. I thrust into her *hard*, fisting her hair and pulling it with one hand while I slap her on the side of her thigh. She gasps, moaning a little, and then her arms stretch out along the back of the couch, bracing against my thrusting as I fuck her. We don't make love. Not this time. I do love her, but this is not lovemaking.

I am pissed. I am ashamed. I am… not me anymore.

I'm someone else now.

And I knew this was coming. I felt like it had already happened. So it's not even a surprise that I don't recognize myself in this moment.

Clara's not either, I guess. Because she's not complaining about the new me.

Of course she's not, because while the new me thrusts my hips, slapping them against her ass and jerking her forward, I stroke her from the front, massaging her sweet spot in just the right way.

She likes it, too. She likes the new me. I know this because she's not even *trying* to be quiet. She is not even *trying* to pretend she's not into this. She is moaning, and gasping, and squealing, and she comes, more than once, while I close my eyes and forget what I just did, and who I did it to, and just use this woman up like a man with no future.

Then, at the last possible moment, I slide out of her, pump myself a few times with my fist, and come all over her bare ass with my eyes still closed.

I don't know how long it takes for Clara to try to rise. A few minutes, maybe? But by the time she is ready to stand back up and reorganize her gown, I'm well and truly done. So I let her.

She's still breathing hard as she slips the remnants of her lacy lingerie down her legs, kicking it away from her with a lovely silk slipper, and stands to face me.

Then she sucks in a long breath and slowly lets it out as her eyes finally meet mine once more. "Well." She practically pants this word out. "That was… unexpected."

I grin, the darkness inside me satisfied. For now. I close the small space between us by taking a step forward. Then I place a hand on her cheek and kiss her again. This time, while it's still passionate, it's not angry. It's sweet. And so is my whispered response. "I love you too."

She lets out another breath, dipping her chin down—maybe a little embarrassed by what just happened. But then she squares her shoulders and looks back up, eyes sad again. Because this is a sad night and while the sex was a good distraction, it's just not enough. "You're going to save me, right?"

"What?" For a moment, I'm confused. And my eyebrows knit together. But then I realize she's talking about the god and the tower.

"Finn?" She grabs me by the shoulders, forcing me to

focus. Her tone has changed. She's not sweet or submissive now. My anger is gone, but hers is just getting started. "Please tell me that you will save me. Because it's very, *very* fucking clear that all ten of us are going into that tower."

"Clara—"

"What?" She knows the answer. So really, nothing more needs to be said. "You're not serious! I'm your future wife, Finn." Her eyes are wide and filled with fear, but also anger. "You. *Will*. Save me."

I don't mean to laugh. I really don't. It just comes out. And I'm not laughing at her, or what's happening. I'm laughing at the idea that I have any say in this.

"This is funny to you?"

"No. It's not funny at all, Clara. It's just…" I shrug. "If the god calls you in, you're going in."

"That's your answer?" She stares at me for a moment, narrowing her eyes down into slits. "You bring me up here, knowing full well I want you to save me, then you fuck me like a whore—"

"Please," I scoff. "You weren't complaining. You got off three times by my count."

Clara Birch slaps me right across the face.

Hard.

Hard enough to make my head jerk to the side.

Hard enough to leave a splash of spark sticking to my hot face and a blue trail streaking through the air in the aftermath.

Then she turns on her heel and walks out, leaving her destroyed, silk-lace panties behind at my feet.

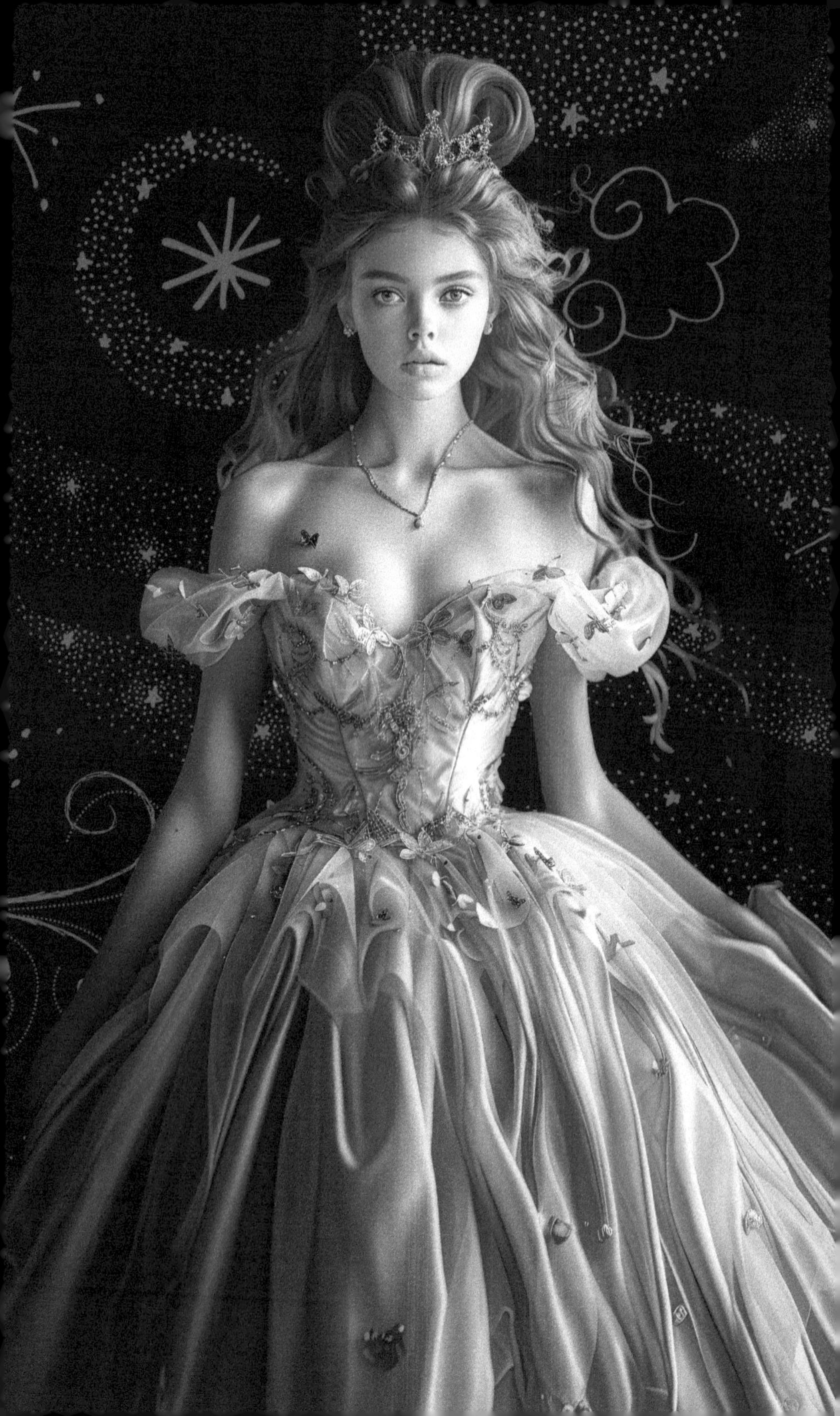

JASINA

CHAPTER FIFTEEN

My *now tired*, overused, overseen—but still gorgeous—blue Choosing dress swishes as Matron Connelly grips my upper arm very tight and tugs me through the empty, quiet corridors of the Maiden Tower.

She grabbed me out of the Little Sister line once the whole lot of us were dismissed from the God's Tower stage after Haryet disappeared through the doors in a spectacular flash of blue light. All the Maidens light up when they go through, but Haryet's light never seemed to shine that bright to me.

"Don't dally, Jasina. Things are happening quickly now and we have very little time."

I hardly think it's possible to 'dally' when she's practically dragging me. But I don't say that, of course. Connelly is not a Matron you mess with, so I don't even bother with an attitude. I just make my silk-slippered feet move a little faster as we cross a bridge enclosed with floor-to-ceiling glass windows.

It is in this moment that I realize I have never seen this bridge before and even though the brightly-lit secondary canal below us is something familiar—Tau City has dozens of them, after all—I don't recognize this one in particular. Or any of the outside buildings that I catch a glimpse of as we swiftly cross and enter a hallway on the other side.

I don't know where I am. "Where are we going?"

Connelly doesn't answer, just flashes me a sidelong stink-eye conveying annoyance.

Of all the Matrons that I had to get stuck with tonight, of course it would be her. She's mean, and big, and built like a man. At least, I think she is. It's hard to tell what her body really looks like under her ten-sizes-too-big blue tunic and cream-colored scapular apron.

She and I round a corner and come into yet another hallway, which looks like every other hallway in the Maiden Tower. But we're no longer in the Maiden Tower, of that I'm certain. We crossed a canal, so… I'm not sure where we are.

It's all very familiar though. Because everything in up-city has the same vibe. Plastered walls that curve up into an arched ceiling—bits of it peeling away in various spots, revealing the stonework underneath—and lit up by electric candles inside sconces positioned about every twenty feet along the passage.

I wouldn't say I've gotten used to the almost free-flowing spark here in up-city, even though I'm an official resident now. But it's no longer such a surprise.

However, I am, and always will be, a down-city girl.

I'm not ashamed of this, either. Even though there are no spark lights where I come from. No elevators—because there are no high towers—no fans to keep you cool during the hot, stifling day, and no vents blowing heat to cozy things up during the frigid, freezing nights.

There is just enough power down-city to run the automated irrigation and heat lamps in the fields, orchards, and greenhouses. We need the power—not 'we' as in down-city people, but the collective 'we,' as in the city itself. The extreme temperature changes between day and night in Tau City prohibit farming to a large degree. And the city does, after all, need to eat.

We, as in the Bell family, weren't always down-city. The Bell-family austerity is partly self-imposed and partly leftover circumstances from deeds done long ago. Punishment, if you will.

My family designed the carillon inside the clocktower. Bellmaker. That used to be our last name. We used to live up in the Tower District as well—which is a privilege that very few families get, even today. But something happened. It was hundreds of years ago now and no one in my family talks about it, so I don't have a clue as to what this something was. It's even possible that they are telling the truth when they say they don't know why we were demoted to down-city.

Matron Connelly stops in front of an arched doorway made of thick, dark wood panels. She grabs the iron knocker and bangs it three times. Then lets out a breath, clasps her hands behind her back, raises her chin, and rocks back on her heels.

The door opens and I find Auntie, staring down at me.

I lower my gaze and curtsey the way I have been

programmed to do from all the Little Sister instruction over the years.

Auntie sighs and spits words at Matron Connelly. "Thank you, Matron. I'll take it from here."

Connelly responds with a deep bow, which I only catch the last of because I'm still straightening up from my curtsey. But it's intriguing because I've never seen a Matron bow to one of her peers before.

Connelly turns with a swish of her tunic and goes back the way we came.

"Come in, come in, Jasina. We don't have all night." Then Auntie steps aside and waves me forward.

The room I enter is... confusing. I stop in the center of it and tilt my head, shaking off my bewilderment and forcing my brain to make sense of what I am looking at.

But... I have no idea what I am looking at. So I simply blink.

"It's a jolt, isn't it?"

I look up her. "What is this place, Auntie?"

"It's a control room, Jasina. These are called switches." She pans a hand at an array of... I dunno. Bits? Bobs? Buttons? Lots of little knobby things positioned on a metal panel that is kind of like a table. But there is a partition with many sections of thick, curved glass coming up out the back side of it.

I look at the... *switches*, then up at Auntie. "What?"

She sighs. It's not a tired sigh, either. It's a 'you're stupid' sigh. "*Switches*, Jasina. To power the images that show up on the televisions."

"Tell-a-whats?"

"Tele—never mind. That's not important. There is something happening right now with the new Extraction Master that we did not plan for. You will be going in. *Tomorrow.*"

"What?"

"Would you please stop saying that! You sound like an imbecile. I sincerely hope you are not an imbecile, Jasina. Because if you are, let me know right now and I'll choose one of your friends to replace you."

I scoff, offended. "No. I'm not an imbecile. I'm confused, OK? I have no access to the Extraction Master. I haven't even been Chosen yet. I don't understand what is happening here."

"Because you're not listening. The god is dying. This is our chance to finish him off once and for all. Why do you think he's calling all those Maidens in?" Thankfully, she doesn't wait for me to answer, because I have no fucking clue. "His spark is weak! He uses them for their spark. He steals it and uses it. Everything you know about the world, Jasina, is a lie. All of it. There is not one thing that you've been told that is true. The Rebellion aims to shatter the illusion these lies have created. We're going to set Tau City free!"

I'm not sure she's done yet, and I don't want to interrupt—or risk sounding like an imbecile again—so I wait.

"Well? Don't you have anything to say to that?"

"Umm… well… what does all that have to do with this room?" I want to stab myself with a fork as soon as these words come out, but oddly enough, this answer seems to please my aunt.

"This room is what we're looking for. This is what we need from you."

"But... don't you have it already?" I pan my hand to the table of knobs and the tele-things.

"No. Not *this* room. Something like it."

"Ooooookay. I'm not sure I understand."

"This room is called a Looking Glass. And inside the Extraction Tower there is another one. This one here no longer functions. It's hundreds of years out of date. But the one in the Extraction Tower should be in prime condition. We think this Looking Glass contains a message from the previous Extraction Master to his son. We need this message. He must not see it. We have it on good authority that he hasn't seen it yet. But the more time passes, the more chances he has to find it. If you were to find it first and perhaps... get rid of it. Well, there would be a place in the history books for your name, niece."

Her stern mouth grows into something that resembles a smile. Except it's not comforting or happy. It's slightly horrifying. "Because something that important at this stage of the game would change everything." Her eyes dart back and forth, searching mine. "It would eliminate a lot of problems. It would give us... more choices. But if you fail." Her smile drops, her mouth grows stern again, and her eyes narrow down into slits. "If you fail, you will compound our problems. Jasina. You will make everything worse. And that too, will go into the history books."

I actually scoff in response. It's kinda loud too. "Auntie, this is a ridiculous task. I am nobody. Not even a Spark Maiden. How the hell am I supposed to get into the freaking Extraction Tower, find a room, find a message, and change the future? I mean... that's setting me up to fail."

She does not like my reaction or my negativity, because she growls at me. "Are we supposed to hold your hand? Are you an infant?"

"No, but—"

"Are you incapable? Shall we call on one of your friends for this job? Which one should I choose?" She taps her forefinger to her chin as her eyes slide up, like she's trying to decide.

"I'm just saying—"

"You're just saying what?" She looms over me like a threat. "That we can't trust you? That you have no ambition? You think this is a joke? You're on the side of the god?"

"No. I don't think that, I'm not on the god's side, and I'm very, very serious about the Rebellion and my part in it. I'm here, aren't I?"

"If you're so serious, then why are you trying to talk me out of assigning you this task? Have you switched sides?"

"What?" I'm shocked that she would even say such a thing. "Absolutely not."

Auntie presses her lips together, humming a little. "You're acting suspicious. You feign bravery. You say you want to be a rebel. But here I am presenting you with an opportunity to make history—an opportunity one of your peers would jump at, and you're trying to talk me out of it. Like you're on their side, maybe?"

This is stupid. She's not even listening to me. It's like I'm not in the room. She's only hearing what she wants to hear. Or she's baiting me, or something.

"Are you a traitor, Jasina?"

"Absolutely not. I already told you."

"What is that girl's name? The one in your group? Ceela, is it?"

"Auntie, I can do this, I swear. You don't have to call on one of my friends."

Her eyes go angry and she directs them at me. "We need weekly progress reports from you from this day forward, Jasina Bell. Do you understand me?"

"Yes, ma'am."

"And we need to know where that room is and if there's a message inside it. If you can't deliver these things by the next Choosing, you're out."

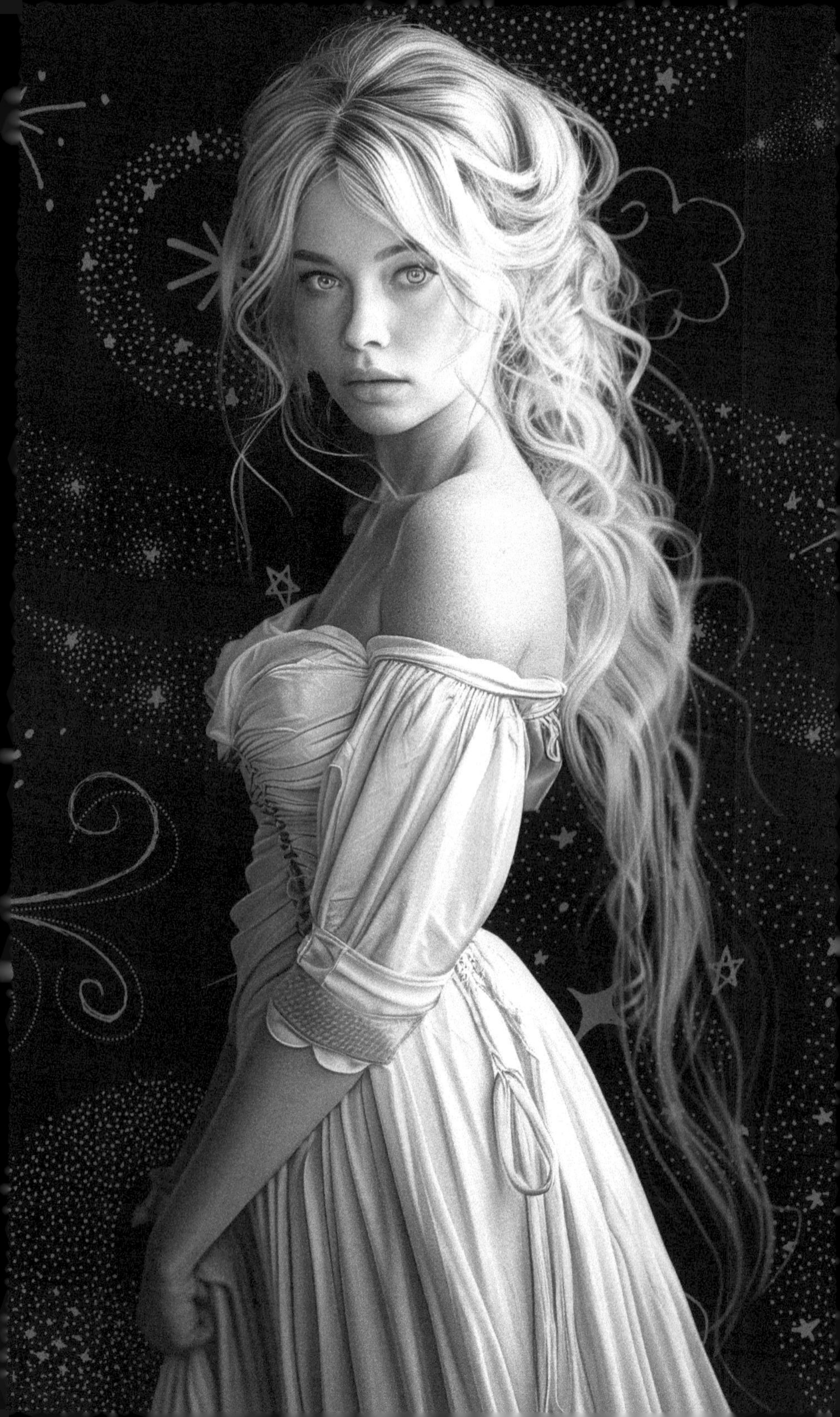

CLARA

CHAPTER SIXTEEN

The moment I open the door to my quarters Gemna is right up in my face, *screaming*. "Where have you been! I was looking for you and you just left me!"

"I'm sorry. Finn—"

"That was cruel, Clara! *Cruel*! We just lost our best friend to the tower and you *left me*!"

Out of some long-forgotten habit, I look over my shoulder, expecting to find a Matron somewhere in the hallways, ready to chastise Gemna for being too loud.

Which is ludicrous. They were around in the early years, especially the first year when we were all so young and rowdy. But that Matron I saw giving the Little Sisters a tour the other day was the first one I can remember seeing actually inside the Maiden Tower since Lucy Fisher took the walk.

Gemna's hysterics are increasing as I stay silent. Her makeup is streaked with tears, her voice is shrill, and when I take her hand, she's trembling. "I'm sorry, Gemmie. I'm *so* sorry! I wasn't thinking. Finn just pulled me away and I… I just… went."

Gemna stares at me for a moment. Eyes wide, like she's

terrified. And this is when it hits me. When *everything* hits me. All eight of the women who came before us have been Extracted. Gone. Lost. Forever. Never to be seen again.

And we're next. We both know it. We feel it in our hearts. This doesn't end until all ten of us are inside that fucking tower.

Which is a shock. Not the sentiment of it, but the reality of it. The realization that I am going to die and I am standing on the precipice of this death in this very moment.

It's not like I had been blocking it out. It's just... I think I was numb, or something. Or possibly conditioned to see these Extractions as something normal. Something common. It's just what happens to the women in the Maiden Tower. One moment they are here, one moment they are not.

And it's wrong.

This isn't normal. It's barbaric. It's a sacrifice. We are sending young women to their death to appease a god we've never even seen. The whole thing could be fake, for all we know.

My arms wrap around Gemna and I hug her tightly, holding onto her like the god himself might appear at any moment and drag her away.

She holds me back just as tightly. Because that bell is going to ring for me. And it could happen in the next minute, in the next hour, or any time at all.

My death is assured. And that means that Gemna will be sitting up here in our quarters alone. Waiting for the bells to toll one final time after I'm gone.

What a horrible way to go out. Not that it's not horrible

for the rest of us, but to be alone when it happens? It's pure torture. And any god who demands this of his followers is evil and no god of mine.

Maybe the Matrons will let Gemna go home? So she could at least be with her family while she waits?

But I don't think so. They don't care about us. Their mission is to keep us in line. To make us poised, proper, and polite. So we don't question them.

So far, it's worked. Because... come on! Eight fucking women have now walked into that tower in the last ten years. And every one of them did it willingly.

Gemna pushes back now, frantically wiping her eyes, smearing black makeup and making a mess of her face. She sniffs. "Did Finn tell you?"

"Tell me what?"

"About the gala tomorrow?"

"What gala? We literally just came from two freaking galas. Why would we need another one tomorrow?"

"I'm not sure, but the Matrons were all lined up downstairs after I came back from the Extraction—*alone!*" She sneers that last word at me.

But I guess I deserve it. It was a really shitty thing to do to her. And the worst part is, I never even thought twice about leaving her alone on the tower stage and following Finn back to his new place. "I'm sorry, Gemna. I really am. I will never leave your side again. It's us, together, until the end."

She stares at me for a moment. Then blinks and takes a deep breath, pulling herself back together. "I don't know what the gala tomorrow night is for, but the Matrons told me not to go anywhere in the morning. That the dressmakers will be here at dawn to fit us. Finn didn't mention it?"

I shake my head. "No."

"Did he say *anything*? Anything at all about what the hell is happening?"

I blow out a long breath, then flop onto the nearest couch, kick off my shoes, and pull my legs up underneath my many layers of silk skirts. "Well, he did mention that there was no way he could help me if the bells rang again."

Gemna sits down next to me, sniffling. "*What?* Why not?"

When I meet her eyes, I see the hope die. She has never said anything about my relationship with Finn or Aldo, never asked a single question in all these ten years. But she was going to ask for help tonight. Was going to beg, maybe, for me to find a way to get us out of our obligations using my connections to the Extraction District.

And now she knows that hope was futile.

"He didn't really elaborate. Just… well, it was a *very* firm no, Gemmie." I shrug. There's nothing more to say.

She grabs for both my hands, holding them in her cold ones, looking me straight in the eyes. "We're going in, aren't we? We're going in and it's gonna happen soon. There are only three more months, Clara. We could have hours, or days, or weeks. But that's it. We're *going in*."

"Yep." It comes out on a long sigh and in a tone of resignation. Matter-of-fact and a little bit lighthearted, actually.

I think this tone surprises Gemna. Shocks her out of her

panic too. Because she sucks in a very deep breath and when she lets it out, she is calm and composed. Chin up, eyes direct. Displaying every bit of her eighteen years of etiquette training. "What do we do, Clara?"

I shrug. "Go out like ladies?"

She locks eyes with me and we stay that way for a long second.

Then we both burst out laughing.

We pause, then it bursts forth again. Soon, we are having a full-on fit with tears streaming down our faces. Not tears of distress. Not entirely, anyway. But tears driven on by hysterics and the sudden, abrupt awareness that not only are we out of control, we never had any in the first place.

It's a manic state. Something that can only end one way.

And so it does.

We hug each other tightly and sob together.

AT SOME POINT in the early pre-dawn hours I wake up and find myself alone on the couch. When I get up and check the time, I realize it's only three-thirty. Gemna is gone. I leave my quarters and go up to hers on the tenth floor, just because I need to know where she is. I find her in her bed, her gorgeous dress left in a heap on the floor, her breathing shallow and uneven. Like she's dreaming.

Or, more likely, having a nightmare. One that involves walking into that black tower at the top of the city.

I go back downstairs and stumble through the darkness as I make my way into my own room, struggling to get the laces undone along the back of my dress. Letting the heavy gown fall to the floor at my feet is a relief until I remember that I left my underwear on the floor of Finn's new palace, ripped to shreds.

How embarrassing. I'm mortified that I allowed Finn Scott to handle me so roughly. He was pulling my hair at one point. And that slap across my thigh—well, let's just say I can still feel the sting.

I cover my face with both hands, willing the memory to go away as the moonlight streams through the round window above my bed, chilling my naked body.

But I'm mostly sad about our tryst last night. Because he's never treated me that way. Our lovemaking has always been careful, and tender, and attentive.

What we did last night had nothing to do with lovemaking.

He was *fucking* me. The way a man might fuck a whore down-city in the Shipping District.

I want to erase the entire encounter from my mind, but as I slip into bed, I find myself reliving every moment. Every harsh grunt. The slap, the hair pulling, and the way he pushed me down over the back of the couch and kicked my legs open.

Then his fingers...

I let out a long breath, shaking my head and closing my eyes.

Don't think about it, Clara. Don't think about it. He wasn't himself. You weren't yourself, either. He didn't mean it. It wasn't a reflection on you. It was stress, and... fear, and... well. All the emotions.

The last time you trysted it was perfect, and soft, and slow.

Think about that time.

It takes several minutes, but I do manage to wipe our last encounter away and replace it with the other one. I close my eyes, steady my breath, and recite the relaxation mantra that I learned long ago, when I was still a Little Sister.

This is my path. This is my life. This is my destiny.

This is my path. This is my life. This is my destiny.

This is my path and I must accept it.

Because Finn Scott is *not* going to save me.

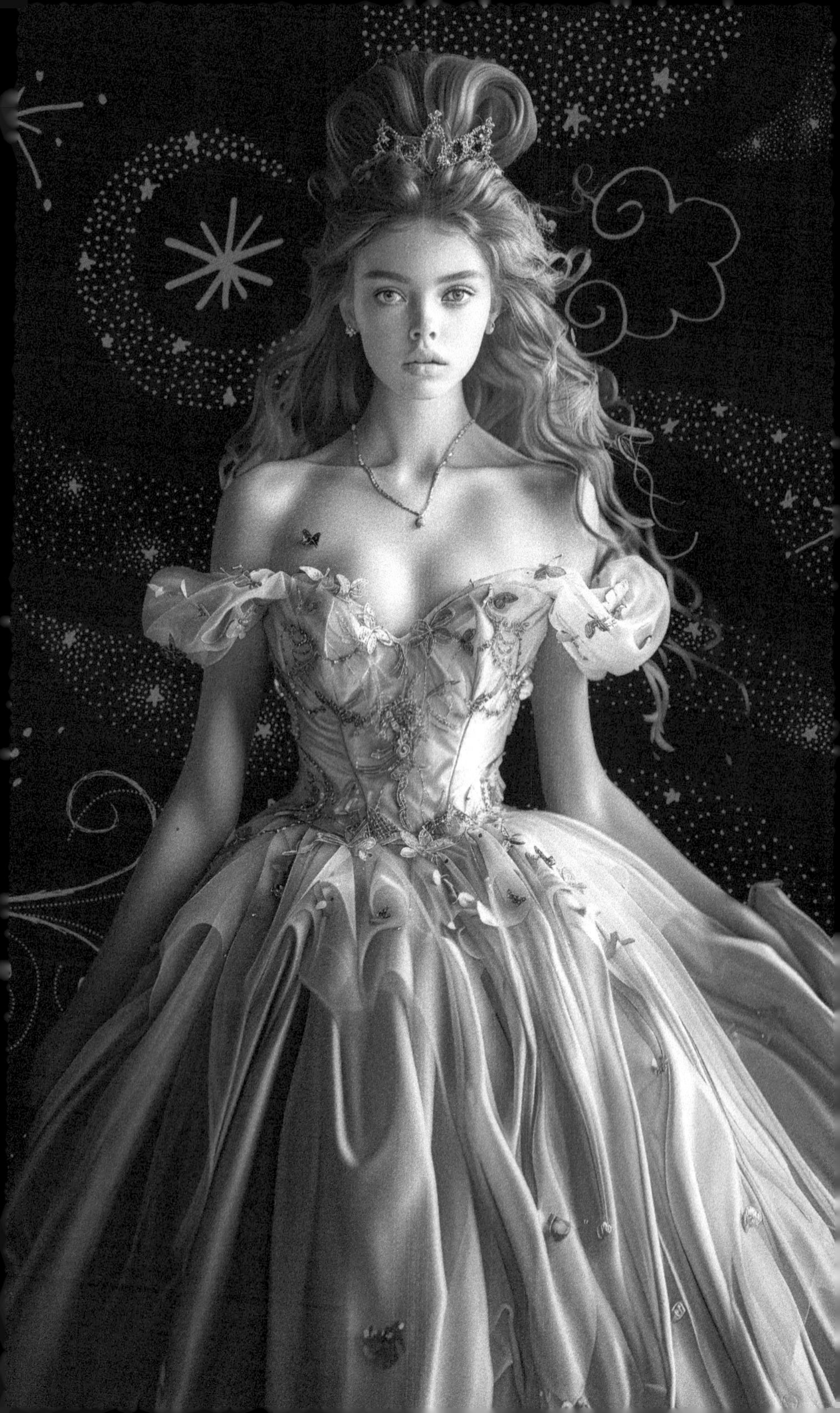

JASINA

CHAPTER SEVENTEEN

"*D*o you understand, Jasina?"
 I'm replaying Auntie's words back in my head as I lie in bed, trying to put the whole night out of my mind.

I nodded with determined assurance. "Yes. It's not going to be easy, but I can do it, Auntie. You can count on me."

I wasn't really feeling this determination, or assurance, but I forced it out. If I didn't, Auntie would berate me until I projected the level of confidence she was looking for.

The hour was already late. If I left right at that point, I would be lucky to get two hours of sleep before the Matrons woke us for Little Sister duties, and I was *so* exhausted, my vision was blurring. I never expected my time in the Little Sisters to be so… monopolized.

I smile, chuckling as I snuggle down into my soft, downy pillow, the warm comforter all wrapped around my body. I had counted on some good times here. One more gala gown, at the very least. At this point, I'm ready to burn my Choosing dress and forget those butterflies ever existed. It's actually starting to stink, I've worn it so many times.

"*Child.*" After all her huffing, and puffing, and threats Auntie had placed a wrinkled hand on my cheek. It was surprisingly soft. "*We're counting on you. Do you understand how important this is?*"

I didn't. Still don't. Not really. Up until this very meeting, being part of the Rebellion was just... an exciting prospect for adventure. Something that made me, a poor down-city girl, feel special. Like I was some sort of Chosen One.

And isn't that the dream of every adventure-yearning teenager? That we are the heroes of our own stories? That the world revolves around us? That only we can save it?

"*There would be a place in the history books for your name, niece.*"

But my confusion was the last thing Auntie wanted to hear about, and I *would* like my name in the history books, so I just leaned into it. Fake it 'till you make it. "*I do, Auntie.*" I conveyed my highest possible level of conviction.

"*Good.*" She smiled and sent me on my way.

It was mostly dark inside when I got to the dorm because it was well past lights out, but there were a few nightlights lit up in various places so I could make my way down the stone canal towards the far end where we stay. As I passed all the other girls, I caught a few whispers, but no one was paying any attention to me. They were all talking about Haryet.

When I got to our space there was a bright light in the far back seating area and this was where I found my friends.

They all stood when they saw me coming—wearing different versions of the gorgeous nightgowns that they found in their dresser drawers—and rushed towards me as I entered the common space. There were only a few electric candles burning, so it was still pretty dark, but I took a moment to admire the new nightclothes we'd been given.

They are mostly made of soft, thin cotton, but the seams and hems are trimmed in silk ribbons. My friends looked like completely different people wearing these garments. And I know they felt different too. They felt important and special for the first time in their lives.

This has also been weighing on me since I climbed into bed wearing my own version of the up-city nightgowns.

We are *somebodies* now.

Not because we agreed to be sacrificed, but because we are part of something bigger than ourselves. I *must* do a good job. I *must* make sure we succeed. Not to please Auntie, but because this is how I make my life mean something. This is how I make my friends' lives mean something too.

I *must* succeed.

"Well?" Britley had asked. "What happened? Where have you been?"

Lucindy came up and grabbed my arm, tucking it up against her. "We thought something bad happened."

Ceela and Harlow crowded in as well, waiting for my answer.

I took a long breath, held it in for a moment, then slowly let it out. "Girls." I looked at each of them individually, trying to be the leader I was meant to be. "It has started."

They held their own breaths then. They didn't squeal, or

giggle, or do anything stupid the way other young girls might when learning a secret.

They didn't act like regular girls because they're *not* regular girls.

None of us are.

We are the Rebellion.

"Help me out of this dress, sisters. We need our rest. God knows we didn't get it last night. We'll talk more after the sun comes up."

They murmured their agreements. And then all their hands were busy unlacing me, and pulling skirts down, and unhooking my corset.

My first breath after that happened was nearly orgasmic, that's how good it felt. And then Ceela was slipping the nightgown over my head, and Lucindy was brushing my hair, and Britley was pulling my bedcovers back as Harlow fluffed my pillow.

So, ironically, my chaotic day ended with more attention and luxury than I could've ever imagined three days ago. And I can't help but wonder, after my friends are are all back in their nooks, tucked into their beds as well, if this wasn't the reason that the Spark Maidens of yore all agreed to be sacrificed for the last thousand years in the first place.

Life is hard when you're only given the minimum. When you have just enough to live.

Luxuries and comfort change the way a person sees the world and it happens quicker than most would like to admit.

But after everything that's happened to me today, it's too heavy of a topic to dwell on now.

I snuggle even deeper into my pillows, wrap the fine comforter around me even tighter, and let out a cavernous yawn as I turn on my side and settle in for a good, deep one-hour sleep.

My eyes close, my mind drifts, and then…

The bells start ringing.

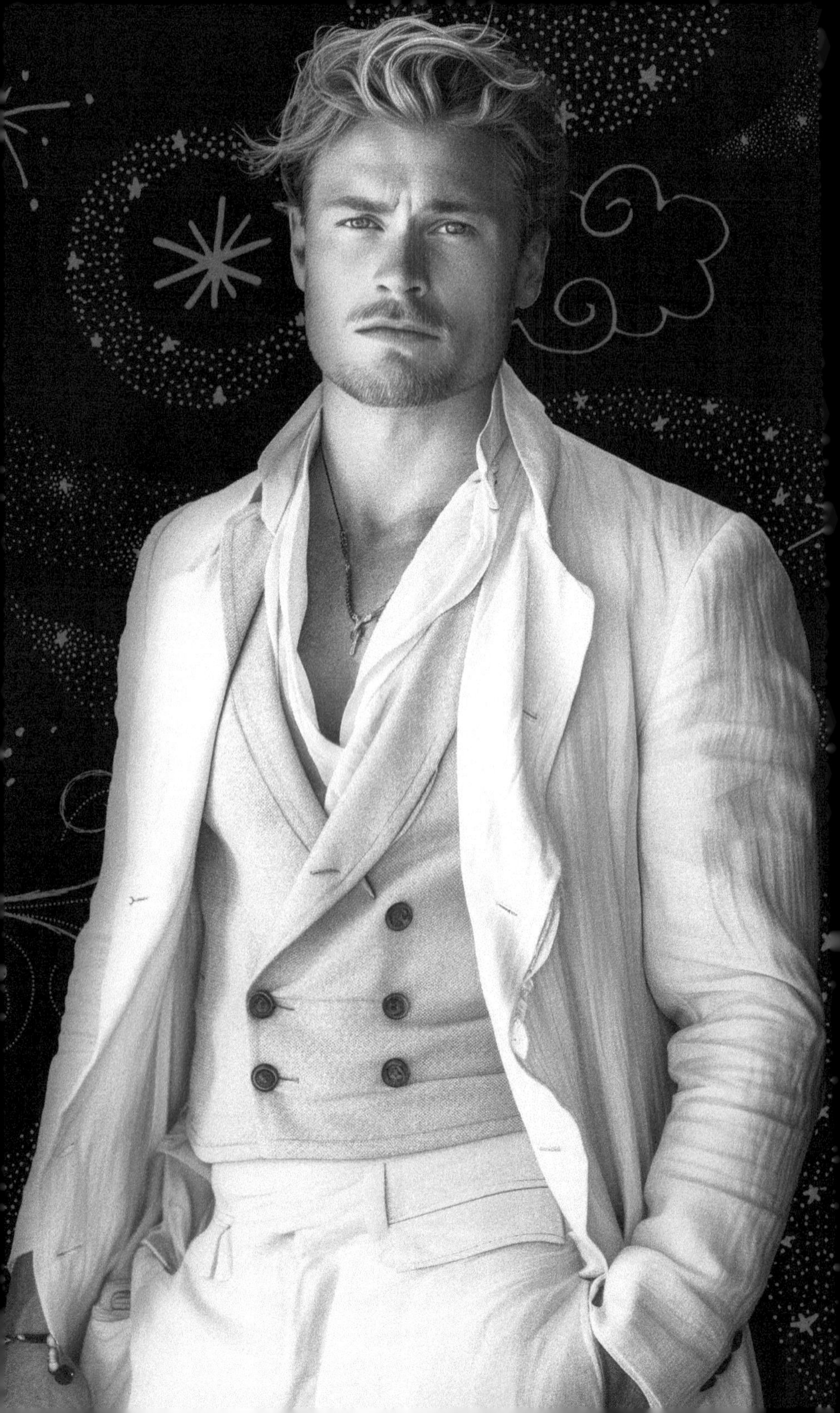

FINN

CHAPTER EIGHTEEN

In my nightmare the bells are ringing. A low, deep resonating thrum that seeps into my brain and shakes my skull. Then pounding. Just pounding and pounding...

"Finn!"

I sit up, blink, trying to make sense of where I am and what's happening. Then I jump up, because while my mind won't accept the bells, it understands that Mitchell is pounding on my door, screaming my name. "Finn!"

I'm still half asleep, groggy and confused, when I open the door and Mitch comes rushing past me. He stops in the middle of the ridiculously large room with his back to me and looks down, pausing. Like he needs to take a breath. Like he needs a moment.

And of course he does. Because those fucking bells are ringing.

But it takes me another second, a second in which Mitchell turns to face me, wide-eyed and mouth open, for me to fully understand what the tolling bells *mean*.

"I'll go get her. Do you want me to go get her?" Mitchell comes at me, grabs both my shoulders, and looks me straight in the eyes. "Focus." He shakes me a little. "Do you want me to go get Clara?" He says these words slowly and deliberately. Like I don't speak his language.

Or… like I might be in shock and having trouble processing.

I shake myself—my head, at least—then remember to breathe. "No. I'm going to her myself. She will be hysterical."

I turn in place, looking around, then down at myself. I'm wearing a pair of loose-fitting linen pants and nothing else. I look around the room—a bedroom I barely recognize because I don't really live here and this is actually the first time I even bothered finding a bedroom to sleep in. So my mind can't make sense of it.

I'm thinking this and I'm not sure about my clothes, or where I now live, or where I might find a tunic. I mean… I was wearing one earlier, but the maids have been here while I was sleeping and the tunic I discarded an hour ago on the floor has been picked up.

This is just the start of things that are unsettling me right now, because somewhere in this palace I can hear the clanging of pots and pans and other kitchen noises.

Cooks, I guess. Making breakfast, I suppose.

This is when I realize it's not even dawn.

I turn to Mitch, panicked. "What time is it?" If the bells ring before dawn then the Maiden is due at midnight tonight. Not tomorrow, *tonight*.

Mitchell, of course, has already figured this out. And his voice is low and somber. "Four-fifteen."

Four-fifteen.

Four. Fifteen.

We've got one day.

Less than a day.

Fuck the tunic, fuck the boots.

I turn to Mitchell. "You don't have to come."

"The hell I don't. Those Matron bitches are not gonna let you in that building."

He's right. I might be the Extraction Master, and so-called king of this district. But I'm nothing across the canal. I cannot order a Matron to let me into the Maiden Tower.

But with Mitchell, we could compel them. Even if it means we do it by force.

"All right, let's go. Where's Jeyk?"

"He went home. I stayed—I had a bad feeling, so I sent him home and kept watch outside your door. But I'm sure he's on his way. We'll probably see him downstairs."

We enter the hall and Mitch rushes ahead to call the elevator, but the doors are already open. The lift attendant looks scared when his eyes meet mine. "I figured…" He shrugs. "I figured you'd want to go to her."

I grab his shoulder and give it a quick squeeze as I enter. "You were right. What is your name?"

"Dodge."

"Dodge, you're getting a raise. And you have officially been promoted to"—I make up a title—"lift captain."

"Oh!" A breath rushes out of him as he works the lift controls while looking at me over his shoulder. "Thank you, Master! Thanks!" Then he turns back to his duty and watches the floor counter move on the display panel in front of him as we descend.

Mitch leans in to me, whispering, "There's no such position, you know that right?"

"There is now." And for some reason, these words come out mean. Angry too.

'For some reason,' Finn? The reason is that the love of your life—the woman who has been planning your wedding for a decade and the only woman you have ever been intimate with—is going into the tower tonight.

And there's nothing you can do to stop it.

The elevator halts, the doors open, Dodge calls out the floor, "Ground level," and Mitch and I exit, making a sharp left towards the central canal. The frigid, night air hits me suddenly because I am half naked and shoeless. But I welcome it because it shocks me into a higher state of alertness.

Once we hit the main walkway, the Maiden Bridge is only a few steps away.

Jeyk is waiting for us at the bridge.

"Are you gonna get her, Finn? Are you gonna hide her? You're not gonna let her go in there, are you?" Jeyk is wound up, his eyes wide, but not the way Mitch's were when I opened the door for him. Mitch is cool under pressure. Composed. He's a thinker.

Jeyk is all instincts. And his instincts right now are telling him that Clara needs saving.

"We'll see," is the only answer I give him. Because, of course, there is no way for me to stop what's happening. I don't have the power.

Well, I guess I could just not show up—keep Clara in my new palace, or make a desperate attempt to leave the city and cross the expanse of desert sands in some kind of hopeless escape—but it's a fantasy.

If I don't have the ceremony... all those Little Sisters. Plus Clara. Plus Gemna...

Of course, this all might be bullshit, but... what if it's not?

Escape isn't possible. There's nothing out there in the sands. It's nothing but wasteland. Every year-four student in Tau City knows this because that's the year they make us run the wall. A twenty-mile marathon that children must complete, in some way or another. You don't have to run the whole way—you can walk or skip or crawl if you want, but you *will* circle the city on the wall before they let you go home. Because they want us all to understand that this is *it*. There is nothing out there. It's dust, and wind, and sand and nothing else.

We've been walking across the Maiden Bridge as I think all these things and now we're on the other side, the Maiden Tower looming large right in front of us.

Amazingly, there are no Matrons waiting for us at the door. Though there is a guard. For a moment I think that guard is gonna stop us, but as we approach, he just steps aside, looking the other way.

Mitch pulls it open as Jeyk and I walk through, then he follows us inside.

But we don't even reach the main staircase that winds up the center of the building before those old nags come rushing out from every direction, their blue tunics fanning out behind them.

"No!" one of them is barking. "No! No! *No!*" She points

her finger right in my face as she approaches. "You do not belong here."

I slap her finger away and she gasps. It is forbidden to fuck with a Matron. They aren't in charge of anything but the Maidens, but if you piss one off and end up in front of the Council, they take the Matron's side every time.

Personally, they've always kind of scared me. They cloister themselves back there behind the Maiden Tower, almost never participating in anything outside of this district. But they are imposing and mean. As children we are taught to never question them. Never even talk to them, actually. Especially if you're male. They shun the opposite sex in a way that comes off as... *personal*.

But I'm not a little boy anymore. I'm the Extraction Master. I might not be in charge of them, but it goes both ways. They are not in charge of me, either. No one—not even the Council—has any sway over me. So these bitches can go to hell for all I care.

In the back of my mind though, I see my mother. Not as my mother, but as one of them. This thought is enough to make me shudder. It also reminds me that I know much, much less about this city, and my place in it, than I thought did yesterday.

One particularly tall and broad Matron steps in front of me, hands up in a full-stop gesture.

"Get out of my way, you bitch." I snarl these words out, making the big woman recoil. Which gives me an opportunity to push past her and head for the stairs. I don't even know where Clara's room is. I have literally never, not once, been inside this tower. But I don't care. There are two

Maidens left at this point. Fuck 'em. I'll just yell her name until she answers.

"Clara!" So that's what I do. "*Clara!*" My shout echoes off the high ceilings ten floors above.

Mitch and Jeyk are still behind me, but both of them are yelling threats and insults at the Matrons, who are following us as we climb the central staircase.

We've reached the third floor and I'm still yelling, but there is a sudden commotion down below and I pause, leaning over the railing to see if it's Clara. I had always assumed she lived up at the top somewhere, but hell, she could be in the basement for all I know.

But it's not her, it's the Little Sisters—haphazardly dressed up in their pretty white nightgowns, all of them in different states of confused disarray and looking like nubile virgins with their tousled hair, and sleepy bedroom eyes, and no corset to keep their breasts from falling out all over the place.

I stop and just look at them. I mean… there is no way I can't *look*. It's… quite something to behold.

Mitch kinda guffaws as he leans far over the railing to gawk as well.

Jeyk mutters, "Holy fucking shit. Look at them." Like he's never seen a half-naked girl before.

The appearance of the Sisters confuses the Matrons. They split—half of them barking orders at the girls below, half of them still trying to follow us up the stairs.

But some of the Matrons are old. Many of them, in fact. And we are not old. We are in our prime.

"Come on." Mitch grabs my arm, pulling me up the next

level of stairs, probably coming to the same conclusion because we're going fast now and the few Matrons still giving chase are falling behind.

I start yelling again. "Clara!" And after a few more times of this, I hear a shout back.

"Finn!" My name comes out as a sob. And when I look up, I see her about three floors above me, leaning over the railing. Her long, blonde hair hangs down, almost covering her face completely. She feels much too far away, but at the same time, I can see every emotion as they flash through her mind and then manifest as an expression.

It is fear, and anguish, and hopelessness.

This is how I will remember her. I know it. I will not think of her as the once fun-loving and playful girl that I grew up with, or the mature, intelligent woman she grew into, or even the way she looked in all those beautiful gowns she's worn over the years.

It's this image of her that will be burned into my memory until the day I die. This moment, as the bells toll incessantly, when she realizes that our dream of forever will never happen.

Gemna is there too, when the three of us arrive on the ninth floor. She and Clara are holding each other. Crying, hysterical, faces buried in each other's necks. And even when Mitch and I try to pry them apart, they cling to each other. Like if they could just hug each other tight enough, then maybe the nightmare will go away. But if they let go, they know they will lose everything.

Mitch is the one who finally manages to pull them apart.

Replacing himself with Clara, he hugs Gemna tightly and Gemna hugs him back.

Clara is then instantly in my arms. Just sobbing uncontrollably.

Jeyk must be intercepting the Matrons on the stairs because that's all I hear—sobbing—as I hug the only woman I've ever loved. The only woman I will ever love.

Jeyk won't be able to fend them off for long, so I push Clara off me and hold her at arm's length. "Where can we go?"

She's a mess, but she's paying attention, because she points a finger down a hallway.

"I'm staying with you. All day, do you understand?" I push her wild hair out of her face so I can see her eyes. "Let's go."

She stares at me for a moment. Like she can't quite snap herself out of the shock. But then Mitch says, "Come on!" And he's dragging Gemna down the hallway.

I grab Clara's hand and follow him. Gemna is slightly more in control than Clara, but that's probably because her bell has not yet tolled.

But it will, dear Gemna. It will.

That god in the tower has an insatiable appetite. And he will feast on you as well.

This revelation, that Gemna will not be spared just because she is the last of them, gives me a sense of evil satisfaction and this realization fills me with shame for a moment.

But the anger inside me has been building over the last few days. Ever since someone murdered my father and set this whole fucking thing in motion, I have been living in a controlled state of rage.

And now I fear that my desire for control is waning.

I don't want to be in control. I want to lose it right now. I want to break things. I want to destroy things. Most of all, that god in the tower. Or even just the tower itself.

I want to bring the whole fucking thing down.

We end up in a common room filled with cream-colored couches, and curved plaster walls with river-stone peeking through in some places. Chandeliers hang from the domed ceiling dotted with skylights that perfectly frame the clear, starry sky above us. There are thick, luxurious rugs on the sandstone floors, and all three corner fireplaces are burning so there is a glow of light flickering across the walls and floor that makes the massive room feel obscenely opulent, but also cozy.

This pisses me off. That this is where they live. Not because it's a place fit for a princess—Clara deserves the best. All the Maidens do. That's not what makes me angry.

It's that it's a trick at best and an outright lie at worst.

Because the women who live up in this tower—the Tau City Spark Maidens—they aren't celebrities, or role models, or princesses.

They are *sacrifices*.

Offerings to a hungry god.

And this lie being told by the serene décor of the community room is, quite honestly, the grossest thing I've ever seen.

Mitchell stops in the middle of the community room and turns to look at me. "The Matrons are still coming."

Then he looks at Gemna. "Do you have a private room that locks?"

Gemna nods.

"Let's go. Lead the way." And then they are heading further into the space, towards a door.

I turn to Clara, but she's already heading in another direction, pulling me along behind her. I follow her inside a room and she closes the door, turns a key in the lock, then removes it and places it on a little stone table.

When she faces me again, she breaks, nearly falling to the floor. If I wasn't here to catch her, she might've. But I do catch her. Then I pick her up, cradling her in my arms, and carry her over to the bed. I gently place her on the covers, but she didn't faint, so she's not unconscious. She's grabbing at me with a desperation I've never seen before.

Under normal circumstances Clara Birch is a model Spark Maiden. Poised, proper, polite.

But this is the end of her life and she is completely and utterly lost. Babbling, begging. "Please, Finn." She gets up on her knees, refusing to lie back on the bed, and grabs my shoulders. Her nightgown—a beautiful garment made of the finest cream-colored satin, silk and lace—is hanging off one shoulder, revealing most of her breasts. Her hair is a tousled mess. Tears pour out of her eyes like rivers. Her normally pale cheeks are flushed pink.

And for some reason, I'm turned on by it. By her anguish, by her vulnerability, and by her begging.

"*Please*, Finn. Do not make me do it! Do not make me! *Please!*"

I'm sitting next to her, wearing nothing but my own

nightclothes—a simple pair of loose linen pants, but barefoot and shirtless—and all I can think about is *fucking her* right now. Taking every bit of her as mine before I have to hand her over to the god in the tower.

I can't save her. So I don't even bother trying to answer her. Instead I grab her nightgown and pull it down over her shoulders, all the way down to her waist, until both of her breasts are exposed. I look at them, licking my lips as I imagine taking her tight, peaked nipples into my mouth. And then I'm doing it. Pushing her back on the bed. Nipping, and sucking until she's moaning and slipping her fingers into my hair.

There is a loud banging on the door. Yelling from outside as the Matrons demand to be let in.

But we ignore them. I pull back, grip the bodice of her nightgown with both hands, and rip it open. She makes a noise that is something between a moan and a squeal, and instinctively her arms come up to cover herself.

I stand back up and then reach for her arms so I can pry them away from her body.

Then I just stare at her.

We have made love plenty of times. A couple dozen over the years, at least.

But until earlier today, these trysts were carefully planned and executed.

I was gentle. Treating her like something sacred and special, which of course she is.

But I don't want to treat her like something sacred and special right now. I want to flip her over and fuck her from behind the way I did earlier.

Instead, I get a hold of myself and take a deep breath. Then I push my night pants down, revealing my thick, hard cock. She looks at it, tender mouth slightly open, then looks up at me.

"We're not gonna talk about this, Clara." I place a hand on her cheek while slipping the other one around to the back of her neck as I take a step forward.

She knows what we're gonna do instead. She knows what I want. She has put that pretty mouth of hers on the tip of my cock before, kissing it tenderly. A promise of more to come—some day.

But she has never wrapped her lips fully around it and fully taken me in.

And I want that now. I want all of her now. Because this is it. This is the end of us. 'Some day' is never coming. I have been a patient gentleman for over a decade and all the things she promised me are now impossible.

None of the ways in which I have imagined myself with her will ever happen.

This one day is all I've got left. And I haven't gotten my fill. I. Want. *More*.

I don't ask. I just use the hand I've placed behind her neck to guide her forward. She resists for a moment, looking up at me. Questioning me. Questioning herself too.

So I explain. What better way to get what you want than to ask for it? "I want all of you, Clara. You're mine, and I'm yours. And today, we're going to take each other in every way possible and we are going to live our dream."

She knows what this means. She knows this is the end

and that she will be walking into that tower at midnight tonight.

I see all the questions in her eyes as she stares up at me. Still crying with tear-stained cheeks and red, puffy eyes.

She's trying to decide whether or not this is something she will agree to.

There's a moment here when I figure she's not going to agree, but in the next moment she takes a breath and decides I'm right. Her resistance to my encouragement fades. Her face comes forward, that pouty mouth of hers open. And when she wraps her lips around the tip of my cock, my head falls back, my hips go forward, and I press her forehead into my stomach.

Immediately, she pulls back, tilting her head up to look at me. Breathing hard and eyes filled with confusion.

It's too much. I'm asking too much. I am aware of this, but at the same time I don't wanna stop. So I place my hands on her shoulders and gently urge her to lie back on the bed again.

She resists, but only for a moment. And the moment she gives in, I reward her by dropping to my knees, spreading her legs open, and lowering my face down between her legs.

"Finn." My name comes out on a shaky breath.

I answer her by dragging my tongue down the middle of her silky underwear. Her back bucks up and her fingers are back in my hair, twisting it up and gripping it with closed fists.

If I want more than she's willing to give, then I have to give her more than she thinks she wants. I grab her underwear with both hands and rip it off her just like I did her nightgown. She gasps, grasping onto my head with both hands and trying to sit up.

But I'm ready. My hands spread her knees open, my tongue slips between the soft folds between her legs, and this is enough to calm her down. Enough, at least, to make her lie back and begin to relax.

"Oh, my god, Finn. What—"

That's as far as she gets. Her head is moving back and forth as I hit the pleasure center and then, suddenly, she's writhing and gripping my hair, and all those inhibitions and insecurities she was feeling just moments ago disappear.

Given a choice, Clara Birch would like to be made love to. Touched tenderly. Worshipped and pampered. She wants it slow and soft.

And I like that. I mean, up until earlier today I hadn't even tried to be more forceful with her. Hadn't even pictured it, though I've heard Mitchell brag about how he is with his women over the years.

But Mitch likes down-city girls. Girls who did not pledge themselves to the god in the tower as a Little Sister when they were twelve. He fucks girls who like men to do naughty things to them in the dark. Not that they aren't nice and sweet in their own way, but they weren't raised to be poised, and proper, and polite.

Mitch likes girls who wriggle in his lap at the seedy clubs in the Shipping District. Girls who charge him gold coins to get naked, and get on their knees, and don't mind being told what to do.

And though I have never once been with a woman other than Clara, I have had fantasies over the last decade.

Fantasies of making Clara do those things too. Not in a club, of course. Alone, in the privacy of our own bedroom. And while this isn't our bedroom, it's all I've got.

It's all I'm *ever* going to get.

Because that piece-of-shit god in the tower is going to rip her from my life and all our hopes and dreams will die right there as I helplessly watch.

If that's how this ends, well… then I'm gonna get everything I ever wanted from Clara Birch before I lose her.

It's a selfish thing, but I can justify it if I give her everything she's ever wanted from me first. I ease a finger inside her, making her moan and gasp ever louder. Making her back arch even higher. And just a few moments later, a powerful release makes her whole body shudder.

In a normal tryst I would hurriedly finish up after she had her climax, but this isn't a normal tryst and so, instead of getting myself off, and instead of letting her relax and fully enjoy her orgasm, I grab both her hands, pull her up, and then get her back on her knees in front of me. She's naked now except for the scraps of nightgown hanging on her arms, but she lets them drop to the floor as she raises her chin to look up and meet my eyes.

Hers are half-lidded. Bedroom eyes. Just-fucked eyes. And she is far, *far* more willing to give me what I initially wanted than she was five minutes ago.

I don't even have to encourage her. She takes me in her hands, gripping my shaft in a tight fist, and then she begins moving them up and down. I grit my teeth and almost let my head fall back to enjoy the pleasure, but it's not enough. Not tonight.

I want more and I want her to know that.

So instead, I place both my hands on her head and urge her forward as I lean my hips in.

She takes me into her mouth and this time, she tries a little harder. When the reflex to gag comes, she pauses, breathes through it, pulls back a little—but not completely—and then tries again.

This alone is more than I ever thought I'd get from Clara Birch. Even after years of marriage. She's not a prude—she's just poised, proper, and polite. And it's enough. I'm so overwhelmed with desire for her—so completely taken by her willingness to please me—I go stiff, fisting her hair tight as I hold her still in preparation for what comes next.

Just as I close my eyes and let go—a fraction of a moment before my come spills out and sprays down her throat—she pulls back and it hits her in the face before she pushes my cock down and I release the rest all over her breasts.

I don't care, though. It's even more perfect like this. I bend down, pick up her tattered nightgown, wipe the come off her cheeks and lips, and then I kiss her long and deep.

We collapse onto the floor, settling together on a luxurious furry rug, and hold each other as we try and catch our breath.

She's still panting hard when she speaks. "That... was... not what I was expecting."

Even though I'm not yet sure if her admission is a good or a bad critique of my performance, I smile. Can't help it. "Did it feel good? Or was it too much?"

She turns her body, pressing her breasts into my chest as

she grins down at me. "Oh, it was good, Mr. Scott. It was very good." Then she's climbing on top of me, straddling my hips.

I wasn't gonna say anything. Wasn't gonna ask for more. Was actually going to let her get some sleep, since I doubt she's had much of that lately. But when you turn your woman on to the slutty side of things and she decides that she's ready for more, you do not discourage her.

I grab at her breasts, fondling them as she lifts up and places me at her entrance. She's slippery wet and I'm still hard—turned on by her assertiveness—so I slide right up inside her and when she lowers herself back down, she takes me deep.

I catch her wincing, so I pause, holding absolutely still as she recovers. And this recovery happens quickly because only a moment later she's grinding into me with hands braced on my chest.

I thrust up, our skin slapping together. And then I'm grabbing her by the ass and moving her back and forth, trying to whip us both up into a frenzy.

This time the climax comes almost immediately and it comes at the same time. We both moan, and gasp, and move even faster, desperate for each little wave of pleasure coursing through our bodies.

When she rolls off me, we're both sticky with sweat and properly exhausted.

We huddle together, arms twined around each other, and start drifting.

I've never spent the night with Clara Birch and I'm sorry about that. Because we have no more nights together. Even now, there is a crack of light on the horizon outside her window. The dawn is breaking, the start of our last day together arriving.

The end is here.

But we've got this day, at least. So I hug her close to me, and kiss her hair, and let my heart slow down with hers. Realizing that at some point the Matrons have given up, because there is no more pounding on the door.

We sleep. Not in a bed, but on the floor.

Not through the night, but through the morning.

And when I wake, the sun is high above us—blazing down through a large, circular window—and Clara is sobbing.

I turn, trying to kiss her. Neck, lips, breasts, pussy—I want to kiss her all over.

But she pushes me away and gets to her feet, completely naked. And this time, when I look at her, she doesn't even try to cover herself.

"What?" I ask, my voice groggy from just waking. "What's wrong?"

She makes a face of confusion. Then she's spitting words at me. "What's *wrong*?" She pauses to let out an incredulous snort. "I'm going to the tower tonight, Finn. Are you really, *really* gonna let me do that?"

I get to my feet as well, and try to pull her into my arms. "Clara—"

"No!" She pushes me away. Two flat hands against my chest. It's a not a hard shove, but I do take a couple steps back just to give her space. "I want an answer. I *need* an answer."

I scoff. "Clara. An answer... to what question?"

"Are you sending me into that tower tonight?"

My mouth drops open and I point at my chest. "Do you think this is up to me? Because it's not. I have no say in this. It's the damn god. Do you have any idea what happens if the Extraction Master refuses to send a Maiden in when she's summoned?"

"No. Because no Master has ever done it before! They're all a bunch of cowards!"

Rage flares up inside of me. Because my *father* was the Extraction Master before me and he was not a fucking coward. But I force my voice to be even and firm when I speak next. "That's bullshit. They have, Clara. Not many of them, because they learned pretty quick that the god in the tower gets what he asks for or else."

"Or else what?"

"Or else he takes you *all*. Not just you, but Gemna too. And not just you and Gemna, either, but all those Little Sisters down there as well."

Her eyes go squinty. She takes a breath. Lets it out. Then replies in a seething whisper, "That's *bullshit*."

"You say that because you've never seen it happen."

"Neither have you."

"No. But I've got a reliable source. Are you willing to chance it?" I'm looking her straight in the eyes as I say this, glaring at her. Pissed off, again. And hating this fact, because this isn't me. But I don't know how to feel any other way right now.

All I can do is try and explain. "Because I'm not, Clara." It still comes out as a growl, but it's not as harsh as it could've been. I am at least a little bit in control. "I'm not willing to chance it. Sending Haryet last night was bad, but you? This is going to kill me, Clara. I might be alive when those doors close, but inside, I will be dead."

I pause here, waiting to see if she's listening closely or not. If she's taking me seriously, or not. And I think she is, because she doesn't reply. Just stares at me with an open mouth.

"I can't kill them all just on the hope of saving *you*! Because you won't be saved, Clara. The god will compel you to walk through the doors. That's why none of the Spark Maidens ever tried to run before. It can compel you. It can make you. And after it makes you do it, it'll make all the others do it too. And there is nothing we can do to stop it. I'm *not* in charge of this."

I pause again, but still she's got nothing to say.

"So now, knowing this, what would you do, Clara? Go into that tower so *they* can all live? Or kill them, and yourself too? Because those are your options."

She gasps. And then she slaps me, the cyan-blue light once again leaking out of her lit-up hands. There are hundreds of glowing symbols on them now, though. Not just her hands, either. I watch as the weird markings crawl past her wrists, past her elbows, over her shoulders—then her whole torso lights up. A moment later, it's covering her whole body. She points at me, screaming. "Get out! Get out right now!"

I grab both her wrists, grip them so tight she winces and cries out, and then I pull her right up to my chest, forcing her to look me in the eyes. "I will not get out." My voice is even now, my tone low and calm. "I will not. Get out. Because I love you. And this is my last day with you. And I'm gonna *miss* you. I'm going to wake up tomorrow and have nothing to live for. Because you, Clara, have been my reason to live since I was a little boy. Everything I've done, I did for you."

She yanks back, trying to free her wrists from my grip, her face still hard and angry. "Is that your reason for fucking me like a whore today?"

I actually laugh out loud. "*Whore?*" Then I narrow my eyes, the heat creeping up my spine as her accusation fully sinks in. The words come out before I can stop them. And the worst thing is, they are easy words that send all the wrong signals. "Well, you seemed to have a good time, so…"

She wriggles in my grip, itching to slap me again. But I keep hold of both her wrists, staring directly into her eyes, as I speak. "Do not ever hit me again." And these words do not come out easy. They come out like a threat.

She recoils, like I scared her, which is not what I was trying to do, so I let go of her wrists. Immediately she turns and walks to the other side of the room, picking up a silk throw and wrapping it around her upper body to cover her nakedness, the glow she was just displaying gone now. She points at the door and speaks very calmly. "Get out."

I shake my head. "No, Clara. I'm not getting out. I'm staying right here. And I don't care if we spend our last day together spitting insults and hating one another, I'm staying *right here.*"

She wants to cry. Her face is bright red and her eyes are glassy and bloodshot. She wants to fall into my arms and sob. And beg for me to save her. And hope that there is some way to stop our dreams from dying before we ever even had a chance. She wants to cry because this is it. This is all we get. This one stupid day. And it's not enough. Especially when we had ten years and all we did was piss them away, thinking we always had tomorrow.

Well, we were wrong. We made all the wrong choices, we prioritized all the wrong things, and the realization that this day is happening right now because of the choices *we* made is a bitter pill to swallow.

After several seconds of silence and staring, Clara lets out a breath. "If you love me, you have a very funny way of showing it." And then the tears once again start falling down her cheeks. She doesn't sob, though. Up until yesterday, Clara Birch was never a woman who felt sorry for herself. She was always acutely aware of her privilege. She was, perhaps, the most poised, proper and polite of them all. A perfect Spark Maiden. Not one black mark against her good name in all those ten years she was on display.

It's just... a lot. The last couple of days have been an absolute nightmare.

And I'm admittedly not handling it well either.

It's my job to keep her steady. It's my job to keep her safe. And I've failed on both accounts. My erratic behavior, my anger, the rough sex—it's done nothing but pile onto the realization that everything she thought was true is not.

I exhale and bow my head. "I'm sorry. I'm making everything worse here. I've said all the wrong things, I've behaved out of character, and I'm just..." I look up at her again. Her face is all crumpled up with sadness now. Not fear, though I'm sure she's still very much afraid of what's coming, just sadness. "I'm just… a huge disappointment and I'm sorry, Clara." I shrug. "That's all I can say."

I have an urge to walk out now. To be alone so I can grieve my dead father and wallow in my own self-pity about having to send the woman I love into the arms of a sadistic god. But that's not me. I'm not a man who walks out.

So I don't. I walk over to her instead, expecting her to push me away, because that's what I deserve, to be honest. But she doesn't recoil. She lets me wrap my arms around her and then she sinks into my chest and just lets me hold her as she cries.

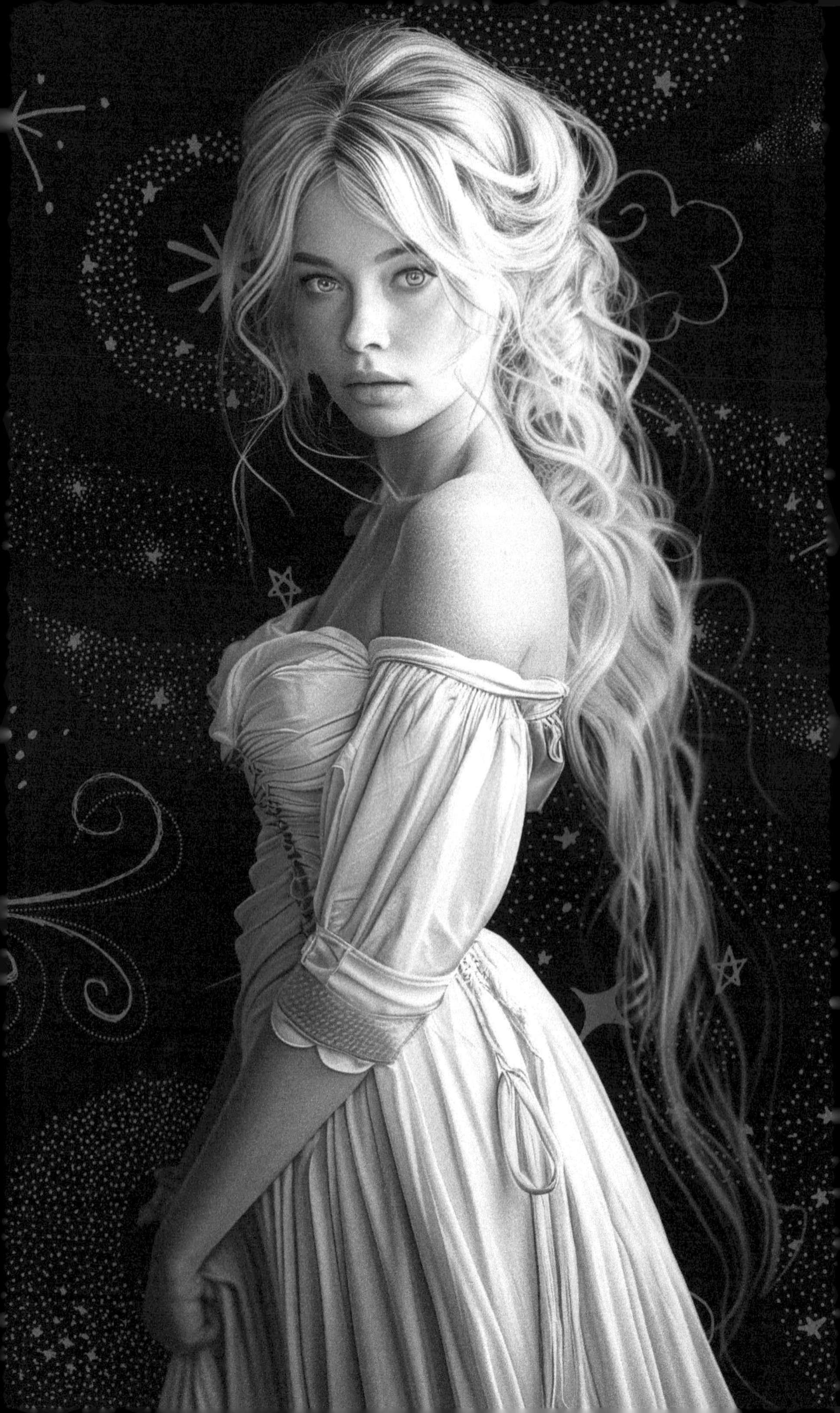

CLARA

CHAPTER NINETEEN

I'm crying, *and sad*, and depressed, and hopeless—I know I feel all these things. But there's a blankness inside me as well. An emptiness. A void begging me to push reality away and concentrate on the dream holding me in his arms instead.

Before I was a Spark Maiden, I was a Little Sister. Before I was a Little Sister, I was a Pledge.

I feel like there has never been a time in my life when the god didn't own me.

My pledge time was only six years because my Extraction happened on my eighteenth year. Some Little Sisters are older, but none are younger than eighteen. If you miss—even by a day—you can't be in that Extraction group. And the upper cutoff is twenty-four. So, there are many girls in Tau City who by chance of birth never even have the opportunity to pledge their lives to the god in the tower.

Twelve-year-old me would've been devastated had that been my case. I was sure—very, very sure—that I was meant to be a Spark Maiden.

Looking back, sixteen years on, I wish it had been the case. I wish I'd chosen another path. One where, yes, I was poor. Sent back down-city to live in squalor after my father died when I was a teenager. Perhaps Finn would've forgotten about me. It would've been a risk.

But it's equally possible that he wouldn't. That he would still choose me. That he would lift me up. That we would not have wasted the past ten years. That we would be married with children by now. Our own home, our own family.

And I feel like such a fool for chasing this stupid dream of independence. Because it was selfish. It was… desire. Lust. For more power and status. For nicer quarters and better clothes.

For coin.

It is a heartbreakingly sober realization that the whole reason I am in this predicament right now is because of *coin*.

I never wanted to go into the tower, but I wanted everything that came with being a Maiden. All the fame, and riches, and comforts.

So it's all my fault that I am here, on the precipice of death, lamenting the scope of all my bad decisions.

I'm crying about it, yes. Because there is sadness inside me.

But more so, there is shame. And anger. At myself, of course, but at Finn too. And Aldo. Why didn't he stop me? If Aldo loved me like a daughter married to his only child, why did he not stop me? Why didn't he take me aside and force me to believe that I am enough for Finn just the way I was?

Perhaps it was not his place? I guess I can understand that.

But then, wouldn't it have been Finn's place? As the man claiming to love me? Shouldn't he have taken me aside and forced me to believe in his absolute, undying love? Forced me to believe that I was enough for him just the way I was?

This idea that I have been wronged lights a fury inside me. Because the truth of it all is staring me in the face.

I am going to die tonight.

My perfectly imagined future was nothing but a dream.

If this was a game of Divinity Cards, this is the moment I realize that I have lost. When I understand that I have placed my bet on the wrong spread and the game is over.

Finn, who has been hugging me while all these thoughts were running through my head, takes a step back, his hands on my shoulders.

It's a confusing gesture in this moment because I can't tell if he wants to get a better look at me—perhaps burn this image of me in his mind as a memory he cherishes, or possibly drives him mad sometime in the future—or if he's actually pushing me away.

His eyes are soft and his mouth sad. So I know it's the first and not the second.

He takes my hand. "Come on. Let's go back to bed. We have time. Let's spend it together, wrapped up in each other's arms."

I allow him to pull me back across the room. I climb into my bed and scoot over to make room for him. Then he's next to me, his arms tightly around me once more, and we both let out a breath.

"Shouldn't we…" I look over my shoulder, trying to see

his face. "I dunno, do something more than sleep our last hours together?"

I can't really see him, but I feel the chuckle inside him because he's got his bare chest pressed up against my back. "Should we make love again?"

I sigh. That was not what I was thinking.

"Kidding," he says. But he wasn't. "Should we… remind each other of the good times?"

I don't answer him, but I do start searching my memory for such a thing.

"I'll go first."

I turn all the way around now. I want to look at that handsome face of his while he talks. I want to memorize his lips, and those eyes, and the curve of his jaw. "OK. Tell me then. Remind me of a good time."

"We were… I dunno. Eight, I think."

I smile because eight was a good year. My mother was not only still alive, but not even sick.

"And we went down-city, remember?"

I smile bigger. Because while I haven't thought about that day in almost twenty years and we used to sneak down-city a couple times a week on a regular basis, I know exactly which one he is referring to. "I remember. We were looking for kittens."

His smile grows wide, lighting up his whole face. "Because you wanted a kitten for your birthday and that was not a present you got."

"So you were going to get it for me."

"Lord Relic."

I almost snort when I picture the grizzled, old, mangy

cat we took back up-city that evening. There were no kittens anywhere, which was probably the whole reason I didn't get one in the first place. But there was Lord Relic, the mouser from the Shipping District who had been around for two decades, if the rumors were true.

"It took us all day to convince his mangy ass we were friendly."

"And then we stuffed him into that flimsy cage and tried to take him home."

Finn is laughing now. "But he was so pissed off, he clawed his way through the canes and escaped."

I'm laughing too. "We were so sure that he would rather stay with us on the boat, we didn't even mind."

"Until he jumped into the canal, threw us a big 'ol 'fuck you' look over his shoulder, and then never looked back."

Finn and I both chuckle. It's a good memory. I was so shocked. It never even crossed my mind that the mangy mouser from Shipping liked his life and would not prefer to come live up-city with me where he would be dressed up for tea parties and pampered like a prince.

"It just goes to show you," I say, "that happiness is relative."

He sighs, but stays silent. Maybe thinking about tomorrow and how I won't be here.

I'm still angry—mostly at myself and not him—but I don't want him to remember me angry. I want him to think about our adventures as children, and our first kiss, and this day too—because I do have to admit, the sex was good.

I guess, if I have to die tonight at the hands of an angry god inside a tower, my last day could be worse.

So I come up with my own good memory for him to hold on to. "My good time was when we were fourteen. I was just starting to get over the death of my mother and I asked you to be my date for the Pledge Gala in my second year."

His face goes sad, which throws me for a moment. Because it was such a great night for me. So great that it never even occurred to me that he didn't have a good time.

"Sorry—did you not have fun?"

His eyes go wide with surprise. "What?"

"It's just... your immediate response came across as... sad."

He exhales, but looks me in the eyes. "I had forgotten about that night. But no, it wasn't sad. It was... heartbreaking and beautiful at the same time."

"What do you mean?"

"I mean... it was the perfect night. It was our first real kiss. It was the first time we went up to the wall after hours."

"That was the part I liked. The first kiss was amazing, of course. Because it was with you and it was everything. But that midnight walk on the wall, under the stars and looking out at the sand was everything. Especially the way you held my hand." I shrug. "I felt like a princess that night in my gala dress. And you were all dressed up too. Like my prince. And it was gonna last forever, Finn. That's how I felt that night. Why did it break your heart?"

He hesitates for a moment.

"What? Tell me."

I can tell he doesn't want to, but after a breath for

courage, he does. "That night, after I took you home, after that first kiss outside your door, I left and I was a hundred percent certain that I was gonna lose you."

"Why?"

"Because you were so perfect, and so beautiful, and… there was no way that the god would pass you up over someone second best. I was sure you'd be Chosen, and I was absolutely sure you'd be number one. So I went home, crying. And my father, he kept asking me what was wrong."

"And you told him."

Finn nods. "I told him."

"And I was Chosen. But I wasn't number one, because your father would never break your heart like that. I was number nine, so it wasn't so obvious. And now look at me. It's my turn to walk into that tower. It's like… that stupid god knew we cheated him. And this is his revenge."

Finn doesn't say anything. He knows I'm right. He knows this is true.

Maybe I'm just making things up to justify my bad luck, or whatever. Maybe I'm making myself more important than I should. Maybe this is my ego, trying to explain things in a way that puts me in the center. Trying to force it all to make sense and have purpose.

But I don't think so.

I think his gut feeling was true. That I was meant to be number one from the very beginning and the whole reason all the girls were called into that tower was because Aldo cheated and made me nine. And that god took it personal.

So this is nothing more than my destiny, finally being fulfilled.

"What will you do, Finn? What will you do with the rest of your life once I'm gone?"

His response is immediate. "What will I *do*? I will get *revenge*, Clara. I will fuck that god over six ways to Sunday and I will make him pay for taking you away from me."

This is the end of the conversation. Even if he didn't tug me up close to his chest and let me bury my face in his neck, it would still be the end.

Because there's really nothing more to say.

It's over.

It's well and truly over.

WE SLEEP FOR A LITTLE WHILE. Doze, really. I have a million things running through my mind, so sleeping isn't even possible. And even the dozing comes with weird half-dreams filled with nonsensical images feeding off my fear and sadness.

But eventually, the peace we've created for ourselves here in my rooms comes to an abrupt end when someone pounds on my door.

Finn gets out of bed, carefully, like he thinks I'm asleep and doesn't want to wake me, and I open one eye and watch him pull his pants back on. He answers the door, barely opening it a crack.

There is a whispered conversation that I can't really follow, then he reaches out with one arm and a garment bag is draped over it.

It's my dress for tonight.

I expect him to let the attendants in—I am always dressed by attendants. But instead, he closes the door and turns back to me. "I told them I would help you get ready."

At any other time, these words might make me blush. Would certainly make my heart beat faster with the thought of Finn helping me into a gown. Standing behind me, pulling my corset tight. Adjusting me. Making me perfect.

But right now, it just makes me sad. It makes me think of all the years we had, and now we don't. How there will be no children. No home of our own. No plans, nothing.

This is it.

He will dress me. We will go to the ceremony. We will feast, and dance, and walk to the tower—probably holding hands.

And then the clocktower will strike midnight and I will walk through those doors, never to see him again.

"How?" I ask, my voice low and husky.

He drapes the zippered-cotton garment bag over the back of an overstuffed chair and turns to me with a face of confusion. "What?"

I struggle, looking for the right words. "I… just… don't understand. Help me understand. How? How could you ever send me in there?"

His frustration comes out as an arrogant huff. "That's not fair."

"I'm *sorry*? What's not fair? The fact that you get to live another day and I don't? Or is the prospect of guilt what's tripping you up?"

"I thought we went over this, Clara. I can't *not* send you into that tower. You'll go whether I send you or not. It's not me! It's not up to me! And if I resist—"

"I get it." I sneer these words out. "I do. I get it. I'm just one woman. Nobody in the grand scheme of things. But…" I huff now too. "How, Finn? How will you live with yourself? Because if the roles were reversed, I could not. And I would not spend your last day pretending everything is fine. I would not"—I nod my head to the dress—"pretend like this offer to dress me is anything other than ritualistic preparation. I would not lie to myself. But you…" I shrug up one shoulder and shake my head. "You are not only lying to yourself, you're doing it so casually and with such indifference it's blowing my mind. It's making me question everything about you. About *us*. Because the man I thought I knew, the one I grew up with, my best friend for as long as I can remember—he would at least *try* and fight for me."

"Even if he knew he would lose? Even if he knew this display of pointless valor would kill people? Is that the man you want? The one who weighs the soul of one against the souls of a hundred, yet still chooses the one? Is that *romantic*, Clara?" These words come out as seething rage.

Which is appropriate, I suppose. Given that I practically called him a spineless coward. But it's out of character. The sex was… interesting. And, not gonna lie, especially to myself, it was good. Very good. But that was out of character too.

Not out of character that it was good. I've always

enjoyed sex with Finn. And it's not even that he did dirty things to me. Or asked for dirty things in return. I've always had a suspicion that Finn was holding back when we were intimate. That he had desires he never told me about.

How could he not? We parted when we were eighteen. We led completely different lives and when we did meet up, we didn't usually have time to explore each other. All our private encounters were trysts scheduled in between appointments and the needs being met during those trysts were more emotional than physical.

We were trying to convince ourselves that we still had a relationship.

We were propping up the idea that we could spend all our new-adult years being two totally different people, on two totally different life tracks, and not have it spoil the dream.

Because I see now that's all it was. That's all Finn ever was.

Just a dream.

But it's just interesting that all of his out-of-character behavior pops up after Aldo died and Finn became Extraction Master. It's maybe not fair to assume that the new title is already contaminating him, but everyone knows power corrupts.

Of course, I might be reading too much into this. It could just be sadness. He's mourning Aldo and soon me. But it's still out of character.

Since I don't answer his last question, Finn decides that he has won the argument and turns back to the garment bag containing my dress. I am in bed, naked, but I throw the covers off me, walk into the massive, luxurious bathroom, and then close and lock the door.

I turn on the hot water, letting steam swirl up around the ceiling, and I stare at myself in the fogging mirror.

I am pretty, but not any prettier than the other Maidens. Perhaps the Maidens, as a whole, are prettier than most women in the city. But... it's basically a beauty contest, so it makes sense that we're all little copies of each other. Slightly different faces, slightly different hairstyles, slightly different heights.

But all the same.

Little copies, doing our duty.

Always poised, always proper, always polite.

In other words: *Don't take up too much space in the room. Don't call attention to yourself. Don't stand out, blend in.*

Finn is like this as well, but in a different way. He is obedient, and passive, and deferential. He is traditions, and habits, and routines.

Which isn't the man I remember in my head.

He was always dutiful, but he was daring too. Always honorable and honest, but unconventional as well.

In the time we've been apart, he's changed. And it's confusing. I guess that's my point. Because of course he's changed. I've changed too.

It just breaks my heart that today, of all days, is the one where I realize I don't know him anymore.

I'm crushed. And I feel hopeless, and helpless, and defeated.

I get in the shower, wash, and get right back out, wrapping myself up in a luxurious cotton towel as I swipe my hand through the fog that has collected on the mirror and stare at my pretty, but ordinary, face.

I'm frowning. And this brings forth a collection of shallow lines around my eyes and mouth that I don't remember being there the last time I looked in the mirror.

Which just makes me sadder. That I gave up my youth to a god in a tower who now wants to take the rest of me too.

A knock on the bathroom door makes me jump. "Clara." Finn's voice comes across as steady, and even, and detached. "It's past six. I need you to come out so I can help you get dressed."

It's past six, Clara. Why are you taking so long? The god is hungry and you need to make yourself pretty for him.

I sigh. Because as much as I want to hate Finn for his… *professionalism,* I hate myself more for not being able to live up to the Maiden motto.

Every Maiden who has gone in to that tower has done it with her chin up. Brave, and steady, and with a sense of purpose.

Do I really want to be the Maiden who goes in frantic, and wild, and delirious?

Haryet was terrified, yet she showed up, she ate dinner, she danced, and then, when the time came, she walked proudly through those black doors.

She was nothing but brave.

"*Clara!*" Finn's voice is louder now and there's a little bit of emotion in it. But it's not desperation or regret. It's anger, I think.

I turn from the mirror and the idea that I have been wronged, even though I've been living like a princess these past ten years, fills me with a new kind of anger. Something I don't recall feeling before. It's packed with seething, turbulent resentment.

I walk to the door and open it up. Finn takes a step back, like he wasn't expecting me to give in so easily. But then he smiles and places his hands on my shoulders. "I know this is hard. But I'm here for you. You know that, right?"

I do. But I can't bring myself to say it. So I don't. I just shrug off his hands and walk over to the dressing area, dropping my towel to the floor. "What about my hair and makeup?"

His eyes are far too busy taking in my body to answer, but when they finally meet mine, they are not thinking about hair and makeup. They are hungry with lust.

I consider the idea that we have sex one more time before the end.

Then toss it aside.

He just... doesn't deserve me. That's my conclusion right now. He simply doesn't deserve me. So it's not gonna happen.

"Finn. Focus." I snap my fingers at him. "I need hair and makeup before I can get dressed."

"Do you want me to call someone in?"

I sigh. He's not good at this. Has he always been this myopic? "You could. But... you could also do it for me."

His eyebrows go up. Then he smiles. "You want me to brush and style your hair? And put makeup on you?"

I mean, what better way to send the love of your life off to be the god's sacrifice? But I don't say that. *Poised, proper, and polite, Clara. This is who you are.*

Finn crosses the room, grabs a robe off a hanger, and helps me into it. Then he points to the hair and makeup chair. "Sit. I'll give it my best try."

I sit, and he putters around for a few moments, then lines up a selection of brushes on a tray. He combs my hair out, talking to me as he works.

"We have three kids."

My eyes shoot up, finding his in the massive mirror propped up against the wall I'm facing. "What?"

"We have three kids. Aldo is still alive, so I'm not the Extraction Master. I told him I didn't want the job. Would never take the job."

A small, startled breath escapes from me. And despite all the horrible things I was just thinking about him, I smile. "What do you do then? Just sit around all day?"

The comb slides through my long, wet hair easily—sending a tingling sensation across my scalp, which turns into chills that make my whole body prickle up, and I shudder.

"I am…" He pauses to think, smiling at me in the mirror. "I'm a scholar."

I laugh. "A scholar?"

"It is funny?"

"Surprising. I never suspected you were an academic. What do you study?"

"The ancient ruins of the desert. The tunnels below the city. I collect artifacts. And we don't even live in a tower."

My mouth drops open. "We've gone rustic? Don't tell me we're living down-city?"

"No. We live *under* the city in the diggers' camp. And our

children run around barefoot and muddy. But they laugh a lot, Clara. And that's the only thing that matters. We laugh a lot too. We don't have any spark, except for the water pumps, and sometimes we crave the sunlight, but we're happy. And there are cave rooms down there with holes in the ceiling where the sun shines through, where plants and trees grow, and the kids can run in the grass. And at night, when they're all sleeping, sometimes we steal away to one of these open-topped caves and make love under the moonlight."

My eyes are swelling up with tears. Because even though this was never my dream, nor his, I suspect, it's such a nice life—such a satisfying future—that I am immediately sorry it will never happen. That we didn't think of this sooner. That we didn't know better than to play a game with a god.

Because there are no winners now.

We both lose.

Finn stares at me for a long moment in the mirror. Internalizing my sadness, I think. Because he starts to apologize. "Clara—"

I interrupt him with a wave of my hand through the air. "Never mind. It's a nice dream, but that's all it is. A dream. Let's stay focused on reality now."

He nods and continues combing my hair until it is smooth and straight, mostly dry. "What do you want me to do with it now?"

I've never had to do my own hair for a gala or an Extraction, so I'm lost for a minute. But then I shrug. "Who cares? Put it up in a pony tail, I guess."

"I think the Matrons would lose their shit if you walked out of this room with a pony tail, Clara."

"Let them."

"How about we just keep it down? Maybe… gather it up like this to keep it off your face?" He pulls up the long strands that hang down the sides of my face and pulls them back behind my head, fastening them there with a gold clip. "Good?"

I nod. Because I don't care.

"And… how about no makeup?"

He's never liked the makeup that I've been wearing since I was Chosen to be a Maiden. And this I do have an opinion about, because I never liked it either, so my voice is low and soft when I answer. "Yeah. No make-up sounds perfect."

"Then all we have left is the dress."

He leaves me in the chair, walks over to the thick, canvas garment bag, and unzips it. I get up and follow him over to the dressing area, taking my position in the center of the room where I usually stand for dressing.

He removes a silk bag first, looking at me with questions in his eyes.

"Lingerie."

This makes him smile as he pulls the drawstring open and removes a pair of frilly underwear, some garters, and some silk stockings.

There's no corset, which means it's built in to the dress.

Finn takes that out next, holds it up and then hangs it on the dressing stand rack.

I narrow my eyes.

Finn comes up next to me, standing at my left shoulder. "What? What's wrong with the dress?"

"It's... got a *blue* skirt."

"Oh. Right. They're always some shade of white during an Extraction, aren't they?"

"Always. Blue is for Little Sisters." And now I'm annoyed.

Finn walks back over to the dress, picks up the skirt and looks at me. "It's pretty though, right?"

"It's an insult, is what it is. And it's slutty. A peasant dress." It is, in fact, a corset dress, the likes of which a man might find on a whore down in the Shipping District. So of course Finn *likes* it. Probably all men would like this dress. But to a woman of my status it's offensive. "I'm not wearing it."

"What do you mean you're not wearing it? Of course you're wearing it."

I give him an indifferent shrug and turn my back to him. "No. I'm not. I have a closet filled with dresses that are a thousand times more appropriate than this one. I'll choose something else."

"You know what?" Once again, his tone is sharp and angry.

I turn, ready for another round of fighting. He has no right to be short with me on this day and I have every right to leave this world on my own terms. So I snap right back at him. "No. *What?*"

"You're..." He pauses. Like he's searching for the perfect word to describe what I am. "You're... *rude.*"

I laugh. Nearly a guffaw. "What?" Then I point to myself.

"I'm rude? Because I don't want to present myself to that evil god in the tower tonight dressed like a slut?"

"Not only are you rude, but you're insecure too."

Another laugh bursts out of me.

"Whatever happened to 'poised, proper and polite,' Clara?"

Is he serious? "What *happened*? Is that a real question? You're sacrificing me to save Gemna and the Little Sisters. You're giving me away—the woman you *love*—like I am a piece of property, Finn."

"Ya know, I was sympathetic of your plight earlier today. But now you're just… unpleasant."

The nerve of him.

"Not only are you unpoised, and improper, and impolite, but you're… a coward, Clara. This is how cowards act. You were the one who wanted to be a Spark Maiden. You were the one who signed up for this. You were the one who spent the last ten years sucking on the teat of that god like you earned it. But you didn't earn it. *Tonight* is the night when you *earn it*. So suck it up, and at the very least, act half as dignified as all your friends who went before you. If not for me or the city, then for the Little Sisters looking up to you. For Gemna, who will be losing her shit tonight, scared out of her mind. And maybe this is what you want? Maybe you're just trying to make sure that you leave us more miserable at the end of the day than when we started it. And you know what? That is the definition of 'coward.' So yeah, you're acting like a fucking coward."

I'm so pissed. Seething mad. Hot with anger. And I'm

just about to banish him from my rooms when he walks over to the door, unlocks it, and pulls it open.

He doesn't even look at me when he spits his next words out. I get a side-eye from over his shoulder, and that's it. "I'll see you at seven at the feast."

Then he slams the door closed, making several picture frames slide down the wall nearest the door and crash to the floor.

I'm too stunned to move. Too angry to scream. Too humiliated to cry.

So I just stand there. For however many minutes it takes for Gemna to cautiously open my door and peek inside.

"Clara?"

I suck in a deep breath. Amazed that my face is not wet with tears.

"Can I come in?"

I look over at her and nod, but I am unable to speak so I don't even try.

"What's going on? Is there some way I can help?"

Now I do cry. Because Finn is right. I'm scaring her. There's still a chance that I might be the last Maiden. That she might escape my fate, and the fates of all the Maidens that came before me.

I'm a terrible friend. Haryet was upset, but in the end, she was the definition of poised, and proper, and polite. She attended dinner, she danced, and she walked into that tower without a fuss.

Just like every other Maiden who came before her.

And I'm going to be the one who throws a fit. I'm going

to be the one who gets hysterical. I'm going to be the one who is selfish and thinks only of herself.

Not only that, I will do all these things looking like a whore.

It's this realization that snaps me out of the pity party I'm currently hosting. What a sight I will be up there on the tower stage, looking like a tramp and acting like a low-class nobody.

Well, some of that is a choice, isn't it?

Maybe I do have to wear the dress they've chosen for me. Fine. I will surrender my body tonight. It does, after all, belong to the god for three more months.

But what I will not do is surrender my dignity.

I pull myself together and turn to Gemna. "Can you help me get dressed?"

Gemna immediately smiles and comes over to me with arms out.

We hug for a long time and I find myself wishing I had spent the day with her instead of Finn.

In the dining ***room*** Gemna and I are now the only ones left at the Maiden table. Everyone has noticed my dress, so I'm hot with humiliation. Gemna held her shock in pretty well when I presented it to her back in my rooms, but I could see that she too was appalled.

It's not that it's ugly or anything. It's not ugly at all, actually. It's not made of cheap fabrics—the cotton is very soft, the silk is divine, and the lace is handmade. It's not even poorly put together. The stitching is some of the finest I've ever seen. The skirts flow in just the right way.

In fact, I look amazing. Especially after Gemna threw my hair up into a messy updo that pulled the look together perfectly and dabbed some makeup onto my blotchy and pale cheeks to try and force my skin to glow.

The whole thing just works and I'm turning the heads of every man in the room.

It's just completely inappropriate because they are looking at me with lust and this is supposed to be a somber evening.

But Gemna did point out that I made a fuss to the Matrons when Haryet was supposed to be getting dressed for her Extraction. I had forgotten about that, but now all those nasty things I said come rushing back to me.

Every one of you needs to get the fuck out. Who gives a fuck what her dress looks like!

That's what I told them, so... yeah. They got back at my insubordination by dressing me like a harlot.

Matrons, one. Clara, zero.

I always knew they were bitches, but this is... catty. And it demeans them in my eyes. Not that it matters, I guess. It's just more proof that this city is filled with charlatans and I spent my whole life living under the spell of liars.

I blow out a breath, doing my best to keep it soft, and

then scan the room. I've avoided meeting Finn's gaze since I arrived. He was already here, but Gemna stepped into protective best-friend mode and steered me clear of him. There are only the two of us left, so we stayed close to each other before the feast was served.

The entire room of upper-city elites seem to have grown immune to the idea that the god in the tower has developed an insatiable appetite. At first, they were quiet and reserved. But as the drinks were served everyone seemed to loosen up.

Everyone but Gemna and me.

This is when I remember that the Little Sisters are up in the balcony, required to be at the feast because of tradition. Their second Extraction event before they've even been whittled down to the top fifty. Which is yet another thing that has never happened before.

I look up and the first face I see is Jasina Bell's. She must've been staring at me because our eyes are instantly locked.

Her hand comes up in a small, timid wave and she sighs. None of the Little Sisters seem to be having fun. In fact, most, if not all, of them look to be on the verge of panic.

Is this what we signed up for? That's what they're asking themselves.

No. It's not what any of us signed up for.

And even though Finn was... *perhaps* correct in his conclusion that I was doing my best to make this night as miserable for everyone else as it was for me—I do not wish this moment on any of those young girls. Not even the haughty Jasina Bell.

So I raise a timid hand back. Which makes her smile. Then she mouths, *The dress...* but I miss the rest, because a hand touches my shoulder and my attention is immediately pulled to the man attached to it. Finn.

"Should we head over to the ballroom?"

"It's part of the ritual, so—" But I stop here, mid-sentence. Because I'm doing it again. Taking my misfortune out on everyone around me.

And that's not how I will go out tonight. I will not be a shining example of cowardice for Gemna or the Little Sisters who will be watching me for any sign of weakness.

I will be poised, and proper, and polite.

My chair slides back, I stand up, and then I look Finn in the eyes as I take his offered hand. "It would be my pleasure."

I hate him. I will never get over this betrayal. I will carry my resentment of Finn Scott into the tower with me and hold on to it as I take my last dying breath.

But I will clutch at this bitterness with grace.

Typically, the Extraction Master is the last to leave the feast so that all the people are waiting for him in the ballroom when he enters. But nothing about this night is typical.

Everyone stays seated as we make our way into the next room and then there is a furious sound of scraping chairs and the swishing of gowns as the rest of the guests follow us.

Finn leads me right into the center of the ballroom, then —while everyone else is still filing in—he raises a hand, signaling for the music to start.

We dance as the room around us gets more and more chaotic, both of us stiff at first, not looking each other in the eyes. But then, once the room is settled—just as my fate is settled—I put my head on his shoulder and he holds me tight. Our feet shuffling, barely leaving the small circle we make in the center of the room.

We dance like this for many songs, and many minutes, until finally everyone decides that we will stay dancing like this until we are forced to leave and make our way over to the tower stage, and so they join us.

Bodies crowd around us and the sounds of swishing dresses and soft conversation fill the enormous room. It's all very cautious and hushed, at first. But things get more relaxed and soon it's a party.

Still, Finn and I cling to each other.

I can't decide if I should stay mad or make up with him.

The only thing I can settle on is the fact that it doesn't matter.

I will go into the tower and my life will be over.

He will stay out here and his will start again.

He will live again.

I don't want to hate him. I don't. I want to love him. I want to be a brave woman in the most challenging moment of my life. I want to be a shining example of what it means to be a Maiden. And I want to go into that tower with as much grace as the women who came before me.

But I can't help the hate, and I don't feel the love, and yes, I do want to be brave, but I do not want to be a shining example of a sacrifice to anyone, let alone those Little Sisters who are all watching me right now. And while I do agree that it would be nice to live up to the standards of courage and grace set by the Spark Maidens who went before me, none of them were sent into this tower by a man who claimed to love her.

It's completely different. Because he is betraying me. I am in distress, I am in danger, and he refuses to step in and stop it.

He didn't even *try*.

All this time I imagined Finn Scott was an honorable, intelligent, capable man. And I believed him when he said he loved me.

How could he love me when he didn't come up with a single plan?

He did promise revenge. And it sounded so genuine at the time. It touched me, it did.

But there was no brainstorming with his friends to concoct a harebrained save-the-girl scheme. Even if it would've never worked, a token gesture along that line would've been a tiny bit comforting. I would, at the very least, feel… valued? I guess?

I don't like feeling this way. I had never thought of myself as small, and petty, and selfish.

But I think I am.

I must be.

Because this is the truth.

This is how I feel.

And I will never forgive Finn Scott for what he is about to do.

The next thing I know it's eleven-thirty, the dance is over, and it's time to go outside and walk over to the tower stage. We hit the chilled air and suddenly the bells are there, ringing, and ringing, and ringing—like they have been all day. But somehow, I had put them out of my mind. Pushed them into the background. Probably because they've been tolling almost constantly for two days and now it's just... background noise.

But the clanging is suddenly too much. And I think it is the sound of these bells that is making me shake. The low, booming peal of the god's call echoes through the air like a disturbance.

My mind is whirring and I feel... *less than*. If that makes any sense. Less than Haryet. Less than Brooke, and Piper, and Lucy, and both of the Mabels, and Marlowe. And especially less than Imogen, who was the first of us.

I'm an embarrassment, that's what I am. And my whole life suddenly feels pointless and shallow. Like I walked through it as a shadow of what I could've been.

If only I'd tried harder or... *something*.

Then Gemna is beside me, taking my hand. And Finn is letting go, hugging me. Kissing me. Meaningless words spilling out of his mouth and into mine.

"I love you." He just keeps saying this as we kiss. "I love you, Clara. I will love you forever."

But it's a lie. It's nothing but a fucking lie. Already Haryet is a distant memory to the people of Tau City. Hell, they probably haven't thought about Imogen in years. Probably don't even remember the name of the Maiden who was sent in twenty years ago.

I know I don't.

Then Finn is all the way across the stage, looking up at

the tower. So I look up too and find that we are one minute to midnight.

One minute. That's all I have left.

The moment this thought ends, the god's bells *stop* and the clocktower bell starts chiming the final countdown.

I watch as the massive black doors begin to open and before I can even make a decision, my feet are walking forward, not under my control.

I'm being drawn in! Like there is a powerful magnet in there and I am nothing but iron.

Which is just funny. Because iron is strong, but I am weak.

And just as I think that, extreme heat fills my fingertips, floods my hands, flows up my arms and over my shoulders, and suddenly my entire body is aglow with cyan-blue spark.

I look over my shoulder, panic building inside me like an inferno. "Finn!" I call, desperate to beg one more time to be saved. "Finn!"

He looks at me, his face unreadable, and for a moment, I think he changes his mind. I think... I think he's leaning forward. Yes! He's coming! He's going to save me!

But just as I think these thoughts, he leans back and that rescue I was anticipating disappears.

"Finn!"

"I can't, Clara! I *can't*!" He yells this over the tolling of the bells. But then, in the moments after, there is silence. It is midnight and I am at the threshold.

There's no way for me to not cross it. I'm not in control anymore. It's like... the god is compelling me to keep walking. This is what sends me over the edge. This is what makes me throw out any thoughts of entering this tower with grace. This is what sends me into a fury.

None of this is in my control. And I know for certain that it's not in Finn's control, either. He can't come rescue me any more than I can rescue myself.

Still, all I have left is fear and rage, so that's what I cling to. "Whatever happened to 'You're my future. And the god can't take you away from me. Not ever?' Whatever happened to that?"

When I look over my shoulder Finn is panicking. But he's not going to do anything and I only have one breath left so I scream, "I will never forgive you! *Ever*. I will hate you 'till the end of time!"

Then I am across the threshold, entering the blackness, and the God's Tower doors slam shut behind me.

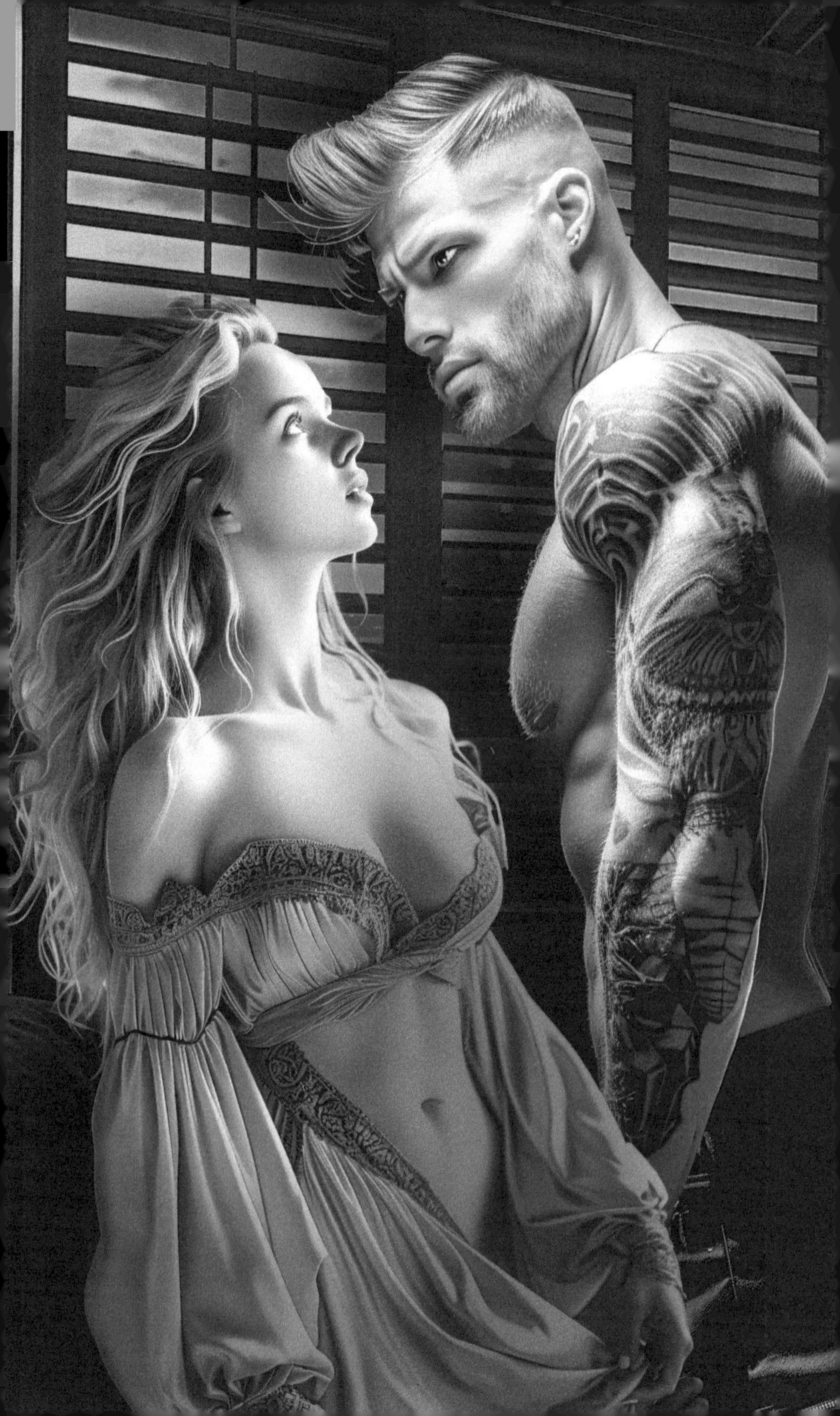

PART 2

"How did we get here? It's a question I ask myself often. How did this world arrive to a place where murderers are celebrated with pretty watercolor illustrations in books? How did we come to a place in time where one half of the line believes the murder of gods is justified? I'll tell you how. We have isolated ourselves. We have split ourselves into two camps—Alpha and Omega. But there's room, folks. There's room for the middle ground here in the Medians where we don't condone the murder of the innocent, regardless of species. At least give them a trial! The Godslayer is a black mark on the name of gods everywhere. Whether they are for or against this genocide, they will all be judged for his actions."

—Maj. Gen. Margorie Garcia, Many-Worlds Recruiting Command, The Medians

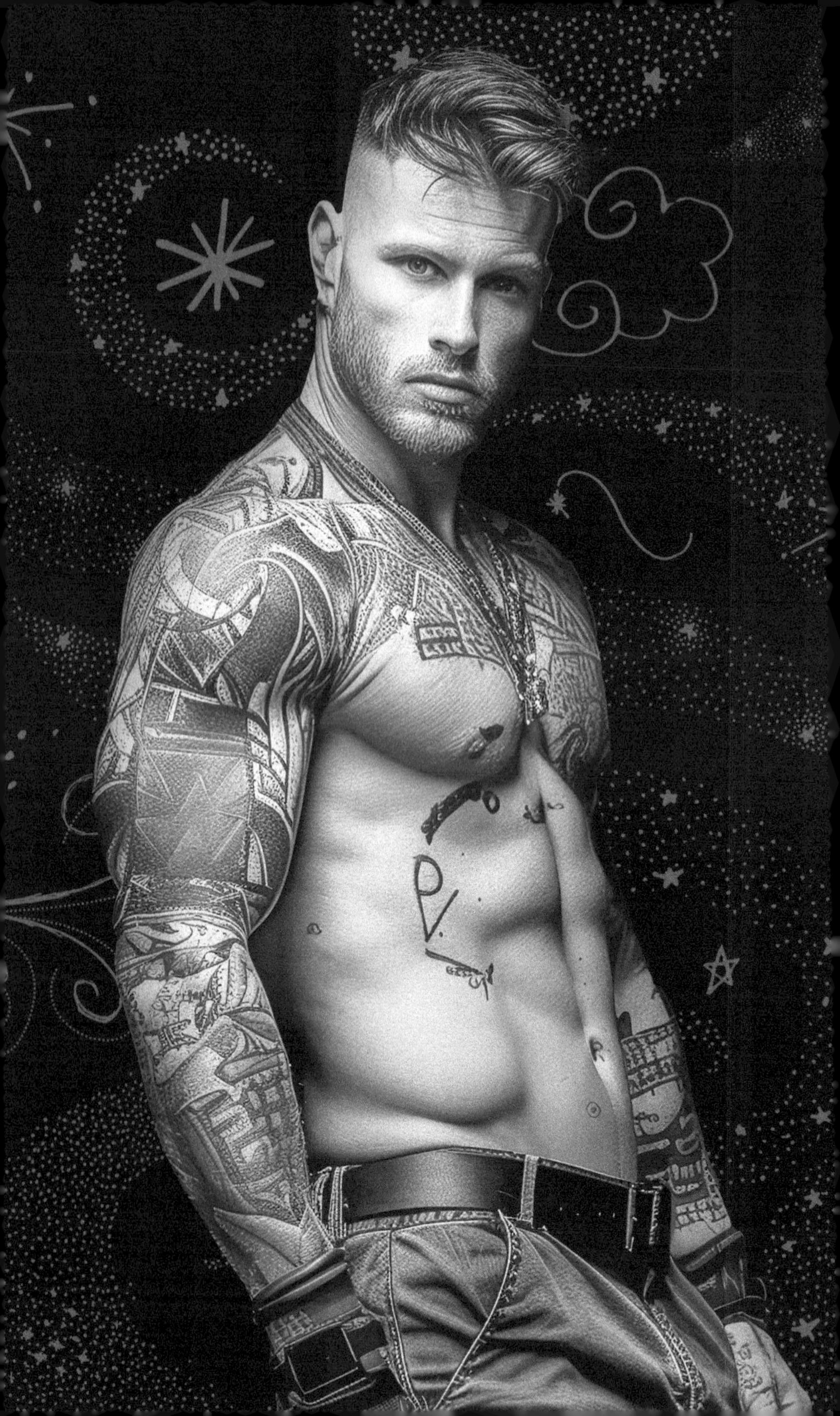

TYSE

CHAPTER TWENTY

*S*omewhere, something is buzzing.

I turn over in bed and shove my head under the pillow, ignoring the buzz until it stops. There is a moment here where I imagine what the buzzing might mean for me, but it's quickly overtaken by the need for sleep, so I just drift off.

The next time the buzzing sounds, I reach over, grab the phone off the nightstand, and throw it against the wall.

This time I drift back to sleep chuckling.

Moments later, there is a pounding on my door.

I sit up, throw my pillow, get out of bed, and stumble over to the door. "Whoever you are, ya had better be ready for a fight because I'm gonna kick the livin' shit outta ya." I throw it open, growling into empty space. Then I look down. "Fuck." A small child. Little girl, about seven. Big brown eyes and mismatched clothes. "Anneeta. What. The hell?"

She sniffles, drags a sleeve across her nose, and sighs as she holds out her hand, offering me a disposable phone. "Someone wants to talk to you." Then she turns those giant brown eyes up to meet mine and smiles, revealing the space where her front teeth used to be just last week. "Would you like to come have tea with me today?"

"No." I feel a little bit bad for being so blunt, but I fell for this once. Tea with Anneeta is a mud-like mixture of boiled weeds scavenged from the outside walls of the tower and the biscuits are made of paper.

I take the phone, then search my pockets for a coin to pay her. But I'm wearing boxers, so I hold up a finger. "Stay right there. Be right back." I close the door on her and redirect my attention to the phone. "Whoever this is, it had better be good."

Stayn's voice comes back at me as a yell. "I've been calling you for five fucking hours, Tyse. And don't try and tell me your phone was dead, because it wasn't. You could've at least texted a reply."

"Sorry. I was sleepin'."

"It's five-fifteen in the afternoon, you worthless bum. I've got a job for you. So get your ass up and get on it!"

"What job?"

"There was a disturbance—five fucking hours ago!—down in the tower's lower levels. I need someone to go check it out."

I rub a hand across my eyes, sighing. "You waited five hours for me to answer the phone so I can check out a couple of vandals in the basement? Why didn't ya just send Anneeta to check it out?"

"Because that location is magnetically locked. No one has been down in that sector since the god left. It's not a *vandal*. It's somethin' else—ya know what? You don't need to know why I want you to go check it out! You just need to get your ass down there and then report back when you're finished!"

I hold the phone away from my ear and look at it because he's seriously pissed off. When he's done, I yawn into the phone as I ask my next question, doin' this just to make him angrier. "What's my take in this?"

"Your *take*?" He's growlin' at me now.

Which was the whole point of me asking the question. I kinda love pissin' Stayn off. He's very excitable. "Yeah. What do I get if I go check out this disturbance for ya?"

He knows I'm just tryin' to wind him up so he gets a hold of himself and blows out a long breath. "How about dinner? Come by tomorrow at seven?"

"Me? Dinner at the Kuiper residence? You're not afraid I'll corrupt your daughters?" I wince and smile at the same time. It's a touch too far, even I know this.

"You so much as look at one of my girls, Tyse, and I'll cut your fuckin' balls off."

"I'm kidding. I'll check out your fuckin' disturbance and report back. And your girls are sisters to me. I'd never."

I hear a semblance of a chuckle on the other end of the line. Then another sigh. "Sorry. I know. I'm just wound up today. Weird shit's been happening all over the city since last night. A power outage, a security hack at the Empire Building, communications are all messed up, and this fucking tower disturbance." He huffs out a sigh. "I'm short men."

"Obviously. That's got to be the only reason you're relying on me for anything."

"Not quite. I can trust you to keep your mouth shut,

that's why I called you. And you live in that stupid tower, so you're close anyway."

"Well, now I'm intrigued. What do ya think I'm gonna find down there that you need me to keep my mouth shut?"

"Not sure. But I don't want to talk about it on the phone."

My eyebrows shoot up. "Whhhhhyyyyyy?"

"Tomorrow. Dinner's at seven. Dress nice. Or, at the very least, take a fuckin' shower. The location coordinates for the disturbance are on the notepad of the phone. Get back to me as soon as you know anything."

The call ends with a single beep as I'm pulling up the notepad. I flip through the options, find the notepad, and read the location. Sector 4, quad H minus 5, floor 2. Fuck's sake. I've never even heard of these locations. Are there even stairs to get down there?

"*Tyyyyyyyse*. I've got to *goooooo*," Anneeta whines from the other side of the door.

I'd forgotten about her. "One sec, kid. I'm coming."

I pull on a pair of tactical pants, grab a coin from a glass jar on the short counter in the semblance of a kitchen, and open the door back up. "Here." I toss the coin high in the air, making her gasp. But this one's got reflexes and that little hand snatches the coin before it can even think about hitting the floor and rolling away.

Anneeta smiles at me, showing off her new, toothless gap, then turns and bolts off down the hallway.

She's one of the few bright things about living in the ruins. There aren't any other kids here. The tower isn't anyone's first choice of residence and while it's true most of its inhabitants are poor, illiterate, and addicted to the spark, they're still smart enough not to try and raise families here. They either get their shit together and get out, or they allow the city to sterilize them for coins and stay.

Anneeta is a special circumstance. A warning for all women who choose this lifestyle to be careful. Her mother's been dead for nearly four years now. Long enough that I doubt the kid even remembers she had a mother.

As far as I know, Anneeta lives on her own, making money running messages inside the tower like the one she just did for Stayn.

But we all take care of each other in here. We are, as they say, cut from the same cloth. Anneeta's edges are just a little more tattered than most, but she's still one of us and everyone looks out for her.

I close the door thinking about the little girl and what a dismal, depressing future she has. It's not her fault her mother was addicted to the spark and was too far gone to take care of the pregnancy one way or the other. Being born under the influence of the spark is a very rare thing these days. Ever since Stayn took over as chief of patrol, and Basil, our friend from the War College, took over as Council head, there have been no births from spark-addicted women living in the ruin.

They sweep the tower every new moon looking for pregnant women, test them on the spot and then take them out by force if it comes back positive. But Anneeta came along before the spark reforms, so she's stuck.

She will never leave the tower. The spark changed her

brain while she was still developing in the womb. She's more than addicted to it now, it literally runs her body.

She can wander the tower and the ruins outside, but if she were to cross that imaginary boundary between the Tower District and the Canal District, she would get maybe three or four steps before collapsing. If she wasn't given a dose of spark within the next several minutes, she'd be dead.

It's an extreme case. All of us inside the tower live off the spark. We're all addicted, but we can leave. There would be sickness if we stayed away too long, but we'd be OK again eventually. Even if we never came back. Total withdrawal would be miserable, for sure, but we would not die the way Anneeta would.

No one knows how long she can live like this, running wholly on the spark. She's the only kid we've got in here at the moment—hopefully the last as well—so it's kind of a case study.

Some do-gooders from outside have tried to rein her in. Tried to make her settle with some of the more responsible adults on the ground floor and live a more traditional life with some schooling and regular meals. But she slips away when anyone gets too controlling. Just... disappears without a trace.

The tower people—the more superstitious ones, at least—think it's the spirit of the tower god protecting her like she's his and his alone. But I think she just knows this place too well to be found. Knows all the nooks and crannies to hide in. Hell, she's probably got a whole road system mapped out in her head that winds through the vents and ducts.

At any rate, the do-gooders have given up on the idea that she can be tamed and now she just does as she pleases.

It's not a bad life if you ask me. Sure, she's missing out on a lot as far as the outside world goes, but freedom always did come with a price.

The phone buzzes in my hand, signaling a message. It's Stayn. *You had better not go back to sleep! I'll come into that tower and kick your fucking balls in if you're not already on your way.*

My smile is wide when I text back, *Who is this?* And when I get a mad rash of messages in reply, I ignore them and toss the phone into the trash. He's just really easy to wind up. Being chief of patrol does that to a guy, I guess. But I don't feel sorry for him. If he didn't want the stress, he shouldn't have taken the job.

I do get my ass in gear, though, pulling on a black tank and the same boots I've been wearing since I was discharged from the Sweep Army seven years ago. Then I fasten my battle belt to my hip and leave, shrugging on a canvas jacket as I make my way towards the central stairwell.

I'm on the tenth floor of the ruined God's Tower. It's only marginally safe as far as structure goes, but it's quiet. Most of us prefer to live down below, closer to the ground. There are maybe several dozen people living above me—the tower goes up fifteen more floors from here—but there are no stairs, only ladders, and the plumbing is iffy on the best of days.

Tenth floor is private enough for my standards. Anything higher is just a nuisance, and I'm nothing if not a practical man. It's the only reason I live in Tau City in the first place. I wasn't ready to give up the spark after I was discharged from Sweep. There's no ruin in Delta, where I grew up. There's a god living in that fuckin' tower. Nasty one, too. Lots of rules and traditions. Which makes for a nice city, I guess, but there's always a tradeoff.

My god came with a lot of expectations, which—after seven years of war—I was no longer interested in accommodating. Tau City not only had a still-functioning ruin, it was close to the base where I was stationed at the end of my service, so I applied for War College and got accepted. That's how I met Stayn and Basil.

Having both grown up here, and coming from respectable families, neither Stayn nor Basil ever got addicted to the spark. But no one in Tau City cares much if ya are. As long as you can still function outside the ruin, it's just another way to unwind. Like a fifth of whiskey at the taverns or a whore on Friday night.

I'm still in control. I do get out of the tower, but not nearly as much as I used to. I've just lost interest in climbing my way up the political ladder the way Stayn and Basil are.

I don't want to lead. I don't want to follow, either. I just want to be left alone.

Living in the tower is free, the spark is free, and it suits me. So why the fuck not?

I do work. Sometimes. Both inside and out.

It's the perfect tradeoff if you ask me.

I nod at some people working on a mural in the wide hallway as I pass by and enter the main stairwell. It's entirely probable that this 'quick job' turns into an all-day thing because I don't even know how to get that far below ground. But if there is a way down there, my best guess is that the main stairwell is where that route starts.

On any given day there are between three and four thousand people calling the tower home. It's a lot when you see them all in the same place, but still a very tiny percentage compared to the nearly two million living outside.

Of course, you almost never get all the tower people in the same place at the same time, but as I descend and the noise becomes increasingly louder, I wonder if they're not all down in the main lobby right now.

When I come around the curve between the second and first floors, I can't believe my eyes. Because it really does look like everyone in the tower is here.

I pause on the steps and lean in towards a man about my age. "What the hell is goin' on?"

"ID's." He doesn't look at me. Just stares intently down at the crowd.

Now that I know this is government business, I can pick out the social workers standing behind a table near the entrance. "They're giving out ID's?" I cross my arms and frown. "Well, that's not suspicious."

"Yeah," the guy says, turning to look at me now. "How stupid do these people have to be to start rattlin' off all their information to the fuckin' government?" He scoffs. "There's no way I'm getting trapped in their tracking system. I just barely got myself out."

I nod, agreeing. Not that I'm out of the system—I'm not. I would have to leave Tau City and start over somewhere else if I wanted to be invisible. Too many friends in high places here.

Everyone in the tower is addicted to spark, that's true. It's an unavoidable side effect. But they're not all here for that reason alone. Some of them just don't want to participate in society. Like me. And ditching your official ID is the only way to do that. That's why no one in here has a phone. It's how they track.

Only disposable phones are 'technically' allowed inside the tower, temporary things that are susceptible to the spark and run out of battery after three or four interactions. But all phones are temporary in here, even if they're not disposable. The city just figured why waste perfectly good phones on the tower people when they can make an inferior product that costs less to produce, charge the same amount for it, and make a tidy little profit off the degenerates who don't want to be good little citizens and participate in the general welfare of society? By which I mean be taxpayers.

No phone, no ID. No ID, no job. No job, no taxes.

No government likes shit they can't tax, including people.

That's why I didn't much care that I shattered my phone against the wall. That's why I threw the one Anneeta gave me in the trash. All phones sold in Tau City have an official tracker on them that allows them to function, including the disposable ones. But they die in less than a day, even if you don't use them for the maximum number of interactions.

There are just as many people in the tower on the run from the patrol as there are true addicts. To them, the offer of an ID and a phone to keep it on is nothin' but a trap, just like this guy said.

The crowd on the stairwell is growing thicker by the second with onlookers trying to decide how bad off they are. Do they need the ID to get a city aid package? Or can they hold out?

There's at least a thousand people down in the lobby below who can't hold out, I guess. Because they are clamoring for a chance to get tracked.

I've only ever seen this done once in the last seven years and it was before Stayn and Basil took over.

So. I guess they're no different from everyone else when it comes to coin.

A part of me always knew they were not any different than the other government officials that came before them, but it still burns. And it's disappointing.

So I sigh and just shoulder my way through the crowd until I make it to the ground level. The staircase does keep going down, but you have to walk around the backside of the stairwell to find the opening for it.

There is a thick crowd of people coming up to see what's going on, same way there was coming down, but after a single floor it thins out. Mostly because that's where the stairwell ends.

I walk a little further into the small lobby so I can see down all eight of the hallways that fan out from the stairwell like spokes, then sigh. Because I don't see any more stairs. Not out in the open, at least. So I guess I'll have to start pulling open doors.

I choose a direction and walk, checking out doors.

Upstairs there are open stairwells at the end of every hallway, plus several hidden somewhere in the middle, and they are mostly marked. But down here, that doesn't seem to be the case.

An old woman is standing in a doorway smoking, her attention fully on the crowd at the bottom of the stairs. But when I stop in front of her, she turns her eyes up to meet mine. "Can I help you?"

"I'm looking for stairs going down. Do ya know of any?"

She points her chin in the direction I was heading. "End of the line that way." Then points her chin the other way. "End of the line that way too."

I'm not sure if this means there is a stairwell at the end of each hallway or not. But I don't hang around to ask because I spot Anneeta staring at me just a few doors down.

"Thanks," I tell the old woman, then walk over to Anneeta. "Are you spying on me?"

She shrugs up one shoulder, unimpressed by my intimidating question. "Maybe. Or maybe I just wanted to watch you get yourself lost trying to find the basement."

"How'd you know I was going to the basement?"

She taps her head. "Doors can't stop me, Tyse. I hear everything."

"That's a creepy answer. You should probably not tell anyone you've got the god inside you."

She scoffs, then full-on laughs. "If they don't already know that, they're kinda stupid, aren't they?"

I laugh too. "Probably right. Anyway. You wanna tell me how to get to sector 4, quad H minus 5, floor 2?"

"No. But I'll show you." She turns and starts running,

weaving her way through people in the crowded hallway. I just watch for a moment, trying to decide if I should play this little game with her. But then she looks over her shoulder and yells, "Come on, Tyse! I'm the white rabbit and you have to follow me!"

A part of me knows this is just another tea party invitation, something I should definitely decline. But it could take me hours to find sector 4, quad H minus 5, floor 2 on my own. And she'll probably get me there in ten minutes.

So I follow, losing sight of her several times when the hallway splits and zigzags. And I realize that the hallway is kind of a ramp. Slowly, very slightly, angling downward. At the bottom of this gradual drop Anneeta is waiting, sitting on a concrete step. Her right arm is raised over her head and her finger is pointing up at the ceiling.

Not all the lights are working down here—the spark must be low—but there are enough still sputtering for me to see that it's not the ceiling she's pointing to, but something spray-painted on the door she's resting against.

It's a circle with a lightning bolt crossing through it from left to right. "What's this?"

"The rabbit hole. Do you want me to go with you?"

I reach for the door handle, find it unlocked, and pull, forcing Anneeta to get up and get out of the way as I open it.

Looking in, I find that it's pitch black and smells stale. "Where does this lead, Anneeta?"

"Down."

"Down how far?"

"Mmmmm." She hums a little, shrugging up that shoulder again. "Maybe... six levels."

"Is that sector 4?"

"Nope. It's Sector 1. All this is sector 1."

"Sector 1 is six levels? Fuckin' hell. How many levels down is sector 4, quad H minus 5, floor 2?"

"Umm..." She shrugs again, but with both shoulders and hands this time. "A bigger number than I can count. A lot. But I can take you, if you want."

"You've been down there before?"

"Of course. I've been everywhere. But down here, mostly in my dreams."

"I'm not sure that's helpful."

"You say that now because you don't dream the way I do. But if you follow me, you will."

"I will what?"

"Dream the way I do."

"Am I gonna get zapped with spark, or something?"

Anneeta laughs, a very childlike giggle. "You've already been zapped with spark, Tyse. That's why you live here."

"Right." I'm suddenly very sorry I agreed to this job. "How high can you count?" I ask just so I can get an estimate of how far I'll need to go.

"Twelve."

I squint my eyes at her. "No one ever told you about thirteen, eh?"

"Thirteen is forbidden. It's bad luck."

"Well, it's still a number. And if you know thirteen, you know fourteen. Then fifteen. Can you see the pattern?"

"Yes. But thirteen is forbidden."

"Whatever. Lead the way. Let's do this." I wave a hand into the darkness, inviting her to go first.

I expect her to balk at least a little. But she just takes off into the black without hesitation. A moment later, just as I'm pulling a torch off my belt, the way forward illuminates.

Again, like back outside, not all the lights are working. So it's a disorienting sputter of semi-darkness instead of actual illumination. "Are you doing this?" I point up at the lights when she looks over her shoulder at me.

She stops, waiting for me to catch up. "No. It's just the god."

"There's no god here, Anneeta."

"Then how do the lights come on?" She falls in next to me, walking again.

"Some kind of sensor? I've seen them before. Where I grew up, there was a god. And there were sensors for everything. All the lights were automated like this."

"Really?" She sounds astonished. "Did you ever meet the god?"

"Oh"—I laugh—"hell yes, I did. I was always in front of that fucker being punished."

"Punished?" She stops walking and looks up at me, hands on hips. "For *what*?"

"For… whatever. He was an asshole."

"What city did you grow up in?"

"Delta."

She's standing right under a light so I get the full effect of her crinkling nose as she stares up at me with squinted eyes. "Where's that?"

"All the way across the sand sea."

"Really? Did you come here in the tunnels?"

"Yep. I sure did."

"One day I'm gonna leave and I'm gonna use those tunnels to do it. Maybe I'll go to your city. Would you like me to say hello to anyone when I get there?"

I grab both her shoulders and turn her around. "Less talking, more walking."

She laughs a little, but does as she's told, keeping quiet and on task until we reach a real stairway. "This is the way down to the lower sectors."

"All right then. You can leave me here, if ya want. I think I can find it."

She shoots me a smarmy smile. Like she wants to tell me I'm full of shit, but she holds that in. "You can go first if you want. But I'm gonna follow just to keep an eye on you."

"Is the god telling you to do that?"

"What god? There's no god here, Tyse."

"Right. Whatever then. Let's go." I start down the stairs, hopping four or five at a time just to see if I can lose her. But she keeps up, jumping onto a railing and sliding down it to pass me, leaping off at the last minute when she gets to the landing. Then she waves a hand, letting me pass.

She's a weird kid. She's always been a weird kid. But I've never had this long of an interaction with her before, so I guess I never realized just *how* weird.

Clearly, she's in control of her situation. Which both makes me feel better and worries me more when I look too closely at what that means.

Everyone knows there's leftover tech in the tower. Obviously, it's how we get the spark. But there might be more going on in here than anyone realizes. And right now, I'm getting the impression that it's got something to do with this child.

But that's a problem for another day because I've been watching the sector numbers as we've been descending and we've reached a door with a large number four painted on it. So I stop and point to it. "Sector 4, right? How do we get to quad H minus five?"

Anneeta looks down into the black stairwell that might go on forever for all I know. Then she looks back at me as she simultaneously counts on her fingers and recites the alphabet. "A, B, C, D, E, F, G, H. That's eight. Which means four floors down, eight quads in."

"How do you figure that?"

"That's just how it works. It's sector 4, level H. Four, four, four."

"What about the minus five?"

"We'll deal with that when we get there."

I squint my eyes at her. "Are you sure you know where you're going?"

She tsks her tongue at me. "Are *you* sure *you* know where you're going?"

I throw up my hands. "Fine. Lead on."

We go down again, three more floors, then she stops at that door. This time the white spray paint says four dash four. Anneeta looks over her shoulder at me, smirking, as she opens it. Again, the lights come on when we enter the new dark passageway. But in here, they do not sputter. Nor are any of them dark.

In fact, I think I can hear a hum. Like… there's a

generator.

And if I didn't know better, I'd think the power was getting stronger.

But that's not supposed to be possible.

Surely Stayn knows how deep this tower is. He did give me coordinates, after all, so he's got some kind of blueprint of the place. Though I haven't seen any indication of them, there must also be security sensors down here, because that's how he got an alert. But does he know there's full-on power? I mean, the whole point of taking out the god was to take out its power. The spark is supposed to be something residual that can do small bits of work, but not with any reliability.

Everyone knows the god's power comes from a series of massive generators deep under the earth and that power can last for generations, even after the god is gone, because each god had thousands of banks of batteries for storage. I've never actually seen one in person with my own eyes, but while I was in Sweep I saw lots of things on vids and a battery bank was one of them. It was like… well, I couldn't really grasp the size of it until a marker was placed to give it perspective. The battery bank was ten times as big as the megalopolis above ground. We were told it could run for several centuries before actually drying up.

The tower in Tau City has been decommissioned for three hundred and twenty-five years, so it should be nearing the end of its life.

Battery banks are normal. Spark is normal. Generators running full-on power three hundred and twenty-five years after being decommissioned is *not*.

I look down at Anneeta and find her wide brown eyes already looking up at me. "Can you hear that?"

She nods, but doesn't say anything.

It's easy to see Anneeta as some kind of unfortunate accident. *Poor girl,* people say. *She'll never have a life outside the spark.* And it is sad, so I kinda agree on this point.

But what if... what if she's *not* an accident? What if there's something going on down here we're not aware of and she's a part of it?

I put my hands on both of her shoulders and bend down, looking her straight in the eyes. "Anneeta, what do you know that you're not telling me?"

She throws me that one-shoulder shrug she likes to do and averts her gaze. Which means she wants to lie, but hasn't made up her mind yet.

"Does the god talk to you?"

She looks back at me. Sniffles. Thinks. Answers. "I told you he did."

"A real god, Anneeta? Or... something else?"

"What else would it be?"

"I dunno. You tell me. What does this god talk about?"

"You."

"Me?" I laugh and stand back up. "Why the hell would he be talking about me?"

Her whole face screws up, like this question has confused the fuck out of her. "Well, it's a game, isn't it?"

"What's a game?"

"The Game of Gods. That what he said."

"The god says he's in a game?"

"No. The god says *you're* in a game."

"Do you know where this god is? I think we have things to discuss. Can you take me to him?"

"I can't *take* you to him."

"Why not?"

"Because. He's..." She spins in a quick circle, spreading her arms out. "He's everywhere. All around us."

"Well, what does he want with me?"

She stops spinning, looking a little dizzy for a moment, then laughs. "He wants you to *lose*, stupid." Then she just takes off, racing down the hallway. The lights above her flashing on, illuminating her way as she runs.

I yell, my words chasing her. "How do we get to the minus 5?"

"Come on! I'll show ya!"

Fuckin' kid. She's cute, I'll give her that. But the weirdness kinda cancels it out and I'm losing interest fast. It's hard to tell how much time has passed since we started this journey, but it's got to be an hour, at least. Which means it'll take another hour to get back up from this point alone. And we haven't even reached our destination yet.

The lights above start flickering off in rapid succession all the way down the hallway, so I have to decide what to do. I could leave Anneeta down here. I'm not worried about that. She can find her own way back, I'm sure. But I'm here. It's got to be close now. It would be a waste to just give up and leave without getting the information I came for.

So I set off after her, the lights coming on to light my way with a kind of sluggish reluctance that I didn't notice when I was watching Anneeta.

"You're imagining things," I mutter under my breath.

"This weird kid is starting to get to you."

Maybe. But I can't deny that I *do* hear a generator and the line of lights above me is rather bright.

Eventually I catch up with Anneeta again. She's lying on the floor now, directly under a light. This is when I notice her outfit. They are always kinda strange. A patchwork of things. She's wearing a skirt—she likes skirts, and they are always kinda poofy and made of weird fabrics only little girls wear—but she never wears *just* a skirt. She's a girl who likes layers. Which makes sense because Tau City has a dynamic climate. It's hot during the day, sometimes extremely hot, but nights are always cold. And the temperature isn't regulated inside the ruins. There's enough power for lights and whatever mechanicals are used for plumbing. You can run a few small appliances, clocks and shit. But there's no conditioned air like there is in the city beyond the ruins. No cooling, no heating. So layers are a must.

But Anneeta's layers are odd. Mismatched things. Discarded things, most likely. Striped tights, fuzzy leggings, or sometimes she wears two skirts at once. One practical layer under, one poofy layer over.

Still, they make her cute and give her a kind of whimsical innocence that stands at odds with the tower all around her. Her shirts are adult size, but cut up to fit her better. And again, she's always got layers on her upper body, long-sleeved Henleys and thermals running down her arms covered by a vest of some sort.

Today she's wearing brown tights, a light-blue ballerina skirt, a long-sleeved tan Henley, and a cropped fuzzy vest.

Her feet are in boots of brown leather that go halfway up her legs. Her hair is long and brown and almost always a mess and her face a little bit pale because she doesn't get enough sun.

But the funny thing is—as haphazard as this all seems—it also comes across as... put together. Like some fashion person personally picked out all these things and dressed her up for a runway show for eccentric children.

It works.

And I don't like that it works. It gives off a feeling that her sloppy put-togetherness has *purpose*.

"Well?" I ask.

She doesn't move. Just lies there in the floor looking up at me, smiling. "I'll leave you here. But I'll wait."

The door has a big white H minus 5 painted on it. I run the coordinates through my head again—Sector 4, quad H minus 5, floor 2. "Is floor two on the other side then?"

Anneeta shrugs her shoulders against the floor. "I've never been in there. Not even in a dream. This is as far as I go."

"You can't come? Or you don't want to come?"

"Can't."

"Why not?"

"Because..." She sits up and looks over her shoulder at the door, her head slowly tipping up to look at the H minus 5. Then her eyes meet mine, flashing a serious expression at me. "There's too much power in there. It will make me sick. Can't you *feel* it?"

I'm about to automatically say no and roll my eyes, but I realize I actually *can* feel it. It's... like... a disturbance in the air. Electromagnetic something or other. Which is a word I don't actually know the technical meaning of, but I've heard it enough during my time in the Sweep to understand that it fits here in this particular situation.

So I nod. "Yeah. I feel it." Then I offer her my hand, which she takes, and I pull her to her feet. "You don't have to wait."

"I know. But I will. It's my job to keep an eye on you now."

"Is that what the god told you?"

She nods. "That's what he said."

It's easy enough to dismiss her talk of gods. Or it would be, if a god didn't actually live in this tower at one time. But I don't dismiss it. I'm not sure what she's seeing, or hearing, or feeling or whatever, but it's real to her.

Which doesn't mean it's real to anyone else. Electromagnetic fields are like that. They can really fuck with your perception. So I make a mental note to ask Stayn —once I report back—if we could maybe get some kind of health care for her.

It's the least I can do after all her help.

"All right then. You wait if you want. I'll be back." Then I open the door and walk through into the dark.

Unsurprisingly, the lights overhead do not turn on when I take a few steps. I had a feeling it was Anneeta doing that on the other side of the door, and now it's confirmed. But it's fine. I just get my torch out and turn it on. It's bright enough to light up the entire length of the hallway—which, from here, makes the next door look very tiny, it's so far away.

When I finally get to the end of the hallway and open the door up, I find myself on a stairwell landing. I'm halfway between two floors. Assuming two is up and one is down, I go up. But the number painted on that door is a one. Then I remember that the numbers are negative, and my assumption was wrong because floor two is below.

I go back down, confirm that the new floor is indeed two, and pull it open. Immediately the electromagnetic humming stops and the new silence is deafening. Not that the hum was loud to begin with. Extremely low frequencies don't have to be loud to do what they are meant to do. But once you get used to the background noise, the absence of it is dramatic.

No lights in here either. This makes sense because if the hum is gone, then the power is too. Which is a direct contradiction to what Anneeta just told me. That she can't come because the power is too strong.

Unless... the hallway is a kind of gate, meant to keep her out.

This seemingly easy job is turning into a spectacular mystery.

I keep walking forward, shining my torch on the walls, looking for another door or... something. This is the end of my coordinates. But it is immediately clear that this is not a hallway that leads somewhere, it's a room. The actual destination.

"Well, fuck." I mutter this, scrubbing a hand down my face in frustration. Is this it? Because all I see is a bunch of tech towers of some kind. About nine feet tall and placed end to end so when seen all together they appear to be a solid wall. I'm not an expert in tech, ancient or otherwise. My time in the Sweep was mostly spent killing people and clearing shit, not studying relics.

But once I take a better look at them, they are familiar. I've been enough places to recognize these towers as something archaic. I was in a firefight once with some Outland deviants in the Outlands Terminal and we were stuck in a room like this for two days waiting for backup. One of the guys with us that day was a techie and he called them server towers. Which was like... a god's brain or something.

These are most definitely powered down. Which just adds to the mystery. Because something has to be going on in here, otherwise why would the sensor go off?

This question snaps me back into a more practical reality and I go looking for that sensor. My torch scans the walls for something that might detect motion.

I find them—hundreds of them, actually—mounted on the ceiling. All aimed down at the maze of walkways that exist between the server towers.

One of them, when I point my torch down at the floor, is ever-so-slightly blinking a blue-green light.

It's in the direct middle of the maze and that's when I realize there's a glow emanating up from the space below it.

My fingertips dance along my battle belt and a moment later I've got the VersiStrike in high ready as I move forward towards the nearest entrance to the cluster of servers.

The Versi comes with its own torch. I tap it on with a practiced fingertip as I slip my other light back in place on my belt. Then I walk forward, carefully and silently, eyes darting around, expecting something to happen.

A maze of server towers really is the correct way to describe the room I'm in. Sometimes when I turn a corner it's a dead end, a looming black tower acting as a wall. So I have to retrace, try again, then again. I've got no idea how long I stumble around trying to find the center because time seems to have stopped. Literally. The display on the Versi where the time should be has no readout.

But it's a while and I'm starting to get frustrated when I see a slight shift in the light levels around a corner and up ahead. Obviously, there is no one in here with me. And no attack is imminent because it should've happened already. So I walk faster but keep the Versi at high ready anyway.

When I get to the corner, I'm just about to turn when everything around me becomes a waterfall of blue. I take a step back in surprise, release a round from my weapon, sending flechette darts everywhere, and then let out a breath, feeling stupid.

I lower the Versi and look at the floor, shaking my head.

My augments came to life. That's all it was. Just my fucking implants. And the waterfall of blue is nothing but commands left over from some old mission or something.

Then, just as quickly as it appeared, it's gone. And in the darkness, the glow I've been looking for is back.

But it's what's in the center of that glow that has me scratching my head.

Because it's a woman.

A scantily dressed woman asleep on the floor of the ruined god's brain room.

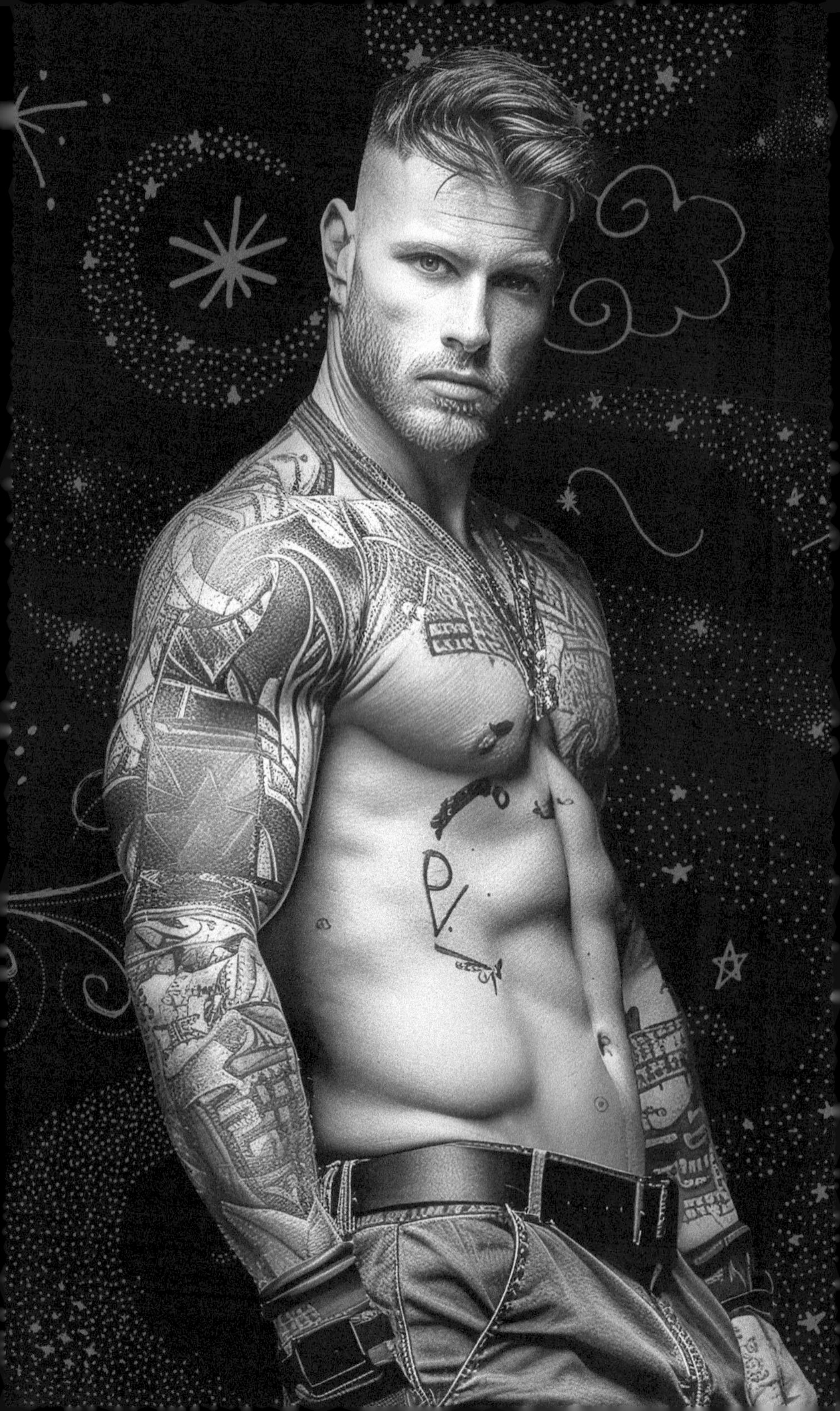

TYSE

CHAPTER TWENTY-ONE

"*Hey.*" I toe the woman with my boot. She doesn't move, so I do it again. "Wake up. What are you doing in here?"

No response. Just... deep breathing.

I wait for an attack, bracing for it. In my experience a half-naked girl lying on the floor in the middle of a place she ought not to be is nothin' but a trap.

But when it doesn't happen, I step backwards, keeping my Versi's torch trained on her as I put some distance between us. And then keep stepping until I bump up against one of the ruined servers.

I'm looking at her—right at her—when the glow that I was following just disappears. This is when it hits me that a minute ago my augments lit up and battle commands were scrolling down my field of vision.

But when I try and tap in and reconnect, it's... dead. Like it has been for the last seven years. Cursing myself under my breath, I shake off the memories that want to creep back in and concentrate on the woman in front of me. She's dressed funny, in sort of a costume. In all likelihood she's a whore and there was some kind of party down here and she got left behind.

It's the simplest explanation, which means it's probably true.

She's alone. I can feel it. I'm going to assume those sensors on the ceiling don't have cameras. Either that, or they stopped working, or maybe never worked in the first place because of the spark or that hum. This means there is a high probability that no one is watching, so I let out a breath, letting solutions run through my mind the way they used to back when I was in the Sweep.

Well, not at all the way they used to back in Sweep. That's the whole reason I'm no longer a soldier and live in a ruined god's tower.

I was first augmented on my fourteenth birthday. Then again, every year after that until I was nineteen. I was meant to be something special. Kind of a… super soldier of sorts.

But the augments never really took. Not the way they should've. I was given a commission as a specialist with computation upgrades. It wasn't a superpower, not at all. But in the beginning, it got me and my men out of a lot of sticky situations.

That didn't last long. My augments started wearing off around age twenty-one. And I was all washed up by the tender age of twenty-three.

That was seven years ago now and I haven't thought about those augments since.

But now—in this very moment—I am thinking about those augments because they were working. A minute ago, two at the very most, they were working. Data was falling down my field of vision in bright blue text. I could tell it was something to do with mission commands, but it was going too fast to actually read.

In the beginning, when the augments were fresh and working pretty good, I didn't need to *read* it to follow along.

Tomorrow's speed, today's mind!

My brain just understood and my body—senses, whole muscles groups, cognitive function—just responded without my input.

Be quick, be smart, be unbeatable!

That was the whole fuckin' point of having them in the first place.

Upgrade to instant reaction now!

Then, one day, the connection was gone and my mind hasn't been able to keep up with the software inside me since I was nineteen.

That's why you need BrainPulse!

So while I did have a couple of years there when I was able to react or form solutions to problems when high-stress situations triggered what was left of my augments, I wasn't in control of it.

In rare instances, users may experience severe side effects such as neural fatigue, prolonged cognitive dissonance, synaptic overload, or short-term memory fluctuations. Prolonged use may lead to dependency on the device for cognitive functioning.

And if *I* couldn't understand what the augments were telling me, then I couldn't trust them. That's the real reason they kicked me out of Sweep. If *I* couldn't trust me, *no one* could trust me.

But it doesn't matter now and this isn't a life-or-death

situation. It's just a stupid woman on the floor. I don't know how she got in here, but nonetheless, here she is.

My disturbance.

You don't need to be an augment to solve this problem. She needs to go.

I toe her again, pushing her shoulder a little, which makes her body rock. "Can you hear me?" I bend down and shake her. "Hey. Wake up. Party's over and it's time to go."

No movement at all. It's like she's unconscious, not sleeping.

Which is just fucking wonderful. She's not a big woman—she's rather small, actually. But dead weight is dead weight and now I'm gonna have to carry her all the way back up to the fuckin' lobby.

Hopefully the social workers are still there. If she doesn't wake up by then, she's their problem.

Resigned to this being the only solution, I scoop her up in my arms and then make my way back through the maze of dead servers, out the door, and back up the stairs the way I came.

After traversing the endless hallway, I reach the door where I left Anneeta. I kick it so I don't have to put the woman down. "Anneeta!" I yell it. "Open the door for me. My hands are full."

It comes swinging open and her little face is looking up at me in surprise. Then she scans down, seeing the woman in my arms. "Who's that?"

I push past Anneeta and start walking. "Dunno. But she was my disturbance. Was lying in the middle of a fuckin' server room, all passed out from partying last night."

Anneeta is trotting to keep up with me. "Party? Down here? I don't think so. I would know about something like that."

"Maybe you don't know as much as you think."

"Maybe you're just wrong?" She runs ahead of me now, making the lights pop on above us. Again, it hits me that they are strong and solid in this section when they should be weak and flickering.

But there's no time to think about that now.

Eventually we get back to the stairwell and then it's a long hike back up.

It feels like it takes forever to get back to the hallway with the lights that flicker, and by this time my arms are aching. I pause, putting the woman down, take a breath, then pick her back up, but this time I throw her over my shoulder to give my arms a break.

Anneeta snickers at me. "If she wakes up, she's gonna be mad that you're carrying her like a bag of flour."

"Who cares? Let her be mad then. That's what happens when you pass out a million floors below ground and trigger security sensors."

By the time we've reached the end of the ramp and people start appearing again, I realize I can't really carry her past the lobby without drawing a lot of attention due to her dress. Which, I've got to admit, is wildly sexy, but completely inappropriate for nighttime. It's below freezing in the tower right now. So I put her down again, shrug off my jacket, and Anneeta helps me put it on her and zip it up.

When we finally make it to the lobby the government ID

people are gone, but there's still a few people waiting in line for dinner services.

I look down at Anneeta, ready to ask her if she thinks the dinner people will take a passed-out woman, but I find her eyeballing the short pantry line in a way that has nothing to do with this woman over my shoulder.

She's hungry. I recognize the look. "Go on, go eat. I'll take care of her."

Anneeta looks back up at me, questions in her eyes. "What are you gonna do with her?"

I blow out a breath, frustrated. The closest health center is a long way off. I don't wanna do it. So I tell Anneeta the only other option I have. "Just... take her upstairs to my place and let her sleep it off, I guess."

Anneeta finds this solution to be acceptable, because she's nodding before I even finish. "That's a good idea. I'm super hungry. Are you hungry? Do you want me to bring you some dinner?"

"Thanks, it's a nice offer. But no. Go eat, then go to sleep. It's past your bedtime."

"OK, Tyse." She yawns cavernously as she talks. "I am pretty tired. And hungry. I'll come check on you tomorrow."

"Hey, wait."

She turns and looks at me.

"Check my pocket." I nod my head down to the one along the side of my leg. "Take four coins. Hell, take five."

Her eyes brighten. "Thanks!" Then she shoves her hand into the pocket, pulls out a handful of coins, counts out five, then drops the rest back into my pocket as she flashes me her new toothless grin. "Now I really will come by tomorrow!" Then she skips off and joins the short line for dinner, looking over her shoulder one more time to wave.

What a weird day. And I've only been awake for the end of it.

I hit the main stairwell, still carrying the woman like a sack of flour, and find that very few people are interested in the fact that I'm hauling an unconscious woman up to my quarters. A few of them make jokes, but most of them don't even look twice.

That's the thing about living in the God's Tower ruin—pretty much anything goes. As long as you don't mess with people, they don't mess with you.

By the time I get home and drop the woman facedown onto my bed, I'm exhausted. It's been a while since I did so much physical exercise and I probably climbed forty or fifty flights of stairs in the past few hours.

Once I've unloaded her, I grab the disposable phone from the trash can, checking for battery. It's at three percent, but that's good enough to shoot off one text to Stayn: *Found your disturbance. All good now. Check in tomorrow.*

It sends, but immediately after, it does the death beep, so I throw it back in the trash.

Then I turn and look at the woman. What now? Wake her up? Is she dying? Should I take her to the health center anyway?

I actually laugh out loud at the thought. It's not happening.

After all that exertion I'm due a shower. So I take myself

over to the bathroom, which is just a tiny space separated from the kitchen by a curtain.

A few seconds later my battle belt is hanging over a chair and my shirt is on the floor. I peek past the shower curtain, start the water—praying there's enough power up here right now to get it lukewarm—and then sit down in the chair and unlace my boots as I stare at the woman on my bed.

She's pretty, I'll give her that. Long blonde hair, nice body... *niiiiice* body. And a little bit slutty. Which is... kinda how I like 'em.

I'm just about to chuckle at my internal monologue when all of a sudden, my augments come to life again. The waterfall of text starts falling, too fast to read. But the moment I think that, they slow down. And I realize it's just one sentence repeating over, and over, and over.

Hide her.

Then it all disappears again. And the moment it does, every hair on my body sticks up on end. The spark.

I close my eyes, shaking my head. I hate that the augments can still affect me like this. And it has been quite a while since it's happened, so I kinda forgot how creepy it could be.

Back when I was younger, at the peak of my augmentation around age seventeen, it was a seamless interaction. I would think something and the augments would contribute. It was a little like a discussion—a brainstorming, maybe. Ideas floated, considered, discarded. But *I* was in charge, the tech was just a tool I controlled. The same way I control my hands and eyes. The blue text scrolling down my field of vision didn't come off as some kind of trespassing personality back then. Those were all my thoughts, enhanced. *It* was me.

This isn't how it feels now. Now these words are an intrusion. A violation, almost. It feels like a parasite. I would've gotten them removed, but it can't be done. Maybe, if you change your mind early enough, like within six months to a year after the tech is first introduced into your bloodstream, they can be filtered out. It takes about two years for them to really implant into your neural network.

But that would've put me at about age fifteen. And at age fifteen I couldn't fucking wait to join the Sweep. There was no way I'd turn back.

Boots off now, I stand up, looking over my shoulder at the woman one last time, then take off the pants. She's still sleeping. Or unconscious or whatever. So I get the shower —the water isn't even close to lukewarm—wash up as quick as I can, then step out with a towel wrapped around my waist.

The next thing I know, I'm staring down the barrel of my own VersiStrike.

I blink at the half-naked woman's glare. She's still wearing my jacket, but it's unzipped now, like she was about to take it off and got distracted. So I can see her whole bare stomach. Her hands are shaking as she points the weapon at me. It was a pretty stupid mistake to leave my battle belt somewhere she could get a hold of it. But in my defense, I thought she was unconscious and even with it pointed at my face, she doesn't come off as threatening.

Not to a guy like me.

I put my hands up, wave one of them, and try on a smile. "Hello. Nice to see you've recovered."

She doesn't say anything, not right away. She stares at me for a moment, eyes narrowed with suspicion. Then she starts stepping back, putting distance between us.

"I'm not holding you hostage or nothin', lady. You're free to leave whenever you want. But if you try and take my Versi with you, I will hunt your ass down and take it back. So why don't you just put it on the bed on your way out the door and we'll call this whole thing even."

Her arms stiffen and she shakes the Versi at me. It's got a hair trigger, that thing. And I can't tell from this angle if she's got the safety off, or what setting she's got it on, but when I used it last night, it was set to flechette. I only keep two cartridges of those loaded at any given time, so she only gets one shot. But it's pretty hard to miss a target standing six feet away with a Versi set on flechette and I can't think of a worse way to end this day than being assaulted with a barrage of tactical darts by a woman dressed like last night's whore.

Especially when I just hauled her ass up a million flights of stairs.

"Who are you?" She's spitting words at me. "Where's the god?" She looks around, like there might be a god hiding in the corner of my tiny quarters. "Where *am I!*" She yells this last part, then starts shaking the Versi at me again.

I put up a hand, trying to remain calm. "Woman. *Do not* shake that weapon. It's very sensitive and if you shoot me, I *will* kill you. Do you understand?"

She takes a breath and narrows her eyes. "Not if I kill you first."

"You get one chance. Got it? And while being shot with a VersiStrike flechette cartridge would be epically painful and cause a lot of scarring, it most definitely will *not* kill me." Now it's my turn to narrow down my eyes at her. "So you will *not* be killing me first. You will just be pissing me off. And I get it, we don't know each other. But take a nice, good, long look at me, darlin'." She does. Her eyes fall all the way down my mostly naked body, then come back up to meet mine. "Do I look like the kind of man you wanna piss off?"

It's a rhetorical question. I'm covered in Sweep tats, battle scars, and even though I've been out of service for seven years now, I'm nothing but muscle. I mean, while it was a bitch to carry her ass up those sixty million flights of stairs, there is a little part of me that's proud I could still do something that physically demanding.

I feel the augments in this moment. It's like a shot of endorphins. And then the blue words are falling down my vision again. They are senseless words this time. Or something more like symbols. Then something really fucking weird happens.

The woman in front of me begins to glow.

I meet her gaze and she gasps, taking quick steps back. She trips over something, the Versi fires, and tactical darts come flying out.

I duck, just on instinct, but luckily, she was pointing it at the ceiling and when I look up there are several hundred scars in the cement above my head.

My gaze wanders back to the woman, who is crouching on the floor, and now I'm angry. I walk over to her, grab the barrel of my weapon, and yank it from her grip. She shrinks back, putting her hands up like I'm about to hit her.

And this pisses me off even more. "Go on, get out if you want. I don't need this shit." I point the Versi at her—it can't automatically reload a flechette cartridge because that was the only one in the magazine, so it's gonna stay empty until I change the setting or meet a very specific set of high-threat circumstances that this woman will never be able to trigger. But I direct it at her anyway just to make a point. "I saved your life. You were passed out a million levels below ground. You would've died down there. So… ya know… you're fuckin' welcome."

"Who are you?" Her voice is shaky now. "What is this place? Where the fuck am I and how did I get here?"

I hold up a finger, ready to make a list. "Tyse." And then a succession of fingers come flying up as I tick off the rest of the answers. "The God's Tower ruin. You're here, inside it. In my quarters. And I already told ya. I carried your ass up a million levels of stairs from below ground. Specifically, sector 4, quad H minus 5, floor 2. Which is, as it turns out, the fucking dead brain room of the ruined god."

"Ruined god?" She looks thoroughly confused. "But… *what?*"

Her face is so contorted with this confusion, I actually laugh. "You must've been really stoned. That must've been some party."

"Party? You mean the gala?"

"Kind of a fancy word for a fucking sparkfest, but OK. Call it whatever you want."

She just blinks at me for many, many seconds. And the weird thing is, she doesn't look stoned. I mean, for someone who was out cold the whole time I was carrying her up those stairs, she looks like any woman who just woke up after a normal night's rest and not anything like one who partied so hard the night before, she blacked out.

I extend my hand and take a few steps forward. She looks at it with suspicion, then up at me. "Your eyes."

"What about them?"

"They're… *blue*."

"So are yours."

She shakes her head. "No. Not that kind of blue."

I turn and walk over to the mirror over the small sink. And sure enough, my eyes are shining an unnaturally bright blue. An indicator that the augments inside me are working at the moment. This is what scared her. That's why she stepped backwards and tripped.

I frightened her.

I let out a long breath, then walk back over to her, extending my hand once again. "It's just the augments. I don't know why, after all these years, they're acting up like this, but it's nothing you need to worry about."

Me, on the other hand? Yeah, I'm startin' to get a little worried.

But I don't tell her that. Instead I say, "Come on. Get up," and shake my offered hand at her.

She hesitates, deliberating. But what other choice does she have? She takes it and I pull her up off the ground.

We stare at each other for a few moments, then she pulls the jacket tight across her half-naked torso, dialing down her slutty factor, but only marginally.

But my slutty factor has been dialed up, I guess. Because I'm wearing nothing but a towel and she's staring pretty hard at me. I chuckle, then turn away. "I'm gonna get dressed and be right back."

I take the Versi with me, stuff it back into my battle belt, and then grab a pair of tactical pants off a shelf by the sink and step into the shower, pulling the curtain closed behind me.

Once that's done, I come back out, expecting her to be gone, but find her sitting in my favorite chair near the steel-shutter window.

I downed all my whiskey last night so I don't have anything to drink but water, there's definitely no food in the cupboards, and she's not here for sex, so... I really don't know what to do with her now that the preliminaries are over.

The chair she's in is the only one I have besides the spindly thing holding my battle belt, but there's a weird vibe floating through this room right now so I lean against the wall instead, silently kinda fuming that she took my chair and is causing all this awkwardness.

"Sooooo." I don't really have anything to say to her, so that's all I've got.

"So," she says back.

"Do you... need coin, or something?"

"Coin?" She squints her eyes at me. "Why would I need coin? I'm in the God's Tower, right?"

"Yeah."

"So… where the hell is he? You're not him, obviously."

"Where the hell is… *who*?"

"The *god*." She says this in a mocking tone. Like I'm a literal idiot.

I chuckle. "The god? The god is *dead*, darlin'. Has been for hundreds of years."

"Dead? How could he be dead? He *summoned* me last night."

My chuckle turns into a laugh. "Did he now?"

"He rang the bells. I'm number nine. He can't be dead. He's been calling us in for nearly a decade now."

"What the hell are you talking about?"

"He's not dead! I'm Maiden number nine. Clara Birch. I'm Clara Birch! He *called me*! That bastard had better not be dead because I gave up my whole fucking life to come into this tower! I gave up Finn! I gave up all my riches! I gave up everything and I wanna see that fucking god, right fucking now!"

She sits there huffing at me. Her face bright red with anger, or frustration, or both.

In my experience, crazy women need to be dealt with in a certain way. You ignore them as best you can depending on the circumstances.

So I ignore the psycho outburst and proceed with questioning. "Is that why you were in the server room?" She shoots me another frenzied, wild look. Maybe she's still high from last night, or something. She doesn't look high, but maybe there's some new drug out there that I don't know about?

"I don't even know what a server room is. I walked through the door, it closed behind me, and I woke up here." She points to the ground. *"In your bed."* She growls those words out. "So what happened to me and how did I end up waking in your bed while you were naked in the shower?"

My laugh is now a guffaw. I point to myself. "Are you accusing me of something? I saved you. How many times do I have to say it? You were a—"

"A million levels below ground. I heard you. But that doesn't seem very likely."

"Doesn't it?" I laugh again. "You're funny, ya know that? I haven't laughed this much in years. You're welcome, by the way."

"You've already said that, too."

"For the coat, I mean. You're wearing my coat. That dress is something else. You look like a whore from the Shipping District."

She sneers at me. "I didn't pick the dress. Obviously, I know I look like a fucking down-city tavern whore. But thank you for reminding me, I feel so much better now."

"Down-city!" My mouth falls open in shock. "Wow. I haven't heard that term since I was Sweeping the Omega Outlands. *Down-city.*" I shake my head. "You're a fuckin' princess, huh? Up-city Clara Birch. Yeah, it kinda fits."

She scowls at me, her face goin' even redder than it was. "Wha... I don't..." Then she blows out a breath. "I only meant that I understand that I look ridiculous. I didn't get to choose the dress. The Matrons did. It was delivered. I had no choice, I just had to put it on! I mean, I did object, of course, but I was trying to be poised, proper, and polite, for fuck's sake! Nine! Nine Maidens!" Her eyes dart back and forth, searching mine for understanding. She takes a breath, trying to calm down, and then her last few words come out low, nearly whispered. "It wasn't supposed to happen this way. I was number nine. Tyse? That's your name?"

I nod.

"I was Maiden number *nine*. Nine chances out of ten that I would not get called into the tower. Ninety-percent chance of total happiness. And I get it—how ironic that the girl who was Chosen, and placed so high because she was in love with the Extraction Master's son, gets what's coming to her." She huffs out a sardonic laugh here. "I bet people were even happy about it. I bet they were saying I deserved it."

I'm not even sure what to say. She's... crazy. Her explanation, if that's what it was supposed to be, made so little sense, I kinda stopped listening back at the first mention of 'nine.' "Uhhhh..." I scrub my hands down my face, absently wondering, *Why me?* "Maybe we should get you to a health center?" I say it very slowly, trying to keep her calm.

"What?"

"For some tests."

"Tests?"

"Look, I don't know what you were smokin' at that party last night. Or maybe... you're like... one of those people who can't handle the spark?"

She wheezes out an incredulous snort. "*What?*"

"But you're not makin' no sense, lady. And I... I'm just the wrong guy, ya know?"

She growls at me. "Wrong guy for *what?*"

"I don't know what you're lookin' for here. Comfort? Sympathy?"

"What?"

"Whatever emotional reaction you're trying to get out of me, it's… just… you know." I shrug. "Not my thing."

"Not your *thing*?"

"I'm just not… the responsible party, right? I don't play that game."

She takes a breath, eyes narrowing down. "I don't need you to *save me*, if that was the conclusion you just jumped to. I never asked you to save me. I'm trying to figure out what happened once I walked through the damn door! And for your information, I can handle the spark, OK? I might be number nine, but I lit up like a fuckin' sun!"

"OK." I don't even know what else to say. But she doesn't elaborate, just stares at me with her mouth open, so I gotta fill up the silence with something. "How about this? I'll take you down to the patrol. I know the chief. He's a friend. In fact, he's the one who sent me down there to look for you. Well, not specifically you. Just to check out the disturbance you were creating. I'm sure he's totally interested in this story you're tellin'. It's just… well, I'm really not."

Slowly her hand comes up in front of my face. And then, even more slowly, she raises her middle finger and shoves it right up to the end of my nose. "Fuck. You."

I slap her hand away. "Ya know, for such an up-city *Birch*, you've got quite the potty mouth going."

Her mouth falls open, aghast. Then her eyes dart past mine, focusing on something. The next thing I know, she's pushing past me, heading for the door.

I wave my fingers at her. "Bye. You're welcome. I'm really fucking glad I saved you by *hauling your ass up all those stairs*! You've been a complete delight."

She grabs the door handle and pulls. But the door doesn't open. She turns to look at me, growling again. "Open. The door. Right now. I want to go."

"So go. It's not locked."

"Bullshit, it's not locked! Look!" She grabs the handle again and tugs. But it won't open.

I walk over, push her out of the way, and pull on the door. But it really doesn't open. "What the fuck?" I try again, but it's stuck. The handle moves, but the door doesn't so much as budge.

Which isn't even possible. Nothing locks in the tower unless you've got a private padlock on it. And I never bothered. I've got a stash of coin hidden here, of course. And it's worth a lot. But if someone were to steal it, I'd just restock. My one really valuable possession is the Versi, but I never leave it behind when I go out and while I know the people in this tower are mostly crazy, they're not crazy enough to steal my weapon. It's literally the only Versi outside the Omega Outlands. They couldn't even pawn it.

All that is beside the point. I kick the door. "Anneeta! Are you out there? Are you doing this?" I listen, but no one answers on the other side. "Anneeta!" I kick the door again. "If this is your idea of a joke, I'll kick your little ass if you don't knock it off right now!"

Just silence from the other side.

The woman comes over, pressing her face to the door. "Help! Someone! Help! The door is stuck!"

"Shouting is pointless. There's no one out there."

"It's not pointless when you do it, just when I do. Is that what you're saying?"

I point at the door. "Can ya hear anyone out there?" She pauses to press her ear to the metal. "No. Didn't think so."

She pulls back from the door and looks up at me with crossed arms. "Then who the hell is Anneeta?"

"A trouble-causing kid, that's who. This is her doing. I don't know how she did it but it's got to be her, 'cause—" But just as I'm saying that, the blue letters are back, again telling me to hide her.

The woman points at me. "Your eyes are doing that creepy blue thing again."

"Thanks for the heads-up."

She huffs. "What's it saying?"

"What makes you think it's saying something?"

She shoots me a look. This look says she thinks I'm the dumbest person she's ever met. "I can *see them*?"

"You can see what?"

"The letters. I just can't read them, they're blurry."

I glance inward at the letters on my field of vision, then expand it out to her. "You can read them?" Then something hits me. "Wait. Are you from the Outlands?"

"The Outlands? No. I'm from Tau City."

I laugh. "You're definitely not from Tau City."

"The hell I'm not. I grew up there. I live in the Maiden Tower. Well, I *did* live there. Until last night when I walked through the God's Tower door."

"This *is* Tau City. And there is no god in Tau City, lady. It's been dead for hundreds of years, I've already told ya that. And I've never heard of a Maiden Tower. There's no Maiden Tower."

She lets out a breath, but her eyes are flashing anger as they look around my small room. "Is that a window?" She points at the window, which is covered in steel shutters.

"Yes."

"Can you open it?"

"We're ten floors up. You can't get out that way."

She hisses her words at me. "I don't want to jump. I want to look out."

I'm annoyed at this request because the shutters are old, and rusty, and a pain in the ass to close after they've been opened. I haven't looked out that window in a couple years, at least. But I go over there, fuck with it for nearly three minutes, and finally the louvers flip open.

I stand aside and present her with the view.

She comes over, lifting her dress up with dainty fingertips, and looks out, pressing her face up to the shutter. She doesn't say anything.

"Well?" I ask, after many silent seconds tick off.

"I don't understand what I'm seeing. It's… very bright."

"Well, it's night so… you know. All the fucking lights are on."

"But even down-city." She looks over her shoulder at me, wincing. "I mean, the lower end of the canal. There's no power down there. Not for lights."

"Of course there's power down there. There's power everywhere. Tau City is a Level One metropolitan area."

"What's that?" She sticks a finger through the louver, like this is gonna help me see what she's pointing at.

I lean in and bend down, trying to follow her point. "What's what?"

"All that down there? Where the up-city towers should be. It looks like... a ruin."

"Well, I'm glad you're finally accepting reality. It looks like a ruin because it *is* a ruin. As I've said several times now, there is no god in Tau City. The tower was decommissioned centuries ago. It's a place for spark addicts now. And... people like me. Who just... kinda hate society and don't want to participate."

Suddenly, she whirls around. Out of instinct I take a step back. "Wait! What about Haryet! Did you find her too?"

"Harriet? Who the hell is Harriet?"

"Har-yet. *Haryet*. She was number eight. She came the night before."

I point to the floor. "Came here?"

"Yes! Two Maidens in two days!" She says these words with manic excitement. But then she deflates with a long breath of air. "Imogen, Marlowe, Mabel P., Lucy, Mabel S., Piper, Brooke, Haryet, and me. Gemna's the only one left."

"Well... I don't know what to say about that. The only reason I went looking for you is because Stayn asked me to. He can't come inside the tower himself. Well, I guess he could, but uptight up-city fucks like him think they'll get addicted to the spark if they even come in once." I chuckle. "I like that term. Up-city. I'm gonna call him that next time I see him."

Clara's face is blank. Like I'm speaking some other language. But she doesn't yell at me again and she doesn't throw a tantrum. In fact, I watch in real time as she gives up, flopping down into my chair.

Which makes me point at it. "Uhhh, that's my chair."

She looks at the chair, then up at me. "What?"

"My chair. You're sitting in it and… you should just sit somewhere else. The bed or that one over there by the shower. But I'm warning you, if you touch my weapon again, I'll break your fingers."

She laughs. Then laughs again.

"What's so funny?"

But she doesn't answer. Just gets up, walks the three paces over to the end of the bed and crawls up it, flopping onto the pillow face down.

I'm not sure what to do next, but I did make a big deal about the chair, so I figure I should sit in it. Which I do. Then put my feet up on the foot stool.

I'm hungry, but there's no food in here. And the door is locked—which is a mystery I really should solve sooner rather than later. But now that I am sitting, the day catches up with me and I realize that Stayn told me that there was a magnetic lock keeping people out of the location where I found Clara.

But there wasn't.

There is, however, one on my door right now. That has to be why we can't open it.

Fuckin' weird.

My head starts spinning a little with all the sudden mysteries, not to mention the fatigue from all that stair climbing. Plus the hunger, and the added stress of arguing with a strange woman, and the sudden rebirth of my long-dead augments.

At some point during the past few minutes the words 'hide her' faded away, but I can still feel the connections. It's not strong, but I've been living with no connections whatsoever for seven years now, so even the slightest bit of spark up there is a major development.

I close my eyes, thinking about this. About the way the blue words fell down like a waterfall. I feel the smile creeping up my face, and the guys all around me. Like I'm there again.

Dusty, it was always dusty. And it was always dangerous too. The Omega Outlands is a lawless place. But there were always moments, in between the deadly ones, when we were all together—me, Jast, Myra, Stepan, and Kirt. And when we were all together like that it was… OK. Maybe not good, but it was OK because we were all still alive.

My smile fades. Because we're not all still alive now.

I'm the only one who made it out and none of this is real.

It's just some dream about some place and a woman who I must hide.

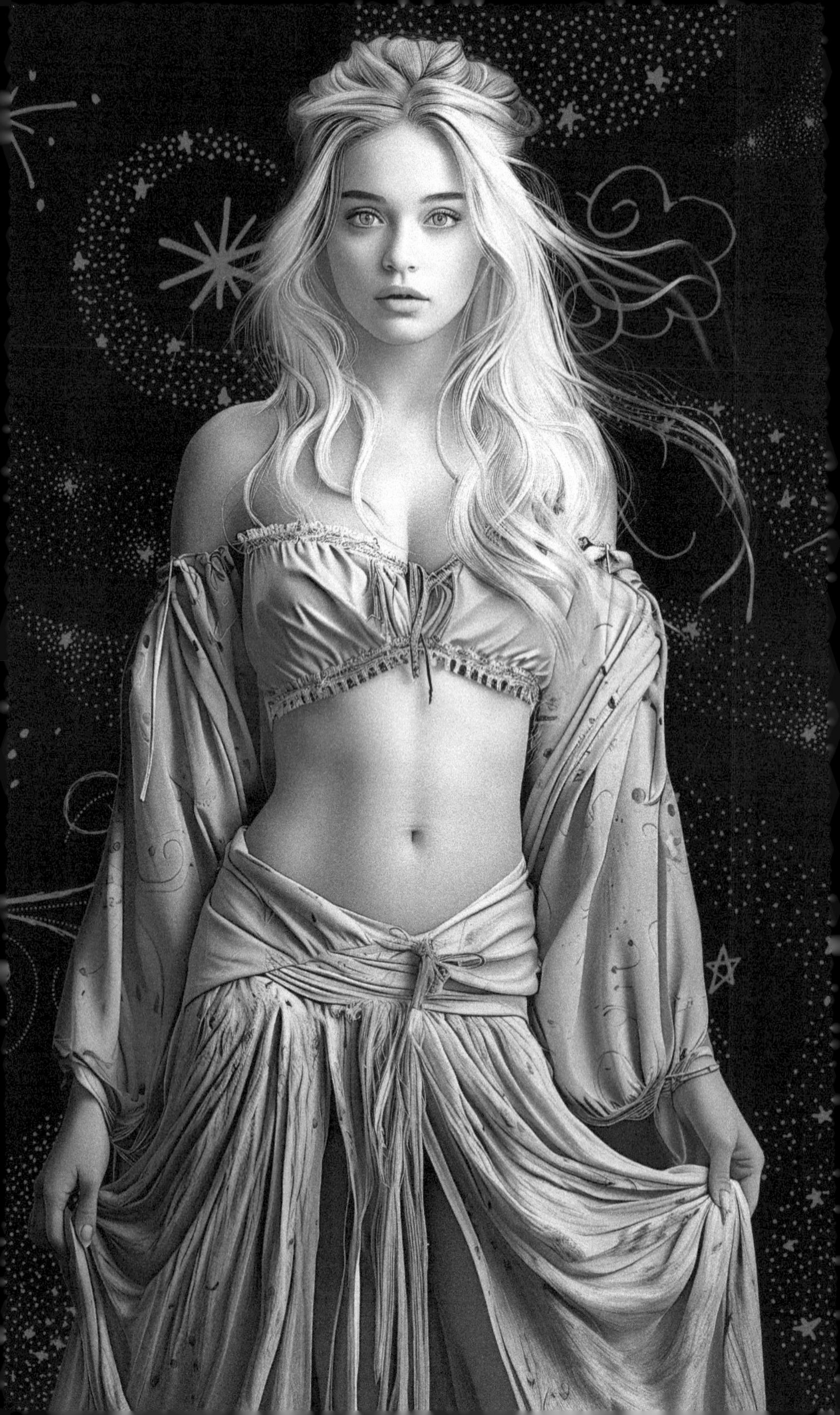

CLARA

CHAPTER TWENTY-TWO

I'm watching him through one open eye as he drifts off to sleep.

I see his eyes close, and his body relax, and then the strange blue light leaks out past his eyelids and he smiles. Like he's hiding a secret.

But then the smile drops and he sighs. A very long, tired sigh.

He's already asleep, I can tell. But he's dreaming or something. Because he's unsettled.

Then the blue light is gone and whatever that dream was, it's over.

I hold my breath, waiting to see if he wakes up. When he doesn't—when he starts breathing deeper—I move around a little. Making some noise. Testing to see how tired he really is. He *looks* absolutely exhausted. The dark shadows around his eyes are a stark contrast to his pale face under the dim lights of the dingy quarters, making him look like a specter.

But he also looks... very... fit. So while he may be sleeping, I'm not convinced that it's deep. So I wait a little longer.

When he doesn't move for several more minutes, I get

up and walk over to the door, trying the handle again. It turns, but the door does not budge.

I press my lips into the doorframe crack and whisper, "Hello?" then look over my shoulder to see if I woke Tyse.

He's out cold. So I try again, this time adding the name he used earlier. "Anneeta? Are you there?" I have no idea who this Anneeta is, or whether or not she's the one responsible for the door locking, but it can't hurt at this point. I need to get out of here. I don't understand what's going on. This can't be the tower. I'm dreaming, or something. Or dead.

That thought sends a shiver up my spine.

But then I think of Haryet. I need to find Haryet. I mean, I get that Imogen and the others—the Mabels, and Piper, and the rest—they're probably dead. Their trip into the tower was years ago. But Haryet was yesterday. Or... the day before. I'm not really sure how much time has passed. But it's two days, max. She has to be here.

Wherever 'here' is.

He says this is Tau City, but what I saw outside was not my Tau City. The towers were so tall. And bright. It was so bright. Like the people down there have never even considered the idea that spark should be rationed. Also, I could only sort of see the canal. It was there, I saw the shimmer that indicates water where the canal should be, but it wasn't bright blue like it is at home. I don't know what's going on with that. It's not even important, I guess.

Haryet is important.

Because there is no god here. Tyse said the god has been dead for hundreds of years. It doesn't matter if it makes sense or why it's happening this way. The only thing that matters is that there is no evidence that a god lives like... *this*.

So I believe him.

And if there is no god here, then my duty is over.

I suck in a long breath, hold it for a moment, and then let it out.

What's in the place of that breath is something I never thought I'd have again.

Hope.

Because if there is no god, and if my duty is over, then I am free to go home.

Which means my dreams of a life with Finn aren't dead.

I still hate him. But... in a I-love-him way, of course. You don't throw away your lifelong love over a trip into the tower. Not when it turns out the whole thing was either a total fabrication or a mistake. If there's a chance to salvage our relationship and make that off-the-cuff dream of him being a scholar, and me being a wife and mother, come true, then I'm here for it.

All I have to do is find my way back to the door. Which, according to the man-baby sleeping in that chair across the room, is a million levels below ground.

But it can't be a million. And while he is a very fit specimen of a man, he's definitely not a god, he's just a regular guy. Of... whatever species he belongs to. With weird blue lights in his eyes. And kinda hot. Maybe even... very hot.

I turn, leaning back against the door, and stare at the man across the room. Standing up, he's extremely tall. But even sitting down, he takes up a lot of space. His hair is something between brown and ginger. That little bit of red could be from the lighting in here—which is a warm tone—but his beard also has some red in it. The sides of his head are shaved, but the rest is long and tied back at the nape of his neck.

Almost his entire upper body is covered in tattoos, but what's not appears to be scarred. I can't see them well from here, but I got a good enough look while we were facing off in the argument.

The tattoos and scars aren't the only notable things about his upper body. He's muscular. He did, after all, carry me up a million flights of stairs to save my life.

Apparently.

I get a little lost looking at him, but shake myself out of it. The point is—going back down those stairs has got to be a whole lot easier than going up them. And that's my plan. Get out of here, go down, find the door, and go home.

I pause to smile. Then a chuckle escapes past my lips. Because I am imagining what the people of Tau City will think when they see me. When they realize a Maiden has returned.

I will have answers for them. We will never send another girl into that tower. The Extraction will be over, Finn and I will be married, and Tau City will live happily ever after.

A small snort comes out with the next laugh. It's a ridiculous dream, I get it.

But it doesn't seem unattainable.

I mean, that door has to be somewhere. All I have to do is find it.

I turn back around and knock softly on the door in front of me, giving it one more try. "Hello? Anneeta? Anyone? Can you hear me?" I press my ear to the cold metal, listening.

But it's completely silent out there.

So I sigh, and look back at the bed. Then at the man sleeping in the chair.

I will admit that he looks dangerous. Like he was in a war. My eyes dart over to that weapon of his hanging in the belt on the chair. It was very heavy. Took two hands for me to lift it. I know Tau City has weapons, but I've never seen anything like that. And those darts it shot—my eyes glide up to the ceiling where the evidence of my stupidity remains.

I could've shot him. I nearly did.

My gaze wanders back down to the man in the chair again. This time I study those scars of his and decide it wouldn't have been the first time he was shot.

This is when I realize I'm still wearing his jacket. I look down at it—trying not to see the slutty dress I'm still wearing—and find there are patches sewn on the shoulders and front. They all look very official, but other than that, they are beyond my comprehension. Tau City had a patrol, of course, but they all wore regular clothes. Certainly nothing like this jacket.

Which is another difference—the clothing. His clothes are very strange. Granted, I haven't seen a good enough sample size of people here to make any kind of fashion determination, but he's definitely not wearing gauzy desert robes or oversized linen pants. His pants are black and have a lot of pockets. I've actually never seen a garment like that and black isn't a common color in my version of Tau City. Everything is a soothing neutral, the colors of sand and sun-bleached blue.

"If you're not gonna sleep on the bed, then I will."

The man's words surprise me. I was too busy staring at his body and studying his clothes to realize he had woken up.

Tyse stands up, rubbing his hands down his exhausted face, and then sighs. "I'm not holding ya prisoner." But just as he says these words, that blue light is back in his eyes. Talking to him. Maybe even disagreeing with him. "If you can get the door open, feel free to leave."

Then, as if that's the last thing he ever expects to say to me, he flops onto the bed, facedown.

I stand still, holding my breath, waiting to see what happens next.

But all I hear is the soft sound of a sleeping man.

Which is just great. I had a bed and now I don't.

I suppose I'll have to take the chair. Because the door is most definitely locked and it's probably that weird time of the night when everyone in the city is soundly sleeping so there's no hope that anyone will wander by outside to ask for help.

The problem is, I don't think I *can* sleep. Not in a strange room with a strange man.

This makes me actually chuckle out loud because that's the least of my problems. I'm in a strange place with no god. A place that calls itself Tau City, but is most certainly not my version of Tau City.

It feels like a... fiction. Something made up. Like a fantasy story in a children's book.

I cross the room and sink into the chair. Then I turn to the side and sigh. I'm not going to freak out. I refuse to be afraid.

If I came here, I can leave here.

And that's exactly what I plan to do.

***

I WAKE to the sound of voices. Lots of voices. Sitting up, I realize the door has been opened and people are out in the hallway. It's what I wanted, but I find myself in a nearly blind panic and unable to move because the reality of my situation feels a lot scarier this morning than it did last night.

I look to my right, scanning for Tyse. But the curtain to the bathroom is open and I don't think his quarters have any other rooms. So he left. And he left the door open so I would know it's unlocked.

Does he want me to leave?

Probably. Most likely he left hoping I'd be gone when he got back so he wouldn't have to see me again.

A man walks by and I catch his eye, which causes him to do a full stop. "Hi." He's turned now, like he's going to enter the room, and I'm about to panic when he's shoved forward so forcefully, he disappears from view. All I catch is the hard thump of a body hitting the floor, then Tyse is standing in the doorway in profile, looking at the man he just pushed.

"Keep walking, Asrel. And if you ever take another peek into my room without permission, I'll scoop your eyes out with a spoon."

Even though that threat wasn't directed at me, the image alone is enough to make me draw back.

Tyse enters holding two brown paper bags. His blue eyes meet mine as he kicks the door closed with his foot. "You're awake."

"And still here, much to your dismay."

He narrows his eyes at me, but doesn't respond. Just brings the bags around to a little table next to the chair. "Don't know what kind of food they've got in your parallel universe, but here in Tau City we usually have bacon, biscuits, and coffee. So that's what's on the menu for breakfast." He points to the bags, then grabs the footstool in front of the chair and pulls it up to the side table, taking a seat.

I open the bag, take out the biscuit sandwiches wrapped up in white paper, and place them both on the table while he opens the other bag and brings out two thermoses of coffee, putting one in front of me and one in front of him.

It's a bit weird to be eating with a complete stranger after spending the night in his quarters. But, actually, that's the least weird thing about my life at the moment. And I'm very hungry, so I concentrate on eating. The food is good. Tastes normal. The coffee is also pretty ordinary. But this just adds to the dissociation I'm feeling. It's all very familiar, but strange at the same time.

Disconcerting is the word I'm looking for.

It's silent for a few minutes, but then he's already done with his food and gulping down his coffee. After that, he leans back on the footstool and braces his elbows on the bed, staring at me.

"What?" I ask, my mouth full of bacon and biscuit.

"You."

I cover my lips with my hand. "What about me?"

"I asked all around about a party down in the dungeon levels, but no one seems to recall one."

I swallow, then take a breath. "I told you. I came through the God's Tower door from Tau City."

"Woman, this *is* Tau City."

I don't know how to explain it, so I shrug. "It's a different Tau City. I don't know. I walked through the door and the next thing I knew, I'm lying on your bed and you're in the shower. That's it. That's all I have."

"Well, you fell and hit your head or something. It gave you a memory hole. That's the only explanation."

"Or," I sneer, "I really did walk through the God's Tower door and woke up here."

He sighs, then reaches a hand into his pocket and pulls out a small device, holding it up to show me. "Should I call Stayn then?"

"Who the hell is Stayn?"

"My friend. The patrol chief. I told you, he sent me down into the lower levels to find the disturbance that was setting off his sensors." Now he points to me. "You were the disturbance. And if you're just gonna lie to me, well, I don't like liars. So I'm just gonna report you and be done with the whole fucking thing."

"I don't know what you want me to say to that."

"I want you to tell me the truth."

"I *did*."

"Well, your definition of truth and my definition of truth don't seem to come from the same dictionary."

I put the bacon biscuit back on the paper and let out a frustrated breath. "OK. Fine. I'm... a... tavern whore. Hence the dress. I was at a party in the dungeon of the ruined God's Tower, got drunk, passed out, and woke up here." I smile. "Happy now?"

He's definitely not happy. "Now you're just fuckin' with me."

"And you're not listening." I get up, take off his jacket, drop it into the chair, and walk across the room.

"Where ya going?"

I don't say anything. I'm so angry. Also scared. And... sad. And... many, many, many other emotions. Confused, and frustrated, and...

He's behind me, grabbing my arm, and pulling me away from the door. "Just stop. Sit down."

But I don't. I yank my arm out of his grip, grab the handle of the door, and pull. I'm kind of expecting it to be locked again, because I'm convinced that he was the one who locked it last night in the first place so I had to stay over. But I'm wrong. It opens right up and all the strange voices that were mostly silent a moment ago come rushing at me.

No one is directly in front of the door, but when I step out and look to my right, there is a small crowd gathered by a large, open stairwell. They are laughing and talking. And when I look to my left, I see that man who peeked into Tyse's quarters at me. The one he pushed away from the door.

This man grins at me, his eyes flashing. Then he takes a good, long look at me, lingering on my breasts, which are mostly visible because this dress wasn't made for an up-city Maiden, it was made for a down-city tavern whore.

And that man down the hall is looking at me like he would like to pay me coin to spend an hour in his room.

I turn away and head for the stairs. I don't know much about anything around here, but I do know that down is my answer.

A few people remark about my dress as I push my way through the crowd and enter the open, twisting stairwell that descends in a wide spiral. We are ten stories up, so that's a long way down. After a few floors I pause and look over the railing, straight down into some kind of lobby far below.

"Clara Birch!" The sound of someone calling my name in this unfamiliar place takes me by surprise. I look up and find Tyse on the tenth floor above me, also hanging over the railing. "Just stop. Wait right there. I'm coming down."

All of these words come out as a command. Like I am someone who takes orders from him. Which just makes me angry. But what makes me even angrier is that he has called the attention of everyone on the stairwell within hearing distance. These people must number in the hundreds, surely. People on the stairs, crowds gathering on the balconies—all the way up and down. And all of them, on every level within earshot, stop what they are doing to look at me.

I glance back up at Tyse, find him shaking his head at me and warning me with a pointing finger, and then restart my escape with more earnest intentions. Feet flying down the stairs, weaving in between slow crowds in front of me and another horde coming up at me, gasping for breath because all of the emotions I possess seem to be building up inside of me at once and I'm trying not to cry.

"Clara Birch!" He yells it *again*. "Stop! Someone stop her!"

"Oh!" This comes out of my mouth as I grab the railing and look up, pointing. "He's trying to hurt me! Someone stop *him*!"

Then I continue my descent as he yells obscenities at me. People have stopped on the steps, confused, trying to sort out what is happening. But in my experience, people only want to know what's happening if it's something they can passively watch and don't have to get involved in. Something they can gossip about later. As soon as you start asking them to actually *do* something, they tend to pretend they can't hear you.

And we have both asked for help.

What to do now?

Even if this Tyse is some well-known, well-respected figure in this place, I'm a woman. Scantily clad, at that. And I'm running away from him.

They're not gonna stop me.

They're not gonna stop him, either. He really does look like a man you do not want to piss off. But I don't care. I've got a lead. And that's what I concentrate on. Getting down these stairs as fast as I can and escaping.

The lobby is suddenly in view. Ground level. A daytime view outside. Hundreds of people, and something that might be a little indoor market that comes off as very down-city.

Then I am out of steps. And confused. Because Tyse said he found me below ground and there are no more steps. I look both left and right, trying to find a way forward in the few seconds I have before he catches up with me, but there are no options but left or right or out of the building.

I head towards the exit, pushing my way through a thick crowd of people waiting in a haphazard line for something at a booth.

Tyse is calling my name again. "Clara! Stop!"

I don't stop. I push past a final crowd and make a dash for the exit. Then I am running under the great arches—and *this* is what makes me halt, turn, and look up.

Because I *know* this archway.

When I last saw it, there was a massive black door covering the opening, but this is it. This is the door to the God's Tower. The very one I walked through.

My eyes slowly crawl up the building, taking in all the familiar details. Then I look around and realize I'm standing on the God's Tower stage, except the smooth, polished stone floor that I remember is now cracked, and crumbling, and looking very ancient.

Then I see the city. I saw it last night, but it was dark, and lit up, and nothing like it looks right now.

I'm so stunned, my mouth drops open. I haven't moved. I'm standing in the center of the archway and people are flowing past me like I'm a rock in a river. But then they start pushing me. Snarling at me.

"Get out of the way."

"Move along!"

Then there is a hand on my arm. And when I look up, those unnaturally lit-up blue eyes are looking back at me. He doesn't say anything, just sighs and pulls me over to the right, getting me out of the flood of people.

I am taken to a spot that I am very familiar with because this was where I stood each and every time I was on this stage watching a friend walk through that same door I just came out of.

The hope dies. Instantly. There is no going back. There is no saving my old life.

I just walked through the tower god's door.

That was my plan, wasn't it?

And this place, this city—it's not my Tau City.

"Here. Sit." Tyse is pointing to a step. Which is the exact same step the Matrons stood on during the Extraction last night.

I don't sit. Instead I take a look around. A good look around. From ten stories up I could tell it was some kind of ruin, but from the ground I see it for what it really is. The Maiden Tower—what's left of it, anyway—is directly on my right. Most of the tower is gone. There's no roof. But the archways above the doors are familiar. I look up, counting the floors. My floor is missing. Just sky. But that's where I lived. Hundreds of years ago, apparently.

I look back down, my gaze wandering over to the bridge that spans the canal—which is not filled with cyan-blue water, but something much darker—and ending at the Extraction Tower on my left. Finn's tower. Or rather, where it would've been. Because this one is just a foundation.

Finally, I look straight down the canal. The banks used to be sandy, and pretty, and lined with sandstone boulders with little waterfalls spilling over them in some places. But these banks are made of some building material I can't even name. It looks unnatural and cold. Nothing but smooth, sharp edges.

Just like the new towers that have replaced the white conical ones with sun-bleached blue domes that I remember. They are tall—very, very tall. Much taller than anything from my Tau City. And they look like spikes. So many of them, all clustered together. So close I get a feeling of claustrophobia just looking at them. Some of them are made of glass and glimmer in the dull sunlight like mirrors. Others are made of that same smooth material acting as banks on the canal. I can count at least a dozen bridges, but they are not the simple ones my feet used to travel across. There are two-wheeled machines I've never seen before with people on them, going every which way.

And the noise. It's distant from here. Beyond what used to be the Extraction and Maiden Districts and well into what used to be the Canal District where everyone in up-city used to shop. So the noises of this city, from where I'm standing, are a bit muffled. But even from here I can tell that there is nothing calm about it. It's a frantic clamor of commotion.

"Are you OK?"

I don't answer him. Mostly because I'm not OK, but also I don't owe him an answer. He's no one to me. He's not even nice. Back in my old life I would not have looked twice at a man like Tyse. Even if we were from the same world, we would *not* be from the same world.

"Look, I don't know what's going on with you, but just take a seat. Relax. Give yourself a minute."

I don't have many options—none, really—so I lower myself down onto the step.

Tyse joins me, leaning back on his elbows and kicking his legs out. Then he sighs. "I've been here seven years and I'm still kinda stunned at it myself. So I get it."

"No offense"—I don't look at him, just stare straight ahead—"but unless you walked through that tower door behind me and ended up in a whole other reality, I don't think you do."

"True. I didn't come through a tower door. But I did come through the tunnels. And maybe it's not another reality, but after spending three years in the Omega Outlands doing shit I can't tell ya about, 'cause then I'd have to kill ya, it sure did feel like one to me."

I turn my head to look at him. "You were some kind of soldier."

He side-eyes me, grinning. "What gave it away?"

I chuckle, despite all the confusion running through my mind. "Well… everything, actually. That weapon of yours. I could barely lift it, it's so heavy. And the jacket. With the patches." I pause for a moment and we stare at each other. "And the tattoos. And scars. You look like you've been hit with those crazy darts before."

"Told ya it wouldn't kill me. They're not meant to kill. Just fuck you up so royally you're out of the game."

"Is that why you're here then? Those darts took you out of the game?"

"Nah. Wasn't the darts. Was this shit, actually." He points to his eyes. "The augments."

"I don't even know what that means."

He blows out a long breath. "Tech. Biotech inside my brain. But it went bad a long time ago so… yeah. That was it for me. All the plans were ruined. All the work, worthless. And then I got on a train, went through the tunnels, and got off here. So that's where I stayed. So I get it. It *is* a different world from the one I came from."

"You didn't assimilate well?"

"What makes you think I'm not assimilated?" He and I stare at each other for a moment. Then he chuckles. "Fine. I'm a little bit antisocial. But I didn't always live in the tower. I went to the War College." He nods his head towards the city in front of us. "That building right there, the one made of blue glass. The Empire Building. That's War College."

"If they kicked you out of the military, then why did you bother?"

"Why did I bother going to War College? It was the best offer I had at the time. But… as you might've guessed, it was not my thing. So I left during the middle of the second year and came here." He tilts his head back, looking up at the tower behind us. "The God's Tower ruin. The spark was free, no rent, and people leave me alone. That's really all I want now. Just to be left alone. Which is why I maybe might've come off as a dick up there."

I'm looking at him as he says all this, but I look away now, focusing on the blue building he pointed out. "You look a little young to be such a cynic."

"Do I?" He huffs and sits up, drawing his legs back so he can rest his elbows on his knees. "Well, in my experience it doesn't take much to be disillusioned with this fucking world."

"I guess I'm in the middle of learning that lesson as we speak."

"Why's that?"

"Because that's the fucking door I came through." I point to the opening behind me, that actually doesn't have a door. "And I just walked back out of it. So… well. My big plan was to do just that. Find the door and walk back through."

"You thought it would… what? Take you back home, like magic?"

I shrug, a little bit defensive. "It sure acted magical when I walked through it the first time."

He's silent for a few moments, then turns a little to look at me. "Clara. It's possible that it happened that way, I guess. But… it's more *probable* that… I dunno, someone hurt you, maybe? And this has affected your memory in some way. Or perhaps the spark fucked you up because you were overexposed and not used to it. You were down there for a whole day, at least. There's an electromagnetic field in the tower. And it's more powerful than I ever thought it could be in the lower levels. A field like that affects your brain. It does, it really does. I saw it weaponized while I was in the Sweep."

"The Sweep? Like the Great Sweep that dusted the Earth with sand?"

"No. Well, I guess they're related. A little bit. The Great Sweep did what you say, but it's the name of the military branch I was in. Sweep."

"Well, sweep, in that context, sounds a lot like killing."

"That was pretty much the idea, I think."

I side-eye him, reevaluating. He's dangerous. Probably *very* dangerous.

But I don't ask any more questions. It's none of my business what he's done in his past.

After a few minutes of this silence he stands up. And I find him looking down at me when I look up at him. "What do you want to do, Clara? Do you want me to call Stayn and report you? Take you down to patrol?"

"Do I have another option?"

He shrugs. "I'll tell Stayn I found a vagrant and it's taken care of. Then we go back upstairs and I'll get you some clothes. You can't wear that dress around here. It's not safe."

"Then what?"

"I dunno. I'll help you figure it out."

"Why?"

"Why what?"

"Why would you help me? According to you I'm an up-city Birch."

He laughs. It's a real laugh, too. His eyes—while no

longer glowing—light up in a different way. "It was a good joke though, right?"

"Birch. Bitch. I guess it was." Then I laugh too. And when he extends his hand, I take it. Letting him pull me to my feet and lead the way back inside the tower.

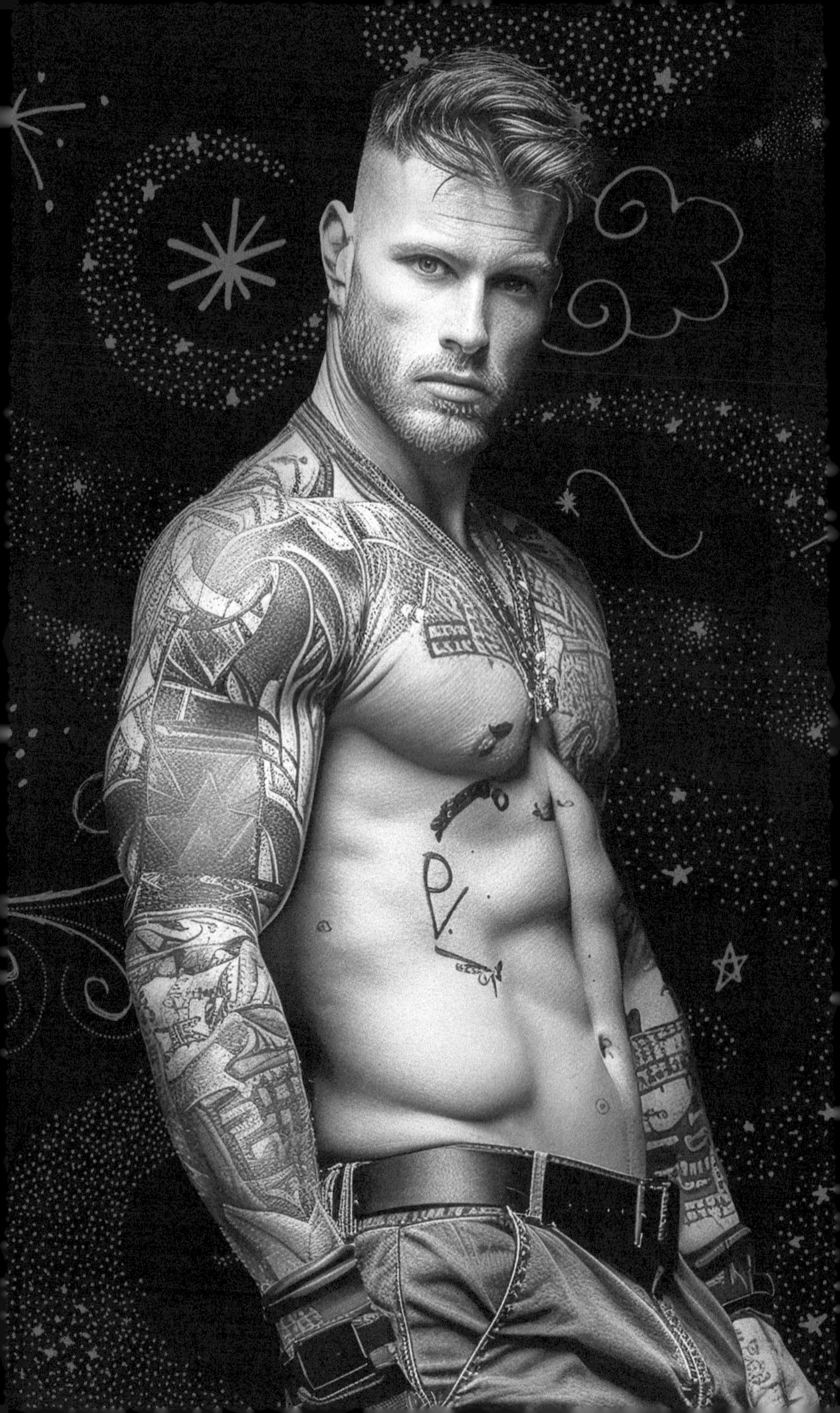

TYSE

CHAPTER TWENTY-THREE

The climb back up to the tenth floor goes far slower than it did going down. But I've had enough stair-climbing to last me a month, so I don't mind the slow pace. Clara seems exhausted too. And by the time we actually get back to my place, she's very out of breath.

"Have a seat and I'll find you something to wear."

She collapses into my chair, then slumps back, frowning at me. "You keep spare sets of women's clothes around, do you?"

"No." I chuckle, checking my inventory of tactical pants. I find an old pair that don't fit anymore, and throw them at her. "They're gonna be too big, of course. But they'll do." Then I get a t-shirt and throw that as well. "You can take a shower if you want. The water will not be hot. It'll be just warm enough to make you feel worse when you get out than when you went in."

"An attractive offer."

When I look over at her I find her staring down at the clothes on her lap, frowning. "Sorry. It's the best I can do. I can take you shopping if you want."

"With what coin? I don't have any. And not to be

disparaging, but you don't look like you have much either." Her eyes dart to my small jar of coins that I keep around to pay Anneeta.

"Well, I was thinking we'd check the big lost and found on the ground level, not *actual* shopping." This makes her laugh. "But ya can't leave anything of real value in the rooms here. People know better than to fuck with my shit, but it occasionally happens that something in here goes missing. Despite the drama last night with the door locking, the doors don't lock in the tower. I'm in the system, though. I've got a pension from Sweep and a digital wallet with the city. That's where I keep my coin. So if you want to look the part of up-city Birch, I'll buy ya something else. But we'd have to go into the Canal District for that."

Her face crinkles up. "Down those stairs again? Then all the way over to the Canal District, then shopping, then back up? No, thanks. I'll make do with these."

"All right. I'm gonna step out while you do that. I'll call Stayn and get a grocery order in."

"You're going all the way back down?"

"No. There's a service hub on Eight. It's got food and some other essential shit. Plus runners who are more than happy to go into the city for the right price. So I won't take long. Then after that..." I shrug. "I dunno. We'll figure something out."

She doesn't agree or disagree. Just sits there, staring off into space.

I leave and head to the stairs, wondering the whole way down what I'm actually doing. Did I just attach myself to this woman? Am I gonna be stuck with her for days trying to figure out what the hell is wrong with her? I didn't see any bruising on her face. There are no obvious injuries to her head that I could tell and no blood in her hair to indicate that someone hit her. But something is definitely wrong with her mind.

I know more than most about how this world works because the Omega Outlands don't exactly obey the same laws of nature as the places outside the Outlands do. But that's different. In just about every way possible.

Her story doesn't even make sense. I didn't find her on the other side of a door. She was in an ancient server room. The party theory is the only thing that adds up. She was drugged. She was down there too long and the spark messed with her mind.

It's the simplest solution, so that has to be it.

The service hub is on the opposite side of the tower from the main stairwell, so I turn right when I get to Eight and follow the curving hallway around to the opposing side of the building.

All floors with a service hub are crowded, and Eight is no different. There are no spare rooms here and so many people sharing them, they spill out into the hallway at times. Everyone wants to be near the action and the action up here is the pharmacals.

Drugs. They're everywhere, of course. But Eight is the only place in all of Tau City where you can get hits of spark. Everyone inside the tower—inside the ruins, actually—we all get a baseline level of spark. It never stops, but it never really changes either. A few volts from the mean, plus or minus, is normal. But that's it. You get what you get.

And eventually, this causes cravings.

So—free enterprise and all that—clever tower people have come up with a way to store the spark. Little batteries that you stick under your tongue to give yourself a jolt.

Or big ones that can deliver a jump directly to your heart—if you've got the coin for that. But that's a rare thing in the tower because no one in here does.

The pharms, jolts, and jumps are only sold on Eight. It's also the only floor that has a dumbwaiter system set up to deliver goods while you wait, without having to hire yourself a private tower runner.

Everything on Eight costs a fuckin' fortune. But everyone pays if they've got the coin because it's convenient.

I've never done a jolt, let alone a jump, so I don't do any business with that crew. I only deal with Rodge, who runs the basic commissary and makes his living off the store and the services he provides tower residents who have plenty of coin to waste. Like me.

There's a thick crowd in front of the door to Rodge's store—which is just three rooms that have had the walls knocked down to make space for inventory. He's the one with the dumbwaiter, a simple rope and pulley system with baskets going up and down nine to five. Down in the ruin Rodge owns another store with his own team of private runners who will go into the city and get you anything you want. For a price, of course.

I need a phone and some food. Normally I'd just get the prepackaged shit that's always in stock up here and call it good. But if I have to send down for a phone—and I do because Rodge can't stock those, the batteries get drained by the tower before they can get sold—then I might as well stock the pantry so I don't have to drag this woman all up and down the stairs every time her stomach rumbles.

There's a long line of people—there's always a long line of people—but as soon as Rodge sees me come in, he waves. "Tyse, friend. How can I help you?" He calls this out from the back corner. Then he stands up and waves me over to his desk.

I'm one of the few people inside the tower who pays with Tau City digital money, which is a lot easier to exchange and use outside the ruins than all those bulky coins everyone else pays with, so he treats me special.

I enter the cordoned-off space he calls an office and take a seat in the chair he's waving at. He sits too, shoots me a wide smile that makes his dark eyes brighten, and steeples his fingers under his chin. "What do you need, Tyse?"

"A phone and some good food."

"Yes, right away. What kind of food?"

"Non-perishable. And enough of it to last a few days."

Rodge is nodding his head as he speaks, always amicable. "Do you want rations?"

"Not really. What other choices you got?"

His eyes kinda sparkle now. "Are you entertaining someone?"

"I've got a…" I sigh. Because I don't know what to call her. "A guest. Temporary."

"Female?" He's smirking at me now.

"Yes. Not that it matters."

"You're entertaining a female. Well, then you need a proper grocery run."

"Well, I don't wanna cook anything."

"Will she not cook for you? Since you are housing her?" Rodge is a traditional guy, originally from Thetaiota, where the gender roles are pretty specific. He doesn't even live in the tower. His place is right outside the ruins on the canal. So he's got city power, which means he's got a kitchen. Which of course he does, because women, where he comes from, cook three times a day like clockwork. It's fucking crazy.

"I don't even know if she can cook, to be honest. But I'm pretty sure that's a no from the looks of her."

He squints his eyes at me. "She's one of *those*, huh?"

"Maybe. I dunno. I don't want anything we need to cook."

"Rations are your only choice then, friend. But there's a new brand out. Made for city adventurers." He pans a hand through the air in a dramatic arc as he says these last two words. Like he's selling me on the romantic idea of luxury camping. "How about those?"

"Fine. I'll take those. Plus a phone."

"No problem. I'll take care of it. It will be delivered within the hour."

I wait as he fills out a debit note and slides it across the desk. I sign it, and push it back. "See ya later." I stand up and turn to leave, but then I stop. "Hey. Have you seen Anneeta today?"

Rodge shakes his head. "No. She hasn't been up here at all."

"All right. If you do see her, tell her I'm looking for her."

"Will do."

I leave the store and hit the stairs. I want to find Anneeta just to see if she's got anything to say about last night, but I'm not walking all the way down to the ground for that. Not after I just paid a premium for my order. So I go back up to ten.

When I open the door to my quarters, I find Clara sitting on the bed, slipping on her shoes. Which I just now notice are more like fancy slippers.

She stands up as I take a good look at her. That long blonde hair of hers is wet and tangled, the t-shirt hangs off her like a flour sack, and the pants are so long, they're bunched up at her ankles.

When I meet her gaze, she sighs and appears uncomfortable, self-consciously looking down at herself, then back up at me.

"Looks good," I lie.

She smiles. "I look ridiculous. But I feel much better. So thank you."

"Well, those are some very nice manners you have there, Miss Birch." I pause here, wondering… "Is it 'miss?'" Which gets me thinking about what Rodge said. Her being one of *those*. Meaning one of those modern women who don't think being a wife is a job.

I have maybe spent thirty seconds of my whole life wondering about the gender roles of women, so my curiosity kinda surprises me.

"It is 'miss.' But I was engaged before all this tower stuff happened. Well, practically. We had three more months before my duty was up."

Some of her ramblings last night come back to me now. "Duty. As a Maiden."

She nods. "That's right. I was Maiden number nine."

I walk over to the chair by the window and sit. The shutters are still open, so there is a spray of unfamiliar golden light shining through the metal louvers, giving the place a cozier feeling than it normally has.

She reaches back, gathers her wet hair into a ponytail, then ties it into a knot on top of her head. After that, there's nothing but silence between us.

It gets awkward quick.

"You don't believe me?"

My shoulders shrug up. "You claim to come from another time. Or… another land. And you were sent here as a sacrifice to a god that doesn't live in this tower. Hasn't lived in this tower for hundreds of years. So… your story makes no sense, Clara. What am I supposed to think?"

She stares at me for a few seconds, her face very serious. "I understand. But your story doesn't make sense to me, either. I wasn't at a party. I mean, I was, but…" Her brows knit together and she sighs, then sits down on the edge of the bed and falls back, looking up at the ceiling for a moment before trying again. "I was at a party, but it was in my own Tau City. The ruins out there were towers. One on either side of the god's tower. It was an Extraction party. I was the Maiden being Extracted. My boyfriend"—she turns her head a little to look at me—"is in charge of the Extraction."

"What's that mean, exactly? He is the one who sent you through the door?"

She nods, but doesn't say anything.

"Well, he's a keeper, isn't he?"

I catch her smiling. "I was *very* pissed off when I walked through that door."

"I can imagine."

"He insisted that there was nothing he could do because if the Maidens are not sent into the tower after the bells ring, the god will compel all the ones in waiting too. And the Little Sisters. And 'are you that kind of person, Clara?'" Her voice changes here. Like she's imitating her man. But she doesn't answer herself.

"Well? Were ya?"

She turns on her side, propping her head up with her elbow. "What do you think? I'm here, aren't I?"

"Yeah. Well, he could've just picked you up and tossed you through."

Her eyes dart down, like she's checking me out, then quickly flick up to meet my gaze. "Is that what you would've done? If you were Extraction Master?"

"If I had the power to kill people or save them…" But I don't finish. I just sigh.

"Well. Your uncertainty has been noted."

"It's kind of a tough decision. Kill one to save more? Or save the only one you love?" I'm not looking at her when I say this. "I guess we know where your man stands."

I expect her to object. Make up some kind of excuse. But she doesn't. She blows out a breath, flops back on the bed, and stares up at the ceiling. "That's what I said too."

"What? That he doesn't love you? It's probably for the best. People in love do crazy shit to keep that love. In my experience, anyway."

"You were in love once and did something crazy?"

"Me? *No.*" I kinda laugh. "I'm not into it. But I've seen lots of men do very stupid things for love. All you gotta do is watch the fuckin' screens. They've got those true crime shows running all the time. There's a bar I go to"—I nod my head behind me—"down there, just past the ruins, and they play that true-crime shit on the screens all day and night. It's a terrible idea if you ask me. They should just put a game on like every other fuckin' bar in town."

"A screen is...?"

I sigh. Because this has to be an act and I feel like I'm getting played. "A TV, a screen, a television."

"I have no idea what you're talking about."

"You've never seen a screen? Your man never took you to the movies and got you popcorn and candy, then kissed you in the dark?" I'm joking, but not really. I am expecting an answer.

"What's popcorn?"

"Really?" I cock an eyebrow at her. "That's your answer? What's popcorn?"

"I've never heard of it, I'm sorry."

"You've never eaten corn?"

"No."

My laugh comes out as a huff. "You're winding me up, now. It's *corn*. It's in everything. It's fuckin' poison, if you ask me. But still, it's in everything. Every city grows corn."

She sighs, like she's tired of this conversation. Or maybe

I'm boring her. "I don't know what to tell you, Tyse. Maybe we have a different name for it, and I would recognize it if I saw it. But I have never heard of corn."

She's not lying. If she is, she's psychopathically good at it. She has either truly never seen or eaten corn or her memory is just fucked. Those are the only two explanations.

Either way, this is bad.

"So, Clara. What do you want to do?"

"I haven't a clue. I don't think I'm going home, though."

"You mentioned friends? Other… Maidens?"

"Yeah. Haryet. But if she were here, wouldn't she have made a disturbance as well? And if that was the case, she would've been in that room with me. Or you'd have been sent to find her instead of me. And you didn't find her. So she's not here."

"Could she, perhaps, be in another room down there?"

"Wouldn't that have triggered an alarm?"

"Should've. But who knows? I sure wouldn't. That's the first time I've ever been down below the ground floor. I got a call from my friend, Stayn, asking me to check it out. It's possible that Haryet is the one who triggered the alarm, woke up, wandered away, and then you showed up after she was gone."

Clara sits up again, her face bright with hope. "Do you really think so?"

"No."

She smiles. Then chuckles. "Then why did you even say that?"

"Because it's possible. I just don't think it happened. But

I don't think you're from some other version of Tau City, either."

She stares me straight in the eyes. "You think I'm lying."

"No. I actually don't. I think… you got hurt somehow and it's affected your memory. I think you need to go to the health center and get checked out. I think you should let me take you there."

She deflates and bows her head, looking down at her fidgeting hands in her lap. Then she sighs and gives in. "OK."

I nod. "OK. The phone and food should be here soon. Then we'll go down." She doesn't say anything or look up. "If you're too tired to walk back up tonight, I'll piggyback ya."

This makes her scoff. "I don't think that'll be an issue." Then, slowly, she raises her eyes to meet mine. "I'm not coming back up here."

"Why not?"

She just exhales again—this one sounding even more tired and defeated than the last—and then crawls up the bed, turning her back to me.

She doesn't say anything else and about ten minutes later, I know why. She's sleeping.

I think about what she said, about not coming back up here. She's probably right. She's not gonna have to worry about that ten-story hike up the stairwell because in all likelihood, I'm gonna take her to the health center, hand her over to the Tau City doctors, and they are going to label her as mentally ill.

They'll keep her there and then I'll walk out and never think about her again.

I sit in my chair silently watching her sleep until the delivery arrives. Then I unpack the rations and shoot a text off to Stayn. I give him the story I promised her I would. *A vagrant, it's taken care of, nice doin' business with you.* By this time, it's early afternoon and I don't see much point in putting off the inevitable.

I pocket the phone and approach the bed, then shake her shoulder a little. "You ready?"

It takes her a moment to open her eyes, then another to remember where she is and what's going on, but finally her gaze finds mine and she sits up, blowing out a breath. "Sure. Let's go."

We leave and descend the tower slowly. Everything about her is a little bit slow right now, her dash down the stairs this morning something akin to a long-forgotten memory.

The stairwell is crowded, as usual, and the lobby is even more of a madhouse than it was yesterday because the ID people are back. They have a whole bunch of tables set up this time and all of them have a massive crowd waiting in line.

We push our way through and go outside. She's walking ahead of me at this point, but she's unsure where to go, so she stops, looking up at me for guidance.

"This way." I point to the stairs that lead down to the east side of the city. "All the government buildings are over on this side of the canal."

She falls in next to me without comment, her mood dispirited. But she does start looking around at the buildings in front of us as we get closer to the edge of the ruin.

I would not say I like it here. I mean, I don't care about Tau City. I've got no loyalty to it. But as a Level One Metropolitan Area it's pretty fucking spectacular. I haven't been to all the great cities, but I've been to a lot of them. And this one right here is definitely in the top three that people should probably visit at least once in their lifetime.

If they can afford the travel, that is. Which most people can't.

But we went all over the world when I was in the Sweep. Especially that year before I was officially accepted into full-duty status. That was the year my augments were outperforming all expectations and I was at the top of my class. I was going places.

The Omega Outlands, as it turned out. Which sounds like a shit deal if you're not aware of what's actually out there. But for anyone in the Sweep, the Omega Outlands was the crowning jewel as far as deployment goes.

When Clara and I get to the very edge of the ruin, right at the boundary of all the new skyscrapers, she stops and just stares at it with her mouth open in shock as she tries to see everything at once.

It's one thing to see it from a distance of ten floors up and five hundred yards back and quite another to be standing at the base, looking up at these towering examples of architectural genius.

Again, I get the feeling that she's not lying. This is not a show she's putting on. This really is her very first time seeing such a magnificent city up close. And it's confusing for me. Because if her story *isn't* true, then what could explain her jaw-dropped awe?

I don't even prod her along. I don't tell her to stop gaping like a tourist or anything like that. I just let her look so I can watch her reaction.

It's real. She is genuinely surprised at what she is seeing.

"Do you like it?" I ask.

A breath comes out of her, like she was holding it in. Then she nods and smiles. "I have to admit, it's... something else."

"Good? Or bad?"

Her shoulders shrug up, practically to her ears. "Both? I'm not sure. My Tau City was much smaller." She points to the water. "The canal was... natural. There were beaches on both sides with boulders and little waterfalls spilling over them."

I look at the canal and picture this as she continues.

"And the bridges. They were not made of that hard-edged stuff."

"Hard-edged stuff? You mean concrete?" I laugh these

words out. Because how does she not know the word for concrete? It's ridiculous.

"Yeah, OK. That." But she's moved on from the bridges and is pointing at the buildings now. "Are these made of glass?"

"Some of 'em. Some of 'em are made of steel. It's just shiny, so it looks like glass when the sun hits it a certain way."

"Well, our towers were tall too. But not this tall. And they were just made of plaster and stone, I think." She looks up at me. "I don't know how to make buildings. They just didn't look like *that*." She points to the skyscrapers. "They looked... natural. Like the canal. Like they fit in with it. All of my city was covered in muted shades of beige and blue. And most of the towers had domes. Sun-bleached blue domes. Almost gray, some of them, because they were so old."

I picture her city, trying to overlay it across this one. There are a lot of traditional cities still out there, Zeta and Rho being two of the most famous. Both of those still have gods, of course. And no train system so hardly anyone ever goes there. I've never gone there. The image I have in my head comes from a textbook.

But Clara's Tau City would be much the same, probably. If it had a god the way she says it does. Because gods don't like change and gods don't like progress. Gods like tradition. Gods like to control the power distribution. Both kinds—the political power and the actual energy grid. Transportation too. Both Zeta and Rho are walking cities. No cars, no bikes, even. Maybe they have horses, but who knows? So this is my next question for her. Just to see what she says. "Did you have a train system?"

Clara reluctantly pulls her gaze away from the skyscrapers and looks up at me. "What?"

"Did you have trains in your Tau City?"

She laughs and looks back at the buildings. "*No*. We had ruins of trains. And tunnels, mostly caved in though. All that was outside the wall." She waves a hand in the air like whatever I'm going on about isn't important to her.

"You had a wall?"

"Yes. It went around the entire city, even the farms."

"What was beyond the wall?"

"Sand dunes. Mountains. Nothing."

Tau City, where we are, has sand dunes and mountains outside the metropolitan area as well. But the metro area is so fucking big these days that if you stand on the viewing platform of the highest, southernmost skyscraper, you can actually see Upsilon City through the public telescopes. So I test this detail out as well. "How far away was your closest city?"

"Closest *city*?" She makes a face at me. "There are no other cities. Tau City is the last one standing after the Great Sweep."

"Huh." A twist in the mystery. But it's not helping her far-fetched story in the least. "So you're from the future?"

"No." She glares at me. "I never said that. I never said anything like that, so don't paint me as crazy. I'm just telling you how it was."

"The simple fact remains, Clara, that your reality and this reality don't match up."

She shrugs. "I don't care. I know what I know. And what I know is that I don't come from here. I walked through the God's Tower door and this is just the place I ended up."

"You're not even willing to consider that you might be ill?"

"I'm not ill."

"So that's a no."

She stops walking and turns to face me. "I never asked for your help."

"No. But you need it."

"Says who?"

"Do you know how to get to the health center? Because if so, by all means, up-city Clara *Birch*"—I bow and mockingly wave a hand at her—"have a nice day."

"It's not funny when you actually mean it, ya know."

I straighten up from my bow. "I'm not trying to be funny. You're mentally ill. I hope you get the help you need." Then I give her a little salute, turn, and start walking back the way we came.

"What if I prove it to you?"

I stop, shaking my head, telling myself to just keep walking. Because this woman, she's a really bad idea. I can feel it. But something compels me to hear her out. So I turn back. "How?"

She thinks for a moment, having not thought this through, I guess. But then she closes the space between us and looks up at me. "I'll go to the health center and let them check me out. Neither of us will say anything about my story. We'll just say I had a fall in the tower, hit my head, lost consciousness, and now I have no memory.

None. And let's see what they say. Let's see if I *do* have a brain injury."

"I think you should just tell them the truth."

"What truth? That I think I'm in the wrong world? No. That stacks the deck in favor of your theory. My story isn't important. If I have a brain injury, they'll find it. And if they do, I'll concede that you're right and I'll get treatment. But if there is no brain injury—no signs at all—then you will accept my story as truth."

"Maybe you're just a liar?"

"Do you think that's all this is? A woman lying to you? To what end? I didn't come looking for you, you came looking for me. What could I possibly need from you that would justify this lie?"

She's got a point. There is no reason for her to be lying. I already came to this conclusion, I just feel like arguing with her for some reason. "Why do you care if I accept your story as truth? You're no one to me and I'm no one to you."

Her eyelids drop into a low and lazy position. Like these words just revealed something about me. Something she doesn't care for. And then there is a marked shift in her attitude. A polite smile appears. A hand extends as her back straightens. "Thank you for your help, then. I can take it from here."

It's in this moment that I see the *real* up-city Clara Birch for the first time.

I don't know who she is. Hell, maybe she doesn't even know who she is. But she is most certainly *someone*. She's got a certain poise to her now that wasn't apparent before I pissed her off with a dismissal. And she's not one of those women who will throw a tantrum or start screaming obscenities—though I have no doubt she's capable of that, given her colorful vocabulary.

She's in possession of herself. Completely in control. And this change is some kind of ingrained training. Something *learned*. Something cultivated. Probably over a long period of time.

I don't shake her hand, but neither does she walk away. We just stare at each other.

There's something going on here.

Some kind of pull between us.

I don't understand it, but it's definitely there.

"Admit you need my help."

She nearly guffaws. "What?"

"Admit you need my help and if you do, I'll agree to this little experiment. And if you aren't injured, I'll help you. Because that's what you want from me. You want my help. You're just too…" I pause, so I can choose the right word.

She squints, ready to be offended.

There are many words to describe my first impression of Clara Birch. 'Egotistical,' 'conceited,' 'stuck up.' But these are actually just insults that I feel compelled to hurl at her because she's fucking with my preconceived expectations.

Better words to describe her are 'composed' and 'confident.' "You're just too proud to ask for it." 'Proud' is the right way forward because there's nothing wrong with being self-reliant, which is the manner in which I mean it.

Clara's expression softens, but she tilts her chin up at the same time, perfectly illustrating my description. "You'll help me get home?"

"If you come out of the health center pronounced perfectly fit, I'll help you. I don't know what that means, but I'll help you."

"Why?" She's squinting at me. "I mean, what's in it for you? You literally just said, like thirty seconds ago, that I'm no one to you."

"You are no one. That's not a lie. But… I'm curious."

"About?"

"Your story, for one. But also… you. Because nothing adds up."

"That doesn't answer my question. Who cares if nothing adds up?"

"I just feel a compulsion of curiosity."

"That's it?" She side-eyes me. "You're not even gonna mention that I'm pretty?"

"What?" And then I smile.

"I mean, that would make more sense."

"What would make more sense?"

"That you want sex."

"That's not it."

"I'm just saying, if it *were*, it would make sense. But you're sticking with 'curious,' huh?"

I force the grin down. Make myself serious. "Yes. I'm sticking with curious."

"Suit yourself. Which way to the health center then? I'm ready."

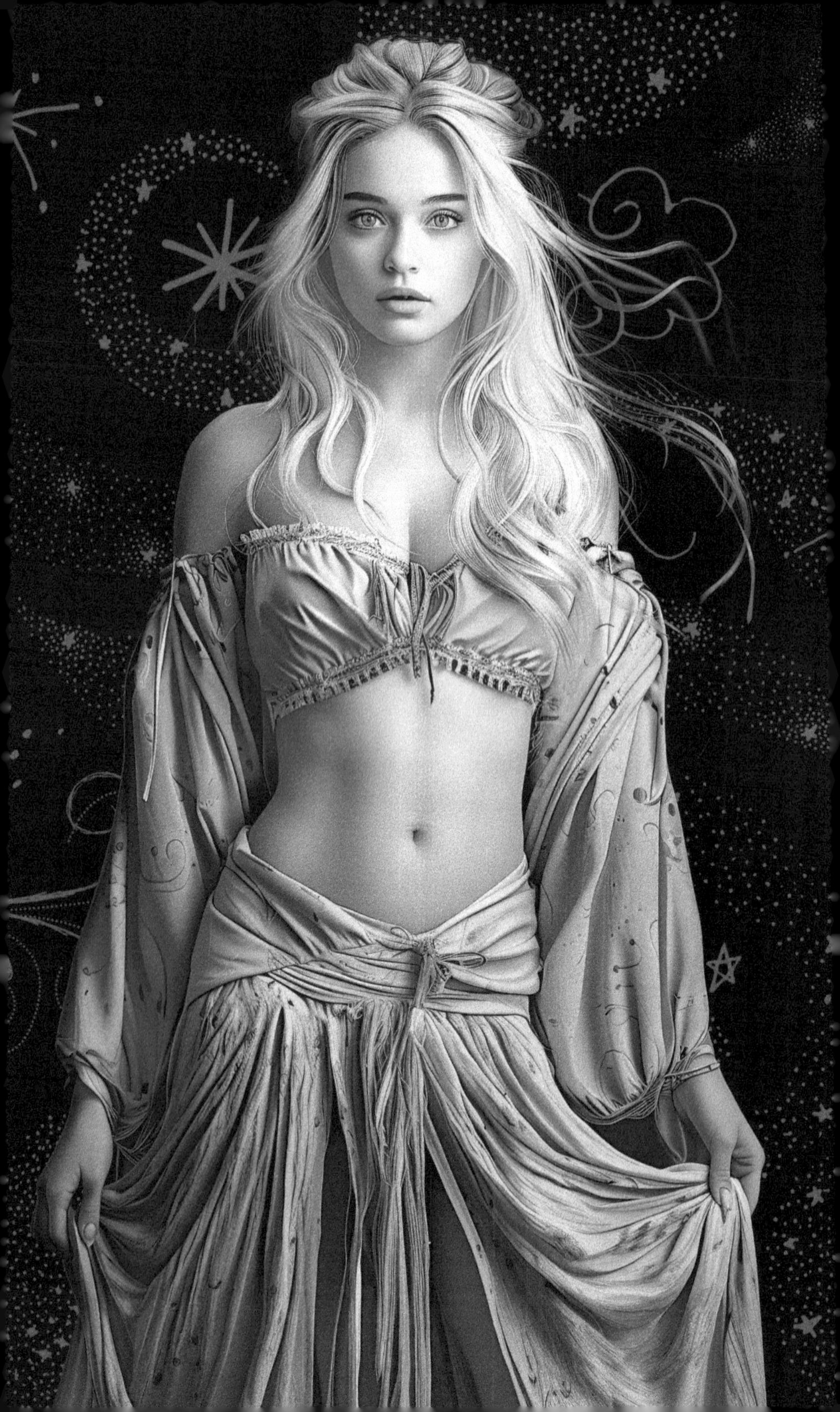

CLARA

CHAPTER TWENTY-FOUR

"Do you have a last name?" We're walking again, just entering the district, when I ask him this. It's not crowded here at the edge, but it will be very soon.

"Saarinen."

"Where do you come from?"

"What makes you think I'm not from here?"

"You sound different."

He smiles, but doesn't look at me. His gaze wandering over the people around us. "I come from Delta."

"Where's that?"

"Long, long way across the sandy sea. On the edge. By the Alphas."

"I have no idea what that means."

He stays quiet for a moment, maybe trying to come up with a way to explain it, and I take this moment to think about him.

Nothing about Tyse Saarinen is anything like Finn Scott. And I do mean *nothing*. He's very tall, for one. Finn is not short, in fact they might even be the same height, but something about Tyse comes off as looming. He's got a lot of tattoos. Finn does not. No one up-city gets tattoos. That's something they do down the canal. And he's not clean-shaven, like Finn.

I've never seen a soldier. We don't have a military in my version of Tau City. There's no need. There's no one coming to invade us because we're the last ones left.

But of course, I've seen illustrations of them in textbooks when I was learning history as a child and Tyse looks exactly like they were depicted in those books. Almost down to the smallest details, including the tattoos. Even his hair. Which is shaved close to his scalp at the sides of his head, but longer over the top. It's not tied back today, so most of the time you can't see that the sides are shaved unless he rakes it all back into place with his fingertips because the longer hair covers it.

Finn's hair was neither long nor short. It was just... hair. About shoulder length. And it's blond, not a dark auburn brown. But it looked good against his desert-tanned skin.

Even though the city does appear to have the same climate—very warm during the day and cold at night—everyone looks less weathered. More sheltered from the sun. Which makes sense, I guess. Since the towers here are so tall, they block a lot of it out.

"The Alphas are like..."

I look up at Tyse as he tries to work out a way to explain the geography of whatever the Alphas are.

"I dunno, a few thousand miles away? Maybe more? Probably more. The Alphas are the ruins closest to the ocean."

"The ocean?"

"Yeah. You don't have one where you come from?"

"I've heard of them, the way I've heard of soldiers. But no. There's no ocean by us. The water we have comes from the god. We have the canals and the lakes, but that's about it."

He lets out a breath. "I think I'd like to see your version. It would be kinda cool to compare it."

"Well, if we find a doorway back, you can come for a visit."

"Right." He snickers a little. "Anyway. The Alphas are far. And Delta City is in that direction. It's on the sea. Which is another word for ocean."

"So you *lived* by it?" I nearly stop walking, I'm so stunned at this development. An ocean, for me, at least, is just a concept. But to him it was a feature of his home.

"Yeah. Swam in it. It's salt water, though. You can't drink it."

"What does Delta look like? Here?"

"No. It's got a god. But it's not the way you describe your home. Maybe something in between a very traditional village and this monstrosity of a place that is Tau City. We have a few skyscrapers, but nothing this wild. And we have beaches too. Not a canal, but a river that comes down from the mountains. It snows up there. You could ski down if you had the coin for that."

"Snow." Again, I know what it is, I've just never seen it. "I can't even imagine what it would be like to live in a place that had snow. What is skiing?"

"You put these long, smooth boards on your feet and slide down the mountain on them."

Just picturing this makes me laugh out loud. "Is it dangerous? Because it sounds dangerous."

"Yeah. It can be. I've never done it. I didn't have coin like that when I was growing up, so I never tried it."

"Do you have coin like that now?"

"I have what I need. And if I wanted to bother with skiing, I could go somewhere and do that."

"So, you're successful."

He laughs. Right out loud. "I live in the God's Tower ruin. My augments failed, I've got no job, I live off a pension, and..." He pauses. Sighs. "And... I'm completely fucking satisfied with this. So, if that's what you mean by successful, then sure. I'm fuckin' flourishing."

"Hm." I hum this, amused at his self-deprecation.

Tyse stops and pans a hand to a building off to the right. "Here we are."

The health center is a relatively short building when compared to the massive towers it's situated between. The whole thing is made out of that hard-edged building material I can now identify as concrete. The doors open automatically when people enter and exit and there are a lot of people here.

"Ready?"

I'm not. But I nod my head to Tyse anyway. I know I'm not sick. I know I wasn't injured. But I'm nervous. Because what if I *was* injured? What if I'm completely crazy and all the things I think are true are lies? Or just a dream, or something? What if Finn never existed?

It hurts my heart to think that. I was angry when I left, but if I ever saw him again, I would not be. I would be thankful, and I would apologize for all the things I said as I was pulled into the God's Tower, and I would beg him to forgive me.

"Come on." Tyse wraps his hand around my forearm, like I might decide to run or something. And he's not going to let me. Not after we made a deal.

I might run, if I had somewhere to go, but I don't, so I give in and let him lead me inside.

And from the moment I cross that threshold and walk into the chaotic lobby, I let him take care of everything. Because I just don't understand any of it.

There are screens with moving pictures on them placed all over the walls. And these screens are on the desks, and people sit in front of them, doing something with their fingers. Writing, I think. But not with pencils. There are chairs with wheels on them, and things are beeping, and people walking around in long blue gowns and masks that cover half their face.

I stand there, silent and confused, as Tyse explains the situation.

We sit for a while as I do my best to take in everything I'm seeing, trying to force it to make sense. I sit very still, rigid and alert, eyes bouncing from one scene to the next, and as I do this, I lose track of time.

But then someone calls my name, and I don't know what to do. I freeze. Unable to stand, let alone walk over to the woman with a screen that is small enough to hold in her hand. She's scowling in my direction, not looking friendly at all.

Tyse stands up and offers me his hand until I take it and stand with him. And then he leads me over to her. There is a small argument here, one I don't participate in. The lady doesn't want Tyse to come with me, but he insists, telling her that I am his wife.

This almost shocks me out of my stupor, only because I want to smirk up at Tyse and give him a knowing look. Curious, my ass. But things are moving too fast for joking and suddenly I'm in a room with machines all around me. Machines I can't even begin to describe because they are things I have no words for.

In the coffee shops we have machines. They make coffee. We have ovens in kitchens. We have pipes and things related to plumbing. We have lights. But we don't have anything like this.

The health center, in my version of Tau City, is a place to *pray*. We ask the god for healing. If the god decides to intervene, medicine appears in syringes. It looks nothing like this.

I am asked to take off my ill-fitting clothes and put on a thin robe and the next thing I know people are poking me with needles—which is at least familiar.

At this point, I don't know what to think. My only option is to just stop participating and let Tyse handle it all. Which he does. But when there's a break in all this commotion, and no other people are close by, he asks me, "Are you OK?"

I nod out of habit. But I'm utterly fucking lost in this place. I just want to go and never come back. Except I can't because this is my reality now. There's no escape. Not a simple one, anyway. And I've made a deal with Tyse. Luckily. I'm so thankful we came in here with that agreement in place because I cannot imagine living through this experience with no one at my side.

I'm desperate now. Desperate to be proven right, and taken out of here, and helped.

Because I will not make it here alone. I will not make it here at all if I have to stay.

If I'm stuck, and there's no way back, I'm going to die in this place. I don't want to be alone when I die.

I'm taken to a new room. It's very cold and this time Tyse is absolutely not allowed to come with me. I answer questions using as few words as possible and then I am told to lie on a table and then put inside a machine. The nurse—that's what these people are called—keeps asking me if I'm OK. And I can hear her, even though she's not inside the machine with me, but in a whole other room.

I don't say anything. Just hold absolutely still until they take me out, put me in yet another room, and Tyse comes back holding up a big brown bag with handles.

I let out a breath after he closes the door. Relieved that the people have gone away, but mostly relieved that he's back.

"They told me it'd be two hours of waiting for the MRI, so I went and got you some clothes that should fit ya better." He offers me the bag.

I'm sitting on the edge of an exam table, but I take it and put it next to me, peeking inside. Then I look up at him and let out a long breath. A breath I feel like I've been holding in all day. "Well? Am I sick?"

"They don't have the results yet. But they said you can change." He nods to the bag. "It all might be too big. But better to be too big than too small." Then he turns back to the door.

"Wait!" This word comes out in a panic. "Where are you going?"

"Get dressed. I'll be right outside." He doesn't wait for me to agree, just slips out and closes the door behind him.

I don't like this place, but I feel like the ordeal is almost over, so I force myself to put the new clothes on and cling to the idea that I will be pronounced healthy and leave here soon.

The pants are the same kind he wears, with lots of pockets and made of soft, thick material. But they are a pale brown instead of black. The shirt is like his as well, short sleeves and made of cotton, but again, not black. More of a cream color. There's even a pair of boots, also like his. Ankle-high lace-ups in brown.

The coat is the only thing different. His coat looks military. Something left over from his soldiering days. The one he bought me is feminine, short, tucked at the waist, comes with a belt, and is made of nice, thick wool the color of the tower domes back in my Tau City. When I slip my arms inside, they glide down the smooth silk lining.

There's a mirror over a desk in the far end of the exam room and when I walk over to it and look at myself, I feel...

well, almost like myself. While this is not an outfit I'd ever wear as a Maiden, it looks like something I could wear back home. At the very least, if I went shopping for this outfit in my Tau City, I might actually be able to piece it together. Minus all the pockets, of course.

Did he do that on purpose? Buy me things in the color scheme I described on our walk over here? Or was it just an accident?

I don't think it matters because the end result is that I feel much, *much* better. I open the door, fearful that Tyse won't actually be out there, but he is. And he smiles as he looks me up and down. "It fits?"

I nod. Then point at him. "We look like we're partners. Except I'm light and you're dark."

He stares at me for a moment, then shrugs. "I've been called worse." Then he holds up a piece of paper. "You've been released. I've already talked to the doctor. There's nothing wrong with your brain. He told me to take you home, make you rest, and come back next week if it hasn't—"

"I'm not coming back. I'm never—"

Tyse puts up a hand, interrupting me. "You don't have to." Then he sighs. "You were right. And I believe you."

It should feel good, this victory. I should feel a little smug, maybe. But I don't. "Just… get me the fuck out of this place."

He smiles, offering me his arm. Which feels familiar, but awkward. Literally hundreds of men have offered me their arm over the course of my Maiden duties. It's a normal thing where I come from. It's just... not something a man like Tyse should instinctively do.

And yet he does.

But maybe I'm reading that wrong. At any rate, I hook my arm into his and let him lead me back outside.

It's dark now and everything I thought I knew about this city is suddenly wrong. It's loud, and there are bright, colorful signs on all the buildings, and it's raining. Which makes the roads slick and dark and splashes of water fly up at us from the machines that transport people around.

I want to ask a million questions about all of it, but I don't really know where to start because nothing about this place is familiar. I want Tyse to explain everything, but I feel like this isn't the time. He's spent the whole day with me and while he wasn't exactly pleasant this morning, he really has been patient. I don't want to push him over the edge and make him regret his promise to help me because there's nothing tying us together now. I'm perfectly fine and we're strangers. A rational person would be looking for a way to cut their losses right about now.

I would, if I were him. So I hold all my questions in.

Then he's pointing at a door and directing me in that direction. "Let's get some food."

I like this idea, if only because a restaurant is something I understand, plus I'm starving. But also, I need to get away from all the stimulation outside. Stopping for food is the quickest way to do that.

When we go inside it's warm and not crowded, so immediately I let out a breath and some of the anxiety I was feeling begins to fade. We are directed to a booth and we sit across from each other. His legs stretch out, bumping into mine, but he pulls them back with a sigh.

I study his face for a moment while a waitress puts menus in front of us. When she's gone, I look down and say, "You're tired of me, aren't you?"

"What makes you say that?"

"Because I would be tired of me, if I were you." I fidget with a napkin, unable to look him in the eyes.

"Why are you so nervous?"

"Why?" This word comes out on a sigh. "Because I'm a stranger here."

"OK."

"And… you're the only person I know."

"Right."

"And you don't have any more responsibilities to me. Not really."

"I did make a deal with you, though." He leans back in the booth and crosses his arms. This time when his legs bump into mine, he doesn't pull them back. Just claims my space.

I don't move my legs either. I look up and force myself to stare into his eyes. It's weird for a moment. They are very blue, but not the unnatural blue they were this morning. "It wasn't a deal. You said you were curious. Which isn't any kind of promise at all."

He stares at me for a moment. Then a small smile creeps up his face. "You like me."

"I don't even know you."

"You think I'm nice."

I think I blush, because my face goes hot.

"Not only that, you need me. More than I need you." His eyes squint a little here. "Which is making you nervous."

I shrug. He's not wrong.

"But it's more than that, isn't it, up-city Clara Birch." This time when he says my name like that, it's not an insult. I can tell the difference now. "I'm all you've got."

I roll my eyes.

"And you think I might leave you here."

Now I look at him again. Because I *am* afraid he'll leave me here. Surely, he's got friends, or places to be, or something.

And just as I think this, that phone thing of his starts making a noise. But we're still looking at each other and he doesn't let the interruption change this. "I'm not gonna leave you here. Ya know why?"

"Why?"

"Because you're pretty."

I laugh out loud unexpectedly.

"So you were right. That's the real reason I'm curious about you." He pulls the phone out without breaking eye contact. "I've got to take this." Then he taps it and puts it up to his ear. "Did you get my message?"

There's a pause while he listens to a faint voice. Then everything about him changes. "Oh, sorry. I forgot. I've been busy all day. Rain check then, yeah?" He listens for a few seconds. "Sounds good. Talk soon." He taps the phone again and slips it back into his pocket.

"What was that?"

"Stayn."

"Did he ask about me?"

"He doesn't know about you, Clara. I didn't tell him."

"Then why was he calling?"

"Because I was supposed to be at his house for dinner tonight and I didn't show. Forgot. Plus, I got a better offer." He doesn't wait for me to smile here, though I do. "The good thing though is that he didn't ask about it. The vagrant, I mean. The whole thing has been forgotten as far as he's concerned."

These words rattle around in my brain for a few moments. It feels like a win, but there's something dangerous about it too. "I owe you."

Tyse grins. "You *absolutely* owe me."

My laugh comes out as a huff. "Well, that's not coy."

"There's no need to be coy. I *saved* you." He leans back and stretched his arms out along the top of the booth, still grinning. "Twice? Three times? At any rate, your debts are piling up, Miss Birch."

I don't know what to say to that. Is he… flirting with me? Because he's got a kinda flirty look about him. Those eyes and that smile, in combination with that rugged, handsome face, give off an impression of flirting.

Or is he seriously keeping track of how much I owe him? I don't know him well enough to tell the difference. And he does come off as rather dangerous. Just because he's been helpful doesn't make him nice. And if he is keeping track—

"Oh, stop, Clara."

"What?"

"I'm joking. I mean, ya do owe me." He grins again. "But I'm not expecting much. Not expecting anything, actually."

"What do you mean by that?"

He shrugs. "Helping people is something you do because you want to. Not because you get something in return. Mostly because people just disappoint ya, so zero expectations is really the way to go."

"Wow. You really are cynical."

He doesn't react. Just stares at me. And after only a few seconds of his full, undivided attention the mood between us becomes heavy and awkward.

The funny thing is, I don't think it's got anything to do with me. Somehow, we've stopped talking about me and moved on to him. And I think he just realized that he gave up some information about himself that he didn't actually mean to.

I don't lower my eyes. I meet his gaze, heavy as it is. "You know what I think?"

"Can't wait to hear."

"I think… I would like to be the one person who doesn't disappoint you. The one person who exceeds your expectations."

"Now why would you wanna go and do something like that?"

I lift up one shoulder in a half-hearted shrug. "Because I can relate."

"Did that boyfriend of yours disappoint ya, Clara?"

I nod as I try and stop the frown, but there's no way I can.

"He sent ya into that tower? Sacrificed ya? For a god he'd never even met?"

I suck in a breath, but my throat is tightening up with an

oppressive sadness. "He didn't even try." I feel the tears welling up in my eyes, and I have a very strong urge to stop them. To pull myself together. To handle this heartbreak with grace, the way I was taught to handle all the other things that came with being a Maiden. But I have to face this truth eventually. Not just let it stew inside me, knowing it's true, but never admitting it. So I keep going and let the tears fall where they may. "That's what hurt me. It wasn't the god or the tower. It was him. Because if I were Finn and he were me, I would've tried. I would've…" I exhale loudly with frustration. "I would've done something daring to try and save him."

"Would ya? I mean, people think that way, Clara, but most of the time, when presented with a situation as out of control as that, most people surrender. Almost no one plays the hero. So before ya give up on him entirely and condemn him to a dark place in your heart, never to be heard or seen again, ya might just cut the man a break, ya know?"

"I do. I get it. And, to be honest, that whole time I was sitting in the health center I was imagining what I would say if I ever saw him again."

"What would you say?"

"Well, I'd apologize, obviously."

"Why obviously?"

"Oh"—I laugh, and my smile is big—"I threw a fit, Tyse." I lower my chin and give him a serious, steely stare. "Absolute *fit*. I cursed him, and called him names, I think."

"You don't remember?"

"I was so mad. I just lost it."

"And now?"

"Well, first, I'm embarrassed about that. But more importantly, I know for sure that he had no choice. And it was the right call."

"How do ya know that?"

"Because when I got within a certain distance of the door, it pulled me in. I didn't walk through of my own accord."

"Why's that matter again? Maybe you told me, but I forgot."

"Because he said if he didn't send me in, the god would take the Maidens-in-Waiting—which is just Gemna now—and then all the Little Sisters too."

"These little sisters are…? Relations?"

"No. Pledges. Prospective Maidens. And there were seventy-five of them. So if Finn had refused we all would've died."

Tyse was leaning forward, his arms on the table, as this conversation played out. But now he leans back. "It's a logical assumption that he was right based on the pulling you described. But that don't make it a fact, Clara. Not that it matters. You should just think a little more critically. Sometimes things aren't that simple."

I don't know what to say to that, so I say nothing.

He's staring at me. Hard. But not in a mean way. A new way, maybe. He's not unwilling to give Finn the benefit of the doubt, but he's not gonna give him a pass.

And he doesn't want me to, either.

That's why he just said that.

Suddenly, everything becomes too much and all the new things I've just experienced start catching up. My whole body goes hot, especially my face, and then I feel tears forming. Because I'm overwhelmed, and sad, and sorry, and stuck. So I don't want to talk anymore.

Luckily, our waitress comes up to the table with one of those screens in her hands. "What can I get for you tonight, folks?"

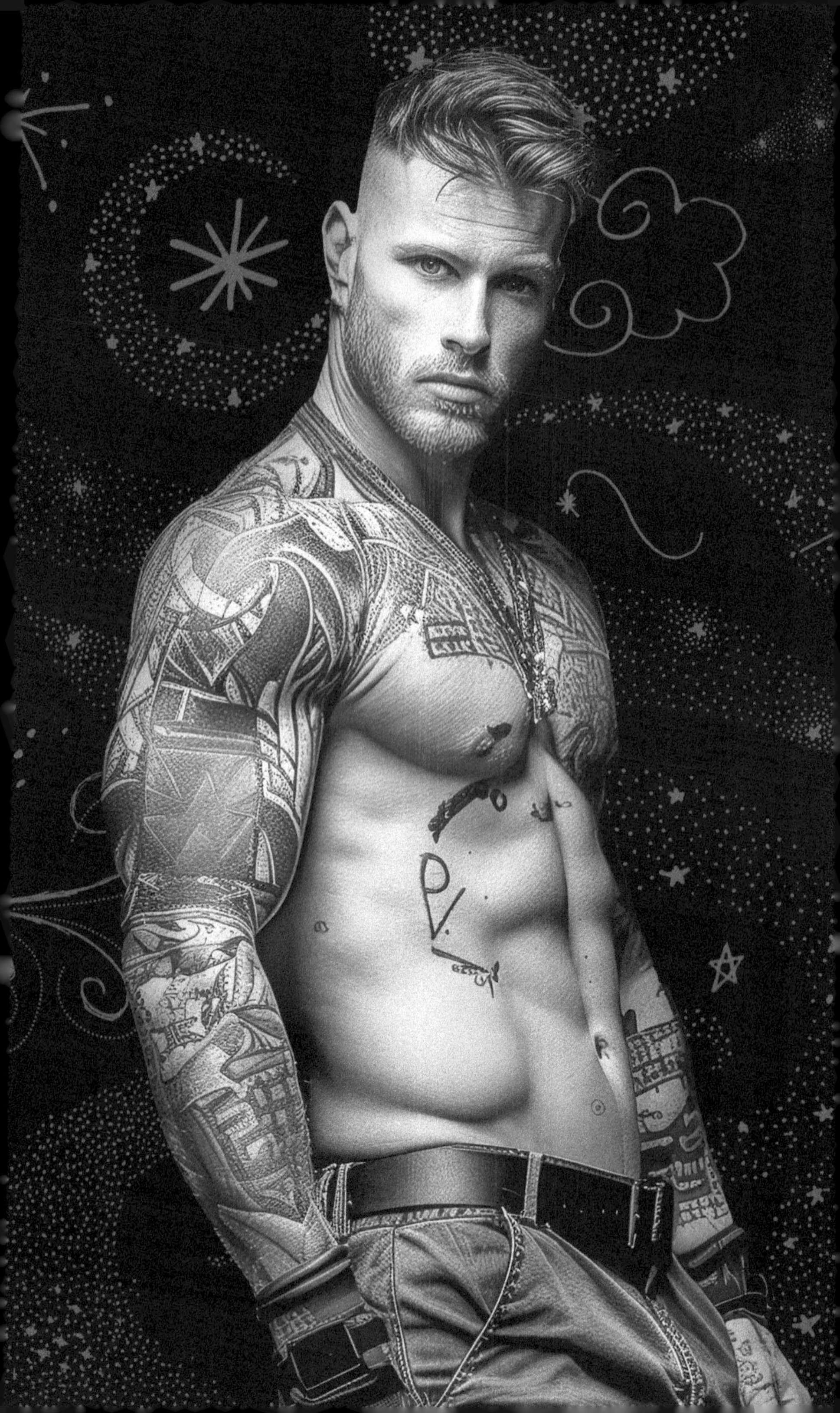

TYSE

CHAPTER TWENTY-FIVE

I *turn to the waitress* and order for both of us. Clara doesn't object, even though I have no idea what she eats. She's not thinking about food. She gives no fucks about what I order. She's trying not to cry and that's the only reason I take control like this. To give her an out. Just a few seconds to pull herself together.

When the waitress leaves and I once again look at Clara, she's wrestled that control back. But she's smaller now. Her shoulders are tucked forward, her hands in her lap. Like she's trying to withdraw into herself.

I decide to change the subject. "Would you like for me to put you up in a hotel?"

"What?" She's surprised by my question.

"So ya don't have to stay in the tower with me."

Her whole face crinkles up and I don't know her well enough to determine if it's confusion or frustration. But then, suddenly, like a switch has been flipped, all those wrinkles smooth out and she takes a breath. "That won't be necessary. If you don't want me to stay with you, I can take it from here."

"No, ya can't."

"What?"

I laugh. "You've got no chance at all of taking it from here, Clara. I mean, you'd pull through, I'm sure of that. But it would take weeks, maybe months, for you to sort it all out and find a way forward."

She huffs. "I don't understand what you're getting at."

"Yes, ya do. Just think about it for a moment. Would you like a hotel?"

Again, I get that crinkled face and I decide it's… annoyance. She's annoyed at me because I'm gonna make her say something here, and she doesn't want to.

"Would you like to stay in the city by yourself?"

Now she gets it. Because her crinkles become furrows and this is anger. "Why are you being a dick?"

"Because it's not up to me, it's up to you. And you're letting me make a lot of big decisions for you right now. It's really not my place. I'm only playing along because I've got no choice."

She scoffs, places her hands on the table, and makes to get up.

I reach out and grab her wrist. "Sit down. It's a stupid question. A really stupid question. And we both already know the answer. So why can't you just spit it out?"

She pulls her wrist out of my grip and leans back. "No. I don't want to stay in a hotel in the city. I want to go back to the tower with you."

"See? Told ya it was easy."

"Now it's your turn. Why are you being a dick all of a sudden?"

"I already told you. You're shuttin' down. And I don't like

it. You can't let me take over. Because you'll get lost if I do. And I don't like lost people. I like people who know who they are. And you... well, you're lookin' for a hero. The conversation we just had about your man pretty much gave it all away, so don't bother denying it."

"Well. So? What's wrong with that? I mean, he's the frickin' man, right? Wasn't it his job to... protect me, or whatever?"

"Dunno. Was it?"

"Well." She huffs. "Yes. Duh. That's the whole point of having a man."

"The whole point, Clara?" I'm smirkin' at her when I say this. Which just makes her angry.

"Why are you being insufferable?"

"Why are you being weak?"

"Weak? I'm not weak. I can take care of myself. If I *have* to. But my point is, when you're so involved with a man that you're practically engaged, should I have to take care of myself?"

"He didn't live up to your expectations. I get it. But maybe you didn't live up to his, either?"

"I'm not supposed to be the hero! *He* is."

"Hm."

She makes a face at me. "What's that mean? That little hum of yours?"

"I'm just reflectin' on your general attitude about heroes. It's kinda dated."

"Dated?"

"Yeah. Out of fashion, so to speak. Women these days just save themselves. But you don't see yourself as a hero because you've never been in that kind of situation. Have you ever saved anyone, Clara? Name one person."

Again, I get a scoff. "Well, who the hell have you saved?"

I hold up a finger, ready to tick off a list. And one by one I do that. "Jast, Myra, Stepan, and Kirt. And that's just my team. Of course, they saved my ass many times as well. But my point is that I've been there. I know what it feels like to make choices like the one your man was presented with and I didn't cave. I didn't give in. I did my fuckin' job. I need you to be the kind of person who doesn't give in and does the fuckin' job. That's the only way you get to the other side of this better than you were when you got here. And forget about your man. He's worthless. We've already established that. He made his choices and that's that. Get it over it and move on."

"You hate him."

"That's stupid. I don't hate him. I don't even know him."

"Then why are you being so difficult right now?"

"He's a complete piece of shit for not trying to save you. Isn't that what you wanted me to say? There. I said it. I'm on your side."

"My side. I don't even understand why we're even talking about this. Why do you care?"

"I care because I need to know where I stand. But you know what's more interesting, Clara? The fact that *you* care that *I* care."

She smiles. Small at first, then it covers her entire face. All the way up to those dancing eyes. "You're acting like a fourteen-year-old boy. But it's kind of comforting that men are the same everywhere. At least I know where *I* stand."

"Yeah? And where's that?"

She sneers at me. It's real too. "The only reason you're helping me is because you expect to get something out of it. You expect to satisfy your *curiosity*."

I simply shrug. "What's so wrong about that?"

"It's not gonna happen."

I sigh and start looking for our waitress.

"Nothing to say to that, huh?"

I look back at her with narrowed eyes. "I don't know why you're being such a Clara Birch to me right now. I'm helping ya. I said I'd keep helping ya. So what are you going on about?"

"You just sat here and spent three minutes forcing me to admit that I wanted to come back to the tower with you. The very least you can do is tell me that you're doing this because I'm pretty and you think you've maybe got a chance."

"Well. I didn't plan any of this. *But*… I wouldn't turn you down." I try and say this with a serious face but it's hopeless. She *is* pretty. I *would* fuck her.

Clara smirks. Like she won a prize.

"There. Is that what you were looking for? That I would fuck you if ya turned your skirts up?"

She tsks her tongue. "You're crass."

"And you're… haughty."

"Haughty?" She's got one eyebrow raised.

"The perfect word for you, actually. 'Haughty.' An attitude only spoiled princesses and bitchy queens can pull off."

"Hmmph." She places her napkin in her lap, pretending to mess with it.

I'm not sure if she's pleased or offended that I put her in the same company as spoiled princesses and bitchy queens.

"Why don't we get back to the conversation?" I ask.

She looks up. "Which is… what?"

"You asking me for help."

Those eyes narrow again. "I already did."

"No. You didn't. You admitted you wanted to come home with me."

She sighs and it's loud and filled with frustration. "So you want me to… what? Beg you to help me?"

But I come right back at her. "And you want, what? Sympathy from me?"

"Well, *yes*." She makes big eyes at me. Like I'm a literal idiot.

So I laugh, because it's cute. "I'm on your side. I already told ya that. I'm helping ya, aren't I? Consider us friends."

"Well, I'd hate to see how you treat your enemies."

I look to my left and side-eye her. "You do not, under any circumstances, want to know how I treat my enemies." Which is probably the wrong thing to say, because she recoils. "I just want you to make decisions. I took over for the hardest part. I let you sleep at my place, let ya take a shower, gave you some clothes, took you to the health center, waited around for your diagnosis, got ya more clothes, and took ya to dinner. I've met all your needs for this day. But I'm not gonna babysit ya, Clara." I'm pushing it here, but I've got a point, so I make it before she really does get up and walk out, because I can tell I'm pushing her limit pretty hard right now. "You need to participate. Otherwise you're just dead weight to me."

Her anger remains for a few moments as she internalizes all my words. But then she gives in and leans back, relaxing into the back of the booth. "Look, I'm... up-city Clara Birch. I... don't know what you're expecting of me. Stop playing games and just tell me what you want."

"Is that how you go through life, then? *Exceeding* people's expectations?"

Throwing those words back at her, when she meant them in the nicest of ways and I mean them as derogatory, makes her completely stop and reassess every word we've said to each other in the past ten minutes.

"I like you," I tell her. "You're very pretty." She doesn't smile. "And I'm in. You need a partner, I'm in. But you gotta pull your weight. You're heavy, Clara. I should know, I carried you up a million flights of stairs. And I'm not talking about how much you weigh, either. You know that. I'm talking about your..." Now I falter for words. Because I've never said anything like this to someone before, but at the same time, I realize I feel this way about all people, not just her. "I'm talking about your sense of self, I guess. Remember that girl I mentioned? Anneeta?"

Clara nods. Her face is slack now, but her attention is fully on me.

"She's seven years old. She was born addicted to spark. Mother died couple years back, at least. She's all alone. On her own. And do you know, even though I *would* help her, without hesitation, she has never asked me for help? She's never asked me for a single fucking thing. If I were putting together a go team, and I had pick of all the people in that tower, I'd take Anneeta with me and no one else. Because even though she's only seven, she knows exactly who she is. And you, up-city Clara Birch, haven't got a clue who you are. You're a liability to me. You're gonna get me killed. And I don't really care about that part, but I want to be in control of my death. I can get myself killed just fine, thank you, I don't need your help for that. So again, I like you, you're pretty, you're welcome to stay with me, and I'll help ya figure out what the hell happened to ya. But I'm not your fuckin' babysitter. I want you to make your own decisions. And if you want any more help from me, then you've got to ask for it. I'm not gonna try and read your mind."

I lift both my arms up and stretch them out on either side of me. "What you see is what you get. I'm an open fuckin' book. And if you and I are gonna be partners—in *any* way—then you will afford me the same courtesy. You will be straight with me and you will not lie to me. Because if I have your back, then you must have mine."

She continues to stare at me for many seconds. But I don't interrupt her silence or try and make her come to a conclusion too soon. I know she wants my help and I know she's gonna give in to my demands. But none of that is the point. The thing I really need from her right now is certainty. Not in me, but of herself.

I've been partners with people, business or otherwise, who take, but never give. And it's not even about the taking, really. It's the sense of entitlement that always surfaces when one person is doing most of the heavy lifting in a relationship, while the other comes along for the ride. And it doesn't take long to create this dynamic. If I had not said anything tonight, this is how Clara and I would be. Me making decisions for her instead of her thinking them through for herself.

And I don't want that. Even if this *were* about sex, I wouldn't want that.

Finally, she lets out a breath. "Can I stay at your place?"

"Sure."

"Can you… maybe… lend me a little bit of coin? So I could buy some things to get me through?"

I hesitate here. Not because I care about giving her money. I don't. But because she left something out. And she remembers this something while I'm hesitating because she hurriedly adds, "I… don't have any skills."

Which makes me laugh. "I wouldn't put that one on your resume."

This, in turn, makes her smile. "No. of course not. I just mean, I was preparing to be a wife. A… a social climber? Maybe?" She winces. Because even she understands this is kind of pathetic. Not the wife part, or even the social climber part, but the fact that she is realizing, in this very moment, that she has no dream. "But I'm smart," she continues. "I can learn. And anyway, coin is not the only way to pay things back."

I raise an eyebrow. "Did you just offer me sex?"

"What? No." She makes a face. "I just meant—you were the one talking about loyalty. So I was offering loyalty."

"Sure, sure."

She closes her eyes, shaking her head. "Whatever."

"I'm kidding about the sex. I know what you're saying.

You can stay at my place and I'll give you some coin to get started. But don't offer that loyalty if ya don't mean it. Because that's worth more to me than coin."

She looks me in the eyes for this last part. All serious now. And she nods. "I understand. And thank you. Not just for taking care of me and giving me what I asked for, but for being so upfront. It's a rare thing, ya know?"

"People being honest?"

She nods. "Yeah."

"Would it have gone over better if that man of yours just told ya outright that he wasn't gonna save ya?"

"Well, he kinda did say that."

"He did?"

"Yes. But… I don't think I was listening."

"Mmm. Yeah. It's a common thing people do when they don't get the answer they're looking for."

"So my circumstances are probably more my fault than his. I mean, actually, it *was* all my fault. I signed up to be a Spark Maiden. I played the game and lost." She gives me a one-shoulder shrug. "It's as simple as that."

"Maybe. Maybe not. I mean, the world, it's stacked against you, Clara. You were never meant to win."

Our food arrives before she can say anything else and the heavy topics we were just discussing fade into the background as we eat.

But on the way home, when we're walking towards the ruins, I recite her words back in my head. *I played the game and lost.*

She's nothing special in that regard.

We all play and we all lose.

It's just the way of things.

WE'RE CLIMBING **the stairs** outside the tower when Clara turns to me. "Can you show me where you found me?"

I stop and pull her off to the side of the door, out of the flow of people. "Why?"

"Because I just want to see it. Haryet had to have gone somewhere. I know she's not gonna be there now, but it's the only clue I have left."

I press my lips together and nod. "Sure. But not tonight. It's a million levels below ground and we've still got to walk up ten flights of stairs."

She groans and looks at the building.

"I'll carry you on my back if you want."

I get a sharp look for that. "No, thank you."

"OK." We walk through the doors and into the lobby, which is pretty crowded still for being nearly ten at night. My gaze sweeps around the first floor, looking for Anneeta, but I don't see her. So we just hit the stairs.

The walk is painfully slow and Clara's draggin'. So I make my offer again as we head up to the third floor. "The piggyback offer hasn't expired yet."

"I'm not unfit, ya know. I lived on the ninth floor of my own tower and I walked up and down those stairs all the time. In heavy gowns, even."

"Let's race then."

She scoffs, side-eyeing me, but skips over my playful threat. "It just felt... quicker. I almost never walked up alone."

"Are ya alone?" I pan my hand at the—literally—hundreds of people all around us.

"No, I mean with my *friends*. We would gossip and stuff. It took my mind off the climbing. Never mind. It was just different."

"Did you just call me bad company?"

I get another side-eye. "Ya know, for a fuckin' cynic, you're awfully sensitive about what people think of you."

"Nah, I'm not. I'm just trying to make a good impression on ya. But I'm not sure it's working."

She smiles, but doesn't look at me. "Well, if that's true, it is."

"You like me."

"You like *me*."

I laugh. "I do like you. Ya asked why I was being a dick? Well, that's why."

"You're a dick to me because you like me. Got it."

"It's not that. I just need to know what you're doing and why. Because I don't get invested in much these days, Clara."

"And you're afraid I'm gonna fuck you over."

"A little, but not really. I haven't got much for you to take. It's just... I haven't had a partner in a while. I don't mean women, either. I mean a *partner*. Someone I count on. Someone who counts on me."

She looks at me now, not smiling. "Your... soldier

friends. That's who you named when you said you've saved people before. What happened to them?"

"What makes you think something happened to them?"

"Because you came here to Tau City to attend War College alone."

"I never said that."

"You didn't have to. It was… understood. So what happened to them?"

"Dead."

She frowns. "All four?"

"All four."

"It was some kind of battle?"

"I guess."

"That's… not a good answer."

"Why not?" She shrugs, not looking at me. "Come on, Clara. Fill in the blanks. Let's see what ya got."

"I don't know much about war. Not enough to fill those blanks in."

"No idea at all then, huh? Your brain is too simple?"

She takes offense to my characterization, but that was the point. "Fine. If it was something to do with war, but not exactly a battle, then… someone made a bad decision and it cost them their lives."

I huff. But don't say anything.

"It was you. You made a bad decision and cost them their lives."

"Keep going."

"Wow. That sucks."

"Keep going."

She thinks for a moment. We're just passing the eighth

floor now, and as we do this, I scan the people waiting in line for jolts and jumps, looking for Anneeta. But she's not here.

Clara thinks for a minute. She answers as we pass the ninth floor. "Those things in your eyes. That make them go bright."

"The augments."

"They don't work right."

I stop, she as well, and then she turns to look at me. "Congratulations." I pan my hand to the space in front of us. "We're on the tenth floor and you didn't even have to think about it."

She doesn't move and neither do I. People come up behind us, parting around us like water, and she narrows her eyes. I'm expecting a question, but not the one she throws at me. "Can I sleep in your bed?"

I grin. "Absolutely."

She turns right towards my door and I come up behind her. When we get to it, she steps aside, allowing me to open it for her. She goes in, but I hesitate for a moment.

Because up-city Clara Birch has somehow gotten a hold of me. She's kinda weak, a little bit clueless, and I would never, not in a million years, be into a woman like her if she hadn't been dropped into my life without my consent.

But I like her and I'm glad she's here.

I step through, kick the door closed with my foot, slip my jacket down my arms, hang it on a hook, take off my shirt, and toss that on the floor.

Her eyes drop down to the floor where it lands, then dart back up to meet mine. She's got questions. I can practically see them running through her head as I watch. But she doesn't say anything. Or step aside.

"I was being a dick earlier," I say, "because I actually think you had unreasonable expectations of that man of yours. Most things are out of our control. And if this is something you've been conditioned to do—have unreasonable expectations of people, especially if you're trying to exceed them at the same time—then I'm gonna disappoint you eventually and it just feels like a setup."

"Wow." Clara takes off her jacket, drapes it over the arm of the chair, and then sits down, kicking her new boots up on my footstool. "You've got baggage, Tyse."

I grin as I take off my battle belt and hang it across the back of the spindly chair. She's not wrong.

"Also, I thought *I* was rigid with my two decades of 'poised, proper, and polite' training. But you? Wow."

I walk over to the bed, the side closest to the chair, and sit down. Then I lean over and start unlacing my boots. "I'm just being upfront with you."

"No. That's not what you're doing. You're… preempting the disappointment. So when that day comes and I'm looking at you like you're a piece of shit for doing"—she waves her hand in the air, huffing—"whatever it is you did, then you don't have to feel guilty about it. You can just point to this night and say, 'See? I told you I was gonna disappoint you.' And then you won't have to take credit for it."

"You mean blame."

"What?"

"You're confusing credit with blame."

I glance up just in time to catch her reaction. It's that crinkled face she likes to make. "Who cares?"

"Language is a precise thing—"

"Oh, my god. *Shut up.*" When I start laughing, she leans back in the chair. Angry now. "Why are you being like this?"

Laces undone, I shrug and stand up and walk over to the door, kicking my boots off. When I turn back to her, she's standing at the foot of the bed. I have a flash of memory of her here. From yesterday when she was still wearing that slutty dress. Which actually wasn't even all that revealing—her stomach was showing, and the dress was hanging very low on her hips, so it was a lot of stomach, and her shoulders were bare, but the dress wasn't sleeveless. It was that off-the-shoulder kind that gets pulled down to look sexier.

The whole thing was alluring, sure. But it looked a little traditional too. Which makes sense if she really does come from a city the way she describes.

Right now, though, dressed like this—dressed in these clothes I got for her—she reminds me of Myra. I never slept with Myra. Not for lack of trying, but she was really into rules and the number one rule of a go-team crew is no sex. And thinking about that suddenly has me thinking about this—"How many, Clara?"

"How many what?"

"Let me guess. Seven?"

"Seven what? I don't even know what you're talking about."

"How many times do you make a man take you out before you sleep with him?"

Her face goes bright red. "*What?*"

"I would just like to adjust my expectations accordingly." My grin is wild.

Her reaction is shock. She sputters for a moment, trying to find the right words to respond. "Because you think I want to have sex with you?"

"Don't ya?"

"Well…"

She kinda looks me over here. Not deliberately, but she can't help it, and it's all kinda funny.

So I smile pretty big. "Ya do, don't ya?"

She sighs, then wipes a hand through the air like she's pushing all these thoughts out of her mind. "I'm not talking about this."

"Why not?"

"Because you don't get to control all the conversations, that's why. I get a say in them too. And it's all fine and good if you expect truth out of me at all times, but that doesn't give you the right to ask any question you want. Nor does it oblige me to answer."

"It's more than seven, isn't it?"

She shakes her head, turns on her heel, then walks into the kitchen, disappearing into the bathroom. There's only a curtain, no door, so I just keep going. "Please tell me it's not more than ten. If so, we could double up on the dates, right? Count breakfast, lunch, and dinner as separate occasions?"

"I'm not having this discussion."

"Why though? Because it's more than ten? If it's more than ten, Clara, we need to talk about the meaning of the word 'haughty.' Because you are absolutely the definition of that word if you demand more than ten dates before—"

She pushes the bathroom curtain to the side with a dramatic swish of fabric and comes back out wearing nothing but the t-shirt. I'm talkin' bare feet and bare legs. She walks over to the foot stool and places her folded-up pants on top of it, flashing her fuckin' ass at me—which is covered in the cutest fuckin' lacy little panties I've ever laid eyes on. The entire back of her bum is covered in ruffles. It's the kind of fancy, over-the-top underwear you put on a child. A child going to a wedding or something. This is not the kind of underwear I've ever seen on a grown woman.

I cover my mouth, trying not to laugh out loud, but though it is stifled, it still comes out.

She whirls around, angry again. "What are you laughing about now?"

"What the hell is on your ass?"

"What?" She twists her neck, looking over her shoulder, trying to see her own ass. "What are you talking about?"

"What is up with that underwear?"

She rolls her eyes at me. "Oh, my god. Just go to bed or something. You're being obnoxious."

"Is that the kind of underwear women wear where you come from?"

She is *so* done with me. "I was being *Extracted*, Tyse. I was dressed up, OK? This is the lingerie they gave me for the occasion. And"—she twists, peeking at her ass again—"it's... I dunno. Just normal underwear for Spark Maidens. If you don't like them, don't look at them."

"Oh, I never said I didn't like them."

Her eyes find mine and she presses her lips together. "I'm not sleeping with you."

"Because it's more than ten, isn't it?"

"I don't even understand what you're talking about there. Seven. Ten. Whatever."

"How many dates did what's-his-name take you on before you slept with him?"

"That's none of your business. My private life is none of your business."

"It was eleven, wasn't it?"

She's about to yell at me, I can see it coming. But she catches herself before any words come flying out. I watch as that same composure she used to dismiss me earlier comes back into play, and again, I am reminded that she is not just some ordinary somebody. She is a very special somebody.

"It was..." Her eyes roll up as she thinks. "A hundred and seventy-three."

"What?" I guffaw at this number.

But the laugh stops abruptly when up-city Clara Birch walks right up to me and places her hand flat against my bare chest. "A hundred and seventy-three."

"That's impossible. No man would wait that long for a woman."

Clara smirks up at me. "He was my childhood best friend, Tyse. We grew up together. We spent every bit of our lives together. We've practically been in love since we were born. When we got old enough, we dated. And right before I was chosen for Extraction, we had sex exactly one time."

"How old were ya?"

"Eighteen."

"How old are ya now?"

"Twenty-eight."

"You've only had sex once?"

"No. Don't be stupid. We met up while I was a Spark Maiden. Every couple of months."

"When was the last time you had sex with him?"

"The day I got here." That smirk of hers turns into a sympathetic smile as she pats my chest. Then she turns to the bed and crawls up it, flashing those ruffles at me.

"I've got no chance at all, have I?"

She chuckles as she slides her legs under the covers and turns onto her side, hugging a pillow. "Not even a tiny one."

Then she closes her eyes and puts me completely out of her mind.

Clara doesn't stir when I get in bed next to her. Maybe asleep, maybe just trying to torture me with her indifference. But either way, she won this night.

Because the only thing on my mind as I lie there, looking up at the ceiling, is her.

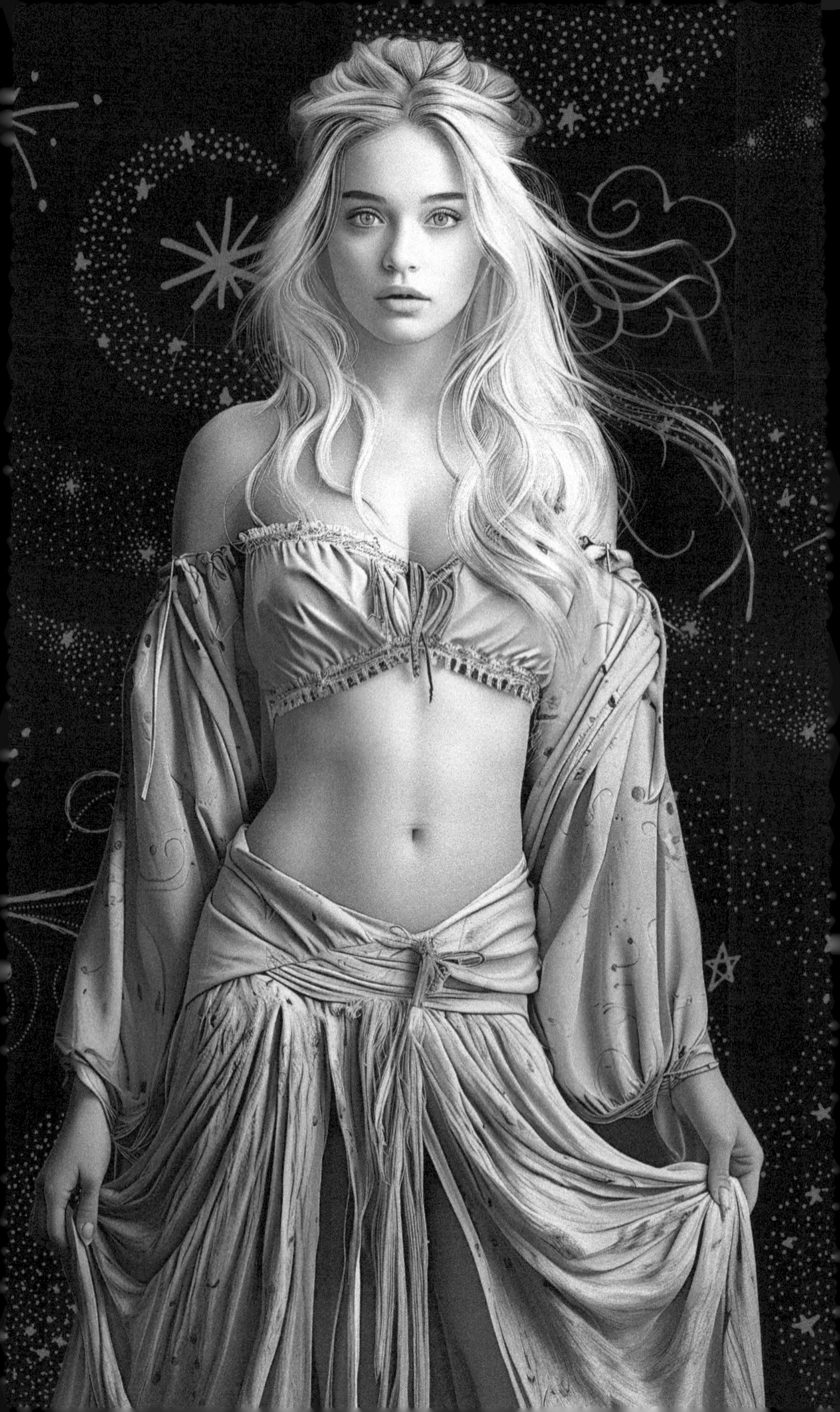

CLARA

CHAPTER TWENTY-SIX

My *dreams are filled* with those last few words of his. *I've got no chance at all, have I?* It even comes through in his voice.

And for some reason, these words bother me. Because in the dream we are clearly together. Laughing, and smiling, and sometimes even arguing like couples do, with the familiar sense that this person you're with can take who you really are and you can be yourself with them without having to fear that they will misread you, or, worse, give up on you.

It's a good dream, but kinda sad too. And I'm not sure why. My mind is spinning with scenarios when I catch the sound of coins clanging against glass. I open my eyes just in time to see Tyse—shirtless and wearing only a pair of boxer shorts—reaching into the jar where he keeps his tip money. When he turns, his eyes meet mine, but he doesn't say anything. Just walks over to the door where a man is waiting and he trades the coins for one of those phones he uses to receive messages.

After the door closes, he turns to me, holding up a finger. "I have to take this." Then he ducks into the kitchen where he proceeds to talk in a low voice.

I look up at the ceiling and realize there's writing and drawings up there. Something very old, probably. Sloppy, and hurried, and faded, the words say 'Sparktopia was here' in large, looping red letters that billow across a white banner that spans an image of a black tower.

Certainly not something Tyse did. At least it doesn't come off as his handiwork, but what do I know? I met the guy two days ago.

I catch him saying, "Be there in a few," in a low voice before turning to me. He sets the phone down on the small countertop and meets my gaze. "I've got work today. I've got to leave and I'll probably be gone until after dark."

"Oh." I'm disappointed and this one word comes out before I have time to rein that disappointment in.

"But I've got an idea for ya. A way to spend your time. A job."

I sit up, pulling the covers around me. "A job?"

"With Rodge. Down on Eight where they have the services. He'll give ya work, he's always short-staffed." Tyse pauses to smile here. "So you can pay me back for the clothes and shit."

Is he serious about the payback? I can't tell. I get the feeling that Tyse Saarinen has more coin to his name than he lets on. Sure, he lives in a free tower with spark addicts, doesn't have a regular job, and is suffering from a biological tech mistake that has clearly derailed his life, but he's not the least bit desperate. There's an air of satisfaction about him and people worried about coin don't act satisfied.

"It's a good job, trust me. Having Rodge on your side is a huge plus in this tower, Clara."

"I'm not complaining. You don't have to sell it to me. I'll do it. What else am I gonna do? Stay here all day and snoop through your shit?" I laugh, because it's a joke, but Tyse doesn't seem to find it funny. "I'm kidding. Geez. Lighten up."

Tyse shrugs. "Whatever. I don't care if you snoop. But ya better be careful, you might not like what you find."

"What does that mean?"

But he doesn't answer me. Just turns, goes into the bathroom, pulls the curtain closed behind him, and a few seconds later all I hear is the sound of a shower.

I blow out a breath, wondering for the millionth time if any of this is real.

It doesn't seem likely that three days ago I had a completely different life in another… world? Time? Not sure. But I was there, in that version of Tau City. And while I had to agree to some seriously unpleasant conditions regarding a certain god inside a tower, in the grand scheme of things it was not all that bad.

I had a boyfriend—maybe not officially, like with quotes around it and shit, but everyone knew that Finn and I were a thing. That we were getting married. I had my own floor of rooms, and my little circle of friends, not to mention more coin than I could ever spend. My social calendar was overflowing with dates, and galas, and dinners, and events. Plus the odd tryst whenever Finn and I could pull one together.

Now I'm living with a stranger in a seedy one-room apartment inside the very tower I just walked into a few days ago, except… it's not that tower at all. I own one set of clothing, have no coin to my name, and my immediate destiny lies with a man named Rodge who is perpetually understaffed.

Which begs the question... *why* is he always short-staffed? Is he a dick? Is he cheap? Does he smell?

A chortle escapes past my lips because it's... insane. That's it. That's the only word to describe my life at the moment. It just makes no logical sense at all.

The shower stops and the bathroom curtain swishes back open. Tyse appears, soaking wet and *completely* naked. His eyes find mine as he reaches for a towel folded neatly on a shelf. But he doesn't smile as my mouth drops open in surprise, just shrugs. "Sorry for the flash, but I don't normally have guests so I didn't properly think this moment through ahead of time."

Then he snatches the towel and disappears back behind the curtain. Only to reappear a few seconds later with the towel wrapped around his waist.

My mouth is still open in surprise when his eyes find mine again. "You're rethinking it now, aren't ya?"

I shake myself out of the shock. "What?"

"That 'not even a tiny one' threat you threw at me last night." He chooses some clothes off another shelf, then disappears one more time to change.

I haven't even recovered from the sight of his 'flash,' as he called it, when he once again reappears, wet, but dressed. He grabs his boots from near the door and then walks over to the chair under the window and takes a seat.

His grin is wide and he watches me as he slips his feet inside his boots and starts lacing them up. "Well?"

"Well what? Am I... *rethinking you?*" I huff. Because... well. I kind of am.

"No. Are ya gonna get out of bed and get dressed? Because if not, I'll leave ya here and you can make your way down to Eight and introduce yourself to Rodge without my help. I'm in a hurry. Stayn's got work for me and it's kind of important."

Well... this is awkward. Because no, I do not want to go down to Eight and explain to a man I never met that I now work for him. But also, I do not want to get out of bed wearing nothing but underwear under this shirt just so he can make fun of me again.

Except I don't seem to have a choice. So I can either be shy about it, or flash him back.

I throw the covers off, swing my legs over the side of the bed opposite him, and let him get a good, long look at my ruffled backside as I slowly stand and stretch my arms up to the ceiling, feigning a yawn.

"I like them, by the way."

I turn to him, smile sweetly, and nod. "I know. You told me that last night. Did you see them in your dreams?"

Tyse just continues to grin as I grab my pants off the footstool, then shake them out and pull them up my legs. He watches me the entire time. Like he's mesmerized.

Which is, not gonna lie, kinda thrilling. Tyse Saarinen is not my type. At all. If he were living in my version of the world, he'd be living down-city for sure. I would not even look at him twice.

Well. OK, if I saw him—as in, had the *opportunity* to see him—I probably would look twice. More than twice, maybe. Because this image he's projecting—it says seedy one-room apartment, dangerous backstory, and if you look too hard, you'll probably be sorry.

But it *works* for him.

The muscles, the tattoos, the facial hair. I was never into the facial hair back home, but that's probably because I never saw Finn with it.

I walk over to the door, get my boots, and then sit on the edge of the bed as I put them on.

Tyse clears his throat. Like he's snapping himself back into the moment. And possibly out of a fantasy about me, perhaps? "Do you think you'll be OK here today without me?"

I side-eye him as I lean over, lacing my boots. "Of course. Why wouldn't I?"

He holds up his hand, one finger raised. "Ya claim to come from another world." He holds up another finger. "I'm literally the only person you know." He holds up a third finger. "Not to sound disparaging, Clara, but you come off as... a bit of a princess."

"Well... thank you. I guess. I am kind of a princess. A haughty one at that. But I'm not stupid, Tyse. And I'm not socially awkward, either. In fact, socializing is probably my only true skill in life—if you don't count dancing and dressmaking, I guess."

"Talking, dancing, and dressmaking. Well. You might just be the most employable person in this whole fuckin' tower." But he's shaking his head and laughing at me as he walks across the room, buckles his weapon belt to his hip, and pans his hand towards the door. "Let's get you busy, then."

RODGE IS a dark-skinned man with a bright smile. Much to my relief, he does not smell, nor is he a dick. In fact, he's quite charming. His accent makes every word that comes out of his mouth sound musical. It's nothing I've ever heard before. Tyse has a weird accent too, but Rodge's accent is different.

I am introduced, we shake hands, and Tyse explains that I am a very smart, capable friend of his and I am looking for work.

Rodge immediately makes an offer. "How about maid? I always need maids. Do you clean?"

Tyse holds up a hand. "No. Not a maid."

"Ooooookay." Rodge's eyes roll up to the ceiling as he rethinks. "How about… runner? You look fit. I bet you could run those stairs—"

Tyse presses that hand forward. "No. Not runner. Something here, on the eighth. Something that doesn't require her to leave your sight."

Rodge makes a knowing expression and he nods. "Ohhhhh. I see." He studies me again. "Well, in that case, you are my new customer helper. You stand there." He points to a space behind a long, wide counter. It's the end destination for the literally hundreds of people in line waiting for service. "And you take orders and fill up bags. Sounds good?" He's not looking at me for approval, though. He's looking at Tyse.

"Yes, that's perfect. And"—Tyse leans in towards Rodge a little—"I do need a maid. My place is a fuckin' mess. Send someone down to clean it all up before she knocks off for the day." Then Tyse looks at me. "Sorry to leave you like this, but I gotta go. I'll see ya tonight."

He turns and walks off, that weapon of his banging against his hip as he leaves.

I turn back to Rodge and smile my biggest professional Spark Maiden smile. "I guess I'm all yours."

---

*I SPEND **the first hour*** shadowing Rodge as he fills order slips. Before the tower residents can enter the store, they interact with a teenage girl at the main entrance, who is Rodge's daughter, Prisha. Residents tell Prisha what they need, she writes it down on a pad of paper and then gives it to them and they move forward in the line so that by the time they get to Rodge and me, all we have to do is fill the order they give us.

It's all very efficient because everyone knows what to expect.

I like that. It's comforting to be in a state of… sameness. Routines are easy. Because as the hours pass, I relax and almost seamlessly start to become one of them. A resident of the tower.

The store is more than basic goods. On the far end of the big room is another room where people do laundry in machines. I can't really see much from behind the counter where I'm filling orders because there are so many people in the way, but every time there is a gap in the crowd, I lean in, desperate to see what a washing machine looks like in this world.

I haven't done my own laundry in a decade, but when I was in charge of it, our machine did not make noise like the ones in there.

"They run off jumps."

"Huh?" I turn, surprised at Rodge's voice in my ear.

"You've been pretty curious about the laundromat all morning. The machines run off jumps. That's how we power them. The laundromat is a joint venture with myself and the gentlemen on the other side of the tower who sell jolts and jumps. I provide machines and labor, they provide the jumps. It's very expensive, but…" Rodge shrugs. "Some residents of the tower have the coin, so we are happy to wash their clothes for them. Tyse always has us wash his clothes. He's got coin, you know. War pensions for augments—even defective ones—are very generous. Don't let his meager existence fool you."

I smile. "Yes. You're probably right about that. But… what's a jump?"

"Oh!" Rodge's eyebrows go up. "You are very new, aren't you?"

I smile meekly and shrug. "Yes."

Rodge continues to work as he talks, taking a slip and handing to me for filling. "Jolts and jumps are packages of spark. It's all around us in here, but just in small bits. The gentlemen on the other side of the tower can collect the spark from the air and package it into potent jolts and even stronger jumps. You're not addicted, I take it?"

I'm dropping little bars of food into the order bag when I answer. "Uhh... I don't think so?"

"Well, if you stay much longer, you will be. So be careful. Maybe you could talk Tyse into leaving when you go."

I turn and hand him the bag, now filled. "Why would I do that?"

Rodge takes the bag and hands it to the resident with a smile. "Five meal bars, five coins, Regina."

Regina—an older woman with very messy gray hair and wearing clothes that look like they have never seen the inside of that laundromat—looks pained as she counts out five coins on the counter. But she doesn't complain and before she turns to leave with her bag of food bars, she even gives us a smile. "Thank you. See you next time."

Rodge gives her a small wave, then takes another order slip and hands it to me, picking up our conversation where we left off. "Tyse doesn't belong here, Clara. He belongs..." Rodge's eyes drift over to the window—which is actually a large cutout in the side of the building, outside of which is the dumbwaiter system that, for the right price, can get any resident of the tower anything they might need from the city. "Out there." Rodge points in a seemingly random direction, which I interrupt to mean Tau City. But then when Rodge adds, "Where he came from," I realize that's not what he means at all.

"He belongs back in..." I search my memory for the

name of the city Tyse said he came from as I start filling up the new order bag. "Delta?"

"No." Rodge laughs. "Not Delta City. The Omega Outlands, of course. He hasn't told you about it?"

"He mentioned it. Kinda of." I just have no idea what he was talking about, but I don't add that part. "It was something to do with his soldiering?"

"Oh, very much. The Omega Outlands is nothing but augments."

"That's the stuff in his eyes," I say, handing Rodge the now-filled bag. "That makes him glow blue and show him words."

Rodge gives me one of his surprised looks—which I rather enjoy because his face is so animated. "You've seen it!"

"Yeah. But… I think it's acting up, or something. He was kind of surprised when it happened."

"Oooooo." Rodge's expression is so comically astounded, I let out a chuckle. "That is something very interesting."

Or, I postulate, something I was not supposed to talk about.

I think he gets this impression as well, because he changes the subject back to our original topic. "Jumps are very big packages of power. The men on the other side of Eight, they sell the spark to people who have been here too long. They need more and more of it to function, so the packages come in different sizes. Jumps are the largest available."

"Define 'too long,' as far as being in the tower goes."

"Well, it's different for everyone. I've been here twenty

years, myself. But I don't live in the tower. My family and I live on the far edge of the ruins outside. So none of us have ever been in the field for more than ten hours at a time. We're addicted, like everyone else on this edge of town. But we can leave and we're not affected much. We even took a vacation back home last year for two whole weeks!" He smiles like he's proud of this. "We could've stayed longer, but Tau City is home now. Thetaiota is where we came from, not where we belong."

"Hmm. Is Prisha your only child?"

"Oh, god, no." Rodge laughs. "She is my baby of nine. But they have all grown and left us behind. That's why I am perpetually understaffed." He pauses to make another astonished face. "Oooh! I almost forgot. I need to send Prisha up to clean Tyse's room. Do you think you could take orders now?"

I nod. "Yes. I can do that. But... maybe *I* could clean Tyse's room? I mean, I am living there now. Plus, it would be a shame to disrupt the flow in here with my inevitable mistakes." I nod my head towards Prisha. "There's always a learning curve, isn't there?"

Rodge is not convinced. "Tyse instructed me to keep you within my sight. If you go up and clean his room, I would not be able to see you."

"But I'd just be in his room. I would close the door. No one will come in, it's *Tyse*."

Rodge laughs. "He's quite intimidating, isn't he?"

"He certainly can be." But my mind flashes back to Tyse standing over the bed last night, looking down at me. *I've got no chance at all, have I?* He didn't look intimidating at all in that moment. He looked almost vulnerable.

And the fact of the matter is, I'm stuck here. After walking outside yesterday and realizing that there is really no way back, I've come to terms with it. This is my new life and, by luck or destiny, Tyse is now the man in it.

Which means he *does* have a chance. I mean… Finn *sent me into the tower*. He literally gave me away. It wasn't to Tyse, it was to the god. But it might as well have been Tyse. Because he's what I found on the other side of those black tower doors.

"Well." Rodge has been considering my offer, and now he lets out a sigh. "It would be more practical to have you clean, since you live there. And I do believe you would be safe. I will walk you up and drop you off, and then I will have fulfilled my promise to Tyse."

I beam a smile at him. "Perfect."

Rodge hands the filled bag over to the resident, collects his coins, and then points to the next resident in line. "Be right back."

I am loaded up with a rack across my shoulders with buckets hanging off the edges, perfectly balanced so I can carry them. Each bucket contains cleaning supplies, plus fresh linen and towels.

Then Rodge walks me back up to ten and deposits me inside Tyse's room. "I'll be back in three hours to walk you back down and close out the day. Good?"

I nod. "Very good. Thank you, Rodge."

It's not that I'm eager to clean—god, it's been a decade

since I've done that too—I just want to snoop. I did, after all, get permission to do that.

This permission also came with a warning: *Ya better be careful, you might not like what you find.* But there's not much in this place.

Whatever personal items I find, they will be small.

So how bad could they be?

MAYBE I HAVEN'T CLEANED my own rooms since I moved into the Little Sister dorm over a decade ago, but I have been watching the maids that whole time. Which doesn't make me an expert or anything, but I have a general idea of how to start this whole cleaning-a-room process.

I am not a snoop by trade or habit, so I don't start there. Discovering things should happen organically. While dusting, probably, since I will have to pick up every trinket, personal item, and scrap of paper in order to clean under it.

So I begin with stripping the bed and replacing the sheets. Then I sweep the floor, wipe up the 'kitchen'—which is really nothing but a countertop—and then wipe down the bathroom.

Once all the gross stuff is out of the way I start on the fun stuff—all the little things he's collected over the years.

Which is a considerable time if he's lived in this same room since he stopped soldiering.

Unfortunately, there's really not much to find. He's not messy, per se. There are no old food bags lying around or anything like that. His personal items are mostly useful things. I find quite a few dead phones. Two lost in the cushions of the chair alone. Also, a lot of notes. Not anything fun, like a love note. Mostly they are just scraps of paper with a few words or numbers scribbled on them. Appointments, I think, because they often have times attached.

I don't throw any of the notes away, just find an empty jar on a kitchen shelf and stuff them all inside just in case he was saving them on purpose. But I don't think he was. I think Tyse has his room cleaned by Rodge's daughter, Prisha, quite regularly because there's not even a lot of dust.

At this point, the sun outside is beginning to set and I've pretty much given up on the idea of learning secret things about Tyse from snooping. Then a knock at the door startles me.

I just stare at it for a moment, wondering who it could be.

Maybe… his friend Anneeta?

But also, maybe that creepy guy down the hall who was caught looking at me and got a very hard shove for his troubles?

"Clara?"

I walk to the door, open it, and find Prisha staring back at me. "Father says it's quitting time. He's sorry he didn't come back two hours ago, like he promised. We got swamped. Do you have dirty linens for me?"

"Oh. Yes, I do." I put them all in a pile on the floor when I stripped the bed, so I load them back onto the bucket contraption and take it back to Prisha. She reaches for it and expertly balances it across her shoulders like she's been doing this sort of thing her whole life. "Did I take too long, Prisha?"

Prisha cocks a perfectly arched eyebrow at me. "Take too *long?*" She's not wearing a lot of make-up, but she is wearing some. And it is very clear that she does not live in this tower. Even if Rodge didn't inform me of that fact, I could tell. Her dress is simple, but a very fine, high-quality linen in a pale yellow that looks very attractive against her dark skin. It's a straight dress with long bell sleeves and ends just above the knee. Every seam is trimmed in light blue silk ribbons.

It's not fancy, but it's also very far from plain and it reminds me of something I might've worn to a luncheon with the Canal District ladies in my past life.

Prisha is also wearing a lot of jewelry. Gold bracelets, earrings, and a necklace. I would be a little hesitant to wear all that treasure on my person in a place like the tower, but I guess if you're Rodge's daughter, people know better than to mess with you.

Prisha might work in a down-city tower, but she is up-city all the way.

"Yeah," I say. "The day is over and I barely just got done. I was too slow, wasn't I?"

Prisha chuckles. "Dear Clara, no one expects you to

work. Tyse has asked my father to watch you. Having you work is just how he fulfills that request. It's the same for me." She shrugs up one shoulder, like she doesn't mind.

"But you are very efficient. I saw you this morning."

"Because what else do I have to do? If I have to come to work with my father every day, I might as well be nice to people and do things expeditiously. Oh! Before I forget. Here."

This is when I notice that there is a small package wrapped in brown paper tucked under her arm. She thrusts the package at me. "And this too." Then she reaches into a pocket and withdraws a coin, holding it out for me on her palm. "Don't spend it all in one place."

I take the coin, then point to the package. "But… what is this?"

"A gift from Father. He likes you and he's very generous to people he likes. See you tomorrow!" She waves, then turns, walking back towards the stairs.

"Thank you!" I call. "See you tomorrow!" I close the door then sit down on the chair and place the package and coin on the footrest. One coin. Is this what I can expect from a day's work? I'm not sure, but it doesn't matter because it belongs to Tyse, anyway. I owe him for the clothes I'm currently wearing. Not to mention the dinner last night and whatever else he's keeping a tab of.

The package is medium-sized and squishy, so I'm prepared for there to be clothes inside before I open it, but I am not prepared for the quality of garment I remove from the packaging.

It's a dress, nearly identical to the one Prisha was

wearing, but dyed the absolute lightest shade of desert green and trimmed in silk ribbons the color of sand.

My smile is big when I lean back in the chair, holding the dress to my chest, because this dress makes me both satisfied and happy in a way I don't really have an explanation for.

I have been given many gifts over the last decade. Too many dresses to count. But all the gifts that came from being a Spark Maiden felt like... well, I hate to say bribes, but that is how they felt. 'Insincere' might be a better way to describe it. Meant to kindle my favor in some future transaction. In other words, they were all tied to an expectation.

None of those gifts or dresses were special to me personally and all of them were taken for granted.

But this is not a transaction, it's a true gift from a man who knows I have nothing to give in return. So I do not take this one for granted and I hold it up again so I can take in all the details, feeling truly happy in a way I never expected, I squeal as I kick my feet against the footstool like a new Little Sister who just got her first look at the dorm.

This kicking sends the footstool tipping over backwards. And this tipping of the footstool is how I accidentally discover Tyse's first secret. Because the top of the footstool flips open to reveal a hidden compartment inside. I place the dress on the freshly made bed and get down on my knees to have a peek.

Inside the footstool is a wooden box about the size of my palm. I pick it up, find it to be heavy, and weigh it in my hand as I deliberate the pros and cons of looking at the contents.

If I look, my curiosity will be satisfied and I will undoubtedly learn more about Tyse.

But then his warning comes back to me. *You might not like what you find.*

Fuck it. I open the box and find stacks and stacks of gold coins tightly packed together with a clear piece of glass, or something like it, over the top of them. They are packed so tight I get the impression that the box was made to hold coins specifically, because they do not jiggle at all. Not even after the box was tipped over with the stool.

The only other thing inside the box is a small circular silver disc, even smaller than a coin, that has been taped to the inside of the lid.

I huff. Well, this was a bust. But that's when I notice that the little disc has writing on it. I squint, but the tape obscures the message just enough so I can't read it. So I carefully peel the tape off and grasp the outer edges of the disc between the tips of my forefinger and thumb as I hold it up to the light. It says 'Capt. T. Jarvinen' on the first line and the numbers one-seven-one-seven-two-three on the second line.

Immediately, my face scrunches up into a frown. "Well, this is yet another a big fat nothing." Then I pinch the flat sides of the disc, ready to put it back, when a spark shoots through my body, forcing me to stand up and release it.

My mouth is open in stunned surprise as I watch the little metal disc roll across the floor and into the kitchen, where it teeters and falls over on one side.

"What the hell?" I look down at myself, checking to see if I'm OK, then draw in a long breath as I try and work out what just happened.

That thing *shocked me*. With some kind of power. I can still feel a tingle in my fingertips from where I touched it. But when I look down at my hand, there's no sign of a burn or anything.

"Static," I say out loud. Even in my world we have static. Little bits of power that hide in the air and collect on windy days. So when you touch certain things—like fabrics—the little bits of power are released and a tiny shock can be produced.

But this was more than a tiny shock. It was... a *jolt*.

Immediately, Rodge's words from this morning come back to me. *"The gentlemen on the other side of the tower can collect the spark from the air and package it into potent jolts and even stronger jumps."*

That's how they sell the spark.

This must be one of those. A jolt or a jump. And Tyse must've been saving it up for something, that's why it was in the box.

Shit, I hope I didn't just use it all up. Rodge said it's all very pricey. That's all I need, more debt to Tyse. It's already gonna take me forever to pay him back if I'm only getting one coin a day.

I need to put it back and pretend I never found this box or his secret hiding place. That way, he'll never know it was me who used his jolt.

Stepping away from the footstool, I eyeball the disc cautiously. How do I pick it up without shocking myself again? This is when I realize the edges must be insulated. Because it didn't shock me when I held it on edge between my fingertips. Only when I pressed the pads of them on the flat sides to put it away.

Is that the secret to holding a jolt? Touch it only on the edges?

Should I go down to Rodge and ask?

But Prisha said the day was over so he's probably gone. And even though I wouldn't admit it to Tyse, I am a little bit scared of the people in the tower. Especially that guy down the hall. I would not want to run into him again without Tyse or Rodge with me.

The thing is the size of a button. Surely I can handle it.

But I eyeball it as I walk towards the kitchen, picturing in my mind's eye how I will grasp it just along the edges and place it back under the lid of the box, put the box away, and pretend this never happened.

When the little disc is at my feet, I let out a breath and bend down, hesitantly reaching for it. The shock it gave me wasn't horrible, but it wasn't pleasant, either. And I'm not eager to experience it again.

I position my fingers, lower them down, and pinch the edges.

Immediately, I'm shocked again, but the shock is already gone by the time I realize it's happened, and a burst of animated light takes its place.

I let go and the light disappears.

Then I just sit there on the kitchen floor, mouth open and eyes blinking, trying to make sense of what I just saw. "What was that?" These words come out in a whisper.

Light. I know that much. But it was more than light. There were... people in that light. And they were moving.

I stare at the little button of trouble, wondering what to do now. Just leave it there and wait for Tyse to come home? Is it some kind of jump or jolt? And did I use it all up?

Definitely not. I did not use it up, but I also don't think it's a jump or a jolt. It's something else. Something...

I reach for it again before I talk myself out of it. And the moment my fingers touch the edges, the light springs out again. This time, there is no shock at all, confirming that this is not a hit of energy for spark addicts.

Then I hear voices and they are coming right out of the light.

Without dropping it, I scramble to stand up. And as I move, the... image—that's the only word I have for this light, because that's what it is—the image moves with me, but maintains a certain proportion. Which is not exactly true to life. Bits of the image are stretched out in some places and squashed in others.

"Attention," someone in the light says. "Discharge number A-14-7-TJ, Captain Tymothy Jarvinen."

Then Tyse's face appears. Big too. So there's no mistaking that this is him. It's just a head, and it's not real, just another light image. I know this because it rotates in a circle and the numbers just recited by the person in charge, I guess, are floating across his forehead.

"Did your advisors explain the proceedings, Capt. Jarvinen?"

When his mouth opens and answers with a curt, "Yes, sir," I am so shocked, I almost drop the disc.

"You are being discharged from the Sweep Army for high crimes against your own team. Was this explained to you?"

What? I lean in. Did I hear that correctly? High crimes?

"Yes, sir."

"This is your official record to be presented to any future employers."

Tyse lets out an incredulous scoff here. "*Future* employers? That's almost fuckin' funny."

The officiator looks displeased at the interruption, but seems to be in a hurry—or maybe it's not his job to correct Tyse—so he just skips over the outburst. "The stipulations of your discharge are very strict and I will recite them now to make sure you understand."

"Trust me, administrator, I'm very familiar with the details."

"You will refrain from comment. This meeting is not about you, it's about procedure. Something you obviously have trouble with."

The eyes on the floating head of Tyse roll in scorn. Clearly these two people are not in the same room. Tyse is somewhere else and his head is being projected into the space where the administrator is. This is not any kind of technology I have seen before, and this assumption about being in different locations would be ridiculous in my world. But after my trip to the health center, anything seems possible in this version of Tau City.

Regardless, the substance of the meeting is clear. Tyse messed up in some major way and he's getting kicked out of the Sweep Army.

Something he sort of admitted to, in a way, but certainly didn't explain to this level of detail. But then again, why would he? I'm a complete stranger. One doesn't go around announcing life-altering mistakes to strangers.

I'm about to let go of the disc and put it back—this is really none of my business, even if he is using a fake name these days—but then a new projection takes the place of Tyse's head.

It's still, not moving, but appears to be the middle of some kind of action. War action. Five people are shown mid-movement, but frozen in time. They are all wearing the same kind of uniform, though small details about it are different. For instance, the one woman has her sleeves cut off. Another man, not Tyse, is only wearing some kind of thick vest up top, but nothing underneath. It looks like they're in a desert cave and something very stressful is happening because all their expressions convey shock, and fear, and pain.

"I was there," the voice of Tyse says. "I remember it vividly. So you can skip the replay."

"Sorry, Mr. Jarvinen—"

"Mr., is it now? What happened to Captain?"

"When this final meeting is over, your ranking will have been stripped and there will be no public record of it anywhere."

Since Tyse's face has been replaced with the soldier scene, I can't see his reaction. But I think he's pissed. Like maybe this part hadn't been explained to him.

"As I was saying," the administrator continues, "this is

procedure. Close your eyes if you don't want to see it, because the replay starts now."

And then all the soldiers spring to life. There is sound, but it's low, so I can't really make out the words. Plus, everyone is in a panic. Something very terrible is happening. Then one of them—the woman—falls to her knees, screaming and holding her head like her brain might explode. This part I do hear, because her screams are so loud, there's no way to miss it.

"It's inside me, Tyse! It's inside me! Get it out! Get it out!"

The next thing I know, her head explodes. Bits of bone and blood just go everywhere. I'm so shocked, I almost drop the little disc. Not even sure how I manage to keep hold of it.

Because whatever she meant by her last frantic words, whatever was inside her head—that wasn't what exploded it.

It was Tyse.

The scene switches to another point of view and there he is, with some kind of weapon, still smoking from the discharge, pointed where her head used to be.

Then another soldier is screaming. A man, the one wearing only that thick vest. And he's saying similar things. *It's inside me. Get it out.* The other two soldiers start up as well. And then Tyse discharges his weapon three more times and all the heads explode.

He puts the weapon up to his own head and I gasp. Even though I know he didn't kill himself, it's still shocking to me. Then he waits—eyes closed and gulping down breaths

—for whatever invaded his team's minds to invade his as well.

The scene ends and Tyse's floating and rotating face is back. His eyes are closed here now too. Like maybe he didn't watch the replay.

"You were accused and found guilty of murdering your own team. This is a high crime in the eyes of—"

"I *had* to." Tyse cuts him off, spitting these words out between gritted teeth. "They were *infected*."

"The trial is over, Mr. Jarvinen, so save it. The conditions of your sentencing and discharge are the following—"

I let go of the disc and the image disappears.

He killed four people. Just… blew their heads off.

Of course, as a soldier, he'd have killed many people. Dozens? Hundreds? Does it matter?

The take-home message here is that Tyse Saarinen is lying about his identity and he's a convicted murderer.

I pinch the disc again, the image appears again, and I watch it all the way through again.

Then again.

And again.

And again.

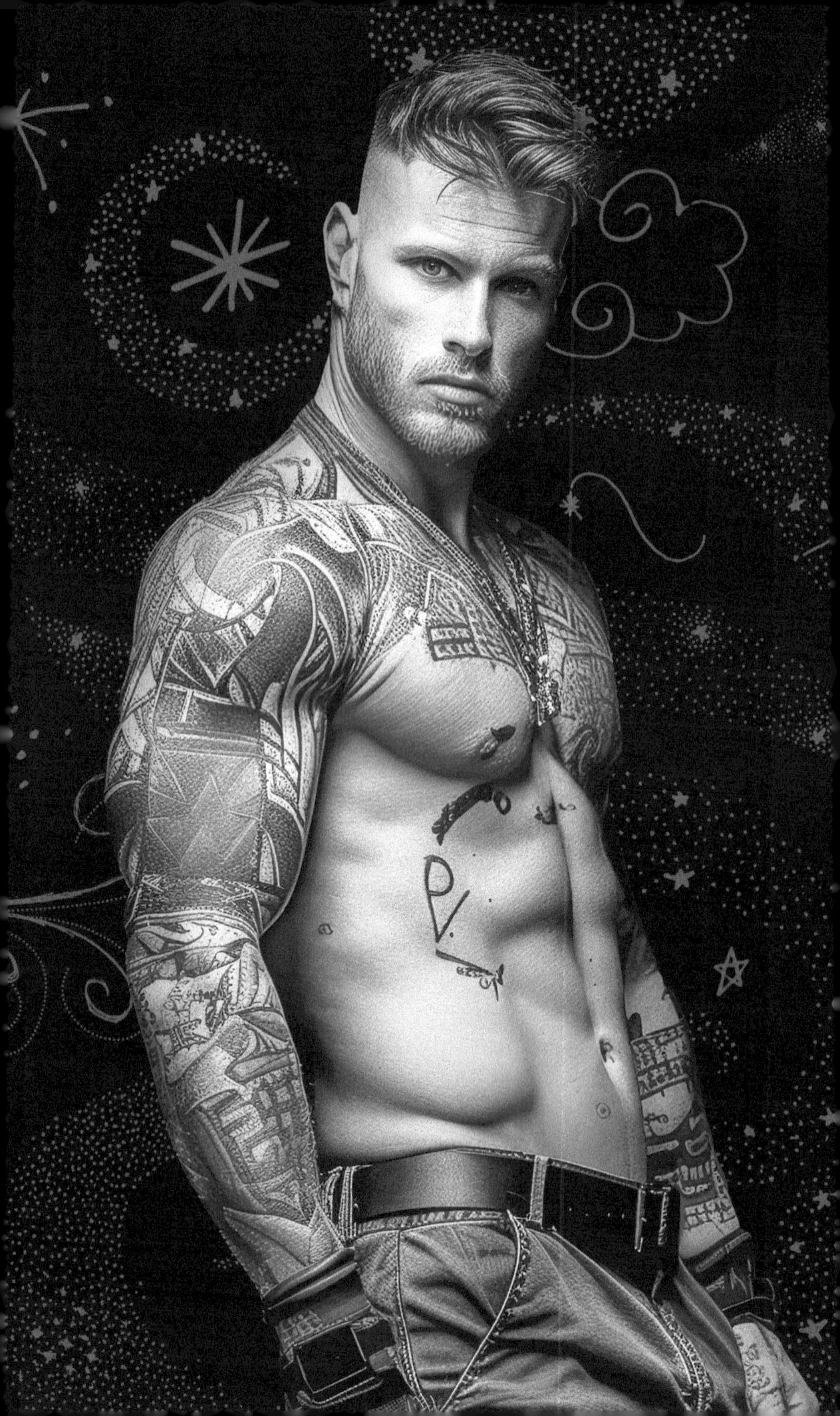

TYSE

CHAPTER TWENTY-SEVEN

*T*he job offer from *Stayn* for this week is security. Most of the time Stayn hires out his off-duty patrolmen for private bodyguarding when important people come into Tau City for meetings or whatever, and doesn't bother calling me in. But there's a big political thing happening this week and all his off-duty guys are busy.

I'm always the last one on the list when it comes to jobs he needs done, but I don't mind because nine out of ten times when he makes me an offer like this, I don't even take it. I've gotten used to the retired life. I like calling all the shots and have little interest in being accountable to people for coin.

But I feel the need for space after last night's conversation with Clara about her boyfriend. Actually, it's not *all* about her boyfriend, it's more that I need time to think about who she is because I think my first impression of her was wrong, so this job is a reason to get myself some space.

I don't make many mistakes when it comes to figuring people out. Normally, I have a highly refined sense of intuition and these instincts have saved my ass in the Omega Outlands on more than one occasion.

But it turns out that there's more to up-city Clara Birch than I first thought. Maybe even *much* more. It's not surprising that she has a boyfriend. She's pretty, she's young, and she's smart. Not to mention the hot body. Which is all I thought she was—the body—when I first found her down in the lower levels of the tower.

I'm still not sure what was up with the dress she was wearing, but she alluded to it being out of her control, and that makes sense. Because the Clara Birch I have started to get to know is not a tavern wench. Not even close. She's some kind of princess. Not in the literal sense, though maybe she is, for all I know. It's possible the Tau City she comes from has royalty. But it doesn't matter if she's got the blue blood or not, she's... refined. And you only have to spend a few hours with her to see it. Slutty dresses cannot hide the things she is inside and if there's one thing that's certain to me now, it's that Clara Birch is intrinsically *polished*.

Anyway, the part about her boyfriend that bothers me isn't the fact that he exists. It's not even the fact that she still has feelings for him. The part that bothers me is their history.

Childhood friends, teenage sweethearts, first loves.

That's a hard act to follow, even if he did send her into the tower as some ritualistic sacrifice. Given the choice to go back or stay, she would go back.

Which shouldn't bother me—she and I are nothing to each other—but it took me three hours to fall asleep last night after I got in bed with her. She had no trouble whatsoever putting me out of her mind and sleeping through the night. She passed out like a baby within minutes.

And then the first thing I started thinking about when I woke up—even as I was getting out of bed and opening the door for the phone delivery—was *her*.

Her. A woman who is no one to me.

And how I am nothing more than the inevitable… *rebound*.

Which kinda pisses me off.

I'm kind of a big deal. Well, *was* kind of a big deal. Yes, I am a failed augment, but being an augment at all puts me in the top point zero-zero-one most intelligent people of the known world. I have a pension, for fuck's sake—which most augments never even get because they *die*—and I'm only thirty years old.

I've got my whole life ahead of me.

Kind of. *If* I were interested in living somewhere other than Tau City Tower, and I'm not. Not at the moment, anyway.

This is another thing that's bothering me. She said no to the hotel offer last night, but she's probably rethinking that decision in the light of day. And once she gets some coin in her hands, she'll be doing more than thinking about it. And I guess that's my fault because I'm the one who set her up with a job with Rodge. But I can't just leave her on her own all day. It's the tower, for fuck's sake. It's not a bad place most of the time. But the people here… they're the farthest thing from up-city we have in this place. Someone needs to keep an eye on her and no one's gonna do it for free. The job with Rodge was the only choice on short notice.

So she's gonna get coin. And as soon as she figures out that she can pay her own way, that's what she's gonna do. She's gonna go get a room. Her own room. One with electricity, and heat, and AC, and screens. But the most important thing is that it will be a room she doesn't have to share with me.

Because let's face it, we're just a couple of fuckin' strangers who got stuck with each other simply because I stumbled into her on a day when she either lost her mind or walked through a dimensional portal.

And now that work's over, this is all I can think about.

I was pretty busy all day because the man I'm running security for is a politician from Lambda. He's got his own team staying close to him, but Stayn says he doesn't trust the politician—does anyone trust a politician?—and wanted me to follow him. I'm sure the man was thrilled about that, but what can he say? It's not his town, is it? If he wants to be here, he's got to put up with me.

But I'm only working days. Stayn has someone for the night shift, so it's just a little past seven when I walk back into the Ruin District and start climbing the outside steps to the tower.

Anneeta is waiting for me at the top, once again looking like a child model in a fashion show for eccentric small people. Her skirt today is a ballerina tutu in pink and everything else—tights, shirt, boots, vest—is all different shades of tan and brown. The only other thing that's pink are the ribbons in her haphazardly plaited hair.

She's cute as fuck, this kid. But every time I see her all I can think about is how she *shouldn't* be cute as fuck. Because she's a homeless seven-year-old so addicted to spark, I'm not even sure she's technically human.

Of course, I'm one to talk. As an augment—failed or not—I'm not technically human either. But I look the part of failed augment. Anneeta here looks like... an avatar. Something artificially generated for virtual space. A little too smooth and perfectly imperfect.

"Hi, Tyse."

"Hey. Where ya been? I've been asking around for ya for two days now."

"Here and there. How's the lady doing?"

"Good, I think. Haven't seen her all day."

"She's working for Rodge."

"Yeah. Did you go up there?"

"I passed by on my way doing something else. I didn't say hi, though. Are you working now?"

"Kinda. For the week."

"Well, I was thinking... I could be her friend. If that's OK."

It should be OK. I mean, she's seven. No twenty-eight-year-old woman wants to hang out with a seven-year-old. Clara will be polite and say hello—because something tells me that being 'polite' is kind of a thing for Clara—and then she's gonna forget all about the kid.

So it's gonna go something like this: Anneeta will be all, *Hi, I'm Anneeta, the resident tower sparkplug. Would you like to have tea with me?*

And Clara—because I will have warned her ahead of

time about the tea party invitation—is gonna be all, *Very nice to meet you, small person, but I will have to decline your tea, for I hear it is atrocious.*

And that's probably gonna be the end of it.

But I have questions. And giving Anneeta permission to hang out with Clara while I'm at work this week feels like a good way to get a few answers. Plus, I can keep an eye on Clara with Anneeta's eyes. It's pretty much a win-win for me.

So I pretend to think about Anneeta's request for a few moments, then sigh. Like I'm being put out. "Well, probably it's gonna be OK. But…" I crouch down on one knee so I can be eye level with the kid, then lean in, like I'm gonna tell her something secret. "When I ask her if she wants to be friends with you, she's gonna wanna know who you are and where you came from. Plus, if you do anything weird, it might scare her."

Anneeta is shaking her head before I even finish. "I won't do anything weird, I promise."

"Well, where should I tell her you come from?"

Anneeta looks confused. "I come from the tower."

"Yeah, but how that's work?"

Her eyes narrow with suspicion. "How's *what* work?"

"See, she's gonna ask questions about you. And I'm gonna have to tell her you're the one who led me to her."

"Oh."

"Yeah. Which is weird. So what do I tell her? I mean, about how you know everything about the tower."

"Well…" Anneeta tries on a smile. "We could lie."

I chuckle, then point at her. "We could. But we shouldn't. I like Clara. I don't want to lie to her."

"Oh." She's confused again. "Well. My head, you see?"

"Mmmhmm." I nod, rolling a hand for her to keep going.

"It sees things. Inside and outside. Well, of course outside. But it's different. You know what I mean?"

Here's the thing. I *do* know what she means. Because as an augment, I've experienced these inside pictures as well. Not to mention the outside ones, which is a whole other thing than actual reality. But Anneeta here is not augmented. She's *seven*.

And when she talks about seeing things inside and outside, she's talking about *the veil*. Something no one outside of Sweep even knows exists.

So seven-year-olds, who would never be augmented, should not be able to see the veil in the outside world or communicate with it inside their heads.

"Yes," I say. "I do know what you mean. But *how* do you see these things inside and outside of your head? And was it always like this? Or has it been changing over time?"

"You sound like a doctor, Tyse."

Oops. She's catching on. "Sorry, don't mean to. I'm just trying to find a way to explain you to Clara. In easy-to-understand terms. And if you tell me, I'll take you upstairs and introduce you to her right now."

Her suspicion fades. "You will?"

"Absolutely. She's gonna be thrilled to meet you. I bet you'll be having tea parties together by tomorrow."

I think Anneeta is lonely—she's just programmed herself not to think about it so it comes out as confidence—because her eyes immediately go wistful and fill up with longing as she pictures tea parties with Clara.

I almost feel bad about lying to her, but understanding Anneeta's relationship to the decommissioned god's tower feels pretty critical in this moment—I do, after all, have a world-hopping woman claiming she was sacrificed to this very same tower god living in my room with me—so I push that guilt away.

Anneeta leans in closer to me, then looks over both her shoulders like she's checking her peripherals before meeting my gaze again. "I didn't always see things the way I do now."

"No?"

She shakes her head. "No. It just happened one day last year."

"Last year?"

"Yep. I saw a lady."

"What kind of lady?"

"She looked like Clara, but... different. And she walked out of that tower." Anneeta points to one of the ruins.

I look at the ruined tower for a moment. It's not completely gone but it's not completely there, either. "Then what'd she do?"

"Just... walked away. And when she got to the edge there?" She points to the imaginary boundary that separates the Ruin District from the Canal District. "She disappeared."

"What do you mean, disappeared? Like... into a crowd of people?"

"No. Just... poof." Anneeta makes a poof gesture with her hands as she says this. "Gone. Like she was never there. And that's when the other place showed up."

Well, now we're getting somewhere. "What other place?"

"That place." She points off to my right. At the ruined foundation of what used to be an ancient tower, opposite the ruined tower she was previously referring to.

I look at the foundation, confused. "I don't get it."

"It's there. Can't you see?"

"What's there?"

"The tower, of course." Then her gaze lifts up and she stares at the sky.

My gaze lifts up to the sky too. The... *empty* sky. "There's no tower there, Anneeta. It's just air."

"You can't see it because you're not me. But there's a tower there, Tyse. And when I climb the stairs and go all the way up to the top, there's a secret room too. A room where people go to see me the way I see them."

I look up at the sky and replay those words in my head. Because I know exactly what she's talking about. She not only sees the veil—which presents to augments as a kind of shimmer. A break in the fabric of reality. Or, rather, the possibility of one—but she *interacts* with it too.

In Sweep, I could see what she's describing. I could also travel across the veil and visit places where the spark was still very powerful. Everyone on my team could. That's the whole point of being augmented. And the whole point of having augments in the Omega Outlands was to manage these places. The details of which are complicated, but not specifically important at this moment.

But there were no people there. At least, that's what we were told. I certainly never saw any, though. It was just a *place*. A bad place, even for augments because it's gone 'amok'. Which is actually a technical term in the Sweep, stupid as that sounds.

I turn back to Anneeta, place both my hands on her shoulders, and wait until she's looking me in the eyes with her full attention. "Anneeta. Can you *see* that tower? Like actually see it?" I nod my head at the empty air where the tower used to be, but isn't now.

She nods.

I let out a breath and stand up. Then I let my gaze wander up to where the tower would be if my augments were still working. There's not supposed to be any veils left outside the Omega Outlands. They were cleared hundreds of years ago.

Did they miss one?

No. That's not even possible. That was the whole point of augments in the early days. To clear the veils in all the tower cities. And even if they failed back then, the augments ran the cities for decades after sweeping. *Someone* would've seen it. Even now, plenty of augments come to Tau City for leave. *Someone* would've seen it.

Hell, seven years ago, *I* would've seen it. I still had some vision when I was discharged. Maybe I wouldn't be able to see an actual tower, like in my prime, but I would know *something* was there. Even if I couldn't see the overlay, I would've felt it, at the very least.

It can*not* be here.

But it is. I know it is. And it's got something to do with Clara.

"Anneeta, could you see this tower before you saw that first lady?"

"No. But I could feel it. And I couldn't see other ladies before her, either. She was the first one I ever saw. But then, after she disappeared, when I turned back to the ruin, it was all like this." She shrugs and opens her arms to indicate all the things I cannot see.

"How many towers do you see?"

She looks around, her lips moving a little as she counts. "Five. But not all of them are tall. Just this one"—she points to the empty space we've been talking about—"and that one." She points across the canal, to the other side of the Ruin District.

Two towers on either side of the God's Tower. Just like Clara described to me.

"Sometimes"—Anneeta points to the space in front of the God's Tower now—"there's a lot of people out there. That night we found Clara—well, the night before that, actually—there were a *lot* of people out there. And the night before that, too."

"What kind of people?" Because this... I don't understand. "Like... *that* kind of people?" I point to all the people in front of the tower right now.

Anneeta shakes her head. "No. Those are real people. The people I see are ghosts. And that night before Clara came, I saw ghosts. I saw *her*."

"Wait." I stare at the tower, trying to picture this. Then I look back at Anneeta. "Did you see her, the ghost Clara, walk through the tower doors?"

Anneeta nods. "I did. I followed her—I always follow them—but she wasn't inside when I got there."

"You always follow... *who*?"

"I mean." She turns away, not looking at me. "I *don't* see them."

"But you just said you saw the lady last year. And the crowd—"

"Well, yeah! I do see *them*!" She's turned back to me now and her voice is higher in pitch and a little bit frantic. "But that's it. That's all I see."

She's lying.

I think about this for a moment, then decide this is as far as I can push her. She's said too much and she's backtracking now so any more discussion is pointless. It's all gonna be lies. If I want more information—that's true, anyway—I need to give her space. "OK." I look down at Anneeta. "Thanks. For the info. Come on, let's go meet Clara."

Anneeta might not trust me enough with the truth, but she might trust Clara. And the three of us need to have a very serious conversation about what is happening here.

Anneeta follows me into the tower and up the stairs, hanging back a bit, like she's nervous or something. Which is out of character for her, so I'm thinking about these possible reservations when I walk up to my door and reach for the handle.

This is when I hear voices. I flip the handle and kick the door open, Versi already at high ready, then just stand there, unable to react because I'm so stunned at what I'm seeing.

A hologram floats in the middle of the room. A hologram of me. But not just me. Jast, Myra, Stepan, and Kirt are all dead on the ground at my feet, holes in their heads the size of my fist, because this is my discharge proceedings and it's playing the worst moment of my life right out in the open.

"How?" The word comes out before I realize that Clara is on the other side of the hologram and I can just barely make out the spectra she's holding between her fingertips.

Still, even though the hologram is playing and she's holding the spectra up, I am still unable to figure out what the hell is actually going on. Because... there's no spectra player. I don't even own one. I keep the spectra because... well, it's mine. My time in the Sweep was two-thirds of my life, if you count recruitment and augmentation prep. I couldn't just toss it aside like it meant nothing.

Clara's eyes find mine and she startles, dropping the spectra, and the hologram disappears

I glare at the woman on the other side of the room. "What the fuck are you doing? Where did you get that?"

Immediately, she's apologizing. "I'm sorry! It was an accident. I kicked the stool over and the top opened up and—"

"You found a box. My box. Which you then opened! Ya had no right!"

"I didn't know what it was. And I tried to put it back, but it shocked me! And then it rolled away and when I picked it up the next time, that... that... *picture* appeared in the air! Like magic! I didn't do anything! It just appeared!"

I force myself to take a breath and calm down. Of course she has no idea what a spectra is. She can't even find a word to describe the hologram she was watching. But nothing about what she just said makes any sense, either. How did she make it play? It's not supposed to play just by touching it.

"Here." She bends down, reaching for the spectra.

"No!" But this command comes out too late. She's already pinching it between her fingertips. The hologram springs open again, and my team—my *dead* team—once again fills the room. I want to rip it out of her hand, but I still can't make sense of why it's playing. All she's doing is holding it. Like she's... "Oh, fuck."

"Take it." Clara thrusts the spectra at me. "Just take it!"

I step forward and reach for it, desperate to make my past disappear, but instead of disappearing, something else happens when our fingertips touch. A massive jump of spark bursts through me and suddenly the entire room is covered in *veil*!

It shimmers for a moment. But when I withdraw my hand from Clara's, it all disappears. "Make it come back!" I say this while looking Clara directly in her eyes.

"Make *what* come back?"

"Ya didn't see that? Ya didn't see the veil that appeared when our fingers touched? It was all over the room!"

"I don't know what you're talking about! Just take it!" She thrusts the spectra at me again, but this time when I reach for it I use both hands, clutching at her so she can't drop it or withdraw. And again, when we touch, the veil appears.

Only this time, it's not just a shimmer. It's an overlay. A complete fucking overlay of the room. With stats, and labels, and everything. Like I'm back in the Omega Outlands clearing a ruin.

"What are you doing? Let go of me!" Clara struggles to get out of my grip, but I hold tight, just looking around, amazed, and afraid, and… relieved all at the same time.

"You're doing this," I tell her.

"Doing what? I'm not doing anything!"

"You're…" It takes a moment for all my training and experience in the Sweep to come rushing back, so I don't have the right word for a few seconds. But then it's all there. All the data I was used to is falling down my field of vision like a fucking waterfall.

Clara struggles harder, her eyes wide in shock.

My augments have come to life again and my eyes are throwing off a blue light so bright, it lights up the dim room, casting eerie shadows across the chair and the bed.

But I don't care about the eyes, or the color, or the hologram, actually.

I am *working* again.

This is when I notice that there's blue light coming from between the cracks in the metal shutters over the windows. I walk over there, dragging Clara with me because I've still got a hold of her hand, and look through. The overlay is covering the entire Ruin District. "Holy fuckin' shit."

Clara leans in, trying to peek through the shutters. "What? I don't see anything. What do you see?"

The ruins are whole again. Tall towers, but nothing like the towers just beyond, in the Canal District. They are maybe… ten or fifteen floors up. And they are not made of shiny metal or glass, but plaster, or mud, or something primitive like that. The tops are domed and the domes are blue.

But the most incredible thing about what I'm seeing is the canal. A bright blue line with beaches on either side that runs straight down the city, just like Clara described it.

There are people down there, too. Just walking along stone paths, talkin' and shit. Having a normal life or whatever. Wearing clothes I've never seen before. Like... desert clothes. Loose things, long things, in every kind of neutral color.

"*What?*" Clara says again, her voice more desperate now. She's looking all around, leaning in and back, trying different angles to see what I'm seeing. "What's out there?"

I let out a breath and take a step back. Then I look her in the eyes. "It's your city, Clara. That's what's out there."

"What? How?" She leans in, once again looking past the shutters. "I don't see anything."

"That's because you're not augmented. You're not programmed to see what I see. But you're programmed to do something else though, aren't ya? Who sent you here?" Then I hold up her hand, the spectra still pinched between her fingertips. "You're doing this, aren't you? You're powering it somehow. *How* are you doing this?"

Clara shakes her head at me, denying it as she renews her attempts to wriggle out of my grip on her hand. "I'm not, I swear!"

"It's not her."

I turn, and Clara gets loose, dropping the spectra into my hand so the hologram disappears, and with it goes the veil and the overlay and the waterfall of data.

Anneeta, who I had forgotten about, steps into the room still looking very much like an unreal little girl.

"What?" I ask her.

"It's not her. Not all of it, at least. It's me, Tyse. I'm the one powering this."

The silence is thick after Anneeta says these words. Mostly because Clara and I are both very confused, though for different reasons. I take another deep breath, trying to slow my heart rate, and then point to the chair. "*Sit.*" I'm looking at Clara. She doesn't even object, just does as she's told, perching on the edge of the cushion in an upright position. Though I think if she wasn't so confused and had her wits about her, she would definitely object to my commanding tone.

Then I turn to Anneeta and point at the bed. "Close the door and you sit too."

Anneeta sighs, but doesn't resist. She closes the door, then walks over to the bed and sits down, looking up at me with those big, brown eyes of hers.

I pace the room, still trying to even out the rhythm of my booming heart, and then, after a couple seconds of this, I stop between the bed and the chair, looking back at them.

Clara has no clue, so I direct my first question to Anneeta. "What did you do?"

"I didn't do anything. I can't help it if the spark lives inside me and comes out whenever it wants."

"Spark did this?" I pan a hand to the room, which is now empty of all evidence of what just happened, of course. Because I am holding the spectra and for whatever reason, I can't power it up the way Clara did. "How, Anneeta? How did spark play the hologram on my fuckin' Sweep discharge spectra when Clara touched it?"

"Well…" Anneeta does a little shrug here. "She's…" Her eyes roll up, like she's thinking. "It says she's a conductor. But I don't know what that means."

"*Who says that!*" This comes out way too loud and both girls jump.

"The… god?" Anneeta's voice is small now. Like I scared her.

I exhale in frustration, then rub both hands down my face, trying to stay calm. When I look at her again, I've got more control over my tone. "There is no god in this tower, Anneeta. You and I both know this."

"You keep saying that, but you see all the evidence of him. It's all over the place. You heard the generators in the lower levels. You saw the power, remember?"

"I do, and I did, but there's still no god here. If there was, don't you think he'd be a little pissed off that several thousand uninvited guests are living in his fuckin' tower?"

"Don't you think he *is*?"

Anneeta and I stare at each other as these words of hers sink in.

I break away first. Then turn and look at Clara. "Tell me what happened."

"I told you. I found that disc by mistake. I picked it up, it shocked me, so I dropped it. And the next time I picked it up that picture appeared. The… hologram, or whatever."

"You can't blame her, Tyse. It's your fault too."

I turn to look at Anneeta. "Explain."

"You're the augment. Without you, I can't make a veil. And without her"—she points to Clara—"you can't see the veil I make. So." She shrugs. "It's all of us."

I stare at her for a few moments. Then my gaze travels down to the floor where the footstool is still overturned. My eyes dart up to meet Clara's and she pleads innocent with her hands.

"I told you, Tyse. It was an accident. I didn't mean to see that stuff. Your… that… hearing, or whatever."

She watched my discharge hearing. And she saw what I did to my team.

I upright the footstool then position it in front of Clara and take a seat, looking her in the eyes. "You can leave, if you want. I'll still pay for a hotel. I'll even walk you into the Canal District."

Anneeta stands up, objecting. "She can't leave! We're gonna be friends! You said so!"

"You…" I point to her, annoyed. "Go home now. Wherever the fuck that is."

"But you promised!"

"Tomorrow, Anneeta. OK? *Tomorrow*. I need to talk to Clara."

Anneeta's eyes find Clara's now. "Don't go anywhere. We're friends now."

Clara sighs, then forces a smile. "I won't."

"Promise you'll be here tomorrow. *Promise*." Anneeta is not convinced. But honestly, neither am I.

Clara nods, her body language more compelling this time. "I promise."

"Fine." Anneeta walks to the door, pulling it open. But before she walks through, she shoots us one more look over her shoulder, directing her words at me. "You'll figure it out, you know. Probably soon." She smiles at me, revealing that gap in her teeth.

Before I can ask a million more questions about what she just said, she's gone, the door closing softly behind her.

I turn to Clara. "I'm serious about the hotel. I won't make a big deal about it. And I'll still help you. In whatever way I can, at least. I saw your city, Clara. It was just as you described. I saw your canal and everything. The towers with the domes. And people walking around in traditional desert clothes."

"Oh, my god!" Clara jumps up. "What?" Then she goes back to the window and peeks out. "You saw it?"

"I did." And now I know for sure that she's not lying. I know I said I believed her, but that was just something you say when the only other choice is to call someone crazy. I didn't wanna do that, so I said I believed her. There was even evidence. A bit of it, anyway.

But this? This is something else entirely.

"I don't see anything, Tyse. Make it come back!"

"Didn't ya hear? I'm not running this thing." I point to the augments in my head. "Anneeta is. She's a child of the spark. She was born in it. She's not right. It affected her brain. But there's no denying that I saw what I saw. She made my augments work. She's not lying and neither are you."

Clara peeks back out the window, still hopeful for a glimpse.

"Sit down, Clara. We need to talk."

She keeps looking for a few moments, but finally sighs and sits back down in the chair so we're facing one another. I'm struggling for words, my mind spinning with the idea that she saw me kill my team, and what she might think about that. Which is a stupid thing to worry about after what just happened, but there it is.

Clara finds her words just fine and starts asking questions. "What was it then? Can you tell me that? I mean, you said you believed me."

"I did. Kinda. But the overlay"—I nod my head to the window—"that's irrefutable evidence."

"Evidence of what?"

"The veil."

"And what is that, exactly?"

"It's…" It's hard to explain is what it is, but I think back to how it was explained to me the first time I saw it. "It's like a mirror, only instead of seeing a reflection, you see past it. Into places that should stay hidden."

"And you're sure it was Tau City?"

"Yeah. It looked… familiar. From your description. I know different worlds exist. I've seen them before in the Omega Outlands. But they're dead. There are no people there, Clara. And I know this isn't a lie because I was there for years. I know what's there. And it's not people. It's just ruins, and remnants, and… other *things*. The Sweep sends us there to clear the veils because if we don't get rid of them, bad energy seeps through and infects this world. Well." I blow out a breath. "Not here in the cities. Only in the Outlands. The veils haven't been in this part of the world for hundreds of years. But forget all that."

"Forget all that? Nothing else matters but that! My city is right out there!" She points to the window.

"Not exactly. But anyway, I meant what I said about the hotel."

Her whole face scrunches up. "What?"

"I know what's on this spectra, Clara. I know you saw what I did."

Finally, some of the tension flows out of her in a long exhale.

"So like I said. I'll take you down to a hotel—"

"Why would I do that?"

"Why the hell wouldn't you? You saw what I *did*. You know I'm lying."

She sighs, looking down, then laughs. But it's one of those incredulous laughs that only comes out when things have spiraled so out of control you've got no other choice than to give in and accept it.

She looks up and meets my gaze and she is fully in control of herself. This is up-city Clara Birch speaking to me right now. "My boyfriend, the love of my life, he sacrificed me to our tower god. Real or not, Finn did that. That's the first thing. Which… honestly, I'm over it because he was confused, and scared, and trying his best with the knowledge he had."

I figured as much, but I don't say this out loud.

"But the tower god is bullshit, I don't understand this world or my place in it, and the only ally I have is a murderer who didn't even tell me his real name when we made introductions."

Her polish is sparkling right now, that's how careful she's being with these words of hers.

"Sorry about that. It's just I haven't been Tymothy for

years now. It never even occurred to me, Clara. I'm just not him anymore. I'm Tyse."

She puts up a hand. "Let me finish, please."

"Of course. Continue."

"It's a lot to process. The betrayal, the inexplicable dimensional travel, or whatever. And the man I'm now seemingly connected to via this... spark magic. Nothing about it makes any sense at all. But it must. It has to." She stares at me with those blue eyes, almost begging me to agree with her.

"Why do ya say that? I mean, *does* it have to make sense?"

"Is the world logical? Does it have rules?"

"Your guess is as good as mine."

"Well, my guess is that it does. Everything obeys the laws of nature."

"Do they? Because that hasn't been my experience."

She hesitates for a moment. Then lets out a breath. "I was afraid you'd say that. Because you're right. The rules don't make sense. None of this makes any sense at all. But that's because we're missing critical information. If we could just find this missing information then it *would* make sense. It *would* follow rules. Like that thing. What happened with that disc?" I'm still holding the spectra in my hand, so she takes that hand and pries open my fingers to reveal it in my palm. She doesn't pick it up. "What is this?"

"It's a discharge record—"

"No. I understand that part. What *is* it?"

"A hologram. Which is like a video, but it plays in the air because it's made of light. However"—I hold up the spectra between my fingertips—"it needs a player. It's not supposed to just play by itself."

"So why did it?"

"You."

"Me *what*, Tyse? I didn't do anything but touch it."

"You've got spark in you, Clara. Like Anneeta does. Wherever you came from, it must be overflowing with spark if it's such a part of you that you can hold technology in your hands and make it work."

"Well, of course I have spark in me, Tyse! I'm a Spark Maiden! But in my world, I was a weak one." She holds up her hand and wiggles her fingers at me. "It's mostly just in my…"

She doesn't finish. She doesn't have to.

"Well," I say, "Critical information obtained. I guess that's one mystery answered. Whatever a Spark Maiden is, it's a pretty powerful thing if you can store it inside you and use it whenever you want. Like you're a human-sized jump, or something. See if you can make it happen again."

She hesitates, but can't fight the curiosity. Her fingertip barely connects with the silver casing of the spectra before the hologram springs to life.

I look around, waiting for the augments to kick in like they did before, but there's no overlay of the veil between worlds and there's no waterfall of data falling down my vision screen. It's just me, shooting my team in their heads.

Clara gasps when she realizes which part of my discharge hearing is actually playing, then withdraws her hand, making the hologram disappear. "Did you see it?"

"The overlay? No. Anneeta was right. She's the one

powering my augments. Well, it's us, I guess. The three of us..." I stop, trying to think of an easy way to explain it. "We're like a circuit."

"But what's all that *mean*, Tyse?"

"Fuck if I know." I blow out a breath, frustrated with myself because it's not entirely true. So I take another stab at answering her question. "I guess it means... we've been given power and we should probably do something with it."

"Do something like what?"

There's only one clear answer here. It sucks, if you ask me, because I'm starting to get attached to up-city Clara Birch. But it's rather obvious, so I just say it. "Get you home, that's what. And if you still trust me, after watching what I did to my team, then I promise, I *will* get you home."

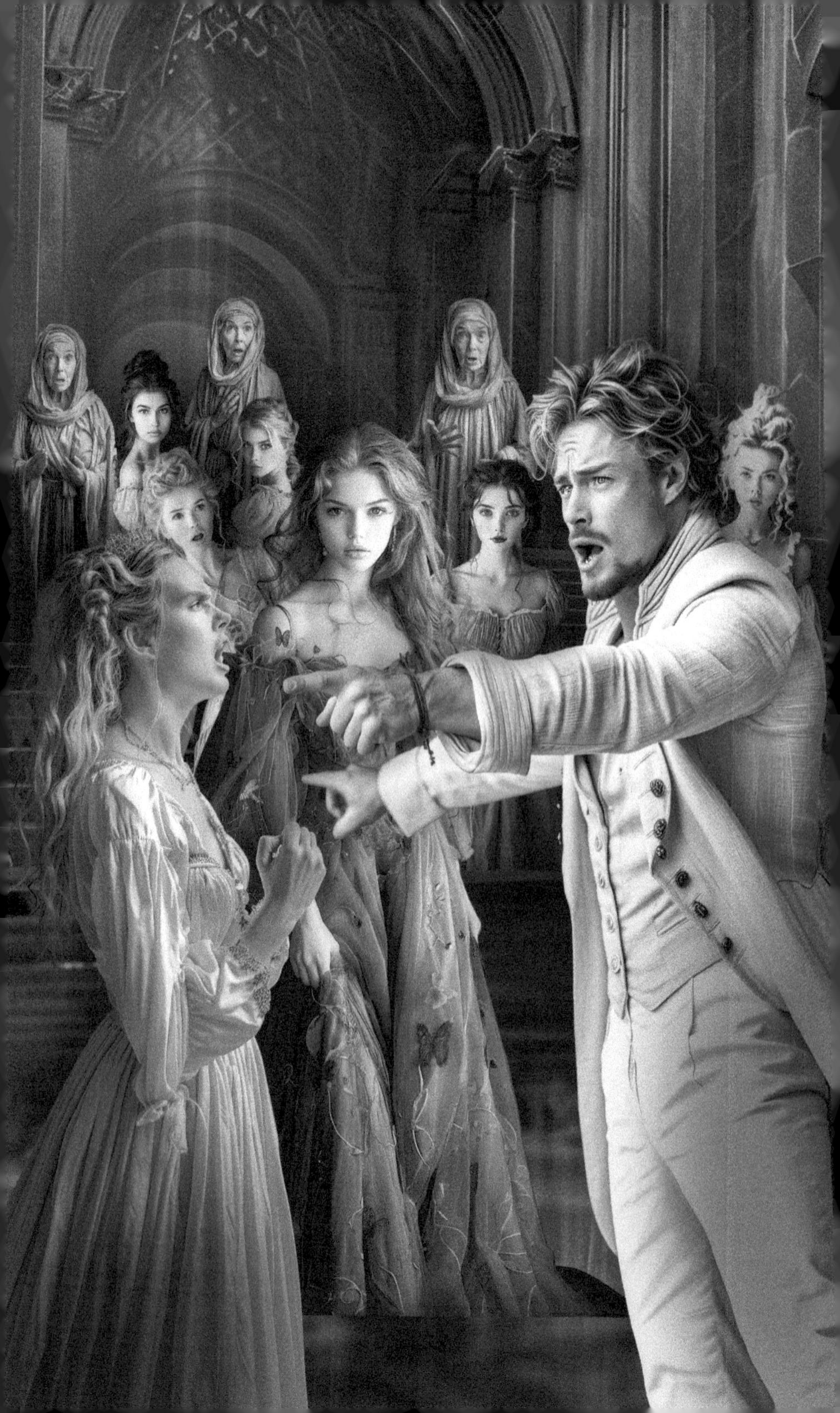

PART 3

"He's not one of ours. He's never been one of ours. We've never even heard of this 'Godslayer.' We will not allow our good name to be dragged through the mud over a man who has never been associated with our recruitment, training, or campaigns."

—Gen. Del Anderson, Chief of Staff, Sweep Command

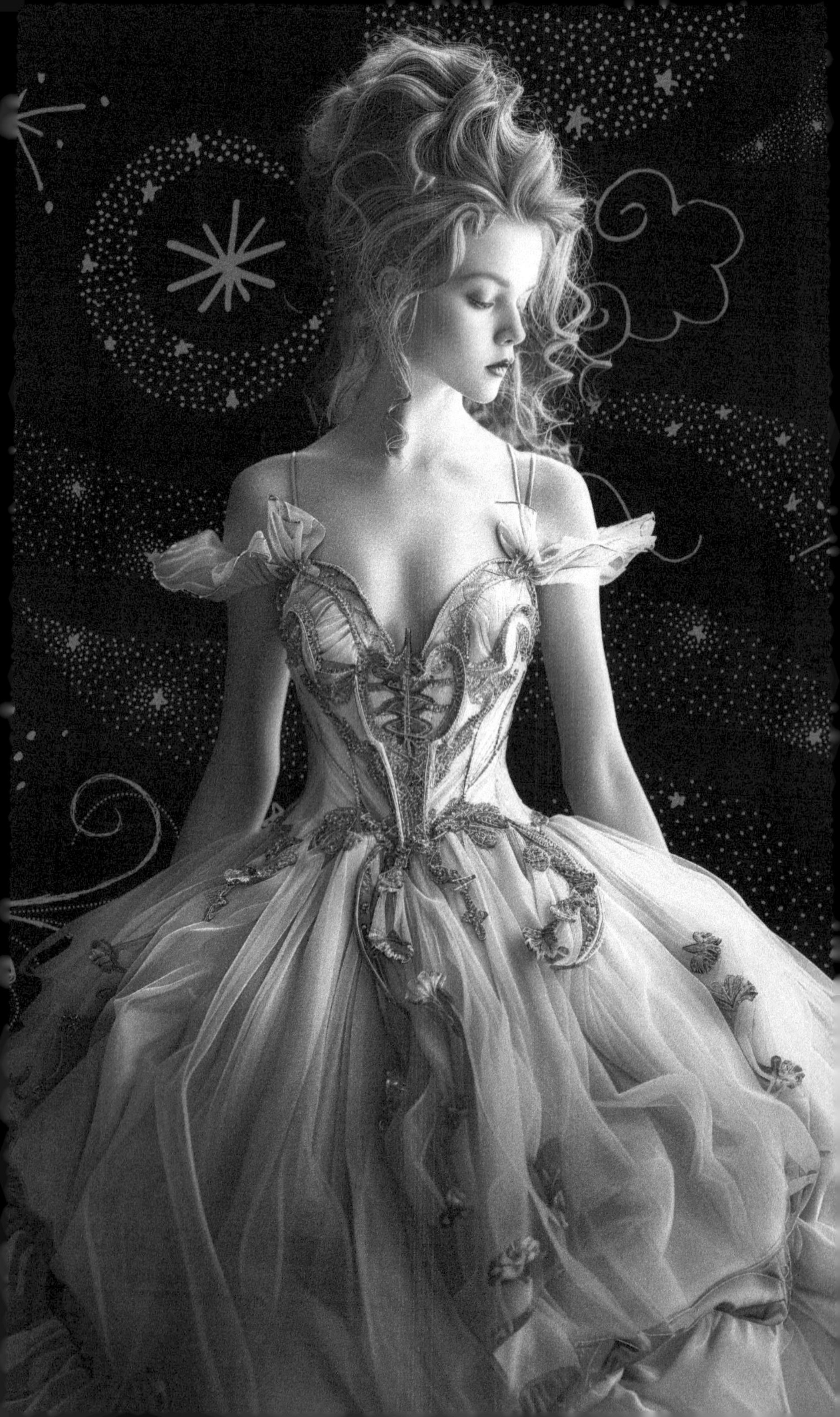

JASINA

reason, his gaze locks with mine as his words spill out. "You're next, you know."

I point to myself, mouth open in shock. "Me?"

"Not literally, of course. But then again, who knows? Maybe it *will* be you? Maybe I should just choose right now?" He turns to the crowd of important up-city people wearing all their fine clothes, with their fancy hair, and their sparkling jewels, and their prim attitudes. "What do ya say? Should we just pick her now? I can pick all ten, if you'd like. Then we can stop pretending this Choosing is anything other than a culling for slaughter. They might as well just be pigs. Hell, all of you might as well just be pigs."

I think all of up-city chokes in horror at this comparison. Some of them start whispering.

Then Finn's friends, Mitchell Davies and Jeyk Ward, come up on either side of Finn, leaning in to him, whispering as they grab him by his upper arms and try and lead him off the stage.

Finn resists. "No, I won't shut up. And no, I won't go home! This is fucked up, you guys. This whole thing is *fucked up!*"

Gemna steps forward, looking every bit the part of a Spark Maiden who knows her place and her value. Because her back is straight, her chin is up, her shoulders square, and her eyes are flashing. "When?" She crosses the stage, walking towards Finn as she speaks. "When, Finn? When did you first realize that this was a sacrifice? When Imogen went through? When Marlowe went through? When the Mabels went through? At which point in this culling did it occur to you that this was a slaughter? Oh." She smiles sardonically as she taps her chin with a single, perfectly manicured fingernail. "No. It wasn't until *Clara* went through that you decided to take a closer look at what the actual fuck was happening here."

Finn closes the short distance between him and Gemna and growls at her. "That's not fair. I wasn't in charge until three days ago. That's *not fair*." He's very tall, but Gemna is not a tiny woman the way Haryet was, so while they are not eye to eye, she in no way looks cowering.

Lucindy leans in to me. "What the hell is happening?"

"I don't know."

Mitchell starts yelling, pointing at Gemna. Then he snaps his fingers and Jeyk has grabbed her by the arm and is pulling her off the stage. She's screaming at Finn now. "Coward! You only care because you lost something this time! You never cared about anyone but yourself and Clara!"

Everyone starts yelling at once. And then we're surrounded by Matrons ushering us backwards in the direction of the Maiden Tower and the Little Sister dorm.

What happens next is hidden from my view, but the commotion continues behind us until we're all back inside the building, making our way through the hallways.

Britley and Lucindy are shook up over what just happened, nervously chatting on either side of me as we enter the dorm and make our way down the brightly painted blue canal towards our spaces. Ceela and Harlow are leading the way in front of us, discreetly whispering to one another.

"Girls!" Everyone in the dorm stops and the whole place

goes silent when Auntie Bell's voice echoes off the four-story ceilings. We all turn, almost in unison, because the shuffle of dresses sounds coordinated.

She's standing in the middle of the open double doors, looking down her nose at us with hands folded in front of her. "You will not ever again discuss what happened after the Extraction tonight. Not even whispers. Do you hear me?"

"But Matron Bell," one of the more popular up-city girls says, "they were so disrespectful of the god and our tradition. Both the Extraction Master himself, and *our* Maidens."

She makes a point of stressing the word 'our' here. Because technically, the Spark Maidens are the property of Tau City. It's all paid for by Tau City. Which means it's paid for by us. Well, not me—I'm not a taxpayer—but that's not the point.

The point is that Gemna acted in a way unbecoming of a Spark Maiden. She was not poised, proper, and polite tonight. Neither was Clara. Not at all. And all of us saw it.

Neither was Finn acting much like the god's master of ceremony. Calling people pigs! What was he thinking?

"It was a stressful night, Little Sister Maylyne, wouldn't you agree?"

The up-city girl nods, reluctantly. "Yes. But they're all stressful. No one wants to go into the tower, but—" She scoffs here. "The nerve of her. After ten years of mooching off city taxpayer money—"

"*Enough!*" Auntie nearly blows her top over the boldness of this girl's statement, cutting it off. "You heard my order.

There will be no discussion. Not even whispers. Now quickly get to bed. You'll be up before sunrise for your first official day in Little Sister training. Lights out in five minutes."

I'm looking at Auntie when she says these words, and she's looking directly at me as well. Her eyes narrow and she gives the slightest of nods. *Get to work, Jasina.* That's what that nod says. Then, with a swish of her tunic and scapular apron, she turns and walk out the doors.

I blow out a breath, because I'm exhausted. Like never in my life have I ever felt this tired. And that little nod was a gentle reminder that my nights are not for sleeping.

We all turn back to the dorm and I make my way to my space at the end of the canal. I'm not even undressed when the lights go out and I end up pulling my nightgown on over my head by the glow of the dim floor nightlights.

There's a chorus of whispered goodnights weaving their way along the gently curving walls and hallways and as I stand in the middle of my space, I say them as well.

But I don't go to bed. I don't make any move at all. I just wait until I hear the gentle sound of Britley's snoring. She's the closest one to me and this snoring is my signal to get to work.

So, in my nightgown and bare feet, I make my way to the back rooms, go down the stairs, passing by many, many empty bedroom spaces, and then find the stairs that go up.

A nightgown is not the most appropriate outfit for spying, but after living through the most chaotic start to the Choosing in recorded history, there are more important things to be concerned about.

It's a pretty nightgown, though. As are all the clothes made for the Little Sister experience. They're all white, of course, and the cotton is soft and light with a little bit of pastel silk ribbon trimming each hem. They're meant to be identical, but since they are handmade, there are slight differences. Mostly in the color of the trimmings.

I didn't even get a good enough look at this nightgown to notice the ribbons, but oh, my gods. Why am I even thinking about this? *Who cares, Jasina?*

There is the door.

This is the only thing I can think to do tonight. This door is the only out-of-place thing I've found during my short stay.

It's a long shot, but I'm taking it. Because my only other choice is to stay in bed and get some sleep. And while I would prefer that choice, I don't think Auntie would be very forgiving if I came to her with nothing the next time we meet.

I need something.

This door is my something.

I let out a long sigh as I walk over to it, then mutter, "At least it's a start," as I take a pin out of my hair and pick the lock. Even if I wasn't part of the Rebellion, I would know how to pick a lock on a door like this. Everyone down-city knows how to pick a simple lock.

It only takes a few tries, then I hear the telltale 'click' of the locking mechanism releasing.

I take one last look behind me, then pull the door open.

It's dark inside, but when I move forward a little, small lights pop on along the floor. Just a few. Just enough for me to gather my nerve, look over my shoulder one last time, step in, and allow the door to close behind me.

My heart is beating wildly at this point, so much so I'm nearly out of breath even though I'm standing still.

Fear, Jasina. That's fear you're feeling.

I don't like the fear, but I can control it. So I take a moment to close my eyes, slow my breathing, and think of the mission and what I'm actually trying to accomplish here.

The standard line is freedom. That's what we're after. To be free of this god and his tower. To stop the Extractions. To make the future brighter for all the people of Tau City.

Normally, most people don't think about the Spark Maidens. They have been tricked into accepting them through the use of this clever Choosing campaign and by celebrating, as well as envying, the luxurious decade of extravagance that will be bestowed on the nine women who will be spared.

But this time it's not going well, this delusion Tau City has talked itself into. Nine women have been ritualistically sacrificed to the god in the tower and people are beyond nervous now. They're on the verge of panic, as is evident from the outbursts on the tower stage tonight by Gemna and Finn.

Of course, Tau City should've been this unsettled about Imogen and all the other number ones who came before her. But people are slow to accept that they are stupid. And I suppose the god has done us a favor by calling all the Spark Maidens in like this. It puts the whole thing right up in people's faces.

When I open my eyes again, my heart has slowed and my feet move forward.

The lights pop on as I move. I've seen them act this way in a few places up-city, so while it's not common, it's not completely foreign to me.

The lights are helpful. Especially when I come to a stairwell leading down. As I descend, I can detect a hum. And by the time I get to the bottom, the hum is more of a rumble. Like there are machines down here.

I'm barefoot, and the ground down here is flat, and hard, and a little bit wet. When I look up, there are pipes—some of which are leaking, and explain the wetness. The passage at the bottom of the stairs only leads one way. I take a moment here to orient myself and decide that I am under the canal and the passage leads across it. Not a bridge, but a tunnel.

Right to the Extraction Tower?

Makes sense, so I follow it until I come upon another stairwell, which goes up. A long way up. And after climbing many flights of stairs I realize that there are no doors to exit out. There are no choices to make, so I keep climbing.

Finally, when I am winded, and exhausted, and ready to just sit down and take a nap—damn the consequences—I realize this is the end of the stairs. I'm at the top. And when I arrive on the landing, there is a door to my right.

I pause, catch my breath, try to stop the fear, fail, and then just keep going. Walking right up to it and reaching for the handle.

What is on the other side of this door? I have no clue.

But I push it open anyway. Just a crack. Just enough for a tall, thin beam of light to enter my darkness.

I hear voices. Muffled, but recognizable. It's Finn and his friend—or whatever he is these days—Mitchell Davies.

Finn is being loud. "She's gone, Mitch. And I did that!"

"You had no choice, Finn. Just... you're tired, man. You're beat. You need to rest. It's been a really fucked-up week. And the next Choosing will be here before—"

"Fuck *that*." Finn doesn't even let him finish. "Fuck that, Mitch. I'm not doing this."

"You're not doing... *what*?"

"The Choosing. It's not even gonna matter. The Council told me—" But he stops.

I can't see them—they are in another room across the open space in front of me—but I don't need to see Finn's face to deduce that he just said something he wasn't supposed to.

"The Council told you what?" Mitch sounds pissed. Possibly at being left out.

"Never mind. It's not important. Just go, OK? Go and take everyone with you."

"But the cooks. It's nearly breakfast time. They're already—"

"I don't care!" Finn yells this. And it is followed by a long, dramatic silence on Mitch's part. Then he's there, in the doorway of the room across the room, and I slink back, letting the door I'm holding open close to just a sliver as I watch Mitchell Davies leave by way of a staircase going down.

About a minute later I can just barely make out his voice

somewhere else in this building, telling the cooks, or whoever, to get out and go home. The Master would like his privacy.

What do I do now? Leave and go back to bed? It's what I want to do. Desperately want to do.

But I can't decide if I've found enough information. And just as I'm thinking this, Finn appears in the open door of the other room, holding a bottle of whiskey. He leans against the doorjamb, his eyes unfocused as they travel up a massive wall of windows with the most incredible view of the night sky, not to mention the God's Tower.

He sighs. Drinks. Sighs again. Then he clumsily turns, walking back into the room, kicking the door closed behind him.

Is that the room I'm looking for? Is that the room Auntie told me to find?

Maybe. But it doesn't matter. It's the only room I've come across. This is the Extraction Tower. I'm here. That goal, at least, has been met. But it's not enough. I need a yes or no on that room Finn's currently in, one way or the other.

That's actual information. Not good information, but what I've gathered so far amounts to a whole bunch of nothing.

It's so close. There's no way I can leave now. I need to get in there. Just a peek. That's all I want. Just to see it one time so when Auntie asks for a progress report, I will have information she needs.

Finn is drinking. Probably well on his way to being drunk. The odds are pretty good that he's going to pass out in that room. Which sucks, because that means I won't be able to get in there and look around. But there is a lot to see here aside from that room. I must explore. I must have *something* to take back to Auntie.

"Finn!" Mitchell's distant voice floats up from downstairs and I go absolutely still. "I'm leaving. Everyone's gone, but we'll all be back just after dawn."

I wait for the door to open again and for Finn to appear and answer his friend. But he doesn't. There's nothing but silence.

"Finn?" Mitchell calls up one more time. Then I barely make out, "Fuck it," as all the lights flip off somewhere down below. A door bangs closed.

I wait, listening for any noises that might indicate that people are still here, but when I don't hear anything after counting out a full minute, I push my door open wider and take a cautious look around.

The first thing I notice is that this is not a door. At least, not on the interior side of things. It's a bookcase filled with books. I'm just about to turn away when a spine catches my eye. *The Godslayer and His Courtesan.* The same book I found in the sewing room back in the dorm.

How odd.

I pull it out and look at the cover, examining it carefully. Taking in the details. It's a nice illustration, though old and the colors are fading. The Godslayer is portrayed as a beautiful man and his courtesan an even more beautiful woman. Behind them is a desert background because the most popular of the tales take place during the Great Sweep when the winds dominated the world and covered it in sand.

I have an urge to open the book and read it, but it's a stupid urge because it's the middle of the night, I'm spying on the Tau City Extraction Master in my nightgown, and if I get caught, my life is over. So I put it back on the shelf.

Anyway, a soft voice inside me says, *there's another copy in the dorm. You can read it any time you like.*

Right now, I need to gather as much information about the Extraction Master's palace as I can. Then I need to get the hell out of here and get as much sleep as possible before dawn breaks and the new day starts because I will not have a single moment to myself until dinner.

Even though the lights are out, the windows are so massive that all three moons in the night sky find a way to shine across the room. Cautiously, I start exploring, walking over to the stairwell first and peeking over the side of the railing. It spirals down another three levels.

But I don't even consider going down there. The room I need tonight is up here, so whatever is happening downstairs can wait.

The problem is, there's not much up here. It looks like an observation deck. There's a desk, the door disguised as a bookshelf, another bookshelf on the opposite side of the room, and a scope that I know from school is used to observe the night sky, but that's pretty much it. I do carefully, and quietly, riffle through the desk drawers, but there's nothing in there but writing paper and pencils. No personal items of any kind.

I really need to get in that room. It's not just for Auntie's approval, either. It's for the greater good. I have been chosen to make a difference in the lives of the people of Tau City. *Me.* Jasina Bell. I am the Rebellion's secret spy. My name—if I succeed—will go down in history. I will be the reason why the Rebellion triumphs over the evil god. People will talk about me far, far into the future. I don't even care if I die trying, either. Would I love to mooch off the taxpayers of Tau City for ten years the way Clara Birch did? Yes. Yes, I would. I would take that life if that's what I was handed.

But I feel like things are progressing in a weird fast-forward way. In fact, I'm starting to get the feeling that there will be no next Extraction. I mean, Finn was pretty clear tonight. First the outburst on the God's Tower stage and then, plain as can be, he told Mitchell Davies that he wasn't going to go through with it.

This is when I remember that he almost spilled a secret tonight. A secret about something the Council told him.

Yes. Things have changed around here. I could feel them changing—slowly—as the Maidens were uncharacteristically called into the tower over the years. But Clara Birch's Extraction tonight is most definitely a turning point and things seem to have reached a precipice.

As far-fetched as it seems, there might not be another Extraction. And if that's the case, things will fall apart very quickly. Three months, that's all we have. That's when the next Extraction Maidens are Chosen and number one is supposed to walk through those tower doors.

Two weeks ago, if you had told me that the Extraction was on the verge of being obliterated, I would've agreed—

because that's my mission as a rebel—but I would not have believed it.

Tonight? Tonight it feels not just possible, but inevitable. The wind has turned. The sands have shifted.

The Rebellion could end this in a matter of weeks. And I might be the one to make all that happen.

Forget the gowns, and the coin, and the galas. I need to take every risk. I need to make every sacrifice. I need to be the one who takes down Finn Scott, Tau City's last Extraction Master. And I don't care if I die doing it—at least my life will have made a difference.

So I'm going to check the room. Just a tiny peek. It's not even a risk. Not really. He's been drinking and by the way he was slouched against the door, it was obvious that it was affecting him. He's probably already passed out.

Before I can talk myself out of it, I walk to the door, grasp the handle, and, ever so slowly, twist. It doesn't squeak and when I apply a little pressure, it opens just a crack. Just enough for me to see what's inside.

I gasp. Not loud, but Finn, who is not sleeping, but only hunched over on the… desk—I'm not sure if that's the right word for circular piece of glass in the middle of the room, but there's no time to really take in what I'm actually looking at—because he stirs, straightens up, and is just about to look over his shoulder when I pull back, leaving the door slightly ajar, and start running across the room, back to the bookshelf.

I'm just reaching for it when behind me he says, "Clara?"

I stop, holding my breath. *Clara?* How could he mistake me for Clara? Not only do I have red hair and she has blonde, but he just sent her into the tower like an hour ago. Is he *that* drunk?

A smile creeps up my face. Maybe he is.

"*Clara.*" Her name comes out sharp this time.

"Yes," I answer. But I do not turn.

He exhales. "I knew that was you."

I hold my breath in, not daring to move. Am I caught? I'm not sure. He's wasted. Not sloppy wasted, though. He's not slurring his words like the men down-city in the taverns where the whores work. But I can smell the whiskey from here. Plus, there is no way to mistake me for Clara Birch if one is not completely smashed. Forget about my red hair, we're not even the same height.

When I hear footsteps coming towards me, I nearly panic and run. I could outrun him, I'm sure of it. There are a lot of stairs. He'll probably trip and fall if he gives chase. My chances are good. But it's too late, because he grabs hold of my shoulder and for a moment I think he'll spin me around and there's no way he's drunk enough to mistake my face for hers.

But he doesn't turn me. He presses his chest into my back, slips his hands over my hips, leans his face into my neck, and urges me to step forward. I don't know what else to do, so I just comply. But I soon realize there's a couch in my way. The back of one, actually. It's facing the windows, like he and Clara might've spent their nights up here stargazing.

When I reach it, I expect him to stop pushing me forward—because obviously, there is nowhere else to go.

But instead, he places his hand between the middle of my shoulder blades, pressing and urging me to bend over.

"Remember when I bent you over this couch the other night and fucked you, Clara?"

Um. What the hell is happening? More importantly, what do I do?

But again, I don't have much of a choice. I mean, I could scream or something. Wriggle away, possibly. But he's pretty insistent. And if I do either of those things, he'll snap out of whatever delusion he's currently existing in and I'll be… I don't even know. Caught, obviously. Punished. And I don't think Auntie would come to my defense, either. It's too risky. We've come too far. The Rebellion is infinitely more important than one teenager who was stupid enough to get caught on her very first assignment.

I would be kicked out of the Little Sisters, disgraced, and sent back down-city to spend the rest of my life regretting my stupidity on this night. Harlow or Ceela would probably take my place as lead infiltrator, and that would be that. My life's work over before it started.

Fuck that. I will not scream and I will not run. If he wants to think I'm Clara, then that's who I am. "Of course I do, Finn, darling. How could I ever forget that? It was amazing."

He huffs out a small laugh, pulling me back up into a standing position. "You liked it. You slapped me, but you liked it. You came three times, didn't you?"

"Mmmmhmm," I hum. But for freak's sake, what the hell? I am not a virgin and I've had my share of boyfriends over the past couple of years, but... yeah, I don't know what to do with this. They're into dirty talking?

I dunno. I'm having a hard time picturing Clara Birch dirty-talking. Or even being on the listening end of it. She's so... I mean, I don't actually know her, but 'uptight' is the first word that comes to my mind. She's rigid and prim.

And Finn, right now, seems very much the opposite of that.

His fingertips slide up over the curve of my right hip, pausing for a moment before gliding around the front of me. His other hand finds my bare arm—nearly stiff at my side from the shock of his touch—and slips down to circle my wrist. Like he's afraid I'll run, and if I were to try, he would stop me.

"Clara. You know I love you, right? You know I didn't have any choice tonight, right?"

I nod my head but can't seem to find any words. And anyway, I'd rather not speak if I can help it. He's immersed inside this delusion at the moment, but I doubt it would take much to bring him out of it. One wrong step, I imagine. So I'm going to stay silent.

The hand on my stomach inches up the center of my ribcage, the other still threatening to hold me captive. His fingertips spread across my front until his entire palm is between my breasts.

I hold my breath as he leans into my neck, an explosion of chills erupting all over my body when he whispers, "Do you want me to make you feel good, Clara? Should we do it like we did that night?"

My eyes are wide, a war of desires wages in my mind, and I shudder.

"You do, don't you?" He kisses my neck.

And I swear, I don't mean to moan, but it slips out. I can feel him smiling against the tender skin just under my ear.

"It was fun like that, wasn't it?" *Fun like what?* He continues the thought, as if he's reading my mind. "All bent over the couch. Your ripped underwear on the floor." His hand slides back down my belly, grabs the cotton fabric of my nightgown, and his fingertips slip underneath it. Inching down inside my underwear. "Your legs were all spread open for me. You were ready for it, weren't you?" And just as he finishes those words, his fingertips are between my legs and it is very apparent that I am, indeed, ready for it, because they slide all over the place.

He chuckles against my ear, his hand moving back and forth between my thighs.

"Bend over again, Clara." These words are whispered so softly, I close my eyes and almost melt. Then his hand is between my shoulder blades again. Not pushing this time, though. "You do it. I want you to want it, Clara. Bend over and show me you want it."

Do I want it? Or am I still pretending that this is just part of my job description as Rebellion infiltrator? Do I care at the moment?

A smirk plays across my face. Not really.

I haven't spent much time thinking about Finn Scott, but there's no denying he's handsome. A little too pretty and clean for my tastes, but that dirty mouth of his has me reconsidering.

I bend over, telling myself that it's an opportunity. One I can't pass up. That this is just what's required to get the job done.

It's a lie. Even in this moment I know this. But I tell myself the lie anyway. I can introspect the fuck out of this decision tomorrow—if I still care about the moral implications. But right now, I just want him to keep going.

He chuckles behind me as he pushes my nightgown up my back, his fingertips making little circles down my spine until they come to that dip where they meet my underwear.

"Slide them down over your ass, please, Clara. So I can see how pretty it is."

I gulp air, but don't hesitate. I reach behind me and begin to pull my underwear down, but his hands grasp mine, stopping me when they reach the top of my thighs.

"Leave them right there for me, please. They're so pretty tonight. So plain and white."

There are many seconds of silence after this. Like he's expecting me to say something back. Does Clara talk dirty back to him? Should I be doing that? To... like... convince him that I'm her? To keep him in the delusion?

I bite my lip, trying to think of something to say, then blurt out, "I put them on just for you." My voice is husky and deep with desire.

I can't see his smile, or feel it—not literally. But I *know* he's smiling. And while I'm thinking this his foot knocks against my ankle, kicking my leg open. I nearly fall over, but he grabs my hair in his fist, steadying me.

This shocks me. I don't know why, of all the things he's been doing for the past few minutes, it's the hair pulling that makes me reconsider what my goals are here—but it is.

Mostly because it makes me moan. Not cry out in pain because a boy yanked on my pigtails in school. But actually... *sexually* moan. Like I want him to do it again.

This is some kind of signal to him. It must be. Or it gets him off or something. Because suddenly the fingers between my legs are pushing up inside me and I'm wriggling. Not trying to escape, but out-of-control wriggling because it feels so damn good. It's almost too much. It's like he just lit a fire inside me. Ignited a passion within me that I never even knew existed.

I've had hands between my legs before. The hands of boys who didn't really understand what they were doing. But this is the hand of a man who knows *exactly* what he's doing.

The initial wave of the climax bursts out of me as a tightly controlled squeal. My mouth clenches together, as I am desperate to control it. But the second wave is like an explosion. Like the fireworks on Extraction Eve. And there is no hope of stopping the scream that flows out of my mouth. So loud, it echoes off the ceiling.

Finn laughs, yanking my hair that is still in his fist. His laugh mingles with my moans as wave after of wave of pleasure fills me up until I feel so out of control, a sob escapes past my lips and my eyes tear up.

It's not fear and it's not pain, so it's confusing. I don't understand what I'm feeling because I've never felt anything like this before. No boy has ever made me squeal like an animal.

But this man did. And everything about what just happened feels primal and dirty.

But the most humiliating thing is… I want him to do it again. The pleasure is still coursing through me—my thighs trembling, the wetness of my orgasm running down them—and all I can think about is how I want him to do it again.

He's still laughing. Thrusting his hips forward, grinding himself against my upturned ass. And then hope fills me—replacing the humiliation of lust—because he hasn't finished yet.

There *will* be more.

He lets go of my hair, grabs my hips with both hands, and thrusts again. But his pants aren't open. And I'm suddenly unsure. Is he just going to play with me like this? Or is he going to put himself inside me?

"Are you tired, Clara?"

"No." It comes out before I can think about it. Because I don't want this to stop. I want it to keep going. I want it to last forever.

"I am." He sighs these words out as he reaches forward and grabs my shoulders, guiding me to stand back up.

My eyes close and my shoulders drop as a sigh of frustration escapes before I can stop it. Hope drains. Desire blooms. And this is it. Maybe he's too drunk to finish.

I'm no stranger to this outcome. The boys my age need the drink to get the nerve. And they don't understand that line between too much and not enough.

But I do.

And I know how to get what I want out of them, even when they don't.

I want Finn Scott inside me tonight. And I need him hard in order to satisfy this lust of mine.

I reach behind me until my fingertips find his belt. His lips press up against my neck, his mouth kissing my earlobe as he whispers encouragement. "Yes. Keep going. Make me want you."

Once the belt is unbuckled, I unbutton his pants, opening them up. He's rock-hard inside his undershorts and I pause, closing my eyes as I let my hands explore his tight bulge.

Finn becomes impatient, breathing heavy into my ear as his hands take over, pulling himself out and placing the full length of him between my palms. He squeezes my hands, forcing me to squeeze him. Then my head falls back onto his shoulder as we both begin the back-and-forth rhythm of sex.

He's kissing my neck, driving me crazy, and my hands go faster, making him moan. He nips the tender skin just below my ear and I hiss, but this just makes him chuckle.

I want more. It's almost an uncontrollable need. So I bend back over the couch and spread my legs as far as they will go with my underwear still binding my thighs. Almost cutting into my flesh.

Finn lets go of my hands, then takes each of them and spreads my arms wide across the back of the couch. I'm panting, waiting, lusting, grinding my hips and thrusting them backwards, inviting him to enter me.

But he laughs, and I recognize the sound of a man pleasuring himself. "Oh, you are very fuckable, aren't you?

And I would love to. But if I give you what you want tonight, Clara, you might not come back for more."

Then the hotness squirts all over my back, and he's moaning, and my own fingers have to slip between my legs and move through the slippery wetness because I refuse to leave here without another climax.

There is combined moaning, and writhing, and then he's spinning me around, kissing me. His mouth hard and forceful against mine. He grips my breasts, walking me backwards around the couch, and then he shoves me down into it.

"Yes," I moan, looking him straight in the eyes.

"No." He looks me straight back. Then he collapses into the couch cushions, his arms around me as he slides to the side, lying down. His pants open, his dick still hard, semen on my backside, my underwear still at my thighs, the wetness practically dripping down my legs.

And he holds me like this—captive, willing, mostly satisfied, yet craving more—and falls asleep.

I stay absolutely still, wondering how humiliated I would be in the morning if I rubbed myself against his thigh and got off just one more time before I leave.

In the end, I don't. I get up, straighten myself out, not even caring if he's watching—but he isn't. He's out—and walk over to the room I came for.

The door is still slightly ajar, but I push it wide open and look up and around at what I know to be the Looking Glass.

I memorize it. The sleek black glass of the circular desk in the middle of the room. The glass panels in the shape of triangles that cover every bit of the circular room as well as the domed ceiling. It's very different than the room Auntie showed me, but that's good. She said that one was outdated and this one wasn't.

It's certainly looks to be in working condition to me. Though, what it does, I have no idea. But I'm not supposed to know what it does. I've only been tasked with finding it. And that mission had been accomplished.

As for the message she wanted me to find? Well. I think maybe she had wrong information. There is no paper in here. There are no pencils. I did find that stuff out in the desk but there were no messages written on the notepads.

So I'm not sure what the message is all about.

Still, I feel like this is enough.

I have found the the room she was looking for.

I have succeeded.

My name will be in the history books.

Everyone will remember Jasina Bell—the young rebel who found the Looking Glass, which is… well, who knows? It's probably the thing that changes everything.

A smirk grows on my lips and a chuckle escapes my mouth as I walk over to the bookcase and open it up.

Everyone but Finn Scott will remember, that is.

Because he's too drunk to even know I was here.

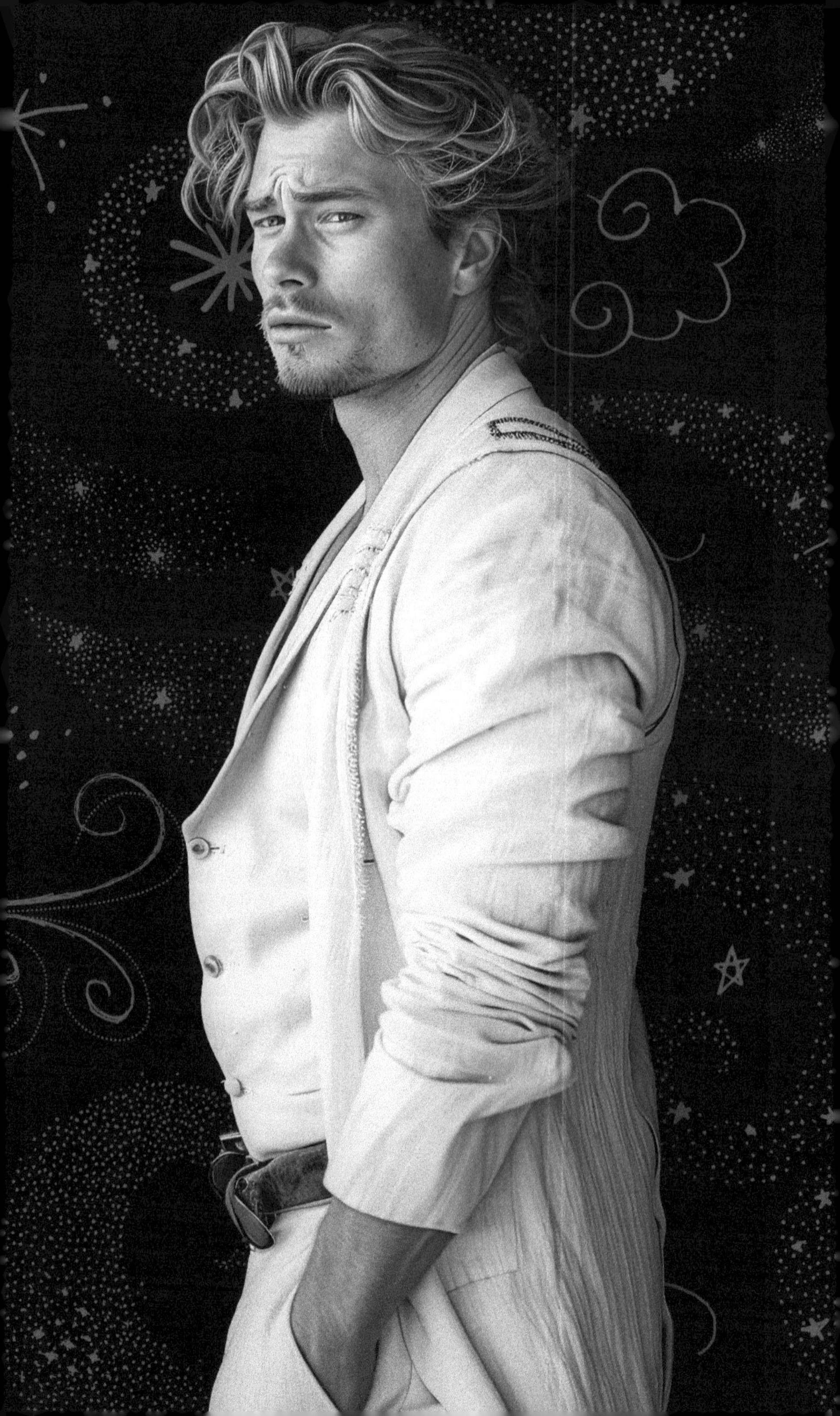

FINN

CHAPTER TWENTY-NINE

The sound of voices wakes me, but when I immediately sit up out of instinct, I am met with a pounding in my head the likes of which I have never experienced before. I hold it in my hands, thinking about long-ago days when drinking myself sick was a proper way to celebrate after semester exams. I smile here, despite the hangover, and push the drinking aside to recall how much easier life was back then when we were young. And I know we're not old, not even thirty yet. But this last week has aged me into another generation. Or so it feels. Maybe I'm being dramatic?

I lift my head up from my hands and open one eye. A tried-and-true method when the room starts to spin.

It's not spinning. That part of the binge happened last night, probably when I was asleep, and then—

There is an abrupt end to whatever thought was coming next because I suddenly remember what I was doing last night.

Or was it a dream?

It has to have been a dream.

I look down, find my dick practically hanging out of my

pants, and suddenly I can *smell her*. It wasn't a dream. There was a woman here. In my mind, I'm calling her Clara, but also in my mind is the image of a redhead.

I stand up, suffer the consequences for nearly a minute with my eyes closed as I put my dick away, and then open them as I let out a long breath, looking around. "There was a woman here, I can smell her."

"What? That's ridiculous. There was no woman up here."

I turn and find Mitchell on the other side of the room sitting at my desk furiously writing something. "What are you doing here?"

He looks up at me, scowling. "You smell. Take a shower. I'm writing your schedule for today's Little Sister bullshit. We're three days behind at this point. You can't miss it, so don't even try me right now."

I just stare at him, trying to understand the implications of his words. "What time is it?"

"It's time to take a fuckin' shower, that's what time it is."

I pinch the bridge of my nose, sighing. Annoyed.

"It's nine-thirty." Mitch doesn't even stop writing. Or look at me again. "Your first meeting is at eleven."

"What meeting?"

Now he looks up. His expression says—well, it just comes right out of his mouth so I don't really need to interpret it. "Why are you such a pain in my ass? Have you forgotten everything? It's day one, Finn. Snap the fuck out of it."

Our eyes are locked at he says this and I'm still processing when he looks away, apologizing. "Sorry. I… that was too soon and… thoughtless of me. I'm just trying to keep going here, Finn. We're behind with the Little Sisters and the schedule is a complete mess. But there's no way to skip this day. You have to meet with each one individually and give them initial scores. The people are… well, they're handling all this change about as well as you are. Which means they're *not* handling it. There was a mob of people outside when I came back this morning."

"What? A mob? Why? What did they want?"

"They want to talk to you about last night and how you acted. They want to know how you're gonna punish Gemna for talking back. Traditions are important in Tau City and last night was…" He shakes his head. "Fuck, who am I kidding? Tradition went awry several years back now. It's just they didn't notice. Well, after last night, they've taken notice."

I walk over to the desk and pour myself a glass of water from a pitcher, then guzzle it down before continuing the conversation. "Who was in this mob?"

"All of the Council. The mayor. A bunch of wives. And a few scholars from the College of Philosophy and Logic."

"The War College? Why?"

"Because… well, everyone thinks the god is pissed off at us. And it's the duty of the War College to predict irrational behaviors."

"Of the god?"

"Who else?"

"Did they predict last night?"

Mitchell laughs. "What do *you* think?"

"I think they got it wrong. I think they got it all wrong. I think everyone got it wrong."

I'm looking at Mitch when these words come out so I watch his expression change into deep worry before my eyes. "You said something last night. Something you didn't finish."

"Well"—I chuckle and rub my forehead—"I'm sure I said a lot last night."

"This was about the Council. And the Choosing. And how... nothing matters. What did you mean by that?"

Shit. How drunk was I? *Come on, Finn, you were wasted. You thought you were with a woman last night when really all you were doing is jerking off like a freak.* There was no woman up here. Just me and my hand. I scoff, then walk over to the windows and draw in a deep breath when I look down and see all the Little Sisters milling about along the canal. They will line up soon so I when I leave my tower I can get a good long look at them.

Inspection day. It's like a meet and greet. But the whole city is invited to gawk. They can't ask them any questions—well, I guess they could, but the girls are not allowed to answer. It's literally just an inspection day. They are not wearing gowns, but the Little Sister uniform, which is the same as a Matron uniform—blue tunic and cream scapular apron—it just looks a thousand times better on the young women than it does on the old.

One would not think that a tunic and apron could be tantalizing, but it is.

Mitch comes over to the window and looks down, nodding his head in appreciation. "They look like a bunch of virgins waiting to be fucked, don't they?"

I laugh as I turn to look at Mitch. "What are you talking about?"

"Them. You know. They're all young, and tight, and… just… I'd fuck them all. At once, if I had the chance."

I scoff. He's such a fucking dog. But as I look at them, I see Clara. I remember her inspection day and I am a thousand percent sure that my father and his valet—who was Clara's father—were not up here talking about fucking these girls. "Knock it off, will ya? Have some respect."

"Well, excuse me, Extraction Master. I was stating the obvious."

I will hate you 'till the end of time. That's the last thing Clara ever said to me. And she will, too. I'm certain of it. Even if she's dead right now, she will hate me forever. Because what I did to her last night was unforgiveable.

Mitch must sense the mood change because he grabs my upper arm and turns me around. "Come on. Go shower. Let's try and be on time. The Council—everyone—they're all uneasy. And uneasiness typically translates into anger. We can avoid that by sticking to the schedule as much as possible. I've eliminated day two and day three of the Little Sister schedule because they really didn't have anything to do with you. It was mostly stupid contests between the girls for rights to fabrics and… whatever sewing bullshit they need to make their next gown. But day four—which is tomorrow—also includes a minor Choosing. You need to have dinner with one of them. I've made you a list."

He leaves me to grab the paper he was writing on earlier and bring it back. "This is my ranking of the girls with a little note next to their names. And I put a star next to the ones I'd invite to dinner tomorrow night, if it were my choice."

When I look at him, he's grinning wildly. So I interpret this to mean that these are the ones he'd like to bed, given the chance.

I take the paper and glance down at it, then hand it back. "Thanks, Mitch. Seriously. I don't know what I'd do without you."

"You'd fail miserably." Then he claps me on the back. "Go. Shower. You really do smell. I'll be downstairs handling things. All your notes will be waiting for you in the Maiden Tower main hall."

He retreats without further comment. But this is when I remember that I do actually smell a woman's scent up here. "Hey?"

"What?" Mitch stops on the stairs to look at me.

"Did you… did you send a woman up here for me last night?"

"No. You were a drunken dick. You made me kick everyone out. I kept a guard outside though. Why?"

"Nothing. Never mind. I was just… missing Clara, I guess."

He nods sympathetically, then resumes his retreat.

I go down one level as well because that's where my new bedroom is, and then I take a long hot shower. Jerking off to the image of a sexy redhead as I stand under the water.

"ARE YOU NERVOUS?" Mitch and I are riding the elevator down to the ground level for the mandatory meet and greet. "Don't be nervous. Trust me, these girls are so nervous, they probably all wanna throw up right now." He leans in to straighten my Extraction Master stole.

It's light blue and the ends are trimmed in gold fringe. It's part of the Tau City official dress uniform. Everyone on the Council, plus the mayor and I, all wear them for formal functions. Though the Extraction Master has the only blue one, I guess because it matches the Little Sisters and they are, technically, under my control.

I swat Mitch's hands away. "I'm not nervous. Why the hell would I be nervous? I'm the one in charge."

"I know. But some of them are really fuckin' hot, friend. If you play your cards right—and don't Choose them, of course"—he points at me, winking—"you could keep one. Ya know?"

"They're like ten years younger than me. I don't want a fuckin' Little Sister. I wanted…" I don't finish. I don't need to.

"You know I'm not serious, right?"

I look at Mitch, doubt written all over my face.

"I'm just trying to take your mind off things, that's all."

"Whatever. Where's Jeyk?"

"Babysitting Gemna. She's a mess, man. It's been non-stop sobbing since last night. I finally ordered a Matron to sedate her. So Jeyk is making sure she doesn't like… fall asleep and never wake up. That would go over great."

I shoot him a look.

He shrugs with his shoulders. "What?"

"You're so cold these days."

"I'm not cold. I'm… practical."

"It's the same thing."

"Yeah, well, my practicality will save your ass one day, mark my words."

"Whatever. I should go talk to Gemna."

Mitch puts up a hand. "Nope. I would table that for now. For whatever reason, she's blaming everything on you."

I scoff. "That's not fair."

"We all know it's not fair. She knows it's not fair. But she's scared. And sad. And scared, sad people have justified stranger things than this. Let Jeyk handle her. At least for a little while. I'll make sure he keeps me up to date each night and if there's anything you need to know, I'll fill you in."

The elevator doors open and before us, on the other side of the lobby glass, are two lines of beautiful young women. All waiting for me to inspect them.

Mitch squeezes my shoulder. "Concentrate on them." He nods his head to the girls. "They're the nicest distraction you're gonna get. That's for sure."

I shrug his hand off me, straighten the stole, and take a deep breath and walk forward. A guard opens the doors and Mitch hangs behind as I step out to the fanfare of music. A tune that used to make me feel proud to be a Tauian, but now only sounds sad.

I was here—behind my father the way Mitch is behind

me—when Clara stood on one side of the canal bridge for her inspection. I remember winking at her. She was stoic. Took it all so seriously. But her eyes did flash and meet mine after that wink.

In this time—a time where Clara does not exist—I don't wink at anyone. I don't even look at them. I cross the canal and enter the Maiden Tower where I am directed to the main hall where all the Little Sisters will sit for first brunch. I will sit at the head of the room, alone, so that one by one they can all be called up for a short interview. It's a blink of an eye for them—just one or two minutes—but for me, it will take the whole day.

The room has been prepared in the traditional blue and cream colors of the Little Sisters and all the tables set for fine dining. Crystal water glasses, and gleaming silverware, and delicate glass plates spun from the purest sands outside the city walls.

I sit down at my table and, since I'm the only one in the room aside from staff, Mitchell takes the Little Sister chair across from me. I meet his gaze and find questions. "What?" I'm already irritated about having to be here, so this comes out in my tone.

"What did the Council tell you?"

"What?"

"Last night you let something slip. I knew they told you something because your attitude took a turn that day, friend."

"My father was murdered. Of course my attitude took a turn."

"But that's not everything. You're hiding something from me. How can I protect you if you're keeping secrets?"

I don't like that he's pressuring me like this. But if our roles were reversed, I'd be nagging him the same way to get his secrets. And anyway, why should I keep the Council's secret? It's not like they have a plan to stop the god from dying.

"They said…" I take deep breath. "They told me that none of this matters because the god is dying and Tau City is gonna go with it."

Mitchell's face doesn't even twist.

"You knew." I don't even bother asking it as a question.

"I knew."

"Were you gonna tell me?"

"Probably. But it wouldn't do any good."

"Do you at least know why he's dying?"

Mitchell lets out a long sigh. "Honestly, Finn, I was hoping you could tell me. I was hoping you'd found some kind of… communication, or something, from your father."

"Why would I find something like that? It's not like he knew he was gonna be murdered."

"Yeah. Right. But most people leave instructions, ya know?"

"He did. You read the Extraction Manual written in his hand to me just two days ago. So what are you really looking for?"

But before he can answer me the massive double doors to the main hall open and we both glance in that direction as the Little Sisters begin to file through in neat lines.

Mitch looks back at me, standing up. "We'll talk later,

but I do know more." He doesn't wait for me to say anything back, just turns and walks away, leaving me alone at the head of the room. When I look out at the Little Sisters every pair of eyes is on me.

The Matrons are in charge of this event so I don't really have to do anything. Just sit here, stand when the girls approach, then sit down and have a quick chat. Mitch has left the notes for me, so I glance down and read them off. *What's your name? Why are you here? What would you do if you were Chosen as number one?* It's all very simple. It's just gonna take all day because there are seventy-five girls here.

In a little over two weeks' time I will eliminate twenty-five of them. Three weeks after that, twenty-five more. Then, at the final Choosing three weeks later, we will have our top ten. Number one is chosen on the actual Extraction Day.

So they don't have time to panic, I guess.

LITTLE SISTERS COME **up to the table** one by one. All bright-eyed and pretty, and wearing those tight tunics and scapular aprons that should cover up their curves, but only end up making them even more alluring.

I try to focus on each of them. Their first meeting with me is a big deal, after all. I am the man in charge of their futures. Do they still think that this is a good thing? That being a Spark Maiden is the pinnacle of success for a young, beautiful, social-climbing woman? Is it still a chance to change one's fortune and future, maybe for generations?

Well, I hate to break it to you ladies, but you're the end of an era, not the beginning. None of you have a future.

"Extraction Master?"

"Hmm?" I look back at the brown-eyed teenager sitting across from me. She's probably the youngest of the bunch, having only just turned eighteen the day before the deadline. Barely squeaking in by the width of a hair.

"Am I... boring you?"

"Of course not. I heard everything you said. Your story of perseverance through the written tests was"—I force myself to say the words—"simply inspiring." Then I smile big at her and stand up. Which is a signal for her to leave now.

She is unable to hide her disappointment. But she does get to her feet when a footman appears behind her to pull out her chair and she murmurs out a less-than-polite, "Thank you," as she wanders off.

The Little Sisters are not allowed to line up—they must stay in their seats until it's their turn—so I have no idea how far into this ordeal I am. All I know is that it's not over because yet another young woman stands up from a table and turns in my direction.

She is a redhead. Little bits on the side are braided and tied back to reveal her pale, heart-shaped face, but the rest is left to fall down her back like a cape, nearly to her waist.

Her blue eyes are locked on mine and... what is that

emotion flashing across them as she makes her way up the center aisle of the room towards me? Recognition?

For a moment I lose my breath. I can't think. I can't even move. Because I *know* her.

She comes up to the table, eyes cast down, and curtseys. "Extraction Master." It's an overly long curtsey. Like a full two seconds too long. But I don't care that her etiquette is imperfect—even though I should because this is the whole point of the today's fucking meeting—I'm just glad for these extra seconds so I can stare at her, then pull myself together before those eyes find mine again.

"Please." I pan my hand to the chair behind her as the footman approaches. "Sit."

She does and I follow, finally interested in what is happening around me. Because this is the girl from my dream. The girl I thought was Clara.

Well, no. That's not true. I knew she wasn't Clara, I just didn't care.

I see her, in my mind's eye, bent over the back of the couch. Her nightgown pushed up almost to her neck—exposing her round ass and creamy, white thighs.

We stare at each other, wasting some of the precious few moments allotted for this meeting. Then I snap out of it. Because this girl, she was in my private quarters last night.

And she knows I remember her, because she looks terrified.

I lean back in my chair, slouching a little. "Do you have a name?"

"Oh… I… sorry." She blows out a breath, unable to meet my gaze now. "Jasina. Jasina Bell."

"Bell?" My gaze darts to the Matrons hovering all over the place. "Isn't there a Matron Bell?" She looks up at me, mouth opening, ready to answer, when I put up a hand. "Never mind. I don't even care. You were in my quarters last night." My eyes narrow down in the ensuing silence, and I glare at her, daring her to lie.

"So what?" Her chin is tipped up in defiance. And she is glaring right back at me.

I scoff. "*So what?* I could have you kicked out, you know."

She shrugs. "So do it." I'm just about to snap my fingers for the footman when she leans in and says, "But if you do, then I won't be able to come back tonight and let you have your way with me again."

The guffaw comes out of my mouth before I can stop it, drawing the attention of the entire room. Especially the Matrons. They start rushing towards my table, but I put up a hand and dismiss them. They are not pleased about this, or my outburst, but what can they do? I'm the fucking Extraction Master. I might as well be the god in that stupid tower, that's how much power I have around here.

I look Jasina Bell straight in her blue eyes. "You brazen little whore."

"I'm not a whore."

"No? Then why the hell were you bent over my couch last night?"

"Because you put me there."

I laugh again. Not as loud this time. "Fair, I guess. But how did you get there?"

I wait for the lie. Fully expect a lie. Because there's something going on with this girl. Something secret.

Something dangerous, maybe. Like… was she sent to seduce me? Kill me? Both?

But she doesn't lie. Because the most fantastical words come spilling right out of her mouth. "There's a secret passage on the top level of your tower. On the inside, the door looks like a bookcase. But it opens up."

"And where does this passage lead?"

"To the Little Sister dorms."

"How did you find it?"

"I guessed. I mean, it was a strange door in a strange part of the dorm. It looked out of place. So I opened it and found you at the other end of a long walk and a long climb."

"Keep going."

"So I decided to enter and take a look around."

"Did you find anything interesting?"

"Well." She smiles at me, but it's an uncertain one. "I found you. If that counts."

"Did you like what I did to you?"

She bites her lip, but doesn't answer.

"Well?"

"Excuse me?" The girl and I break eye contact and look up to find a Matron has approached my table.

I'm annoyed. I was very much interested in hearing Jasina's opinions on what we did last night. Eagerly anticipating her squirming. "Yes?" My tone is curt and was in no way meant to hide my anger. "What is it, Matron?"

"Is there a problem here?" The weird thing is, the Matron is looking at Jasina. Not me.

"Why would there be a problem?" I am, however, the one who answers.

The Matron drags her poisoned gaze away from Jasina and directs it where it should've been all along. Is that... *contempt* I see in those eyes? And actually, do they have the same eyes?

"What is your name?" I ask the old woman.

She presses her lips together and huffs air through her nose. "Matron Bell."

"Bell?" I smile at the creamy-thighed girl across the table from me, raising my eyebrows. "As in Jasina Bell?"

"My niece."

"Your aunt?"

Jasina shrugs, but doesn't say anything.

"Well, Auntie Bell, I hate to disappoint you, but things are just fine."

Matron Bell, however, flat-out ignores me. "Come along, Jasina. Your time is up."

I stand up, point at Mitchell—who is watching this whole exchange, since that's his job—and he comes over. "What's up?"

"I'm not done here." I nod my head towards Jasina. "Can you escort Matron Bell a suitable distance away so this Little Sister and I might finish our conversation?"

Mitch's eyes are dancing, his brows up. He really wants to ask me what the fuck is happening here, but deep down, he's a professional. So he doesn't. Instead, he bows to me. "Yes, Extraction Master." Then he turns to the Matron, grabs her hand, and hooks it on his arm as he turns her around. "Have I ever told you the story of how I became the Extraction Master's valet, Matron Bell?"

I wait until he's a good distance down the center aisle—

which is plenty of time for Matron Bell to shoot me not one, but two death glares—before sitting back down at the table.

"Now, where were we?" I look at Jasina. "You were in my quarters."

She stares right back at me. "Your fingers were between my legs."

Ohhh. She wants to play, does she? "You found a secret passage."

"You have a Looking Glass."

My eyes narrow. "What do you know about it?"

She shrugs up one shoulder. "Nothing. Not really. I was shown something similar in the Matron Tower. But it's… well, completely different, actually."

"You're a spy."

"I'm the Rebellion."

"Why are you telling me all this?"

"Why haven't you told your bodyguard about it?"

"I asked you first."

"Fine." She draws in a deep breath. "Because I don't think you want to do this. I think, given the chance, you'd be on our side. I think you regret—deeply—the fact that you sent Clara into that tower. And I think, if you had a choice, you would not be Extraction Master."

"So you think I'll take your side?"

She huffs. "Which side would that be?"

"You tell me. You're the rebel."

She and I just stare at each other again. I'm interested in this conversation. I want to keep it going. But at the same time, I want to think about what happened last night. It's not all clear in my head—probably because I was drunk. But I think I liked it. I think she liked it too.

Finally, she says. "I don't know which side that is."

"Don't you think you should figure that out before you make any big moves?"

"I want to see your Looking Glass."

I nod my head towards her aunt. "So you can report back to her?"

"Well…" Jasina falters. "That was the original plan. But it doesn't have to be the only plan. I mean." She sighs. "What I really want is to make a difference. And I want people to remember that I made this difference. I want to be in the history books." She shrugs. Like that's all there is to it. She wants to be famous.

"Why would I tell you anything? Especially about that. I mean, I don't know what this silly Rebellion is all about, but even I can see the obvious. You don't like the status quo? Let me guess. You're one of the down-city girls."

"Yes and yes." She leans in. "But you can't tell me you're satisfied, either. You killed the woman you loved. For what? For a god who doesn't exist?"

"How do you know she's dead?"

"How do you know she's not?"

"What makes you think the tower god doesn't exist?"

"What makes you think he does?"

"Because he's dying. And if he wasn't real, he wouldn't be dying."

"So it's true."

"I don't know. Is it true?"

She sighs and leans back in her chair, nearly slouching.

Which is very unbecoming of a Little Sister. "I don't know either."

"You want to see the room?"

"Yes."

"Why should I show it to you? You'll just feed all my hard-earned information to your spinster aunt over there."

"What if I didn't?"

"Come on, Jasina. Why wouldn't you? This whole conversation is just a ploy, isn't it?"

"A ploy?"

"Yeah. So I'll give you information. You came to my quarters, in the night, of course. And wearing that see-through nightgown, of course, of course. So I would…" I smirk and shrug up one shoulder.

She fills in the blank with a straight face. "So you would… what? Finger me and get me off?"

"Wow."

"What? I thought you liked the dirty talk? You were certainly candid last night."

"I thought you were Clara."

"You did not. You *wished*, maybe." Jasina tips her chin up. "But you knew I wasn't Clara and you didn't care."

"So?"

"So I told you something real. I told you pretty much everything I know, actually."

"How loyal are you?"

"To you?" She scoffs.

"To your cause."

"Well, I want things to change."

"What if I told you that you didn't have to do anything to

make things change because change is coming whether we want it or not?"

She squints at me. "Is that what you're telling me? The god is dying and everything is about to change?"

"Yep. That's what I'm telling you. And no one wins, Jasina. The game is over." I stand up. "And now, so is this meeting."

The footman has rushed over and is hurriedly pulling out Jasina's chair so she has to stand as well. She does her curtsey and then, a moment later, she's gone and the next girl is sitting down across from me.

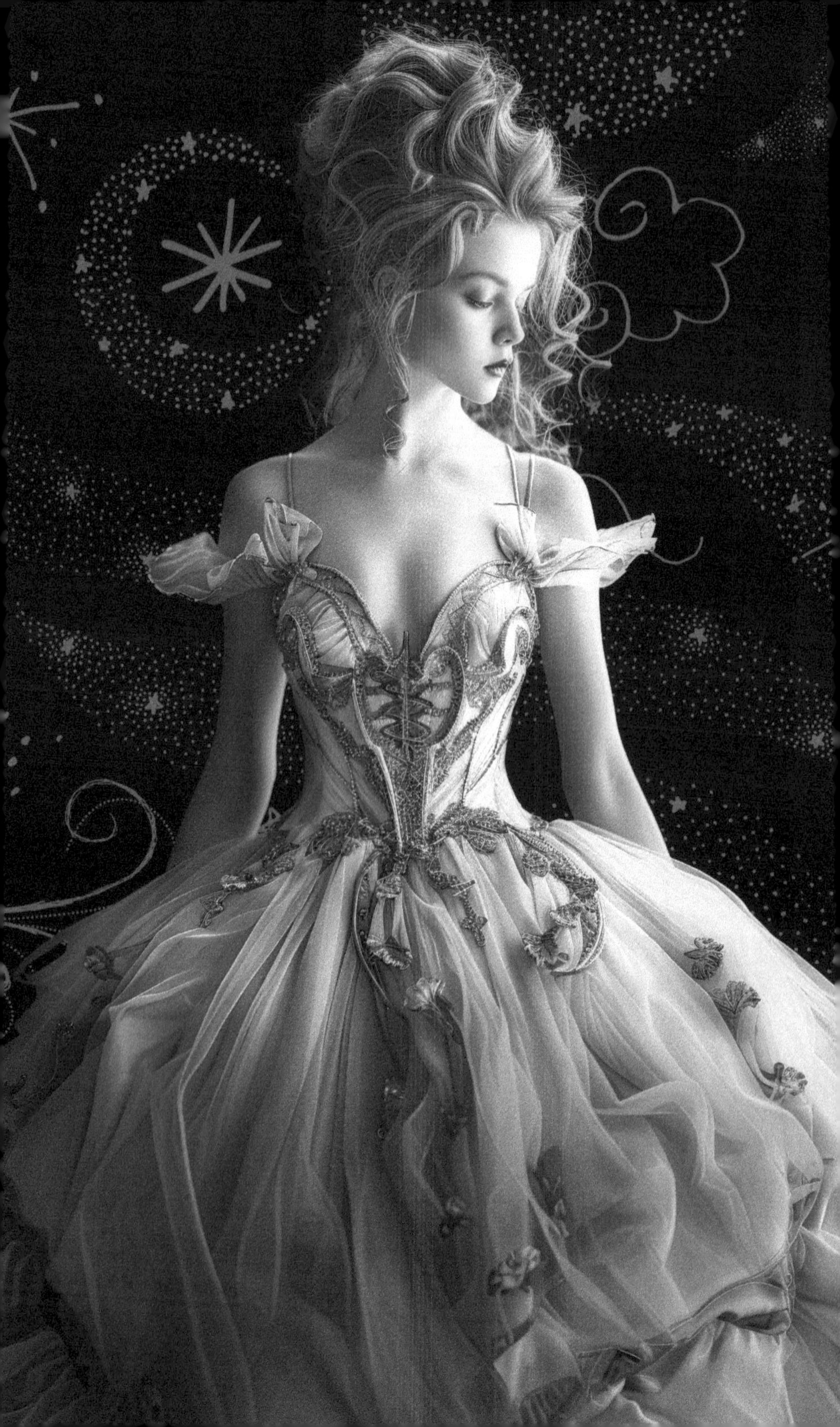

JASINA

big secrets to Finn Scott. So I suppose their suspicions had cause.

Donal offers me his arm and I dutifully hook my hand around it the way I'm supposed to with an escort. We start walking, turning corners and traveling along one of the many, many, many twisted passageways inside the Maiden Tower.

He remains quiet, nodding his head at every Matron standing guard at each hallway intersection. The thing about Donal that tends to win people over, aside from his brown-nosing, of course, is his good looks. He's tall, and broad, and handsome. Not only that, he knows how to be charming. I mean, he's never been charming with *me*, but he's been trained up as the legacy for the Tower District, so proper etiquette has been ingrained into him since birth. His manners are impeccable, there's no denying it. But he's so ugly on the inside.

"What do you say, Jasina? Should we steal away for a little quickie before I take you back to the dorm?"

And right there is the perfect example of this ugliness. We are not familiar in this way. He has no right to say this to me. I look up at him, disgusted. "Keep dreaming. The Matrons are watching, you idiot."

"They are. Until they're not."

And this is when I realize that they *aren't* actually watching. In fact, there are no Matrons at all along this passageway.

The next thing I know he's pushing me into a dark nook. I make to scream, but his hand is firmly across my mouth. It's so big, and he's pressing so hard, a panic floods through me. Not because of his reference to a 'quickie' and what his immediate plans might be—though I'm pretty sure he is intending on having his way with me—but because I can't draw in a breath.

I've been paired up with this jerk for nearly five years now and a girl doesn't have to be a genius to see this moment coming. I'm ready because I've practiced for it, so on instincts alone my knee comes up and gets him in the balls so hard, he immediately doubles over, coughing and sputtering.

By the time I'm back in the main corridor, he's retching his guts out behind me.

I turn the corner, find a Matron—who is very surprised that I am alone—and before she can ask the obvious question, I provide an answer. "He's getting sick in that nook back there. You might want to take him to the health center."

There's a commotion of Matrons after that. All the ones along this corridor go rushing past me to render aid while I just continue my walk back to the dorm in peace.

What a dick. Of course it pisses me off that he pulled this stunt, but I'm angrier about being paired up with him in the first place. If every girl knows that Donal Oslin is this way, how is it possible that every Matron doesn't?

They do. They just don't care.

And that's the nicest conclusion to come to. Because it could be that they know and they *do* care. In other words, they've placed Donal with me on purpose, knowing full well that this would happen.

It's this belief that I grab onto for two reasons. The first is to ease my guilt about what I just told Finn Scott. I am not a traitor. I am loyal. I, as much as anyone, want this evil god in the tower gone. I want this barbaric ritual of Extraction to be over. Spilling all those secrets wasn't in the plan. I didn't actually have a plan—not after last night, at least. But Finn revealed a part of himself to me by mistake. He doesn't want this either. Why should we be enemies when we can be allies?

Of course, that's not the only reason. The way he touched me held a lot of sway in the end. And I get it. He's missing Clara. He wants Clara. I was nothing but a convenient substitute. But when he came out of the building this morning and walked across the bridge, I saw him in a new light. Vulnerable, regretful, and not the monster I had made him out to be in my head all these years.

He loved Clara. He doesn't want to do this. He said that. And I believe him.

So he's not on their side. He's not even aware there *are* sides, from the way he tells it. So why should he be our enemy? Why couldn't he help us?

Then there's that. The term 'us.'

Because when Auntie came up to the table during our talk, I suddenly stopped feeling like part of her 'us.' Why was she so confrontational? I wasn't doing anything weird. Does she suspect that he and I...? No. Surely not. Why would she jump to that conclusion?

Unless... she was somehow watching.

No. It's not possible. If Auntie was able to spy on Finn in his quarters, why would she need me?

I turn the corner of the last hallway and come face to

face with her and Matron Connelly. "Auntie!" I nearly skid to a stop, that's how surprised I am to find her right in front of me. "What are you doing here?"

Better question is... how did she get here? Wasn't she just behind me, back in the dining hall? I'm sure I saw her there before I left. Didn't I? Maybe I just thought I saw her.

"Come with us, Jasina."

"OK." I start walking, but suddenly they have both grabbed me by the upper arms and they are practically dragging me down the hallway. "What's going on? Why are you acting so weird?"

"Shut up, niece. We will talk in private."

I am dragged like this down many passageways and then, once we enter the same interior glass bridge I was in the other night, I realize we're going back to the Matron Tower. A tower where no one is permitted except Matrons. Which didn't bother me much last time, but last time I was being treated like the Chosen One and right now I'm being treated like a prisoner.

We end up at the same place—the door to the control room. And this is when I realize things are really wrong, because Auntie dismisses Matron Connelly with a wave of her hand. There is no discussion.

The door to the room where the tele-visions live opens and I am shoved through by Auntie's firm hand. I stumble forward, and turn, just as she slams the door closed behind her. "What were you doing up there, you little witch?"

My mouth drops open. "What?"

Auntie stares straight at me, and my instincts are good enough that I see the threat, so I shrink back. But it's not enough. The slap across my face is quick, and hard, and angry.

I'm so stunned I can't even move. My cheek stings like I was punched, not slapped, that's how hard the blow was.

"Answer me! Right now! What were you talking about at the Extraction Master's table?"

"He asked me about my family! He asked me about you! Because of our names!"

The hand is coming at me again. And again, I am too slow. It has still not fully registered that I have become this woman's enemy. The second blow sends me stumbling sideways and I'm so off balance, I end up on the floor. I put my hand in front of my face as I stare up at my aunt, wondering what the hell is going on. "Why are you so angry?"

"Answer me. What were you talking about?"

"We were talking about Clara, OK? I said I was sorry that he was forced to send her through the tower! It was just a ploy!"

Finn's word comes flying out of my mouth. Thankfully. Because it is this word 'ploy' that changes Auntie's anger into something else. Not regret, that's for sure, but possibly... confusion.

I grab at this turn, getting to my feet. "He's vulnerable, Auntie. Don't you see? I'm trying to get close to him. To make him like me."

Her confusion solidifies into something else now. It's hard to read, but I'm hoping it's acceptance. "To make him like you. No. To make him *want* you. Sexually."

"Yes! Of course!"

She smiles. Then sighs. "I apologize, then. I should've realized you'd resort to sex to complete the job."

"What the hell does that mean?" I didn't intend to say that out loud, but out loud it comes.

"You've always been a whore, Jasina. How many boys have had their hands up your shirt, hmm? Maybe the better question is, how many of them have had their hands up your skirts? Well, I am not surprised. I always knew you'd resort to sex. But what do I care? It's just your nature. And it benefits the Rebellion, so… carry on then."

Wow. Once again, my mouth drops open in shock. Such a shock, I can't even speak. A *whore*? I would not call myself a whore. Not even by the laziest standards, let alone the strictest ones. Ceela has been with many more boys than I have. Sure, Lucindy is still a virgin, but she's a prude. Even Britley has been with two boys and she's nearly as chaste.

Auntie snaps her fingers at me. "Stop wasting my time, Jasina. Report your progress."

Report my… is she serious? She thinks she can just abuse me like this and I will… what? Submit and cower? I'm about to lay into her good—hundreds of colorful insults on the tip of my tongue—but instead, I take a breath and pull myself back under control.

Matron Bell is not a woman you mess with. She is mean and dangerous, but more importantly, she is powerful. I've always taken this power for granted, but only because I thought I was part of the inner circle. We're family, after all. We're on the same side.

At least I thought we were.

This display today tells me something different. I am

nothing to her. She might call me niece, but in her mind, I am nothing but a servant. I am not anything special. I am not some prophesized Chosen One who will save the day.

I am a whore, apparently. Well, I guess it's better to know where I stand than to go on thinking the people I care for care back.

And actually, Auntie's betrayal cancels out my own betrayal this afternoon with Finn Scott. He might lust after me, but at least he doesn't look at me with disgust the way she is right now.

What did I do, though? What triggered this?

It must've been Finn. It's the only possible explanation. I quickly run the meeting back through my head, but from Auntie's point of view. I picture Finn and me at his table, leaning into each other like we were telling secrets. Like we were… intimate.

OK. I guess, if I were the one in charge of a political coup and my highest-placed spy was looking cozy with the enemy, I might jump to conclusions. I might even become paranoid.

But this meeting with Finn today was mostly innocent.

Wasn't it?

I mean, I hadn't planned on betraying the Rebellion. Not at all. Everything I did last night was to get more information. At least, it was until he started touching me. Then… well. I don't have time to parse all those feelings right here in the moment, but it hadn't even entered my mind to switch sides, that's for sure.

"Jasina!"

I jump. "Yes."

"Report!"

"Right." I take a deep breath and talk. "I got in, but I got caught. That's why we looked familiar back there."

"You"—she scoffs, blinking her eyes at me like she's astounded by my idiocy—"were *caught?*"

"Yes." I'm already on thin ice with her, now is not the time to lie. So I spill everything. "He was drunk, he mistook me for Clara for some reason, and then he... he... he kissed me."

That's as far as I'm willing to go. I will not tell her about how he had his fingers between my legs. And I'm definitely not telling her how it made me feel.

"So he came to his senses at the table today?"

"His senses?" I scowl. "What the hell does that mean?"

"You are no Clara, Jasina. She was the perfect Spark Maiden." She smiles and places the back of her hand along my still-stinging cheek in a caring gesture that is at odds with the words spilling out of her mouth and the look of pity in her eyes. "You will never be a Spark Maiden, my dear. You haven't got the breeding."

My whole face screws up in confusion. "Well, you were a Maiden, and I'm your niece. So I'm failing to see—"

"You're a mongrel, Jasina. I was born in the Tower District. You are nothing but"—she crinkles her nose here. Like I smell bad—"a lowly, third-generation, down-city slut."

Wow. For the second time in five minutes.

"What is the plan going forward?"

Well, now that I think about it, I actually do have a plan going forward—it's to sabotage this entire Rebellion. Fuck these people. Who the hell does she think she is that she can just insult me like this and expect me to play good little spy for her? No. No way. I'm done.

But of course, I don't say any of that to evil Auntie Bell. Instead, I start a new ploy. I'm starting to like that word. "I think I can get inside that Looking Glass room tonight. I think he's interested in me. He told me to come back. That's what we were talking about at the table."

That's not actually how it went. But when I offered to come back he certainly didn't object.

Auntie smiles here. A very wicked smile. "He wants to fuck you."

I do not cringe, I simply shrug. "Maybe?"

"There's no 'maybe.' You're a whore. He wants to use you and throw you away. You will let him do this, Jasina. But if he throws you away too soon, my dear, you will be discarded by us as well. I expect a report tomorrow about the Looking Glass room. Do you understand?"

I nod enthusiastically. Because I feel like this meeting is coming to an end and I desperately need to get the hell out of here so I can sort through everything that just happened. "I understand. I will have details tomorrow. Important details that will further our goal of toppling the tower god. I promise, Auntie."

I turn, so ready to retreat, but I am yanked back by my hair. So hard, I nearly fall backward on my ass. I stifle the scream and the insults—not to mention the tears—and cower in front of Auntie as I turn.

Just bow to her, Jasina. Just grovel. It's what she wants. And if you give her what she wants, she will let you go.

"Please, Auntie." I whimper these words, more angry than afraid. But she doesn't want a strong woman, she wants a weak one. She's always wanted a weak one. That's what I am to her. Something... pitiable. Pliable. Disposable. A mongrel. So I become that girl. I put up my hands, like I'm afraid she might strike me, and project a sense of weakness and cowardice—the complete opposite of how I see myself. Or how I thought of myself before this encounter, anyway. "I'll get the information. I swear!"

Auntie Bell seems to grow bigger above me. Like my fear—pretend, or maybe not—is enough to build her up. "You'd better, Jasina. I'm warning you. Do not cross us. The consequences will be catastrophic for you."

I nod, breathing heavy—some of which is not entirely faked—and stand back upright, though careful not to look her in the eyes at the same time. I hunch my shoulders and move towards the door again. She's still got a hold of my hair and for a moment, I'm not sure she'll let it go. Maybe she plans on walking me back to the dorm like a dog on a leash?

But then I'm free. And I don't walk away calmly or with any kind of dignity, I take off running.

When I get back to the dorm, Ceela, Britley, Harlow, and Lucindy are already there, busy sorting fabrics for dressmaking. Our next gala is in three days, so that's how long we have to make our gowns.

Lucindy looks up from a pile of silk. "There you are! Where did you go?"

I shake my head. "Later, Lucindy. I need to..." But I don't have a word ready for what I need, because what I need is... clarity. Time. A fucking drink and maybe even a pipe filled with sunweed. "I need to use the restroom," I say, because it's the only thing that will get me some privacy without question. "Be right back."

I force a smile as I slide past, into other spaces, and I just keep going. Not towards my own nook, but around more corners, and down more hallways, and into more sunken spaces, and up more empty stairwells, and again, I have to wonder why the hell this place is so palatial with enough beds for hundreds of girls when there are only meant to be seventy-five.

It doesn't make sense. But then again, nothing about my world makes sense right now.

By accident—or maybe not—I find myself standing in front of the doorway that leads to the secret passageway and I have an almost uncontrollable urge to pull it open and run to Finn.

But he's not even there. There were dozens of girls in line after me. He'll be busy until late afternoon, I'm sure.

Jasina, you're an idiot. My self-deprecating words slither around in my head like a serpent. *Running to him is a mistake because you outed yourself as a freaking spy!*

That was really stupid. In fact, that henchman of his—Mitchell Davies—is probably on his way to collect me right now. Then what? I'll be kicked out of the Little Sisters and—

Stop. That's not how it's gonna go, Jasina. If Finn was going to out you today, he would've done it right there at your meeting.

This calms me because it makes sense. He wants something from me. He didn't exactly invite me back, but he didn't tell me not to when I made the offer. Mitchell Davies is not coming to get me. Not yet, anyway.

I catch my breath and I look at anything but that door.

I turn back to the stairs and go down, looking for a bathroom so I can wash my face and then slip into the sewing room and get to work on my next dress. But that's when I see that book again. The same spine that was sticking out of the stacks the last time I was walking around this space.

I pull off the shelf and stare at the cover. *The Godslayer and His Courtesan*.

I know the story. The kids' version, not this one—which is something much more than a child's tale because this is a thick tome and not a picture book. Actually, the best clue is the subtitle, which reads, *The Untold History*.

Interesting. Because this implies that it's not a myth, the way it was portrayed in the children's book I had as a child, but something more.

The tale of the Godslayer and his Courtesan isn't just one story, it's dozens. They are all different—they even happen in different places. Even different periods of time.

But they all have a common theme—the Godslayer's love for his Courtesan.

But they also have a common conflict. Every tale starts with them being separated. The Courtesan is kidnapped, the Godslayer loses his memory. She falls into an alternate reality, he has to go on a mission. Of course they always reunite in the end. But if I recall correctly, some of the tales were rather dramatic close calls.

This is the common theme for all the stories, but how he breaks free and reunites with his one true love has several dozen versions. But eventually, they come together and spend eternity destroying the god towers and reuniting the liberated gods with their spark goddesses.

He's more of a tower-slayer in these stories, if you ask me. But… no one asks me anything.

I pout, holding the book to my chest as I look down at my feet. I'm still upset. Still in shock from the absolutely denigrating attack I just suffered from my own aunt. Who, up until just a few minutes ago, was a person I looked up to.

What did I ever do to her?

What did I do?

"Jasina?"

I turn, startled, and find Ceela standing in the entrance that leads to this space. "You scared me."

She lifts up one shoulder in a half apology. "Sorry. I just got worried when you didn't come back from the restroom. What are you doing?"

Her tone started light enough, but that last question… I dunno. Maybe I'm just being paranoid, but it came out accusatory.

I hold up the book. "I saw this on the shelf the other night. *The Godslayer and His Courtesan.* Remember that one?"

She smiles, but… is it fake? I can't tell. Auntie's words are now rumbling through my head. *If he throws you away too soon, my dear, you will be discarded by us as well.*

Ceela would take my place as lead. Even though I consider her a friend—I do, I really, really do—she is… bold. Like I am. Like I was, at least. Until I nearly got raped by the boy assigned as my escort and then got slapped around by the woman I trusted most in this world, that is.

Ceela is a natural ringleader. So I need to be careful about what I say here. What if Auntie has already offered her my job if I should fail?

Might Ceela have an interest in helping me fail?

"Remember when we used to read this book together when we were kids?"

Ceela makes a face. "What are you talking about? I never read that book. I hate fairy tales."

"It's not a fairy tale, it's a myth. And of course you've—"

"I said I didn't, Jasina. Why are you arguing with me?"

"What?"

"You're acting weird. What are you doing in here?"

Again, I hold out the book. "I just told you. I wanted this book." I snap these words at her the same way she snapped her words at me.

But she's preoccupied, busy scanning this space for clues as to why I might be here that don't include this book, and I'm counting my blessings right now that she didn't find me upstairs in that space where the door is. Because she would've figured it out.

Finally, she blows out a breath. There is nothing to see here. It really is about a book and she has accepted it. But her words are still terse and they come with a look of high suspicion. "You're testy today."

I scoff, clutching the book to my chest, then push past her and start walking back to my nook. "Yeah, well, you would be too if Donal Oslin tried to rape you in the hallway and Matron Bell slapped you across the face for not making progress."

"What? Jasina! Why didn't you say something?" Finally, she sounds nearly normal again. Her silk-slippered feet patter behind me as she hurriedly catches up.

"Because I was shaking, Ceela. And confused. And I wanted a stupid fucking book to make myself feel better. And then you come along, trying to accuse me of something—"

"I didn't! I wasn't!"

"Whatever. I'll be in my nook."

"But our dresses!"

"*Fuck* the dresses." I make my way back to our space, then disappear around a curve of a wall that leads to my nook. I stop, pressing my back against the plaster, trying to not to hyperventilate as I listen, to determine if Ceela is following me.

But she's not. A few seconds later, I do hear her whispering, though. All four of them, actually.

So that's it, I guess. She's turned them against me somehow. What a great day. I lost my aunt and all four of my friends.

I have nothing left but this job.

A job I don't even want to do anymore.

I continue into my nook, flop down onto my bed, open the book and start to read.

But I can't even see the words over the tears that spill out of my eyes and flow down my cheeks.

***

I stay curled up in bed with the Godslayer all afternoon and evening. I don't even get up for dinner. I just listen to the sounds of Little Sisters all through the dorm. They are busy, busy, busy sewing dresses because tomorrow is a prize day and someone gets to have to have dinner with the Extraction Master tomorrow night.

They all want to be Chosen for that. They all want to be Chosen for everything because they are stupid and don't see the Choosing for what it is. A way to make them buy into the idea that being fed to the god in the tower is a fun, once-in-a-lifetime chance that can't be passed up.

Even my former friends are buying into it because they are dutifully sewing their stupid dresses, hoping for the chance to sit across from Finn Scott tomorrow night at dinner. To have his full attention.

I wonder if he will stick his fingers between everyone's legs before he's done here?

At this point, nothing would surprise me.

None of my former friends came check on me when I didn't show for dinner. Tonight is the first night the dining room on the very top of the Maiden Tower is open for us and we had planned to go together.

It's like I'm not a part of them anymore.

They don't even say goodnight to me and when the lights go out, I don't get up and go to Finn.

I simply cry myself to sleep.

Because I'm all alone now.

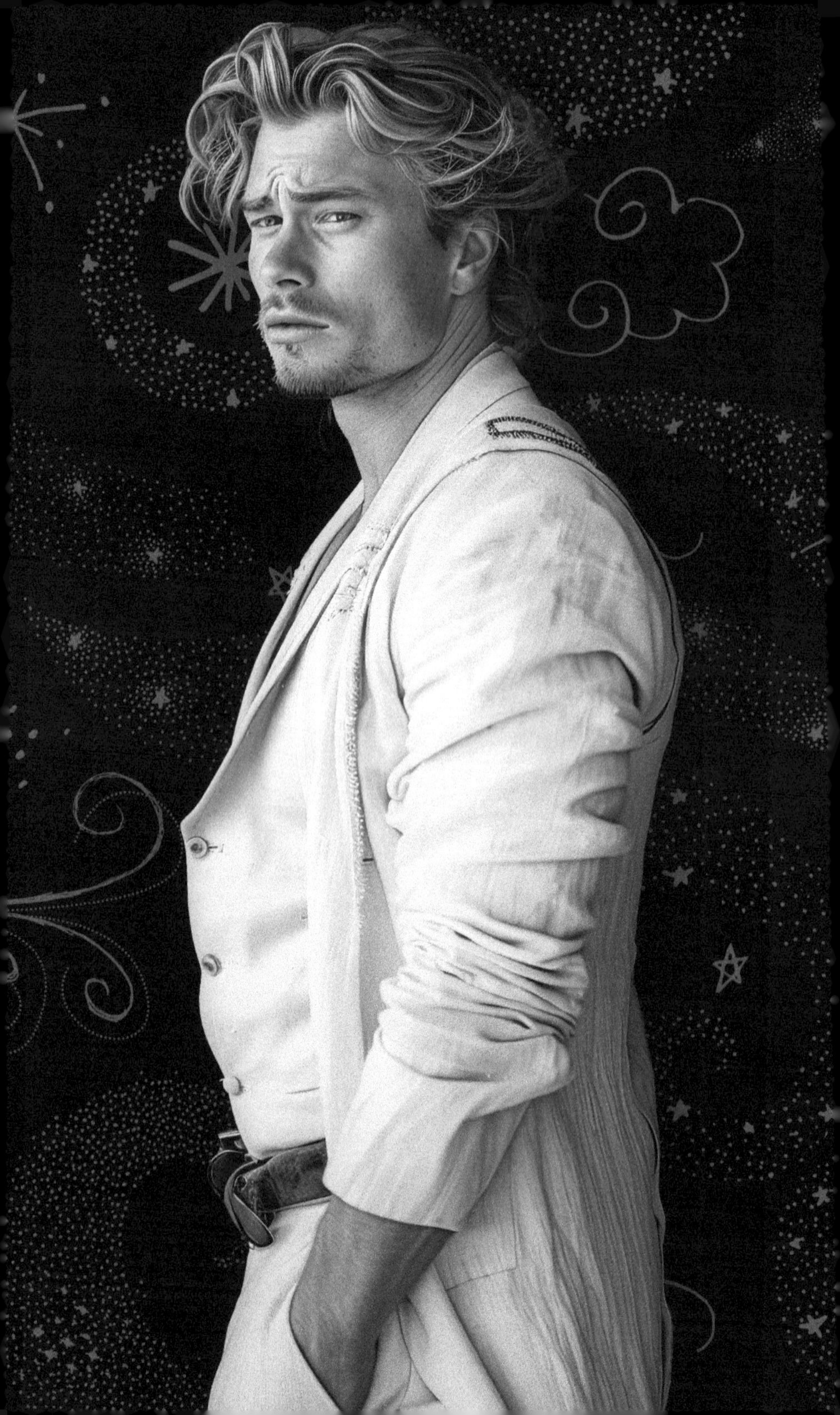

FINN

CHAPTER THIRTY-ONE

*S**he doesn't show.*
    I wait on the couch up on the top floor, just staring at that bookcase, until well past midnight. I even open the bookcase up, go all the way down the stairs, pass under the canal, go up the stairs, and *almost* open the door that I know leads to the Little Sister dorm and drag her sexy ass out of bed and bring her back here.

After a few agonizing minutes of deliberation, I actually do open that door, but I'm presented with so many different places she could be, I don't even bother looking for her. Just retrace my steps and sit my ass back down on the couch and stare at the bookcase.

In fact, when I wake up in the morning, that stupid bookcase is the first thing I see.

"Did you sleep up here?"

I blink the sleep away and look up at Mitch, who is looking down at me like I'm insane.

"Are those yesterday's clothes, Finn?"

Obviously, both of these questions are rhetorical, so I don't bother answering.

"What's going on?" His tone is terse now, so I have to say something.

"What do you mean?" Deflection probably isn't the best choice because it just makes him angrier.

"What do I mean?" He's staring at me again. Not like I'm insane, but like I'm... lying. "You're acting weird. Is something going on that I don't know about?"

"Mitch, I don't know what you want from me. I tell you pretty much everything, but that doesn't mean I owe you everything. And you wanna know why I'm acting weird? I mean, what kind of question is that? Have you already forgotten about Clara?" Mitch shrinks back from this accusation. "I know the rest of Tau City has. *Thank god*, they're saying to themselves. *Thank god that Maiden is gone, and the bells have stopped ringing, and I can go on with my life pretending that none of this is happening until the next time the bells ring.*" I shoot him a sneer here. "I had higher expectations of you."

He starts stuttering. "No, I didn't forget about Clara. Of course not!"

"Then why are you acting like I should just get back to normal? Nothing's going back to normal, Mitch. Nothing. Ever. She's gone. My life is over."

"No. No, it's not, Finn. You're having dinner with a Little Sister tonight. I've made a list of five that I think are suitable. You should just—"

"Move on?" I raise one eyebrow at him.

"Fuck one. I was gonna say fuck one. Just... to make things easier until... time heals the wound, ya know?"

Time is not gonna heal my wound. But it's pointless to

argue with him. Besides, this dinner might actually be my answer to the current melancholy. "Who's on the list?"

Mitch smiles like this is me agreeing to his 'fuck one' plan. Then he pulls out a slip of paper and hands it over.

I scan it, but Jasina's name is not on the list. Still, Mitch isn't the one in charge here. I am. So I hand it back and look him in the eyes. "I want Jasina Bell. She's my choice."

"What?" His face is so scrunched up in confusion, I almost laugh. "I mean, she's fuckable, for sure. And that display at the opening gala was pretty cool. But… *down-city*, Finn." He shakes his head. "She's got a really bad rep as a whore."

"I don't care. I like her and I want to spend time with her tonight. If I can't have Clara, I at least want someone interesting. Throw in a spa day and new dress, as well. Tell the cooks I want the dining room set for dinner at seven."

I turn to leave, so ready for a shower, but Mitch grabs my arm. "Wait. Finn. Come on, man. You can't… I mean. OK, fine. I'll get you Jasina. But there's no spa or new dress included in this day."

I shrug off his grip on my arm and look him in the eyes. "There is now. Get it done. I'm taking a shower. Tell the cooks I'll be down for breakfast in twenty minutes."

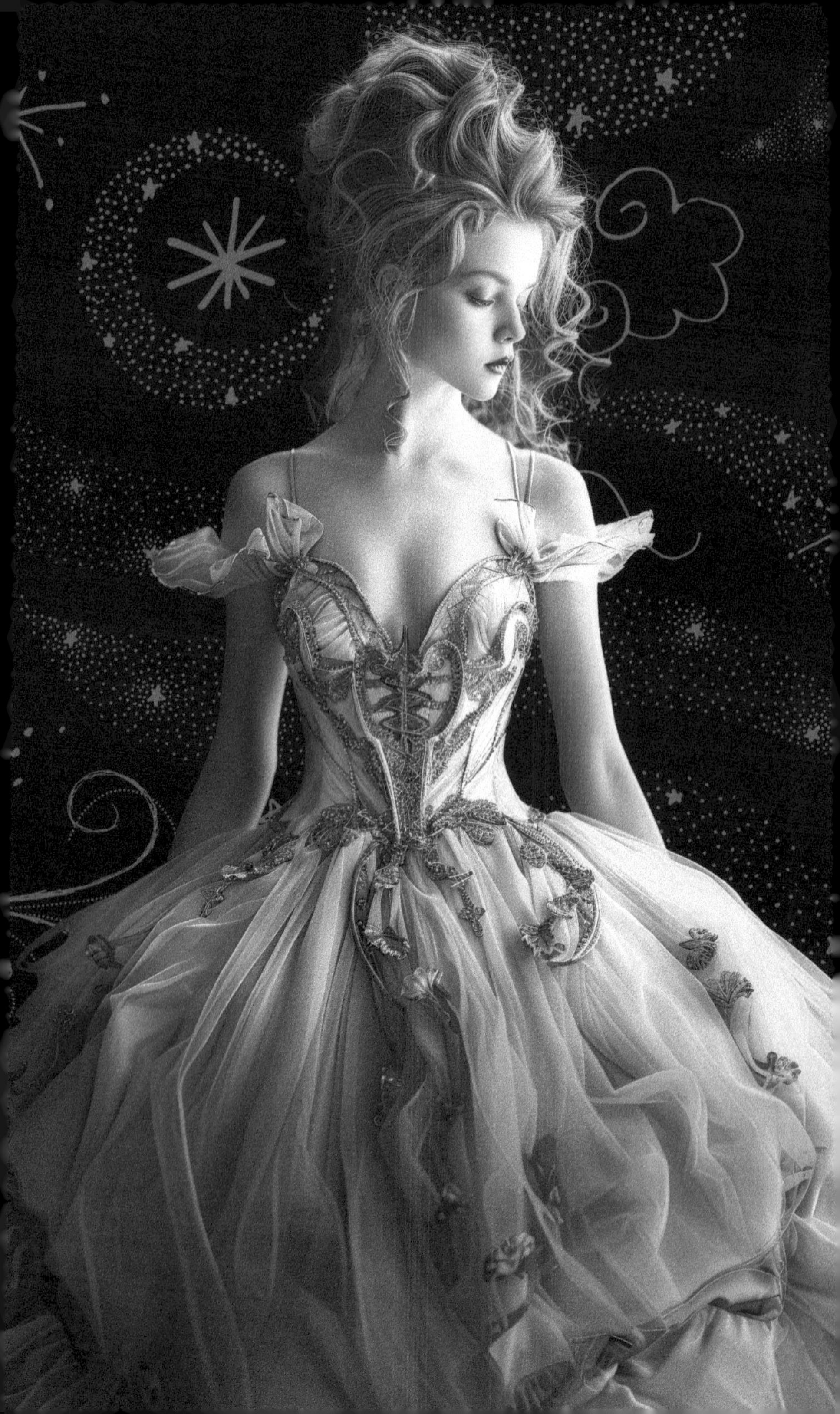

JASINA

If I have to stand alone, I will do so with grace.

The Matron, who is not one I recognize, waves me forward. "Hurry up, then. There's a lot to do. First, you must stand for the couturier."

As I walk up the fake canal the other Little Sisters start whispering. Probably wondering why Finn Scott would choose me, of all people. There's a little part of me that realizes that it is dangerous to arouse suspicion among them. There will be gossip. They will hate me.

But they already hate me. And anyway, once I leave the dorm and arrive at the Maiden District couturier's boutique, I've forgotten all about them. Because this room is filled with the most extravagant fabrics, and intricate lace, and opulent silk I've ever laid my eyes on.

This, I decide, is why we volunteer. Because this is the height of luxury.

And I get the distinct feeling that, as a Little Sister, I am not supposed to be here.

The dressmaker is quite tall so when she looks me over, she's literally sneering down her nose. "You are pretty, but your body has curves. Too many curves. You should mind the weight. It creeps on and never comes off. As it stands, you're at least a size eight with that ass."

I *could* be offended. But why bother? I am a size eight. And anyway, my ass is definitely one of my best assets. Pun intended. And this bitch has to make me a dress. *Has to.* As in has no choice. So why should I let her bad attitude ruin my day?

I shake my head and raise my chin. Then I start

demanding things. I am a rather good dressmaker, and while I am not up to her standards, I have opinions.

She balks at my demand for a sweetheart neckline ball gown. But after I demonstrate that I am not a completely uneducated dressmaker-in-training, she gives me off-the-shoulder sleeves, a dropped-v waistline, and a bare back. Sensing I might challenge her about the waistline, she adds, "I don't have time for glass beads, even if I commandeer every seamstress in the district. But… it will be entirely made of silk." Then she winks. "And I won't make it blue."

I leave the couturier's boutique feeling happier than I have all week. Then it's spa time. And I get the full Spark Maiden treatment. Steam sauna, massage, body scrub, bubble bath, facial, manicure, pedicure, haircut, hairstyle, and makeup.

By the time I arrive back at the couturier's boutique, I feel like yesterday never happened. Of course, I know it still did. I know that this day isn't going to fix anything, it's just going to make it all worse once it's over.

But I don't care.

Because when the ladies' maids finish dressing me and I look in the mirror… well, I'm absolutely certain that even if this night with Finn ends in disaster, it will be worth it.

It is… *almost* how the couturier described it to me before I left. It is off-the-shoulder, but she has made sheer armlets, giving it a more refined look.

There is a dropped-v waistline, but it comes with a faux corset that hugs my curves and has the most beautiful gold hooks running down my front. I almost can't stop looking at them.

The back is open, like she promised, but the dress comes with a stole made of so much silk, I could wrap it around my whole body, twice, hiding every bit of skin, should I choose to do so.

And true to her word, none of it is blue. It's champagne and the lightest of pinks. Just the feeling of these luxurious fabrics draped across my body sends a tingle all the way down to my toes.

This dress is beyond my imagination, let alone my skill. It's so much more than I ever expected. Especially with just one day to pull it together. I look at the couturier and bow my head as I dip into a curtsey. "Thank you. I am undeserving."

She comes over and taps my shoulder, making me straighten up. And when I look her in the eyes, she says, "I think you might be the prettiest girl I've ever dressed. Everyone calls you a slut. Do you know that?"

My face goes red hot.

"Dear, do not be embarrassed. Do you know why they call you these names? It's because your beauty is a threat. To women. To men. To entire power structures. Whatever it is you do in your private time, Jasina Bell, has nothing to do with the names they will call you. So I made the dress a little bit slutty, because all men like that. But I only did it because your body can pull it off. You like it too, right? It's still elegant, don't you think?"

I let out a breath, nodding. "I've never seen anything so beautiful in my life."

She gently places her hand on my cheek and smiles. "Neither have I."

I leave there a little bit confused by this last comment. Did she mean she's never made a prettier dress in her entire career?

Surely not. I've seen the dresses the Spark Maidens wear. They're all gorgeous.

But then... then she must've meant... she's never seen a prettier *girl*.

I have never thought of myself as ugly. I have eyes. But... I don't see myself as something that threatens power structures.

She must've just been being polite.

It doesn't matter though. Because I am filled with the feeling that tonight is something meant for me, and only me. And even if everyone in that dorm hates me when I go home tonight, I won't care.

If I must stand alone, I will do it with grace.

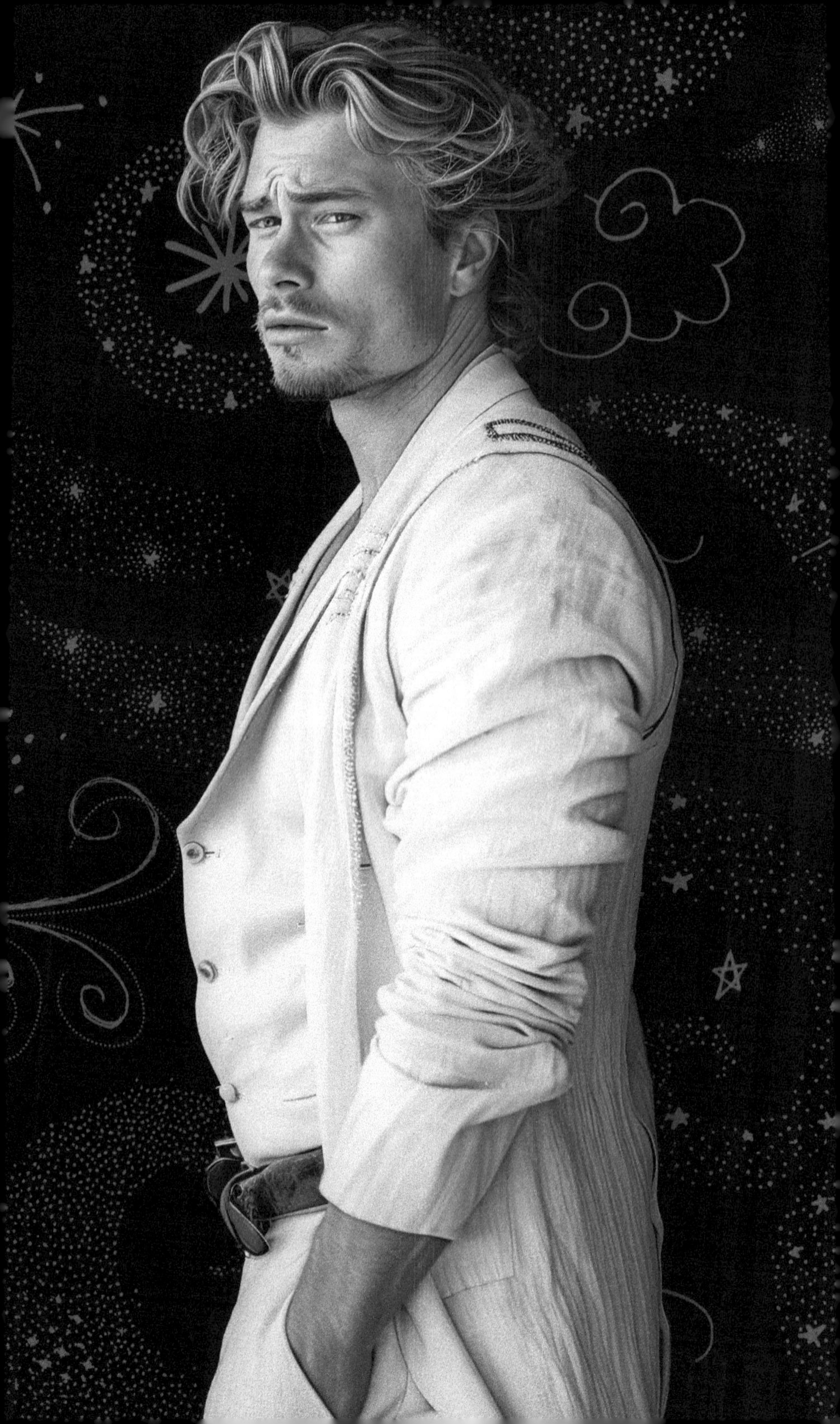

FINN

CHAPTER THIRTY-THREE

At five minutes to seven I'm dressed and pacing the front room, waiting for Mitch to deliver Jasina Bell. I'm not nervous. I would not call it nervous. But... the fact is, I haven't had a first date with a woman since Clara and I were fourteen years old and she asked me to be her escort to the Pledge Gala in her second year.

And it occurs to me now that we even talked about that night just before she went into the tower. It was her favorite memory with me.

But is this night with Jasina a date?

Or is it just a dinner with a down-city girl who won a Choosing contest?

I can't decide.

It could be something more. If there was any sort of future in my future.

But at the very least, I'm gonna be seeing her for the next three months. I know this for sure, because I'm the one in charge of Choosing and I'm gonna make sure Jasina Bell makes it through every one of them.

If this place lasts that long, that is.

Because I don't know what it means for the god to be

dying. The only thing I took away from the Council meeting that day my father died was… hopelessness.

Suddenly, the doors open and I turn just in time to see Jasina's face light up in surprise as Mitch escorts her inside.

She's been here, of course. But only upstairs, not down here. And she's impressed.

I walk over to her and Mitch backs off as I take her hand, kiss it, and smile. "Welcome. Welcome to my home, Miss Jasina Bell."

She blushes, which is a nice touch if it's fake and downright sexy if it's not. "Thank you." She curtsies, bowing her head. And this is when I notice how mature and refined she looks tonight.

It's the dress. It's gorgeous. And big. A gala dress, for sure. Not what I was expecting, but I can't complain about the bare shoulders or the way the neckline plunges to reveal cleavage. "You look lovely."

This makes her smile and draw in a big breath. "As do you. I mean." She blushes again. This time it's absolutely real. "Your suit is stunning."

I turn to Mitch, find him leering at her cleavage, and shoot him a look when he finally manages to meet my gaze. "You can leave now."

Mitch looks confused. "You want me to leave?"

"And you can take the cooks and servers with you."

"But… Finn—I mean, Extraction Master—it's five courses. Who will keep the food hot? Who will serve?"

"I've got it, Mitch. So please." I pan my hand at the door. "Dismiss them and go."

He lets out a long breath, wanting to argue with me. But

he won't. Not in front of Jasina. Instead he does a little bow, then retreats in the direction of the kitchen, barking orders as he walks.

Jasina and I look at each other. She's nervous, but there's a little bit of sadness in her expression as well. Why though? Because I dismissed everyone and we're going to be completely alone?

No. She's nervous because... she likes me?

Or... she had a bad day? That can't be it. She looks amazing. She had a day at the spa and the Maiden District couturier's full attention.

She had a bad *yesterday*. That's why she didn't come. Something happened.

Mitch comes back leading a train of servers and cooks. When he opens the door and steps aside, they file through. He sighs one last time, then backs out of my palace and closes the doors behind him.

I turn to Jasina. "You're sad."

"What? No." She smiles, still nervous, but also still sad.

"Yes, you are. What is it? What happened yesterday?" Her face falls into a frown and I knew it. I knew I was right. "Come on." I take her hand and tug her in the direction of the dining room. "Let's eat before everything gets cold."

She doesn't resist. Simply allows me the privilege of taking her into the dining room where two places have been set and enough food has been put out to feed a party of eight. "I told them to just cook it up and we'd eat buffet style."

Jasina nearly snorts. "Oh, my god. Were your cooks furious?"

"Probably. But they get the night off. What do they care? Grab a plate, fill it up, and tell me who made you so sad you didn't want to come see me last night."

She grabs a plate but doesn't meet my eyes. "Why do you think that's what happened? Maybe I just don't like you?"

"Please. You like me. Tell me you don't."

She's putting little bits of food on her plate, so she doesn't say anything for a few moments. Not until she's picked out what she wants and can no longer avoid it. Her blue eyes are a little bit glassy when they meet mine. And this is when I notice that they are not the cyan-blue color of the canal like Clara's.

They are royal blue. The blue of ancient kings and queens. The blue of sapphires. The blue of butterflies.

She opens her mouth and I'm expecting another excuse or maybe an apology for looking sad. But instead, she tells me the truth. The whole story about Donal Oslin pushing her into a nook and her aunt slapping her across the face comes spilling out right there as we stare at each other from across a spread of food.

When she's finished, I look her straight in the eyes and make a promise. "She will never do that to you again. And as for Donal, I know his father. I will—"

"No." Jasina puts up a hand. "No. I don't want you to say anything. To either of them. Just… let it go."

"Fuck that. No. He needs to pay for what he did. I don't have any power over Matrons, but she's not gonna have another reason to slap you ever, Jasina. Because tonight, you and I are gonna figure out that room. And then we're gonna tell her everything we know."

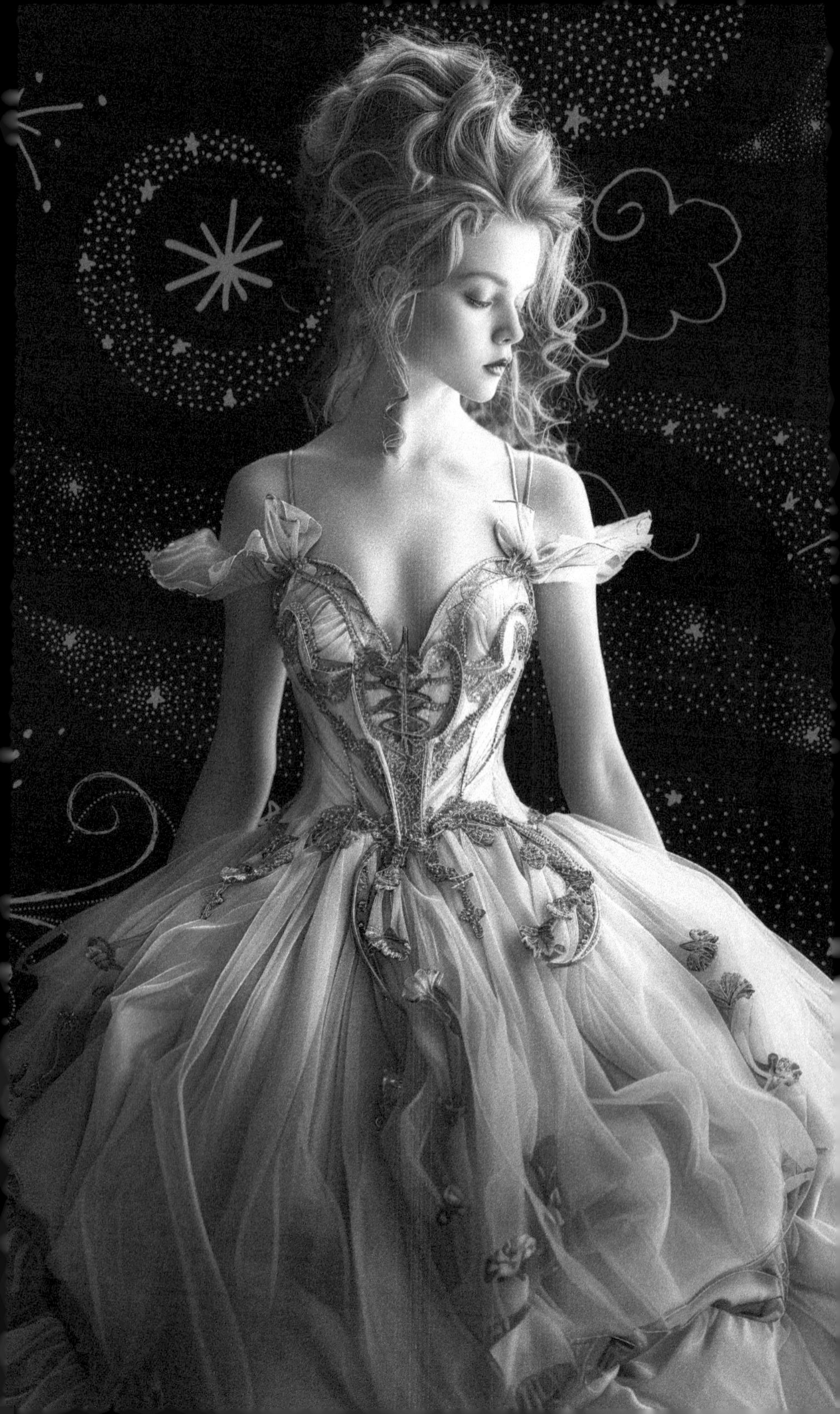

JASINA

should

spa day this morning. I think my auntie turned them against me."

He sighs a little, then shrugs up one shoulder. "OK. Fine. We don't tell them shit. But you want to know what that room *is*, right?"

"Why do you even care what I want?"

"Because... well... you're like this teeny, tiny ray of red-haired hope leaking into a pitch-black room from underneath a door, Jasina. I've lost the only three people I ever considered family. First, my father died, then I found out my mother's part of the Matron cult, and then I sent the woman I love through the tower doors. The only people I have left are Jeyk and Mitch."

I make a face at the mention of Mitchell Davies, which Finn does not miss.

"What? What's that look for?"

"Nothing. It's none of my business."

"No, tell me."

"I just don't understand why you're friends with that guy."

"Which one?"

"Mitchell Davies."

"Mitch is my number one. He's been my best friend since we were like six."

I scoff. "Have you ever been down-city with him?"

"Couple times. For drinking." But Finn holds up a hand. "But not for the whores. I never cheated on Clara. Until you, she was the only woman I was ever with."

"Well, if you left before the whores then you missed the

big show. Because Mitchell Davies has a reputation down-city as a man who likes to hurt people."

"What are you talking about?"

"Specifically, young girls. He pays them. To be quiet. But if you agree to spend a night with Mitchell, then you ask for the coin to make up for not being able to work for a week because he's gonna blacken your eyes and split your lip."

"That's bullshit, Jasina."

"Sometimes he breaks their ribs."

"Stop it. He does not. I'd have heard about it."

"But you just said you never stay."

"Someone would've told me."

"Why the hell would someone tell you that? For what reason? You were the Extraction Master's son. As up-city and privileged as they come. For all they knew, you're just like Mitch. You just do it in private."

There's a silence here. A silence filled with Finn's deep thoughts about himself and how he actually might be more like his friend than he realized. Because he was rough with me. He didn't hurt me, but it's not a stretch of the imagination to believe that he *could*.

He shoves his hands in his pockets and lets out a sigh. It takes him a moment to look me in the eyes, but when he does, I find sincerity. "I want to know things, Jasina. I want to understand what's happening to us. I'm tired of the lies and I want the truth. I think it's up there in that room. And if you want the truth as well, then I would like you to join me so we can find it together."

I smile. And it's a big smile. Maybe the biggest smile I've ever smiled in my life.

"Is that a yes?" He's not sure what my smile means. But I am. "It's a yes."

WE LEAVE **the food for later** and climb the stairs to the fourth floor. The door to the Looking Glass room is closed, but not all the way, so Finn just pushes on it and it swings open to reveal the domed room covered in weird white triangles, that are so shiny, they look to be made of glass.

The triangles are positioned in an interlocking, top-to-bottom way so as to allow them to curve with the ceiling. This is not the first time I've seen them, of course, but it's the first time I have my wits about me and really take a good look.

"What?" Finn asks. "What's so interesting about the ceiling?"

"They cover the dome."

"So?"

"So there has to be a purpose for that."

"Maybe they're just ceiling tiles?"

"Maybe they can do two things at once?"

He smiles. "But what is their other job?"

"Well." I blow out a breath and look around the room again. "There is a control room in the Matron Tower like this, but it doesn't look like this at all. It had glass plates or something that can show images. It also had a desk with a bunch of switches. So I'm thinking that these triangles are a different kind of glass plate and this thing"—I point to the circular desk in the center of the room—"this is where the switches live. My Auntie said that room was outdated but the one in the Extraction Tower wasn't. This is just a newer version of that old room."

He looks around, up and down the walls, reflecting on my statement.

I look around too, and this is when I notice that the open door makes a break in the seamless triangle tiles. So I walk over there and push it closed. But it pops back open.

I lean in, trying to see what the problem is. "What's wrong with the door?"

Finn walks up behind me. "What?"

"It won't close. Look."

"Oh. Yeah. We broke it trying to get in. I didn't have a key."

I look up at him. "Can you fix it? I think it needs to be closed. Look. There's a little smooth thing here on the side of the door and it matches this smooth thing here on the doorjamb."

"Huh. Like they have to match up or something."

"Yeah. It's some way to signal that the door is closed and… I'm not sure. Like maybe a connection is made."

Finn studies the door for a moment, then points. "This plate is bent on the lock. Let me go find a tool and see if I can get it to lie flat."

He leaves and I go over to the circular desk in the center of the room, then step into the ring and stare down at the black top. Which I now realize, once I take a closer look, is not completely black. There are faint outlines. Circles, and squares, and rectangles.

"Found something." Finn is back and he starts working on the bent plate on the side of the door.

But my focus is on this desk. Because I can actually see a hint of letters under the black glass. Suddenly it hits me that it needs a light behind it. That's how we see the words and shapes. It needs a light.

The moment I come to this realization, Finn stands up. "Got it." Then he pushes the door until it closes with a click.

The lights go out. And in next moment, the entire room comes to life.

I gasp as the desk around me lights up, just like I guessed it should.

"Holy shit. Is that the night sky?" Finn is looking up at the ceiling, his face glowing a faint gray-blue color.

I look up too and sure enough, it's like we're standing outside on the top of the Extraction Tower dome, looking up at the stars.

"We did it!" Finn walks over to the desk and enters the ring, slipping his stomach right up to my back because this desk was really only meant to hold one person at a time. But I don't tell him to back off. I like it when he's close. "It's beautiful, but..." Finn hesitates. I can almost feel him frowning behind me. "But what's it mean?"

I look up, tipping my head back, trying to get a look at his face. "I don't know."

"The night sky is cool, right? But who cares? This can't be all it does."

"No. The desk is how you control it. Look. There's all

these… switches." They don't look anything like the switches I saw in the Matron control room, but it's the only word I have to describe them. "I think you tap them or something."

"Oh, fuck. I think you're right. Because when Mitch was in here with me, he was tapping on the glass like crazy, but nothing happened."

I turn—which isn't an easy thing to do since we're so pressed together and my gown is quite voluminous—and look up at Finn. "Mitchell Davies was tapping on it? Like he was pressing buttons, or something?"

"Yeah."

"He *knows*. He knows how to use it."

"What makes you think that?"

"Well, was your first instinct to start tapping on the glass?"

"No."

"No. Because you had never seen this before. But he had. He knew how it worked. He just didn't know how to make it work."

The light in here is dim and I've got a weird view of his face, but I'm pretty sure Finn Scott is rethinking everything he ever thought he knew about Mitchell Davies right about now.

"It's a terrible thing to be betrayed. Trust me, I know. But he's not what you think, Finn."

"Yeah." Finn sighs and rakes his fingers through his thick, blond hair. Then he looks down at me. "Yeah, you might be right." He leans both hands onto the glass, like he needs a moment. And I'm just about to exit the ring desk and give him this moment when suddenly the night sky above us disappears and the room blinks a bright white.

He and I both gasp, but then the white is gone and the night sky is back.

"Oh, my god. What did you do?"

Finn shrugs. "I didn't do anything. What did you do?"

"I didn't move at all. But you…" I look down at the desk and see two rectangles on either side of me. They're just plain black inside, but there's a glowing blue outline around them. "You put your hands on the desk," I say, pointing at the rectangles. "You put your hands there. Do it again."

It takes Finn another moment to catch on to what I'm telling him, but then he leans over, just like he did, and presses his palms into the black spaces outlined in blue glow.

Once again, the night sky disappears and the white light is back.

Finn gasps, and when I turn to see what he's looking at, I gasp as well.

Because it's his father.

Aldo Scott's face is big, and bright, and smiling as he looks down at us from the curvature of the interior dome.

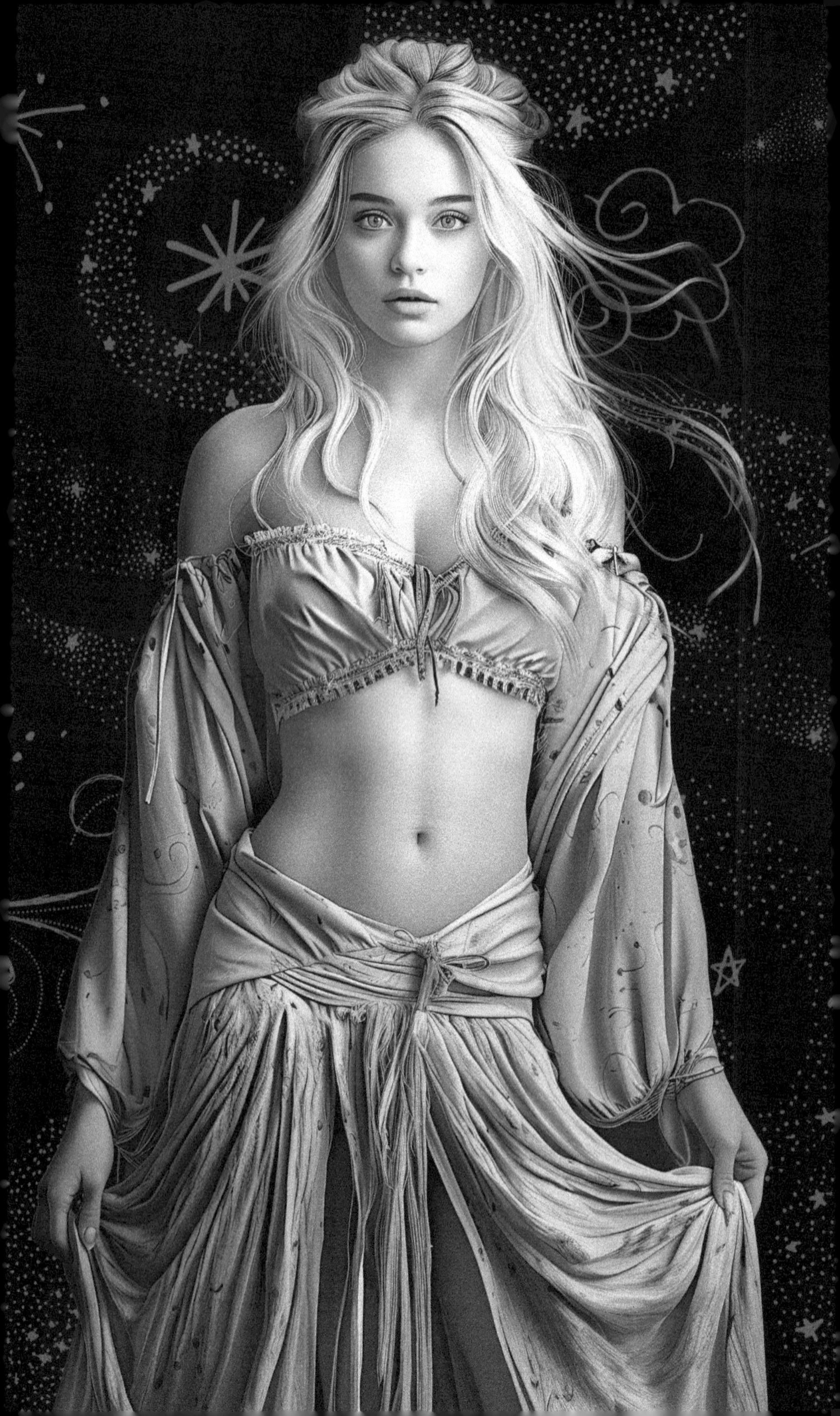

CLARA

CHAPTER THIRTY-FIVE

*G*et you home.

That's what Tyse said last night.

Get me home.

I don't think it's possible. I really don't. I think whatever it was that happened to me is permanent. So I'm not obsessing over this statement of his. It didn't keep me up that night for hours and hours while Tyse slept soundly next to me. Almost as if this new mission of his is reassuring. Unlike me. Because I might be feeling unexpectedly unsettled.

Which is stupid because I'm not unsettled. Why would I be unsettled about the thought of going home?

Tyse is in the shower, getting ready to go to work. I need to get up too, but I'm so exhausted from absolutely not obsessing over how he wants to get me home, I can't think about spending another day down on Eight with all those people and all those noises.

I feel like I need some space. Some time to think.

"Hey?"

I open my eyes and watch Tyse come out of the kitchen, dressed, but wet. "Don't you believe in towels?"

He squints at me. "What?"

"You're always wet when you come out—never mind. What were you gonna say?"

He's still squinting at me. "Did you sleep well?"

"No." It comes out as a pout.

"OK. Well, I was gonna say, I don't think you should go down to Eight today."

"Done."

"What?" His squint is deeper now. He's even cocked his head.

"Done. I don't want to go down to Eight today either. But just for the sake of argument, why should I not go down to Eight today?"

"Oh. I just think you should stay inside. Until we figure out what you are."

"What I *am*? What's that mean?"

"Well..." He tries on a smile. Like it just hit him that I'm in a bad mood and he's about to do his best to navigate around it. "Clara. We don't have Spark Maidens here. It's not a thing. And this is what you tell me you are. So I'm thinking that you're maybe... special." He smiles bigger, believing this to be the way forward.

"Special?"

"Yeah. Like... you know. A genius or something."

I sigh. "Whatever."

"What's wrong with you?"

"Nothing. You're going to get me home. What could possibly be wrong with me?"

Again, he squints. Then he smiles. "You like me. You're

gettin' attached, aren't ya? And you're gonna miss me when you leave and go back to loverboy."

I huff.

But when I don't refute any of his statements, he points at me. "Noted. And I like you back. So I want you to be safe. That's why you should stay here all day and I'll tell Rodge you're not coming on my way down."

I sit up in bed a little, not wanting him to go yet. "What time will you be home?"

"Sixish, maybe?" He sits down on the footstool so he can lace up his boots. "I'll bring food. But there's rations in the cupboard. They're supposed to be the best there is. I bet they're really tasty."

He gets a side-eye from me for that remark. But it's not enough to break his mood, because he winks. Then he stands up, hooks his weapon belt around his waist, and shrugs on his jacket as he walks towards the door and pulls it open. I get one more glance from over his shoulder before he leaves. "Stay out of trouble."

Then he's through and the door closes behind him.

A whole day to myself doesn't sound as interesting as it did yesterday. Yesterday I was going to snoop. That kinda backfired.

A sharp knock on the door startles me right out of bed. I hesitate, then call, "Who is it?" Because I know it's not Tyse. He would not knock.

"It's Anneeta." Her voice is chirpy and she drags her name out like it's a song.

I walk over and open the door. Anneeta is a small child of

about… eight, maybe. I'm really not an expert in children, but I do like them. With long brown hair and big brown eyes, she's very cute and her personal style is off-the-charts whimsical. So I brighten. "Hello, Anneeta. What can I do for you?"

"We're friends now because Tyse said so. And he said I could come keep you company since you're staying home alone today."

"Oh. Well, this is a nice surprise. Come on in." I leave the door open, then walk over to the chair where my clothes are draped and start pulling on my pants.

"I like your undies. Ruffles are my favorite."

I blush, even though it's not Tyse commenting on my underwear this time. "Thanks. They're the only pair I have, so I'm a little bit sick of them, to be honest."

"Oh. You need more clothes?"

"Yes. Desperately. But the only coin I have is right there." I point to Tyse's jar of coins. I added my own coin to the collection last night. "Does that buy much?"

Anneeta walks over to the coins as I put on my boots. She takes the jar down and gives it a good check. "Yes. That's Tyse's tip jar. It's quite a lot. Especially with the groat in there. Does he tip people groats?" She frowns. "He's never tipped me a groat."

"Is that the odd one? No, I earned that yesterday working for Rodge."

"Oh. Well, I was right. Tyse doesn't tip groats."

"How much is it worth?"

"Fifty of the little coins."

"Wow. Did I work that hard yesterday? To earn that?"

Anneeta shrugs. "You must've. Or else Rodge really likes you."

"Hmm. So maybe I *can* afford new clothes. Do you want to go to the Canal District shops with me?"

"Can't."

"Oh." I deflate a little. "Not even if I buy you something sweet on the way home?"

"I would love to go, but I really, really can't. I can't leave the ruin. I'm a spark baby, you see."

"A spark baby? What in the god's name is that?"

"I was born here in the tower already addicted. They can't take me out because I would die."

My mouth makes an o-shape, but no sound comes out. "I… I'm so sorry. I'm very sorry to hear this. Tyse did mention that you… but… I guess I didn't put it all together."

She shrugs. "It's OK. I'm OK. I like the tower. But you know what? They don't have proper shops here, but they have a lost and found. If people don't claim a lost thing within three days, they put it on sale and all proceeds go to feed tower people who can't afford to pay. We could shop for your new clothes there."

Up-city Clara Birch would laugh out loud at this suggestion. But tower-ruin Clara Birch suddenly feels like beggars can't be choosers. "That sounds perfect. Let's go then. Let's spend all my coin at the lost and found."

Anneeta claps and beams with happiness as I fish my groat out of the jar and put it in one of my many pockets. Then we leave and start the journey downstairs.

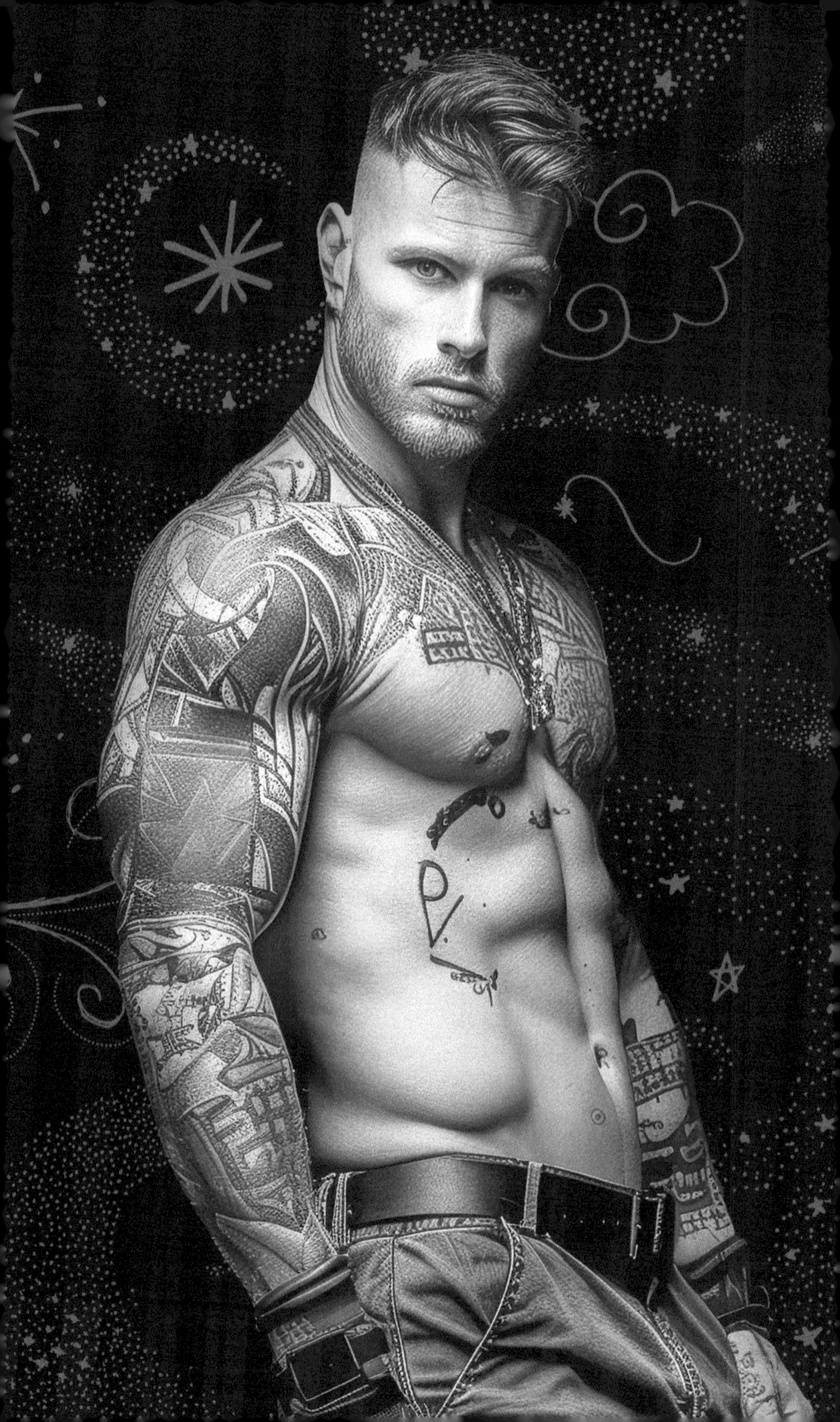

TYSE

CHAPTER THIRTY-SIX

The sun is just starting to set when I make my way back up the tower steps with bags of fried meat and rice. It was a boring day and I'm glad this job is over tomorrow. I'd quit already, but I don't like breaking my word to Stayn. Or anyone, actually. It's kind of a thing with me.

This thought leads directly to the woman currently living in my room. I made that promise to get her home because I was embarrassed that she saw my discharge spectra and all that entails. I thought for sure she'd want to take me up on that offer of a hotel room in the city.

But this morning's bad mood is an indication that she's less than enthusiastic about my promise to get her home.

She does like me.

I smile up the last flight of stairs and then make my way to my door. But I pause here because I hear laughter inside.

When I open it up I find Anneeta and Clara sitting on the floor with a coffee table between them—a table that was not here this morning—hovering over a game of HoloHops.

Anneeta sees me first. "Tyse! You're home!" She jumps up, beaming a wide smile at me. "Look at what Clara can do!" She points to the HoloHops board where the little game pieces—which normally take batteries, and which also normally do not work here in the tower for more than a few minutes—are projecting pictures of animals a couple of inches up into the air.

But that's not the amazing thing Anneeta is going crazy about. At least, not the only one. The crazy thing is that Clara Birch is lit up with blue spark from her fingertips to her shoulders and little patterns of shapes, or letters, or something are dancing across her skin.

I look over my shoulder just to make sure no one is passing by in the hallway, then kick the door closed with my foot. "Holy fuck, Clara! What are you doing? Put that shit away!"

The smile on Clara's face drops and immediately the light disappears, her skin back to normal. "Sorry."

All the holo pics of animals that were projecting above the game board also disappear and this makes Anneeta whine. "Why did you do that? I like HoloHops! And I was winning!"

I'm furious, also wondering how many times today Clara did this, so my tone is less than friendly when I start peppering her with questions. "Did you do that anywhere else but here in the room? Did anyone see it?"

Clara stands up, wiping her hands on her pants like she's nervous. And these aren't the pants I bought her, nor are they a pair of mine. "No! I only just did it now because we can't use batteries here."

"Where did you get those pants? Where did this table come from?" And as I look round, I realize that there are quite a few things in this room that weren't here this morning. A yellow rug, which I am standing on. A small wooden chest of drawers. Some curtains hung up over the rusty louvers—also yellow. And four throw pillows on my bed with birds embroidered on them. "What have you done to my room?"

When I look at Clara, she wrings her hands a little, then shrugs up one shoulder. "We went shopping at the lost and found. All of this for just nine coins! Can you believe it!"

Anneeta squeals out her contribution to the day's events. "And we had a tea party!"

But I'm looking at Clara when these words come out and she makes one of those quirky, slanted smiles that indicate things with the tea party might have gone awry.

I laugh just picturing it. And this laugh cools me down a little, even though I am still worried that Clara was displaying her… *power*, or whatever, when I came in. If anyone finds out what she can do, the government will get involved. And that's the last thing we need. "Clara, it's not a good idea to show anyone that light of yours."

"Did you bring food?" Anneeta rushes over and relieves me of the paper bags. "I'm starving. I can stay, right?"

I say, "Yeah, you can stay." But Clara and I are still looking at each other.

Clara shakes her head. "I won't. I promise. I won't do it again. And no one saw. We only just got back a little while ago, and I only used it to power the game. I swear."

"She swears." Anneeta is digging her fingers into a container of fried meat and stuffing it into her mouth. "She won't do it again."

"Who taught you to eat?" I grab the container and the bags from Anneeta and point to the sink. "Wash your filthy hands, at least. And get forks for everyone."

Clara hurriedly cleans up the table, putting the HoloHops game away, then shoves the box under the bed. "See?" She points to the table. "Now we have somewhere to eat."

I plop the bags down on the new table and then take off my jacket and hang it up. By this time, Anneeta is back with freshly washed hands and she's pulling soda cans out of the bag with excitement.

Her mouth makes a big o-shape. "Soda! The meal people don't like to give me soda. They say it makes me hyper. There's six here, so that means I get two, right?"

I grab the soda, pull one off, and offer it to her. "One."

"One? But there's six! That means we each get two."

"Well, I'm gonna drink three, so you only get one."

"That's not fair!"

I pull the can back just as she's reaching for it. "Your share can be nothin' if ya want."

She tsks her tongue at me. But makes her face sweet. "Please, may I have one soda? I promise to be content with one soda."

I let her grab it this time, then sigh.

"Well." Clara is still nervous, because she wipes her hands on her pants again. "How was your day?"

"Boring. But yours wasn't. I thought I told you to stay inside?"

Clara sits back down on the floor and starts doling out

food. "I needed clothes. And the lost and found?" Her eyes go wide as she stares at me. "Oh, my god!"

"It's a fucking treasure trove." Anneeta laughs. "She said that like two million times when we were shopping."

"Mouth, kid."

"Sorry, Tyse." But she's not sorry because she snickers these words out.

"Anyway." Clara sighs. "It was a pretty good day. How about you? Tell me what you did."

I shrug. "Same old day."

"Are you gonna sit?" Clara is still doling out food and she puts a container in a space that I think is meant for me.

"Sure." The coffee table is positioned between the end of the bed and the wall, so it's a small space to begin with. It's also low to the ground and getting my legs underneath it to sit on the floor is a chore. But I manage because I'm intrigued by this little scenario that's playing out in my room.

I spend quite a few unoccupied minutes thinking about last night. The overlay, the veil, Anneeta and Clara. And the spectra she found. I'm trying to figure out where this might be heading, because clearly it is heading somewhere.

Anneeta has always been a mystery. There's just something about her that doesn't add up. I just can't put my finger on it. And Clara, well, where to start? She claims to come from another dimension. And since I have not only seen this place, but have also witnessed the way she can store up spark in her body, I've got no choice but to believe her.

"Tyse? Are you listening?"

I look over at Anneeta. "What?"

"Did you bring dessert? I'm already done."

"No. Sorry." I lean over, trying to see into her container because she can't have eaten that fast. But nope. It's empty. "Were you starving?"

She smiles and nods. Then gets to her feet. "I'm gonna have second dinner downstairs. Do you want me to bring you guys back anything?"

"No," I tell her. "That's cool. See ya tomorrow."

"Yep." Anneeta looks at Clara. "Tomorrow. Tea party at nine. My place. Don't be late."

Clara points to her. "You're on."

"Bye!" Anneeta waves and then slips through the door, closing it behind her.

Clara and I both sigh and look at each other. I'm not sure where to start, but it doesn't matter. Her mouth opens and words just start spilling out.

"Oh, my god. The tea party?" Clara's eyes are wide. Like she still can't believe she got sucked into that.

"I should've warned ya. I meant to, but I forgot."

"She fed me some kind of boiled mud and little pieces of grass."

I nod, laughing. "Yep. I fell for it once, too. Ya should not have promised to go again. She'll be expectin' ya."

"Oh, no. I will not be going. But anyway. What do you think of the new decorations?" Clara does a little thing here. Something very girlish and flirty. She looks over her shoulder and tilts herself in my direction as she tucks her chin. Her smile a little bit shy, her eyes a little bit mischievous. "It brightens the place up, don't you think?"

I look down at the rug—which I am not sitting on—then up at the curtains. "Yeah, it's fine."

"It's fine? It's better than fine. And for nine coins! Can you believe it?"

"Where'd ya get nine coins, anyway?"

"Oh, Rodge. He paid me a groat for yesterday."

"What? What'd ya do down there, a striptease?"

She laughs. "No. Just… helped fill orders, then I came up here to clean your place. He overpaid me, didn't he?"

"Way overpaid you."

"He gave me a dress too."

"What?"

"A dress. Like the one Prisha was wearing yesterday."

"Well." I lean back against the end of the bed. "He likes you. That's handy."

"Yeah. So a groat is worth fifty of those coins in your jar."

"Yep."

"So." She shrugs. "I bought all this stuff, plus a whole new wardrobe."

"So that's where those pants came from."

She stands up, modeling them by turning around and giving me a nice view of her ass. "They're OK, right? I mean, I know they're ripped. But Anneeta says it's fashionable."

She's wearing a pair of faded denim jeans that are least one size too big for her. They've got all strategically fashionable rips in all the right places. Knees, thighs, and a small one on her hip. "They look good."

My opinion makes her smile. "They do, huh? I don't

know what this magic fabric is, but it's soft and these pants are comfortable."

"What else did ya get? Fancy a fashion show?" I wink at her and she blushes.

"Oh, a whole bunch of stuff. But I gave it to Rodge to wash in his machines."

"Well, there goes all your coin, right? It was nice while it lasted."

"What do you mean? He didn't charge me."

"What?" Now I'm just confused. But also suspicious. "Why not?"

"Why do you say it like that?"

"Because washing machines require jumps to power them. And a single jump costs four groats. You can make it cheaper by putting your clothes in with someone else's, but it's still gonna be at least thirty coins."

"He said don't worry about it."

This is when it hits me. He's billing me. He's not giving her any of this for free, he's just putting it on my tab. I chuckle, because it figures. "Anyway." I change the subject. Let her think she's his favorite person in the whole world. What do I care if it makes her happy? "What else did you guys do all day?"

"Anneeta took me to her place."

I'm taking a sip of soda when she says this, and I nearly spit it out. "What?"

"Yeah. She showed me where she lives."

"Where? What does it look like? It is a room?"

"Well, it is a room. But not one with a door like this. I'm not sure I could find it again because first we had to go through something called an access panel. She could walk, but I had to crawl. Then, after I had a good crook in my back, we ended up in some kind of... water room?"

"Water room?"

"I don't know what to call it. Anneeta called it the cooling cell. It was just like... a lake of water, only inside. There was a little walkway around it with a mostly functioning railing, and we followed that to the opposite side of the lake and on the other side of that wall was her place."

"What did it look like?"

"Small, cozy, cool. The water made like a mist in the air. So even though it was hot as hell outside, it was pleasant."

"Where does she sleep?"

"Oh, she's got a bed. It's actually a really nice room."

"Really?"

"Yeah. It was all decorated. I mean, I'd sleep there if I was here. There were even rugs. Nice furry ones."

"*Really?*"

"Really. And a fireplace."

"Shut up."

"I swear. It was something right out of an up-city house, in my opinion. There was no window—not a real one—but she had something that looked like a window, but it was really a painting. She got new curtains too."

"Speaking of... I wasn't aware they had matching décor sets in the tower lost and found. What's up with this stuff? It looks new."

"Oh, it is new. I found it in Anneeta's personal shop."

I squint at Clara. "Her what?"

"Yeah. Down in the lost and found, there's a whole room down there filled with things specifically for Anneeta. Everything has her name on it. She said I could buy this set because she's so over yellow."

"Huh. Well, it's nice to know that the charities are taking care of her. Sometimes I worry, ya know?"

"Oh, it's not charity. It's the city. She's even got her own personal shopper."

I squint "Like a runner?"

"Yeah."

"Where does she get the coin for this?"

Clara shrugs. "I don't actually think they charge her for anything. She just takes what she wants."

"That must be how she gets those clothes."

"They're cute, right? She's got a very well-developed sense of fashion."

"But why? That's what doesn't add up here. Why does the city pay for this? And why didn't I know about it?"

"I dunno. Maybe you never asked."

It's true what she says, I never had asked anyone about Anneeta. But it's weird to me that everything is free for her. I mean, it's good. It's nice. It's generous.

But cities aren't known for being good, and nice, and generous.

"Did she do anything weird?" I ask Clara.

"Define weird."

"Anything."

"Well, she calls herself a spark baby."

"Yep. She was born in this tower."

"So I think she's like me, Tyse."

A chill runs up my spine. "What makes ya say that?"

"Because she did something and I don't think it was conscious. She was walking along that railing in the lake room and she was dragging her fingertip along the wall. And it left a trace of cyan-blue light behind."

I picture this and a sick feeling creeps into my stomach.

Suddenly, Clara's hand lights up. And she points a finger into the air. I watch, stunned, as she draws a heart. But the cool—or maybe disturbing—thing is, the heart lights up blue. Like she's using a digital marker on a tablet instead of her finger in the air.

She draws some more things. Clouds, and arrows, and spirals. Then she smiles at me. "This was my display in the Choosing. No one had drawn things in the air like this before, so even though it's a stupid trick, it was unexpected and people liked it. Back then, when I was eighteen, it could only last a few seconds, then the light would fade. But as I got older, I could make the light stay all night if I wanted. It was fun, for a while. Until my Extraction turned into a living nightmare and all my friends started disappearing through the tower door. Then I just forgot about the spark. It stopped being important, I guess. But here, Tyse, *here*, in this version of Tau City, I discovered I can do *this*."

She touches me and before I pull away, my entire arm lights up blue with light and a shock shoots through my system. So powerful, I jump up, breaking contact, extinguishing the light, and spilling soda cans all over the table.

I get to my feet—Clara as well—and we stare at each other with just the small coffee table between us.

"Sorry. Did that hurt? I did it to Anneeta and she said it felt good."

I'm still trying to figure out what happened, so I don't answer.

She, of course, interprets this negatively. "Oh, my god. I'm so sorry. I fucked up. I should've never done that."

I let out a breath. "It's fine. You just... surprised me. I've never used a jolt or a jump, so I'm not sure what it feels like. But I think that's what you just did to me."

She pouts. "I didn't mean to. Anneeta—"

"Yeah, well. Anneeta isn't exactly normal, is she?"

This is when it occurs to me that Anneeta shares a lot more characteristics with Clara—and Clara with her—than either of them do with me.

And I've been neurologically altered, so I'm less, or maybe the right word is *more*, than human.

Which means both Anneeta and Clara have even less in common with the general public than they do me. And by general public I mean... *humans*.

Again, my silence makes her nervous. "I'll clean up." She drops some napkins on the spilled soda and starts shoving takeaway containers into bags.

"Hey." I grab her arm, making her stop. I note that it's not me touching her that starts the spark reaction, but her touching me. "It's fine. It is. You just surprised me, that's all."

She doesn't say anything for a moment. But then she lets out a breath and gives it a try. "I think I'm... like her." I nod. "I think I was a... spark baby." I nod again. "I think I'm not like you."

I force a smile. "Thank god, you're nothing like me. I'm

ruined. Like this tower. But you, Clara Birch, you're a very bright and shiny thing indeed."

She manages a small smile. "I scared you."

I want to deny it, but she knows she did. So instead, I joke. "Yeah. And that makes you one of the most badass people in this whole city. Because I'm a pretty scary guy myself."

Finally, I get a real chuckle. "I was just very excited. I mean, about meeting her and realizing that I'm not some freak, ya know?"

"Oh, I know."

She studies me for a moment. Then nods. "Yeah. You're pretty freaky too with those eyes of yours. Did you see anything when you got shocked?"

I shake my head. "No. But I think it needs to be all three of us in order to activate the augments."

She's about to say something, but before she can open her mouth there's a knock at the door. I stare at it, my hand already on my Versi, ready to pull it out.

"Oh. That's my laundry." Clara smiles at me, then pushes her way past to answer the door. Sure enough, it's a runner from Rodge with several packages wrapped in brown paper and tied with twine, plus another, smaller bag, with the name of a boutique printed on the side. She thanks the runner and pulls a coin out of her pocket to tip.

Then she takes the packages and the bag, and closes the door with a kick of her foot. When she turns to me, it's like she's forgotten everything that just happened because her smile is wide and real. She brings all the packages over to the bed and drops them, making them tumble across the mattress. Then she starts untying the twine and unpacking her new-to-her clean clothes.

But it's the little boutique bag that I pick up. "The Cheeky Goddess?" Despite all the weird shit that just happened, I smile. "You ordered underwear from the Cheeky Goddess?"

"Well, look. I am not against second-hand clothes, once laundered. But second-hand underwear is a hard limit for me."

"But... the Cheeky Goddess?"

She shrugs. "So? I don't know what that means."

I snicker, then peek inside the bag. "Oh, I'm dead. These are amazing."

"Shut up. What is the problem? And why are you so fascinated with my underwear?" She snatches the bag from me and looks inside. "Oh."

I snicker again. "Fancy a fashion show? Because I'm up for it."

"Just forget you ever saw it. I'll return it tomorrow and get something more practical."

"*Forget*...? Clara, I'm gonna be dreaming about that underwear all night. And you will not return it. You can't just flaunt Cheeky Goddess underwear in front of a man and think you can *return* it. The damage is done."

She blushes, but it comes with a smile. "I'm taking a shower." Then she grabs a couple of things off the bed—plus the bag of underwear—and disappears behind the bathroom curtain.

I stand there, looking around the room, wondering how, in the span of three days, my life has turned into something that has throw pillows. Not to mention a bed covered in freshly laundered women's clothes and the woman they belong to sleeps next to me at night.

It makes almost no sense. A change this dramatic shouldn't be possible.

Yet here we are.

When I come back from throwing the trash down the chute Clara is freshly showered and putting all her clothes away in the small chest of drawers she bought. She has also moved the coffee table to a dark corner, so there's more room now.

She looks at me when I enter. "You're not mad, right?"

"What could I possibly have to be mad about?" I mean, she's wearing a fucking nightgown. White. Cotton. Trimmed in satin lace. And it's not entirely opaque when the light is shining behind her. I can actually see that fuckin' underwear. Also, she's not wearing a bra. She doesn't even need to be backlit for me to figure that out.

Clara straightens up and starts to look nervous, because I've been staring. This is when I notice there's steam wafting out from the kitchen area. "Was the water hot?"

"Oh, yeah. It was amazing."

"Huh. Well, I might take advantage of that." I take my

shirt off and toss into the empty corner where I normally let the dirty clothes pile up. Except now it's not an empty corner. It's a wicker basket.

I just shake my head and unbuckle my battle belt as I walk into the kitchen. I drape the belt over the chair, then reach in and start the water. "Fuck. It's freezing. Not even lukewarm."

"No?" Clara comes over, and then, when she's standing next to me, it turns hot as it runs over my hand. "Well, it sure is steamy."

"You did this?"

"I did what?"

"You're making it hot."

"I am?" She points to herself.

"Do me a favor. It's been years since I had a hot shower in this place. Just stay right here. I won't take long."

She narrows her eyes at me. "You want me to stand here on the other side of the curtain, mere inches away from your naked body, while you get clean?"

"Yeah." Then I drop my pants and walk into the shower. The water starts to go cold again, so I know she's walked away. "Come on, Clara. Be nice to me. I brought dinner home. I saved you. I literally carried your ass up—"

"A *million* levels of stairs," she calls back. "I know, I know. You won't stop talking about it."

"Come on. If you spark me up a hot shower, I promise to make it worth it."

She does come back because the water goes hot again. "Make it worth it how?"

"Whatever you want."

"No. That's a lazy promise. You have to come up with the reward. It was your idea."

"OK." I grin, because I can think of a lot of very nice ways to reward her for this. "But… I don't know the limits."

"What do you mean?"

"Loverboy. Your man who gave you to the god. You're infatuated with him. Which is fine. I respect that. But how can I give you something really nice and satisfying if you're just gonna misinterpret it?"

"Did you just offer me sex in exchange for hot water?"

"See? I did not. But you *interpreted* it that way."

"You did so."

"Well, *do* you want sex in exchange for hot water? Because that's a done deal as far as I'm concerned."

"No."

"You're sure?"

"Yes."

"How about a foot massage?"

She hesitates. "Foot massage?"

"Yep." I can barely contain my snicker.

"I can't tell if this is sexual or not."

I pull the curtain aside and look out at her, grinning. "Do ya want it to be sexual?"

"No."

I shrug, withdrawing back into the shower. "OK. Then no. It's not."

"But is it normally?"

"Your man never gave you a foot massage?"

"No. We didn't spend time together like that."

"Like what?"

"Like… you know. We didn't linger with each other. We didn't share a space. Or a bed."

I pull the curtain aside again. "So this is a first for ya? Living with a man?"

She cocks a hip, folds her arms, and narrows her eyes at me. I withdraw back into the shower once again, grinning.

"Don't get excited, Tyse. I'm a grown-up. I can be in the same room with a man without sleeping with him. Trust me, I've gone on hundreds of dates with gentlemen while I was in service to the god. *Nothing* happened."

"Yeah, but… I'm not a gentleman." The water goes cold and I laugh. "Hey! Come back!"

She doesn't answer. She doesn't come back either, so I'm drenched in cold water. But it was worth it.

I like up-city Clara Birch. She's serious, and smart, and strong.

But tower-ruin Clara Birch is positively delightful. And that's who she is right now. A woman high on her own spark, and matching yellow décor, and a boutique bag filled with very sexy underwear that I'm a hundred-percent certain she bought by mistake.

I'm still grinning when I get out of the shower with a towel around my waist and take my dripping wet and nearly-naked self over to the chair, where I plop down.

She's still putting her clothes away and she does her best to ignore me, but I'm kinda hard to ignore. "Oh, my god. Why must you walk around wet?"

"I like to air-dry."

She wants to be mad, but she smiles despite herself.

Though she does turn her back to me a little, so I can't watch her too closely.

"Hey."

She doesn't look at me. "What?" She just continues to fold her clothes and put them neatly away in her new chest of drawers.

"It's nice to come home to you."

She stops what she's doing, going still for a moment. Then she looks over her shoulder at me. "Yeah. It's nice to be here when you get home."

"Your man—"

"Finn."

"Right. That guy. What's he look like?"

She snickers a little. "Picture the opposite of you. That's an easy enough way to describe him."

"Short, fat?"

"No." But she smiles. "You're a little bit taller, but not by that much. But you've got way more muscles. His hair is blond. Kinda shoulder length. And he's got blue eyes."

"We're nearly a perfect match."

"Yeah. But no. People in up-city don't get tattoos."

"So you're slummin' it with me?"

"No. I'm just saying. He's very up-city. He wears tailored clothes and his manners are impeccable. His father was the Extraction Master."

"Which is?"

"The person in charge of sending Maidens into the tower."

"Ah. A bloodline thing. Poor guy."

She stares at me for a moment. Then lets out a breath.

"Yeah. It actually is unfortunate. I can't imagine what he's feeling right now. I can't imagine what's going on back home, either. Chaos?" She shrugs. "Or... did they just forget about me, like they've forgotten about all the others? Did Gemna get called in? And if so, are they just relieved that all ten of us are gone and it's over now?" She shrugs again. "I just don't know."

Here's where things get interesting. She places the last of her clothes inside the drawer, closes it, then takes a seat on the bed, facing me. Like we're about to have a very serious talk.

But she must not know where to start, because she just looks down at her feet for a moment.

"You're allowed to be mad at him, ya know."

She looks up. "I know. Trust me, I was."

"You *were*. But you're not now. Because you're OK. Nothing bad has happened to ya. So you think... *I should be grateful. I should let it go. I should forgive.* Because that's the grown-up thing to do. That's the mature thing to do. But you know what, Clara?"

"What?" Her voice is very small all of a sudden.

"It's fine to forgive him. Because that's forward momentum on your part. But you don't ever want to forget that. *Ever.* Because when you get home—"

"How do you know I'll get home?"

I laugh. "Because... well, if I say I'll get ya home, then you're just going home. Somehow, some way, we'll get it done. And when you get there, and you see him, it's totally fine to love him again. But Clara, you can't ever *trust* him again. Not after what he did. He failed, mate. He *failed*. And he didn't do it honestly, ya know? Like ya said, he didn't hatch some harebrained scheme to save you that would never, ever work. He just... gave up."

Her eyes have been locked with mine this whole time and this is how they stay when she speaks. "You wouldn't give up, would you?"

"Well"—I smile here—"I've fucked up my life plenty, you saw it all on my discharge spectra. But I do my best, at least. I tried to save them. And when I couldn't, I did the right thing. Even if everyone else says it was wrong."

"Can I ask you questions about that?"

I blow out a breath. I really don't want to talk about that day. But if I don't, she'll just wonder about it. And this wondering will fester and turn into resentment, which will pop up at the most inopportune time. That's always how it happens. So I might as well just say yes.

I lean back into the chair cushions and shrug. "Sure. Ask away."

"What were they infected with?"

"Code."

"What's code?"

"It's like... a neurological virus made specifically for augments. It doesn't affect humans. If you were there, it couldn't get inside you because you're not wired like me."

"Even if your stuff doesn't work anymore, it can still infect you?"

"I don't know, actually. I had a whole team of cyberneurologists look at me afterward and half of them thought I wasn't affected because my augments had already failed."

"What did the other half think?"

I chuckle. "The other half thought I was a traitor. That I had found something there on the other side of the veil. Something that protected me, but that I was keeping secret. And that I set the whole thing up to kill my own people."

Her face goes very crooked as she thinks this through. "How in the world could they come to two completely different conclusions like that?"

"How? Well, that's just simple human nature right there, Clara Birch. The nature of the whole universe, I think. There always has to be an enemy. Ya can't ever have peace. It's one against the other."

"We had peace. I mean, in my Tau City, there were no conflicts."

"I doubt that. But maybe it's true. It's just far more likely that ya never saw the conflicts. Ya see, it's just the way of things. There's always two sides. And both sides lie. That's the whole problem with choosin', ya know? You're never on the right side because they're both nothing but a bunch of liars."

"So that enemy you were fighting when your team got infected?"

"What about it?"

"Who were they?"

"Who?" I think about this for a moment. "Well, they weren't exactly a 'who,' but more like a 'where.' Ya see, in the Omega Outlands the veil is thin, but also heavy. It can poke through."

She squints her eyes at me, trying to figure out what I mean. I let her, because she's smart, and I like watching her brain fit things together. "It's like the overlay here. My world and this world kinda… colliding."

"That's exactly what it is."

"But what are these places? The future, the past?"

"Maybe. No one is certain because while we can be pulled through, no one has ever come back."

"Then why do you think I can go back?"

"Because wherever you're from, Clara, it's *not* the Omega Outlands. Trust me. That place doesn't have people. There are no people there. Especially people like you."

"But—"

I put up a hand to stop her, because she really doesn't need to know any more about the Outlands. "Ya know, it's kind of a heavy topic. How about we just get back to talkin' about fun things like foot massages and smutty underwear?"

She smiles. Then laughs. Then agrees with me. Not directly. But she does turn and crawl up the bed, aiming for the open covers. "You better get dressed, because you're not coming to bed wet and naked."

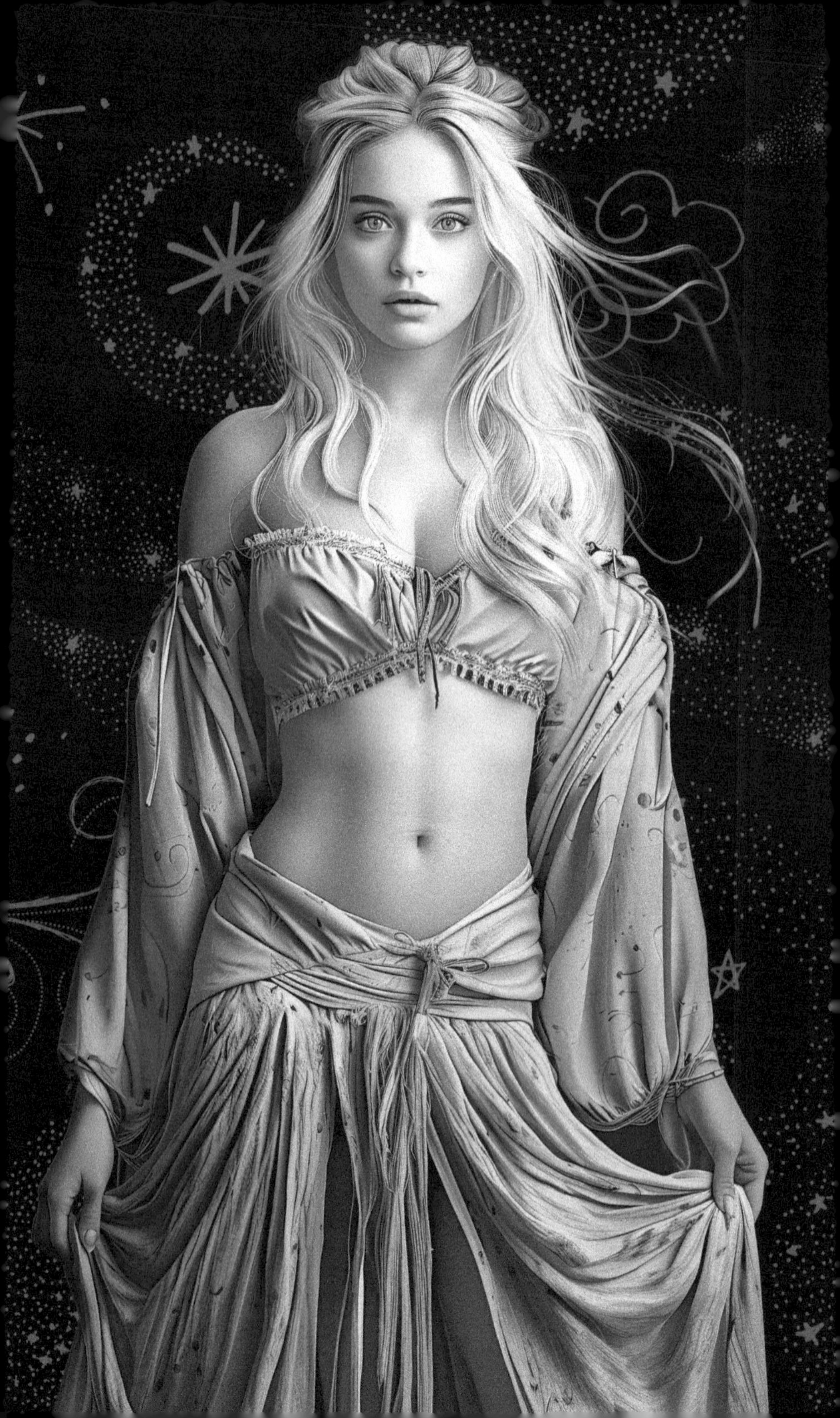

CLARA

CHAPTER THIRTY-SEVEN

Tyse gets up and goes back into the kitchen. He keeps his clothes in there on shelves next to his towels. I can't see that part of the kitchen from my position on the bed, he's just out of my line of sight.

So I spend the next minute running everything he just said through my head. Of course, this is not enough time to come to any kind of conclusion about any of it, but it does keep the ideas and words fresh so I can think about what it all means later.

He comes back shirtless and wearing a pair of loose pants. I get a good look at the tattoos when he climbs into bed. Some of them are words, but I don't have enough time to read them. I do have time to notice, however, that a lot of the tattoos are covering up scars.

He notices me noticing and points to the ceiling. "I've been shot with the fuckin' darts twice. The tattoos are just a way to pretty it all up."

I look up at the darts that are still lodged in the ceiling from when I tripped and shot his weapon. They are almost all inside the weird painting of the Sparktopia tower, making it look like a target. I imagine what it might be like to have them sticking out of my body. "Twice?" I look at him. "Why?"

"War. Anyway, we're back on foot massages. Turn and lie that way"—he points to the foot of the bed—"and put your feet in my lap."

When I hesitate—because I'm suddenly trying to come up with reasons why this foot massage doesn't need to happen—he takes my pillow and throws it down at the foot of the bed. "Come on. Do it. I promise, you'll be thanking me later."

I don't see a good way out of this without coming off as childish, so I change position, my head on the pillow at the foot of the bed, and put my feet in his lap. "This is crazy."

"It's not crazy. This is spa treatment, tower-ruin Clara Birch."

I smile, despite how uncomfortable I feel.

But then he takes my foot into his hand and I nearly jump out of my skin, the sensation is so unexpected.

"You're ticklish?"

"I don't know." I'm suddenly out of breath. "I never thought I was."

"Ya learn somethin' new every day. Now keep still. You'll get over it. I'm not trying to tickle ya."

I close my eyes, wincing when he presses his fingers into the fleshy arch of my foot, doing my best not to squeal. It does feel good, but it's almost too good. Like I want to scream and laugh at the same time.

"Holy shit."

"What?"

"Open your eyes, Clara."

I do, and then sit up, gasping as I look down at myself. My whole body is glowing cyan-blue. And not only that, all the designs are there too. The swirls and symbols. Hundreds of different designs cover every inch of my skin. I look like… well. I look like there's a story written on me. Except it's written in a language I don't read.

"Can I ask you questions now?"

I prop myself up on my elbows and look at Tyse. He's still pressing on my foot, but he's staring right back at me. Intently. Just watching me. "Sure."

"What does it say?"

I shake my head. "I don't know."

"Really? You have no idea?"

"None."

"No one from your city ever tried to read it?"

"No. Why would they?"

"Because it's clearly saying something. Don't you think it's odd that no one was curious enough to decipher it?"

"Well…" I sigh. "I guess I never thought about it before."

"Did all the Spark Maidens have symbols written on them like this?"

I squint my eyes and press my lips together, trying to think back. "I'm not sure. I don't recall. But they weren't always there. You have to develop your spark. And when I first started, I could draw things in the air and that was pretty much it. The spark was in my fingertips. But over the course of my Choosing, it grew. This is normal. And that's when the symbols came out."

"And no one thought it was weird?"

"Well, I see what you're saying. But in our defense, spark

presents in many different ways. Hundreds, probably thousands of ways. And all of it was just considered… normal."

"What do you think it says?"

I look down at myself again. This is when I realize Tyse can see my whole body underneath my nightgown because of the blue light. When I look up at him again, he's watching me very carefully. So I decide to watch him just as carefully back. "I don't think I need to go home."

He grins. "That's what you think it says?"

He's joking. I know this. But he's also serious. I nod, so he knows I'm joking but also serious as well. "Yeah. That's what I think it says."

Then I pull my foot from his hands, grab my pillow, and return to the normal sleeping position, but with my back to him.

He reaches over and flicks the light off, then settles down under the covers.

But a moment later, and without a word, or even asking, his arms wrap around me and he tugs me up close to him.

That's it.

That's all that happens.

And I fall asleep calling him a liar in my head.

Because he actually *is* a gentleman.

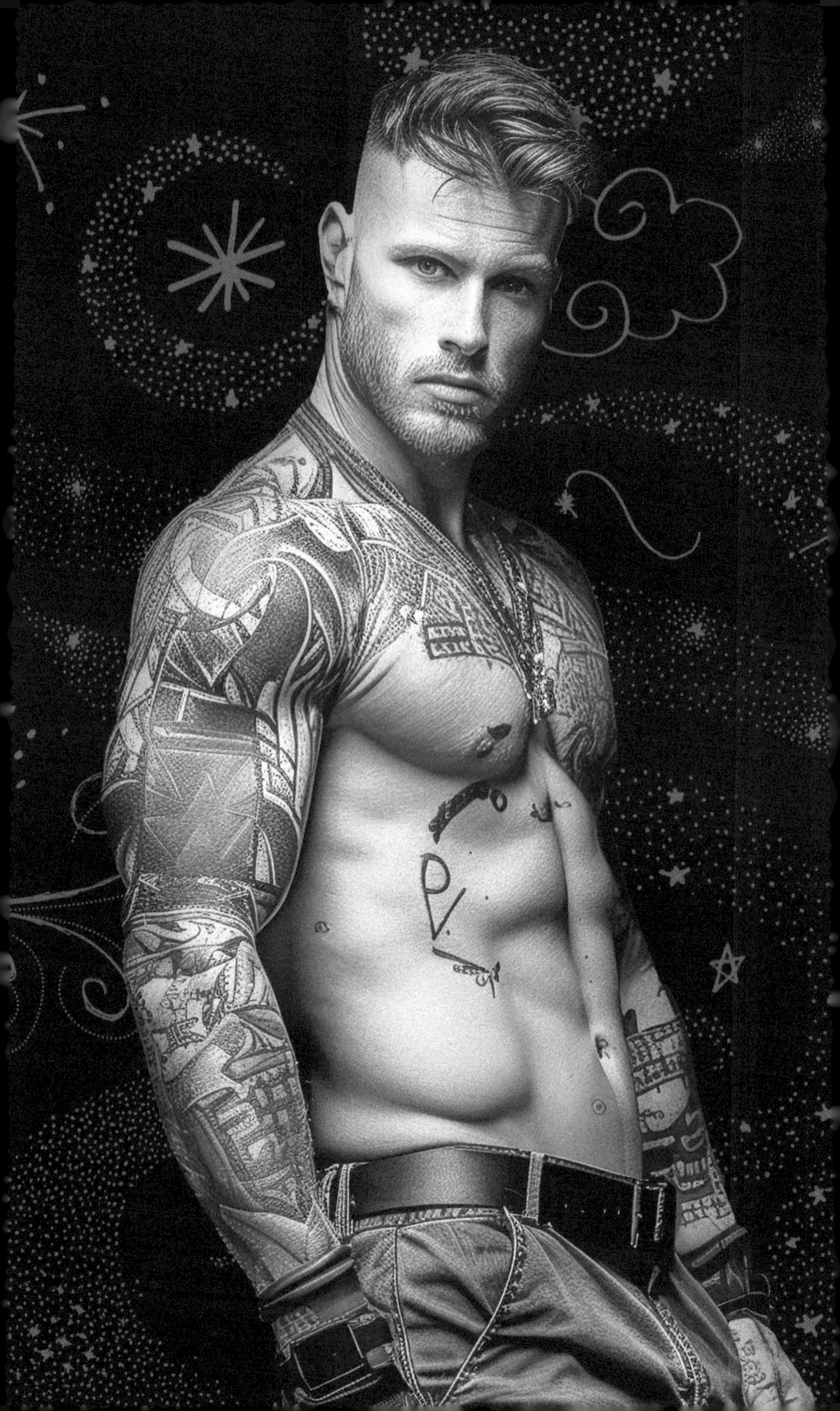

TYSE

CHAPTER THIRTY-EIGHT

The out-city politician Stayn asked me to follow leaves just after lunch, so I get off early. I'm just about to shove my city-issued patrol phone through the little gap under the glass in logistics when a text buzzes in. I hold up a finger for the clerk. "One sec." Then I take the phone back and check the message.

It's from Stayn. *See you tonight.*

Tonight?

I shove the phone back through check-in, sign my name, and then go find Stayn to see what the hell he's talking about.

Logistics is in the basement because of security, and Stayn is a top-floor kind of guy these days, so I have to ride the elevator all the way up to the seventy-fourth floor of the skyscraper to see him. But I haven't ever been to his office, so stepping out facing those western floor-to-ceiling windows is kinda worth the trouble.

Fucking hell. So this is why guys do it. The view.

I turn away, make my way to reception, then wait as I'm announced, then directed through a buzzing door and told to turn left.

I find Stayn behind not one, but two sets of double doors, at the end of the hall. His office is... well, let's just say my room could fit in here ten times, easily.

Stayn gets up from his desk when I'm let in. "Well. I wasn't expecting to see you up here. Ever."

I grin, get a little lost in his eastern view on the opposite side of the office, then turn back to him, my gawking under control. "I got your message as I was turning in my phone. I thought the job was done."

"It is."

"So... why are you expecting to see me tonight?"

He laughs, claps me on the back, and points to his bar. "Do you want a drink?"

"No. Just an explanation."

"You got big plans tonight, or what? Because you said raincheck on dinner last week, remember?"

"Oh, shit. I forgot. Did we say that was tonight?"

"We didn't. But you're already in town. And now that you're here, you might as well come home with me. I'll leave early. We can go now. Janice and the girls are dying to see you again. It's been months since you've come by."

"Ah, I can't, Stayn."

His face furrows up into confusion, but then he turns to make me a drink I don't want. "Why the hell not?"

"I've got... well, I got a girl. Waitin' at home."

"What?" He actually spills some of the drink when he turns around to face me again. "You... you're... in some kind of... relationship?"

"Are you surprised?"

He bursts out laughing. "Oh, my god. You're in a

relationship. When did this happen? Who is this woman? Better question"—he points at me with the drink—"why is she dating you?"

I don't have a backstory prepared for Clara, so I have to make up something general on the spot. "She's one of those vagabond girls. A traveler. Just came in from..." I falter here. "I don't know. One of the median cities."

"And you found her... how?" He's not suspicious. It's genuine curiosity. Because he's never seen me with a woman. Well, not one I'd take home.

"We bumped into each other last weekend."

"Last weekend? Things are moving fast if she's living at your place."

"It's a temporary thing. She's outta here in a couple days. That's why I can't come tonight. Maybe next week, when she's gone."

Stayn claps me on the back again. And he might be wearing the widest smile I've ever seen. "Well, you just bring her along."

"Oh—"

"No." He shakes his head. "No. Janice will not forgive me if I don't make you come. You're coming. Seven. You've got plenty of time, so... don't forget to take a shower. And here. Your drink."

I want to protest, but... it might be fun to take Clara over there. Stayn, regardless of his sell-out political job, is a friend. And his family is big, and good, and his home is one of the few places where I feel comfortable outside the tower. So I give in, take the drink, down it, and leave.

All the way down to the ground floor I picture this

night. Clara and me sitting in Stayn's dining room. The walk there, the walk home. The sudden realization that this is a date. And not only that, it's a good date. A good second introduction for us. One that paints me in a slightly better picture, if only because of the company I keep.

BY THE TIME I get up all the steps and I'm pulling my door open, it's nearly four. But I'm still a couple hours early, so I walk in on a party.

A tea party, to be exact.

Clara, who is sitting on a velvet cushion that was not here this morning, jumps up from the little coffee table, turning to me with a smile. "You're home! We weren't expecting you."

This is when I notice that Anneeta is also sitting on a velvet cushion at the little coffee table. "What is going on here?"

Clara points to the table. "This, my good sir, is a proper tea party. You see, I"—she places a hand across her chest—"have hosted at least a hundred of these fuckers over the last decade. And I wanted to make sure that our little friend here has a better perspective of what an actual tea party looks like."

"We got finger sandwiches, Tyse! Do you want one?"

The whole table is set for high tea. Like… I actually feel like I'm back in the Delta god's tower, being served tea as I wait for punishment because that's the kind of asshole god he was. He'd soften ya all up with cucumber sandwiches and get ya all loose with hot tea as the scent of lavender lingers from the fresh flower arrangements. So then, when he appeared for your little 'talk,' you think he's a good guy. But he's not. He's always been an asshole. And you only make this mistake once. The next time you're there, you don't even look at the tea.

But this Clara's tea party and it's… delightful. Just like her.

Nothing in the tea set matches. Not the plates, not the pot, not the cups. All the little spoons are every different kind of metal and almost everything is chipped. But the table is dressed up with a yellow cloth that matches the rug, which matches the curtains, which matches the throw pillows.

And she's wearing… "Oh, my god, what are you wearing?"

"Do you like it?" She spins for me. "This is the dress Rodge gave me." She pauses to think here. "Or maybe it was Prisha? I'm not sure, but I love it. And it's perfect for tea. Don't you think it's perfect?"

Not only is it perfect for tea, it's perfect for dinner. I was a little worried about Clara showing up in jeans and boots. But this dress works. It's a light green color and… well… not slutty. "It's perfect. In many ways. Because I've got us a dinner invitation tonight."

I'm expecting her to balk at this dinner. Most girls I've

dated in the past—if you could call it dating—would not be the least bit interested in having dinner with the patrol chief of Tau City.

But up-city Clara Birch was made for dinner parties. And she's all smiles when this invitation comes out. "Really!" She presses her hands together and sighs. "Oh, I can't wait. I was starting to feel a little—" But she stops mid-sentence and suddenly remembers we're not the only ones in the room. She looks over her shoulder at Anneeta.

Anneeta looks *crushed*. Even I can see this and I'm no expert interpreting the moods of little girls.

Clara steps in to mitigate. "It is OK with you, Anneeta? If we go to dinner in the city tonight? I'll bring you something back. Something very sweet or something very pretty. Your choice."

Anneeta goes into a full-on pout mode now, crossing her arms and everything. "What about these sweets?" She points to the little cookies stacked perfectly on a tarnished three-tiered silver tray. "And the sandwiches."

"We can have another party tomorrow," I say. "We'll have it out on the ruin steps and everything."

Anneeta makes a face at me. "They'll be soggy by tomorrow, Tyse."

Clara intervenes. "We'll get new sandwiches and sweets, of course. And I'll pack these up so you can take them with you and they won't go to waste."

"How's that sound?" I ask. "Fair trade?"

Anneeta huffs. "I *guess*." But she is not happy about it.

Clara takes over, packing up the food and putting it back into a very fancy box that came from the city via runner, while Anneeta starts dumping tea out into the sink. It's real tea, too. I can smell it. I bet Clara got it hot with her spark. And I kinda wish I was here to see that.

Finally, after several minutes of bustling about, everything is packed up and Anneeta is sent on her way with promises of tomorrow.

Clara shuts the door, then turns to face me as she presses her back against it. "Hi."

"Hi, yourself."

"Did you have a good day at work?"

I shrug. "It was… whatever. Good news, though. The job is over. So I won't be gettin' up early to go into the city tomorrow."

"You can sleep in then?" She walks over to me, then takes a seat on the bed.

"Sleep? Sure." I smile at her.

She points at me. "I missed you today."

My eyebrows shoot up. "You did?"

"I did. I feel like you're a tea-party kind of man."

I just laugh. Then I get up and start taking off my battle belt. "I'm gonna jump in the shower. Could you…"

"Stand nearby and heat the water for you?" She's got a wild grin on her face. "And if we had gotten past this preliminary point already, I'd just attack her right now. Throw her down on that bed and make her squeal.

But… we're not there yet. So I just shrug. "If you don't mind."

She gets up, walks over to the shower, turns the water on, and then turns her back to me. "Hurry up then, get in."

I strip and do as I'm told. But the whole time I'm

washing up, I'm staring at her cyan-blue hand, a little bit mesmerized by the swirls of patterns on her skin. They're pulsating tonight. Like they've got energy to burn.

"So tell me about these people we're having dinner with?"

"Stayn is a friend."

"This is the one who sent you to find me down in the lower levels?"

"Yes. He's the patrol chief. He's got a nice family, though. A wife and three daughters."

"You know them well?"

"Yes. I've spent the holidays with them every year since I arrived in Tau City. And odd dinners in between. Like this one. This is actually my payment for going to find you. He promised me a dinner."

"And that's the one you forgot about because I was in the health center?"

"Yes." I'm done now, so I turn the water off. By the time I open the curtain and pull a towel off the shelf, she's already walking away.

I don't go out wet. Instead, I dress. I don't wear fancy clothes. I don't even own fancy clothes. But I've a lot to choose from because apparently someone did laundry while I was at work. I already know that Rodge is billing me for all these expenses, but I ask anyway. Just to see if she's figured it out. "You did laundry?"

"Oh, yeah. You don't mind, right? Prisha came down and asked for it. She said she was gonna put it in with another load."

I'm not sure what to make of this answer. So I pull a

shirt on and go back out to the main room. "How are we paying for it?"

"Oh, she said it was a gift from Rodge."

I grab my boots and sit down on the chair. "Why the hell is he giving us free laundry services?"

Clara doesn't seem to understand how dear this service is. Because she just shrugs and changes the subject. "Should I change? Or is this dress good?"

"It's good." I smile at her. "But I told him you're a vagabond girl. So maybe add some layers. Like Anneeta dresses. To make it all eccentric and shit."

"A vagabond girl?" She tilts her head at me.

"Yeah." But this one word comes out with a really big, stupid grin. Because she's so damn delightful. "It's a term we use to describe… free-spirts of the female persuasion. Girls who like to travel and have experiences instead of settling down with a man."

Clara turns to her little chest of drawers and takes out some very long, beige-colored socks. She sits on the bed and starts rolling them up her legs, all the way over her knees. "Hmm. Travel wasn't a thing where I come from. How will I make conversation? What should I talk about?"

"Just make it up."

"But how? I haven't been anywhere."

"Neither have they. They're all born in Tau City. Tau City is a place you go, it's not a place you leave. Everyone wants to live here. They don't travel much. But if you're worried about it, talk about the traditional cities. The closed ones with strict gods. Like Zeta and Rho. When we get into the Canal District, I'll get a phone and you can look at some pics to get an idea. Just... whatever you do, do *not* light up with spark."

"They've never been to those cities?"

"No. You need permits."

"So how the hell did I get there?"

"You were born there, of course."

"OK." She shrugs and reaches for her boots. "All right. If you're not worried about it, I'm not worried about it."

Right on the edge of the Ruin District is a whole slew of shops that cater to the tower people. There are lots of quick food places, coffeeshops, and laundromats—that run off real power, not spark, so they are super cheap. And every single one of these places sells phones.

So as soon as we leave the Ruin District, I stop at the first shop and get one for each of us. Then I program our numbers, call her phone, and give my number a name.

"Look." I hold Clara's phone out to her. "This is the keypad, this is the menu, and this is where you can search for things." I do a search for traditional god cities and pull up some images. Then hand her the phone. "There. Now you can get an idea of what they look like."

Clara blinks at me, stunned. "You can ask it anything? Anything at all? And it will just give you answers?"

"Yes. Pretty much, anyway. You always need to take into consideration that each city has its own info rules."

"What does that mean?"

"They scrub the databases of things they don't want you to know. But I don't think the traditional cities will be a problem."

"OK." She nods her head with resolve. "I will study as we walk so I can be the perfect dinner date." Then she hooks her hand into my elbow—an old-fashioned gesture that actually lends credence to the idea that she's from a traditional god city—and looks intently at the phone as we walk.

She reminds me so much of Anneeta tonight, it's crazy. Because after only two days of hanging out together, Clara has adopted Anneeta's eccentric style. She's wearing her new green dress from Rodge, but she's layered it with a long-sleeve brown Henley that kinda matches her thigh-high brown socks. Not stockings, *socks*. Made of cotton and ribbed. And she's not wearing sexy high-heeled boots like the city girls, but the combat ones I got her when she was at the health center. Her jacket is something from the lost and found and resembles mine, but olive green instead of black. It's cropped at the waist and covered in flower patches instead of deployment badges. She's even got her hair piled up into something that falls between a plait and a bun. It's very messy, but in all the right ways.

She is a textbook description of a vagabond girl and the whole fuckin' look is sexy.

Maybe too sexy? Is it too sexy? This is when I notice that everyone we pass on the sidewalk is looking at her. Not casually, either. I feel like the women are memorizing her style so they can copy it tomorrow, but the men will definitely be undressing her in their minds tonight.

Stayn's girls are gonna love her.

"OK." Clara looks up at me. "There are two cities to choose from. Zeta and Rho. Which one am I from?"

"I'd go with Zeta. No news gets out of that place. It's zipped up tight."

"Well, how did I get out?"

"It's not a prison. You just left."

"Do many people do that?"

"No. But vagabond girls come from all over. So you got on a train for an adventure. You'll go back one day. Probably. But you're young and enjoying your youth."

"So why did I stop here?"

"You ran out of money and you're using me for my pension."

She laughs, leaning into me a little. "Tyse Saarinen, you make me happy."

For some stupid reason, and even though the night is very cold, a warm feeling floods my body. I smile, looking down at her. "Well, I would like to go on record that you, up-city Clara Birch, are a complete delight."

She leans into me again, hugging my arm a little. But she doesn't say anything else. And though the rest of the walk over to Stayn's house on the banks of the main canal is silent, it's the perfect kind of silence. Filled with moments that are neither too empty nor too full.

"*Wow.*" Clara is looking up at Stayn's canal-front house in complete awe. "I've never seen such a building in my life. This is a house, you say?"

"Yes."

"One family lives here?"

"Yep. And it is over the top, but in Stayn's defense, he is the chief of patrol. It's a very big deal. There are literally fifty thousand men under him. He's like the general of his own private army."

"He's in charge of the Canal District?"

"No, the whole city."

"Hmm. It sounds dangerous to give someone so much power. In my city there was a head of each district and they were like… you know, powerful, and rich, and stuff. Like Finn—he could command a lot of people, but not the heads of other districts. And he had no say whatsoever in the Maiden District."

"Well. Power, when not checked on a regular basis, flows up. Not down."

"I'm not sure I know what that means."

"It means… it consolidates, ya know? Away from the people in general and towards heads of departments, like Stayn."

"Is he a good guy? Or a bad guy?"

I'm slightly ashamed to admit that I have to think about this for a moment. "Well, he's my friend, so I like him. But if he wasn't, and all I saw was the power play and the politics, I would definitely consider him a bad guy."

"That's a good note. I will keep it in mind when I mingle."

"I get the feeling dinner parties are second nature to you."

"Oh, Tyse. I'm in my element here. I am so ready to go in there and compliment strangers while eating canapés, drinking champagne, and enjoying this evening to the fullest." She pauses and looks up at me. "You do have canapés here, right?"

"If you mean gross-looking finger foods made of crackers, paste, and cheese on silver plates, then yes."

She nods and lets out a breath. "I'm going to eat one of everything."

We go to the door and ring the bell. It opens almost immediately, and then Janice, Stayn's wife, is there in her fancy dress, and her perfect hair and makeup, and her lipsticked mouth moving a mile a minute as she greets us warmly and ushers us inside.

There is a whirlwind here filled with teenage girls in frilly dresses, and politicians with their arm-candy wives, and even a couple of dogs that are way too big to be house pets, but since when did rules ever stop rich people from doing impractical things?

Coats are taken, I feel very underdressed next to the power players in coats and ties, and Clara morphs into a Spark Maiden—minus the spark—right before my very eyes. Her smile is big, her voice is soothing, her eyes are bright, and she even leans in and lightly touches people on the arm when she speaks to them. Like everyone in this room is an old friend.

She is at home, to say the least. Like she has attended thousands of dinner parties in alternate dimensions and this one, at the Tau City patrol chief's home, is no particular big deal.

We are separated, as is the way of things. It's just… I've never come to dinner here with a date before, so I never noticed how weird it is that men are ushered into Stayn's office, while the women gather in the living room.

Cigars are passed out. I sit on a tufted leather couch and then exhale smoke as I accept a glass of brandy on the rocks from Stayn. He takes the chair to my right and immediately, the conversation turns to Clara.

"So. Where the hell did you kidnap this one from?"

"Is that an insult? Are you insinuating that she is too good for me?"

Stayn laughs. "Brother, she is…" He decides to stop here so he can choose his words carefully. *"Delightful."*

I raise my glass in his direction and we do a mock 'cheers.' "She is, isn't she."

"Keep this one. You're gonna keep her, right?"

I just smile over my glass as I take a drink.

"OK, OK," a rotund, older man says as he approaches us. "Enough about your man's woman, Stayn. I only came to one of your stuffy parties to discuss the Looking Glass. What news, friend?"

"What's that?" I ask Stayn.

Stayn ignores me. "Not tonight, Richard. This is not a

business meeting. I told you that. It's a dinner party. Janice will kill me if we start talking about work at the table."

"All the better to do it now," the portly man says.

"What's a Looking Glass?" I ask again.

For a moment I'm sure that Stayn is gonna blow me off. But he gives me a side-eye instead. Like he's reconsidering. "Well, if I tell you, you have to keep it secret."

The big guy takes a chair to Stayn's right and sits. "I thought you said the man was an augment?"

I shrug. "I am. But I have no idea what we're talking about."

"As an augment, you've seen this stuff. Hasn't he, Stayn? He's the reason I'm here. You told me he has information about this kind of thing."

I look at Stayn again, this time with suspicion. "What the hell is all this about? You invited me under false pretenses?"

"No. Well..." Stayn smiles. "Not originally. It was payment, remember? For the disturbance in the tower."

"Right. And now it's what?" I'm getting a really bad feeling about this. Because while I do not know what a Looking Glass is, after what happened with Clara, I can take a good guess.

"Yes, let's talk about that disturbance, young man."

I direct my gaze to the older guy, then look around and realize every man in this room is watching us. Waiting for whatever comes next. Like I've got answers and they're gonna get them out of me. I look back at Stayn. "What's going on?"

"That disturbance," Stayn says. "It was..."

"A vagrant. I told you that. There was a party down there and someone got left behind."

"Right. Well, here's the thing, Tyse." Stayn actually sits on the edge of his seat, leaning towards me, like this is some kind of secret, when obviously it's not. "After analyzing the vibrational fingerprint of said disturbance—"

"Just spit it out, Chief!" the old man interrupts. "It matched the signature of a Spark Maiden from Dimension 702. And we weren't expecting another delivery for three more months. So we need you to be real specific about what you found down there in the tower, son."

I can't even speak. I can't even come to terms with the fact that this fucker just used the words 'Spark Maiden,' let alone the fact that they have… ordered one? In the past? And have one… what? On hold? For the future?

Also, in the back of my mind, I'm processing the reality that I just brought said Spark Maiden to *dinner* with them.

And this is when it occurs to me that we might not actually make it out of here.

One thing. One slip-up. One little spark.

That's all it takes.

And it's over.

Me and Clara. The overlay, my augments, and Anneeta.

It's all over.

A HUMAN MAN **would panic here.** Unless he was highly trained in stress warfare, he would not be able to react appropriately.

But I'm not really human. And the moment the panic begins, it also ends. Because my augments kick in. Stayn sees it. Hell, everyone sees it. Because, of course, there's a blue light in my eyes to indicate that I've been turned *on*.

All of them gasp, even Stayn. And then the three of us who were sitting are now standing.

"Are... you OK, Tyse?" There's not just suspicion in Stayn's voice now, there's a hint of alarm.

"I thought you said he was decommissioned? What the hell is going on here?" The old man is about to overreact.

So I play it all down with a smile. "That's a good question." But then I look straight at Stayn. "What *is* going on here?"

He repeats the old man's concern. "You... *were* decommissioned, right? I mean, that's why they discharged you, right?"

"Of course."

"Then what is happening inside that head of yours, Tyse? Because from this side of things, you look very much like an operating augment. And you know as well as I do that all operating augments have to be registered as non-human active warfare weapons."

I sigh, then set my drink down on a side table. I can feel the augments dial back, but they don't completely turn off. There's an internal overlay now with a few stats, but nothing else. I look at Stayn, then all of the men in the room. They don't look frightened anymore, they just look like they want to lock me up somewhere in a lab and never let me see the light of day again.

The smile is fake, but warm. "Well, I see that a lesson in augmentation is in order here. As you know, we are chosen as kids and the process starts when we're about fourteen. My brain isn't entirely human anymore. The augments can never be removed, as I'm sure you've heard. Nor can they actually be turned off."

The room is suddenly filled with murmuring.

"That's not what your discharge spectra said."

I meet Stayn's gaze. "It was part of my deal. New name, pension, and official 'off' status. But before you guys all overreact, they don't work. They haven't really worked since I was like nineteen. It took a few years for it to really show, but they don't work, Stayn. They're there, and sometimes they flash a little blue light, but there's nothing happening inside my brain as far as the augments go."

"Why should we trust you?" This comes from some guy I was introduced to, but can't recall his name. "You could just be lying."

"I could. But do you really think Sweep would let me out if I still *worked*?"

There's mumbling now. But they can't deny this. There is no way in hell Sweep would discharge me if my augments were functioning.

"You have something on them," Stayn says. "What is it?"

"What makes you think that?"

"Come on, Tyse. Don't bullshit me. A new name, a pension, and official 'off' status? It's the definition of a fresh start. You know something. Something they want you to keep quiet. But more than that, you know something so big, they can't just kill you to keep it secret. There's some... dead-man's switch, or something. And ya know, what? Good for you. If you found a way to use this information to keep yourself alive, total respect for that. I don't care. But I want to know what you know. What is it?"

They're looking for something. Something I don't have any actual knowledge of. Stayn is right—I did bribe my way back into civilian life—but he's fuckin' batshit crazy if he thinks I'd spill this secret to *him*. The Sweep would pick me up so fast, my head would spin. And I'd be dead within a day. Probably less.

No one, outside of a god, maybe, will ever get that secret from me.

Still, I gotta say something or Clara and I aren't going home tonight. So I look at the old man now. Because this is the only way the lie works. "I know about the Looking Glass. I know what it is."

The room erupts in excitement.

But I put up a hand to hush them. "I saw it. I saw lots of things in the Outlands. I know where it is."

"Where?" The old man's hands are in the air, like he's about to throttle the answer out of me. But I shoot him a cautionary look that comes with a flash of blue light, and he pulls them back.

"It's in the Omega Outlands, of course. You don't really think they'd let that thing inside some city, do you?"

"That's not what we heard." This comes from another man whose name I don't recall. "We heard that every tower has one. And that the new god needs—"

"That's *enough*, Edward!" Stayn's roar echoes up into the high, coffered ceilings of his office, making everyone shut up at once. He stares hard at Edward, then straightens his tie and looks at me, smiling. "OK. Well, this is not proper dinner conversation. Let's pick it up on Monday. How about nine AM?" Stayn looks around the room as they all agree. Finally, his gaze lands on me. "You good with nine AM, Tyse?"

I shrug. "I'll be there."

It's the best possible ending, in my opinion. Because they have forgotten all about the Spark Maiden vibrational signature from Dimension 702, or whatever, and have refocused their attention on some Looking Glass thing I've never even heard of.

EVERYTHING THAT HAPPENS NEXT IS *fake*.

We smile, we clap each other on the shoulder, we joke, we dine, we drink, we make polite conversation. Clara is a perfect dinner party guest. She listens attentively, she smiles politely, and she uses all the right forks at all the right times.

But I am counting the seconds until it's eleven-thirty because this is the earliest I figure we can escape without looking suspicious.

Janice and Stayn walk us to the door. We're not the first

to leave, so our jackets are ready, held out by the butler and a maid so we can slip our arms into them.

Janice and Clara say their goodbyes. There's air kissing going on and lots of smiling.

Stayn leans in to me. "Monday, right? Nine AM in my office? Oh, and your woman is a keeper. You'll bring her back, right? Janice loves her."

"Yes, I'll be there Monday. And of course we'll be back. Can't wait."

We shake hands and then Clara and I escape into the night.

But even though we're out, we're far from safe. There is no way they're not watching us. Even if they've forgotten about the Spark Maiden, I have some kind of critical information they need.

So I play it cool on the way home. "Wanna get some coffee?"

Clara thinks about this, but declines. "Nah. It was such a nice evening. I'm already wound up enough. I just want to go to bed." She looks up at me, smiling. She's got her hand around my arm again, like she's never walked a city in her life without an escort. And hell, maybe she hasn't. Because clearly, she is a dinner-party kind of woman. She's been talking about her night since we left. She loves the girls and if we were gonna be in this city on Monday, I guarantee Janice would be her new best friend.

But we will not be in Tau City on Monday.

We're getting the fuck out of here tomorrow.

I just can't tip off Clara—not until we're inside the tower, at least. Because everyone outside the ruin is tracked and monitored. Especially through the phones in our pockets.

I can't throw them away, not yet. Not until we're in the tower, because the cameras are watching and I'd bet my life that Stayn is up, right now, in some secret room in his massive house, watching us walk home. Looking for any sign that I might run.

"You didn't have a good time?"

I look down at Clara. "What? Sure I did."

"Well, you're super distracted. What did you talk about with the men while I was chatting up the women?"

"Oh…" I blow out a breath. "Nothing much. Boring work. But not my work, so really boring work."

"You have a meeting on Monday, though?"

I want to end this conversation and I'm trying to think up some kind of plausible way that won't arouse suspicion when Clara suddenly stops and gasps out loud.

"What? What's wrong?"

She lets out a breath, then looks around. "We just came back inside."

That's when I realize she's right. We just entered the Ruin District. In other words, we just entered the spark. "Clara? Look at me."

She tilts her head up, but I can see the panic in her eyes. I can almost see the blue, as well. Maybe I'm just imagining it, because I know that she wasn't ready for the extra spark and now she's feeling a little bit full.

It used to affect me that way too, though I never lit up blue from it.

And that's exactly what she's about to do.

Stayn—or someone, at least—is still watching. Probably leaning into the screen to get a better look at what's going on right now. And if I don't do something fast, they're about to get an eyeful.

Clara is panicking. She knows this is bad. There are hundreds of people out here around the tower and if she explodes with light, everything changes.

And not in a good way.

I grab her and then I kiss her. And when my mouth touches her, all her extra blue spark starts spilling into me. It's cold at first. Ice cold. But then, as the kiss continues and she relaxes with the realization that it's going to be OK, it turns warm.

And then it's pouring into me faster, and faster, and faster until I explode…

Except I don't explode.

I float up, and up, and up. And it's not me doing all this floating, but the augments inside me. Because when I look down, there I am. Standing just inside the Ruin District kissing up-city Clara Birch in front of the whole city.

But… it's not *my* city.

It's *hers*.

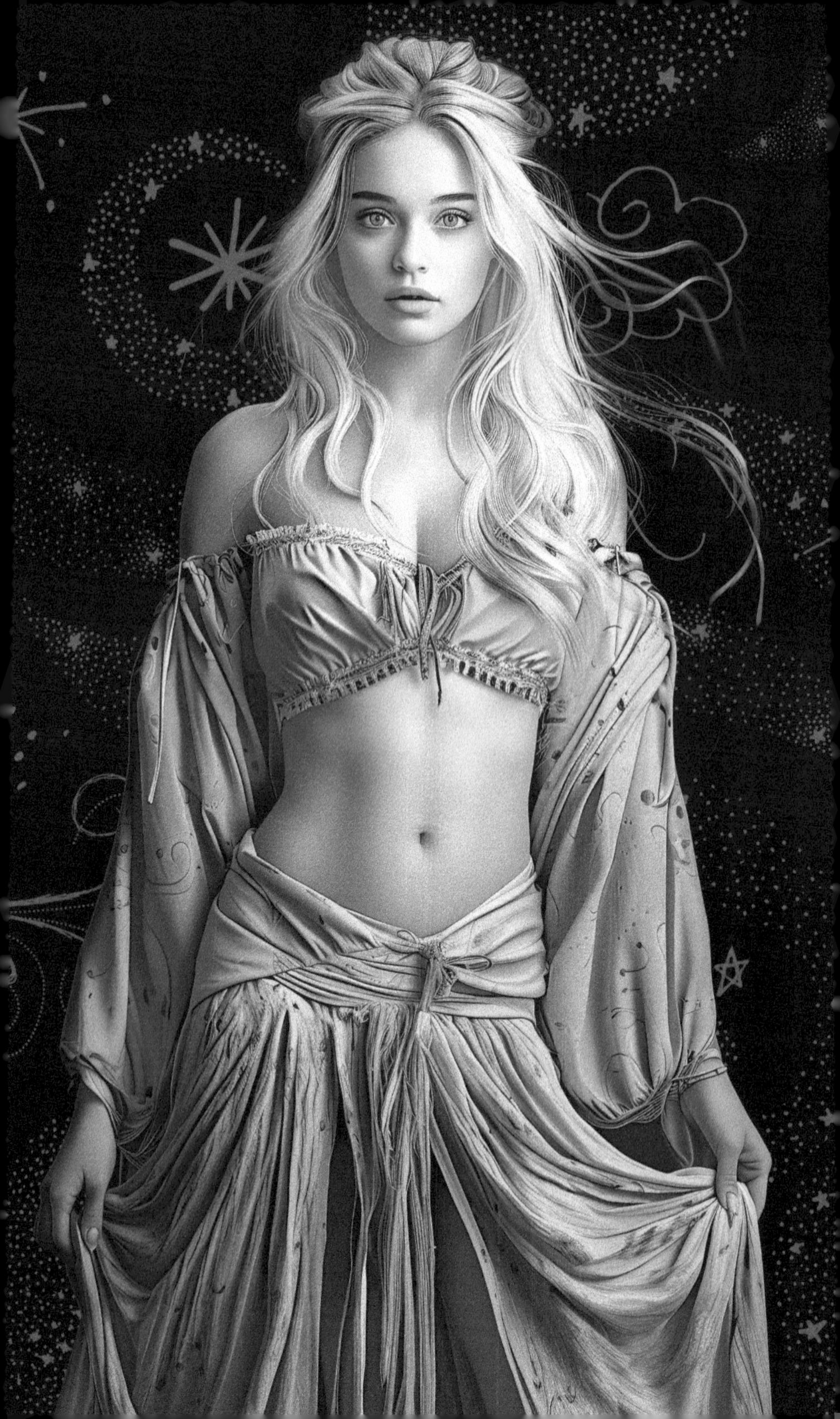

CLARA

CHAPTER THIRTY-TWO

*I*t's *my first kiss*—not ever, of course, but my very first kiss that is not Finn. And it does not disappoint. I realize that he only did it to ease the build-up of spark inside me so I didn't literally explode with it in front of the whole city.

But it feels way too good to care why he did it.

It's everything I never knew I wanted. When I walked across that imaginary line between the Canal District and the Ruin District there was an immediate expansion of spark inside me. Even when I was a Little Sister and I was practicing my spark display several times a day, it never filled me up this way. And being here, in this Tau City where spark isn't everywhere, all at once, but contained within a very specific and defined area, it feels very all or nothing.

I didn't notice much difference when I left earlier in the evening. But as the hours passed inside the patrol chief's house, I could feel... an emptying. A space inside me.

A space that was flooded with spark once I came into the ruin.

Also a new feeling.

Overwhelming, actually.

And it was complete genius on Tyse's part to dissipate the building spark by taking some of it from me through a kiss. It would've never occurred to me that I could *share* it.

When we pull back and I look up into Tyse's lit-up blue eyes, they look vacant for a moment. And there's a small panic inside my chest that I might've hurt him in some way.

But then he blinks, looks up at the sky for just a quick second, then down at me.

I am flooded again, but not with spark this time. It's just... I don't know. I don't think I've ever felt this way before. It's warmth, and it's a sense of safety, but also it's just this overwhelming feeling that I would do anything for him.

Anything.

His hands are still on my shoulders and he gives them a squeeze. "Are you OK now, Clara?"

I nod. "Yeah. Yep. I'm fine. That was..."

"Weird?"

"Um. Noooo. It was..." I smile at Tyse and do a stupid flirty thing with my head here that I didn't plan. "It was... my first kiss. Well, you know. That wasn't Finn." His eyes dart up to the sky for a moment, like he's thinking about something, and I immediately regret what I just said. "Sorry. I should just shut up about him now."

He lets out a small laugh. Then looks back down at me. "Come on. Let's go home."

And then he takes my hand and leads me into the tower. Home.

I think about that word as we climb the steps in silence. Well, the tower isn't silent. There are hundreds and hundreds of people all around us. But we are. And I'm glad. Because... *home*.

His room does feel like home.

He feels like home.

The climb goes fast, like it always did back in the Maiden Tower when I was climbing with Gemna and Haryet. And as we come up to the tenth floor and walk over to his door, I suddenly have something to say.

We go inside and he closes the door behind us, and then he turns to me, and I decide it's now or... no. It's just now. I need to say this now. "Tyse, I don't want to go home. This place is strange, and big, and loud, and a little bit scary, and I know I did *think* I loved Finn, but I'm just not sure—"

Suddenly the space between us, and he's holding my face in his hands, and looking me in the eyes when he says it. "Fuck. Finn."

That's what he says. That's all he says.

And then he's kissing me again. Only this time, it's much different. Better, if that's possible. Because he's determined, and a little bit forceful, and he's sliding my jacket down my arms, and pulling my dress up over my head, and then I'm standing in front of him in my Cheeky Goddess underwear, and my socks, and my boots, and the smile on this man's face as he looks at me is nothing short of hunger, with a tinge of amusement.

But he doesn't say anything. He just takes a step forward so I have to take a step back. And because this room is so small, I'm already bumping into the side of the bed.

A bed we share.

A bed where we sleep next to each other.

He takes another step and this time I can't really do anything but sit.

I have a flash of panic here. It's fleeting, but it's real. Because this position—me sitting down and Tyse towering over me—it's reminding me of the last time I was with Finn. And despite the fact that the sex felt good, it wasn't *good sex*. It was… fear sex. It was desperate, and sad, and vulgar.

Tyse squints his eyes at me, like he's reading something on my face. And immediately he bends down, placing his hands on my knees. "What's wrong?"

"Nothing's wrong."

"You're lying. We don't have to—"

"That's not it."

"Then what's wrong?"

"I'm thinking about Finn."

He almost stands up again, but I put my hands over his to make him reconsider. Which he does. But he also spells it out for me. "I don't wanna compete with that guy."

"You're not. He's not even here."

He taps a finger to my head. "I mean, in there. I don't wanna compete with him in there."

"Trust me, he's not in there."

"Then why are you thinking about him right now?"

"Because I just remembered that he was…" But I suddenly can't say it out loud. Because I hadn't even admitted this to myself before this very second, and it's so hard to believe that I start to wonder if I just got it wrong.

Except I didn't get it wrong and my eyes are filling up with tears, because I got it exactly right, and my heart is broken over this new awareness.

"He was what, Clara?"

"He was *mean* to me."

"Mean to you how?"

Then I'm crying, and I feel stupid, and I don't know what to say.

"Mean to you how, Clara?"

"He treated me like I was some down-city tavern whore. He wanted things… things I had never done before. But I did it. And still he didn't save me. And he said things…" I let out a breath. "Forget it. The important part is that when I walked through the tower door, I hated him." I look up and meet Tyse's eyes. "I told him I would hate him 'till the end of time. He was someone else. Something happened to him after his father died."

"When did his father die?"

"The day the bells rang for Haryet."

"And you went in the day after Haryet."

"Yeah."

"Well, that's all pretty stressful. Maybe he—"

"*No.*" I stop Tyse right there. Before he can defend Finn. Because it's not true and I don't want to hear it. "That's not why. Yes, it was stressful. But the change in Finn was something else. It wasn't stress, Tyse. It wasn't. It was something *else*."

Tyse stands back up and this time I don't stop him. Then he takes off his jacket, hangs it up, then removes his weapon belt, draping it over the chair in the kitchen. And then takes off his shirt and walks over to the chair to take off his boots.

It's a pattern with him that I've come to recognize.

I lean over, take off my boots too, and then grab a

nightgown out of my little chest of drawers. It's a lot like the one I wore last night. White. Cotton. Soft. Girly instead of sexy. And I feel very young in this moment. Like… immature. Which is not how I felt in the Maiden Tower. There, I always felt so grown up.

But I think it was an illusion. I don't think I ever grew up. Not until I came here.

When I turn, Tyse has already taken his pants off and is standing in his boxers. But this is just how we sleep so I don't know if we're going to keep going, or this is just… sleep.

"What do you want to do?"

Did he just read my mind? "What do you mean?"

"You want me to… find the door and go kick his ass? Because I will."

I just blink at him for a moment. "What?"

"That Finn fucker. I'm pissed. Can you tell?"

"Not really."

"That's how ya know I'm pissed. I'm a quiet kinda pissed. And after what you just told me, it's my new mission in life —well, after tomorrow, which we are not gonna talk about tonight—but after tomorrow, it's my new mission in life to find that fucker and make him pay. And by make him pay, I mean… in *every* dimension. Because I'm gonna hurt him in his *soul*."

"Oh. Well… I was actually just wondering if we were gonna have sex tonight."

His face goes blank. Then a small smile lifts up his lips. He chuckles. "OK, then. We're gonna table the revenge scheme for a couple days and just concentrate on the sex. Acceptable?"

A sense of joy transcends my sour mood and suddenly the world is all right side up again. "You're very serious when you're working, ya know that?"

He nods. "I am. And I do. And I've got a lot of work coming up. But I'm trying to remind myself that I'm off-duty right now so I'm doin' my best."

Well. If ever there was an invitation to remind a man that he's off-duty, that was it. I grab the front of my nightgown with my fingertips and lift it back up over my head. As soon as it's off, I make eye contact with Tyse again.

He's smiling now because whatever work thing that's on his mind, he's truly put it aside at this point. "What are ya doing?"

"I don't like the nightgown anymore. It reminds me of that place I used to live."

Tyse presses his lips together. "I see."

"In fact"—I reach behind my back and unclasp my bra—"I don't like these undergarments, either." I let the bra slide down my arms and then I step out of my Cheeky Goddess underwear. I do not break eye contact with him. And, to my surprise, he doesn't break eye contact with me, either. "So I'm just gonna sleep like this."

Then I pull the covers back and slip into the bed.

I'm looking him right in his blue eyes when he reaches over and turns the light out. For a moment it's completely dark. But then there is a blue glow emanating up from my skin and I can see Tyse as he drops his boxers—lit-up eyes locked on me—as he gets into bed.

His body eases in up next to mine, his hand on my stomach. But he slowly slides it down between my legs. "One day... I'm gonna *read* you, Clara Birch. I'm gonna get that story your spark is so desperate to tell, and I'm gonna know you better than anyone else in this fuckin' universe."

And then he kisses me, and while he's kissing me he puts me on top of him. My legs straddling his hips. My hands sliding under his arms and gripping his shoulders like I don't ever want to let go. He's got one hand between my legs, and the other is around the back of my neck, holding our lips together as our mouths work in unison.

But a moment later, he's inside me. And this is nothing like the sex I've ever had before. Because my entire body is lit up with spark, and it's so powerful that it lifts off me the way those butterflies did on Jasina Bell's dress. The whole room is blue, and the spark is floating all around us like snow falling in mountains I have never seen before, and this man underneath me is moaning sweet things into my ear as we make love.

And this too is new. Because it's *slow*. So slow. It's lingering and the pleasure isn't some instantaneous climax, but a sustained sense of pure delight that goes on, and on, and on.

He holds me close to him, my breasts pushing against his chest. But after the first climax, I sit up and we keep going. Even slower this time. His face is lit up blue from my glow and when I tap his chest, my spark comes right out the end of my fingertip and leaves a mark on his skin.

I draw a heart around his heart. I write my name on his

stomach. I trace his tattoos in cyan-blue and little by little, he takes it in.

The glow I leave behind becomes his.

Like a gift.

And while I'm doing this he's tracing my story. The one written on my body. And all I hear as I make love are his words. His promise to me. *One day I'm gonna read you, Clara Birch.*

And I think to myself… *Well, of course he is.*

Because whatever is written on me—whatever story this is—I know one thing for sure.

It's the story of us.

*T*IME IS WEIRD IN DREAMS, so I don't know how long I've been standing at the window of our room looking down at what used to be the God's Tower stage. I only know the moment when I realize where I am and what I'm doing.

Which is watching an Extraction outside.

Imogen's Extraction. She's far down below, but I recognize it because of the blue sphere of spark she makes around her body as she walks through the tower doors.

This scene is superimposed over the ruin, but I can see it quite clearly. Not like it happened ten years ago, but like it's happening right now in this very moment and I'm up in the tower, looking down on the old Tau City where I used to live.

Everything goes black for a moment.

Then there is another Extraction. And even though I don't remember what kind of display Marlowe Hughes did when she walked through, I know this is Marlowe.

Another darkness. Another scene change. And yet another Extraction. This time it's Mabel Paice. It keeps going like this. Darkness. Lucy Fisher. Darkness. Mabel Shaw. Darkness. Piper Adley. Darkness. Brooke Bayford. One by one they walk through the doors and disappear underneath me.

Darkness.

Then nothing.

I lean in, squinting. But there's nothing but blue mist out there.

"Haryet!" I yell it. Just in case she's lost. Because she's next. And I want to see her so bad, but she's not here. "*Haryet!*"

Then it all disappears and I find myself sitting up in bed because someone is pounding on our door.

Tau City

PART 4

"Yes, everyone agrees that the Godslayer is disgusting. But I find his Courtesan to be the most repugnant woman in the history of females. What a tool she is."

—Glenda Washington, Dean of Women's Studies, Dupont College, Phi City University

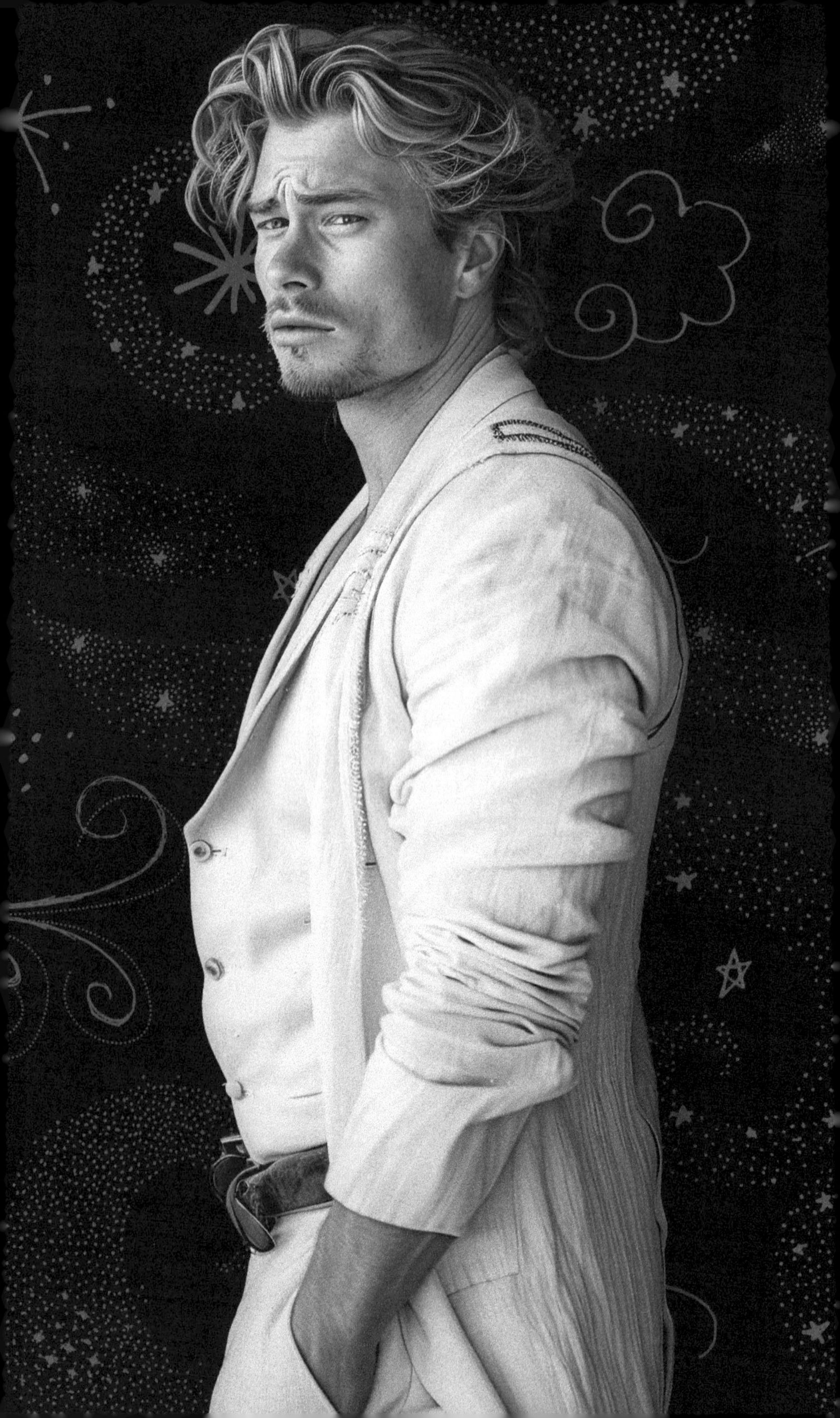

FINN

CHAPTER FORTY

"*Hello, son.*" Just the sound of my father's voice is enough to make my whole chest hurt. I wouldn't call him my best friend. I wouldn't call him a friend at all, actually. He was my *father*. And that's so much more than a friend.

He was my whole world. And I miss him. It hasn't even been a full week, but in this moment, I feel like it's been a thousand years since I talked to him last.

"If you're watching this..." He pauses to smile and chuckle a little. "Well, things must've gone terribly awry. I'm probably dead. But"—he puts up a hand—"don't worry. If I died trying, it still would've been worth it. Because I can't live with the lies. I did it when I was your age because... well, my father assured me that it was the right thing to do. And I trusted him, just like you trust me. But it's not the right thing to do and I wouldn't be able to live with myself if I told you otherwise. I'm not going to talk you into it the way he did me. You're better than that, Finn. You're better than me. You're better than any of the other Extraction Masters that came before you. And I am truly happy to make that ultimate sacrifice if it means you have the information you need to make a different decision. So if I'm dead right now, know that I did not die in vain. Because you will do what I could not."

Jasina turns her head to look at me. "What is he talking about?"

"I'm not sure. Just listen. I don't want to miss anything."

"What I'm going to tell you now is the truth," my father says. "And if you tell anyone, they will call it lies. They might even convince you that I'm crazy. Or that you misheard. I hope that your trust in me is still solid. Because the truth is the only way out.

"First of all, the tower. The tower is many things but it is not a god. It's not alive, it's not sentient, it's not in control of anything. You see, the Extraction Master is what controls the tower."

"What?" Jasina looks at me again. "I don't understand."

"Just *listen*, Jasina." I don't mean to snap at her, but this is too important for interruptions.

"Are you listening, Finn?" my father asks.

Shit. He's asking me a question. "Am I supposed to answer him?"

"Finn?" My father's face shows a look of confusion.

I'm so confused. "Is he... *in there*?"

"Oh, I'm sorry. Are you asking me a question? Am I allowed to talk now?"

I shoot her a look. "Don't be a child, Jasina. This is important."

She huffs, frustrated with me. But then decides to simply answer my question. "No. He's not in there, it's just... like...

it's *him*, but not him. I don't know how to explain it. But he's not in there."

"If that's not him, then why is it asking me questions?"

"Maybe… it needs… prompting? To continue? Maybe it needs to hear your voice?"

"So I should answer it?"

"Well, it stopped talking so I think it's waiting for you. Just tell him you're listening."

"I'm listening."

My father's confused look changes to satisfaction. "Good. This was a security check." Jasina makes a noise of satisfaction in front of me, but doesn't remark about her good guess. "When I ask you questions from now on, you will be required to answer. Your voice is the key to the truth. Do you understand?"

"Yes."

"Excellent. In addition to unlocking the truth, your voice is a key to all Looking Glass rooms. You are an Extraction Master and your security protocols were automatically programmed into the mainframe upon my death. Remember this for later."

"That's it, I'm taking notes." Jasina forces her way out of the circle and then starts tapping on the glass until she finds whatever the hell she's looking for. I don't even bother asking, because my father is still talking.

"The first thing you need to know is that the gods are real. There is no god in that tower but they do exist in other places. Spark Maidens are food for these gods."

My head starts spinning. There is a terrible, awful ache

in my chest, and for a moment, I think I might actually pass the fuck out. Because he just said... *food*.

I fed the woman I love to a god. I really did. And I knew this was a possibility, but it was something far-fetched. Something inconceivable. Something... *impossible*.

And now it is not only conceivable, it is *real*.

"Finn? Are you paying attention? I'm trying to write as fast as I can, but it's taking too long to find the right letters!"

I turn and realize Jasina is the tapping out words on the glass. She is frantically trying to write down everything my father is saying by tapping on letters that are lit up on the glass.

She yells at me. "*Pay attention!*"

I turn back to my father and force myself to listen.

Something about trains. Something about tunnels. There are other places outside of Tau City. And men who aren't men, but something called augments.

"And the bookshelves, Finn," my father continues. "The ones outside this room. They are hidden doors to secret passageways that lead to towers. One to the Maiden Tower —it opens up into the Little Sister dorm—but the other one leads to the God's Tower. This is the important one and here is what you need to do..."

I LISTEN and Jasina taps behind me. My father goes on at length, taking great pains to give me details, most of which I can't make sense of. But I trust him and I know that if I do as he says, one day I will understand.

When he finally stops, after he says a final goodbye and the triangle ceiling tiles return to the view of the night sky and a clock appears counting down ten hours, I let out a long breath and turn to look at Jasina. She's still tapping on the glass, trying to get the last of his words down, so I wait until she stops before asking, "Can we watch it again?"

She looks bewildered for a moment. Her hair is a bit messy, her face is pale, and she's slightly out of breath. "Let me try."

If she wasn't here, I'd be lost right now. There's no way I'd have figured out this glass top, not the way she did. I'd have missed the message. Hell, I'm fairly certain it would've never occurred to me to take *notes*.

"I don't think so, Finn. I think the clock up there?" We both look up at the countdown. "It was a signal that the message was over."

"Yeah, I figured."

"But I need a notepad and a pencil. Oh!" She holds up a finger. "In your desk." Then she's rushing to the door and pulling it open. The night sky disappears and so does the countdown, but we know that's because the door is open and that seal has been broken.

I follow her out. "How do you know what's in my desk?"

But she's not at the desk. She's staring at the window. And when I turn my gaze to the window, I realize why.

There is a bright cyan-blue light floating up from down below.

"What the hell is that?" I walk over to the window and look down, squinting my eyes, because...

"Is that... Clara, Finn? Kissing some man?"

It is. But not. It's... like an outline of Clara made of spark. And she is kissing a man, also just an outline of blue spark—in fact everything is blue spark down there. I've processed this for barely a second when movement above draws my attention to a bubble of spark rising up past the dome of the Extraction Tower. There is a man floating in the middle of this bubble. The same man who is kissing my Clara in the apparition down below. Only he's not an outline, he's... like *real*.

We lock eyes. His narrow. Then they suddenly light up—like there's spark inside him.

And then, even from all the way up here and from behind glass, I begin to hear the crowd.

Dozens of people have gathered and all of them are watching Clara Birch kiss a man who looks nothing like the god I imagined inside that tower.

Who isn't a god. Can't be a god. Because my father just told me that there are no gods in the tower.

Did he actually say that? It's... life-altering, this revelation. And yet, it's like it hasn't hit me yet. I can't seem to make any sense of things. Especially this *man* floating out in front of my tower.

But he's not a man, either.

My father made that clear as well. And even though his

speech didn't come with a picture of what this man is, I don't need a picture.
I *know*.
Men who aren't men, but something called augments.
He's an *augment*.

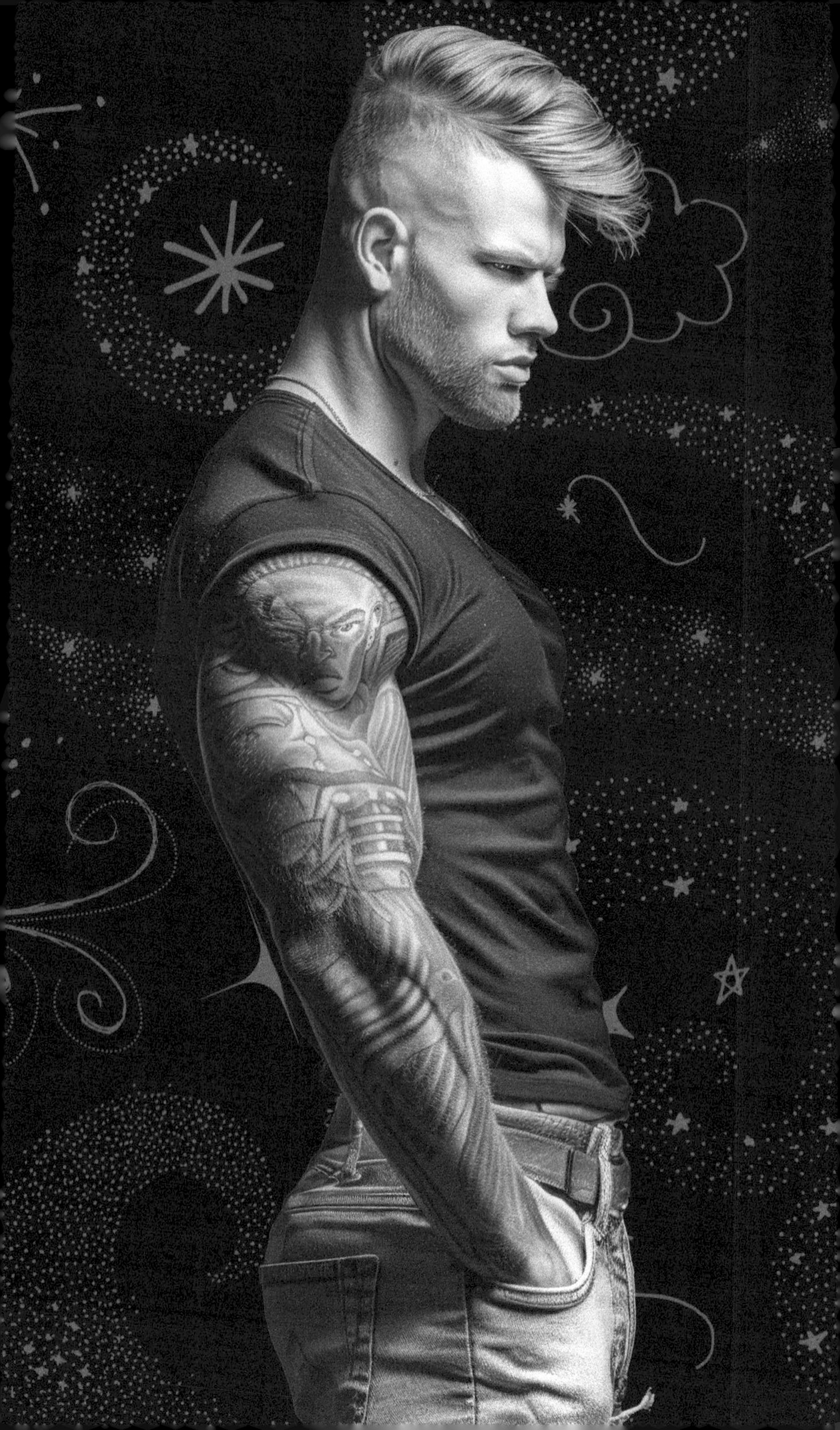

TYSE

CHAPTER FORTY-ONE

I know it's *Anneeta* at the door before Clara calls out, "Who is it?" and Anneeta answers, "It's me."

I know because the moment I open my eyes, the overlay is back. Not like it was the first time, but like it was last night when Clara and I were kissing outside the tower.

The spark is floating all around us like snow. It has a fairy-tale quality to it, but not the fluffy kind of fairy tale. Not the prince on a horse with a happy ending kind of fairy tale, but the dark ones. The ones where you know there's witches in the forest and wolves waiting to eat you.

"Hold on, Anneeta." Clara turns to me. Smiles. "Good morning."

But I'm still in the overlay. Reliving last night when I was floating above the kiss Clara and I had outside in front of the tower ruin and the town down below wasn't mine, but hers.

I saw him. Her Finn. He was in the top floor of the missing tower. Only, of course, it wasn't missing in Clara's city. He and a redhead girl were looking out the window that was tinted blue. And then I looked down and saw that the hundreds of people who were there in our world had dwindled to dozens in theirs.

And they could all, every single one of them, *see us*.

They saw us.

He watched us. *Her* Finn. As I kissed *my* Clara.

And then his eyes came up and met mine. He saw me too. Both of me. The one kissin' her and the one floatin' in the air looking down.

We looked right at each other. And I saw it in there. The *mean* in him. I saw it.

That's why, when Clara started telling her little story about how he treated her that last day, I went all hot with anger.

He was *mean* to her.

I thought he was a dick from the very beginning, but... *mean* to her? How the fuck could anyone be mean to this woman? She's like a fuckin' lion cub. She's got power inside her that could probably destroy a fuckin' city and she's got no clue. None at all. It's never even entered her mind that she might... *do* something with that spark that pours out of her hands like magic.

"Tyse?"

I blink and the overlay goes with it. "What?"

"Anneeta's at the door. We should... get dressed?"

I let out a breath. "Yeah." I swing my legs out, stand up, grab her nightgown, and toss it to her. She's giggling. And I'm... *so angry*. But I force a smile and pull on my pants.

Then I turn my back to her as I stand in the center of the room and rake my fingers through my hair. Because today is real.

We are leaving.

We are gettin' on a train and we're going as far away from here as we can get. Because there's something really fucked up going on in this tower. Hell, in this whole city. I never thought much about why they just let us squat here. Why they feed us. And have a nice little lost and found where we can get new things for cheap. Or why they don't care that we're not paying taxes.

You know there's evil lurking when a government isn't grabbing those fuckin' taxes everywhere they can.

And now, after hearing those men talk at Stayn's last night, it's startin' to make sense. Just a little bit of sense. I know I don't have the whole picture, but the tiny bit I do understand is dark. And wrong. It's comin' for us. And if we don't get the fuck out of here, it's gonna get us.

There's a loud thump on the door, which I decipher as a kick. And then Anneeta is complaining. "Are you gonna open the door or what? I have something, you know. Something important."

Clara is out of bed now and she's the one who answers the door, not me. "Sorry, Anneeta. We were sleeping. What have you got there?"

I lean to the side to see past Clara and get a look at Anneeta. She's all dressed, like usual, looking like a fairy-tale kid trapped in a tower.

But she smiles at me, revealing that gap in her teeth. Then she holds something up to Clara, answering her last question. "I have a book."

"For me?" Clara's surprise, as well as her delight, isn't fake. And this is what I mean. She's a kitten.

And he was *mean* to her.

Anneeta sighs. "It's for you, yes."

"Come in. Come on." Anneeta is ushered inside the room by Clara, and this is when I see the book. I recognize it. A child's picture book called *The Godslayer and His Courtesan*. It's a popular book here and I've seen Anneeta carry it many times, though not recently.

Clara shuts the door.

As that is happening Anneeta's eyes find mine. "You have to make a promise, Tyse."

But I say, "No," before she even finishes.

"What?" Clara turns to face me. "You can't say that, Tyse. Not until she tells you what she wants."

I'm looking straight at Anneeta now. "I already know what she wants." Then I narrow my eyes and just say it. Because this day is whatever it is. It's the beginning, it's the end, it doesn't even matter. It's happening, right now, and we've got to make choices. "She wants forgiveness. Don't ya, Anneeta?"

"Forgiveness?" Clara is laughing. But that's because she doesn't know yet.

She doesn't have any idea what this child is.

Because she didn't hear Edward's slip-up last night in Stayn's office. *"We heard that every tower has one."* And he was talking about the Looking Glass. Which I was lying about. But it's what he said next that clued me in. *"And that the new god needs—"*

But that's where Stayn stopped him.

"Why would she be asking us for forgiveness?" Clara is looking bewildered.

I point to Anneeta's book. Because I remember now. I remember why she carries it around. It's got a picture of her mother in it. "Show her, Anneeta. Show her why you need to be forgiven."

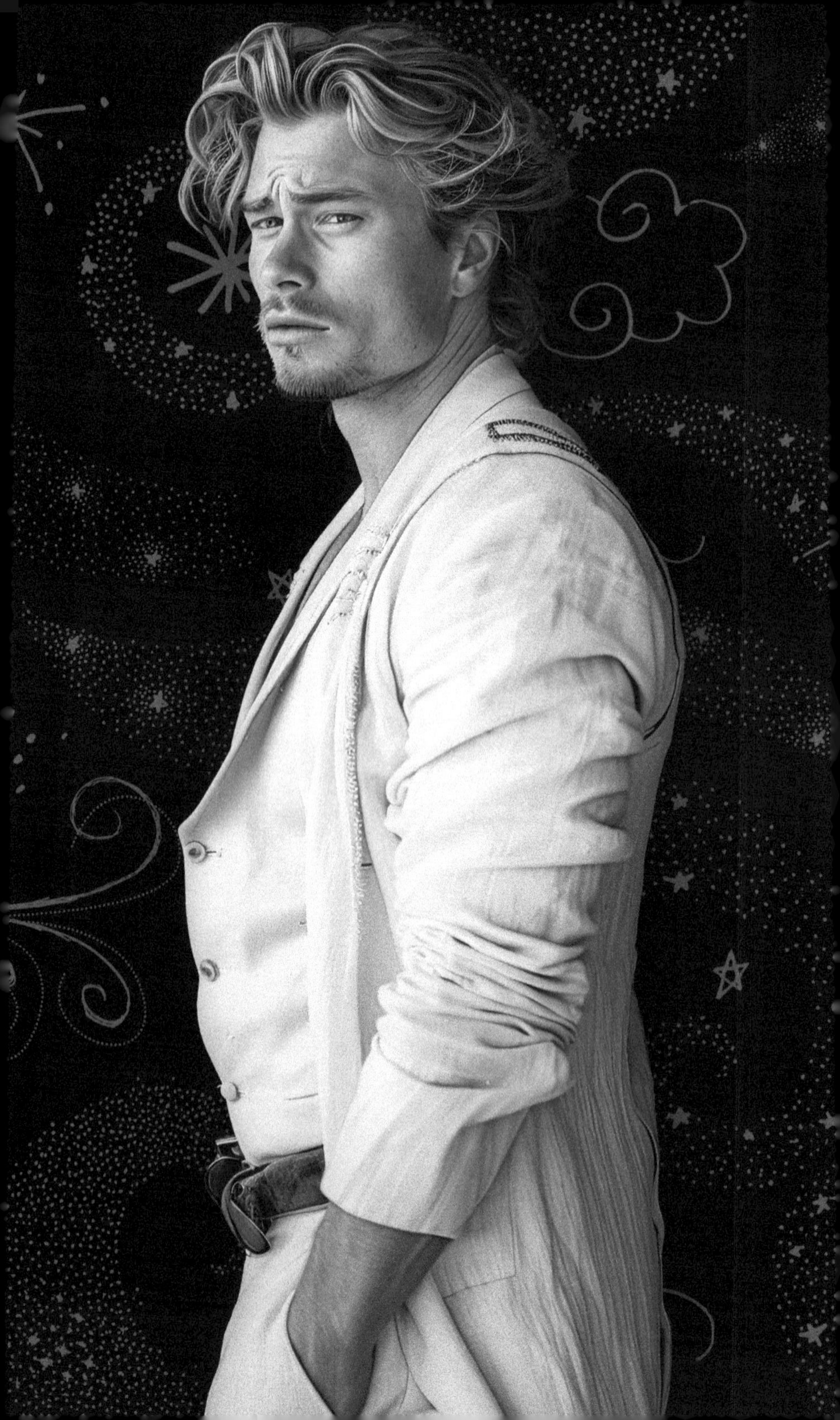

FINN

CHAPTER FORTY-TWO

The augments live in towers, my father said.

They have powers, he said.

They walk between worlds, he said.

They do God's work, if God's work was that of the Devil.

I mean, it goes way, *way* beyond that. But this is the take-home message for me. Jasina can sort the details, she's the one with the fuckin' notes. But this is all I need to know.

It's nearly one in the morning now. Jasina has been writing, and rewriting, and outlining, and paraphrasing everything my father said since we saw the blue man hovering above our city like a threat.

He has my Clara.

He has my Clara.

That's the real message. The only one I can concentrate on as Jasina does all her busywork with her notes.

I'm not delusional. I understand that I bear some responsibility for what's happening. I gave her to him. I handed her over.

But it's much easier if the enemy is not me so I table all

thoughts about how badly I fucked up and concentrate on what's coming next instead.

I go back into the room, close the door, and look at the countdown. We've got five hours, forty-seven minutes, and sixteen seconds. Which doesn't seem possible.

Where the hell did five hours go?

I exit the room, leaving the door open, and pace in front of the windows, trying to sort out all the many, many things I have learned tonight.

There's still a crowd down in front of the god's tower even though the blue sphere of spark, and the couple kissing inside it, disappeared last night and didn't return.

I'm surprised when Mitch doesn't come back to escort Jasina home. But then again, not really. Because if all that I've learned about Mitch is true, he's panicking. And it's got nothing to do with the down-city girls.

It's because he *knows*.

He knows about all of this.

He knows what this room does, he knows what the tower is, he knows there are devils pretending to be gods, and he knows that the augment we all saw kissing my Clara last night is something that's neither human or machine, but both.

And the augment has Clara.

But even more importantly, as far as Mitch is concerned, the whole fucking city now knows that Clara Birch is alive. Not *here*, but alive. And not only that, they think that man was the god.

They think they saw *God*.

They are not panicked, they are celebrating.

And this wasn't in the plan.

Neither was I, actually. I was just some dumb fool whose father kept him in the dark. Was he protecting me? Was I a ploy? Or did he just realize that his life's work was about to be upended by this false god, and I was his last-ditch effort to save his legacy?

I guess I'll never know. It'll haunt me, I'm sure. I'll probably write a book about it one day and it will be filled with nothing but spite.

Neither here, nor there.

Because the motivations of the last Extraction Master aren't important. What's important is that in five hours and however many minutes and seconds, Tau City will be gone.

I know this because that's what the countdown is. It's set to blow the Extraction Tower, but taking out the tower takes out the Looking Glass. And my father was very clear on what, exactly, this Looking Glass does.

"Firstly, the Looking Glass controls the tower doors. It opens them. But more importantly, it communicates with the god's world, Finn. Without the Looking Glass, there is no connection. And without this connection, the city will die. The explosion of the Extraction Tower won't be enough to take out the whole of Tau City, but it will mark the beginning of the end of everything. And I know what you're thinking, son. You're thinking… this is a terrible idea. But you only think that because you are unable to imagine how much worse it could get. There is no easy way out. The time for an easy way out is long past. This must be done or the worlds will never be the same again. We will never have this chance again. We must end it, Finn. *You* must end it."

The end.

The end of us, yes.

But more importantly, the end of *them*.

The god in the tower, his augment, and my Clara as well.

Which I have made peace with. If I can't have her, neither can he.

"OK." Jasina joins me at the window tapping her pencil on her notebook. "Do you want to hear the breakdown?"

"Is it any different than the last one you gave me?" I don't even look at her. I just stare down at the people in their post-holy-moment celebrations.

"Well." Jasina shrugs. "It's more succinct."

I actually smile. Just a little. Then side-eye her. "I'm sure it's perfect." I turn now, placing my hands on her hips, pushing forward, grinding against her.

She blushes. "What are you doing?"

"I feel like our… *date* got interrupted."

"Yeah, well…" She wriggles a little, like she wants to back away. But I hold onto her hips, unwilling to let go. "Things kind of… went off track, true. But maybe now is not the time—"

"*Jasina*. The whole thing blows up in five fucking hours. Now is the only time we have."

"Yeah." She sighs. "I get that. But… there's a lot to do, don't you think? I mean, your father was very specific. Number one—"

"Are you really making a list?" I whisper these words right up against her ear, causing her to shiver.

"Number one is get out of here. Not have sex. Number two—"

"Jasina, come on."

"Number two was destroy this tower."

I lean in, kissing her neck. Her shoulder shrugs up, but not because she's pushing me off. It's because my kiss is tickling her. "That's already in progress. The countdown is happening whether we like it or not. And there's five hours. Plenty of time to have sex first, find the trains, and get the hell out of here."

"And number three—after the tower explodes you have a mission!"

"Fuck the mission. I don't care about what comes after. And neither should you. All I care about is how much I crave you right now. And how badly I want to be inside you."

She doesn't protest, but she doesn't say anything, either. She wants to say no. But she's not going to.

"I'm not Mitch," I tell her, whispering these words in her ear. "I'm not going to hurt you. Or force you. Or anything like that. But Jasina, you're mine now, don't you see? You're mine, and I'm yours."

She looks up at me, sapphire-blue eyes wide. "What?"

"You heard me. We're partners now. It's you and me, Jasina. Forever. Don't you get it?" I take my kisses higher. To the edge of her dainty jawline. Then I've got her lips between my teeth. I nibble on them, gently, but also with intention.

For a moment she doesn't kiss me back. But when I persist, and start hiking up the many layers of silk that make up her elaborate skirts, she gives in just a little.

But it's not until my hand finally touches the soft skin of

her inner thighs that she really surrenders. Her head drops back when my fingers slide between her legs and she moans when I push one inside her.

I take my time here. I go slow because she wants it slow. Clara always wanted it slow too. Women want to be cherished and loved. And they want you to show them how much you cherish them and love them while you put things inside them. Cocks, fingers, tongues. Whatever.

That's where Mitch got it wrong. You don't need to force them. Ever. Not if you do it right. And success is so easy. All you have to do is make them feel cherished. And I do cherish her, in my own way. I want her to enjoy what I'm doing to her because after she's done, and she's post-climax —all flushed with those soft feelings that make her pliable— I want to do it my way.

I want to enjoy it the way I like it too. And they don't care if you get a little rough. If you pull their hair, or slap their asses, or pinch their nipples.

This is what Clara taught me that last day we were together.

She doesn't care if she's been… primed correctly.

So that's what I do.

I prime my Jasina. Because she is mine now.

But then, when she is moaning, and panting, and writhing, and her hair is plastered to her face with sweat, I take her by the shoulders, whip her around, push her against the window so hard, it rattles. And then I lift up all that silk, grab her hair in my fist, and enter her from behind.

We could die when the countdown reaches zero.

And maybe we will.

Then again, maybe we won't.

But if I have to live in this lie of a world, she's here for the duration.

She will be my comfort.

She will be my toy.

She will be my reward.

I come, and she comes with me, and the whole time I picture doing this to *Clara*.

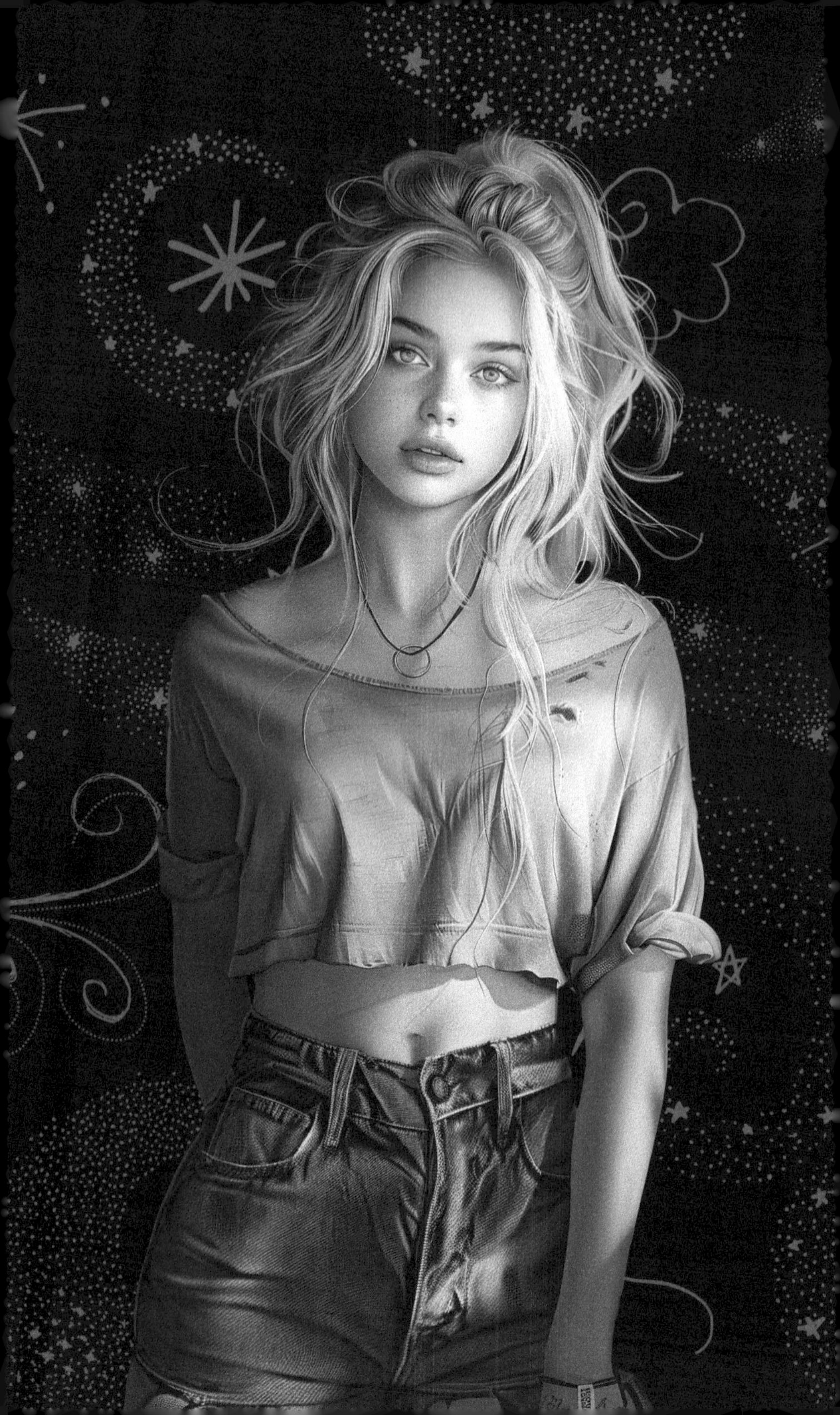

CLARA

CHAPTER FORTY-THREE

"*S*how her, Anneeta. Show her why you need to be forgiven."

"Tyse!" I'm a little bit shocked at his tone, so I'm not sure what to say here. "What—"

"Clara. You don't understand. Go on, Anneeta. Tell her."

I look down at Anneeta and find her frowning. But it's more than just a frown, it's sadness. "What have you got in the book?"

"Show her, Anneeta. Show her what you keep inside that book."

Anneeta's frown deepens. Then she takes a big breath, opens the book, and pulls out a piece of paper. She extends her hand, offering it to me.

"What is this?" I take it. "A photograph?"

"My mother."

"Your mother!" I smile at her, but when I glance down at the picture, the smile drops and my heart begins to race. Because it's... Imogen. I look over at Anneeta. "Your mother was..." I look over at Tyse. "You knew?"

He's shaking his head. "I didn't. I mean, she's... not right, ya know? You can see it, can't ya? Her clothes, they're—it's just the whole thing is wrong. She's not addicted to spark, Clara."

Anneeta stomps her foot here. "That's not true! I am so!"

But Tyse points at her. And he's mad. "You're *made* of spark."

"So is Clara!"

I gasp. "No, I'm not! I mean... I have it inside me but—"

"You're made of it! Just like *me!*" Anneeta squeals these words. Like a child. Like any child throwing a tantrum. But with this squeal comes a burst of spark so powerful, it crashes towards me as a wave, nearly knocking me sideways.

And also with this squeal comes the blue light in Tyse's eyes.

"Stop it!" He comes at her, grabbing her shoulders, shaking her. "Stop it right now!"

"You want the augments!" Anneeta screams. "You like them! You miss them! You *want* them! I'm just giving you what you want!"

He lets go of her and turns to me. "What's her name?" He points to the picture.

I can't think for a moment. My mind is doing calculations—Imogen has been gone for nearly ten years, this child is... not ten. So... what exactly is happening here?

My mind has gone blank.

"Clara." Tyse isn't trying to be mean when he says my name. He's trying to snap me out of my shock. I get this. But it's terse. Like we're in a hurry or something. "*Clara!*" He says it again. Louder now.

"Imogen," I say. My voice is soft and sad, the complete

opposite of his. Because I don't understand what's happening. I don't like what's happening. "Her name was Imogen Gibson."

Tyse turns back to Anneeta, his blue eyes lit up so bright now, he's casting shadows across the room. "What happened to Imogen, Anneeta? Hmm? What happened to her? Tell Clara. Tell her everything or we're leaving right now and you're staying behind."

"You can't go!" This isn't a squeal, it's a loud, echoing shout that comes with vibrations and another wave of spark. And this time, Tyse and I are both blown backwards, crashing into the bed.

I blink, stunned at the sudden violence. And when I look at Anneeta, her hair is standing on end. The room is filled with spark.

Tyse recovers, stands, and offers me his hand. I get up as he points at Anneeta. "You need us."

She crosses her arms and then there is a clicking sound at the door and even I understand what this click means. She's locked it. The magnets, or whatever. And we're stuck until she decides to unlock it.

Tyse crosses his arms too. "We can't trust you. And locking that door, keeping us prisoner, just makes it worse."

Anneeta closes her eyes, takes a breath, and all the static, spark, and light disappears. When she opens them again, I see it.

She's not a little girl.

She's nothing close to a little girl.

And when she speaks, she is calm, and mature, and completely in control. "Fine." The door clicks again. Tyse walks over to it, pulling it open to check and make sure it's unlocked. Because clearly, she cannot be trusted.

He doesn't leave though, just closes the door again and turns to Anneeta. "What happened to Imogen? What happened to your mother?"

Anneeta looks at me, frowning. There is a slight hesitation, but then she just spits it out. "I ate her. When I was three years old. I ate her."

For a moment these words do not make sense. Because I'm picturing this child—this adorable, big-brown-eyed child with missing front teeth—trying to gnaw on an arm while wearing a pink tutu, brown tights, and a Henley.

It's so ridiculous, I laugh right out loud.

"Clara?" There's worry in Tyse's voice. It's warranted. Because I think I'm losing my fucking mind. "Clara?" He grabs my shoulder and shakes me.

"Right. I'm fine. It's just..." I look at Tyse. "She said she *ate* her?"

"Not like *that*," Anneeta growls. "I ate her spark. That's how I live. It's not my fault. It's like eating adventure bars. It's just food to me."

Suddenly, my dream comes back to me. The one I was having before the knock on the door. I saw them all come here. One by one. "What happened to the others, Anneeta? What happened to Marlowe, and Mabel P., and Lucy, and Mabel S., and Piper, and Brooke? Did you eat them too?"

Anneeta lets out a long sigh. "I didn't know they were your friends. I didn't even know it was wrong. All I knew is that I needed the spark."

"What about Haryet, Anneeta? What happened to Haryet?"

Anneeta shrugs. "I don't know. She didn't come to me like the others."

"The others came to you?" Tyse bends down and places his hands on her shoulders. "Tell the truth now, Anneeta. There are no secrets if we're friends. You can't lie and you can't hide things. We need to know everything."

Anneeta nods. But then she looks up at me. "They just came to me. They were sleeping when they arrived. And it's not even like I had a choice. When I need the spark, I need the spark." She shrugs with her hands.

"You didn't eat me, though. How come?"

"Because I'm not hungry for it. I don't need it yet."

Tyse stands back up and paces the room, rubbing his hands down his face. Both Anneeta and I stay quiet as he does this, but I'm just starting to get impatient when Tyse looks at me. "Pack a bag. We're leaving."

"What?"

"*No!*" Anneeta squeals again. But this time, there is no spark display. She respects him. Maybe even fears him. Because she has her emotions under control. "You can't go!"

"We have to." Tyse isn't looking at Anneeta. "I didn't tell you last night because we were… having a good night, ya know? You were happy, and you had fun, and I didn't want to spoil it. But they know a Spark Maiden came through."

"It wasn't me!" Anneeta yells. "I swear on myself that I didn't tell them!"

I'm confused for a moment, but then I figure it out and look at Tyse. "*She's* the god?"

He nods. "She's the god. A new one, I guess. They're trying to grow a new god for the tower and they needed Spark Maidens to get her to mature."

"That's why they kept ringing the bells." I look at Anneeta. "They were feeding you."

"And when you say 'they,' Clara," Tyse continues, "you understand that the 'they' is Stayn and all those men who were at the party last night? They let some things slip. They don't know it's you, not yet. But they've been thinking about it all night now. And I've got a nine AM meeting on Monday morning. What do you think he wants to talk to me about? We need to get the fuck out of this city today. Like right now."

"You can't leave!" All of Anneeta's bravery disappears with these words. And part of me understands that she's not a child, she's some kind of god. And she's very in control and not at all confused and conflicted. She knows what she needs—the spark. And she knows the tower is the only place to get it, so she's stuck here.

At least she was, until I showed up.

But she plays this part of innocent child *very* well.

"Tyse!" Anneeta walks over to him, looking up. He is a tower compared to her. "You don't understand. We are *something* together." She points to me, then herself, then Tyse. "We are the Looking Glass."

"What?" That's Tyse.

"What?" That's me.

Tyse bends down again, placing both hands on her shoulders. "What do you know about it?"

She looks him in the eyes. "I know everything. I'm a god, remember?"

"Then explain."

"The Looking Glass is a way to see things. It covers all worlds at once. That's where you come in. You're the overlay, Tyse. Because you're the augment."

Anneeta directs her gaze to me. "But the overlay is only visible inside the spark. That's you. You're the spark."

Then she points to herself. "But you have to have a god to interpret the symbols. I'm the only one who can read it. So you see, to have a Looking Glass you need all three of us. Once those men figure out that we're the Looking Glass, they'll come for you. For both of you. Because they will already have me. I'm trapped here. It's much easier to find an augment and a Spark Maiden than it is to grow a god. They will never let you go if they have me. They will always have hope. They will hunt you until the ends of the world and they will never stop."

Tyse and I are both silent. Because we understand this is probably true.

"But if you take me," Anneeta continues, "to the right place, then they will lose all hope and they will give up."

Tyse sneers. "Right place, huh? And where, exactly, is this right place?"

Anneeta smiles at Tyse. "A place you already know. A place with a god who will let you in."

"Delta?" Tyse is shaking his head. "You want us to take you to Delta and give you to my old god?"

Anneeta shrugs. "He's not a little boy. He doesn't eat spark anymore, he *makes* it. And he will let us in because you belong to him. You'll always belong to him. There is no one in Tau City who could hurt him and that means if we're under his protection, there is no one in Tau City who could hurt *us*."

Tyse huffs. "Your plan has a critical flaw in it, little god. You can't leave the tower."

"But I can." Anneeta smiles at me. "All Clara has to do is feed me along the way."

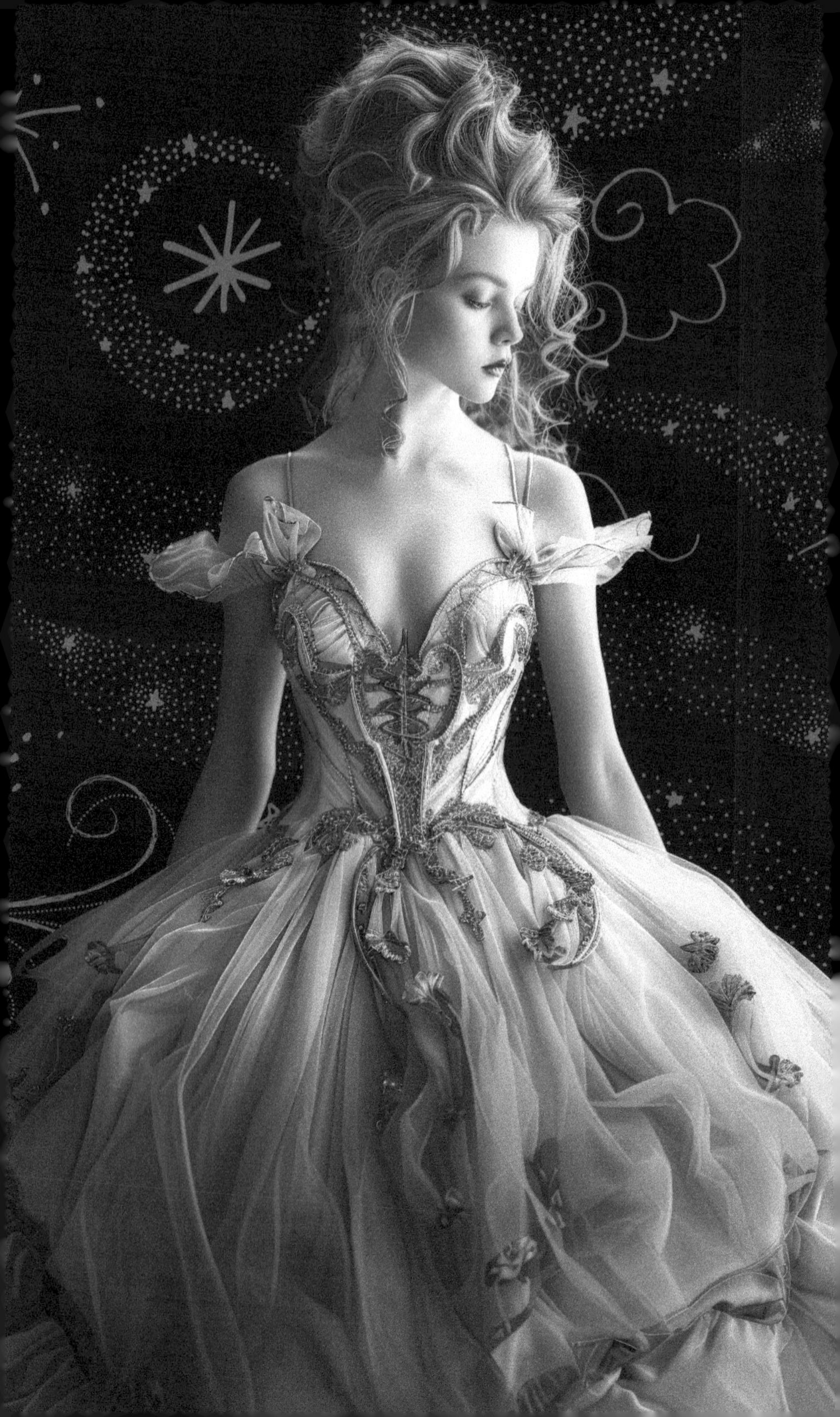

JASINA

pledged myself, not only to the god in the tower, but to the Rebellion.

Finn does whatever he wants with me as the rumbling of the crowd down below lessens, then stops completely. He puts me on my knees, he bends me over the couch, he pulls my hair.

And I can't even complain. Not really. Because it feels good. It doesn't matter if he's thinking of Clara while he's fucking me. It really doesn't. Because I don't love him, either. I don't even *like* him.

I just want his attention.

I just crave his touch.

But I could substitute anyone for him, really. Even Donal, if he was all I had. Even Mitch. That's why those down-city girls do it. They want the money, sure. But they want the attention too. It's a sickness for girls like me. Girls who lift our skirts up anytime someone so much as looks my way.

My auntie was right. Donal was right. I'm a slut.

The thing is, I don't care. I don't care about any of *that*. I care about the history books. I want people to know who I was. I want them to say my name a hundred years from now. I want them to turn my tale into something bigger than life.

Jasina Bell—the young rebel who found the Looking Glass.

Not only that, I found the message that Auntie was looking for. I'm sure Aldo was picturing Finn alone while he watched the message. He certainly wasn't picturing a particular red-haired rebel. But I was there. I heard everything. While Finn was shutting down, in shock, and unable to process the information spilling out of Aldo's mouth up on the wall, I was taking notes.

I wrote it all down so I don't forget? Sure. Fine. It's a good reminder.

But that's not why I wrote it down. I wrote it down so there would be a record of this night. So that Aldo's message would be preserved for all eternity.

Leave the tower.

Blow it up (already in progress).

Get on the train and go down the line.

There were also a few warnings. When leaving the tower by the secret staircase that leads under the god's tower, keep going and do not stop no matter what you see. Which is a bit creepy. And concerning. Is there a monster down there?

But the weirdest thing was the second caution. *Do not talk to your mother.*

Not my mother, of course. Finn's mother.

This is when I remember Finn telling me that his mother had joined a cult. Which, obviously, is the Matrons. So while this caution was not meant for me, it's very helpful. Because it means I should not talk to my auntie. I will never tell her about this message from Aldo. Ever.

I had some reservations about destroying the Looking Glass. Before the countdown, at least. My first impulse was… no. No way. I'm not destroying the Looking Glass! That's my legacy. But then I realized that this has been my goal all along. Because my goal was to free the people of Tau City. And if this Looking Glass is destroyed, there will be no more Extractions.

Mission accomplished.

Anyway, that's not even the point. The countdown has begun. Aldo didn't take any chances that we might be swayed over to the dark side, so to speak. The end of the message was the trigger. Whether we want this Looking Glass to blow or not, it's goin' up.

There has been a shift in my perception here. In my view of my place in history.

As Finn fucks me, I think about this, warming to the idea.

And there is a bigger, better way to go down in history.

The Glassbreaker?

Not as catchy as the Godslayer, but it'll do.

When Finn's done with me, he slaps my ass and falls into the couch cushions. Closing his eyes as he smiles his way into sleep like his father didn't just give him a directive. Like he couldn't care less. Like ending tyranny and slavery just aren't on his list of things to do today.

I straighten my gown. Finn started ripping it off me at one point, so it's practically a miniskirt right now. Then I walk over to the desk and pick up my notepad.

I read my succinct summary of what Aldo Scott told his son to do. Then I look over my shoulder at a passed-out Finn and decide... he doesn't really deserve this honor.

The countdown for this Looking Glass has already begin. I couldn't stop its destruction, even if I tried. Aldo Scott set the Looking Glass up to play a single message for Finn. Just the one, just the one time through. That's all he wanted him to know about the room. That's the only information he gave up.

However… my gaze darts to the bookshelf on the right side of the room. An exact replica of the one on the left side of the room. Which is the one that leads to the Little Sister dorm.

I'm slightly ashamed that I didn't notice it immediately because it's so obvious that if one bookshelf was a hidden door, might the other one be too?

Of course, this one leads to the tower. Which leads to the tunnels. Which leads to the trains. Which leads to… outside. Places that are not Tau City.

This is Finn's mission. Leave here and repeat this act in every city where the train stops.

I take one more look at Finn, sleeping soundly on the couch. So satiated and satisfied.

And I decide that he deserves to die. If he is this apathetic. If he is this shallow. If he is this unconcerned that the tower he's sleeping in is going to explode in just a few hours, then fuck him.

Let him die.

I tuck the notebook securely into the bodice of my dress and have only one regret as I open the bookcase and slip inside and onto the landing of a dark staircase. I wish I had boots. Because silk slippers are really not the most appropriate footwear for the end of the world as I know it.

But a girl plays the hand she is dealt, and honestly, who could've predicted the twist this night took?

I focus my attention away from my shoes and back where it belongs. The stairwell. When I descend, I notice that no nightlights pop on to help guide my way. In fact, there are no lights at all. Just a faint glow from the room beyond the bookshelf door.

For a moment I wonder if maybe I should go into this new life more prepared. Pack a sack or something. Find those boots, though where I would get boots at this hour— *oh, for fuck's sake, Jasina! Concentrate!*

My hand wipes through the air as a way of casting all these thoughts aside and I resume my descent. Carefully, slowly, I creep down, down, down. It's like fifteen levels to the ground floor of the Extraction Tower, but I'm counting as I round each landing, and this stairwell goes down further. There is no canal on this side of the tower, but there is a small lake. And in the center of the lake is the God's Tower event center. Which is not where I need to be. I would check my notes, but I can't see them. So I just keep going until there are no more stairs. There is a faint light here. It's a lit-up sign that says 'exit' in red letters.

But there are two passageways—a literal fork in the road —and I can't decide which way the exit sign is pointing. So I hesitate.

And that's when I hear it. The faint sound of *breathing*.

I turn, gasping, desperate to see in the dark. But that small amount of light from the sign isn't enough to make out anything other than a large, looming shape slowly coming towards me.

"This is the problem with you slutty down-city girls, Jasina." These words come out slurred and angry. "You think that the rest of us are all dirty, stinking, stupid peasants like yourself."

The shape forms up into something recognizable when Donal Oslin steps directly under the exit sign.

He's laughing now. Because he's got me. Fool him once, fine. But not twice. There is no way I will get his balls again and he knows it. "It didn't even occur to you that we would have sensors guarding this stairwell?" He tips his head up, smiling. I can't afford to take my eyes off him, so I don't look up, but I know he's looking at a very faint glow of light that belongs to the top floor of the Extraction Tower. "Thanks, by the way." He sneers these words at me. "For leaving the door open. I've been trying to break into that tower since I was fourteen."

Then he lunges at me. And a moment later, he's got a hold of my hair and he's pushing me down to the ground.

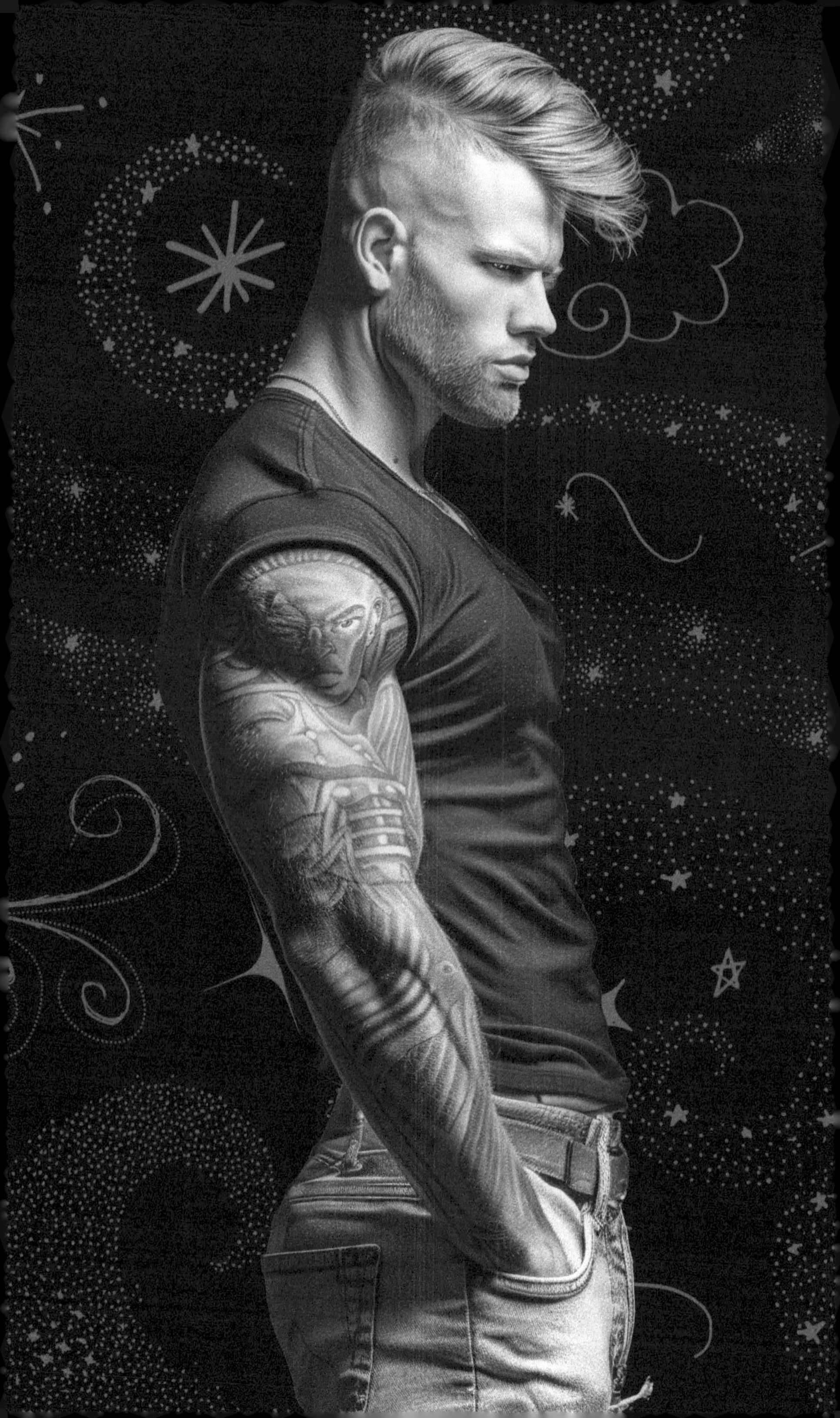

TYSE

CHAPTER FORTY-FIVE

All Clara has to do is feed me along the way.
It's not a stupid plan. It's not even as sinister as it sounds because the guys down on Eight pack up spark into jumps all day, every day. It's a thing.

I'm thinking this in my head, but in the same moment Clara is saying it out loud. "We *can* actually pull this off."

"Clara." I shoot her a look. But we haven't known each long enough for her to catch my subtle side-eye that, to me, is screaming *shut the fuck up*.

Because she doesn't shut the fuck up, she keeps talkin'. "Yeah. I mean"—she shrugs, looking me straight in the eye—"those guys downstairs package up jumps, right?"

I look at Anneeta and she's beaming. I point at her. "You, go. Now. I need to talk to Clara."

Anneeta narrows her eyes at me. And even though I don't even have any lights on in here, the shadows flicker dark. Like I'm pissin' this baby god off.

"*Don't.*" I'm still pointin' at her when I say this. "Don't you fuckin' dare threaten me. Because I'm gonna tell you something right now, I'm not afraid of you. If you're so damn powerful, why can't ya leave?"

She cowers a little. But I can't tell if it's genuine or if she's just a really good little faker. If I was placing bets, I'd say faker.

"Tyse." Clara walks over to me and takes my hands in hers, lookin' me in the eyes. "We can't leave her behind. We're… kind of a team. Right? I mean, we can *see* other worlds. Well, *we* can't, but you can. And she's part of that. We don't know what it means yet."

"That's exactly my point. Just because we *can* do it doesn't mean we should. And maybe she's tied to this tower for a reason, ya know?" I look at Anneeta now, narrowing my eyes. "Maybe baby gods are too dangerous to be let loose on the world."

Anneeta cocks a hip and sneers at me. "How do you figure I'd be 'loose?' Because the way I see it, I need Clara to do anything."

"Right. And that's a very short-term solution. I don't think there's another fuckin' tower in the whole damn world that sells jumps, Anneeta."

"Right! Yes. That means it's fate!"

"Fuck off. Fate, my ass! It's luck, kid. *Luck*. And those jumps are heavy. How many can we realistically carry? Even by high-speed, non-stop train, Delta is fourteen hours away. Do you know how long one jump will last ya?"

She huffs. "No."

"Exactly. You don't know shit. You know less than Clara and she's not even from here."

"OK." Clara steps between us, facing me. "Should I remind you of your little speech the other day? What happened to 'If I were putting together a go team, and I had pick of all the people in that tower—'"

I put up a hand to stop her. "That was *before*, Clara. She's a fuckin' god. And she's a little liar too. I don't like liars. I can't trust liars."

"I didn't lie about anything!" Anneeta is reverting back to her childish ways, which I'm OK with, because it proves my point.

"Nah? Well, leaving things out on purpose, important things like, 'Hey, Tyse, I'm a baby god and I eat Spark Maidens for breakfast,' is just as bad as lying."

Oh, I get a look for this one. She is mad. Her arms come up, crossing in front of her, and her eyes are narrowed into slits. "Fine. But you left things out too. You killed all your team members. How do Clara and I know you won't just kill us one day? Maybe you're the one we can't trust?"

I'm about to walk over there and choke her out, but Clara is in my way. "Tyse. Calm down."

"She's baitin' me. And I don't like it."

"You're baiting her."

I scoff, looking down at Clara. "You're joking, right? We have every reason not to trust her. She ate your friends!"

"I didn't know they were her friends! I didn't even know it was wrong! I need the spark and my mother gave me spark. What was I supposed to do? Ask her if eating is wrong? If your mother gave you grapes and then one day you find out grapes are people, then you'd know how I feel right now."

Clara turns to face Anneeta. "Wait. Do you mean that Imogen told you to eat the Spark Maidens?"

"Well, of course!" Anneeta even stomps a foot when she says this. "I was a baby. How would I know what I'm supposed to eat?"

Clara turns to look at me again, but now she's the one giving me 'the look'. "She didn't know. Now she does."

"You're not even the least bit concerned that she will drain you dry and leave you on the floor, a withered-up corpse?"

"No." And she's serious too. I can see it in her eyes. "And ultimately, it's my decision, right? If I want to help her leave, then it's my decision. And I want to help her leave. Think of it this way, Tyse. If we leave her behind, what happens then?"

"You're trying to make me feel sorry for her because she's gonna starve?"

"No." Clara shakes her head. "Think about it. She's not going to die. I think it's way past that point. She might be hungry, she might not grow and mature, but she's going to live. And what kind of god will she become if we leave her behind and let the city raise her?"

"Yeah," Anneeta huffs. "Think about *that*, Tyse."

Clara turns to her. "You shut up. You're making things worse."

Anneeta pouts, but she doesn't back-talk Clara.

I have to admit, though, if the little god Anneeta must exist, it's better to have her as an ally than an enemy. And that's what Clara is really saying.

So I throw up my hands. "Fine. It's your decision. I'm outnumbered, I guess. So fine. We'll pack up as many jumps as we can and then we'll get on the first train to Delta."

As soon as these words are out of my mouth, someone is pounding on my door.

I point a finger at Anneeta and make a zipping motion over my lips. "Who is it?"

"Runner! I've got a delivery for Tyse Saarinen."

I walk to the door, open it a crack, and then trade the runner a coin for the little package. He tips an imaginary hat at me, then takes off down the hallway.

I close the door, turn back to the girls, open the bag, and look inside. It's a phone. And when I take it out, I find a text message from Stayn.

Call me when you get this. The meeting can't wait. I need you to come in now.

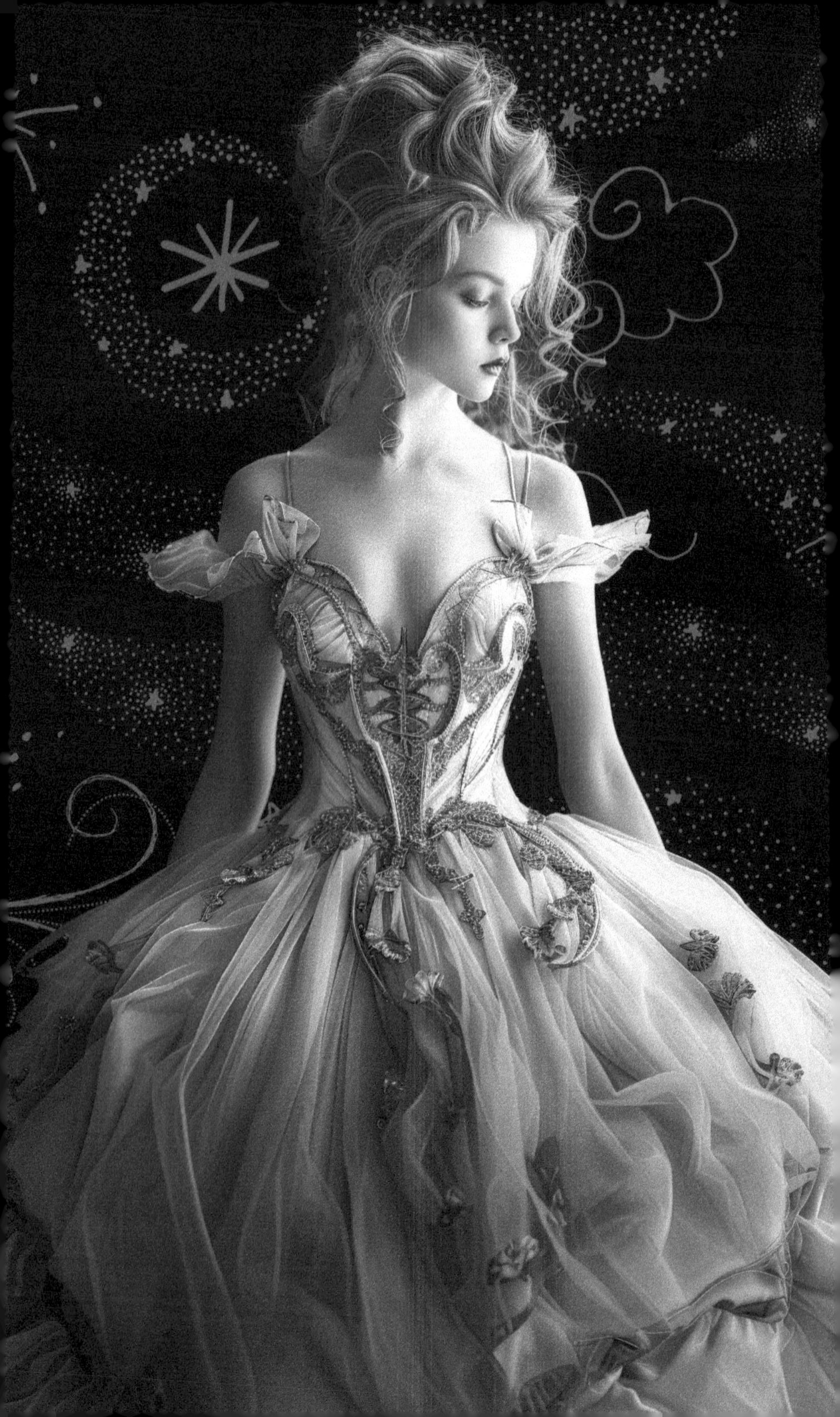

JASINA

mean. She knows he would kill me right now if she wasn't here.

But Auntie Bell doesn't care about me. She has never cared about me. I am... a tool. Nothing more than a hammer. Hell, hammer is far too lofty a role for me because a hammer implies power. And I have no power. It becomes very clear to me as I lie on the ground, looking up at Donal as he considers the idea that he might just stomp on my face anyway, that I am a nail. Something to be hit.

But then Auntie is there, pulling him back with her two strong hands on his shoulders. "We don't have time for this, boy. You need to get into position."

"She came down from there!" He points down the hallway, indicating that I came down the stairs from the tower. "We can get in now."

"It's far too late for that, Donal. That Looking Glass is out of our reach. But this one—" Auntie motions down the left-hand passageway with her head. "This one can still be coaxed into working. We must proceed with the plan." Then she pauses to look at me. "And we need my niece here. She has spark in her. We need every bit of spark we can get our hands on."

Donal huffs. "She's a traitor. She needs to pay for what she's done."

Auntie places a hand on his cheek and smiles. It's... a touching smile. Like she actually cares for this evil boy. "What do you think happens to her next, dear boy?" An evil grin plays across Auntie's face. And when I glance at Donal, I see a matching one on his.

"Get her up off the floor and bring her along, Donal. It's time."

Donal comes at me so quickly, I flinch and cover my face with my hands again, fearful that he will get in one last blow before submitting to my aunt's demands. But he doesn't hit me. He grabs me by the hair and starts dragging me along the hallway after my auntie.

I scream, and he stops, turning to sneer. "One more sound out of you, and I'll rip all this pretty hair out of your head. Auntie doesn't care about your hair, do you, Auntie?"

"Come along, Donal!"

"Auntie?" I whimper. What does he mean?

Donal sneers at me. "Oh, you didn't know? How fun! Your Auntie isn't a Bell, Jasina. Bells are down-city half-breed whores like yourself. She's an Oslin."

"What?" He's still dragging me by the hair, but I've got a hold of his arms now, so it doesn't pull so much. And I manage to get to my feet and stumble after him.

"That's right, Jasina. She's my auntie, not yours. She's not related to you at all. She only married your great-uncle because the Matrons told her to. They needed to breed you, ya see." He stops walking so he can lean down into my face and spit his words out. "So I can *eat ya*."

"What?"

"Donal!" Auntie yells this time. "Keep up, boy. We need to get this started!"

Donal yanks me and starts running, so I have to run too. But I trip and fall and he keeps going. So when we get to the end of the hallway, I enter a large room filled with people being dragged across a smooth shiny floor by my red hair.

Suddenly there is a lot of murmuring and Donal lets go, walking away from me like I never mattered in the first place.

I sit up, my head burning and my body already sore from the attack, and look around. But it takes whole, long seconds for my mind to even form thoughts that can explain what the hell I am looking at.

The people are the easy part. There are—well, every Matron who ever existed appears to be in here with us. And the Little Sisters are all here too, all wearing their blue tunics and cream aprons.

"Jasina!" Auntie barks my name so loud, all the hushed murmuring immediately stops. Like just her voice is enough to scare the piss out of people. "Get in your line!" She points to the Little Sisters, who are backed up against a wall on the far side of the room.

I scramble to my feet and stumble in that direction, looking for friendly faces. All of the up-city girls turn their gazes away from me. But I was expecting that.

What I wasn't expecting is for my friends to do the same.

"Lucindy," I say, still stumbling as I reach out for support.

"Don't!" she snaps at me. "Don't touch me, Jasina."

"What?" I look at Harlow. And she doesn't even bother with words. Just shakes her head. Then I look at Britley. "Brit?"

"Jasina, just shut up and stand in line."

"Here." Ceela moves over a little bit. "You can stand by me."

I want to say thank you—should probably say thank you

—but this isn't a genuine offer. I've known Ceela too long. I know her too well. But I slip into the space anyway because there's no other place for me.

As soon as we're shoulder to shoulder, she starts in, her words just a whisper so as not attract the ire of Auntie. "You're in big trouble. And don't look to us to save you, Jasina."

"What did I do?"

"What did you *do*?" Ceela turns to side-eye me, her lip actually curling up to show her teeth. "Are you *joking*? You're a traitor! You—"

"Listen up!" Auntie Bell roars, her voice echoing off the high ceiling of the underground room. "Matron Lightly and Matron Scott are going to explain your roles in the ritual. Do not speak, or ask any questions. This must be done and you all are here to do your part in saving this great city."

The word 'ritual' is what snaps my attention back to the room I'm in. It didn't make any sense to me at first, because I didn't have the proper context for it. But now I see.

It's a *church*.

We have chapels, of course. Places where we pray to the god. But the church of the Tau City tower god is… well, the tower. Only Extraction Maidens enter the tower, so it's not a place for regular people.

But we're *in* the Tower District. It's above us, but we're still in it. And even though I've never seen a proper church, this is a church. There are symbols everywhere. Circles with stars inside them. Not stars like the five-pointed ones that kids draw, but even simpler than that. Just eight lines radiating out from a central point. They are all over the room in every size imaginable. And when I look up at the ceiling, it's painted to look like a night sky.

I squint my eyes, trying to get a better focus on the stars above me, when suddenly, they twinkle.

"What the..." I whisper. "That's not... paint. It's..." No one is paying attention to me. Ceela doesn't even snap at me to shut up, she's so engrossed in what the old Matrons are saying about the city. How great it is, or whatever.

It's not paint on the ceiling. And I'd bet coin—all the coin I have—that if the lights came on right now there would be a dome covered in white triangle tiles on this ceiling. And they would be blank. Just like the Looking Glass Room up in the Extraction Tower.

This is when I start listening again. Because I realize that Matron Scott is Finn's *mother*.

Finn!

I know I left him behind, but... shouldn't he be here? I mean, everyone who's anyone in Tau City is in this room right now. Something big is happening.

It's practically treason to not invite the Extraction Master.

"The god is dying!" These words, said by Matron Scott, refocus my attention on what's happening around me. Mostly because all the Little Sisters gasp in unison. They didn't know.

I am not surprised, of course. But I'm keenly interested in what follows this revelation.

"But don't worry, good people of Tau City." Matron Scott smiles—and wow, even as an older woman, she is still very beautiful. It's her beauty, I think, that settles the traumatized Little Sisters. Not so much her words, though her tone is soft and comforting.

Until the next part comes out.

"You don't need to worry about the dying god because we have grown a new one." She pans her hand to... my mouth drops open.

"No." I even say it out loud. "No way."

"Donal Oslin," Matron Scott says, "is our new god. As the only young resident of the Tower District, he has lived his entire youth inside the spark and this unique upbringing will allow him to ascend to god status. This morning's ritual will elevate him and everything you love and enjoy about Tau City will be preserved."

There is a sigh of relief from many of the girls around me.

But there's a hefty level of skepticism too. Because... why are *we* here, if it's all going so well for Donal's ascension into godhood?

"There is one small thing we need from each of you, however."

"Well, here it comes," I say.

Ceela elbows me in the ribs. Not gently, either. "Shut up. Listen!"

"Listen to what, Ceela? Don't you understand what she's saying? They *need* something from us? Are you that stupid? What do you think that something is?"

Her cheeks go bright red. But she doesn't look at me when she growls her words out. "You are the most selfish girl."

"What?"

"That's right." Ceela looks me straight in the eyes for this part. "You want all the glory. You want to be the Extraction Master's courtesan. You want to be the Rebel who does it all. You want everything, Jasina!" These words seethe out of her like poison. "You are selfish, narcissistic, and you will get that glory over my dead body."

She *really is* that stupid. "Ceela." I use my mature-leader tone of voice. "They're gonna take our spark. They're gonna drain us and give it to Donal, who is, obviously, *not a fucking god because he's an evil teenage boy!*"

I scream this last part. Which is a mistake. A very big mistake.

Because my scream interrupts two things happening at the same time.

The ancient Matron, who I have never ever seen before —Matron Lightly—is in the middle of saying Gemna's name. And a large, heavy curtain is being pulled back to reveal a room separated from us by glass so thick, you can see the woman screaming on the other side, but not hear her.

This screaming woman is Gemna. And she is somehow hovering in the middle of a radiating star circle that is easily twenty feet in diameter. Her arms and legs are spread wide, attached to rays with chains and cuffs. And she's wearing a gala gown. Like this is one of the most important events of her life.

"Well, I see we have our first volunteer." The ancient Matron's voice cuts through the silence like a hot knife through butter.

I look over at the Matrons and realize everyone is looking at me. "What?"

"We need two Little Sisters to help Gemna prime the Looking Glass. And Jasina Bell has just volunteered!"

She starts clapping. And then everyone is clapping.

And the next thing I know, Donal is coming at me with a wicked grin on his face.

I step back, trying to disappear into the crowd of Little Sisters all around me, but they push me forward and a moment later, Donal has me and he's dragging me over to the massive glass room. And now I see that there are two more circles in there. Two more spaces on either side of Gemna, where two more women should be.

It couldn't be more obvious who belongs inside this trio of circles even if they had engraved brass nameplates.

The radiating circles were meant for Spark Maidens, not Little Sisters.

Except these days Tau City is two Spark Maidens short of a trio.

This is when I realize what Aldo *really* told us last night. He did mention that the Extraction Master controls the tower doors. But he neglected to specifically spell out that *he* was the one who called Haryet and Clara inside.

Which I get, I guess. It makes sense. Because he *knew* they had this Looking Glass down here. And he knew it needed three Spark Maidens to work. He knew that, even if he destroyed the Extraction Tower, they could use this one to… well, I'm not really sure what they're doing. But he didn't approve and he made sure that even if they used it, the result would be unpredictable.

Aldo sent Clara into the tower.

Aldo ruined his son's life.

I wonder if Finn figured this part out yet.

I wonder if Finn is even awake.

Suddenly, I understand why he's not here. They were calling me a traitor. So Finn was a traitor too. They cut him out because they saw us as a team.

And then I cut him out too.

Now I'm sorry about that. I'm sorry for leaving him up there to die. And not because I'm stuck here inside this nightmare where Spark Maidens are drained to feed an evil teenage boy who thinks he is a god, but because Finn and I actually *were* a team.

They are going to drain me of spark until I die and give it to Donal for his ascension. And the ironic part is... it's all my fault.

"All of you, of course," Matron Scott is saying, "will be used in the ritual. You will *all* give him your spark, but you will not be consumed in the reaction like Gemna and Jasina. We still need one more girl. One more Little Sister who would like to go down in history. Who will it be?"

Well, the irony is overflowing today. That's what I get, I suppose. I wanted my name in the history books, didn't I?

It's not exactly playing out the way I had hoped.

Suddenly, there is a voice above the murmur of others. "I'll do it! I'll volunteer!"

It's Ceela. And I wail, "No, Ceela! No! Don't you see? Don't do it!"

Donal slaps me. "Shut up, Jasina. It's an honor to give me spark for my ascension!"

Ceela has stepped out of the line of Little Sisters and is walking towards us as the Matrons praise her for her unselfish ways.

I want to throw up, but we're at the door to the glass room now, and when it opens all other voices and noise is drowned out by the screams of Gemna Hatley.

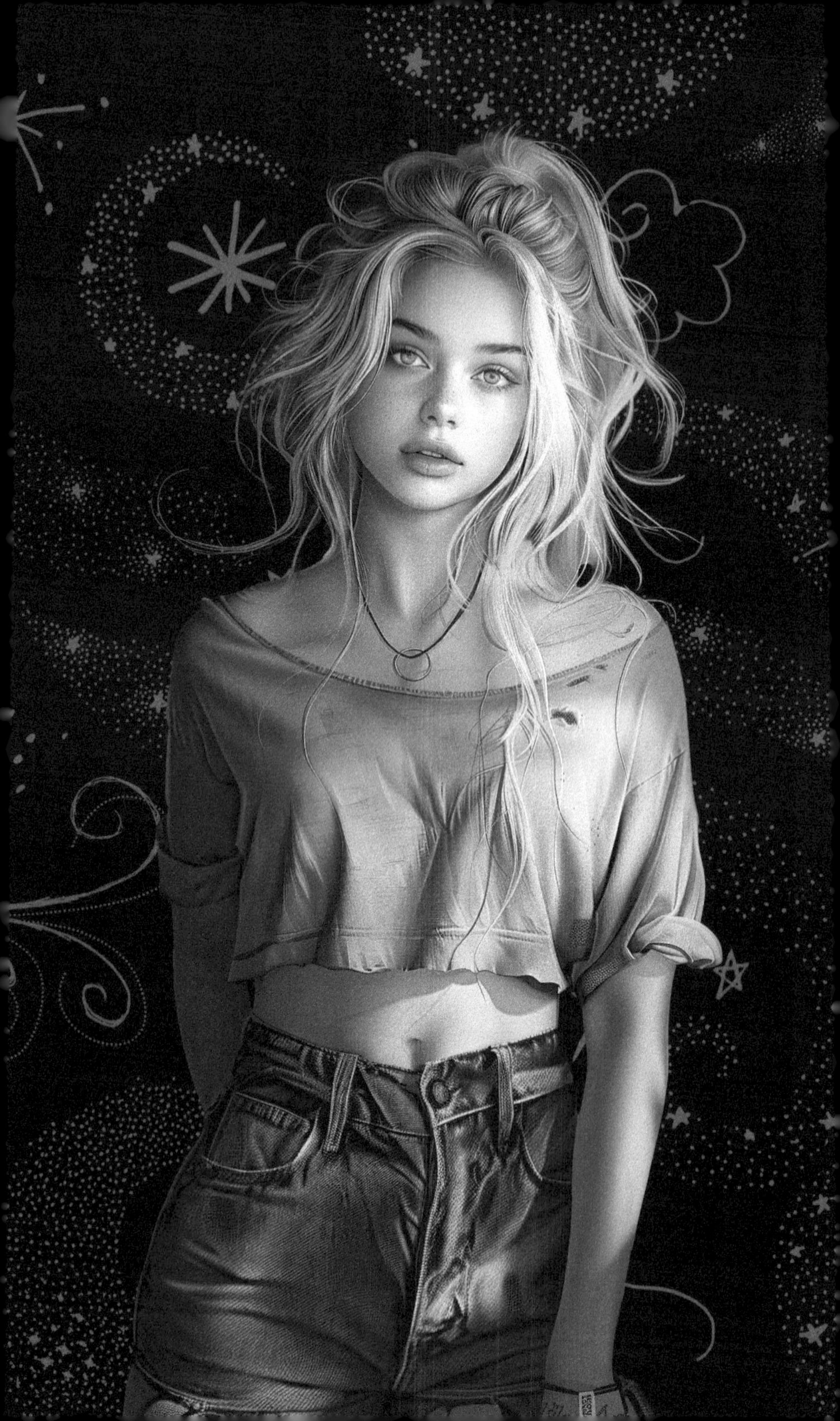

CLARA

CHAPTER FORTY-SEVEN

I watch Tyse as he reads the message on the phone that was just delivered. "What's it say?"

He sighs. "'Call me when you get this. The meeting can't wait. I need you to come in now.'"

"What are you gonna do?"

He scoffs. "Fuck him. I don't have the whole story here, obviously. But we're leaving. And we're leaving right now." He directs his gaze to Anneeta, narrowing his eyes. "I'm warning you, Anneeta, if you do anything to hurt Clara—"

"I won't! Geez! How come you don't believe me?"

"Because you're hiding things. And you need Clara to live. Do you think I'm fucking stupid or something? If it comes down to you or her, you're gonna save yourself. And I'm going on record right now to say, if you do that, if anything happens to Clara, I will take you out." His eyes narrow down even further now to indicate the threat is still incoming. "And it would be a very big mistake to think I couldn't make good on this. Do you understand me?"

Anneeta is frowning, but she doesn't talk back. Just nods her head. "I do. I understand."

"Good." Tyse turns to me. "OK. Let's go talk to Rodge.

I'm sure the runner has reported that the phone was delivered, so I figure we've got a couple hours, maybe, before Stayn starts to panic and does something stupid."

The three of us leave the room and head downstairs to Eight. We pass right by the spark dealers and go straight to Rodge's store. It's early, so there aren't a lot of people in line, but there is a line and we have to push through to get inside.

Rodge sees us and waves us past the people. "Come, come," he says. "My favorite customer. Come tell me what you need, Tyse." He's smiling at us as Anneeta, Tyse, and I go behind the counter.

"Rodge, I know you're busy, but can we have a chat in private?"

"Sure, sure, sure," Rodge is saying. "Come into my office."

Which isn't an office, but it's on the far side of the room, so I guess it'll do. Anneeta and I stay where we are. Prisha is here, and I wave to her, but she stays at her position near the door, collecting orders.

"We should try it."

I look down at Anneeta. "What?"

"You. You should try giving me spark. Just to make sure we can do it."

"Let's wait for Tyse." But before these words are even out of my mouth, she's got a hold of my hand. I try and jerk away, but it's too late. Immediately, I am losing all strength in my legs. She drains so much spark out of me in just a few seconds, I nearly fall over.

She lets go.

It takes me several seconds before I can even speak and many more before I can stand on my own without holding on to the counter. I side-eye her. "I said *wait*."

"Sorry. I just needed to know if you could do it. Because if not, then I would have to go hide. Stayn is coming for me, Clara. Not you. Not Tyse. *Me*."

I'm angry. Taking my spark like that feels like a very personal violation. But I'm scared too. Because it was very easy for her. Way too easy for her.

Fourteen hours. How will I get her to Delta City without killing myself?

I'm not even sure it's possible now. Not after that little display.

I want to say more. I want to tell Tyse. But if I do, he'll put a stop to this right now and we'll leave without her. I *know* this. And I'm not ready to let her go. Not yet. Not until I understand what we are. Because clearly, we are something. Something powerful. And while I have spent much of my life feeling quite pretty and privileged, I have never felt... *valuable*.

Yes, sure, I was chosen as a Spark Maiden. But number nine? I wasn't considered anything special, just someone who squeaked in. Anneeta and Tyse make me feel... special. I want to figure this out. I want to understand, not just what I am, but *why* I am.

I want Anneeta to come with us so we can figure it out. Because nothing is making sense at the moment. A whole lot of things about my life feel like lies.

I'm tired of it.

I want the truth and the truth requires Anneeta.

Rodge and Tyse leave the little corner office and come back our way. Rodge looks at me, smiling. "Yes, we can do this. All you need is coin." He looks at Tyse now. "And your man has it. Let's go set it up. Prisha!" He yells this across the room. "I will be right back. Ten-minute break, everyone. Ten minutes."

A groan arises from the people in the room, but what can they do? If Rodge says he needs ten minutes, then Rodge gets ten minutes.

We leave through a back door and make our way to the other side of the tower where the spark guys are. Rodge leads the way in, telling Anneeta and me to wait near the door while he takes Tyse over to the man at the counter. Unlike Rodge's place, this waiting room is small and there are walls and doors that lead to other rooms. There is no machinery in here. Nothing that looks like a spark extractor. Not that I've ever seen one of those.

But then Tyse and Rodge disappear into one of these other rooms and it makes sense that it's all done behind the scenes. I'm not sure how one pulls spark out of thin air, but it must be a highly guarded process.

Rodge appears after a few minutes. He doesn't stop to talk, just says, "I'll be right back," as he passes.

Both Anneeta and I blow out a breath. She doesn't try and touch me again.

Many minutes go by before Rodge returns, handing me a pack. "There are ID's in here, train tickets, and robes. A veil for you. From my traditional city of Thetaiota. No one will bother you and you won't have to show your face."

"Oh. Thank you." I let out a long breath as I take the

pack. Because this is getting kind of complicated. I hadn't thought about disguises and this change in clothes makes everything a little more serious than it was a few seconds ago.

"You're going to be OK," Rodge says. "I have to get back to work now. But you'll be fine. And when you get there, you send me a postcard letting me know just how very fine you are, OK?"

I soften when he places a gentle hand on my cheek. "I will. Thank you." I say it with more feeling this time. "I don't know why you're so good to me, but I want you to know I appreciate it. You've made my time here better."

"I like you, Clara. I see your spark. Not the kind that goes into jolts and jumps, either. But the other kind that lives in your eyes. Tyse sees it too. And I know that you will make it."

He gives Anneeta a glance now, then nods at her, but he doesn't say sweet things the way he did to me. "I've always known what you were. And I hope that the people of the tower have taught you things, little god. Because if you want to be a good god, you have to care about your people."

Anneeta, unexpectedly, is speechless. She just gazes up at him with big brown eyes that, I realize now, are deceptively innocent.

Rodge doesn't wait for her to find her words. Just gives me another smile, and leaves.

Tyse appears holding onto several heavy packs that he slings over his shoulder. "Come on, let's go. There are patrol officers outside the Ruin District. I don't know what they're doing here, but it's not a good sign. Is that from Rodge?" He points at my pack.

"Yes. Train tickets, ID's, and clothes to change into for a disguise."

"Good. Anneeta." He looks down at her. "We can't risk going down the stairs. Is there another way to get to the train tunnels?"

"Follow me." I think she's actually happy that she's got something to offer in the way of escape, because she takes off with light feet, looking over her shoulder at us with a smile, just to make sure we're keeping up.

She stops at a door, which, when Tyse tries to pull it open, is locked. "Don't worry." Anneeta taps her head. "I've got the key."

The next time he pulls on the door, it opens. We enter a stairwell and start our descent.

Anneeta stays almost a whole floor ahead of us, which gives me time to ask Tyse a few questions. "Are you sure this gonna work? I mean… I hadn't thought about all the details. The ID's, the tickets, the clothes. It feels a little unreal."

Tyse huffs. "It's all we've got, Clara. The only way out is through now. We don't have a choice. Stayn knows what you are. He probably knows I'm playing a part too. And he definitely understands what Anneeta is. They're trying to grow a new god for Tau City. This is a very dangerous thing. There's a reason why gods were decommissioned hundreds of years ago. None of them are good. Not even the one in Delta. He's an asshole. Trust me, we won't be trustin' him."

"Then why are we even going there?"

"Because Anneeta is right. I'm his. All the people in god cities belong to the gods. They don't keep us prisoner because they're not allowed—it was part of the Sweep Accords. But everyone in Delta is marked, including me. If we tried to take refuge at another god's city, Delta would consider me a defector. Worse, since I'm an augment, I'd be a traitor. He'd find a way to kill me for sure. One way or the other. So we have to go to him if we want any chance of getting out of this alive."

"What about the train? I mean... disguises, Tyse? It's fourteen hours. How are we going to get there?"

"Stayn has no power outside Tau City. The trains are governed by a neutral patrol made up of representatives from all the leftover god cities. They are impartial. So no one will fuck with us on the train. The problem isn't the train, Clara. The problem is Anneeta."

I sigh. I want to tell him what happened when she took my spark upstairs, but I don't. I will have to find a way to endure it. So instead I redirect the conversation. "How many jumps did you get?"

"Thirteen."

"Thirteen." I look up at him. "Will it be enough?"

He shrugs. "Less than one an hour? Let's hope so."

Suddenly, the relative quiet in the secret stairwell is broken by a faint, crackling voice, floating up from down below. Anneeta stops on the stairs below us to listen.

"*Tyse Saarinen! There is a warrant for your arrest. Come out, unarmed, and no one gets hurt.*"

"It's Stayn." Tyse lets out a breath. Then looks at

Anneeta. "I hope you know where you're going. Because they're inside now and we need to get to the train tunnels without running into them."

Anneeta looks frightened for a moment. Then she lets out a long breath. "I do have a way. But..." She directs her gaze to me. "I don't think you're gonna like it."

"Why not?" I ask.

"Because..." She looks up at Tyse now. Her voice is small and soft. "It's where I fed."

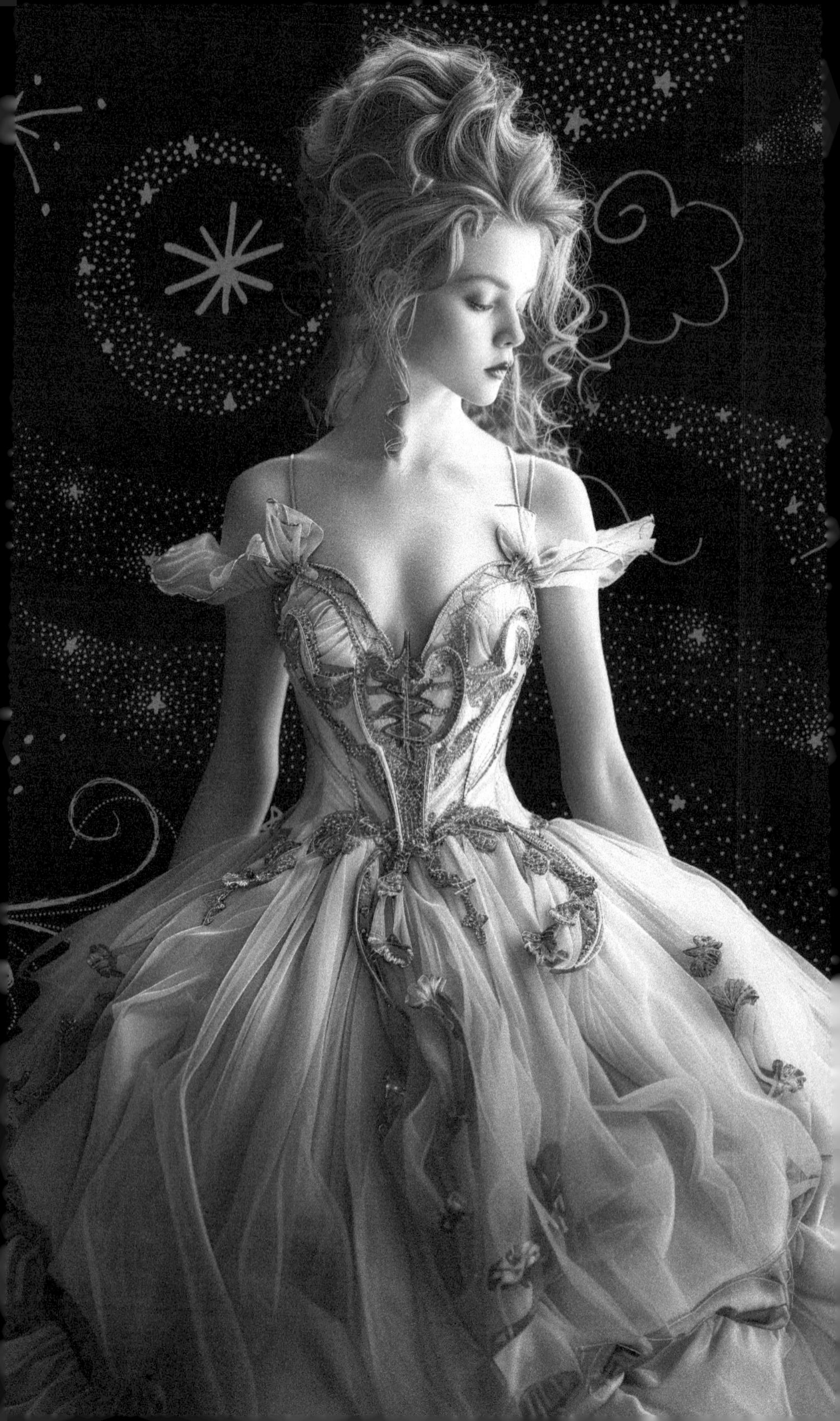

JASINA

Then there is laughter. And it's not Donal.

I look at the door where Ceela is still frozen—scared shitless, I guess, and unable to move. But there's someone behind her.

She is pushed out of the way and Mitchell Davies appears. He's looking right at me when he speaks. "*Save her?* He's not gonna save her, Gemna. I mean, come on." He looks at Gemna now. "Finn didn't even have the balls to save Clara. You think he's gonna stand up for this tramp? Listen." He walks over to Gemna, his eyes gleaming with degeneracy. "Just give in now. For fuck's sake, everyone is sick of your blathering. Show some fucking grace. What happened to 'poised, proper, polite?' There's no way out of this. In fact, this is what you signed up for. You should be proud that you can give your life for all these others."

Gemna towers above him on that circle, but this height difference in no way diminishes Mitchell. If anything, it makes him look more powerful, more in control, since she is a prisoner tied to a ring and he is not.

But at the same time, Gemna is no teenage girl. She's a Spark Maiden. She might be number ten, but she is, by far, the most powerful person in this whole room.

Maybe the Matrons have more power. I mean, it stands to reason that they do. But no one ever talks about them. No one pays any attention to them at all. Which, in hindsight, feels like a big blind spot on the people's part.

Gemna stops her screaming and makes a menacing growl when she speaks. "You're sick. All of you are sick! You're going to kill us to turn him into something"—she glances at Donal—"inhuman. An abomination. *You're not a god, Donal!*" Gemna's calm fades with these words. They are piercing and I suddenly have a headache.

"Fuck off," Donal says. Then he's got me by the arm and he's dragging me over to the circle on the other side of Gemna.

At the same time, Ceela starts protesting, finally coming to her senses. "Forget it! I don't want to do this. I take it back."

But it's too late. Mitchell Davies has her by the arm and is dragging her to the circle on the near side of Gemna.

By the time I refocus my attention on myself, the cuffs are already going on. I resist, and my feet are still on the floor, so I even try and run, but Donal is pulling on a chain now and I am yanked backward, falling so hard on the glossy stone floor, I hit my head and everything goes blurry for a moment. Then I'm being hoisted up by my arms, the strain on my shoulder joints too great to resist. I stand, getting in position in the center of the circle, which allows Donal to put cuffs on my ankles.

The next thing I know my legs are yanked open and my feet are secured to the radiating star.

I'm caught. I'm trapped. And there's nothing I can do about it.

This is really happening. They are going to drain all the spark out of us so they can… what?

I look around, desperate for answers.

Even if I can't escape, I'd rather die knowing what is happening than being completely left in the dark.

It's a Looking Glass, I know that.

But what are they doing?

I don't understand.

Donal finishes with me, Gemna is still screaming like a wind from the Great Sweep, and Ceela is demanding —*demanding*—that she be let go as Mitch finishes cuffing her ankles to the radiating star inside her circle.

Donal is done too and both he and Mitch walk to the door, open it up, and leave us.

But it's what happens next that starts to unravel the mystery of this ritual.

For the first time I notice a chair in front of the glass room. But it's not any kind of chair I've ever seen before. And when Donal sits in it, Matrons appear with a crown of some sort with all kinds of metal wires attached. They place the crown on his head and plug the wires into the glass wall. On this side there is a metal panel and more wires, each leading to one of the circles.

This is how they will drain us.

Our power will be sucked out, sent through those wires, and delivered to the crown on his head.

When all but Matron Lightly back away from Donal's chair, I brace for it. They are going to… flip some switch, or something, and that will be it. We will be ended.

But that's not what happens.

There is no way to hear what's being said on the other side of the glass—even if Gemna wasn't still screaming her fucking head off—because the glass is too thick.

But I can see just fine. And all the Little Sisters are starting to panic. This panic lasts for several minutes while Matrons, and that fucking degenerate Mitchell Davies, all try and calm them down.

Maybe the girls are OK with this, or maybe they are just being threatened. Regardless, they calm down. And then one approaches the center of the room. I don't know this girl's name, but she's from up-city. She is directed to stand in a certain spot marked by a pattern inlaid into the stone floor and then Mitchell puts another crown on her head, just like the one Donal is wearing.

I don't mean to scream when the process starts, but the cyan-blue lights that comes out of her in a long, pulsating line scares the hell out of me and it's just an instinct. Her body goes rigid and for a moment, I think she will fall to the floor. I think she needs a chair.

But I'm wrong. The spark is holding her up as it is drained. And it's not until she is empty, and pale, and lifeless that she finally crumples like a used-up piece of paper and slams face first onto the floor.

I know the girls are screaming. Hell, even Ceela is screaming now.

But then the girl stirs. Her cheek is bloody when she finally lifts up her head and her nose might be broken, but she's alive.

And I can almost hear the sigh of relief in all the Little Sisters out there.

Something terrible is happening to them.

Something evil and gross.

But they're not going to die.

Not like us.

And so they form up in a line. Waiting their turn to feed the new god.

No one is coming to save me.

That is what I say in my head, over and over, as the seconds, and minutes, and hours tick off as each girl gives her spark in the name of Donal Oslin.

No one is coming to save me.

It takes a little while before I snap out of the hopeless stupor. But eventually, when the line of Little Sisters is half as long as it was when we started, I finally understand what they're doing.

They're not opening a Looking Glass.

Whatever they needed the one up in the Extraction Tower for, that's over now. And anyway, it's been rigged to blow up by Aldo. They couldn't use it even if they wanted to.

This room is also some kind of Looking Glass, but it's more than that.

That's when I finally get the answer I was seeking.

This is a *door*.

This is a door that leads to… wherever it is that Spark Maidens go when they walk into the tower.

They are going to destroy Tau City by draining it of all its spark and then they are going to leave. They are gonna walk through the tower doors and leave tau City to die.

Does Donal know?

Or does he really think they're trying to turn him into a god?

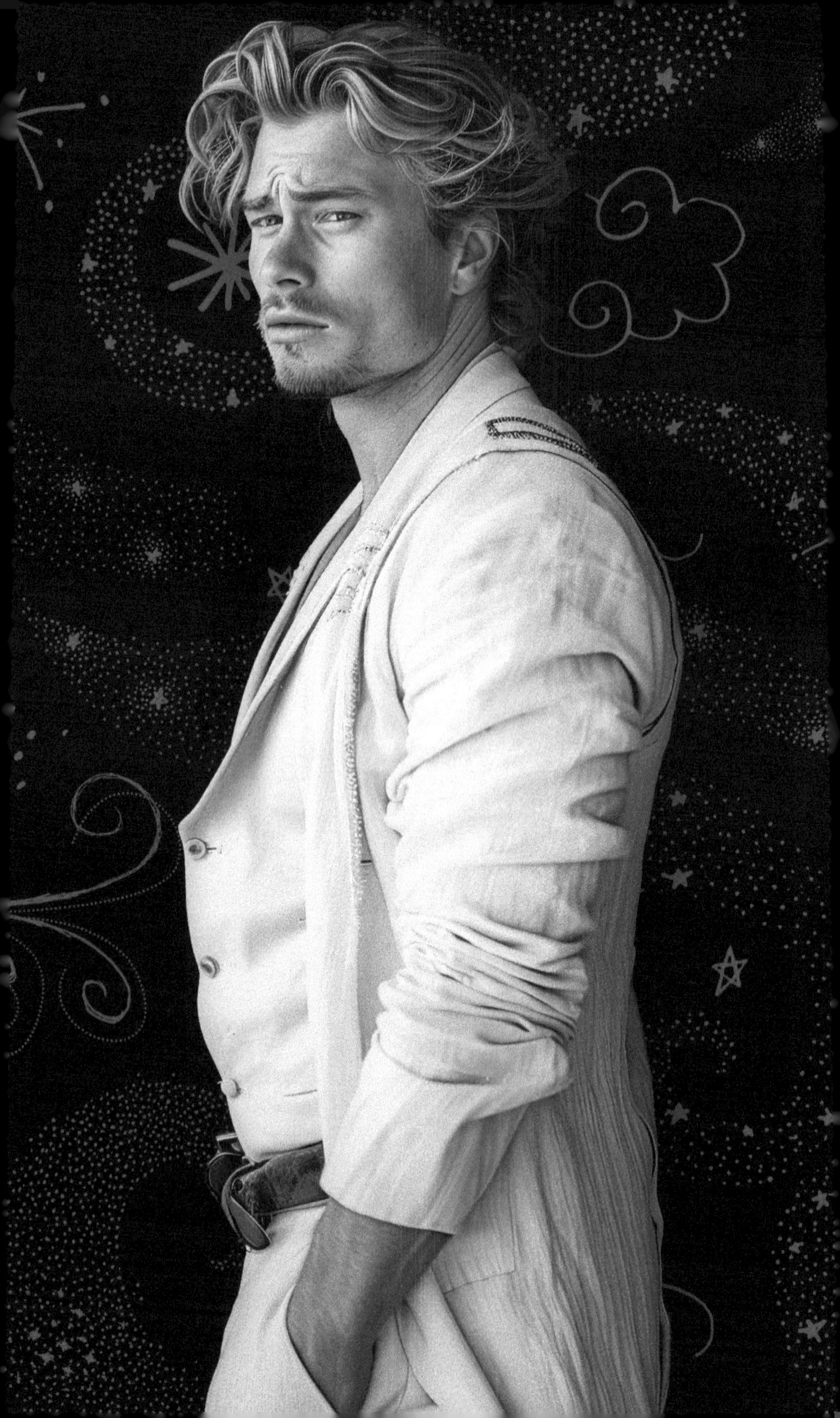

FINN

CHAPTER FORTY-NINE

A low hum reverberates through my body, waking me from a dreamless sleep. My eyes open, but everything is blurry. For a moment I can't remember who I am, or where I am, or what that noise is.

The first thing that comes back is Clara. It's a happy memory of us in my bed while the Choosing festival goes on in the city down below.

It's a comfortable feeling. Like sitting in front of a fire on a frigid night.

But then all the other things that have happened since that day come flooding back.

Father's dead. Mother's in a cult. Clara... *oh, Clara*. My eyes are closed but I squeeze them tighter, trying to make it all go away. I don't want to wake up. I don't want to feel the loss. I don't want this to be real.

But it doesn't end with Clara. The Looking Glass, the secret stairwells, the message from my father.

And Jasina.

This is what makes me open my eyes again. *Her*. Because she's still here.

I sit up, swing my feet over the side of the couch, and

spend a few seconds rubbing my fingers against my temples. But that hum is still there and it's annoying. I stand up—shirt untucked, pants open—and pull myself together as I walk over to the massive windows and peer down.

The hum is a chant and the chant is coming from a riot of people down on the God's Tower stage. They have gathered in the very spot where Clara Birch was kissing a man who is not me inside a ball of spark last night.

Last night they were celebrating. So what the hell happened to transform this crowd into a riot?

I turn away from the window—I couldn't be more uninterested in the complaints of the common person of Tau City right now if I tried. Whatever they are angry about, they definitely didn't send the woman they love into the tower. Their father didn't leave a secret message, only to be murdered for it. When did that happen, I wonder? When did he make that message? A day before he died? Hours? Minutes?

It was recent, that's all I know. It set something off. Not the countdown, either. Something more than that. Everything started changing around here the moment he died. I *felt* it.

It was very hard for me to concentrate on details of the message while it was playing so I don't feel like I got the full significance of what he was saying.

Which should panic me, but Jasina was taking notes.

This is when I turn and find that she is not here.

"Jasina?" I wait, listening. Maybe she went downstairs? "Jasina?" I say it louder.

Nothing.

So I walk over to the stairs and peer down. "Mitch! Are you here?" He should be. All week he's been here before breakfast.

But I don't smell breakfast. "Is anyone here!" I shout it as loud as I can.

No one answers.

They must all be at the riot.

Blowing out a frustrated breath, I turn. And this is when I see that the hidden door leading to the Tower District is open a crack.

I quickly cross the room, open it all the way up, and look down.

It's dark. And when I step in, no lights come on.

"Jasina," I mutter. She went to the tower. She left me. "Oh, shit!" I say this right out loud, then rush over to the Looking Glass room, go inside, close the door, and when the triangles light up all around me, I read the countdown that's circling the room in bright, blinking blue numbers.

One hour, three minutes, thirty-two seconds.

One hour?

How long was I sleeping? Which is a rhetorical question because all one has to do is count backwards to figure that out.

Better question is... when did Jasina leave?

And why? I mean, we had the whole 'teamwork' thing going last night. Not to mention the hot sex. Did she really leave me here to die? Or might she have gone exploring and gotten herself in trouble?

Could go either way, I suppose. And it doesn't really matter. This tower *is* going to explode and if I'm still in it, so am I. I go over to the desk, grab a torch light out of the drawer, and then walk through the bookcase, closing it behind me.

I know it's going to be a long climb down because, clearly, I'm at the top of the tower, so I force myself to try and remember the basics of my father's message as I descend.

There were two parts to it and the first part was my mission. Get out of here, which I am in the process of doing so... check. Then destroy the Extraction Tower, which he initiated for me with the countdown so... check. And lastly, find the train underneath the Tower District, get on one, and do this all over again in the next city down the line.

A train that leads to another city.

This part of the message tripped me up for a good two minutes while I was listening to my father, so I missed most the details. But in my defense... *trains that work? And can take me to the next city?*

These things should not exist.

I'm about to get lost in my thoughts about all that once again, but then I remember the second part of his message.

"You might see things down there, Finn. Ignore it. Do not interfere with anything that is happening below the Tower District. Just get on the train, take it down the line, and cut all ties with the gods by destroying their Looking Glass in the Extraction Tower."

And then he said something so shocking I completely missed everything that came after. Because he said, *"Do not, under any circumstances, talk to your mother."*

My mother?

"She's the enemy."

I'm ready to dismiss this last comment as absurd, but I can't. Because she's one of them. She's one of those culty Matrons. And the last time we spoke, she was walking away from me. Not just... like... moving to another building or whatever. Not just... going on a little retreat to pull herself together.

She was walking away from *me*.

Like I meant nothing to her.

Like I was a job.

And like, with the death of my father, that job was now over.

I stop my descent and stand in the dark stairwell dazed and confused. Shattered, maybe. With the realization that my life has been a lie.

Then something else hits me. An idea. An... explanation. An answer. One I wasn't particularly looking for, but which presents itself nonetheless.

The first thing my father started explaining was the opening of the god's tower doors. *"The Looking Glass controls the tower doors,"* he said. *"It opens them. But more importantly, it communicates with the god's world, Finn. Without the Looking Glass, there is no connection."*

Which was pretty clever, now that I think about it. He told me the important part first, but then distracted me with the part about the connection to another world.

Another *world*? I mean, in my defense, it's a life-altering thing to say. So it's no wonder I succumbed to his distraction.

But the real betrayal didn't come from my mother and

her allegiance to a cult of dried-up Spark Maidens. It came from him.

If the Looking Glass controls the tower doors and the Extraction Master controls the Looking Glass, this means... the Extraction Master *opens* the tower doors.

I lean on the metal railing, looking down at the darkness. My head spinning with the realization that my father is the one who called Clara into the tower.

He took her from me.

I don't know how, but he did. He rang the bells. He called her in. And now that I think about it, this is probably why he was murdered. I mean, he made the message. He set up the countdown for the Extraction Tower's destruction. But that's not all he did. He set up another countdown. One that would ring those bells and force Haryet and Clara to enter the tower.

And someone killed him for these things.

There's a part of me that understands that something bigger than me and my love for Clara is happening here. That my father was doing something important. That he didn't call Clara in for no reason.

But there's another part of me that doesn't care about why he did it.

I just want to hurt him the way he hurt me.

Which is dumb. Because he's dead.

So I force myself to straighten up and continue my descent.

There was a lot of other stuff in the message but this is all I can remember. Jasina took notes, though. She also took them with her when she left, so I need to find her. I need those notes.

I pause, because I'm at the bottom of the stairs now and there's a faint glow up ahead. I shine my torch at it and find a sign that says 'exit' in red letters.

But the tunnel splits here, right below this sign, leaving one uncertain as which way to go. Which is stupid and I spend a moment being annoyed because doesn't that defeat the whole fuckin' point of an exit sign?

Now I have to make a decision. And I'm not prepared because fuckin' Jasina has the notes. My father gave very explicit instructions on how to reach the trains, which is literally my only goal, and if she were with me, we could just look it up.

But *noooo*. She had to go exploring all by—

My internal complaining screeches to a halt when I spy something small on the ground to my left. I shine the torch on it as I walk over and pick it up.

It's Jasina's slipper.

Which is another thing. Silk slippers? For a job like this? We should've prepared a pack or something. At the very least, she really needed a different pair of shoes.

Then again, if she did have a more appropriate pair of shoes, one would not have fallen off her foot. Which means I would not have a clue as to which direction I should go.

And now I do.

I turn left, looking for more clues. Who knows, maybe she's leaving a trail of clothing behind so I can find her? Maybe when I do find her, she'll be naked and we'll have a little tryst—which would be pretty exciting considering the fact that we've got like forty minutes before this whole place blows up.

Kind of a fun way to end things, but then again, I'm annoyed.

This is when I hear chanting. And at first, I'm thinking this is the riot of people on the God's Tower stage because I figure I'm pretty close to being right underneath it.

But it's too loud for that. And the words are all… weird. They make no sense.

I turn the torch off, shove it in my suit coat pocket, and then creep forward, sticking close to the wall, so I can peer around it when I get to a corner.

I'm a hundred-percent committed to stealth when I do this, but I don't know what I'm looking at, so I have to step out to get a better look.

There are women—Matrons, all dressed up in that crazy outfit my mother was wearing the day of the funeral, but this time their faces are hidden by hoods—and they are in a giant circle, lined up along the perimeter of the room.

They're the ones chanting.

But there are a lot more people in here than just Matrons. It's filled with Little Sisters. Some of them are standing in their tunics and aprons, looking nervous. Some are even crying. But most of them, like a good fifty girls, are sprawled out on the floor, moaning and gasping for breath.

I'm not understanding what I'm seeing. Nothing makes sense. Why are they chanting? Why is no one helping these girls?

Then I look at the far side of the room and it all starts to make sense.

The first thing I see is a glass partition separating this room from another one. Then I see Gemna, strapped to a circle standing on end with arms and legs open. Then I see Jasina!

She's strapped to another circle. And a third girl—one I certainly met, but don't recall her name—is also attached to one of these circles.

I can tell they are screaming, or crying, or maybe just talking because their mouths are moving. Especially Gemna's. But I can't hear anything. And it's not because of the loud crackling of spark that is being pulled out of a Little Sister and directed towards... I pause to squint. Is that Donal Oslin? The Tower District governor's son?

I'm confused, but that doesn't matter.

Because the cautionary part of the message my father left for me suddenly comes back to me. *"You might see things down there, Finn. Ignore it. Do not interfere with anything that is happening below the Tower District. Just get on the train, take it down the line, and cut all ties with the gods by destroying their Looking Glass in the Extraction Tower."*

It feels like good advice.

I know Jasina has the notebook, but... I remember most of it. I don't need the notebook, not really. So I'm about to turn and take my father's advice.

But that's when I see my mother.

And again, my father's voice is in my head *"Do not, under any circumstances, talk to your mother."*

What the... I blink. Take a moment, even though my moments do not number in the many right now, and try and sort out what is actually happening.

I look up, see that the ceiling is painted like the night sky, and then it hits me.

It's a Looking Glass. Like the one upstairs. But then again, not like the one upstairs at all—for obvious reasons, of course. But the one thing that separates this Looking Glass from the one in the Extraction Tower is... its location.

I look around, trying to orient myself, and realize that we are probably directly underneath the god's tower doors.

As in the very doors that Clara, and all the other Spark Maidens before her, walked through.

I suddenly understand what they are doing. They are opening the god's tower doors. Not the ones above and outside, but right here in this room. Somehow, some way, this thick glass can be turned into a door. And then they are going to walk through.

What will they find on the other side of that door?

A god?

A new world?

Clara?

I'm looking right at my mother when she turns and suddenly, we lock eyes. She smiles. Her whole face brightening up, like she's happy to see me. Like she didn't join a cult and walk out. Like maybe I wasn't just a job that ended with my father's death.

"Finn! You're here! Come." She beckons me with open arms. "Come, my son. Join us as we begin anew."

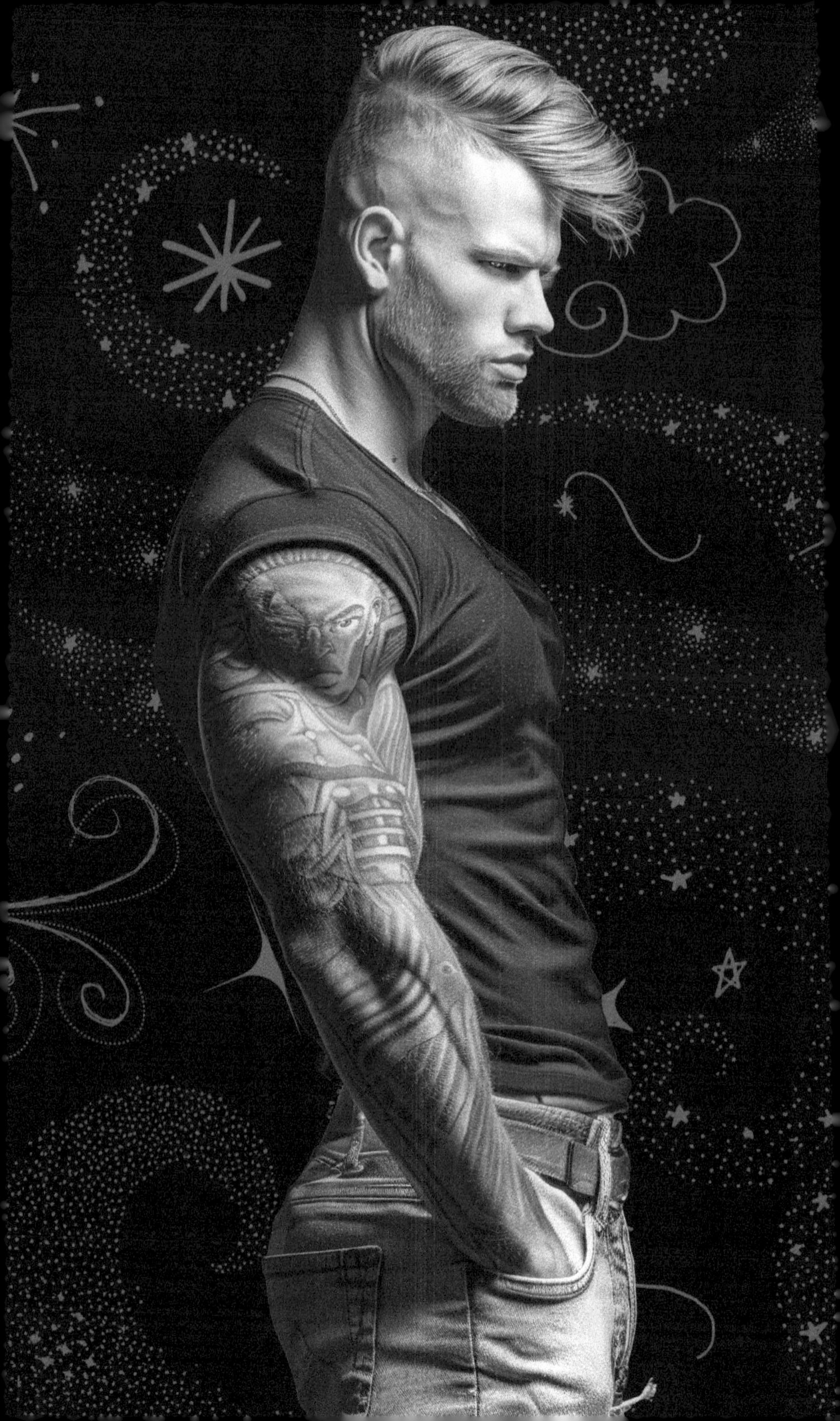

TYSE

CHAPTER FIFTY

"*It's where I fed.*"

These words come out of Anneeta's mouth and it's so honest and innocent, that it actually takes several seconds of silence before I am able to put it all together.

She *ate* them.

Literally ate them? Like… chewed them up and shit?

Or drained them of spark?

Not that one is better than that other in the grand scheme of things, but given the choice, I would prefer the latter.

It's Clara who finds her voice first. "You *ate* them?" I think she's mad. But Clara Birch has been trained somehow. Trained to be… polite, or something. Manners have been ingrained into this woman in a way I can't even relate to, so that's all she says. One question, three words, loaded to the hilt.

Anneeta is not going to answer. And if I were her, I wouldn't answer that question, either. There is no good way out of this, it's done. We are in the middle of running from the Tau City Patrol and we're not even close to safe.

So I decide to take control here. "Take us, Anneeta.

Clara, we can discuss this later, but right now we need to get the fuck out of this tower and onto that train. So whatever's in this room where we need to go, close your eyes and take my hand until we get through it."

Clara looks at me, squinting. Her gaze migrates over to Anneeta without breaking the squint and, in fact, she narrows her eyes down further until it becomes a glare.

Does she want to change her mind about feeding Anneeta spark so we can take her with us?

Maybe.

But it's too late now. Anneeta is the only way we get out.

So I say, "Please, Clara." And just as those words come out, the voice of Stayn echoes through the building. He's got some kind of megaphone, or something. A PA system, maybe. And he's talking to me.

"You're surrounded, Tyse. There's no way out. And we're not after you, you know that. We just want Anneeta and Clara Birch. If you hand them over, you're free to leave. Hell, you're free to stay if you want. This has nothing to do with you. It was a mistake that you got involved. And everything will be just fine if you hand them over."

"Are we going, or what?" I'm looking at Anneeta as she says these words and her mouth is an angry sneer. "If so, follow me."

She doesn't wait for me to make a decision. If I'm going to betray her, she's gettin' the hell out of here first. Clara and I look at each other. She shrugs. "If you want to—"

"Fuck off, Clara. I'm not turnin' ya in."

"I'm just saying—"

"If that's all you got to say, then say nothing. Let's go." I grab her by the hand and pull her along at a run, trying to catch up with Anneeta.

Anneeta is waiting on a landing in front of a door a couple floors below. She doesn't look too sure of herself, so her little attitude was a bluff.

But when I glance down at Clara Birch, she's smirking like a girl who hasn't got a care in the world. "What the hell are you smilin' about?"

She really is smiling. And it grows bigger now. "Just… even if it doesn't work, I want you to know… I appreciate the effort."

Which makes me smile too. "Hey. What can I say? I'm a fighter."

I get an even bigger smile—which actually comes with a blush. "Yeah. And trust me, I'm taking notes for later. When a man pledges to save me, it come with a reward regardless of whether or not he succeeds."

"Oh, my god," Anneeta moans. "Can you two save it for later, please?"

I pan a hand at the door. "Lead the way, ya little spark-sucker."

She pulls a face at the insult, but Anneeta doesn't say anything else. Just opens and leads the way into a dark hallway. The lights do not come on, but there's power in here. Indicator lights on unseen pieces of equipment let off enough glow to allow us to see shadows.

When a weird smell hits my nose, I understand why there are no lights. Anneeta's keeping the them off on purpose because she doesn't want Clara to see the remnants of her friends. Whether they are shriveled-up skin suits, decaying meat sacks, or just bones—Anneeta knows better than to divulge this dark part of her inhuman soul.

If she even has a soul. Which, according to some—most, actually—gods do not. Because they are made by man and not created with spark like the rest of us. That's why she has to feed. To fill up the empty spaces inside her that make Anneeta something... *other*.

And again, I can't help feeling the connection between her and I. I was born human, but I was made into something else. It's not the same, but it might as well be.

Clara is sniffing the air as we walk. She knows where we are. She's right in front of me, Anneeta leading us both, and I've got my hand on her shoulder, urging her forward around and past the dark shadows.

But suddenly, my augments come alive. It's so unexpected and such bad timing that I take a step back. Then, without warning, the overlay is everywhere and when I look, I see that Clara is standing a little bit apart from us with one hand raised in the air. It's lit up with cyan-blue symbols and there is spark leaking out of her like a trickle of water might leak out of a hose.

If a trickle of water could defy gravity, that is. Because her spark is aimed upward. And there's only one reason for this.

She wants to light up the room.

She wants to *see*.

"Clara..." But there's nothing Anneeta can say. Not at this point. So she doesn't get past Clara's name.

Clara, to her credit, is in complete control of her emotions. And once again, I see that training she's had. It goes far beyond politeness and manners. It's self-restraint, and composure, and discipline.

Any other woman—hell, even a man, probably—would be losing their shit right now if they were looking at the remnants of their friends on the floor and they didn't have her training.

Anneeta sighs. Then, unexpectedly, she gives up. "Forget it. You two go. I'm staying."

I'm ready for this. I'm all for it. So I'm not about to argue with her. I reach for the hand Clara's not holding up in the air, but she shakes me off and turns to face Anneeta.

I hold my breath, wondering what she's gonna say.

Anneeta looks up at her and then breaks. Starting to cry. Because what is there to say?

There are bodies on the floor in different stages of decomposition. There are bones. There is skin. There is some flesh.

Still, Clara hasn't decided what to say yet. She just stares at the hungry little god like she's running scenarios through her head the way I used to when I was in Sweep.

Hell, what do I know about Spark Maidens? Maybe they can run scenarios in their heads?

Clara sighs. Then looks over her shoulder at me. "One of them is missing. Haryet is missing."

"I told you!" Anneeta is overreacting. Like a child might. Which, of course, she is. So these words come out too loud and with too much emphasis. She's also sobbing. "I didn't see her! I didn't feed on her! *I'm not even hungry!*" She screams this last part.

Clara does not so much has flinch. She is the definition of

temperance. She takes one step towards Anneeta and points at her. The spark is still spilling out of Clara's finger, but it doesn't reach all the way to Anneeta. "I believe you." Clara's words are calm. Soothing, even. "We're never gonna talk about this again. But I'm making a rule right now. If you *ever*"—I can't see Clara narrowing her eyes, but I know she is—"*ever*—steal spark from someone, I will end you. I will fill you up with spark until you explode. I don't care if it happens next week, or next year, or next life time. You have a new rule, Anneeta the god of Tau City Tower Ruin. And your rule is you will never, ever again take someone's spark without permission. That's what *animals* do."

Anneeta recoils, gasping.

I might have things in common with her, but I don't know what kind of existential crises a little god might grapple with. If I had to guess, though, I'd imagine there'd be a lot of angst inside this girl about what she *is*. And more importantly, what she *isn't*.

"Do you understand me, Anneeta?"

Anneeta has been knocked so far off her high horse, she can't even speak. She just nods her head at Clara as tears stream down her frowning face.

The spark disappears from Clara's fingers, my overlay switches off, and we all let out a breath as the near-darkness surrounds us once again.

"Come on," I say, pushing past Clara and taking her hand at the same time. I saw the door when the spark lit the place up, so we're out of here. Anneeta follows, sniffling. Trying to get herself under control.

I pull the door open and suddenly I'm lit up with lasers.

The Versi comes out of the holster on instinct. Even before Stayn has a chance to say, "Drop your weapon!"

There isn't a chance in fuckin' hell I'll *ever* drop my weapon. And it's too late, anyway. Everything about how I use it is automatic and Stayn knows this. Because he *knows* what I am.

I think something, and the weapon reacts. It can even pick rounds. Flechette for moments when ya just wanna make a point. EMP for when the machines are comin' at ya. Time disruptors when the Omega dimension breaks through the veil. And lasers when you want a former friend to understand that if he targets you, you're gonna target him back.

"Hold your fire!" Stayn yells this. But their lasers still dance across my chest.

There is a connection between the Versi, and my arm, and my brain. A connection that was, up until last week, rather degraded. So much so that I had completely forgotten what it was like to be connected to the Versi in this way.

But a lot has changed in a week and let's just say, my memory has now been jogged.

There's a reason for the hair trigger that almost got me shot with flechette darts when Clara was waving the Versi around. It's because it's part of me. And sometimes—lots of times, actually, at least in the last seven years—it goes off without my permission. It could even be used by someone else.

But this connection I feel right now—it's like I'm

nineteen again. Like I'm in my prime. And this makes me smile.

Stayn recoils. Then starts his bargaining. "Tyse. Listen to me."

"I've got no intention of listening to you. Get out of our way."

He hesitates. Then looks over his shoulder, like he's trying to gauge what he should do next. I do not follow his gaze. I don't need to. The Versi knows everything happening in this hallway right now. It's practically alive at this point.

"OK." He puts up a hand. Lowers his weapon. "Targets off." The red lasers dancing across my chest blink out one at a time. "There. We're all calm here, right?"

"Some of us more than others. But I'm not fuckin' joking with you. We're leaving and you're gonna forget about us."

"Tyse." Stayn laughs. It's a nervous laugh. "That's not even possible. I mean... the woman." He nods his head to Clara. "She's... *ours*. We paid for her."

I don't react externally, but inside, there are all kinds of what-the-fucks running through my brain. Paid for her? What?

Then a memory of the party last night. *We weren't expecting another delivery for three more months.*

This is a transaction to Stayn. That's it. She's just... a *product*. Something bought and paid for.

"And Anneeta, Tyse." Stayn laughs again. Like this whole idea of me leaving with these girls is absurd. "She's our... she's our *god*. I know you figured that out. I know how smart you are. She can't even leave, Tyse. You're gonna kill her if you take her out of the tower."

"You don't own me!" It's a childish thing to say. But it's comin' out the mouth of a baby god, so entirely appropriate. "And you don't own Clara, either. She's *mine*."

It's a risky move, but up-city Clara Birch knows better than to take that bait. She waits it out like a pro.

Stayn ignores Anneeta, unconcerned about whatever powers she may have. "We grew her, Tyse. We've paid for all the spark. It's all factory direct, on the up and up. We've got all the paperwork—"

"She's not a product, Stayn. She's a…"

He laughs. "Don't you dare. Don't you *dare*. You, of all people, know better. You've been to the Outlands."

"And you haven't," I retort.

"But I've been briefed. You know there are… *things* out there that aren't right."

"Things like me, Stayn?" I stare right into his eyes. And I know mine are lightin' up because there's a spark of fear in him. "You as much said so last night, right? All operating augments have to be registered as non-human active warfare weapons. Sound familiar?"

"Well…" Stayn forces a chuckle. "Of course. But you're not operational, remember?"

This statement has two meanings. One. I am, of course, operational. So he's telling me that I do indeed need to be registered as a non-human active warfare weapon. But he's also saying that I could just agree with him. Say I'm not operational and he would look the other way.

Are most people really this spineless? That they would sell out so easily? With just the promise of safety?

Maybe they are. It's a sad thought. But I barely qualify as people, let alone most people, so it's not gonna play out that way with me.

When I don't say anything Stayn keeps going with his bargaining. "That little god belongs to Tau City. And how far do you think you'll get?" Anneeta whimpers when Stayn takes a step forward, but in the same moment a shield blast bursts out of the Versi as a warning. But it's a very serious warning because the acoustic pressure wave is strong enough to make Stayn stumble back six feet.

Stayn puts up his hands. "OK. Look, I'm not here to fight with you, Tyse. I know what you are, I know what you and that weapon can do, and you've got a very serious do-not-fuck-with-me face on right now. But listen. You don't have all the facts. There's a reason we need this god. The rules have changed, and if you leave here with her, you're gonna find that out real fuckin' fast. There's a war. The Game of Gods. Ever hear of it?"

I haven't, but I don't say nothing.

"It's a real thing. And every city needs a god if they want to play. And trust me when I say this, we don't have a choice. We play or we die. If you take her, you're sentencing everyone in Tau City to death. Death, Tyse. Millions of people for what? One god? You can keep the woman." He nods his head towards Clare. "We'll order another Spark Maiden when the time comes. We get them from a factory. They make hundreds of them every year. She's not even ripe. There are much better ones out there than her. We'll get ourselves a ripe one and in a few months we'll feed our little god, she'll level up like she's meant to, and it'll all be fine. So take the woman, but leave the god. That's all I'm asking. It's fair. You know it is."

I don't say anything. I'm still sortin' out this Game of Gods thing.

But the coolest thing about being an augment with a genetically assigned VersiStrike is that I have this luxury. I don't have to pay attention. I have time to think my way out of things.

Too bad for Stayn he takes my distant look as negligence.

Big mistake.

Because he comes at me, and in the same moment, the Versi lasers are targeting eighteen men in a wide arc, at the same time.

"One more step!" I warn him. "One more step, Stayn, and you're done. It won't even be up to me."

His lip curls up and his words come out as a growl. "Well... I think you're a fuckin' liar, Tyse. I think you're playing big. Acting like you're still in Sweep. But we both know you're washed up."

I sigh. Because he doesn't understand. And it's sad. I liked him. I did. But he's gonna get himself killed here right now and there won't be a damn thing I can do to stop it.

"One more step," I warn again.

And once again, he curls that lip like what I just said was nothin' but a dare.

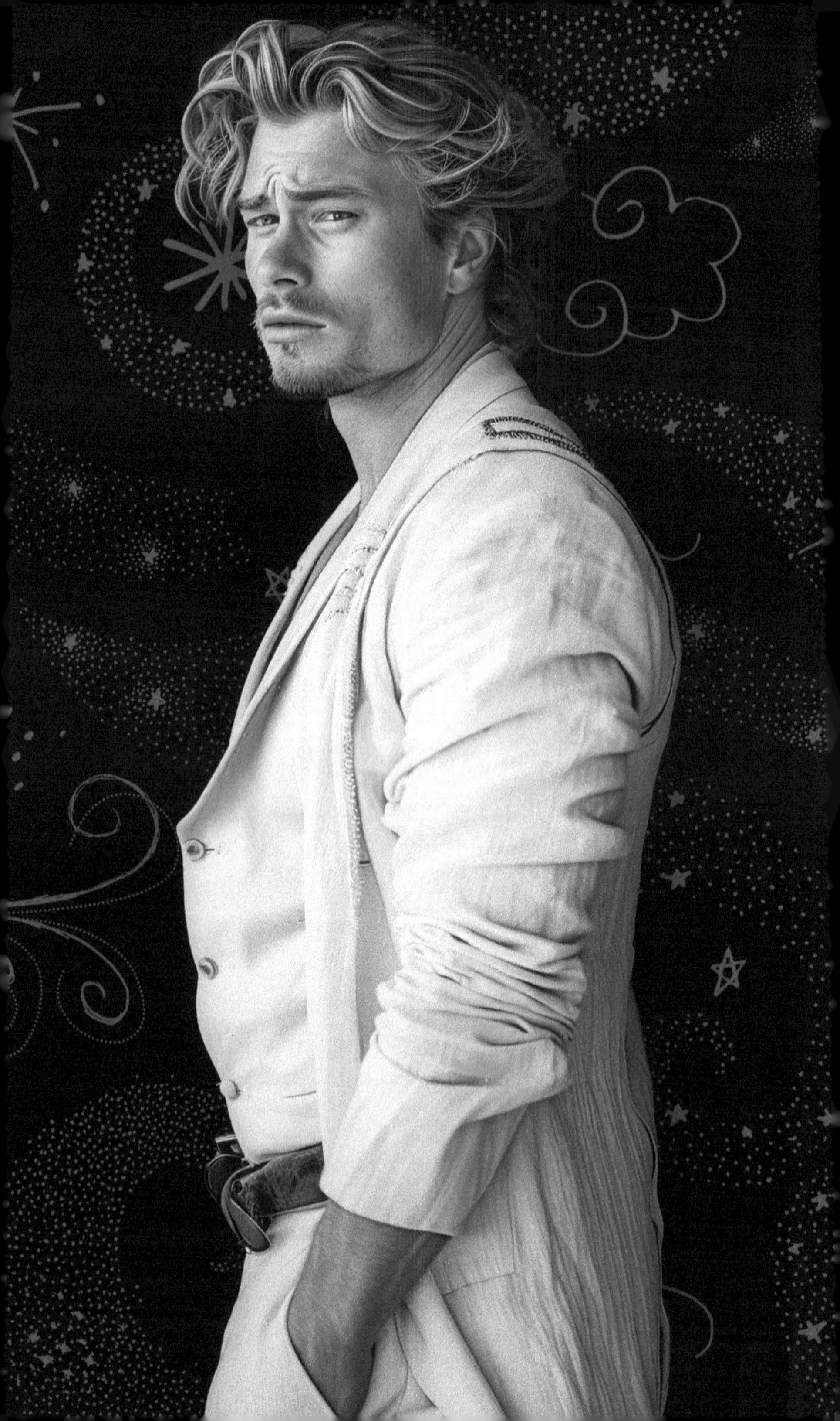

FINN

CHAPTER FIFTY-ONE

Join us as we begin anew?

"Finn?" My mother's smile is cautious as she comes towards me with arms extended. She takes my hands in hers. "You have questions, I'm sure."

The only response I have is a huff.

"I know this is all very unexpected. It's your father's fault."

Suddenly I have words. "How the hell do you figure that?" It comes out angry. Which is becoming a familiar feeling for me since my father died, but is completely at odds with who my mother thought I was.

So she hesitates. Reevaluates.

"He called them in, you know that right?" Her blue eyes are searching mine when she twists the knife in my back. Figuratively, of course. Though it doesn't feel at all figurative in my opinion. "He called them in, Finn. Both Haryet and Clara. He rang those bells. He made those tower doors open. He sent her through. He did this to you. And do you know why?"

I sigh. Because this isn't a surprise. I'm not shocked because I already figured it out.

If the Looking Glass controls the tower doors and the Extraction Master controls the Looking Glass, this means that the Extraction Master opens the tower doors.

"Do you?" My mother's tone is sharp when she asks me this.

"Do I know *why*?" I scoff as my eyes scan the room because... yeah. I actually *do* know why. Gemna, Jasina, and the other girl are chained and cuffed inside a circle made of some kind of metal. The Matrons are lined up along the perimeter. The Little Sisters are standing in line to feed a teenage boy who dreams of raping girls in hallways or have already passed out from the stealing of spark. "Of course I know why." I sneer these words at her. Because she thinks I'm stupid. Not only that, she thinks I'm disposable. "This is a door, *Mother*. One you can compel to open if you've got enough energy."

My mother leans in, smirking. But also whispering as she side-eyes the room. "Keep your voice down, son. We don't want to scare the Little Sisters. But you're right. I don't know if this is just a good guess or if your father left you some kind of message..."

"He did."

She lets out a breath. Stares at me for a few seconds, then again, she sighs. "So you know. You understand. The god is dying."

On a very basic level, this is accurate, I suppose. But it's also deceptive. I wish I could remember what my father said exactly, but I can't. I need Jasina's notes. So I say nothing. Which forces my mother to continue her deceit.

"There's more, Finn." My mother takes a breath. I don't recognize this woman standing in front of me in her ceremonial robes. She cannot be—is *not*—the same woman who baked me cookies and helped me do homework. "Because the real truth is, there is no god, Finn."

I reach up and scrub my hands down my face, pushing the heels of my hands into my eyes.

"There's no god, but," my mother continues, "they might as well be gods."

I pull my hands away from my face and look at her. Because I think this was the part of my father's message that I missed. Maybe she isn't lying? Maybe I'm wrong? Maybe the world isn't ending right now? "What do you mean, Mother?"

"They control us, Finn. They control everything. We're… *prisoners.*"

"Who?" I stare at her, mouth open.

"The gods who are not gods, of course."

I blink at her as some my father's words come back to me now. Workers, he said. Something about Workers.

"They control everything, Finn. Everything on the other side of those doors. We don't have a say in any of it, so yes. I guess they are gods in their own way. Because they have god-like powers over us, that's for sure. They need us, for now. But very soon, they won't. They are building something on the other side of those tower doors. They are making something. And if they succeed, and it looks like they have, then we will become obsolete. One more Extraction, if we're lucky, and then it's over. We are on the edge of dereliction. We will be abandoned. They will starve us and while it will feel slow and painful, it's really just a few months. They will come in, they will sweep us up, clean up the city, and shut it down. So we have no choice. We must enter that world through these doors, otherwise we all die. Which means… we need Gemna and the Little Sisters to get enough spark to complete this task."

I turn and look at the thick glass. At Jasina, who isn't paying any attention to me, but talking to Gemna or whoever that other girl is.

"It's your father's fault, Finn. It's entirely his fault that we are using up Little Sisters like this. If he had just… let us do it our way—"

I whirl back around. "Your way?" I scoff. Thoroughly disgusted. "If you had your way, Mother, it would be Clara up there in that circle next to Gemna. It would be Haryet as well. He sent them through the doors so you couldn't *have* them."

My mother's face softens and her eyes go… I dunno. Weepy, or something. Like she's sad. "It has to be done, my son. It must. If your father had agreed to our plan, he would still be alive today. And perhaps Haryet, and Clara, and Gemna would all survive the opening of the door? You don't know. And the reason you don't know, and Clara is now gone, is because your father was selfish."

Would still be alive today?

Did she really just say that?

I don't even have the ability to respond I'm so stunned.

She did it.

She murdered him.

Or, at the very least, she sanctioned it.

"Finn? Did you hear me?"

"Of course I fuckin' heard you, Mother! Just... give me a moment, OK?"

My mother puts up her hands and this gesture is obscenely ceremonial-looking because of the robes she's wearing. She takes several steps back. "We don't have much time, but of course, you must process."

I turn a little, not looking at anything in particular, just thinking. I picture myself as a small boy in our family home behind the Extraction Tower. Our cozy, brightly lit, neutrally decorated six-room house. I picture myself standing between my mother and father. My mother, smiling down at me with her pretty face and warm smile. Extending her hand to me, along with her invitation. *Come, Finn! Join us as we begin anew.*

My father standing opposite, his face stern like it was in the Looking Glass room. *Don't interfere with anything that is happening below the Tower District. Just get on the train, take it down the line, and cut all ties with the gods by doing what we discussed.*

I picture myself as a teenager taking Clara Birch to her gala in her second year of Pledge. Her favorite memory with me. Clara. Good, honest, loyal Clara. Poised, proper, and polite Clara.

I thought for sure she was dead. But then a miracle. I see her and that man she was kissing last night. Somewhere, through the Looking Glass, she is alive. I know this now. It's a fact, not a guess. And if I cross over, I could find her.

But as I'm thinking this, I turn a little more and my gaze

wanders to Jasina Bell on the other side of the massive glass wall. She's still talking. Not to me. I'm not even sure she knows I'm here. She's talking to Gemna, who, now that I look closer, I think is screaming. She's talking to the other girl, too.

Jasina. The girl who shows up with not just questions, but answers. The girl who takes notes. The girl who wants to make history. The girl with a plan.

She's got a plan.

I don't know what it is, but tying her to a circle that is clearly meant to drain the spark out of her in order to power a portal to another world isn't enough to make her give up. She is plotting something. She's always plotting something.

And she left me to die.

They all left me to die, actually. I'm not even supposed to be here. I'm sure they thought I'd sleep right through their secret ritual under the Tower District.

But that's neither here nor there.

Jasina is the one who matters now. She took my father's notes and left me to die.

In my sleep.

So she could... what? Take my job assignment? Did she really think she could just replace me in this whole scheme? *I'm* the Extraction Master, not her.

It's like... next-level balls. On someone who doesn't even have balls.

It's audacious. It's bold. It's... *brave*.

Stupid, as well. But there's something to be said for dodgy escape schemes.

And as I'm thinking all this, cyan-blue light begins to seep out of Jasina and Gemna. Gathering around them like a cyclone wind.

I turn to my mother and smile. "What do you need me to do?"

Her relief is so immediate, it comes out as a breath of air the color of spark.

I've never seen my mother display spark. It never even occurred to me that once upon a time, she was a Spark Maiden.

But of course she was.

She's the Extraction Matron.

And there is only one way to become a Matron. Ya gotta be a Maiden first.

"You don't have to do anything, my son." My mother lets out another breath, and again, it's spark. It swirls around in the air between us. Then she steps forward, making it disperse as she passes through it. I am fascinated as the little particles glitter in the air like stardust, but no one else seems to notice.

I want to look at Jasina one more time. But I can't. I can look only at my mother as she comes towards me and, once again, takes both my hands in hers.

They are cold. And it's weird. Because all my life I've felt only warmth from her.

"The Little Sisters are almost done." My mother turns, panning a hand at the short line of still-standing Little Sisters in front of Donal Oslin—who looks like he's been in the down-city taverns all day. He's drunk on the spark that he's stealing from the girls.

There are only five left. And he's taking the spark pretty fast because he finishes one in the few seconds that we're watching.

"One he's taken them all," my mother continues, "the glass will be primed and he'll power it up. And once that happens, the door will open and we will all walk through."

She lets out a breath of spark, but this time she pans her hands to the people waiting in a dark corner. The Council, of course. All the district Masters, including Donal's father. And the Matrons who are not directly involved in the stealing of spark.

But there's another face over there. One more staring back at me.

Mitch.

Not Jeyk, but Mitch.

He gives me a weak smile when my gaze meets his.

I turn away and find myself looking at Jasina, and Gemna, and the other girl behind the glass. Whatever Jasina's plan is, it's working. Because there is a firestorm of blue spark filling up the room beyond the glass.

Everyone must see it at the same time because the room suddenly erupts in a chaos of panic.

"Turn it off!" someone is yelling. "We're not ready! He's not ready!"

I think it's Donal's father. Indeed, Donal is not yet done with the last of his girls. There are still three waiting in line. I have an idea what this is about. But honestly, my understanding of the situation hardly matters.

Because Jasina Bell is here. And whatever she's planning

on the other side of that glass, it happens now. The blue spark coalescing between the two women builds to a dramatic climax and suddenly the Looking Glass explodes.

I laugh as I'm blown backwards and the ceiling falls down on top of me.

Because of course it explodes.

I would expect nothing less from the willful, redheaded girl filled with blue butterflies.

I LOSE TIME, I'm certain of it, because when I wake up there is nothing but sparkdust in the air. Glittering, beautiful, cyan-blue sparkdust all around me.

Everywhere I look there is broken glass. People are bleeding, and screaming, and running. The ceiling is creaking and croaking like it's about to completely collapse.

But I get up.

I don't know the plan. I don't give a fuck about the plan. I have one job here. Just one.

I cross the boundary that used to be made of thick glass, heading for the circular contraptions that are no longer there. And I should be worried. I should be panicking. I should be saving myself. I should be on that train and getting the fuck out of here because we're not done exploding things yet.

The Extraction Tower explosion is still very much on countdown.

But I'm not leaving. Because I know she's alive. And *this* is my one job.

To save Jasina the way I could never save Clara.

Jasina Bell or Clara Birch?

It's not even a fair contest.

Clara is my past.

Jasina is my future.

I FIND **Jasina Bell** buried under a pile of rubble. After removing some rocks and thick shards of glass, I find her pale, her whole body speckled blue with spark that seems to be attached to her in some way. Sometimes floating off her body like the butterflies on her dress, but more often it appears to be inside her. Glowing from within. But she's breathing, just like I knew she would be. And that's all that matters.

I look around and the next person I see is Gemna. She is alive as well. No one came to save her, but she didn't need saving. She got up and is now taking stock of the situation. Her dress is tattered, her face smudged with dirt, and like Jasina, the spark is all around her body. Much thicker. Deeper too, I think. Her skin looks translucent and her long blonde hair is wild and alive with static that makes her look like a beautiful monster.

She is *mad*.

I'm gathering Jasina up in my arms when Gemna and I lock eyes. Hers narrow. She hates me. I think she might want to kill me. "It's gonna blow," I say. "The Extraction Tower is rigged and it's gonna blow. If you want to save anyone, now is the time."

It's a little bit selfish, me redirecting her anger like this. Because I just want her to leave me alone so I can get Jasina the hell out of here. But I don't want Gemna to die. She's made it this far. I don't know what they were doing behind that glass. I don't know how they got themselves free and made it all explode. But I can take a good guess.

It was the spark.

If these up-city assholes can use it for their evil ends, why couldn't the Maidens control it even better?

Maybe that's why they had all those stupid Choosings, and galas, and parties? Maybe that's why they kept them in a tower and took the prime years of their lives? Maybe it was never about coin, or men, or celebrity?

Maybe they just wanted to make sure the Spark Maidens never had the opportunity to understand who and what they really are. Never had the opportunity to realize their full potential.

"Jeyk wasn't here." She says this over the clamor of injured and frightened people like we're just having a normal conversation.

"No. I didn't see him either."

Gemna nods, pressing her lips together like she's come

to some sort of conclusion. "He's not one of them." Then she lets out a breath, turns away, and starts walking across the rubble.

"Gemna!" I yell it. She doesn't turn, but she stops. "You heard me, right? It's gonna *blow*."

She side-eyes me from over her shoulder, a glint of cyan-blue spark in her eye. "Don't worry. I've got this." Then she starts walking again and disappears behind some rubble.

This is when reality catches up and the clamor all around me becomes panic. Fresh and filled with fear. People are crying, and wailing, and screaming.

But when I look around, I realize that most of them are Council members and Matrons. Privileged up-city assholes who were gonna leave this place, regardless of the damage they caused. And now they're not.

It's sickly satisfying.

Almost all the Little Sisters were passed out on the ground after being milked of spark. They were crushed by weaponized glass and falling debris. They never had a chance.

I don't care about the ones who lived. The Matrons and Council members can go fuck themselves.

I've got the only thing I care about.

"Hold on, Jasina. We're leaving now." I whisper this into her ear as I carry her back down the tunnel I came through earlier. There's a lot of rubble at first, but the spark explosion was localized and there is almost no damage ahead, so my pace quickens.

I pass by Jasina's slipper and have an urge to pick it up so

I can present it to her, like a gift, when she wakes up. But the ground begins to shake beneath my feet and I know I'm out of time.

So instead, I turn into the other tunnel that leads to the trains and I *run*.

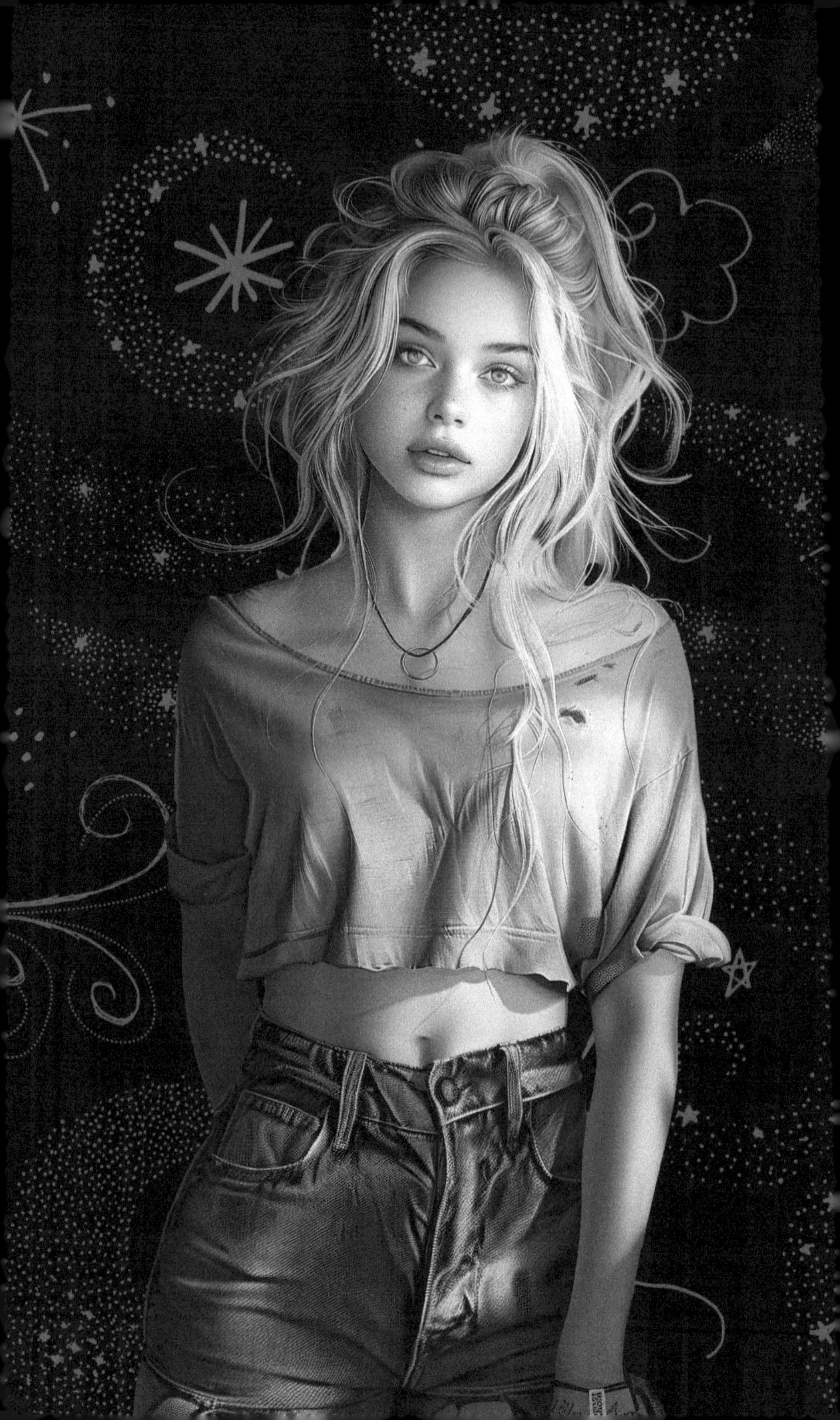

CLARA

CHAPTER FIFTY-TWO

"One more step, Stayn. I'm not fuckin' around." Tyse is in front of us, that weapon of his pointed at the men who are blocking our way out.

Anneeta reaches for my hand—an innocent gesture. But as soon as she makes contact, spark lights up my body, filling me up, and then the overlay comes alive all around us.

I'm looking right at Stayn when this happens and he's not surprised. At first, I think it's because he knows about it. He's got some kind of inside information.

But that's wrong. He just can't see it. It's just the three of us who can see it.

Suddenly, the overlay is reacting. To Stayn, or his men, or the weapons, or maybe it's just Tyse. I'm not sure.

All I know is there's a distortion in the air in front of Tyse and then everything in front of him is blown backwards. Like toy soldiers on the sand, they fall backwards. At the same time, a bright blue bubble forms around us. Protecting us from the barrage of fire coming from the enemy.

Everything goes quiet for a moment. But the moment

feels long. So I watch as Tyse turns in slow motion, his mouth opening, no words coming out, but I don't need the words.

Let's go!

Time speeds back up as he grabs my hand and Anneeta is still holding onto me, so we are pulled through the passageway by Tyse. Down some more stairs, through more hallways—and the whole time, the overlay is with us. The spark is with us. And I know we're gonna make it.

But as soon as those thoughts are out of my mouth, the ground begins to rumble and Anneeta begins to scream.

Tyse stops, picks her up, looks me in the eyes. "We're at the tower boundary. You've got to feed her now."

For a moment I can't think.

And we don't have a moment.

"Clara!" Tyse snaps at me. Not because he's angry, but because I'm shutting down and if he allows me to do that, everything, all of this, is for nothing. "Take her hand. And run!"

I do. I grab onto Anneeta's hand as Tyse begins to run down the passageway.

Anneeta, who was screaming just a moment before, settles and the screams turn into sobs. I can feel her taking the spark from me. It's a little bit repulsive and I have to control the urge to pull away.

We haven't even made it onto the train yet. There are fourteen more hours of this.

But I can't think about it. All I can do is give her what I have and run.

The ground is no longer rumbling now, it's sliding back

and forth. Shaking everything. We crash into the walls as they begin to crumble.

The overlay begins to react again, and that's when I see him.

Finn. Running up ahead of us. Carrying the redhead girl, Jasina Bell, in his arms.

"Keep going!" Tyse sees him too. I know he does.

But they're not here. They're *there*.

And we don't have time to worry about them or there.

Because something above us explodes, forcing the bubble of spark to form around us again, and all that's left is us and here.

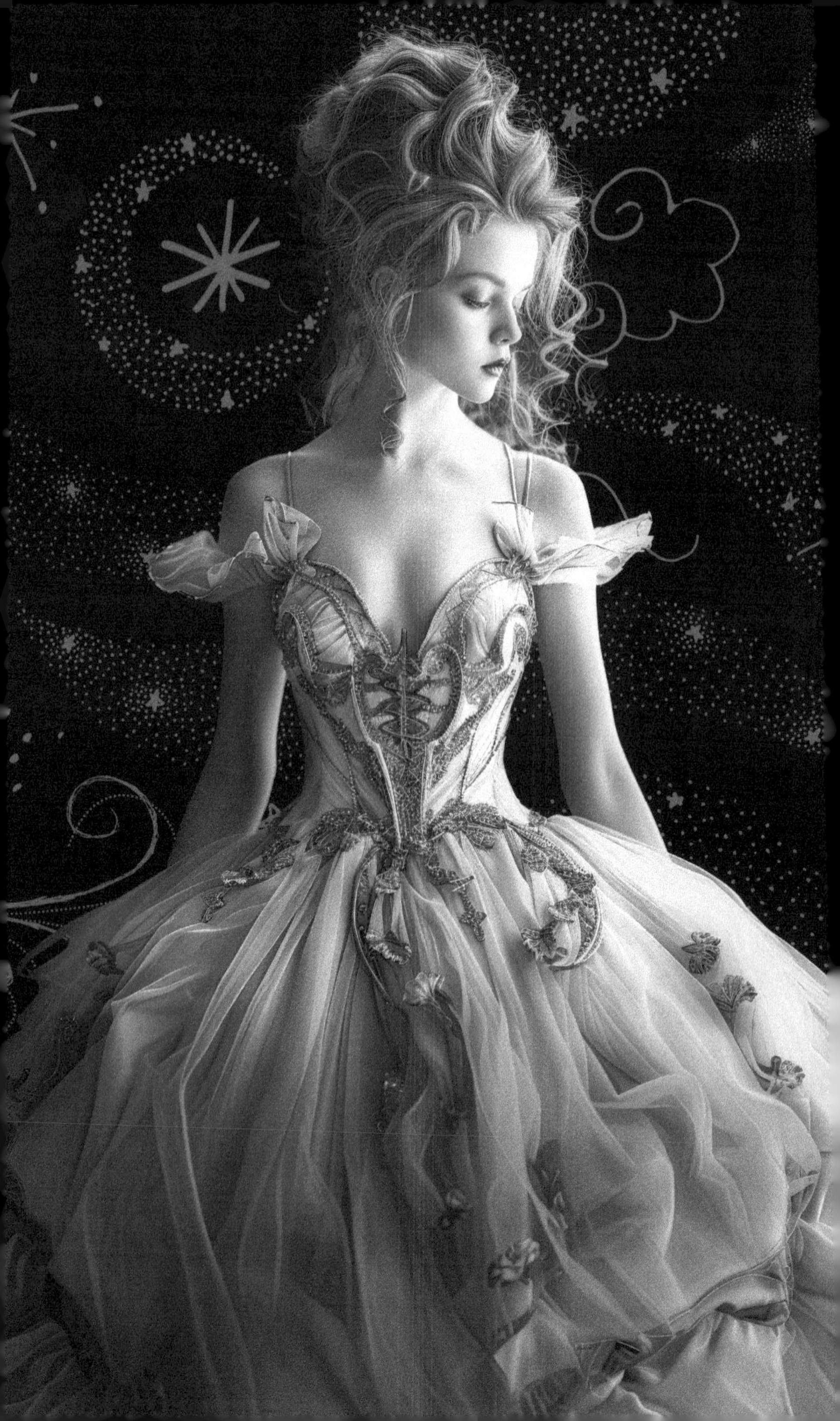

JASINA

Master, because his father never died. He's just an apprentice. And we wait, in love, while I serve the god in the tower as a Spark Maiden. I get rich, and marry him, and we have a family.

The Matrons never start a Rebellion to usurp the gods that live on the other side of the Looking Glass.

The Council never rounds up all the Little Sisters so Donal Oslin can eat their spark and open the door to another world.

Nothing explodes and there's no such thing as working trains.

We just... keep going. We go on like we always have.

Living, and laughing, and drinking coffee. Eating pastries, and walking on the sand, and having parties. We live in towers or in the cute, winding, canal-front neighborhoods behind them. We have children that we dote on and spoil.

They grow up. Our girls pledge. Then pledge again.

And it's *fine*.

One Maiden must die, that's all. Just one.

It's worth it because we get to grow old, we get to die, and it's OK because there's always someone coming up behind us to take the burdens we leave behind.

We live in ignorance and it is nothing but bliss.

"Jasina." Finn is whispering into my ear and for a moment I'm in bed with him. There's a festival down below. People celebrating because it's Choosing Day. And I have been Chosen. "Jasina? Can you hear me?"

But it's not me in bed with him. It's Clara.

She's the one he loves. She's the one in bed with him. She's the Spark Maiden. And he waits for her.

"Jasina? Can you get up?"

I let out a long sigh. Because what's the point? What's the point of any of this?

"I knew you'd be OK."

OK? I don't know what world he's living in right now, but I am not OK. Ceela is dead. She couldn't help us when I came up with the plan to overwhelm the system with spark. It killed Donal. And when I think about it—how his body went stiff and blue light started burning holes where his eyes were—it makes me happy.

"Come on, Jasina. We have to go."

I am pulled to my feet, eyes still closed, because I do not want to open them and see the truth. I've seen enough truth, thank you.

They're all dead.

All those Little Sisters. I mean, maybe one or two survived—but it wasn't Harlow, or Lucindy, or Britley, or Ceela. Ceela died when she didn't push out her spark with Gemna and I. We simply—burned her up. Not as badly as we burned Donal, but the last memory I have of Ceela is of her blackened body still strung up on that circle as the cyan-blue spark coming out of Gemna and me danced against the glass.

She was the first to die, actually. And even though we were falling apart at the end, I would not wish that death of hers on my worst enemy. Harlow, Lucindy, and Britley were in the middle of the line. So when Gemna and I broke the Looking Glass, they were already passed out on the floor.

They're probably still buried there now.

They might stay there forever.

"Jasina! Do you understand what happened? The Extraction Tower blew. We're done here. We need to go! For fuck's sake, pull yourself together!"

This is what makes me open my eyes. Rage courses through me like a disease in my blood and I look at Finn Scott straight on. He's a mess. His face has burns on it, and it's all smudged with dust and ash. His shirt and suit coat are in tatters.

And this startles the anger right out of me.

Then I look down at myself. Half a dress, one slipper, blood all over my legs.

But that's on the outside.

On the inside... on the inside I am... *butterflies*.

The spark dances under my skin as a shimmering, blue glow.

I look back at Finn feeling more like myself. And when he lets out a breath and smiles, I feel his relief so acutely, I'm conflicted. "You wanted *her*."

His smile drops. "What?"

"Clara. She's the one you want, not me."

He places his palms flat on my cheeks, staring at me intently. "Why the hell would I want *her*?"

"Why the hell wouldn't you? She was your life. I'm nothing but..." I don't wanna say it, because when I do, it all becomes real. But ignorance isn't really bliss. And anyway, it's time. "I'm nothing but a down-city whore. A sad, substandard replacement for the only woman you ever loved. I am nothing but... the fucking *Courtesan*."

He looks confused for a moment. Then he smiles. And then laughs. "You're crazy." He's still holding my face in his hands. "Clara was my worst failure. You, Jasina? You're the only damn thing I've ever done right. I didn't save Clara. I saved *you*. And as for you being the Courtesan, well... who wouldn't want to be the Courtesan?"

I huff. "She's a whore."

Finn scoffs. "She's not a whore."

"Well, she's not the Godslayer's wife."

"No." He shakes his head. "She's not. She's... she's his *choice*. Don't you get it? The wife is an obligation. The Courtesan is the true love. The woman he risks everything for. The woman who has his heart. And even though I never got the whole story, I'm like... absolutely fuckin' sure that the Courtesan takes notes. So when her man fucks up, and boy, he fucks up a lot, she can save him back."

"My notes!"

He pulls a notebook out of the waistband of his tattered pants and holds it up. "I saw this falling out of your dress while I was carrying you." Then he does a mock scoff. "I can't believe you left me to die."

I plant my hands on my hips, suddenly angry again. "You called me *Clara*."

"When?"

I make big eyes at him. "When? During sex."

"I didn't."

"You did."

"And that's why you left me to die?"

I tilt my chin up, ready for a fight. "Yes. That's why."

"Because I mixed you up with the woman I failed?"

"Are you trying to imply it was guilt? Because it's just... it's not gonna work."

"I'm sorry. OK? I'm sorry. I can't change that. But I promise, it was the last of her. I don't wanna find Clara, even though I think I could. If there's one door, there's another. I think that's the moral of this story. She's out there, kissing a man who isn't me—"

"So you *settled*. For me."

"I didn't settle. I chose you, Jasina. You and I spent our last night in Tau City together because I *chose* you. And I chose you because you were the one I trusted. Even though I could've confided in Mitch and I could've figured it all out so much quicker. And had I done that, I'd be in that other world right now and you'd probably be dead. Or worse, in the hands of an evil teenager who thinks he's a god. But it's more than that now. I *need* you. It's us against them. And there's nothing you can do that will change it. We're destiny, Jasina. You're my future and our love is destiny."

I don't know what to say about this declaration. And while the conflict is swirling up inside me like a turbulent river, Finn Scott uses my confusion as an opportunity to kiss me.

It's a long, slow kiss. And the whole time he's whispering, "I choose you. You're the only thing I've done right. We will not fail. Because we are the Godslayer and his Courtesan."

When he pulls away, I'm smiling. I look like shit, I feel like shit, and the spark inside me is doing shit I don't understand, but... I still smile.

Because maybe we are?

Maybe we're destiny?

And while I had imagined my name written up in a history book and not a child's fairy tale, it's still in print, right?

It feels like a win.

I allow Finn to lead me out of the rubble. This is when I notice we're in some kind of tunnel. There's even a train here. Of course, it's been crushed by rocks and debris from the Extraction Tower explosion, and doesn't look anything like how I imagined it. It's sleek, and white, and… very out of place.

But it's a train and we made it.

Finn stops to look at it, then turns to me. "Obviously this one no longer runs and we'll have to walk to the next station, but if you can't walk, Jasina, don't worry. I'll carry you."

And that's it, I guess.

He wins.

Because if I can't walk, he'll carry me.

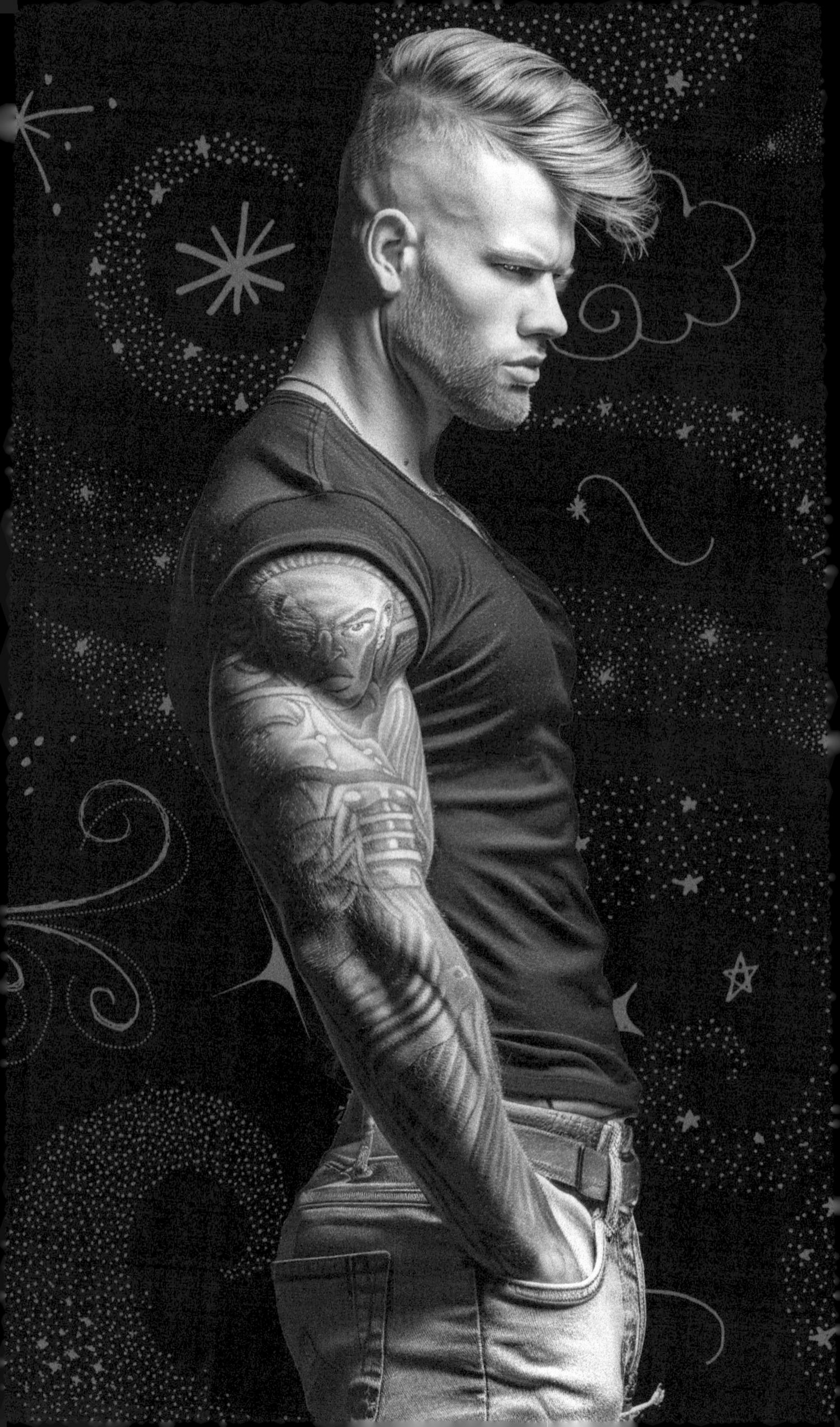

TYSE

CHAPTER FIFTY-FOUR

*B*eing inside the spark when the explosion happens is a trip, to say the least. It's like being inside a translucent blue bubble that repels anything and everything that comes hurling at us.

It's chaos.

But at the same time, it's poetry too. Because the overlay is on, and my augments are working, and inside the bubble, Anneeta isn't dying. She's just fine.

It doesn't last, though. None of us understand what we are or how we're connected. Which means we can't control this power we have. So naturally, it fades away and leaves a new reality behind.

A reality where I'm on the run from Tau City, I've kidnapped its god, and I've partnered up with a Spark Maiden straight out of a fairy tale to keep the god alive so we can deliver her to another god in a city that is nearly four thousand miles away.

It's something out of a fiction.

Whatever that explosion was, it has taken out the train station just north of the tower so we have to walk to the next stop. But there are at least fifteen stops before you even get out of Tau City, so it's only like half a mile.

I'm still carrying Anneeta, who passed out just a few minutes after we left the safety of the bubble. Clara stumbles along beside me. There is a large crowd up ahead when we approach the next station, so we stop and I help Clara put on her traditional desert robes and veil that Rodge packed for her. It's a good disguise. Mine as well. Though, of course, I don't have a veil. Just a head covering.

No one dresses like this in Delta City, but they do in other places so no one pays us much attention when we come up on the crowd. They ask us if we're OK, and we say a few words, then keep going. The trains aren't running here either, so we have to walk to the next station along the crowded pedestrian walkway that lines the tunnel.

By the time we get there, hand over our tickets, get settled in our compartment—first class, that was nice of Rodge—Clara can barely walk.

I've been carrying Anneeta this whole time, but Clara has been feeding her spark. Holding her hand as we walked. She's exhausted when she sits down on the leather bench in our compartment, too tired to even open her eyes.

I set Anneeta down next to her, then take off the pack with the jumps and pull one out. I've never done a jump, but the guys I got them from showed me how to use it. I know we brought these for Anneeta, but I give the first one to Clara instead. There's a sensor that fits under the tongue and when you activate the jump, it shocks you.

I empty the entire thing into her and the color starts to return to her face. It takes a few more minutes before her eyes open, but eventually they do open and she forces a smile. "We made it."

"We made it."

Of course, we haven't made it. The train hasn't even left the station yet. It's actually very late. The whole plan—fourteen hours—it's all bullshit because of that explosion. At first, I thought it was related to the VersiStrike because it used an acoustic weapon the last time it fired. But that explosion was huge. It wasn't my weapon. It was something else.

It was Finn. A little voice whispers that inside my head. *It was Finn.*

And it was. I saw him in the overlay. He was carrying a woman with red hair through a tunnel. And I think the explosion happened in that world, not ours.

Which is a troubling thought, to say the least. Is the veil that thin in Tau City?

Must be.

I feed Anneeta a jump too, just to see if she'll wake up like Clara did, but she doesn't. Doesn't even stir. But she doesn't look dead, either. Not that I know what a dead god looks like. I've got no clue.

So Clara just keeps feeding her spark, and I keep feeding Clara jumps, and the train finally gets on its way, and an hour later, we're speeding through the tunnel at top speed.

But I can count. I know how long it takes to get to Delta.

I know how many jumps I've fed them.

I know how many we've got left.

And it's not enough.

Eight hours in, I have to make a decision because Clara, even when I feed her jumps, is no longer conscious. She's gonna die if I let Anneeta take any more spark. And we only have one jump left.

It's hopeless.

So I have to choose.

Lose one?

Or lose both?

Anneeta is lying down on the bench, her face sweaty and red. I'm sitting next to the window and Clara is slumped against my chest. About an hour ago I made it so that Anneeta and Clara can no longer hold hands. I allowed Anneeta's head to come in contact with Clara's leg, but over the course of the hour I've repositioned them a dozen times, at least, so that the contact is as light as possible. Right now, it's just Anneeta's *hair* touching Clara.

It's not enough. But it's still too much. Any more contact than that, and Clara dies.

I give Clara the last jump because I've made my choice.

I'm going to save her, not the little god.

But an hour after that I give up and just look out the window, trying my best to come to terms with a world where neither Clara, nor Anneeta, are in it. Because we're all out of jumps and Delta City is still nearly five hours away.

The train is angling up now and it comes roaring out of the tunnel at full speed, running parallel to the sea. I haven't been back to Delta since I was fourteen and they took me away for augmentation.

On that trip I didn't get a private compartment on a high-speed train. I was packed into a Sweep cargo train, like all the other boys they were pickin' up around the world, and we sat shoulder to shoulder for seventeen hours. No windows at all.

But this is nice. And even though the two girls I was countin' on having a future with are unconscious next to me, I just stare at the scenery as it goes flashing by. The sea is so blue, the sky is so blue, and the sand is nothing like the sand out in the desert between cities. It's black, not tan. And I know from experience that it smells like fruit. Oranges, to be specific.

I think back on my childhood when we used to run these beaches and each time my foot would hit the sand that scent would float up into the air. We used to run, and run, and run—just for the fuck of it. Just so we could smell it.

Every kid in Delta knows why the sand smells like fruit. Tiny, microscopic crustaceans live in it. And when you step on the sand, you're just killing them. Millions at a time. The scent is just them dying. That scent is nothing but death.

I sit up, startled, when suddenly the overlay comes online. It's the familiar sweeping waterfall of symbols that I can no longer read.

Except it's different now. It's... slow. And I realize I *can* read it. It's spitting out information about the landscape rushing by. Data and figures scrolling down my field of vision. And something else, too.

Somewhere else, actually.

Because the veil has disappeared, at least through my eyes, and it's like being back in the Omega Outlands where I could see it all. Only more. Landscape over landscape over landscape. World under world under world.

I turn, checking on Clara and Anneeta, because this is a good sign. If the overlay is working, then they're helping me.

But they're not. Anneeta is still red-cheeked and sweaty. Clara is still slumped against me, unconscious.

The only thing that's different now is that my overlay is inside the compartment too. There are people in here with us. Two men and three women, one of whom is a teenage girl. They are talking, and laughing, and they are made of spark.

The overlay is stealing their spark. It's coming out of them like…

I stand up, jostling Clara, walking right through one of the men. I know this phenomenon, but I have to search my memory for the right word because it was not something I ever learned to use as an augment.

It's *plasma*.

There are lines of plasma bursting off their bodies. It stretches, crackling and snapping, like tendrils reaching out for me. They touch my body, and it doesn't feel like anything. Not even a little bit of wind. But it makes me glow under the canopy of the overlay.

I just look at my hands, all lit up blue, and I know what to do with it.

I'm still not sure about Anneeta. I can't trust her. It makes me sad, but she's been lying. So I don't feed her. I just feed Clara. I sit back down, trying my best to ignore the ghosts of another dimension sharing the space with us, and I hold Clara in my arms, giving her life back one second at a time.

BY THE TIME *the train* starts the long slowdown that will take us into Delta City, Clara is mostly awake. I've been giving her constant spark for hours now, but it's just barely enough to keep her alive as Anneeta sucks it right back out.

The ghosts in the compartment with us are sprawled out on the benches and on the floor. Tongues rolling out, faces red with fever. So much sweat dripping off their bodies, their clothes are soaked. They're not dead yet, but they will be soon.

And I feel terrible about it, I do.

But it's us or them. And they are no one to me.

So I just close my eyes, and pretend they aren't there, and allow my heart to sync with Clara's as we pull into the station.

We're barely stopped for a minute before the Delta City

Patrol comes rushing in, pounding on our compartment door. They don't wait for me to get up and open it. I couldn't even if I wanted to because the ghosts are dead, the overlay is gone, the food is gone, and Clara is practically clawing at me for more in her delusional state of spark deprivation.

The patrol breaks down the door, comes in yelling all kinds of official things, and starts separating us. Pulling Clara off of me and picking up Anneeta.

I don't bother fighting. It's not even them doin' it.

It's the god called Delta.

Of course he knew we were coming.

Of course he knew we had a god with us.

And anyway, it's a relief.

Because I'm so exhausted, I doubt I could even draw my weapon.

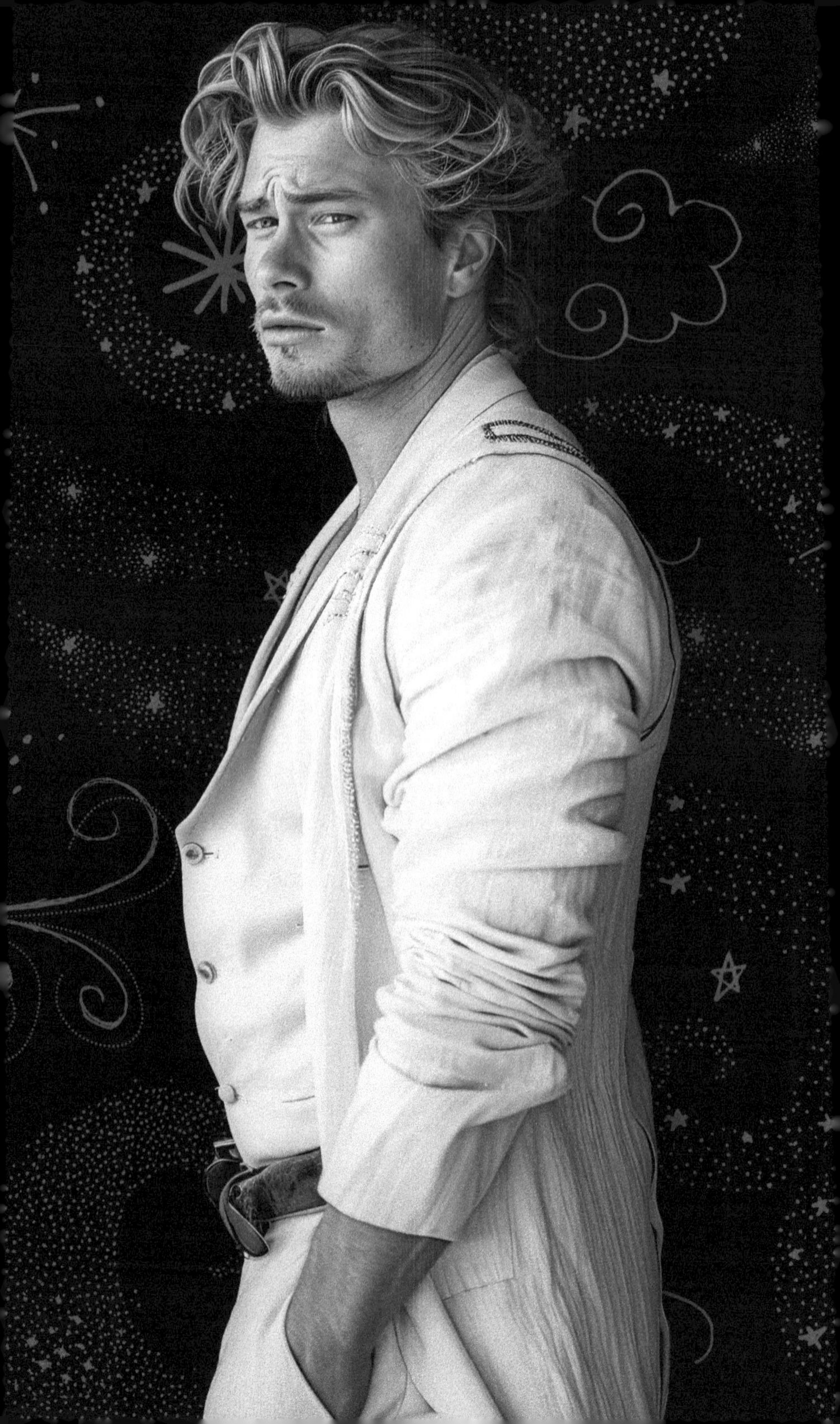

FINN

CHAPTER FIFTY-FIVE

There's no way to count days in the tunnels. It's just one long underground hole with barely enough light to see by. But we walk for a long time. I do carry Jasina some of the way. But when she gets too tired, or her feet get too sore—that one slipper of hers was more of a detriment than it was worth—we just stop and sleep. We're probably dying of thirst at this point, but after all we've been through, neither of us is willing to give up now.

So we walk. Stumbling, most of the time. Until finally, there is a bright light up ahead.

"Oh, my god!" Jasina turns to me, grabbing my shoulders, shaking me. "Is that—" She starts laughing and it's a mixture of relief, and hysterics, and disbelief that she suddenly can't control.

It *is* what we've been looking for. It's a station. It's a city. My father was right. There are more places in the world than Tau City and this quest we're on, it's real.

We've been in a pretty dark place for a lot of hours now and both of us were starting to think the whole thing was bullshit.

But it's not.

"Holy shit!" Jasina stops dead in her tracks, her feet bloody because she's been walking barefoot most of our journey. We tried tearing up pieces of her dress and wrapping her feet. When that disintegrated, we used my suit coat. Then my sleeves. I gave her my boots, but they were too big and her feet were already too torn up, so the pain wasn't worth it and she just went barefoot. She looks at me, smiling. "We made it. And look! They're just how your father described them."

Honestly, if she wasn't with me, and she didn't take those notes, I'd be freaking the fuck out right now. Because I have zero memory of my father describing the things we're looking at as we walk towards the bright light of the train station.

They are... *machines*. But they look like men. If men had white, gleaming bodies and no faces. They are Workers.

Do not bother with them. They are Workers. That's what Jasina wrote in the notebook. *They will not bother you. They cannot even see you. Just walk past them, follow the tunnel—you'll recognize it because you traveled through one just like it when you left Tau City—find the stairs that lead up to the Extraction Tower, enter the top floor of the Extraction Master's quarters, and, using your Extraction Master credentials, activate the self-destruct for the Looking Glass. Then leave the way you came, get on the next train, and go to the next city down the line.*

We start this process, walking right past the oblivious Workers.

But Jasina pauses just outside the door that leads to the tunnel beneath the Tower District so she can read a sign.

"Sigma Factory—Dimension 702." She looks at me, frowning. "What's *that* mean?"

It's pretty obvious what that means. But it's really hard to say it out loud. Still, it needs to be said. "It's… not a city. It's a… well, factory really is the only word that properly describes where we come from. They make you, Jasina. They make Spark Maidens. They produce you. You're a… a *product*. And I'm nothing but a Worker. Some other kind of Worker than these machine men that can't see us. It was fake, you see? A lie. Tau City was nothing but a lie. And so is this one." I look at the sign and read it. "Sigma City is just another Tau City. A factory that belongs to someone else. You, and all the girls with spark inside them, are something to be sold. That's why the bells ring. That's why the doors open. Someone *bought* you. And when you walk through the doors you leave this world and go to another one."

A world where Clara was kissing a man called an augment.

But I don't say that out loud.

There's a lot more to this story—a lot of questions we'll probably never get answers to—but I'd just be guessing and there's no point in continuing. We're not walking through the doors. We're here to do a job and we're damn well gonna do it.

Jasina doesn't argue, but she doesn't agree either. She just stares at those words. *Sigma Factory*.

If the Tau City station hadn't blown up, there would've been a sign there too. *Tau Factory—Dimension 702*. Maybe the train travels along some break in reality? A line so bright you cannot miss it?

No. A line so bright you cannot even see it.

But the facts are the facts.

We were... prisoners. Like my mother said. Except that's not quite the right word.

We were... *livestock*.

We were *pigs*.

I almost laugh here. No wonder the Council and Matrons were so horrified when I threw that insult at them after Clara walked through the doors.

But we're not a part of the factory anymore. Jasina's not a pig, she's the Godslayer's Courtesan. And we're gonna blow the whole thing up one Looking Glass at a time.

WHEN WE GET INSIDE, we set the self-destruct first, but it's got a ten-hour timer, just like the last one. So we loot the tower. We take water, and food, and boots, and packs while the Extraction Master and his family sleep. We don't wake them. We don't even warn them.

If this plan is going to work, there can only be one Extraction Master left at the end.

And that's me.

We don't stay for the explosion. We leave, heavy with plunder, enter the train with the Workers, and we rest, sitting on the floor in the back, drinking our water, and lacing our boots, and eating our food.

We feel it, though. The whole train shakes when the Looking Glass blows.

But it's a relief and soon after, we're curled up together on the floor, letting the rhythm of the train lull us to sleep so when we stop, we can get up and do it all again.

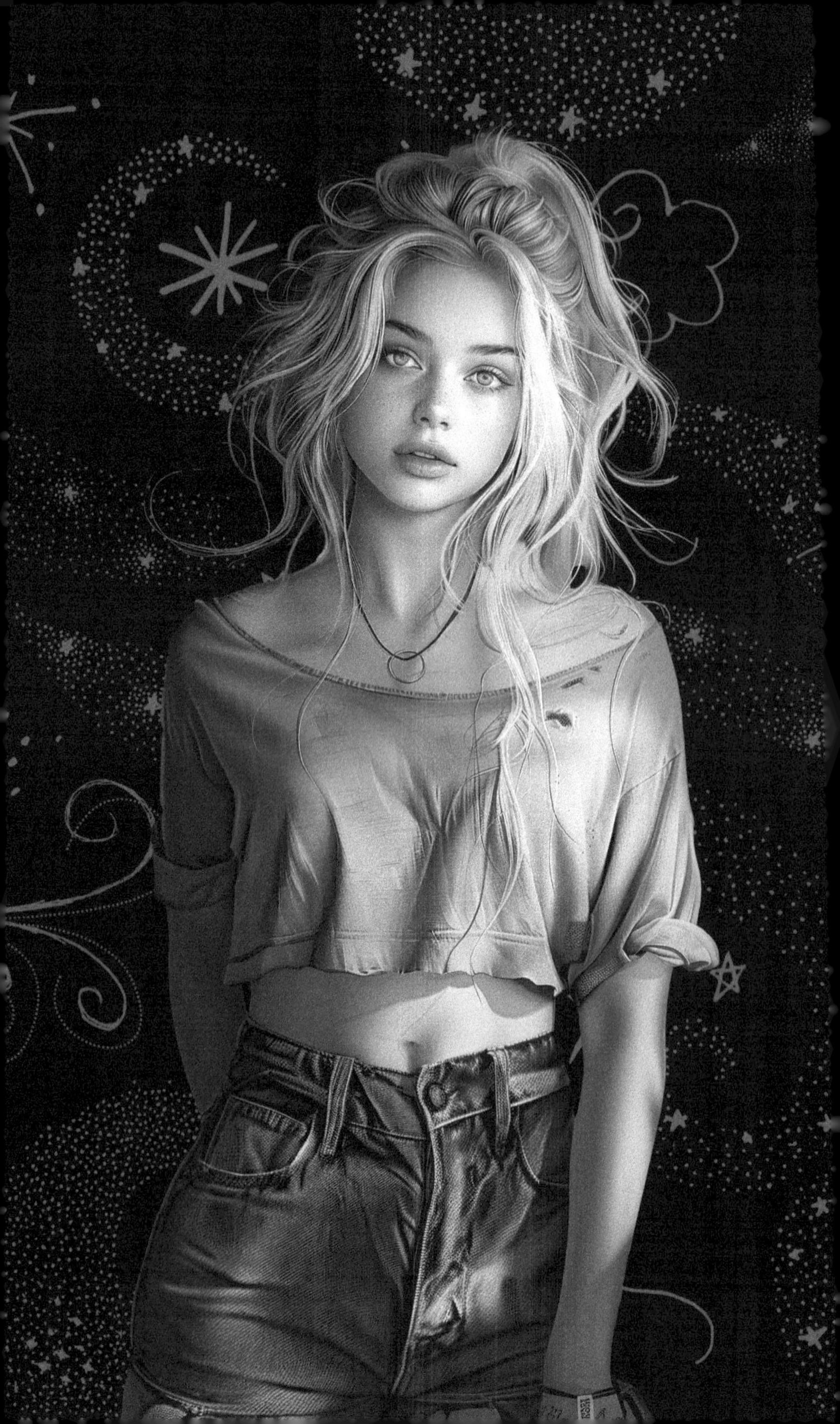

CLARA

CHAPTER FIFTY-SIX

I'm not awake, but I'm aware. That's the conclusion I came to as we were traveling towards Delta City. I knew I was feeding Anneeta and Tyse was feeding me. She was getting spark and I was getting jumps. But at some point, that ended.

At some point, *I* ended. And right now, I'm sitting in a… nothingness. An emptiness. Except everything is white.

"I died?"

The man kinda shrugs. "In a way. But like all things, it's relative."

I squint at him. "What do you mean?"

"We'll get there, don't worry. But you were saying…?"

"Was I saying something?"

"You were. It was about your friend, Haryet Chettle."

"Oh. Yes." I blow out a breath. "It's so frustrating these days. My mind is so scattered."

"It's normal."

"Who are you again?"

The man smiles at me. It's one of those indulgent smiles. Like he's answered this question a million times. "Delta."

"The god."

"Correct. Maybe we should start over again?" He doesn't sound mad. He doesn't even sound impatient. But I'm getting the feeling that he's tired. Like I'm wearing him out. "Do you know where you are, Clara?"

I'm opening my mouth to say no, because I actually don't. But then, in the next instant, it comes back to me. "I'm in the Delta City Health Center."

"That's right."

He's a nice-looking guy. For a god. Not that I have any idea what male gods look like—the only one I know is a child with a wildly whimsical sense of fashion. But he's easy to look at. In fact, he reminds me a little of Finn. Older. Late thirties, maybe early forties. But he wears his age well, if that's what it is. Age.

"Do you remember how you got here?"

"The train."

"But this building specifically? Do you remember that?"

His voice is so soothing, it kinda relaxes me. "I was taken from the train and brought here. But... we were talking about Haryet, right?"

Delta smiles at me. No teeth, just wide lips and bright eyes. "We were. Shall we pick it up then?"

"Yes. Because I saw her."

He leans in. And this leaning is *almost* imperceptible. But I catch it. "You saw her... where?"

"In my dream. It was... like the overlay thing that Tyse can do?"

"Tymothy?"

"Yes, I guess that's his real name, isn't it?"

"Real, like death, is also relative. I haven't spoken to him yet, so... he prefers Tyse now?"

"I would think? But don't quote me."

"So you saw your friend Haryet inside an augment's overlay. Do you think it was Tyse's overlay?"

"No."

"Why not?"

"Because he wasn't there. This was in that space of time on our way here when I was... dead?"

"Relative term." He swipes one hand through the air, dismissing my question. "So you have the abilities of an augment?"

"What? No, I don't think so."

"So, Clara. This is what I'm having trouble with. If you can't make an overlay, and you're positive this overlay you saw didn't belong to Tyse, then where did it come from?"

"We've had this conversation before, haven't we?"

"*Hundreds* of times."

"This isn't real, is it?"

"Real is—"

"Stop. It's not relative. You know what I'm talking about. We're inside my mind. *You* are in my mind."

"I'm sorry if this upsets you. It's merely a thing of convenience for me. Would you like to wake up now? We can talk about this another time. I don't think you have the answers I'm looking for anyway."

It's kind of a loaded question. Because, obviously, I do know more than I've said. I just can't figure out how to put it into words. And he knows this. That's why he sat through this interview hundreds of times. He wants what I know.

Implying that I don't have these answers prompts me to try harder.

"I had another dream. Back in Tyse's Tau City. I saw all the Extractions."

The god sneers out a laugh. "Is that what they call them? Extractions?"

"Yes. I mean, that what we called it. But…" This is when that final exchange between Stayn and Tyse comes back to me. "But we, the Spark Maidens, we were… ordered?"

Delta nods, but doesn't say anything.

"Like one might order a dress from the couturier?"

He nods again.

"That Tau City where we just came from, it placed an order for me to feed their little god. And there is paperwork proving that it's legitimate."

"This is all illegal, by the way. Here in the Alphas, we do not tolerate such things. There is spark here, of course. I make it. I don't eat it, Clara. I'm old. Thousands and thousands of years old. I came into being long before the Great Sweep even thought about destroying the world. There are a few others like me. But in the Omegas—and I know that Tau City doesn't consider itself to be part of the Outlands, but it is—in the Omegas they have turned your spark—*our* spark—into a commodity. Like apples, or wheat, or tin. The Tau City you came from shared a space with the Tau City Tyse came from. It's not the past, it's not the future, it's the present but along another dimension. There are many worlds like this. Tyse, as an augment, can see these worlds. Here, not so much. The veil is not thin. But out there, in the Outlands, and when he's working properly, he's like a…"

"A Looking Glass."

Delta points at me. "Precisely. But the reason I'm telling you all this is because you, as a Spark Maiden from the illegal Tau Factory in Dimension 702, you cannot see through worlds. You are not a Looking Glass. You are just a power source."

"So when I saw Haryet, and the other Extractions, it wasn't real?"

"And we're back to this. Real is relative. So, while I would love to dismiss this as a stupid, pointless dream, I cannot, Clara. Because I fear you are much more than you realize."

"Much more than what?"

"Much more than a *battery*." These last words come out with the most frustration he's showed me so far. Though still, they are calm. "Which is why"—he stands up—"I'm glad you're here."

"Wait. You're just gonna dismiss me? What about my answers?"

"Maybe they'll come to you, maybe they won't. In the meantime, enjoy your stay."

Three things happen at the same time.

He disappears.

Everything goes black.

I open my eyes.

"Hey." Tyse is smiling down at me. "I thought you were waking up. How do you feel?"

I sit up and look around. It's not a bad room. Nothing

like the health center in Tyse's Tau City. In fact, the soft corners and neutral décor reminds me of home. I peek under the covers and find that I have been dressed in a loose linen gown, which causes a bit of longing.

"Clara?"

I nod. "Yeah. I'm good. I think." Then I smile, trying to push everything that came before out of my mind so I can just be... present. "We made it. Anneeta is OK?"

"She's fine. They've got her in a special housing unit. Apparently, I'm not the first augment to steal a god and bring her home."

I raise an eyebrow. "Well. That's..."

"Concerning?"

I laugh. "To say the least. Did your god... plan this?"

Tyse blows out a breath, sighing loudly as he looks out the window to my right. "Do you want to see the ocean? We've got black sand here. It smells like oranges when you step on it."

He's changing the subject. Which means he's pretty certain that Delta did plan this, but he doesn't want to talk about it.

And I don't want to talk about it either.

When a god tells you to enjoy your stay, well... it's probably a bad idea to disappoint him.

I get up and walk over to the window, smiling so big my cheeks start to hurt. "It's the most beautiful thing I've ever seen."

Delta City is something out of a dream. Kind of like the way my Tau City was. All the houses and buildings are white, which contrasts against the black sand, but it's not just the sand that's black, all the dirt is. Everywhere you look and you see ground, it's black.

And the ocean is cyan-blue, like the canals from home. A different, lighter color than the sky.

Tyse walks up behind me, slipping his hand around my waist like we've done this a million times already.

Like it's always been us. Like he's always been my happily ever after.

Like he's always been my dream.

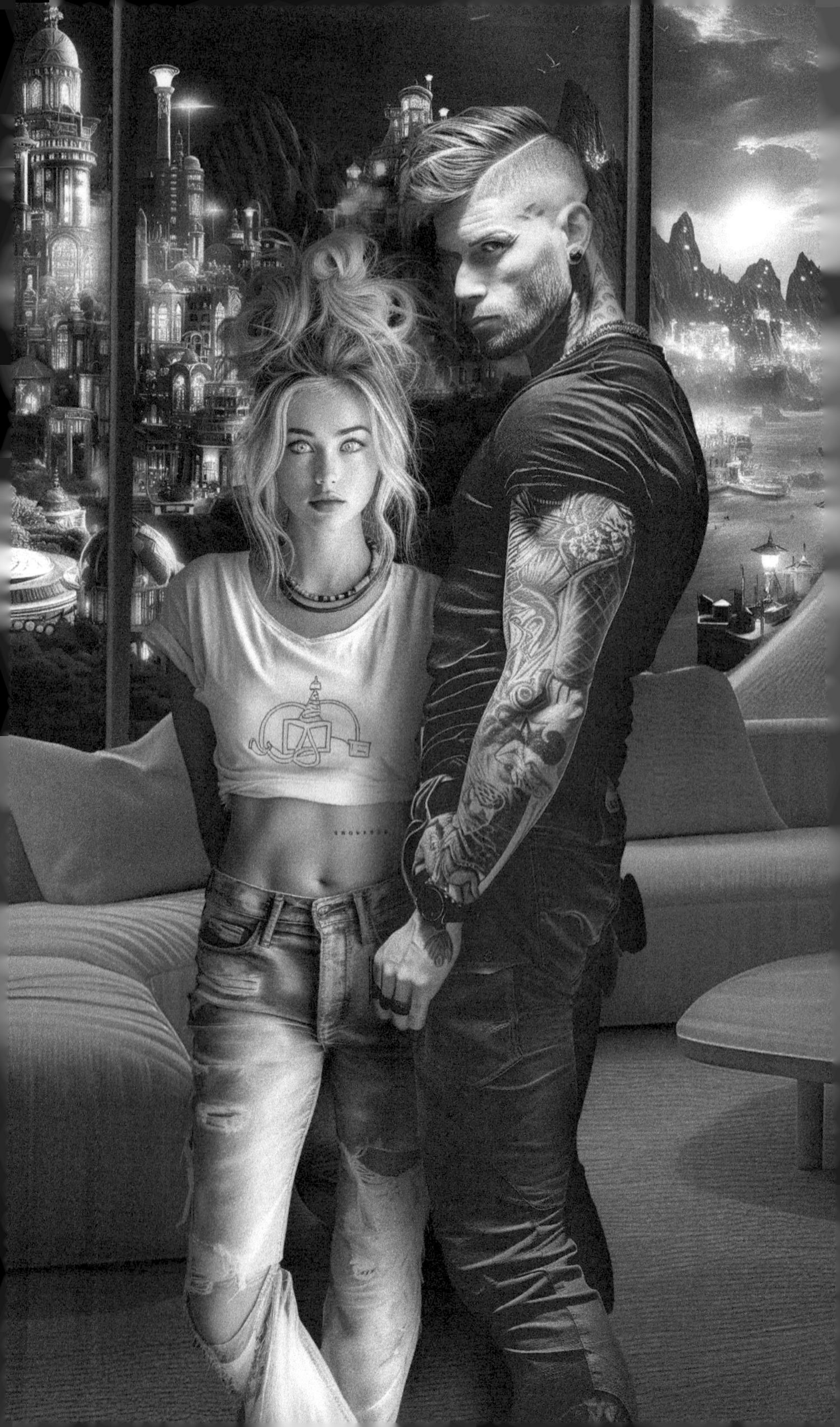

EPILOGUE

"This so-called Godslayer, as well as his Courtesan, are inarguably the most hated figures in all of human history. Their violence is repulsive. Their complete lack of regard for the inhabitants of other worlds is revolting. And though the history books do not yet reflect it, they will spend eternity burning in Hell for their actions. Mark my word on that."

—William Morton Smith, Department Chair, College of Historical Violence, Upsilon City

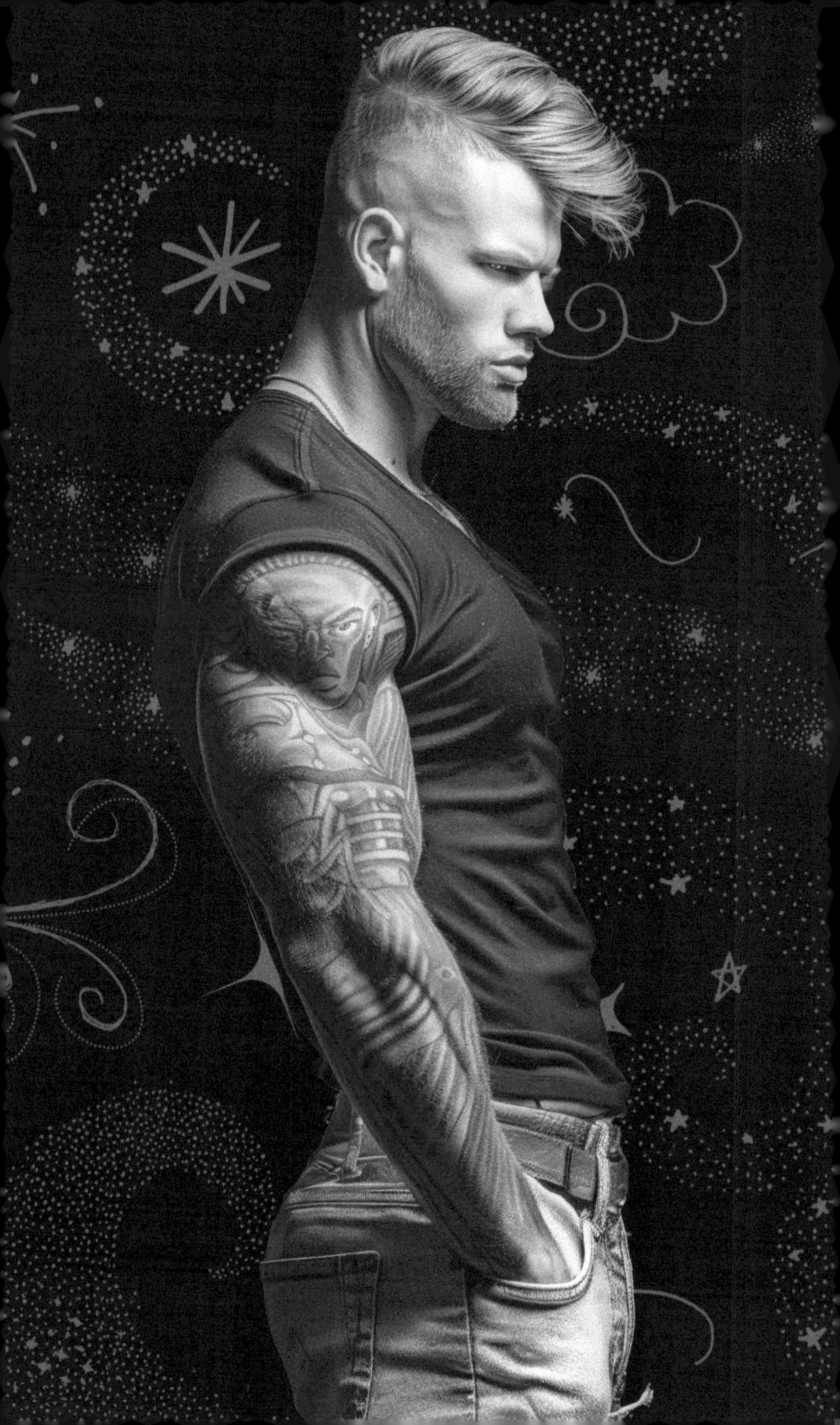

TYSE

TYSE

*I*t's been more than three weeks since Clara, Anneeta, and I arrived in Delta City and so far the god hasn't called me into the tower. It's off-putting, in a way, because I know he wants to talk to me. There's no way he doesn't want to talk to me. How many boys leave here every year to be augmented? Two? Maybe three. Certainly never more than three a year.

And how many of them come back?

I don't actually know the answer to that, but it's got to be a rare thing. Why would they come back? If they lived through deployment, they would be thirty-four years old once they earned their pensions. Twenty years. Why would anyone come back after twenty years?

Unless, of course, all Delta's augments are out there appropriating spark from across the veil, charming Spark Maidens into being their partners, and stealing baby gods.

Which might actually be a thing since Anneeta isn't Delta's only mini-sparkplug. He's got quite the collection of little gods in a school down on the beach.

There's definitely something going on here that I haven't been filled in on. But it's not bad being home. Clara and I have a nice place on the top floor of a building. It came furnished and it's a thousand times better than what we were living in back in the tower ruin.

Clara says it reminds her of home. And it's the same for me, obviously, since this place is literally my home.

I'm not exactly sure how the coin works here in Delta because I was a kid when I left and I didn't pay for anything back then. I didn't have parents, either. I was always in consideration for augmentation so as a child, I lived in a special home on the beach with other boys in the same situation.

Kinda like the school they have Anneeta in, now that I think about it.

I didn't earn any money as a kid. That I know of, anyway. I wasn't expected to pay for anything. And that's kind of the vibe I'm getting here now.

That I am... kept.

Which is a familiar feeling since I was in Sweep. I was kept there, too. Didn't pay for nothing. Not even when we went on leave. Both the whores and the booze were paid for with coin from the unit accounts.

So I'm not bothered about the money situation.

I'm bothered because Delta hasn't called for me yet and I was expecting to see him on day one.

My gaze scans the room of people and lands on Clara. She's talking to another woman who is about her age, so I get to stare at her unnoticed. There are a lot of pretty people here at this party. Clara started dragging me out for social engagements on day five. It's her thing. She likes people. She likes being around them, and talking to them, and showing off her body, and her hair, and her clothes.

And why not? If you've got it, flaunt it.

But she's still got that same self-possession she had back in Tau City. She's very polite and easy to talk to. Our first day out after fully recovering from the train ride in, she made three friends standing in line for coffee. It's like she was born to network.

She's got a phone now and there are twenty-seven contacts in it.

How do you make twenty-seven friends in a new city in just three weeks?

I've got a new phone too and Clara is the only number in there. I don't even have Anneeta's number yet. But this woman, she's got twenty-seven new friends.

The funny thing is, it's got nothing to do with the people or the city. It's just who she is. And these people *like* her. They don't tolerate her. They don't see her as the new shiny thing they need to get in on. They like her.

Clara finally feels my gaze and when those spark-colored eyes of hers meet mine, she smiles. She doesn't display, though. It's weird. Even though the air in Delta is filled with spark, she's in control of it now. Like somewhere along the way she mastered the subtle art of spark-witching without even joining a cult, or whatever.

There's so much spark in the air here in Delta City, even I can see it. I don't even need the overlays anymore. I just concentrate a little and kinda feel for it, and then... there it is. Floating all around me. Like I'm standing in a whole sea of spark.

People walk through it like they don't even know it's there.

I haven't asked anyone yet, but I'm pretty sure they *don't* know it's there.

It's like a secret world just under the one we live in.

My augments have come back online, little by little, ever since the train came roaring out of that tunnel and at three weeks out, I'm fully functional. Like I'm nineteen again. Which is crazy, because even if I didn't lose my capabilities ten years ago, at thirty years old I'd still be nearing operational termination.

Nothing lasts forever, after all.

Except me, apparently. I seem to get better with age.

This makes me smile and I hold up my glass of champagne to Clara. She holds hers up back, duplicating the gesture from across the room, then turns back to her friends so she doesn't come off as rude.

She's such a fuckin' kitten.

"Excuse me, are you Captain Tymothy Jarvinen?"

I turn, annoyed, and look at the man who's askin'. "I might be. Why?"

"The god would like to meet with you."

"Hmm. Tonight, of all nights?"

The messenger just shrugs. He's got no idea of the subtleties playing out here. He doesn't care, either. "Who can explain the whims of gods."

I feel like this is his standard answer. Something he has learned to say without even thinking. So I just let it go, down my champagne, set the glass down, and invite him to lead the way with a wave of my hand.

He leads and as I follow, I text Clara and let her know I'll come back to walk her home once my meeting is over.

She sends me a kissing smiley face as a response. A month ago, she didn't even know emojis existed. Today, she sends me text kisses.

Life, man. It's a fuckin' trip.

IT HAS BEEN **sixteen years** since I last took this walk to the God's Tower at the edge of Delta City and it just now occurs to me that I've lived away from him two years longer than I lived with him.

I got augmented. I got deployed. I worked in Sweep. I saw between worlds. I killed people. I saved people. I got kicked out. Brand-new name that came with a pension and a brand-new life.

And still, I'm back here. Right where I started.

Did your god plan this?

Of course he did. Was it from birth? Dunno. But there's no way that the set of circumstances that put me through all those things lands me right back here without some kind of divine intervention.

Did Delta get me accepted for augmentation?

Certainly. Yes. There's no way I'd be one of the chosen if my god wasn't on board. So that's a given.

But did he kill my career just when it was taking off?

Did he infect my unit so I was forced to kill them?

Did he feed me secret information so I could use it against Sweep command and demand a new name and a pension after I was discharged?

This one feels like it should also be an obvious yes. I mean, it shouldn't have happened that way. I was court-martialed and found guilty. Dishonorably discharged with the fuckin' spectra to prove it.

So, maybe it wasn't Delta. But it *was* someone, that's for sure.

There's a war, Tyse. The Game of Gods. Ever hear of it?

No. I hadn't heard of it actually. When Stayn said those words to me I had no idea what he was talking about.

Of course, three weeks on and maybe I don't understand much, but I think I might be in this game.

MY GOD LIVES on the top floor of his tower. The rest of it is empty, as far as I can tell. I mean, I've never been given a map or anything, but once you enter it's very clear that this building is really nothing but empty space.

It's just a hollow shell that contains one thing—a massive, winding staircase that leads to the top. The messenger leaves me at the front door, closing it behind me as I enter.

I look up, trying to see the top. Already tired and the climb hasn't even started yet.

But this is what I wanted. This is what I've been waiting for. So I start the journey.

I go slow because pacing is everything. And while I had been living on the tenth floor of another god's tower, and I did carry Clara up a million flights of stairs when I saved her, the trip out of Tau City was draining, to say the least, and I just don't have the stamina I did the day I left.

Eventually though, I do make it to the top. I take each step very slow on that last bit of the ascent because there is a lot going on up here and I'm trying to listen in before I make my appearance.

When I arrive at the little stairwell foyer at the top the first thing I see is the tea spread. Silver trays holding tiny sandwiches, several tea pots with steam pouring out the spouts, and a whole set of matching china. There's even a bouquet of flowers in the center of the fuckin' table.

Of course, I do not partake. I walk right past it, but then stop short just outside the entrance to the god's room because I realize I'm listening to a meeting of people. Many people because there are at least half a dozen different voices.

I catch a few words, but it's not anything dramatic. More like backstage minutiae of city politics. When I finally step out of the little stairwell foyer, the first thing I see is the overlay.

Except it's not my overlay. It's Delta's.

There are nine people up here, except they're not people. Well, maybe they are. But in this tower, they're holograms. The overlay is conducting a meeting. I've only ever seen something like this a handful of times while I was in Sweep. And it was mostly just walking past glass-walled offices while in random administration buildings. I've never actually been inside one.

For a moment I'm not sure what to do. Wait here? Announce myself? Leave?

But then Delta looks at me and steps aside—splitting himself in two.

The other eight... gods, because let's face it, that's what they are—they don't seem to notice that my god has left the meeting. But that's because he hasn't. He's talking to them in his other body even as he's walking towards me, extending his hand in greeting. And as he does this, he stops being a spark hologram and turns into flesh and blood, wearing a cream-colored linen suit, nice leather shoes, and a smile that makes his spark-colored eyes brighten. His hair is slicked back, so I'm not sure if it's long or short, and he's got a ring on. I notice the ring because when I shake his hand, it's cold against my skin.

I've never actually interacted with him in human form like this and it's a little bit disconcerting. When I came up here as a kid—always because I was in trouble for... whatever—he was a giant face of code on the screen at the far edge of the room.

This human body was there, always, but it was sitting at a desk, its back to me, furiously writing things down in a book. Which feels like a really weird thing now that I'm a man, but as a kid, I didn't even care. I interacted with the code face. Which was like forty feet high and twenty feet wide, so it was very intimidating and standing in front of it as a five-foot-tall child didn't give me much time to look around and wonder about shit that didn't concern me.

"Captain Tymothy Jarvinen."

We finish shaking hands and so I withdraw mine before correcting him. "It's Tyse Saarinen now. I'd appreciate it if you'd let everyone know."

"Right." He smiles again. "Tyse." His eyes light up with spark. "Done. Tymothy is dead. All records erased and replaced."

I sigh. "Well." I sigh again. "Nice to see you, I guess."

"Oh, you're not here for a social call, *Tyse*. It's business. But come, let's get away from this boring meeting." He turns and starts walking away.

I take one more look at the gathering of gods made of light, then follow.

We end up in a room behind the massive, dark screen and it's kind of a relief when I enter and he closes the door behind me, making the many voices go away.

"Have a seat, Tyse." He gestures to a large cream-colored leather chair situated in front of a massive desk made of glass.

I sit and he takes his place behind the desk.

"How was your trip?"

"My trip in?"

"Trip out, trip in, either-or. Here and there. All of it. I want to hear everything."

I raise my eyebrows at him. "You want my life's story?"

"The highlights will do."

"Don't ya have that on record?" I tap my head to indicate his AI brain.

"Of course I do. But it's rude to assume things you haven't told me yet."

"How about we just cut the bullshit, Delta. Tell me what's going on."

"I always did like your directness. I knew you were the one. The moment you were born I pointed at you and said, 'He's the one.' And look. Here are you. The actual one."

"For fuck's sake. One what?"

"The Godslayer, of course."

I laugh. "The Godslayer? The storybook guy? From the fairy tale?"

"Oh, it's not a fairy tale. It's a myth. A prophetic one. Well, it was. And then you were born, and... well, here we are smack in the middle of it. But there are many versions of the prophecy. It's always like that, isn't it? I mean, in the world we live in, secrets are impossible. The key to secrecy these days is disinformation. Confusion, is a better way to say it. Many versions make many questions. Many questions make many answers. So that's my long-winded way of saying, yes, the storybook guy, with an asterisk at the end."

"OK." I'm not sure what to say to that. He just smiles at me, his hands folded on the desk, like he's waiting for me to say something else. "So... what the fuck do you want?"

His smile grows into a chuckle. "I have always admired your rebellious attitude, Tyse. What do I want? Well, I want you to kill some gods, obviously. It's completely out of control." He pans a hand to the door. "Hence, the meeting."

"I don't understand. Aren't you collecting gods?"

"Yes. And"—he puts a hand up, palm first, like he's warding off my next question—"don't worry. Anneeta is just fine. All the baby gods are. You see, if we get them early enough, it works out. The babies aren't the problem. It's the teenagers." He rolls his eyes. "Fucking teenagers. Am I right?"

I shrug. "Yeah. I guess. They're always a bunch of assholes."

"Exactly. So… yes. We need to kill them. And that's where you come in. You and your partner will be deployed."

I stand up. "*What?*"

"That Spark Maiden? Oh, she's lovely, Tyse. And the two of you? The way you worked together to save that shit-stain little spark plug? No offense, but Anneeta is…" He blows out a breath. "Quite a challenge. She had absolutely no supervision, did she?"

"Um. No. Not really."

"This is our problem. Anneeta will learn, I'm confident of this, and she will grow into a responsible god. Eventually. But there are so many of them out there now, Tyse. So many little shit-stain gods running around these towers. We can't have it. We simply can't have it. So the Alphas and I"—he nods his head to the door to indicate the other gods in the meeting outside—"well… it's war."

"War?"

"That's right. Well, it's a game as well." Delta smiles. "It's all just a game, isn't it?"

Is it though?

Stayn's words as we were escaping from Tau City come back to me now.

There's a war, Tyse. The Game of Gods. Ever hear of it?

It's a real thing. And every city needs a god if they want to play.

We play or we die.

Delta must read my hesitation as confusion, because he stands up and starts tapping his desk. "Let me fill you in on what's been happening."

I'm already standing, so I just step forward and look down at the glass that has now turned black and is lit up with a map.

"This is the line." Delta points to a line that runs right down the center of the map. "It's a line we do not cross. It's a line in the sand, literally and figuratively. It's a line so bright, you cannot miss it."

"It's the... train?" I look up at him, confused.

"Indeed it is. The train is our line. It's a waystation between worlds. You can't cross worlds—well, *you* can, because I had you augmented. But people riding the trains can't cross. They are in the world they are in."

"I'm not following."

"We live in a world of many worlds. They are not copies, per se. They are not anything like that tired old theory of the fucking 'multiverse.'" He does air quotes when he says 'multiverse.' "That theory was ludicrous to begin with. There are no doppelgangers, Tyse. There are no other 'yous' out there. There is just one of everyone. But the worlds are many. And the gods… well, as I have said, it's gotten out of hand.

"We, the Alphas"—again, he nods his head towards the door to indicate the gods out in the meeting—"we're old, Tyse. Thousands of years old. We've earned our right to exist. We Swept the worlds clean with dust and remade them in our image for our own purpose. That's why we're gods. We live on the line in the central cities. Alpha, Beta, Gamma, Delta and all the way down the alphabet to the Omega." He's pointing at the map as he talks, tapping on each city along the line. "But above, and below, and between the line there are many worlds. You can see them. I know you can see them."

I consider lying, but it's pointless. "Yeah. All right. I can see them. So what?"

"Well, that makes you very special. Because if you can see them, you can cross over. You can interact with other worlds. You've done it. I know you've done it." His smile drops here. "That's how you kept Anneeta and Clara alive."

I don't admit it, but he doesn't really need me to.

His smile returns and he taps the map again. This time it changes to something else. Something similar, but not exact. "This is our problem dimension at the moment. This is the one you will be clearing first. This is the factory world. They make Spark Maidens here."

I stare at the map, then look up at him. "That's Clara's world."

"Yes. All gods have Spark Maiden factories, Tyse. We all use the spark. But we don't all use it in the same way. None of this is the point, though. The point is that these factories, they're rebelling. And there is one particularly annoying Worker—from Clara's home factory, actually—who is blowing up the Looking Glasses in that world. He and one of the products are travelling the line and cutting ties with this world. The home world. This is not something I can tolerate."

It's Finn. He's talking about Finn. And whoever that redhead girl is he was carrying when things exploded back in Tau City.

"You're going to get ahead of him on the line, cross over, take over the factories, and you're going to kill any pseudo-gods you find inside the factories. Every single one of them until they are gone. And of course, put an end to this rebellious Worker and his product. When you're done with that, we'll talk again." Delta taps the glass and it all disappears.

I wait, but apparently this meeting is over because he comes out from behind the desk and offers me his hand, looking me straight in the eyes as we shake on it. "You leave in three days. Prepare your Courtesan, she's going with you. All gods need food. Good luck and Godspeed, Godslayer."

I open my mouth to ask just what the fuck that means, but he disappears, right before my eyes, like he was never here.

All gods need food.

And there it is. Confirmation.

I'm in the game.

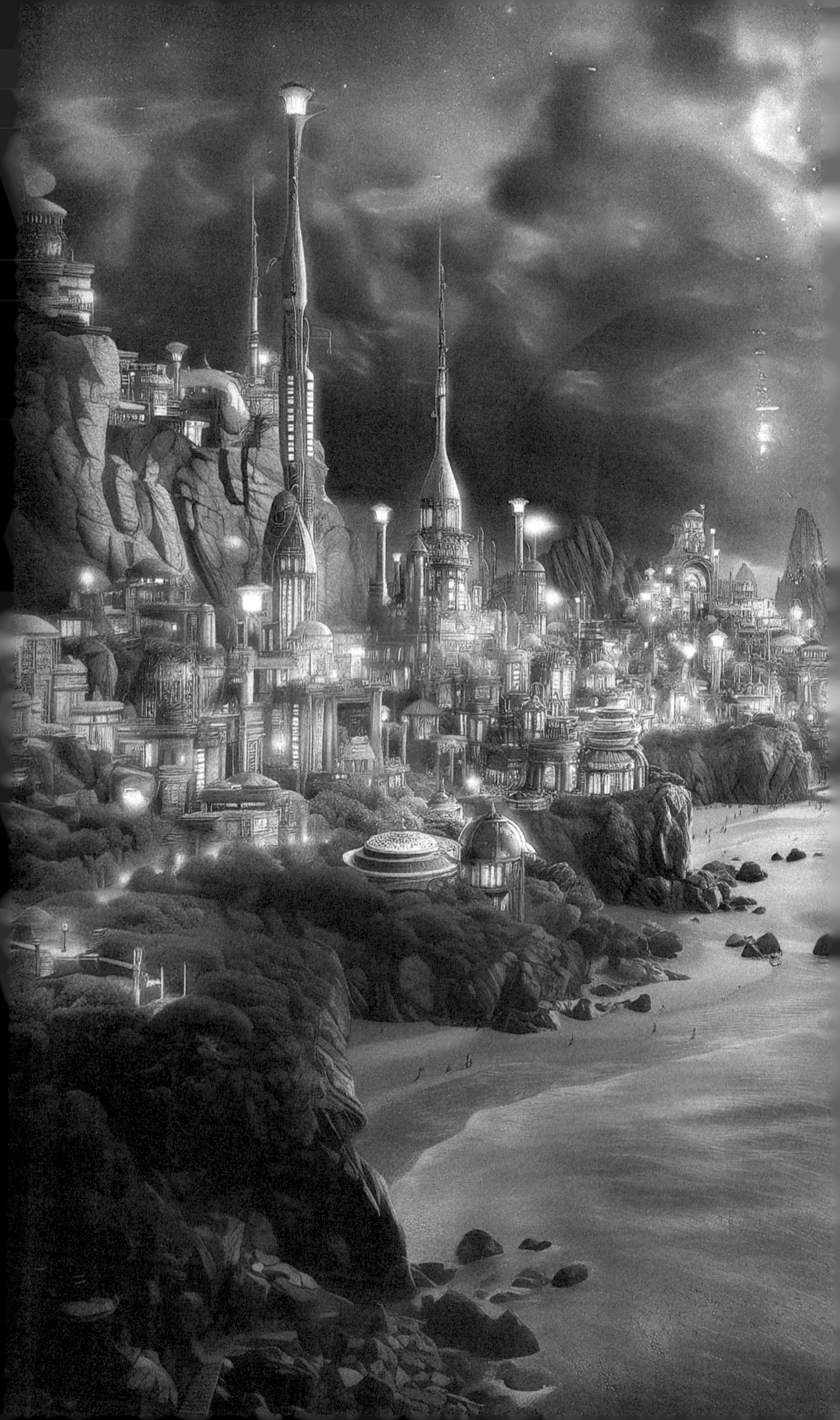

END OF BOOK SHIT

EOBS

Welcome to the End of Book Shit. This is the part of the book where I get to say whatever I want about what you just read.

I actually have a lot to say about this book. First of all, it took me four months to write. Which is a very long time for me to spend on a single book without stopping to work on something else. I worked on this book exclusively from August 13, 2023 until December 17, 2023.

I wasn't gonna write this one next. I put up a post on my author Facebook page early summer 2023 (I think) listing a bunch of projects I had on my list. Sparktopia was one of them but I was calling it 'Dark Romantasy' back then.

People had all kinds of opinions on what I should write next but one comment stood out to me. She said that I should write the one that sounds the most fun, or would make me happy. Something like that. And the comment stuck because Sparktopia was the one on my mind.

I had only come up with the idea a few weeks before. And I think I actually came up with it while I was on a zoom call with the guys for writing sprints. And all I had was the 'high concept'.

And this is exactly what that was:

"There is a god in a tower in the center of the city.
He is not good; he is not bad; he just is.
But, like all things, he has desires.
Every ten years, ten Maidens are chosen.
But only one is presented to the god in the tower.
Until now."

By the time I sat down to write this story in August I had a little more than that:

"Unexpectedly, the god starts demanding more Maidens for Extraction and one by one they are called inside the tower. Now Clara stands on the precipice of her turn and her dreams of living life with the man she loves are threatened.
But there is hope. Clara's childhood sweetheart, Finn, is in charge of the Extraction. Surely, he will save her from the insatiable desire of this mysterious god. Won't he?
At the same time, a rebellion is brewing. The forgotten underclass has a plan in place to finally put an end to the tower and the god. But there is a price for freedom. And it might be more than they can afford to pay.
When Clara is forced into the tower against her will she discovers something very unexpected.
The thing inside the tower is not a god at all.
He's just a man.
One who will destroy the entire city to get what he wants.

Her."

I almost NEVER follow the plot presented in the "before book" blurb. It's just a way to get started or fill in a field when putting a book up on pre-order. And I thought for sure that I would have to abandon this blurb when I was about halfway done.

Which is fine. I did write another one. Several, actually.

But looking back I don't think the 'before book' blurb is too far off. Of course, we now know that Anneeta was the god in the tower and she had nothing to do with Clara's Tau City at all. At least we don't think so at present. So that's kinda off. And I had envisioned Tyse being a little more... mean, I think. But he didn't present that way and I don't like to twist characters into something they're not just to fit into my initial expectations.

So he's not mean. But he is a little bit rigid.

Anyway, I want to talk about the characters one by one in this EOBS and Tyse is last, so I will save any further comment for that.

First up is Clara. She is pretty much exactly how I imagined her in my head when this idea came to me. She and Finn stayed the same throughout. Their struggle changed a little because, believe it or not, I didn't have the spark magic system set up before I started writing. I don't even know where the whole 'spark' thing came from—it's just one of those weird things that pops out while you're writing. And I'm pretty sure that didn't show up until I started Part 2, so I was a good 50,000 words into this story before I had the magic figured out.

Then, of course, I had to go back and add it all in.

So while Clara's character arc didn't change, her intrinsic qualities did. The Spark Maiden thing was there from the start—but it wasn't a 'Spark Maiden' it was just 'Maiden'. (As you can see from the 'before book' blurb.) She IS a princess. She IS haughty. She is up-city all the way. And she's never going to apologize for this, either. This is what makes her special.

It was her 'Poised, Proper, Polite' upbringing that molded her into the woman she is today. She is in control of herself. And this, my friends, is a superpower. Just look around. Look at all the people losing their shit in real life. Out-of-control emotions have been the downfall of more than one king.

Not this princess. She's wears her crown and it is not crooked. She had her moments at the end of Part 1, but I like that she lost control. She had never seen herself like that. It was a shock. Not only that, it was a reminder that she chose this "Poised, Proper, Polite' lifestyle. And even though none of this is one the page, at some point she decided it was worth hanging on to. If I had to guess it was in that restaurant talking to Tyse after her trip to the health center.

Finn was never going to end up with Clara in this book. I had planned a few other scenes with the two of them but it didn't really fit the plot. So maybe in another book. There is a lot of set up for future books between Clara and Finn, I will say that.

I know there will be some book bitches complaining about Finn's early character or whining about the lack of trigger warnings with him—but I don't care. Finn has the most growth in this book of all the characters. Even Clara, and she went to another dimension. He's not perfect. He's very far from perfect, but he's not evil and he's not stupid, either.

He chose to save Jasina. Why? To ease his guilt about not saving Clara? I mean, maybe. I don't, not for one second, think he's a 'changed man'. Not at all. But he's progressing. He's learning. And I'm really looking forward to Finn's part in the next book.

Jasina was kind of part of the initial plot. The Rebellion was in the 'before book' blurb. But I didn't know I'd have four points of view until just before I started writing the book. It took me a while to figure out how to structure this book. It's definitely not some simple 'her-chapter-him-chapter' like most dual POV romance books.

I'm bored with those, so I'm trying to find ways to make story more exciting again and carefully planned 'bouncing pov's' is one of the ways I'm experimenting.

But I love, love, love Jasina Bell. She's amazing.

I love everything about her. I love that she is unapologetically… slutty. Not in the strictest sense of the word—as she even said in her own words—but she knows she's pretty, she knows the men look at her. And while she does have brains, what's wrong with being the classic femme fatal? Especially if she's bringing her brains to the table. Not to mention her note-taking skills.

Then we have the tower people. This was a complete surprise. I remember taking to the guys during a writing zoom and telling them that Clara just walked through the tower doors and I had NO IDEA what came next. I mean, I had a general sense of what I wanted to happen, but those tower people showed up and bam, my world shook. I didn't even know Anneeta was in the story at the beginning of Part 2. Even when she knocked on the damn door and woke Tyse up. I didn't actually make Anneeta the god until way later in the story. Though, she was always Tyse's little helper in trying to get to the lower levels to find his 'disturbance'.

I think I knew pretty early on that Tyse was gonna be a washed-up super soldier, but the augments... that was in the moment. Everything about the Omega Outlands was in the moment. Rodge was born out of the need to not make Tyse walk down ten stories of stairs just to get some fuckin' food. As far as the guys selling spark, I have no clue where they came from.

But I do know this: ALL OF THAT WAS ALREADY WRITTEN when it came time to save Anneeta and take her out of the tower. I didn't have to go back and add in a single thing to make that plot point work. It was always there.

Like this is the exact story that was meant to be put out into the world.

This is what I love about writing books. I had this little idea—which basically boils down to:

A magical woman in the verge of her happily-ever-after is sacrificed to a god by the man she loves.

And four months later I have this long, twisted, complicated story about four people and a little god looking for their destiny.

To say I am proud of Sparktopia is an understatement. I am beyond proud of this work. I love the worlds, I love the characters, I love the premise, I love the mystery, I love the 'gods', and the train that slides along a split in dimensions.

And the cover. Oh, my god, I love the cover.

If you don't already know this, I do ALL my own graphic design. Every cover, every teaser. I made about five covers for this book trying to get the image in my mind onto my Photoshop canvas. It took a long time but it was worth it. I absolutely adore the cover.

And the interior images took months to pull together. In fact, I made at least thirty compositions for the interior paperback images. Not all of them made it into the book, but it was a massive undertaking. In fact, I just put the final images into my formatting program like 10 minutes ago and I'm sending it off to the printer tonight or tomorrow. I had an early, early copy printed up last year, but I replaced every single one of those images for new ones in the final edition.

I really love graphic design so I do it all myself. And I guess I should say something about AI image generation here because, obviously, I did not paint all these images. I used Midjourney.

I have very specific opinions about AI. But they are changing. It scares me sometimes how much they are changing. I have reservations about a LOT of it but I never had any reservations about making my own images.

I'm not stealing some graphic artist's job because I'm the graphic artist. And to me, Midjourney—which I pay for—is a replacement for the royalty-free stock art website subscription I used to pay for. And it's half the price for more images.

Midjourney is a tool for me. And if people don't like that, I don't really care. I do things my way.

So regardless of what people think about AI, I'm using it for graphic design. And I'm not going to apologize for that any more than I would apologize for using Photoshop.

It took several THOUSAND iterations of images on Midjourney to come up with the assets to make the compositions that you see on the pages of this book. Thousands of iterations.

The last time I looked I was up to nearly 122,000 generated images (the VAST majority were all for this ONE book). And MOST of them were total SHIT. Like 99% of them are unusable for various reasons.

It's actually not that easy to use AI for graphic design, it's an actual skill. I mean, every once in a while, it will spit out an image that doesn't need to but cut out and modified in Photoshop, but it's a rare thing. All the compositions in this book were made from assets. Not a single image was made solely by AI.

With that said, I agree that AI is not good for humans. But the only way back now is the complete removal of the internet. I don't see that happening. And if it does, our world has collapsed. It's just that simple.

I know people are going to be asking about a hardcover version because all I've made is a paperback. I'm holding off on that for now but I do plan on having one. Probably it will be ready by the time the second book releases.

It's August 3 right now and I'm a little over halfway through my current book—which is American Vampires #3—and then I'll be starting the second Sacred Trinity trilogy.

But as soon as those are all done—I'd say November '24—I will start this second book in the SPARKTOPIA world and I am aiming for a summer 2025 release.

Anyway, I am off track - back to the end of book shit…

I don't think I've ever written a book where I loved every single character so much, I can't pick a favorite. All four of these players bring something very special and unique to the plot and the whole thing falls apart if one was missing.

Which brings me back to Tyse.

Boy, do I ever love a super soldier. I really, really like them. So Tyse already has a very special place in my heart and I can't wait to see where he goes in future books.

Just in case you weren't paying attention to the Godslayer story being told in the "Parts" - Tyse IS the Godslayer and Clara IS his courtesan.

And how fun is that? That these two very likable people turn into the most hated figures in human history?

I can't wait to get that story. lol

How did sweet Clara end up being one half of that? Well, I have a pretty good idea that her path started in that restaurant, after her health center visit, and Tyse laid out his "conditions of partnership" in VERY Clear terms.

> "What you see is what you get. I'm an open fuckin' book. And if you and I are gonna be partners—in *any* way—then you will afford me the same courtesy. You will be straight with me and you will not lie to me. Because if I have your back, then you must have mine."

And if these two actually do end being the most hated figures in human history, then I guess we know how series Clara Birch and Tyse Saarinen take their their pledges of loyalty.

I'm really anxious to write more in this world and I hope you are just as anxious to read more.

I also love AI characters.

If you're new to me, this is not my first book about AI 'gods'.

My career started with a science fiction thriller series that had a sentient house called HOUSE. (I am Just Junco, 2012)

Then I wrote about SHEILA and the upgraded Alphas in the Anarchy Series (2015).

And of course, ALCOR, under my KC Cross pen name in the Harem Station Series. Not to mention his doppelgangers and modified humans. (2019)

Plus, that sneaky little GREGORY in The Ro Bro. He was an unexpected bit of fun. (2023)

So I've been writing AI characters for over a decade now and I feel like AI has finally become so ubiquitous that you can pop one into a story without it even being science fiction.

But for sure, Sparktopia IS science fiction.

It's also fantasy, and thriller, and mystery, and of course, romance.

In other words, it's typical JA Huss.

And I hope you love it as much as I do.

Thank you for reading, thank you for reviewing, and I'll see you in the next book.

Julie
JA Huss
August 3, 2024

The Godslayer and his Courtesan

ABOUT THE AUTHOR

ABOUT JA HUSS

JA Huss is a scientist, *New York Times* Bestseller, *USA Today* Bestseller, and a cowgirl who rides English. Several of her audiobooks have been nominated for the Audie and SOVA Awards and the one time she entered a book for RITA consideration, she was a finalist.

Five of her books were optioned for TV/film, and she co-wrote a pilot with actor/screenwriter Johnathan McClain.

In her seventeen years as a self-published author, she has written hundreds of non-fiction science workbooks for children and nearly a hundred adult novels—mostly twisted, spicy dark romance, with a bit of romantic fantasy and sci-fi romance as side projects.

JA Huss enjoys experimenting with tropes and genres, almost always delivering unexpected twists while still meeting reader expectations. She never writes the same story twice.

For her, the creative process is filled with sleepless nights and endless angst, which leads to perfect endings. Plot and pacing are things she takes seriously, worldbuilding and characterization are her trademark strengths, and she loves taking big risks that sometimes pay off.

She lives with her family on a ranch in central Colorado and posts daily updates about her horses, donkeys, dogs, goats, and chickens on Instagram.

She has a Patreon now where every single one of her books is released early for members, even the audiobooks. So if you'd like to check that out you can find it here:

www.patreon.com/AuthorJAHuss